OLLIE'S CLOUD

CALUMET EDITIONS

Minneapolis

Second Edition December 2022

10 9 8 7 6 5 4 3 2
ISBN – 978-1-960250-25-4

Cover art and book design by Gary Lindberg

OLLIE'S CLOUD

GARY LINDBERG

**CALUMET
EDITIONS**

Minneapolis

ALSO BY GARY LINDBERG

FICTION

Sons of Zadok
Deeper and Deeper
Ollie's Cloud

NONFICTION

The Power of Positive Handwriting
Letters from Elvis
Brando On Elvis
The Roots of Elvis

OLLIE'S CLOUD

PART 1
BUSHRUYIH, PERSIA 1823

CHAPTER 1

Two boys, each twelve, lay on a blanket of warm Bushruyih sand, heads nearly touching, eyes fixed on the clouds. Ali, younger than his friend by a month but taller by three inches, squints as the sun emerges from behind a luminous mountain of nervous vapor, then his eyes widen.

"Do you see it? Right there!" Ali points toward a small pinched cloud near the peak of the white mountain. His friend, Jalal, tries to follow the aim of that rigid finger. "It's the Prophet Muhammad, in the clouds," Ali exclaims.

"How do you know? Have you seen the Prophet?" Jalal smiles. "Maybe it's the Promised One."

"The Qa'im? No, it looks like the Prophet. He's come to me in my dreams."

"Then maybe *you* are the Qa'im."

"Don't be disrespectful!" Ali barks angrily, a pious reflex hammered by a careless remark. He can barely believe that Jalal would say such a thing. Anticipation of the coming of the Promised One, the Qa'im, the Islamic messiah, is stirring in Persian hearts. It has become a religious passion, enveloping the minds of small children, middle-aged merchants, old mullas, camel drivers and muleteers and rice farmers and harem eunuchs, seizing their dreams and shaping their lives.

"It is said the Promised One may already be among us," says Jalal. "There is a Tradition that says, 'His cause will appear and His name will arise in the year sixty'."

Ali's eyes narrow. On the Islamic lunar calendar, 1260 coincides with the Gregorian year 1844, only 19 years away. He says, "If he's born in 1260, how could he be among us today?"

Jalal sits up and drops a handful of sand in Ali's hair. "Sometimes I wonder about you. How can you grow up to be a great mujtahid if you pay so little attention to details?" He takes a sip of water from a gourd slung over his shoulder.

Ali shakes the sand from his hair and jostles his friend with a bony elbow. "You didn't answer my question."

"All right, the Tradition says that His *Cause* will *appear* in the year sixty. And so if He were thirty years old by 1260, He would be our age right now. He could be *you!*"

Ali flinches at the suggestion. The thought makes him tremble. Could he be the Promised One, the *Qa'im*, and not know it? Had Zoroaster or Jesus or Muhammad known His true station when He was twelve years old?

Jalal stares at Ali momentarily and then laughs. "I was joking!"

Ali realizes that he has been caught in a terrible fantasy. Even to entertain the slightest notion that he, of all the youngsters in Persia, could be the Promised One of God is to have committed the sin of pride. He kicks Jalal in the leg and then stands up, stomping a few steps away with his arms folded angrily in front of him.

Jalal rubs the pain from his leg without complaint. "I think it's safe to say you are not the Qa'im."

"Of course not!" What is this new feeling that has overtaken him? *Disappointment!* He is disappointed that he is not the Qa'im, that he was not chosen to be the Promised One.

"Ali, forgive me if I said something to hurt you."

In a silvery flash Ali sees that Jalal exhibits the qualities that one would expect in the Qa'im. Never has this boy shown anger or violence. He seems possessed of spiritual insight far beyond the other twelve-year-olds in the village.

Ali turns to face his friend, who is smiling, and in that youthful countenance Ali sees the flickering of something—a mirage perhaps, or a glimpse of... what? Could it be the reflection of Allah in the mirror of this boy's gleaming face?

A dagger stabs at Ali's heart. Had he kicked the Promised One? He feels suddenly hot and prickly. He drops to his knees as if sword-struck, then raises searching eyes. He touches his friend's arm lightly, leaving a trail of sand and goose bumps.

"What's the matter?" asks Jalal.

Ali Qasim feels caught in a vortex. The world is tilting. History and prophecy, once rivals, embrace. He is ether, a feather on the desert breeze, a beetle floating on the froth of time. He cannot speak, can only stare at his friend's face, which eclipses the sun. He is dazzled and frightened. Filled up like a new wineskin. Completely unprepared for the prospects that are unfolding. Dreaming, perhaps!

Jalal bends and speaks. His words like riprap break the waves of hope and terror. "Ali—I am not the Qa'im either."

Ali sits. Sighs. Of course! They are both just twelve-year-old boys. In the sand. Playing. Imagining great and wonderful and terrible things. Minds affected by the heat. Just boys. "Yes, I know," he says. But he is still not quite convinced.

The sun is too much for them now. The boys crawl to the shade of a small clump of mulberry trees that breaks the monotonous flat horizon outside the city walls. Their horses, sleek and strong Arabians with bridles but no saddles, are tied to one of the trees. To the west, the Salt Desert stretches beyond the curve of the earth, beyond Ali's imagining. But the boys' gaze now is toward home, Bushruyih, which lays a half-mile west of the mulberry trees, a grimy, sun bleached village that seems to have been heaved up ungenerously from the desert floor. This is their home, in the mighty region of Persia called Khurasan.

Crumbling mud walls mutely encircle the village and guard it from Turkoman marauders, invading armies, hostile neighbors, evil spirits, all that is unknown and uninvited, which is almost everything. Ali wonders why a village would waste precious water making mud for walls. He tries hard but cannot think of anything in Bushruyih worth guarding.

The wooden city gate in the southeast wall is massive and ornate, serving as both warning and greeting. Mountains form a wall beyond the city. And beyond them Ali has heard there is an even greater ocean of sand. He has never been beyond the mountains, or past the Salt Desert to the east.

The dwellings inside the walls of the village are built of mud-coated stone, marl, or brick, carelessly whitewashed. From a distance they look like rotten teeth. The larger habitations of the merchants have flat roofs and tall *badgeers*, wind-towers that capture the wind from any direction and guide a refreshing breeze through channels into the dwelling below.

Dusty, twisting Bushruyih streets follow ancient footpaths. In some places they are too narrow for two people to walk shoulder to shoulder. In one quarter of town the graveyard overlaps the main street, its flat tombstones providing sparse pavement.

Through the city gate Ali can see the glimmering white abode of Mirza Hasan Qasim, Ali's father and the *kelauntar,* or mayor, of Bushruyih. Ali can also see the chief mosque of Bushruyih, a shabby mud and brick edifice that is undistinguished except for its large size. From this joyless structure, the *mujtahid*—the chief Muslim cleric of Bushruyih—oversees the spiritual life of the residents.

A hundred steps behind the mosque is the flea-infested caravanserai, an inn for travelers and their animals. Tall arched entrances open onto a square yard surrounded on all sides by two stories of squalid, bare rooms. A gallery on the upper floor serves as a hallway and passage to the rooms used by travelers. Camels, mules, and horses are quartered in stables below these rooms.

The colorful and noisy bazaar is across the street from the caravanserai. Behind one of the largest shops, which offers a rainbow of exquisitely colored and patterned fabrics, are the dying rooms of Jalal's father, Haji Mulla 'Abdu'llah. Some say that this cloth dyer's way with colors is close to alchemy. The title *Haji* before his name identifies him as one who has completed the Haj—a holy pilgrimage to Mecca. Because he leads prayers at the mosque, Bushruyis also call him *mulla*, a respectful title for learned men and religious scholars. 'Abdu'llah's shrewdness has helped him become one of the wealthiest residents of the village.

Ali and Jalal continue to stare peacefully at the village. The rhythm of Islam courses through their veins, beating a steady cadence. In a moment, just a moment, the *mu'adhdhin* will summon the faithful to their noon prayer with a voice like the breath of angels, and Ali will shiver in the heat, press his moist forehead into the sand, empty his mind of all but the Will of Allah, resonate to the spiritual impulses, and recite the prayer that he has spoken so many hundreds of times.

The wind shifts as the call to prayer begins. A cool mountain breeze wafts across the village toward the mulberry trees, toward Ali, carrying the golden melody of the *mu'adhdhin* to his ears, into his mind and his soul. He is a pilgrim on a mystical journey, a traveler who has never left home, a seeker. If it pleases Allah, *let him be the one to find the Promised One!*

The mesmerizing chant of the *mu'adhdhin* ends. Ali raises his head. Sand rains from his face like tears. A single thought invades his mind: *he had not recited the prayer.* He had disobeyed the commandment of Allah and selfishly pled his own cause. What a sinful, prideful, self-seeking person he is!

Jalal is seated in the sand, staring at Ali. "I have something to confess," he says.

Ali shakes his head knowing that he should be the one to confess.

Jalal continues: "I asked Allah to appoint me to find the Qa'im."

Ali's guilt is swept away by something else—*competition*. Perhaps it was not selfish to volunteer for a divine mission. Maybe it was an act of courage. Now they would see who Allah favors!

Ali stands, feeling suddenly tall and strong. The clouds above have disappeared, like veils parting. Looking up, there is nothing between Ali and Allah.

"Someone is coming!" Jalal is looking south. A shape with many legs, made wrinkled and warped by the rising mirage heat, seems to float on the watery glare of the desert floor. Slowly the shape swells into something more distinct—not one shape, but many shapes. Men on horseback. Silhouettes against a boil of dust.

A hot and crampy ball of fear explodes in Ali's chest. All strangers here are scorpions. Every child has heard the frightening tales of the Turkoman nomads of Anatolia and northeastern Iran. *Turkoman* is the most feared word in Khurasan. They raid and burn Shi'ite villages, kill the women and elderly, and take the young men to Bukhara or Khiva to be sold as slaves. Of course, it has been many months since a Turkoman party ventured so far from the northeastern frontier as Bushruyih. But just last year the vulture-shredded carcass of a lone Turkoman—identified by his black sheepskin cap and scraps of his billowing trousers and shirt of coarse linen—was found in the desert barely five miles from the Bushruyih gate.

Like Ali and most Persians, the Turkoman nomads are Muslims, but of another stripe. Shortly after the death of its Founder, Islam was cleaved into two warring camps—Shi'ite and Sunni. Each camp accused the other of heresy. Mutual hatred grew so intense that Sunni mullas legalized the killing and looting of Shi'ites. Attacks on Shi'ite *infidels*, they said, would please God and His Prophet, wash away one's sins, and provide sure entry into Paradise. Such beliefs fan the flames of brutality already raging within Turkoman breasts.

What frightens Ali is that even one Turkoman was so close to Ali's home. There were enough perils to keep one awake at night—snakes and scorpions, evil eyes, demons... and Turkoman raiders. Of course, these barbarians would never venture so far over the Persian border if they did not possess the finest breed of horses. A horse is to the Turkoman what a ship is to the pirate; it carries himself and his fortunes. The saddle is his fortress. It was known that some Turkoman horses could go 600 miles in five days!

As the undulating shapes come nearer, Ali and Jalal cautiously retreat to the mulberry, untying the horses and desperately grasping the bridles. The boys are breathing heavily, but neither wants to be the first to bolt. Ali fingers a small silver charm that hangs among many others from a chain around his neck. This comforting object, which looks like a tubular needle-case, contains pieces of paper inscribed with verses from the Qu'ran. Wearing the Qu'ran is a great protection.

"It's probably a small caravan," says Jalal hopefully.

"Yes, probably." Ali is prepared to agree with any theory that does not involve the Turkoman.

"There is not much sand being kicked up, so there can't be that many of them."

Ali grips the bridle more tightly. "Probably just a few."

He speaks bravely, but Ali cannot shake his fear that the menacing, shape-shifting shadow moving toward them is Satan manifested as a band of Turkoman raiders on the strongest, fleetest horses in the desert. He imagines that they are the horses of the apocalypse that he has learned about from Gordon Cranston, the roving Christian missionary who sometimes teaches English to Ali and his mother.

Ali has always been proud of the Arabian stallion that his father had given him for his tenth birthday. It is a magnificent animal, pure white except for a mane and tail dyed deep orange with henna. The tail is proudly tied up in a knot.

Ali judges the distance to the Bushruyih gate. Yes, he could make it there safely on his Arabian if the Turkoman began their charge at full gallop.

Jalal squints and cocks his head, trying to straighten the rippling figures. "I'm trying to see if they're carrying flags," he says expectantly.

Ali does not understand. Why would these horsemen be carrying flags?

"I'm looking for the Black Standards," Jalal says. "Certainly you know why."

"No."

"The Black Standards—flags of pure black. They are symbols of the promised Qa'im."

"How do you know these things?"

"I read." And then Jalal punctuates the desert air with an exclamation: "Yes! I can see the Black Standards hoisted aloft."

He leaps onto his Arabian stallion and repeats the words of the prophecy. He leans forward in the warm arch of the animal's back and digs in his heels. The horse rears with a snort and lunges toward the jagged string of travelers.

Ali instinctively follows. He mounts his horse and slaps the huge beast into a fierce gallop. He cannot let Jalal be the first to reach the Black Standards! It is a race. If Ali is to be chosen for this divine mission, *let his stallion grow wings.* Flashing hooves chop at the ground. Flared nostrils drink the fiery air. A muscled neck rhythmically thrusts forward and back, cadenced by Ali's heartbeat, which grows faster still. He can no longer feel the bone-jarring thump of hooves striking the ground. The gallop smoothes into an airy glide. He and the stallion are one. If he would look down, surely the ground would be falling away, his shadow growing smaller.

The first jarring sound is like a finger snap, a dry mulberry twig breaking. Ali recognizes it at once—a rifle shot. The second sound is a loud jumble of Farsi, the native language of Persia. Someone—many people—are yelling for him to stop. *Come no closer!* Jalal reins his stallion to a halt and Ali almost runs into him.

The mysterious figures ahead are now close enough to be clearly seen. There is no Black Standard. Instead, a man is propping up his dark cloak with a stick to shield his head from the sun. And there are no Turkoman horses, only mules and seven men. Two of the men are old, with white flowing beards. Three ride mules. Four walk, and one of these is aiming a rifle at Ali.

The men are tense. They squint malevolently in Ali's direction. At last they seem to identify the interlopers as two unarmed boys. The man with the rifle laughs coarsely and lowers his weapon.

Two large white encasements, like mummies, are bound with thick ropes to each side of the baggage mules. Ali now understands what he is confronting—a small caravan carrying corpses to be buried near the Holy Shrines in Najaf or Karbala. The old men, bent and sagging on their mules, are going there to die. For a moment, everything is still and silent except for the chiming of bells suspended from the collars of the mules.

Approach! A hoarse voice intrudes.

With a pinch of knees, Ali and Jalal nudge their horses forward. The men begin slapping their sleeves and chests, making clouds of dust. One of the old men raises a water gourd to his lips, finds it empty.

The boys stop a few yards from the caravan of corpses. Ali sniffs the air, expecting a foul smell. The corpses are so tightly wrapped that even the desert heat cannot leach out the fetid, stinging odor of death. Except for the vaguely human shapes, these enshrouded cadavers may as well be rolls of silk or linen on their way to the market in Mashhad. Ali counts sixteen corpses, two per mule-side.

The man with the rifle points toward the city walls, then opens his parched lips and speaks. "What is this village?"

"Bushruyih," answers Jalal.

The man nods. "There's a caravanserai?"

"Yes. Have you been traveling long?" Jalal seems at ease with these strangers.

After a long pause, the man with the rifle lets out a long sigh that seems to reduce his size by half. He squats to stretch his long leg muscles. "About five days," he replies at last. "We come from Khur to the south. A band of Turkoman attacked us two days ago. They spared our lives when they saw the corpses. Not out of pity—the Turkoman have no pity—but as slow torture, I suppose. They left us with the burden of carrying our dead, but with no money or provisions for ourselves."

"I have some water," says Jalal. He unslings his water gourd, sloshes the water inside to show that it is not empty, and then tosses it to the old man with the empty gourd.

Ali finally finds a voice. "Did you fight them?" he asks.

"You want to know if we fought the Turkoman?" The man with the rifle stands and walks menacingly toward Ali, eyeing the boy's gourd. Ali hands it to the man, who smiles.

"Thank you." The man takes a long drink and hands it to another man. "We chose not to fight. There were at least twenty Turkoman, heavily armed with blades and muskets. We surely would have been killed and our dead relatives left to rot out here in the wilderness. On the day of resurrection, they would have been very surprised to rise from their sandy graves and look upon the barren desert instead of the Holy Shrines."

The men find this very funny. They laugh heartily.

The man with the rifle looks up at Ali and smiles. "And so, my little friend—my name is Sadiq Muqaddas. These are my mules." Sadiq is the *charvadar*, or chief muleteer, who has provided the small band with mules for about six tumans each.

"I am Ali Qasim."

"Will you lead us, my friend, to the caravanserai?"

"But how will you pay? If the Turkoman took all of your..."

"My father will see that you have food and water," interjects Jalal. "No man who lives through an encounter with the Turkoman should go without nourishment."

Ali had not thought to offer hospitality to this ragged band of travelers. He has much to learn if he wishes to be chosen for the sacred mission. Deciding it is not too late, he adds: "My father, too. He is the kelauntar of Bushruyih."

Sadiq smiles. "Thank you, friends. But if you can show us to the caravan-serai, we can take care of ourselves."

"Rest a while," Ali says. "Then we'll accompany you to the caravanserai."

Ali glances at the two old men seated shapelessly on their mules like sacks of grain. The life seems already drained from them. Ali wonders if they can make it as far as the city gate. Long before reaching Karbala—another seven hundred miles or so—they will probably end up as another pair of mummified corpses hitched to the sides of a mule. Ali watches as Jalal's horse gently walks over to one of the old men. Seated high on the stallion's back, Jalal looks down at the old man who is hunched on a mule. The man, who has been staring at the sand since the encounter began, slowly lifts his gaze and smiles at the boy. His face is long and brown. Thick white eyebrows seem to be holding up the weight of an immense striped turban that is a puzzlement of folds. Upon seeing the youth, his slumped body straightens.

"Can I get you anything?" Jalal asks. His voice is a whisper, almost lost in the gusting desert breeze. Ali strains to hear.

"Nothing for myself, thank you."

"You are going to Karbala?"

"Yes. With my wife." The old man sadly turns his eyes to one of the en-shrouded corpses. "She wanted to be buried near the tomb of Imam Husayn. It was her greatest wish."

"It's a great distance."

"Yes, I know, and I am very old and tired. But I am simply honoring a promise to my wife. Some men have many wives, but I had only one." The old man pauses, cocks his head, and stares at the youth's eyes. "And who do I have the privilege of addressing?"

"Jalal."

"I am Muhammad Kujiri."

"What will you do in Karbala after your wife is buried?"

"Ahh—the directness of youth. Perhaps you are wondering if I am going there to die. Such is the reason that most old people go to Karbala, I know."

Jalal is embarrassed.

Kujiri continues: "My reason is different. Perhaps I will die there, perhaps not. My purpose, however, has more to do with something I wish to do *before* I die."

"Pray at the Shrine?"

"Oh, I will certainly do that. But there is someone there I want to see again."

"A relative?"

"You are an inquisitive one," Kujiri says. "I have questions, too. Deep questions. And that is why I must gain an audience with this person. I believe he has the answers."

"A great mujtahid, then?"

"No. Someone even greater than the greatest mujtahid."

This statement mystifies Jalal. Kujiri can see the questions written on the boy's face. For a moment Kujiri considers withholding the answers, but this youth has charmed him.

"Have you heard of Shaykh Ahmad?" Kujiri asks.

"Yes. The mujtahid says he is an *infidel*. Why would you want to see him?"

"Are you familiar with his teachings?"

"We've been told to ignore them because they are false."

"Then how do you know he is an infidel? How can you judge for yourself?"

Jalal thinks about this.

Ali feels suddenly repulsed, as if surrounded by something unclean. This man is a Shaykhi, a follower of Shaykh Ahmad, a known blasphemer and perverter of the teachings of the Qu'ran.

Jalal finally replies. "Since I know nothing specific about this man's beliefs, I cannot judge for myself."

"Well, that is why I go to Karbala," Kujiri says. "I could have paid Sadiq to take my wife to the Holy Shrine for burial. But for myself, I seek the source of those teachings."

"We should be going," Ali says. Maybe Jalal will take this hint.

"One moment," Jalal says. Then he turns to Kujiri. "I have a question about your beliefs."

The old man looks skyward, as if hearing the question before it is asked, then says, "Perhaps you want to know how much longer we must wait for the Promised One?"

Jalal is astonished. He stammers: "Well—yes…"

"And what is your understanding of the Qa'im?"

Ali seizes this opportunity to confront Kujiri and prove his religious knowledge. "The Promised One will come to kill the enemies of true Shi'ites, infidels like the Sunnis and the Turkoman. He will kill so many that a river of blood will reach the stirrup of his horse."

"So the Qa'im is a warrior who will come to fill the world with justice by slaughtering enemies of His true faith?" Kujiri says.

"Yes, and he will bring all infidels to Islam by his sword —Sunnis, Jews, Zoroastrians and Christians." Ali is proud of himself. He feels passion building as he speaks. One day he will become a great mujtahid and use his knowledge and zeal to stir the souls of Shi'ites throughout Persia.

"I see. Very interesting," Kujiri says flatly.

Ali is deflated. His passion has failed to arouse the Shaykhi.

"And you, Jalal, is that what you believe also?" Kujiri asks, his gaze firmly focused on the youth's unblinking eyes.

Jalal blinks once, twice, gaining time to think. Ali's rhetoric, a serviceable condensation of one of the mujtahid's more popular sermons, now sounds skewed, even radical. Could it be that killing infidels is the way to worldwide justice? Hadn't this been tried before without lasting result? Would not the Promised One have some clearer insight, some innovation, some better solution to offer?

"Certainly, the Qa'im may prove to be a great warrior and leader of armies," Jalal says.

Kujiri laughs and says: "You would make a fine diplomat." He turns to Ali. "What can you tell me about who the Qa'im is?"

"Well—he was born a thousand years ago. He escaped from his enemies. And he has been living there ever since, with his wife and some believers, in a city of seventy thousand portals where people speak seventy thousand languages."

"My, it must be hard to have a conversation there!" Kujiri says. "Go on."

"We are told that he has helped many travelers who were lost in the desert. Maybe he helped you survive your encounter with the Turkoman!"

"Yes, perhaps. And young Jalal, do you agree with your friend?"

Again Jalal blinks. His mind whirls. He had heard this story countless times and had never questioned its literal truth. But now, hearing it again…

"How can I say if this is true?" Jalal replies at last. "Perhaps over time the story has gained some decoration. Or perhaps it may have another meaning."

"Ahhh!" Kujiri says, letting the long vowel seep slowly from his lips. "In other words, the story may be symbolic, not literal. In which case, to find the true meaning of the story, we should consider…"

"Ali is right, we should be going," Jalal says curtly. He feels suddenly uneasy with the direction of this conversation. His mind is agitated, his gut rumbling. Never before had he challenged the longstanding teachings of his faith. Or thought to.

Kujiri sighs, smiles, and then sags into his thin saddle. "You are right."

As the small band of travelers ride toward the village, Ali and Jalal, almost in unison, wonder how Kujiri would have answered that question—*how much longer before the Qa'im appears?*—if they had let him. But what does it matter? Scores of Bushruyis solemnly stare at this macabre caravan of the dead as it enters the city gate and passes the mosque.

Seized by the desire to pray, to cleanse himself of the Shaykhi taint, Ali makes an excuse to abandon his friend. He removes his boots, places them near the entrance to the mosque and silently enters.

CHAPTER 2

On the far side of the mosque the mujtahid speaks to a small gathering of robed mullas who sit reverently at his feet. It is a dialogue, with questions thrown to the mujtahid who then dispenses truth and wisdom as he sees it. Mulla Ibrahim Baqir, like all mujtahids, exercises authority to expound his own theories and opinions about religious laws. He is a prominent doctor of jurisprudence and religion, and in religious matters his followers adopt his views, imitate his behaviors and follow his instructions, sometimes unthinkingly. In Bushruyih, Mulla Ibrahim has many followers. The brightest and most serious ones are invited to attend classes in which heated debates are common. As Ali approaches the group, the topic is whether the Prophet Muhammad's urine was ritually clean.

Ali unconsciously stirs, his face a hatchet of smoke in the darkness. The mujtahid sees him. Mulla Ibrahim knows that Ali is the son of the governor of Bushruyih. At first, the mujtahid is angry. It is easy to see Ali as an agent of the despised Qajars. Was he sent here to spy on my teachings? Did I say something that would offend the governor?

The mujtahid bites back an inclination to chastise Ali for interrupting the group, knowing that his powerful father might take offense. He motions the youth forward.

Ali slowly walks through stripes of sunlight that pierce the chamber.

"Ali Qasim," the mujtahid says.

"Yes, Mulla Ibrahim. May your shadow never grow less."

"And to what do I owe this honor?" The mujtahid now seems amused. His smile softens and he cocks his head to listen, favoring his good left ear.

Ali glances at the faces of the mullas. All are staring at him.

"There is a matter on which I need to consult," Ali says. He is no longer certain this was a good idea.

"I see. Well, you have a mosque full of the brightest religious minds in Bushruyih. We can spare a few minutes to resolve any perplexity that you may have." The mujtahid turns to the assembled mullas and then says, "Isn't that right?"

The robed gathering murmurs approval.

"Please, go ahead. What is your dilemma?"

Ali is not sure how to begin, so he mumbles.

"Speak up, Ali Qasim, so we can all hear you."

Ali clears his throat and starts again. "In the desert today Jalal and I encountered a group of travelers headed for Karbala."

"And why were they headed to Karbala? To bury their dead at the Holy Shrine?"

"Yes. And they had been attacked in the desert by the Turkoman, who took all their valuables."

"Let me presume that your dilemma is how to help this unfortunate band of travelers, though the best fortune of all is that they are alive! The Turkoman are not known for compassion."

"That is not what I am concerned about. While we were talking to the pilgrims, I discovered that one of them follows the teachings of Shaykh Ahmad."

These words erase the amusement from the mujtahid's lips. His eyes narrow coldly and his voice drops an octave. "Tell me—did you speak to him?"

"No, I just listened to him talk to Jalal."

"Did you touch him?"

"Touch him? I—I don't think so. No, I didn't."

"And did this caravan continue on toward Karbala?"

"They were very tired, so Jalal took them to the caravanserai."

The mujtahid begins to pace. "It's good that you did not touch him. Shaykhis are unclean, no better than dogs!" He turns to the mullas. "They corrupt the teachings of the Prophet Muhammad and possess the satanic power to mislead those who listen to them."

Ali backs away, feeling responsible for the mujtahid's sudden wrath.

"This youth found the strength to resist their false teachings," the mujtahid continues. "He found the strength to report the Shaykhi heresy that has poisoned our village."

The mullas mumble approvals. Two of them smile and nod.

"Shaykh Ahmad is an imposter, for no man who studies the Qu'ran can reach the conclusions that he expounds."

Several of the mullas rise in anger, shouting curses. One of the younger clerics pulls a knife from its sheath, exclaiming, "I will cut out his blaspheming tongue!"

There are more shouts, more drawn knives. Ali is frightened now.

As the mujtahid continues to pluck the exposed nerves of the mullas with his rhetoric. Now swords are drawn. They glint in the slanting beams of sunlight.

The mujtahid is not finished. He is carried on a wave of emotion. "These infidels are worse than idolaters," he says. "They are heretics and cannot be redeemed. If such a man were in the caravanserai, he must be punished and made to recant!"

Ali tries to envision the old Shaykhi as a powerful agent of Satan, but can't reconcile the images. Certainly the old man was no threat. Ali begins to regret his words and fear for Kujiri. He feels suddenly emboldened. "Excuse me," he says, "but if this man cannot be redeemed, then what would be the purpose of making him recant?"

The mujtahid immediately understands his error. He glowers at Ali's insubordinate challenge.

At last one of the students says: "Even though a Shaykhi cannot be redeemed, by recanting he will demonstrate the power of truth over satanic fancy. Mulla Ibrahim, thank you for allowing us to reach this inevitable conclusion."

The mujtahid's humiliation is reversed. He smiles and says, "This is the lesson I hoped you would learn. We must lay bare the Shaykhi lies and make this evil-doer renounce his infidelity—or die." He unsheathes his sword and carves the air with it. "Let us go find Satan!"

The mullas all rise and shout. With his final words before marching out of the mosque, the mujtahid pierces Ali's heart: "We go in the name of Ali Qasim!"

Ali watches the mullas leave. Their blades are sharp. Ali's head is pounding and perspiration rains from his face. I have no right to question the authority of the mujtahid, he tells himself.

Ali wants to nullify his catalytic role in the coming violence but he cannot find a convincing argument. In the end he knows that he has betrayed an old man who possesses a kind and searching heart. Ali had offered up a sacrificial victim to the ready knives of self-righteousness.

We go in the name of Ali Qasim!

The mujtahid's scorching words sear his heart. Ali has become the banner of bloodlust!

I have no right to question the authority of the mujtahid, he tells himself again. I am just a boy. But his heart does not believe his argument. He can only picture the old man Kujiri. The kind smile. The gentle laugh.

Ali prostrates himself and prays that the Will of Allah be done. It feels like a cheap way out, but it's the best he can do.

CHAPTER 3

The large door to the caravanserai is open, there being no immediate threat to security. Jalal and Sadiq lead the weary caravan of the dead through the gate and into the bright courtyard where they are greeted by Omar, the *dalandar* or entrance-keeper, who is a cousin of Jalal's mother.

"Jalal!" Omar says with smiling eyes. "I have not seen you in quite a while. You bring us business?"

"My friends are looking for the finest caravanserai. Do you have any recommendations?"

"Well, since we are the only caravanserai within forty pharsangs, I suggest they rest their weary bones here."

"Very wise and unbiased counsel. Omar, this is Sadiq, the charvadar."

The men greet each other. Omar takes Sadiq aside to negotiate for provisions.

The courtyard is surrounded by austere rooms—barren cells with straw-covered floors—elevated a few feet upon a ledge. The rooms have no doors and are built in the form of Saracenic arches. Behind the rooms lie the stables.

As Omar and Sadiq negotiate, Jalal watches the men of the caravan slowly walk their mules into a tight knot with Kujiri at its center, as if protecting him. Seated high upon his Arabian stallion, Jalal can see Kujiri's back. The protectors' eyes are darting back and forth, searching for spying eyes.

In a horrifying move, Kujiri suddenly plunges his arm into one of the mummies, the one secured on the right side of his mule. The arm easily slides up to its elbow through a fold in the muslin wrap. Jalal imagines the arm wriggling through the rotting entrails of the corpse. And then Kujiri quickly removes his arm. It is not dripping with the slimy stuff of death. Instead, his unsullied hand is grasping a small leather coin pouch that looks quite full.

Kujiri turns and looks around guiltily. He catches the eye of Jalal and immediately knows that his secret has been discovered. Kujiri raises his index finger to his lips. *Shussshhh! Don't tell.*

Jalal nods. *I will not tell anyone.*

Omar and Sadiq have finished their bargaining for provisions. Kujiri approaches them and the three men quietly discuss something. Jalal cannot hear them, but it looks like Omar and Sadiq are explaining the deal they struck. Kujiri nods politely and then removes some coins from the leather pouch, placing them into Omar's outstretched hand.

The boy climbs off his horse and tethers it. "I thought that was your wife," Jalal says to Kujiri, referring to the corpse.

"My wife is on the left side. On the right is everything else that I possess converted into tumans."

"The Turkoman—they never searched…?"

"Of course not. Who would interrupt the sleep of the dead?"

Jalal hands the coin back to Kujiri, who says: "It is not enough?"

"It is too much. Neither my silence nor my friendship has a price."

Kujiri is touched. "Jalal," he says, "may your face one day look upon the Promised One, who indeed is very near." Kujiri kisses the boy on both cheeks.

The old man goes back to his mule and begins to remove some of his belongings from a sack of coarse haircloth. As the boy watches, Kujiri climbs to a room and spreads out several carpets on the floor. He hangs a curtain in the open doorway and vanishes behind it.

Glancing across the courtyard, Jalal sees Omar in a heated discussion with an Englishman, Gordon Cranston, a Christian missionary who passes through Bushruyih to administer medical aid and give English instruction to the privileged ones including Ali's mother. The mullas tolerate this tall blonde man because he does not try to propagate his religion; if he did, he might be put to death.

Omar whispers conspiratorially to Gordon. "The vizier is in Bushruyih meeting with the kelauntar as we speak. This must mean that they are about to consummate their bargain."

"Then the exchange could take place as early as tomorrow."

"They've been seen at the tea house. My nephew works there. He has very large ears."

Gordon hands Omar some coins. "I need confirmation of when the exchange will take place. Do you understand?"

Omar takes the coins and smiles. "If it can be learned, it will be, I assure you."

"Assuming the worst, I need to be ready tonight. Is that possible?"

"Of course. But I will need to pay for some things in advance."

Gordon understands. He will pay whatever it takes to guarantee that the arrangements are satisfactorily made. Secretively, he hands more money to Omar. The men shake hands English-style, then kiss each other on both cheeks. Gordon marches out of the courtyard.

CHAPTER 4

The cloth dyer's shop opens onto the street that approaches the caravanserai. It is always stuffed full of brightly-hued fabrics neatly folded into soft piles or draped over dowels like rainbows of light to attract the eye. Now, during the heat of the day, the shop is free of customers.

Haji Mulla 'Abdu'llah, father of Jalal, sits on a large Persian rug fanning himself in the oppressive heat. Daggers of memory prick him with the unfulfilled desire of his youth. His body tingles, as it did twenty-five years ago, with the yearning to become a great religious scholar, a renowned doctor of Islamic law.

As if blown away by a faint whistle of wind through the dye shop, the fading remembrance of the boy vanishes completely. 'Abdu'llah drinks in a lungful of hot, dry air. To a desert creature, the warmth is comforting. He knows that the course of his life is established; it makes no sense to wish it were not. But the future of Jalal—ah, that's different. 'Abdu'llah sets his mind on planning the journey he will soon make with his son. In one week they will leave for Mashhad, the most prestigious religious center in Persia. There Jalal will attend the finest *madrisih*, a religious seminary. One day Jalal will be a great religious scholar, a renowned doctor of Islamic law. Perhaps he will return to Bushruyih and replace that bigoted buffoon, Mulla Ibrahim, as mujtahid.

There are still no customers in the shop. 'Abdu'llah decides that this will be a good time to visit Jaffir the blacksmith, who is creating a very special gift for Jalal.

As 'Abdu'llah stands and straightens his garments, his eyes are drawn to a flurry of activity outside the shop. An agitated group of white-turbaned mullas is marching down the street. The loud threats of these holy men offend 'Abdu'llah, who finds violence abhorrent. Though designated an honorary mulla, due to his teaching activities and calls to prayer at the mosque, 'Abdu'llah finds many of the mujtahid's teachings illogical and radical. While Mulla Ibrahim for years has ranted against women's education, 'Abdu'llah married a literate woman and encouraged her to continue education. His wife, Nadja, is a celebrated poet—celebrated everywhere, that is, but in Bushruyih, where her works are unknown.

'Abdu'llah watches the band of mullas charge past the shop. What frightens him most is the glint of steel; the clerics are marching with swords and knives drawn. Blood will flow! 'Abdu'llah steps from his shop and falls into the swelling throng that trails the mullas. Some of these people, too, are now cursing the evil that has entered the village. No one knows what that evil is, but everyone is certain that it will be excised by the clerics.

And then 'Abdu'llah hears words that darken his heart. *In the name of Ali Qasim!* Has some harm come to his son's friend?

'Abdu'llah quickens his pace. He begins to look for his son, Jalal. Weren't the two boys together this morning? If harm has befallen Ali, what of Jalal? The emotion of the crowd begins to excite 'Abdu'llah. Fear overtakes him. Obviously some great peril has been unleashed. He imagines the worst—murder, abduction, an accident. Who would harm a youngster? *Please, Allah, if it be Your will, allow Jalal to be safe.* Soon he finds himself shouting with the crowd. Without understanding why, but with great intensity, he shouts: *In the name of Ali Qasim!*

CHAPTER 5

Mirza Hasan Qasim, pear-shaped and thick-bearded, will be thirty-five years old tomorrow. He is the nephew of Fath Ali Shah, Persia's Qajar ruler. Even though he is only a capillary in the dynasty's bloodline, Qajar nepotism has rewarded him with a major position in a village that is but a flyspeck on the shah's map. As *kelauntar* of Bushruyih, he oversees village security, civic governance, and tax collections, making sure the shah's due is quickly forwarded.

An ever-shrinking government salary stimulates Hasan's creativity in financial management. Tax overages and bribes of every kind find their way into his bottomless purse, allowing for a lifestyle far above the other local desert dwellers. The lifestyle has grown more expensive, however, and the normal spoils of the office have recently fallen short of his obligations. For six months he has short-changed the shah—a dangerous game, but in such an obscure little hamlet who would notice?

Unfortunately, the vizier—who pays attention to such matters for the governor of the province—has an eye for detail and a nose for felony. And like so many in the government, the vizier also has no detectable code of ethics. This is what has brought the vizier to Bushruyih where he sits in the back corner of a teahouse with the kelauntar and discusses the financial dilemma over the steaming brew.

The kelauntar is a bitter man. For seven years he has lived in a wilderness that even Allah surely has forgotten. He sees his appointment as a life sentence in hell and curses his father's name. If his father, the shah's brother, had not jealously competed for the throne, Fath Ali Shah may have shown mercy on his wretched sibling and given his nephew a job in some bearable place.

The kelauntar does not understand moderation. The Qu'ran allows a man four wives, and he has the maximum, plus six concubines. Though alcohol is strictly forbidden for Muslims, the kelauntar surreptitiously imports cartloads of fine Shirazí wine and drinks it alone by the bottle.

He has one other passion: his son, Ali Qasim. His only son. Three wives have born him seven daughters, but only Anisa, a slave-girl purchased from the Turkoman, has given him a son. Anisa is a fair-skinned angel with sandy hair and blue eyes. The kelauntar had been immediately mesmerized by her spotless beauty. She had been thirteen when he bought her and returned to his father's house in Mashhad, the holy city near the Bokhara frontier. She then became his first wife.

The Turkoman had claimed that Anisa was English, that her missionary parents were killed in a Turkoman attack when she was seven. They'd said she was greatly prized for her beauty but was considered stupid because she could not speak any of the languages or dialects of the region. She had been bought and sold, worked hard, used often by the men for their pleasures; and then she'd developed a maddening streak of independence. She had grown less submissive, more aggressive. This wisp of a girl had begun acting like one of the men, making demands and giving orders. Her owner, a shaggy one-eyed Afghani, had wanted to kill her but his brother suggested that the girl's beauty might fetch a fine price. Within a month she had become the property of Hasan Qasim and the Turkoman had acquired a handsome profit.

Besides having given the kelauntar a son, Anisa provides a target for his anger and frustration. Fueled by wine, his fury often erupts in violence. He pummels the poor woman with his fists, calling her vile names and accusing her of unspeakable things, often with his slaves and other wives looking on. He blames Anisa for his wretched existence, his father's sins, his own jealousy. He tries to defile her incandescent beauty, so often the cause of his suspicions. He threatens to kill her, maim her, sell her back to the slave traders. But always he falls asleep in tears before carrying out these threats, awakening in his own vomit. And then he leaves, never with an apology, sometimes for a week or more.

The kelauntar fears that someday his fiscal infidelity will be discovered; many other embezzling princes and officials had been found out and punished. But what could they do to him? Assign him to a lower hell? Here, in a dark corner of this rancid-smelling café, seated on a wooden platform opposite the vizier, he is about to settle his account in a most painful manner.

An enormous striped turban like a monstrous weight seems to drive the vizier's head down into a pudding of jowls, plumping them out into exaggerated pouches bristling with beard. "I presume the details are taken care of," he whispers. "And that I can take possession tomorrow morning."

A server pours more hot tea.

"Of course. Just as we agreed," the kelauntar replies sadly. "And I presume you are prepared to fulfill your end of the bargain."

"Naturally. I am an honorable man," the vizier lies. "May I see the marriage contract?"

The kelauntar passes a document to the vizier, who quickly scans it.

"You are clever," the vizier says. "In the event of divorce, her dowry is almost nothing."

"She was my legal slave when I married her."

"She is the most beautiful woman I have ever seen."

"She is a scorpion—with a fierce sting in her tail."

"Tomorrow morning, after you divorce her, you will sell her to me for the amount of her dowry. No money will change hands. She will become my slave. And then I will marry her so you have no further claim on her."

Persia is truly and gloriously a man's world. The kelauntar's mind races through the simple process of divorce. Three times he will repeat to his wife the words "you are divorced" and it will be done. And yet, as the vizier knows, the kelauntar can recall her twice without further ceremony. But if he divorces her three times, or if she remarries, he cannot take her back. So by marrying Ali's mother immediately, the vizier severs all claims of recall by the kelauntar. The vizier possesses her as slave and wife. It is complete ownership.

"But the boy stays with me," the kelauntar emphasizes.

"It is the woman I want, not her pup."

A year earlier, the vizier had paid a visit to the kelauntar's compound. Violating all Persian custom, the kelauntar had brought the fatted official to the anderun and asked for his wife, his prize possession, to be unveiled before him as if she were a magnificent sculpture. Most women would have swooned in shame, but Anisa had stood proudly, even arrogantly, as the head eunuch removed her veil and exposed her exquisite English features. Covetousness immediately had overwhelmed the vizier and he had pledged to possess this woman. For months he could scarcely think of anything but the magnificent creature that had been revealed to him. Knowing that most village officials were corrupt, he had conspired to find the kelauntar's crime. It was surprisingly easy—and cheap—to obtain the damning records. And then had come the extortion.

"When you have your new wife," the kelauntar says, "you will sign an official statement that my stewardship of the shah's finances is without peer."

"Yes, you'll be free of me. You are a lucky man to have such an astonishing wife to save you from disgrace and punishment."

The kelauntar's mood is sour. He was a fool to have left uncovered the evidence of his graft. He was even more of a fool to have boastfully exposed his wife to the lustful vizier. But what of it? The woman is a scorpion. Her venom is the obsession she incites in men made unattainable by her arrogance. Ali will be heartbroken, but the kelauntar will think of some compensation to give him. Something to ease the pain.

The kelauntar sips the last drop of his tea and stands. "Tomorrow morning, then. At the mosque," he says.

"You have no idea how I am looking forward to it."

The kelauntar steps into the street and begins walking. Like a serpent's tail, his retinue follows in an undulating wave. The local people nod respectfully as they pass, but not kindly. He does not care. He is thinking about going home. He is dreaming about the bubbling *kalyan*—the water pipe—and the opium he has brought from Isfahan. He is dreaming about the bottles of ruby wine that await him. He is dreaming about a few hours of blessed oblivion.

A sound intrudes. There is shouting and cursing. He can hear footsteps, many of them, scuffling over the stony street. He turns to see a group of sneering mullas striding toward him with a swagger, blades drawn. A crowd follows, urging them on. What could this be about? The shouts grow louder, and then the kelauntar hears the words. *In the name of Ali Qasim!*

He is chilled. What does this mean? *What has the boy gotten himself into now?* The kelauntar squints into the sun, shades his eyes, and watches the crowd turn a corner. They are headed toward the caravanserai. *This is a religious matter, I'm sure,* the kelauntar tells himself. The mullas take care of religious business and he takes care of Qajar and civil business. But he is worried. They are shouting the name of his son. Swords are drawn.

The kelauntar begins to trail the crowd, staying a few steps behind so he doesn't look like part of the mob. He feels a tug on his arm and looks down. Beside him is Ali, red-faced and breathing hard.

"I've been trying to find you!" Ali says.

"What is going on? Why are they chanting your name?"

"They're going to kill a Shaykhi at the caravanserai. It's my fault. You must stop them!" The boy is crying.

The kelauntar comes to a halt. Mulla Ibrahim and he had never before crossed swords. There was an implicit understanding between them, a line drawn in the warm Bushruyih sand. The Qajars have power, yes, but at the local level the clergy have the people behind them. The kelauntar is not anxious to test this delicate balance of power.

"What do you mean it's your fault?" the kelauntar says to Ali.

"I told the mullas about a Shaykhi coming to the caravanserai. I thought I was doing the right thing. I didn't think they would want to kill him."

The kelauntar understands the dilemma. He can step in and protect his son from these haunting feelings of guilt, or he can do nothing and preserve the balance of power. As for the Shaykhi, who cares?

"Come with me." Hasan puts his hand behind Ali's back, rubs it gently, then pushes the boy forward. They begin to follow the crowd toward the caravanserai. The kelauntar has no idea what he's going to do.

"The Shaykhi is with Jalal," Ali says.

The kelauntar dreams of the kalyan.

CHAPTER 6

Jalal is seated in Kujiri's room when the noisy mob enters the courtyard. "They've come for me," he says. "Your friend told them a heretic was in the caravanserai."

"Ali? He would not do that."

From the courtyard, the old man and the boy can hear the hoarse voice of the mujtahid, Mulla Ibrahim. "If there is a Shaykhi present here, let him show himself!"

Jalal sweeps aside the thin curtain and steps out onto the gallery overlooking the courtyard. The mob below audibly gasps when they see the youngster. Of all the children of Bushruyih, this boy is thought of as the most pious and spiritually gifted. Fathers hold him up as an example for their own sons, and some even call him the *child of light*.

'Abdu'llah is at the rear of the crowd, stunned by the image of his son standing alone above the mob.

The kelauntar instinctively weaves his way through the crowd, approaching the mujtahid as he tugs Ali by the hand.

Surprised at the appearance of the boy, Mulla Ibrahim takes a step back. "Jalal—perhaps you did not understand. I was calling for the Shaykhi."

"Yes. You believe that he is a heretic and deserves punishment for his beliefs."

Some of the mullas thrust their swords skyward and shout agreement. Mulla Ibrahim gestures for them to lower their blades.

"My child," the mujtahid says gently, "has this satanic force corrupted your thinking? That certainly would be cause for the Shaykhi's execution."

"The Shaykhi is a devout Shi'ite, as you are, my teacher," the boy replies.

Mulla Ibrahim nods graciously, knowing that he has often claimed credit for developing Jalal's spiritual insight. "Perhaps some of the Shaykhi's ideas are different than yours, Jalal continues, "but then, as I recall from one of your classes, you disagree with some of the doctrines of Mulla Fazlollah, the great mujtahid of Fars. And if my memory is correct from another class, you take issue with some of the teachings of other mullas. Are we to pronounce them heretics and sentence them to death?"

Mulla Javad, a student standing near the mujtahid, grasps his sword handle angrily. "The mujtahid's argument with these most learned doctors of law are over minor points!" he shouts. "The Shaykhis insult Muhammad by teaching that the physical resurrection is a fantasy!"

Javad expects the crowd to cheer his words, but there is only hushed silence as everyone waits for the boy's response. Jalal steps to the edge of the gallery and places his hands on the rail. His father sees the boy standing there, as if in the pulpit, speaking to the congregation below with such conviction and authority that even Mulla Ibrahim remains silent. This image of Jalal, preaching at the age of twelve with a man's life on the line, will linger in the mind of 'Abdu'llah for the rest of his life.

Behind the curtain, Kujiri sits and listens to Jalal argue for tolerance of the Shaykhi views. The boy aptly repeats the teachings that Kujiri had given him on the journey to the caravanserai, but creatively weaves in references from the Qu'ran and the traditions to bolster his convincing argument.

As the boy speaks, the mujtahid glances at the kelauntar and begins to appreciate the increasing delicacy of the situation. The villagers are certainly behind the mullas, but ultimate power and authority still rests with the ruling Qajars. If only the kelauntar had not shown up here! The mujtahid suddenly is not anxious to test the balance of power.

"I ask you," the boy concludes, staring at Mulla Ibrahim, "should we punish a Shaykhi for his desire to comprehend the spiritual significance of the Prophet's teachings? If we punish each attempt to discern meaning, whether right or wrong, we may quench the spark of reason and interrogation that you yourself, Mulla Ibrahim, have ignited in so many of us.

He gestures toward the curtain. "The man you seek is behind this curtain. He journeys to the tomb of Imam Husayn to bury his wife, who believed that she would be physically resurrected. This man respects the beliefs of his wife, even though he doubts the need for a resurrection of the body. He and his wife lived in peace for many years, each of them holding fast to their own questions and beliefs. On his way to Bushruyih, this man's caravan was marauded by the Turkomans who took everything of value that they could find. But they spared his life so he could bury his wife at the Holy Shrine. Surely if the murderous Turkoman can show mercy, you can as well. What an example of the Prophet's mercy this can be!"

The hundred or so spectators are stunned by the eloquence of this child. There is not a word spoken until Mulla Ibrahim breaks the silence.

"You have a bright mind, Jalal. It has been a joy to have you as a pupil!" The crowd murmurs approval. The mujtahid smiles, again taking credit for the boy's genius.

CHAPTER 7

The kelauntar's compound is encircled by a windowless mud wall spattered in patches by white pigeon droppings. The cooing, fluttering birds strut along the top of the wall like an army of sentries. Ali and his father, trailed by the retinue, walk along the barren wall and approach a barrel-chested man.

Gholam Reza and three others guard the solitary front door, a massive wooden slab studded by iron bolts. Gholam nods respectfully at the kelauntar, opens the groaning door and says, "The tutor has arrived. He is in the anderun."

Beyond the door and through a short corridor Ali inhales the leafy breath of the garden—a shady oasis of mulberry, walnut and fruit trees, fragrant red and yellow roses, luminous white irises and china asters, sculpted iron benches, fountains fringed with violet leaves.

The house reaches like the thumb and fingers of a hand to grasp the courtyard on three sides. To the left is the *birun* or men's apartment and to the right is the mysterious *anderun* or women's quarters. The house is built of sun-dried bricks thickly whitewashed and glimmering in the leaf-dappled sunlight. Steps lead up to a verandah that stretches nearly round the garden. A dozen two-leaved doors, each capped by fanlights and filled with gaudy-colored glass, provide gay portals to the interior. Numerous windows, like sparkling jewels, catch and fling the sunlight toward the kelauntar as he and Ali walk toward the Judas tree. Four sullen children, Ali's younger half-sisters, play dignified games around the edge of a large water tank.

Hasan and Ali have not spoken a word to each other since leaving the caravanserai. The kelauntar's mind is lost in chaos. He is simultaneously astonished by Jalal, envious of the cloth dyer whose son has captivated the village, ashamed of his own gutless performance at the caravanserai, stung by the vizier's extortion, and deeply craving the opium-rich kalyan.

He slowly bends his cracking knees until he is seated on a bench, and then turns his deep-set eyes toward Ali who is staring at him. He sees in Ali's face disappointment and rejection. After hearing his son's plea for help he had been outdone by a brave twelve-year-old boy. But the final outcome had been positive, had it not? Perhaps if he had intervened the result would have been worse. It may have been the kelauntar's wisdom and maturity that caused him to recognize the virtue of restraint, of letting young Jalal act out his disarming performance.

No, this self-delusion is not working. Under the piercing gaze of his son he cannot conjure success out of deceit. He knows too well the darkness of his own heart, the tortuous pathways of his scheming mind. And he knows that within hours Ali will be torn from his mother.

The boy looks into his father's eyes. They are moist and expressive. He sees in them love, yes, certainly love, but also something he has not seen before—self-doubt. He also sees pain, such terrible pain. He wants to put his arms around his father to return the love, but he is now twelve; he should not act like a child. He is angry, too. Angry that his father has let him down. That his father beats his mother. That his father's affection is deeper for the wine bottle and opium pipe than for Ali.

The kelauntar glances down at his feet and mutters, "Ali, I've made a decision." He takes Ali by the hand. His lips smile but his sad eyes betray apprehension as he says, "I'm sending you to the madrisih in Mashhad."

Is this fair compensation—school in exchange for a mother?

Ali is stunned. He had never been able to muster the courage to ask for such a wonderful thing. After learning that Jalal was going to the famous seminary, Ali had been so envious that he had prayed for forgiveness.

"I'm going to Mashhad?" Ali asks, looking for reassurance.

The kelauntar's eyes smile now. "Yes. I think we can be ready for you to travel there with Jalal next week."

This is pure joy! Ali throws his arms around his father and squeezes as hard as he can.

It has been a long time since the kelauntar has experienced the physical touch of his son, the tactile transfer of affection. It is electric.

Tears gather in the kelauntar's eyes. He knows that he has bribed Ali, but in his emotional abyss even a purchased expression of love is a treasure.

For a blissful moment the kelauntar allows himself to believe that a hug is love, that a son's pardon has been granted, and that a bridge has been built. He knows that when the delusion fades, there is the blessed opium-filled kalyan.

Ali exuberantly rushes toward the anderun to tell his mother the good news.

CHAPTER 8

Abdu'llah strides toward the blacksmith shop. He is anxious to inspect the gift that he is having crafted there for his son. Most of the blacksmith work is coarse and utilitarian—shoes and bits for mules and horses, iron gates and latches, repairs and refurbishments. The simple work suits the crude skills of five sweaty workers. The sixth, however, is an exception—Baqir Muhammad Shafti.

For ten years, Baqir had worked as a master sword-cutler in Isfahan, the old capital of Persia once celebrated for its exquisite manufacture of swords for the Qajars. As with most trades in Persia, the art of sword-making had all but vanished and few artisans were now capable of fabricating blades equal to those of former ages.

Baqir had been working for a maker of fine weaponry when his employer had come into possession of a precious sword crafted by a famous cutler named Assad'u'llah who had lived many years ago. Some of his famous swords, it is said, possess powers that defy belief.

One night the Assad'u'llah sword had disappeared and a frantic search by police discovered it concealed in Baqir's house. Despite his protests of innocence, Baqir had been sentenced to have his thieving hands cut off. His wife, however, managed to sell all their property and with the proceeds bribed the police chief to allow Baqir's escape. He had fled east into the Great Salt Desert, finding safety in the remote village of Bushruyih.

'Abdu'llah came to know of Baqir's tale of woe one evening after the sword-cutler had drunk a bottle of red wine and tearfully confessed his secret past to the cloth dyer. Baqir then had revealed the part of the mystery that had never come out.

Baqir's employer, it seems, had recognized Baqir's immense talent and had commissioned him—for a handsome price—to produce a counterfeit Assad'u'llah sword. The exquisite forgery, from its material and manufacture down to Assad'u'llah's etched signature, was so perfect that no expert could discern the fraud. One evening, the employer had planted the sword in Baqir's house, reporting its "theft" and suggesting that Baqir had been behaving suspiciously. He had hoped to accomplish two things: avoid payment, and ensure that Baqir could never again counterfeit another sword that might devalue the employer's treasure. After the arrest, Baqir could not explain the true circumstances for fear of even harsher punishment. After all, he *had* committed a crime.

A few months after Baqir's drunken confession, while 'Abdu'llah had been pondering alternatives for a gift for his son, the idea of a sword had come to him. Yes, this was it! He would commission Baqir to create an instrument equal to the Assad'u'llah sword. This one would be no counterfeit, however. He would have Baqir inscribe the sword with his son's name.

Baqir had brought with him to Bushruyih several *koors*, cakes of Indian steel, from which the finest blades are made, dreaming that one day he would have reason to use them. That day had finally arrived. With great determination, he'd hammered a gently curving blade out of the koors and then placed it over a low fire all night. The next morning he had removed the blade, smoothed the surfaces, filed it expertly, and then heated it again. At last he had plunged the blade into a trough of castor oil. Over the next several days he had tenderly polished the blade, sharpened it, and fitted the hilt.

His next step had been to bring out the *jowher*, the damask pattern of the blade, a natural design of dark wavy lines produced by the crystallization of the steel. The true quality of a blade is known by the arrangement and closeness of the pattern and the bell-like chime it emits when struck by another hard object. To reveal the jowher, Baqir had cleansed the blade from oil and grease. Then, using sword-cutler's alchemy, he had unwrapped a strange yellow stone mysteriously called *záji shámi* and ground it to a powder in a china cup containing hot water. With a piece of cotton he had painted the solution onto the blade and let it dry, then repeated the process twice. Each time the black jowher had grown more vivid. The pattern was unusually dark and tight, the design exotic. Finally it had been time to engrave the name of Jalal of Bushruyih in gold upon the blade.

Baqir next had turned his attention to the scabbard, which he had fashioned from thin wood laminate, fitting it precisely to the blade. Then he had joined and covered this hardwood skeleton with black leather on which he had stamped a verse from the Qu'ran rendered in his wife's expert calligraphy. On the finished scabbard he had mounted a pattern of gold and gems that he had purchased with the money 'Abdu'llah had paid him for the sword. He had needed no incentive to produce this masterpiece. The opportunity to again apply his artistry had been its own reward. And in his opinion, the quality of this piece exceeded the fraudulent Assad'u'llah sword he had created years ago.

'Abdu'llah strides into the blacksmith shop, beaming with expectation. He looks at Baqir, who smiles broadly.

"It is finished, then?" 'Abdu'llah asks.

"It is ready for its first breath."

The gleaming object rests in a locked cabinet within the blacksmith's shop. Baqir unlocks the cabinet and removes a burgundy satin pouch the length of a sword. The pouch is rigid as Baqir hands it to 'Abdu'llah, who can vividly remember his first sword, pale and lifeless by comparison.

The other workers, none of whom have seen Baqir's project until now, gather around 'Abdu'llah as he anxiously opens the tie that closes the end of the pouch. 'Abdu'llah's hands are trembling with anticipation. Slowly he removes the bejeweled scabbard. The entire group gasps with delight at the exquisite beauty of this object. 'Abdu'llah is stunned. He glances at Baqir with wide eyes. Baqir nods, urging him to remove the sword.

Holding the scabbard in his left hand, 'Abdu'llah places his right hand on the hilt and slides out the glinting blade. Its beauty—the perfection and uniqueness of the jowher, the flawless arc, the golden luster of his son's engraved name—is beyond belief. As he tilts the blade, a flash of reflected light ignites his face. He turns to Baqir in admiration.

"This is truly a masterpiece!" 'Abdu'llah says.

Awestruck, the blacksmiths applaud the artisan.

"There is one other thing you must do," Baqir replies. "Give it life!"

'Abdu'llah understands. He sets down the scabbard and transfers the sword's hilt to his left hand. He tests the blade's sharp edge. It whines against the whorls of his thumb. He snaps a fingernail against the blade and it sings, resonating with the clear voice of an angel.

CHAPTER 9

In the kelauntar's anderun, two people are seated on the floor of the front room, which is used for receiving female guests. The first person is Ali's birth mother, Anisa, so achingly beautiful and porcelain-perfect that it startles to see her move. She reclines on huge satin pillows and clutches an outer robe of pale blue brocade that only partially conceals her billowing skirt and the white stockings that clothe her legs. A creamy-colored muslin veil, bound low on her forehead, cascades down the hair behind. The exquisite beauty of her face is fully revealed to her seated companion, Gordon Cranston, the English missionary who tutors her when he is in Bushruyih.

"So it is confirmed, then?" Anisa quietly asks Gordon in Farsi.

"There is no doubt. If we don't act tonight it will be too late."

"But I'm not ready!"

"This is our last chance. Tomorrow morning you will be the vizier's wife and be on your way to Kirman… without Ali."

"Without my son? You mean he would separate us?"

Gordon shrugs his shoulders. "That's what I've been told."

Anisa gathers her resolve. "How will we be ready in time?"

"I've arranged for everything we need outside the compound. You need to finish our arrangements inside."

Anisa sighs nervously. "Maybe it's better that I don't have time to think."

"Just do what we planned. Everything will be all right. I promise."

Ali thrusts open the door and playfully kicks off his shoes before shuffling inside. He is anxious to announce his good news! At twelve, Ali lies somewhere on the smudged line between childhood and adulthood. He now sleeps in the birun with his father, segregated from the females, but still spends most of his time in the anderun with his mothers and sisters. He enters flushed with his father's promise.

"Ali, you look so excited," Anisa says.

"I have wonderful news!"

"Then come over here and tell us!" Anisa replies. Her silky voice has become excited, breathy. Ali runs to his mother and crashes to his knees, grinning.

The lack of furniture in the anderun focuses attention on the floor. Over thick matting, a large Persian carpet stretches down the middle of the room and overlapping runners cover the sides and top. Beyond this room is the kitchen and blue-tiled bathroom, the slave quarters, and the *sherbet-khaneh,* or sherbet house, in which the samovar and kalyan are prepared and washed. A large sleeping room beyond the sherbet-khaneh also serves as a center for games and other entertainment during the day; floor mattresses, bolster-shaped pillows in bright prints, and wadded blankets are stuffed into alcoves and rolled out on the floor at night.

Anisa looks at Ali expectantly, eyes sparkling with a mother's delight. Seeing her son happy is her greatest joy.

"Tell us, Ali. What is your news?"

"Father is sending me to the madrisih in Mashhad! I leave next week with Jalal!"

Anisa looks away. The light in her eyes is extinguished.

"That's wonderful, dear," she says. But her voice is brittle now, insincere. *It's true then—the kelauntar intends to separate us.*

"You're not happy for me?" Ali asks.

She forces a smile, tight and nervous. "Of course I am," she replies. "But I'm a mother. I'm happy and sad at the same time."

Ali hugs his mother. Nestling his face into her neck, he sees for the first time a bruise on her chin. In his mind he hears the strike of fist on flesh. It sucks the joy out of him. "I won't be gone forever," he says.

As Anisa hugs her son, she looks at Gordon Cranston. A stare, helpless but demanding.

Prompted by this look, Gordon speaks in English: "Ali, how is your English coming along?"

Ali releases his mother and turns to Gordon. For a moment he doesn't understand these words. His brain is stuck in Farsi. But then the sounds become familiar. Yes, the words are English. What do they mean, *How is your English coming?*

Slowly, Ali forces his tongue into the odd shapes demanded by English words and haltingly says, "My English... is... getting better... but... I need... to practice... more."

Gordon smiles and touches Ali on the arm. "You will get more practice. Much more. I promise." Gordon turns to Anisa, looks through her, makes her shiver in the heat.

"It's time for your lesson," Gordon says to Ali. "What shall we read this afternoon?" The question is a little joke between Gordon and Ali because the answer is always the same.

"The *Arabian Nights*!" Ali says. "A tale from *The Arabian Nights*."

Gordon smiles and reaches for two books that are already on the floor. The first is a bound Farsi volume of *The Arabian Nights*. The other is a tooled leather notebook containing Gordon's English translation printed neatly in his own hand.

Like most Persians, Ali loves this adventurous story in which the sultan of an ancient dynasty—betrayed by his unfaithful wife—has pronounced all women wicked. To punish them, the sultan has vowed to marry a fresh wife each evening, only to have her strangled the following morning. On the morning of her execution, Scheherazade—the sultan's newest wife—begins to tell a series of mesmerizing tales that cannot be completed before the time she is to be put to death. Thoroughly captivated by his wife's masterful storytelling, the sultan grants a day's reprieve so she can finish. But each day one tale leads to another that is even more fascinating than the one before. And each day the sultan grants yet another reprieve, saving one more woman from certain death.

"It is my turn to choose which of Scheherazade's tales to read," Anisa suggests. She pauses, but there is no argument. "Tonight we will read *The Enchanted Horse*. I will read in Farsi and Ali will read in English."

Ali makes a face. It's hard work reading in English. He'd rather have his mother simply tell him the story in her gentle, soothing voice, the way she did when Ali was little. In those comfortable days, nestled in his mother's arms, he would imagine that his mother was Scheherazade.

"All right, then," Gordon says. "Shall we get started?"

Anisa begins to read. *It was the Feast of the New Year, the oldest and most splendid of all the feasts in the kingdom of Persia.*

Ali reads the English translation. Gordon helps with the pronunciation of several words.

Anisa continues. *The day had been spent by the king taking part in the magnificent spectacles prepared by his subjects in the city of Shiraz.*

Ali reads the sentence in English.

The sun was setting, Anisa says. *And the monarch was about to retire, when suddenly an Indian appeared before his throne with an artificial horse that looked like a real one.*

Ali looks up at his mother, who is smiling at him. "I don't know this tale," he says.

"It's my favorite," Anisa confesses. "I've been saving it for a very special time. The English, please." Ali reads the translation. Back and forth, in Farsi then English, Anisa and Ali tell the story of the enchanted horse.

> *The Indian apologized for his late arrival, then said: "None of the wonders you have seen during the day can be compared to this horse." The king replied, "It is but a clever imitation of a real one. What is so special about it?"*
>
> *The Indian explained, "It is special because I have only to mount him and wish myself in some special place, and in a very few moments I shall be there."*

If Ali had been watching Gordon, he would have seen the Englishman's eyes memorizing his mother's face. If he had been listening to Gordon's heartbeat, he would have heard it quickening.

The melody of Anisa's expressive voice, her impossibly beautiful features, her golden hair cascading like shafts of sunlight—all this is more than Gordon can bear. He cannot stop worshipping her with his eyes, cannot concentrate on the lesson. Everything he has ever desired seems summed up in this magnificent creation reclining on pillows before him. He fights her magnetic pull, battles the attraction of his body to hers. It is important that he project a detached demeanor for a few more hours.

Anisa cannot prevent her eyes from glancing furtively at Gordon. But when she sees Gordon looking at her she quickly turns away, afraid that the intimacy of their eyes might betray her desire to touch the skin of this Englishman, feel his arms around her, his moist breath on her neck.

> *"Do you see that mountain?" asked the king, pointing to a huge mass that towered into the sky. "Go and bring me the leaf of a palm that grows at the foot."*

Taking a seat on the horse, the Indian turned a peg in its neck and the animal bounded like lightning into the air. In a few minutes the Indian returned with the palm. The king now desired the horse. "Name your price," he said.

Ali's half-sisters, their mothers, even the anderun slaves are beginning to quietly crowd near the English lesson, eager for a moment's escape into the magical world created by the words of their beloved Anisa.

"I can only sell it on one condition," the Indian replied. "The horse was given to me by its inventor in exchange for my only daughter. He made me promise that I would never part with it except for some object of equal value."

The king offered any city in his kingdom. But the Indian declined, saying, "I can only give you my horse in exchange for the hand of your daughter."

Eyes widen throughout the anderun. A startled gasp causes Gordon to become aware of the growing audience. Astonished, he counts fifteen already.

Anisa looks around and sees the many captivated faces. Smiling, she decides to give them what they want—*entertainment*. Her rich voice becomes even more animated as she begins to enact the characters in the story.

Though the king decided the bargain was fair, he insisted that the prince be allowed to test its powers. The Indian agreed and helped the prince to mount the horse. But before he could show the prince how to guide it, the prince turned the peg. He and the horse were soon out of sight.

After a long time, the prince had still failed to return home. The king grew angry with the Indian. "If the prince is not safely back in three months," he said. "I shall have your head." The king threw the Indian into prison.

Meanwhile, the prince landed safely on the terraced roof of a huge palace. Bravely he set out to explore, finding himself at last in a magnificent chamber full of sleeping women, all lying on low couches... except one, who was on a sofa. This one, he knew, must be the princess.

The kelauntar's other wives are intoxicated by fantasies of a gallant prince finding them asleep. The delicious dream makes them shudder with delight. The flame of their silent passion is fanned by the nearness of Gordon, the mysterious foreigner, a man more exotic and beautiful than anyone but Anisa. Gordon becomes their prince, their unattainable prize, their unrequited prayer.

On hot and lonely nights, each of them has longed for intimacy with this handsome Englishman. He is everything the kelauntar is not—kind and gentle, respectful of women, patient, lean and muscular, and so very *very* desirable. Every one of them, at the right moment, would risk her life for one scorching touch of his broad hand…

> *Gently stealing up to the side of her bed, the prince saw that she was more beautiful than any woman he had ever beheld. The princess opened her eyes, and seeing before her a handsome man, she remained speechless.*

It is too much for the kelauntar's fourth wife who suddenly swoons, spins, collapses—her fall broken by a large pillow. The other women rush to her side, fan her, gently slap her face and pinch her cheeks. She awakens with a blush of embarrassment.

Under the cover of this distraction, Anisa again glances at Gordon. This time she does not avert her eyes when they meet his. Connected ever so briefly in this way, Gordon is certain he can read her thoughts. *I want to be with you so badly. But be careful. We have only a few more hours to wait.*

Anisa finally turns away, then takes the hand of the fainted woman and squeezes lovingly. The kelauntar's wives have grown close in the past few years. In many anderuns, wives grow spiteful and fiercely competitive, jealously plotting against their rivals as they seek power and favored treatment. But here the wives have banded together to survive the oppression of the despised kelauntar. Anisa, the beautiful one, is the usual victim of the kelauntar's rage, and the others have come to think of her as their savior, the one who suffers for them. They would do anything for her. And tonight they will have the chance.

The faint echo of the *mu'adhdhin* takes everyone by surprise. The entertainment of the English lesson had transported the audience into a timeless world, but now time has intruded. With momentary chaos, the assemblage comically scrambles into position for the evening prayer.

As Ali prostrates himself, he senses a subtle shift in the constellation of bodies surrounding him. Something is different. He raises his head and peeks around the room. Everyone is submissively prostrated in the act of prayer— everyone but Gordon Cranston, the Christian, who can be excused; and Anisa, who kneels alongside the missionary but remains upright with open eyes, unmoving lips and insolent face. Ali is confused. *What does this mean?*

Ali's questioning stare magnetically draws a glance from Anisa. As their eyes meet, Anisa seems momentarily disturbed. She turns to Gordon, who does not notice, and back to Ali. Then her face becomes serene and radiant. She places her palms together, fingers pointing heavenward. Slowly she closes her eyes and bows her head in the Christian posture of prayer, the pose that Ali has seen Gordon piously adopt many times.

Ali again prostrates himself, but he is not listening to the *mu'adhdhin*. A horrifying thought has come to him. He prays for Allah to forgive his mother because the sin of apostasy, of abandoning Islam for another faith, is punishable by death.

CHAPTER 10

Jalal's family sits comfortably on the floor of their anderun after dinner. A servant clears the bowls as 'Abdu'llah explains to his wife, Nadja, the episode at the caravanserai.

Jalal's younger brothers and sisters listen, bursting with laughter at their father's descriptions.

"I don't know why we're sending him to the madrisih," Nadja says dryly. "He already knows more about Islam than the mujtahid." She chuckles at the thought.

"Don't tease him, Nadja," 'Abdu'llah says. "He's had a rough day defending the entire Shaykhi movement."

Nadja laughs and bows. It is all in good humor. "I will obey my husband—my lord and master. Even though he cannot write a coherent verse without my help."

"Not everyone is cut out to be a poet, my dear."

"And not everyone is cut out to be a master cloth dyer."

The children look at each other. They are quite sure that the parents of their friends do not talk to each other like this. Bibi-Kuchik, Jalal's sister, rolls her eyes and glances at her siblings.

Her brother, Bahram, is confused. He asks a question. "Father, at the mosque we are told that women should be subservient to their husbands. And that girls should not receive education. Are these teachings wrong?"

'Abdu'llah's face grows serious. He turns to Bahram, now just ten years old, and says, "In some areas I disagree with Mulla Ibrahim's interpretation of the Qur'an."

"Without thinking much about them, I might add," Nadja interjects.

"Still, we must live in peace in this hamlet," 'Abdu'llah continues.

Nadja needles her husband: "Your father is saying that it's good for *business* to keep our views to ourselves."

'Abdu'llah ignores his wife and says, "You can see what happens when someone, like Shaykh Ahmad, speaks up with a different interpretation. Most people cannot tolerate a difference of opinion when it comes to religion, and in Islam the role of women is a religious issue."

Jalal speaks for the first time. "But if someone truly believes in something, shouldn't he speak up? I'm thinking of mother, who is not only educated but a gifted poet. Is she not being hurt by our failing to announce her gift and publish her works? Are not many others being deprived of the beauty and elegance of her verses?"

Nadja beams at this unexpected compliment. She takes Jalal's hand and squeezes it. Then she smugly turns to her husband for his reply.

"My son, we cannot change our culture or the attitudes of our neighbors by engaging in defiant, even heroic acts. This would serve no purpose, for our neighbors are not ready for change. Of that I am certain." Like 'Abdu'llah, Nadja harbors fears of retaliation, false accusations of heresy, religious persecution, even loss of business. "Perhaps when the Qa'im appears he will set the matter straight and we will no longer have to disagree with the religious authorities on these matters. They will be better informed, and women will become equals."

'Abdu'llah feels a need to switch topics, so he stands and gestures for Jalal to stand with him. "If I may change the subject... as you all know, in one week I will be taking Jalal to the madrisih in Mashhad. I wanted a special gift to mark this auspicious event. Finally I came up with an idea. I hope you will like it, my son."

'Abdu'llah walks to the other side of the large room and finds the red velvet pouch containing the sword. He carries it to Jalal and presents it to him with a slight nod of the head.

Jalal immediately knows what the pouch contains. With eager hands he removes the wooden scabbard from the pouch and marvels at its magnificence.

"Go ahead, remove the sword," 'Abdu'llah suggests.

Jalal grips the hilt and pulls out the glinting sword. Stunned at its beauty, he drops to his knees, holding the flat blade across the outstretched palms of his hands. He looks up at his father. "I don't know what to say. It's... it's beyond my imagination."

"It's not imagination," 'Abdu'llah says. "It's very real. It was made especially for you."

"And I will never be without it."

This is a Persian boy's dream, to own a sword that will be the envy of all. He wants to take the sword and race to Ali's home. He wants to share the magic of this blessed gift with his best friend. But he knows that the streets are dark and dangerous at this hour.

He stands, holding the heavy sword gallantly in one hand. And then it happens. His hand begins to tremble—not nerves, or fear, but some tremor erupting from the core of his body. Nadja rises, concern turning to terror as Jalal drops the sword and slowly slumps to the carpeted floor, his whole body shaking. Nadja throws herself onto him, trying to smother his convulsions as if they were flames. 'Abdu'llah stands there, frozen, watching. The children begin to shout, afraid for their older brother.

Finally the seizure is over. No one understands the epilepsy that has gripped the boy. Pale and perspiring, Jalal takes a deep breath and in a perfectly normal voice says, "Is the sword all right?"

"What?" his mother says. *How can he be worried about the sword?*

'Abdu'llah picks up the sword and puts the hilt in his son's hand. "No harm done to the sword," he says.

"I'm all right now."

Nadja hugs him desperately.

"Probably the stress of the day," Bahram suggests. But secretly he fears that demons have possessed his brother.

"And the excitement of the sword," 'Abdu'llah adds. "I'm feeling shaky myself!"

Jalal sits up, still clutching the sword. "I was afraid I broke the sword when I dropped it," he says.

'Abdu'llah kneels beside his son and says, "Don't worry. This sword cannot be broken. I promise."

CHAPTER 11

Bushruyíh is dark, a glowing crescent moon the only illumination. Three hours after sunset, no one is allowed to walk the streets without carrying a lantern. Violation risks arrest by the *gazma,* or night patrol, strict enforcers who carry cudgels and straight swords to aid their mission. The city gates are closed, watched over by the dalandar and several heavily armed guards.

Omar is alone on the street. A dim lantern swings in his hand as he walks from his small home and arrives at the caravanserai. The evening entrance-keeper recognizes him and opens the courtyard gate. Inside, Omar finds six men packing mules. It appears that this small caravan will be leaving in the middle of the night.

Omar speaks to one of the men, handing him a goatskin sack full of coins. "You must be ready in an hour. When you receive word, you must proceed at once to the mosque and wait by the entrance. Be sure you all carry lanterns."

The man, obviously the charvadar, stares at his feet, then looks up and says: "When will we get the rest of our payment?"

"As I explained, you will be paid at the conclusion of each stage of your journey."

"This is very dangerous. I'm not sure we're being paid well enough."

"The party who commissioned you will pay a handsome bonus when you reach your destination."

The charvadar nods, accepting the bargain. Omar leaves the caravanserai and walks toward the mosque. From there he can see the kelauntar's compound and he is just minutes from the caravanserai. It is the ideal vantage point to wait for the signal.

The interior of the kelauntar's anderun is one of the few Bushruyih dwellings illuminated at night. The warm glow of lanterns flickers on the walls. Anisa has received a message that the kelauntar will be paying her a visit this evening. She reclines expectantly on soft cushions knowing that when her husband arrives, with wine on his breath, she must play the game exactly right or the plan will fail.

She thinks about how Ali, now asleep in the birun, had seemed to recognize her metamorphosis during the evening prayer. *How will he react?* She mourns her son's loss of innocence; she knows that Ali is protecting her secret, though their pact remains unspoken. Ali will not tell the kelauntar about her affection for the Englishman and her conversion to Christianity.

Voices! She hears the kelauntar enter the anderun. It is beginning.

Hasan sees Anisa reclining on the pillows. He is intoxicated, but not as drunk as Anisa had expected.

She rises and walks over to the kelauntar, tracing her long painted nails on the back of his hand and neck.

He shivers. *She is shameless!* he thinks. But he loves her touch. It drives him mad! She is so beautiful, so desirable... so infuriating. Her English blood pulses with an arrogance that enrages him. After all, she is just a *woman!* Yet she has a power over him, the shame of which can only be broken by harsh punishment. *Will he have to punish her tonight?*

Anisa pulls him to the pillows, pushes him down until he almost disappears in their softness. She looks him in the eye and then smiles gently. "I want tonight to be special," she says. "I've asked the others to leave us alone. Is that all right?"

He nods *yes*. It will be better that way. This will be their last night together.

"Would you like the kalyan?" she asks. He nods again. "I'll prepare it for you."

Anisa appreciates the delights of smoking the kalyan. The perfume of Turkish tobacco relieves the boredom of the anderun and wraps her with sensuality. The fragrant smoke rushing into her lungs can seem like the breath of God entering her body.

She appreciates the kalyan also for its role in her plan this evening. Instead of tobacco, Anisa places a damp wad of opium into the bowl of the water-pipe and tops it with burning charcoal. Then she inserts the end of a snake-like leather tube into her mouth and puffs, making sure the mind-numbing smoke is easily drawn through the bubbling water.

She hands the leather tube to the kelauntar. He inhales, then glances appreciatively at her. He has acquired a craving for the bitter taste of opium. He will indulge himself tonight. Maybe he will put off her punishment until morning.

"Would you like me to tell you a story?" she asks.

He loves the sound of her voice. *Why not?*

"This story is called *The Enchanted Horse*," she says, "from *The Arabian Nights*." She tells him of the Indian and the enchanted horse, the prince flying to a far-off land. She tells him how the prince returned to his father with a beautiful princess, and how the Indian was released from prison only to kidnap the princess in retaliation for his own inhospitable treatment.

The kelauntar listens and puffs, charmed by the story but slowly drifting into another world not populated by either Anisa or the enchanted horse. Anisa continues to narrate her tale.

> *The Indian had turned the horse so that it entered a wood close to the capital of Cashmere. Goaded by the Indian's threats, the kidnapped princess called loudly for help. Her cries were heard by a troop of horsemen.*

> *The leader of these horsemen was the Sultan of Cashmere, and he instantly demanded to know the identities of these two. The Indian said the woman was his wife. "My lord," the princess cried, "this man is an abominable magician who has this day torn me from the Prince of Persia." Believing the princess, the sultan ordered his followers to cut off the Indian's head.*

Anisa speaks with great emotion, watching the kelauntar puff on his kalyan. As she narrates the tale, the irony of it strikes her. She may as well be telling the story of her own life—the English orphan captured and sold into slavery by the Turkoman only to be purchased by the nephew of the shah.

> *The Sultan conducted her to his own palace. Then he bade her repose, saying she should explain her adventures on the following day. The princess fell asleep, flattering herself that she had only to relate her story and then she would be restored to the prince without delay.*

At daybreak, however, the Sultan proclaimed that the woman would become his wife. The princess was awakened early by horns, and then fainted upon learning that the trumpets were the start of her marriage ceremony.

At length her senses began to return. Rather than break faith with the Prince of Persia by consenting to such a marriage, she decided to feign madness. She began speaking absurdities and using strange gestures while the Sultan watched her in sorrow.

The kelauntar turns for the first time toward Anisa. His eyes are cloudy and red, but he stares at her the way he does before going into a rage. She grows nervous. *Keep telling the story,* she tells herself. *Give the opium time to work.*

The kelauntar's eyelids become narrow slits, and then close. Is he unconscious? No. He reaches out and takes her hand, almost tenderly, and rubs his thumb gently over it. She continues her tale.

Days passed. At last the Sultan gave orders that doctors were to be allowed into her chamber one by one to attempt a diagnosis. Many foreign professors flocked into Cashmere, but they were no more successful than the local physicians.

The prince, in the disguise of a doctor, was finally brought before the Sultan who led him to the room of the princess. The young man's heart beat fast for he knew immediately that her madness was feigned, and that it was love of him which had caused her to resort to such a trick. He told the Sultan that the princess's malady was not incurable, but that he must speak with her alone. Once he was with the princess, an expression of joy overspread her face, such as only comes when what we wish for most and expect the least suddenly happens to us.

Anisa stops, testing for consciousness. The kelauntar opens his eyes, takes a deep puff of the kalyan, and hoarsely complains: "Don't stop now." As she continues, he closes his eyes.

The prince returned to the Sultan. "Sire," he said, "during her voyage on an enchanted horse, a portion of its enchantment has

> *contaminated her and can only be dissipated by certain per-*
> *fumes of which I possess the secret. Command the horse to be*
> *brought into the square outside the palace and leave the rest to*
> *me. In a few moments you shall see the princess as sane as ever*
> *she was. To make the spectacle as impressive as possible, I sug-*
> *gest that she be richly dressed and covered with the noblest jew-*
> *els of the crown." The Sultan agreed and the following morning*
> *he arranged for the horse to be brought into the great square of*
> *the palace. A large crowd began to gather.*

The leather tube falls from the kelauntar's lips. Anisa takes it in her hand but continues to speak, afraid that silence may awaken him again.

> *When all was ready, the Sultan took his place on a platform. The*
> *princess slowly approached the enchanted horse and mounted*
> *it. The prince placed around the horse some large braziers full*
> *of burning coals. Into each he threw a perfume.*

Anisa puts the tip of the leather tube in her mouth and sucks, inhaling the bitter opium smoke. And then she exhales slowly. The smoke fills the space between her and the kelauntar.

> *Soon there arose from the braziers a thick smoke which almost*
> *concealed both the horse and princess. Springing lightly up be-*
> *hind the lady, the prince leaned forward and turned the peg. As*
> *the horse darted up into the air, he cried aloud so that his words*
> *were heard by all present: "Sultan of Cashmere, when you wish*
> *to marry a princess, learn first to gain her consent." It was in*
> *this way that the prince rescued the princess... and returned*
> *with her to England.*

The kelauntar is unconscious. Anisa looks around the room. A dozen people are standing behind her—the kelauntar's other wives, the eunuchs from Zanzibar, the children—all of them with moist eyes.

"You must hurry now," says one of the wives. "Get Ali and go!" The wives, carrying Anisa' packed bags, escort Anisa to the birun. The kelauntar's fourth wife takes a lantern and heads for the roof to give the signal.

Omar can see the waving lantern above the walls of the kelauntar's compound. This is it! He turns and races from the mosque and enters the caravanserai. The caravan is assembled and waiting, but the men are asleep. Omar whistles loudly. The men stir slowly, begin to rise.

"Now! Now!" Omar beckons.

From one of the shabby traveler's rooms a tall woman emerges wearing a peasant's chador, the garment worn by Persian women outdoors. Fully veiled by the chador, she walks slowly and awkwardly down the steps into the courtyard and takes a seat on a mule. Omar approaches her and whispers something. Finally the men are at their mules, which stand patiently and fully burdened. The caravan spills out of the caravanserai as Omar hands each of the men—and the one woman—a lantern.

Anisa softly enters her son's sleeping chamber and approaches him. Her mind is spinning. *How will I explain to him why we must go away?* But as she is thinking, she sees Ali looking at her. He is awake! His piercing eyes cut through her.

"What is it, mother?"

She can't speak. All this planning, and now she has lost her voice!

"Does father know you're in the birun? He'll be angry."

"My darling son, there's something I have to tell you."

Ali's eyes begin to glisten with tears. "You're going away with Gordon, aren't you?"

Dear Allah, he thinks I'm abandoning him! Anisa reaches out and takes Ali in her arms, hugs him tightly. "I'm not leaving you, Ali. You and I are going away together."

"But I can't. I'm leaving for the madrisih next week."

"Please—I can't explain right now. But I promise that one day you will go to the finest school in the world. Listen to me now. I know this is frightening and hard to understand, but we must leave right now. There is very little time."

Ali narrows his eyes. "Are we in danger?" he asks.

Anisa hesitates for moment, then says, "Yes, we are in danger. Will you come?"

Ali looks up, studying her face. He can see fear in it. And doubt. And a mother's love. Ali looks around the room and sees two of the kelauntar's other wives staring at him.

"No, I want to stay here," Ali pleads. "I want to go to the madrisih. This isn't fair!"

"Ali—I am going to tell you the truth now. I hope you will believe me." Anisa grabs hold of Ali's arms as if to emphasize the importance of her next words. "Your father is going to divorce me and make me the vizier's wife tomorrow. I will be taken away without you. Do you understand? You will never see me again unless you come with me tonight."

The words stun the boy. But then he stiffens. "This is not true. You are my mother. Father would not separate us!"

"The vizier has given your father no choice. The bargain is already struck. Our only chance is to flee."

Ali's mind races. Leaving with his mother means he will never go to Mashhad. He will never see his father again. Or Jalal. It is too much to comprehend.

"If we flee, they will track us down. They will kill you!" Ali says.

"No. Gordon is helping us. He has a plan. Please, Ali… we must go now! We must place as much distance between us and the kelauntar as we can before dawn. It's our only chance."

Ali looks around the room. The others are nodding. What should he do? Is this incredible story true? Who does he choose to trust?

And then it occurs to him… yes, his father's sudden promise to send him to Mashhad. It came out of the blue. Out of guilt, perhaps. A payoff. Recompense for a future loss. It becomes clearer now. And as it does, Ali slumps onto his bed mat feeling the heavy weight of disappointment, the stabbing pain of betrayal. But sorrow quickly gives rise to anger. Only one course of action makes sense now.

Ali quickly stands up. "All right, I'll come with you."

He snatches up his Qu'ran then hurriedly begins to search for some personal things.

Anisa stops him. "No, just the Qu'ran. We have everything else you need."

This is another blow, another loss. Leaving everything behind. Everything! Can he really do this? Can he totally abandon his life?

"Ali!"

Yes, he can.

The kelauntar's second wife hands him a peasant chador. He eyes it suspiciously.

"You must wear it, Ali," she says. "They must think you are a girl if our plan is to work."

The boy's face flushes with embarrassment. The three women gather around him. Their warmth is comforting.

Giving him no to time to think, they slip the chador over his sleeping garments and push soft sandals toward him. Anisa also covers herself in a coarse chador.

"You must go now!" the second wife says, shoving them from the room and steering them into the garden. Struggling with the bags, the group slowly makes its way to the compound's rear entrance. It takes all of them to lift the heavy crossbar that secures the unused door. With a heave, the door opens, creaking loudly.

Outside the gate is nothing but blackness.

"Where are they?" Anisa says. She is suddenly afraid that something has gone wrong. "They were supposed to be here."

"It takes a little while to get here from the caravanserai," the third wife explains. "If Allah wishes you to succeed, he will guide them to your door."

For a moment they are quiet, listening. And then they hear the faint clop-clop of mules hooves. Anisa' heart pounds faster as the sound grows louder. She prays it is not the night patrol.

An orange glow appears around the corner of the compound's wall. Then another. Five, six, seven lanterns. More.

It is the caravan. Anisa tearfully embraces the other wives before they silently slip back into the compound, closing and bracing the door behind them.

Hidden beneath his chador, Ali feels both exhilarated by the adventure and humiliated by his costume. For the first time he is experiencing Persian life as a girl.

"Ali," his mother says, "do not say a word to anyone. Remember, you are disguised. Don't give it away."

The caravan stops at the compound's rear gate. The charvadar, Nasrullah, gestures to the tall woman seated on a mule behind him. The woman gets off her mule and walks to Anisa and Ali, approaching them closely.

"There are two mules beside mine, one for each of you," she whispers to Anisa.

Ali recognizes the tall woman's masculine voice.

"Gordon?" Ali says.

Anisa grabs Ali's arm and squeezes hard, reminding him not to speak.

The tall woman turns to Ali and nods "yes," she is Gordon.

Ali suddenly feels better about wearing the chador. Gordon has to wear one, too.

Gordon gestures for Nasrullah to get the women's bags packed on the spare mules. It is not unusual for a woman to remain silent when dealing with men, particularly men she does not know.

Nasrullah and four others begin to tie the bags onto mules as Anisa and Ali climb onto their animals. At last the job is done. The caravan starts up, making its way for the main gate of Bushruyih. The spray of lantern light and gentle percussion of hooves in the quiet night makes this an eerie but tranquil escape—except for the rapid beating of three hearts.

Within ten minutes the caravan approaches the main gate, which is closed. The gatekeeper blinks off the fog of sleep and stares at the caravan. It's unusual for a caravan to leave the city at this hour of the evening, but not unheard of.

"Where are you going?" he asks. Not an interrogation, just a question.

"To Mashhad. We prefer traveling in the cool of the evening."

"Well, you have a moon tonight."

The gatekeeper and four guards unbolt and open the large city gate, allowing the caravan to pass through into the desert.

Was it just this morning that Jalal and I were at the mulberry trees staring at the clouds? Ali wonders. *What will my friend do when he finds me gone?* The finality of his decision suddenly becomes more vivid, more real. With each plodding step of his mule, Ali feels his heart being torn from his body. He begins to weep. At first silently, glad that the chador conceals his tears, then loudly and uncontrollably.

Anisa steers her mule closer to his, reaches out and takes his hand. To the men in the caravan, this weeping is just a young girl's melancholy. The weaker sex.

Gordon is lost in thought. How he wishes they could gallop away on Arabian stallions at high speed, putting greater distance between themselves and the search party that the kelauntar surely will launch in the morning. But it is better this way. When the searchers inquire about an Englishman, no one will have seen him. A woman and a boy? No.

As planned, a mile from the Bushruyih gate, where the pale road splits north to Mashhad and south to Tabbas, the caravan turns south. The gatekeeper will say that the only travelers to leave the village were going to Mashhad.

But Gordon's course is set for Tabbas, then on to Kirman and finally Bushire, the port city on the Persian Gulf. In Bushire they will board a steamer and begin a civilized journey to Bombay, where Gordon will collect the belongings he had left at the missionary station there, and then travel on to England. His home. The home of Anisa's family.

Both he and Anisa are returning home at last.

Only Ali is leaving.

PART 2
LONDON 1825

CHAPTER 1

Standing on the rough deck, Ali can make out a dark scuff that mars the otherwise featureless fog into which the Prince Regent sails. From the pointing fingers of passengers all around him, and the excited cries of *England! England!*, he knows that his voyage is almost over. Dressed in English clothes purchased for him in Bombay, he looks like an English child with a tan. His mother stands behind him, her frail arms wrapped snugly around his chest to protect him from the damp air.

His stomach groans and cramps. Anxiety of the unknown. Another encounter with strangeness. *What is this gray streak that stains the horizon just ahead? Where is the sun?* He feels as if he is descending into the first level of hell. The other stops on this journey were temporary interruptions in the flow of his life, but he is told that London is to be his permanent home. Here he will likely spend the rest of his life. Ali looks around, astonished at the expressions of joy on many of the passengers.

Ali remembers the Bushruyih sun and heat, his proud Arabian stallion, the dry desert wind in his face, his friend Jalal. His heart swells with loneliness and regret. He has abandoned everything—his life and dreams, his father, even his God—and he has done so willingly, a full partner in the crime. Weeks ago his life had been filled with purpose. But now there is no madrisih in his future. Never will he be revered by the pious and called *mulla* or *mujtahid*. Praying to Allah will bring only scorn from those who love him.

On each previous day of this tiresome trip, as the mu'adhdhin had called to prayer the Muslims on board, Ali had felt pulled to prostrate himself, plead for forgiveness, offer his life as a sacrifice for the unfoldment of the great plan of Muhammad. But each time such thoughts had intruded, the prayer that tortured him would mercifully end, its faint echo would finally dissolve into the sea, and with it Ali's passion would fade, only to be replaced by feelings of guilt. *How could he harbor such an attachment to the Prophet?* After all, had not the Christians staked an earlier claim to God? Was not Muhammad an immoral and murderous power-monger who invented a counterfeit rival to the Christian God as false authority for his worldly aims?

Gordon's daily English lessons had fully burdened Ali with the sin of Adam, condemned him to eternal damnation, then washed him in the saving blood of Christ. Ali could neither wholly discard his previous beliefs nor completely accept these new teachings. For Ali, the absolutes of Christian and Islamic Truth eventually have merged into a new reality in which there are two deities, God and Allah, siblings who refuse to acknowledge each other. God is the older brother but has grown tired and feeble after leading his people into many battles over thousands of years. Allah possesses the strength and vigor of youth but lacks the authority of His firstborn brother. God is angry; Allah is strict. God loves the Jews; Allah loves the Arabs and Persians. Jesus was God disguised as a man; Muhammad was the Word of God—the Qu'ran—disguised as a man. Jesus died to save mankind; Muhammad lived to lead mankind.

For Ali, the main difference between those who favor God and those who follow Allah seems to be dietary. Christians drink blood and eat small uncooked pieces of God, calling it "communion"; Muslims neither eat God nor pork. Whichever menu one chooses, the final reward is heaven. God's heaven and Allah's heaven are the same place with different amenities. Muslim martyrs, at least the men, are promised seventy-two virgins upon arrival; Christian martyrs either are promised none, or—as Ali suspects—are just too embarrassed to talk about it.

Everyone seems to be expecting a Messiah to appear. According to Mulla Ibrahim, the *Qa'im* would be appearing very soon to renew the world. All Muslims are excited by the prospect. According to Gordon, who also seems very excited, Jesus had died but would be "coming again" very soon to renew the world. The Jews, Gordon said, were still awaiting the first Messiah but remained hopeful that he would come soon.

Perhaps all of these Messiahs are one! What sense could there be in so many "Promised Ones" appearing so near in time?

Anisa pulls Ali closer. They are surrounded by the staccato chant of seagulls. Ali looks for them but can only see shadows gliding through the mist. He peers ahead at the dark scuff now gaining form. Walls are rising up from the dismal sea. Black smoke from giant columns horizontally billows into the air, darkening the already dim sky. Made gauzy by the fog, everything appears shadowy and nightmarish. Rain begins to pelt Ali's forehead. A cold breeze makes him shiver. Surely they are entering the very pit of hell with the fire gone out.

The enormity of this place astonishes him. Compared to the flat, baked-mud houses of the port city of Bushire, the utter magnitude of man-made structure here is both breathtaking and terrifying. The ship moves inexorably toward the maw of this beast and it seems to Ali that the Prince Regent is being swallowed whole by London just as Jonah was inhaled greedily by the whale.

Through the fog Ali can see the busy signs of the port—moored barges rising with the tide, coasting traders wrinkling the water's black surface, Glasgow and Aberdeen steamers unloading goods, skiffs and wherries dancing nervously about like water bugs. And from everywhere the unintelligible curses of coal-whippers and scullers, the hammering and sawing of shipbuilders, the angry grunt and growl of pumps and engines and capstans.

The Prince Regent turns toward the wharf, dodging corroded chain-cables and clanging buoys and threadbare hawsers, then scattering a soggy flotilla of wood chips and splintered baskets before carving through rippling coal scum. Before long the ship pours out its passengers, a kaleidoscopic stream of turbans, fezzes, top hats, veils, robes of all colors and waistcoats and girdled gowns.

Exiting the customs-house, Ali's eyes are drawn to a horse-drawn coach with a tired mare and bent driver. The rain is coming down hard and the driver pulls his slouchy hat down further.

A woman's hand extends from the carriage window and gestures abruptly.

Ali looks up at Gordon, who waves back at the woman.

"It's her," Gordon says.

It's *who*? Ali is confused.

"I'm sure I won't remember her," Anisa says.

"Don't worry, she remembers you," Gordon says.

They slosh their way to the coach and the door magically opens, revealing a dark cavity. From outside, Ali cannot see anyone seated within. And then two firm hands grab him by the waist and hoist him through the doorway. Anisa climbs in beside him. Gordon speaks to the driver, explaining where to pick up the baggage, then pulls himself into the dry cabin with a grunt.

"London, just as I remember it." With a gloved hand, Gordon brushes a pond's worth of rain off his broad shoulders. Then, as if remembering his job, he turns to the woman seated next to him, an old woman who has captured the attention of Ali and Anisa. "Mrs. Chadwick, may I present to you Anisa, your granddaughter."

The old woman extends her hand toward Anisa.

"Oh my!" Anisa sighs. "I was not expecting... I did not think I would be so overcome with emotion." Anisa slowly reaches for the old woman's hand, taking it gently.

Ali detects a false note in his mother's tone, as if she had rehearsed this moment.

Mrs. Chadwick closes her bony fingers around the small white hand but remains silent.

Ali stares at this strange woman with a long, leathery face and a foamy spray of white hair that cushions a small dark hat. The woman's cadaverous skin and splotchy, stringy neck make her look dead, except for her eyes. There is a spark in those heavy-lidded eyes that betrays life inside.

"And this is Ali, your great grandson," Gordon continues.

Mrs. Chadwick releases Anisa's hand and turns to Ali. Yes, the spark is there, fanned now into a glow.

"So this is the boy," Mrs. Chadwick says.

Her voice is much lower than Ali had expected, raspy and labored. When she suddenly smiles, the shock of it forces Ali back into his seat. But there is something about the old woman's smile that warms him in the chill of the cabin. He resists looking into her eyes again, fearing that the glow might woo him. He is not ready to be seduced into a relationship with someone he does not know.

Mrs. Chadwick reaches out to him, both hands freckled with liver spots and knotted with arthritis. As her arms tremble from the effort, Ali looks up at her and sees tears. They do not quench the spark in her eyes, but fuel it, intensifying the genuineness of her offering, her hands.

He does not know what a great grandmother is, or why this withered old woman has touched him emotionally, but he is overtaken by an exquisite sensation of release. He takes her hands. They are not cold, as he expected, but warm and generous. Her thumbs stroke the backs of his hands, stirring the cauldron of his emotions. And then Ali notices that he, too, has tears in his eyes and a hot, crampy ball in his chest. Suddenly he weeps. He weeps for the loss of his father and his friend, the warm familiarity of home, the heat and dust and mothers and sisters; he mourns the evil he has done and the good he has not, his betrayal of Allah, praise be unto him, and the corruption of his future; he cries because he does not know where he is or where he is going.

Mrs. Chadwick leans forward and puts her arms around Ali's neck, presses her forehead against his. Ali feels as if his thoughts are now streaming directly into the old woman. And he awakens to new thoughts, perhaps hers, and they calm him. *There, there, the journey is done. You are with your family. Back where you belong.*

The old woman backs away now, plucks a lacy handkerchief from her velvet handbag, and dries the boy's eyes. "Ali, Ali," she says, trying the name out on her tongue with a hard accent on the last syllable. "I think you should have a proper English name, now that you're about to become a proper English gentleman. Oliver! Yes, Oliver."

Gordon looks at Ali. "Oliver it is, then. We will call you *Ollie*. Not such a change, after all."

"Ollie," Anisa says softly. This is taken as agreement, but for Anisa is something else entirely; it is acknowledgement of her sacrifice, for she knows that she has lost her son to England and Mrs. Chadwick.

CHAPTER 2

They arrive at Mrs. Chadwick's two-story mansion in Belgravia. The rain has finally abated. A doorman opens the coach, helping Mrs. Chadwick to exit first. She stumbles slightly and he steadies her.

"I've grown a little tired," she explains as the others step from the coach. "I'm going to nap for a while. Gibson will show you to your rooms. We'll have dinner promptly at eight."

Ollie's room overlooks a groomed lawn thinly forested with thick trees and ringed with a tall, clipped hedge. *So much green*, he thinks.

He inspects the furniture, opens all the drawers in an enormous rosewood chest, sits on the bed, trying to understand the need for all the clutter. Then he pulls the bedcovers onto the floor and lies down on them. Within seconds he is asleep, dreaming of Bushruyih, and does not awaken even when Gibson enters with his bags.

A knock on the door startles him. It is very dark. Confused, Ollie sits up and tries to reconstruct the past day to determine where he is. Another rap on the door, this one louder. And a disembodied voice: "Oliver, sir, dinner is served in the dining room."

Ollie manages a squeaky "Yes!"—an English word over which he has gained complete command. He stands and stretches. Moving to the window he can see that the clouds have disappeared. Now that his eyes have adjusted to the dark, the room is illuminated by streaks of moonlight.

The open door reveals a dark candle-lit hallway. Ollie can hear faint voices at the end of it. A number of other doors line this corridor and he touches them with his fingers as he walks toward the voices. At the end of the hallway is a spiral staircase that he recalls climbing on the way to his room. Now he descends, still following the voices, which grow louder and echo through the marble-floored vestibule on the main floor. He turns in the direction of the voices and enters a warmly-lit dining room with a long mahogany table and a dozen brocaded chairs. The table is temporary home to an immense crystal bowl filled with fruit, gleaming dishes and sparkling silverware, long-stemmed wine glasses filled with port, and five people. At the end is Mrs. Chadwick in a flowing white gown. Three rows of pearls are coiled around her neck and a gold bracelet hangs delicately from her wrist. Gordon sits at her left in a waistcoat and checkered vest.

Across from Gordon are two other gentlemen. The first is Reginald Pennick, an Anglican priest. He is a blustery balloon of a man of seventy or so with badly dyed hair, a bushy moustache, and a pompous air. To his right is the grinning Herbert Eaton, a pale and wiry contemporary of Gordon. Ollie's mother is absent.

"Ah, it's Ollie!" announces Gordon when he sees the boy appear in the doorway. "Come and sit, lad. Your mother will be present shortly." He pats the seat of the chair next to him. Reginald and Herbert rise as Ollie enters the room and silently takes his seat.

"Ollie, did you rest well?" Mrs. Chadwick asks.

"Yes, ma'am."

"You may call me great grandmamma."

"Yes, great... grand... mamma." Ollie's tongue stumbles over the word.

"Very good," Herbert says. "I understand you've only been speaking the mother tongue for a short time."

Ollie glances at Gordon for help. *Mother tongue?*

"He means the English language," Gordon explains.

Herbert laughs. "Yes, the mother tongue... English. Of course, for you the mother tongue is something else I suppose. Persian?"

"Farsi," Gordon interjects. "But Ollie also speaks Arabic, and his English is more proper than that of many Englishmen."

"Impressive," the rotund Reginald Pennick says, fingering his moustache. "And do you speak Latin, young man?" Gordon begins to insert a comment but Reginald holds up a beefy hand to stop him. "A multilingual lad like Ollie can speak for himself, I'm sure. What do you say, boy? Do you know Latin?"

Ollie looks at the old man for a moment then haltingly says, "I do not know this language... of which... you speak."

Reginald sits back in his chair, satisfied that the boy is no prodigy. "He has a rather odd accent, doesn't he?"

The remark cuts Ollie to the bone. He lacks confidence in English, and now his enunciation is also under attack. He vows to eradicate the Farsi from his English.

"My dear Mrs. Chadwick, if you are going to raise him to be a gentleman he must certainly learn Latin."

"My dear Mr. Pennick," the lady replies, "he most certainly will become a gentleman, and learn Latin, and many other things he has not had the privilege of studying in his native land. He has only been in England for five hours. I think we can allow him another day or two to master the lessons of a civilized world."

The small party laughs politely, all except Ollie.

Mrs. Chadwick notices the boy's sullen expression and addresses it with a wine glass. "I propose a toast to my great grandson, Oliver... *Chadwick*." Until now she hadn't considered the issue of a last name. "Oliver Chadwick, we are delighted to make your acquaintance."

Glasses clink, but before the guests can sip their wine an apparition appears in the doorway. Standing there is Anisa, clad in her finest Persian robe, face mysteriously veiled. "Dear God!" Herbert exclaims, astonished at the sight. Reginald stares, then remarks, "It's true, then. She was a harem girl."

With a sense of drama, Anisa glides to the table, first moving behind Herbert and Reginald, tantalizingly close, her garments brushing against the backs of their heads like a Persian breeze, then to Mrs. Chadwick, taking her hand and kissing it. "Grandmother," she says. A statement.

The two male guests are speechless as Anisa drops her veil. Never have they seen such a beautiful woman. "Gentlemen," she says, addressing Herbert and Reginald. "I apologize for my tardiness." The line is well-rehearsed but she delivers it well. The two men continue to stare, mouths agape.

Anisa proceeds to her chair next to Ollie. At last Herbert finds some words. "I would wager that you have some interesting tales to tell," he says to Anisa.

"I don't know if my tales would interest the English," she replies. "My missionary parents were murdered in Persia. I was captured as a child, taken to Bokhara where I became a slave to many men, and was finally purchased by a Persian prince for his harem."

Ali notices that his mother does not refer to the kelauntar as her husband and has elevated his status to *Persian prince*.

"I understand you were rescued by Mr. Cranston," Reginald says.

"The *gallant* Mr. Cranston," Anisa adds. "And now I am at home with my true family."

"I am certain *The Times* will be very interested in your story, Mrs....uh..." Herbert has stumbled headfirst into quagmire. *How should he refer to this woman? Was she ever officially married?*

"My Persian name was Anisa. My English name is Anne. You may call me Anne." She glances at Mrs. Chadwick for approval, but the old lady's eyes are on Ollie.

"Very good," Herbert replies. "If I may be so bold, Anne, as to suggest myself as a most capable interviewer and writer of articles for that esteemed newspaper. I believe your story will captivate the nation."

Ollie understands the purpose of this dinner. It is not a family occasion. It is business. London is not so different from Bushruyih, except that here the women are unveiled and speak openly to men.

"Perhaps later we can arrange a time for the interview," Gordon suggests.

Mrs. Chadwick claps her hands loudly and shouts, "Clare, our dinner please." Two English servants immediately enter with trays of food.

Over a dinner of pheasant and squash, Gordon peppers Reginald and Herbert with questions about happenings in England since he had left the country eighteen months earlier. An astonishing flow of chatter, incomprehensible to Ollie, pours across the table, marinating the platters of food with news about attempted reforms at Oxford, accusations of new developer intrusions in Kensington, gossip about the monarchy, complaints about the state of politics, and boasting about the growth and widening influence of Reginald's parish. Gordon hungrily devours each morsel of news while Anne tries to look interested.

Ollie picks at his food. The pheasant is good but he longs for lamb kebab and rice. To keep entertained he tries to pluck familiar English words from the unceasing surge of the unfamiliar and then repeat each word in his mind, over and over, *thinking* the odd shape of its sound exactly the way it had been pronounced.

After dinner, Mrs. Chadwick suggests they retire to the drawing room. The men all pat themselves on their bellies to express their satisfaction with the meal, then compliment their hostess as if she had cooked dinner herself. Herbert joins Gordon and Anne for the short walk to the drawing room. Mrs. Chadwick takes Reginald's arm as they follow. Ollie trails them all. He cannot hear the quiet conversation between Mrs. Chadwick and the Anglican priest.

"Reginald, I need a favor," Mrs. Chadwick says. "I want Oliver at the Charterhouse."

"My dear lady," Reginald responds, "Charterhouse is certainly a fine school. I am most aware that your late husband graced that institution with his presence at one time. But its reputation, how should I put it... has been suffering of late. The students are mainly lower- and middle-class riff raff these days. Let me make arrangements for a tutor instead."

"My husband had a great affection for Charterhouse, Reginald. And if I may point out, our son, Augustus, also attended Charterhouse. My husband believed that English gentlemen could not be reared in the drawing rooms of the upper class. Can you make the arrangements?"

Reginald smiles. "So this delightful feast was a bribe, then."

Mrs. Chadwick looks at him slyly. "Exactly."

"Then I will do my best, Emily. And may I say the plum sauce was magnificent."

They have reached the drawing room. From an ornate sterling tray, Gibson serves small glasses of sherry. Gordon and Anne sit next to each other on an overstuffed sofa. Ollie sits at his mother's feet, more comfortable on the floor. Mrs. Chadwick offers Ollie large round chocolates from a ceramic bowl and he takes one but is not sure what to do with it.

"Go ahead, eat it!" Mrs. Chadwick says, smiling.

Ollie tentatively takes a bite and likes what he tastes.

"Mrs. Chadwick, I can't recall ever hearing how your son ended up in Persia?" Herbert, the newspaperman, is holding the sherry glass just under his lips as he speaks. And then it occurs to him what an unfortunate choice of words he has made. *Ended up* in Persia? Perhaps the old woman will ignore his words and...

"He *ended up* dead, Mr. Eaton," the old woman says flatly. Herbert gulps the remainder of his sherry and abruptly sets down the glass as Gordon tries to smooth over the awkward patch.

"I believe he meant..."

"I know what he meant," Mrs. Chadwick continues. "He meant 'what was he doing in Persia?' Well, Mr. Eaton, my son Augustus was a brilliant man who was wholly dedicated to God. What caused him to leave the Anglican church and join the Presbyterians we will never know, but he served the same God as you and I, you can be assured of that.

"After his ordination, he was assigned as minister to a small Presbyterian church near Devonshire where he met and married a fine, upstanding young woman named Elizabeth. They had one child, a daughter they named Anne. But Augustus was not content to serve God in a country church. He petitioned for permission to undertake missionary work in India.

"When they left England, Anne was six years old. While serving in Bombay, Augustus met a trader from Isfahan, Persia, who had learned English in Bombay. The trader filled my son's head with stories about the exotic land of Persia. This was a land in which the Good News of Christ had not been heard. It must have been an irresistible lure for my son. At any rate, he packed up his little family and went to Persia. Three months later I received a letter that he had sent from Bombay. I imagine he was already dead by that time, but we had no way of knowing."

Ollie finds that he can comprehend a great deal of what Mrs. Chadwick says. He understands that this story is about his grandparents, Augustus and Elizabeth Chadwick. But he feels nothing for these people. It is far less interesting than listening to a tale from *The Arabian Nights*.

Mrs. Chadwick stands and walks to a wooden mantle, lifting two small paintings in gilded frames. She stares at them for a moment, hands trembling slightly, and then offers them to Herbert who looks at the faces and passes them on.

"This is a portrait of my son," Mrs. Chadwick says, referring to a handsome, dark-eyed young man who bears a striking resemblance to Ollie. Each person in turn, upon seeing the portrait, glances at the child on the floor to confirm the uncanny likeness.

"And the other one, of course, is Anne's mother," Mrs. Chadwick continues. Young Elizabeth is a plain woman with a nose slightly too large for her face—attractive nevertheless, but with little of Anne's smoldering beauty. "God knows how they died."

"I know," Anne interjects. "I was only seven, but I will never forget. Several weeks after our ship landed at a large port in Persia we joined a caravan. Where we were headed I do not know. I remember that one day we were slowly walking across a large desert when I heard shouting and yelling. The people in the caravan grew very frightened. They tried to form a circle with their animals. The men took out their muskets and started shooting. And then I saw the Turkoman. They were like demons descending on us! I was very afraid. In all the confusion I started running. Suddenly I found myself outside the circle.

"My father noticed that I was missing. I could hear him screaming my name. But I couldn't see him. And then I turned and saw him running toward me. A man on horseback came between us. He raised a big, curved sword and swung it... cutting off my father's head."

Mrs. Chadwick gasps. Anne starts to weep, then says, "I'm so sorry. Forgive me." Anne's earlier displays of emotion had been forced and artificial, but this time Ollie senses genuine anguish. Gordon puts his arm around Anne's shoulders and pulls her close.

Ollie looks over at Mrs. Chadwick, who leans backward in her chair as if dead. Reginald is standing by her, holding her hand and offering a handkerchief. "What a barbaric thing for a child to witness!" he offers. "And for a mother to hear!"

Herbert is mesmerized. He leans forward and asks, "What about your mother?"

"Good God!" Reginald scolds. "Don't ask her to relive another moment of terror."

"It's all right," Anne says, calmer now. "It's been more than twenty years. I've just never... I've never told the story to anyone before except Gordon. After the Turkoman beheaded my father, he pulled me up onto the horse with him. I clawed him with my nails, but he just laughed. Another Turkoman reached down to grab my mother, who screamed and hit his legs with her fists. He tried to pull her up, too, but she fought back and fell to the ground. And then his horse rose up and came down on top of her. The horse started running and its hooves struck her again. That was the last I saw of my mother. They took me to Bokhara and sold me."

For a moment there is a deep silence. Ollie's mind is spinning. He has never heard this tale before. At last Anne looks at Mrs. Chadwick and says, "Perhaps this was not a good time."

Mrs. Chadwick takes a deep breath, dabs her teary eyes with Reginald's handkerchief, and says, "No, my dear, this was a good time to tell your story. For two decades I believed that I would *never* know what happened to my son. And then one day Gordon came calling."

Reginald sits down as Herbert stands. "So Gordon, my good fellow, how did you manage to find Anne in such a despicable place?"

"As you know, I am an Evangelical. Like Augustus, I traveled to Bombay to begin missionary work. While there I became acquainted with some Presbyterians—dedicated people, I must say, although not of my particular religious persuasion. They told me about Augustus and his family, who had left for Persia two decades earlier and had never been heard of again.

"I must admit, the mystery of it intrigued me, and I became interested in Persia. There was so little known about it. And to my way of thinking, there were countless souls there for converting. I could have the whole land virtually to myself. Within two years, while performing medical and spiritual healing among the Hindus, I became relatively fluent in Farsi, taught by a Persian expatriate who had moved to India.

"Finally I began the first of several missions to Persia. I quickly learned that the Muslims—the followers of Muhammad—took a very dim view of Christians attempting to convert their own. If a Muslim changes religions, he can be put to death for apostasy. The one who entices him to convert can also be executed.

"During my wanderings, I arrived in a hamlet called Bushruyih and called upon the mayor to pay my respects. The mayor and I talked for about an hour and then, quite unexpectedly, he told me that one of the slaves in his harem claimed that she could speak some English words. Now if the mayor had been a strict Muslim, he never would have escorted me to the anderun where the women were kept. Fortunately for all of us, the mayor was not a deeply religious man. In fact, he was a nephew of the shah, and so part of the secular order."

"It would be quite some time before I would lay eyes on Anisa's face because of the obligatory veil. But when the mayor introduced us, I can remember saying to her, "Good morning," and being quite startled when Anisa responded by saying, "Good afternoon." She was correct, of course, as it was half-past noon.

"Anisa implored the mayor to engage me as her English tutor. I believe he found the novelty of this idea quite amusing. And he probably found me quite innocuous. At any rate, I began to teach English to Anisa—Anne—and then to her son. I stayed in Bushruyih for about one month. But I had other obligations, so I had to leave and did not return for another three months.

"During our separation, I began to put the pieces together. An English-speaking slave girl, the mystery of the vanished missionaries two decades earlier—well, you see where this was leading me. On my next visit to Bushruyih, I was once again engaged as Anisa's tutor. But this time I prevailed upon her to recall her early years. And I discovered that her parents indeed were the fabled Chadwick missionaries. I can't begin to tell you how excited and terrified I was. Here was a child, an English citizen, held against her will in a foreign land and now grown up. An English child who had survived misadventures and cruelties beyond imagination.

"It became my mission to return Anne to her family in England. When I proposed this to her, she immediately seized upon the idea and we hatched a plot to escape. But my time in Persia was too short and my financial resources too depleted to implement the plan at that time.

"One of my remaining obligations was to return to England for a speaking engagement—a fund-raising tour, actually, for our missionary work. So within several months I found myself in London. I looked up Mrs. Chadwick and told her the story. She contributed a generous sum of money to our cause, which allowed me to shorten my tour and return to Persia. I landed there six months ago, and here we are today."

Mrs. Chadwick suddenly stands straight up and says, "I know this may appear rude, but I have grown very weary. If you don't mind, I'm going to retire. Gibson?"

The entire group stands. Gibson enters and takes Mrs. Chadwick by the arm, leading her out the door and into the shadows.

Herbert turns to Gordon and Anne. "Well, I say, this has been a most gripping evening, but I think I'll shove off as well. May I call you for another conversation? I would like to hear more of the details for the article in *The Times*."

"As you wish," Gordon replies.

Reginald pats Gordon on the shoulder. "An Evangelical, eh? My, my." He staggers out the door without another word.

Ollie is staring at a large oil painting, a portrait of a stern-faced man with brows like a thick hedge, eyes with droopy lids, and pouting lips.

"That is Mr. Chadwick," Herbert explains. "Edward Chadwick, your great grandfather. He was one of the owners of *The Times*. Very powerful, influential... and wealthy. Not a bad family to be born into, my boy. You've done well."

CHAPTER 3

For Ollie, the next several weeks are a tumultuous blur of English elocution sessions, shopping trips to acquire the proper apparel for an English school boy, lessons in etiquette and money counting, evening dinner parties, and tours of London and environs. A series of newspaper articles catapults the story of Anne and Oliver into the public's consciousness.

In *The Times*, drawings of mother, son and rescuer accompany a long article under the headline: ENGLISH HAREM GIRL AND SON RESCUED BY MISSIONARY FROM ENSLAVEMENT IN PERSIA. The *Manchester Guardian and British Volunteer* writes: LONDON PUBLISHING HEIRESS FOUND ALIVE IN PERSIAN HAREM. And *The Observer* announces to its Sunday readership: ENGLISH SLAVE GIRL BROUGHT HOME FROM PERSIA.

Anne and Oliver are the talk of society.

Except for the parties, at which he and Anne are usually the evening's curiosity, Ollie finds himself cut off from his mother. She, too, has been caught up in a whirlwind of activities: interviews with newspapermen, endless speaking engagements at churches and libraries, fund-raising events for the Evangelicals. Despite her tightly packed schedule, Anne seems to thrive on the attention.

Gordon has received a handsome advance from a London publishing house, George C. Boothby & Sons, to submit a manuscript detailing his Persian adventures and the rescue of Anne Chadwick. And he has announced plans to marry Anne.

Ollie is defended from the ferocity of public intrusion by his great-grandmother who personally attends to the boy when he is at home. He finds himself basted with her love and basking in her luxurious favor. The hollow space in Ollie's soul once occupied by his mother has been generously filled by Mrs. Chadwick. At her urging he has begun to call her *Mum*, an endearment he is fond of because it is so much easier for his Farsi tongue than *great-grand-mother*. In his mouth the word *Mum* becomes a hymn of praise, a mantra, a plea, a gossamer thread that binds him to this knobby, wrinkled old woman who makes him feel so warm and happy. The word embodies a power, like the word *Qa'im*, which penetrates vast mysteries and reveals unfolding layers of meaning. *Mum!* The sound of it makes him feel at home and brings a smile to the parched lips of Mrs. Chadwick.

In Ollie's evolving notion of spiritual truth, the two deities of God and Allah both demand worship and prayer. Ollie has solved this dilemma by viewing the five daily prayers of Islam as five individual opportunities for prayer. And so at dawn, when the *mu'adhdhin* of habit awakens him, he prostrates himself for his well-practiced conversation with Allah. The next three prayers are offered to God in the posture of Christianity, on his knees with hands folded. The evening prayer is once again presented to Allah in the attitude of complete submission.

On one particular damp night, Mrs. Chadwick enters Ollie's room to find him prostrate on the floor chanting undecipherable words. She gasps, and the intake of air startles Ollie. He arches his back and looks under one arm, seeing Mrs. Chadwick upside down in the doorway. Hurriedly, he chants the rest of his prayer to himself and then rolls over and sits up.

Mrs. Chadwick still has one hand over her mouth in astonishment. "Ollie, what are you doing?"

Ollie is quite sure that *Mum* will not approve of his praying to Allah, but he cannot bring himself to lie about something so sacred. He decides to tell the truth, even if only part of it. "I was praying," he says. Not at all untrue.

"Praying? But what words were you uttering? Certainly not English—or Latin."

"I was praying in Farsi," he says honestly. "Since I am more fluent in Farsi than English, perhaps my prayer will be better understood in that language." A valid premise. Who is to say?

Mrs. Chadwick wags her head and walks to the bed. She sits and pats the bedcovers with the palm of her hand, beckoning Ollie to join her there. Amusement shows through her oval eyes, which strain to mask it. Ollie climbs onto the bed and lies down on his back, bony knees pointed toward the ceiling.

Mrs. Chadwick places a hand on one of these knees, caressing it like a mother. "Ollie, I know this is confusing, but I want you to know that Christians do not have to lie on their bellies to pray."

"Is it wrong, then?"

"Well, I imagine that no posture could be considered incorrect if one is praying. But it is unnecessary to prostrate yourself, and in some quarters people may think that you are, what shall I say, promoting your piety."

Ollie does not know what piety means, but he says nothing.

"And another thing… God knows many languages. He is omniscient, after all. That means he knows everything, so to speak. So you do not have to pray in Farsi for God to understand you. Truth is, he understands English quite well but prefers Latin. Don't ask me why. Are you clear about these things?"

"Yes, Mum."

"Good. Then we have another issue to go over, something of great importance to you."

Ollie sits up and crosses his legs. Everything that Mum says is of great importance to him.

"Reginald Pennick paid me a visit this evening. You remember Reginald, don't you? The Anglican priest from St. Martin's."

"The fat one, yes."

Mrs. Chadwick's eyes glisten with delight at the boy's candor. "Yes. Mr. Pennick stopped by to deliver some wonderful news. We have received permission for you to attend school at the Charterhouse, a fine boarding school."

"A *boarding* school?"

"Yes, a boarding school, meaning that you will live there also. This is the best way for you to absorb the atmosphere of the school and get to know your fellow students and teachers."

Ollie is suddenly fearful. "But I want to stay here. With you, Mum. I don't want to leave home again. I can learn to pray the correct way."

"Oh, Ollie, this is not a punishment. I'm not sending you away because you prayed incorrectly. This is… a *reward*. You will learn so much there. And you will receive the finest religious instruction."

Ollie wants to register another complaint, but this school, this Charterhouse, is beginning to sound like the famous madrisih in Mashhad. Yes, had not his mother promised that he would soon attend the finest school? She must have meant the Charterhouse. *An English madrisih.* It must be a very good school if Mum were sending him there. And while he is quite certain he cannot become a mulla at the Charterhouse, perhaps he will become a great Christian priest.

His fear evaporates and excitement begins to surge, tempered only by the knowledge that his friend, Jalal, will not be there with him. "Then I am ready to go," he says.

Mrs. Chadwick, amazed at his sudden transformation, simply stares at him for a moment before saying, "Pardon me?"

"I accept your reward. I would like to go to the Charterhouse very much." He speaks with a sense of joy and throws his arms around Mrs. Chadwick as he says, "Thank you, Mum, thank you." He remembers the day that his father gave him permission to attend the madrisih. He has the same feeling now.

Mrs. Chadwick says, "You are very welcome, my son." She embraces him, wraps herself around him, absorbs him into herself, and the years melt away until she is holding Augustus in her arms again.

CHAPTER 4

The picnic had been dreamy. Ollie and his mother and Gordon had romped and played in the sun, cuddled in the cool grass, stuffed themselves with Clare's lunch of bread and cheese and haddock, sipped sweet tea, and then explored the park on foot. They had laughed at bad jokes, recalled stories of Persia, and had even shed a few tears over the memories of friends left behind. Ollie had never felt so safe and loved. His only regret, as he would recall in later years, was that Mum had not been invited. Then it would have been *perfect*. She would have seen that there was nothing to worry about.

As daylight had faded, ominous clouds had begun to stir on the fringes of the sky and a chill had clawed its way through Ollie's coat. The afternoon laughter and chatter had given way to silence as the carriage clattered down the rutted road to a dinner party at Walter Nettleship's home. They had not changed clothes—Gordon had said the party was "informal." But as their clothes had remained unchanged, the gay mood had altered considerably, perhaps due to fatigue or the return of more gloomy weather.

Ollie remembers these things as he sits in a small room stuffed with frayed furniture and the gaudy souvenirs of Walter Nettleship's missionary journeys. Nettleship and nine others, all unfamiliar to Ollie, have joined Anne and Gordon to celebrate Ollie's passage into formal English education.

Nettleship is a brittle stick of a man with trousers too tight and a fat, pasty face that seems squeezed out of a high collar. Dinner had been a buffet of tasteless sandwiches, dry fruit, and flat pastries that crumbled before you could put them into your mouth.

Ollie is glad that dinner is over, but feels claustrophobic as the group gathers in a circle around him.

"So young master Chadwick," Nettleship says, "I understand that you have been a Christian for only a short while."

Ollie looks at his mother, who avoids his eyes, then turns to Gordon who is looking at a chip in the wooden floor. "Yes, sir," Ollie says.

"I wonder if you fully understand what it means to be a Christian."

Ollie feels his blood begin to stir. He knows that he is being challenged, but he does not know why. Still, he had stood up to Mulla Ibrahim in debate, and he remembers Jalal's courageous defense of the Shaykhi at the caravan-serai, so he stiffens in his chair and speaks up: "As you said, Mr. Nettleship, I have only been a Christian for a short time, so I am certain that I do not fully understand what it means to be a Christian. I hope that my education at the Charterhouse will teach me to be both an English gentleman and a Christian."

The group murmurs approvingly. In their experience, it is rare for a twelve-year-old to address adults in such an articulate and forceful manner. Walter Nettleship smiles and says, "Well said, young man. I had expected more of an accent, but your elocution is quite good. My compliments to your tutor."

"Thank you," Gordon says.

"However, your expectation that the Charterhouse will teach you how to be a Christian is misguided. You see, the Charterhouse propagates a High-Church brand of religion that has very little to do with being a Christian."

Ollie is confused by this statement, but then he begins to understand. This man, Nettleship, must be the *mujtahid* of the Evangelicals. He speaks with great authority. And the *High-Church* must be a kind of heresy, like the Shaykhi movement, that threatens the pure ideals and teachings of the Evangelicals.

Nettleship turns to Gordon. In a deep baritone he commands the handsome missionary to speak. "Gordon, have you taught this young man about the sinfulness of human nature?"

Ollie does not like this man, Nettleship, and he does not like the way that Nettleship puts Gordon on the spot in front of the others, so he interrupts: "I know about sin. I know that all men are sinful. If you want to know what I have learned, then please ask *me*."

"So you know that all men and women are basically sinful creatures, sinful from the day they are born, rotten to the core with sin. And you must know, then, that each human being has inherited the sins of his father, and his father's father, all the way back to Adam, the first man. And you must also know that your soul, Oliver Chadwick, is putrid with sin, encrusted with it, oozing the venom of Satan. Everyone here knows that you have grievously sinned."

The room is silent. Everyone looks at Ollie. The blood rushes from the boy's head and his stomach begins to cramp as he suffers under the gaze of the Evangelicals. His father had done many bad things, this he knows. But Ollie cannot understand how he, the son, can be blamed for them. Thinking back, however—yes, he can remember his own sins. He had tried to kick Jalal, betrayed the Shaykhi, coveted a position at the madrisih in Mashhad. His mind had wandered during prayers. He had been prideful and selfish, disrespectful to his parents, less than completely honest with Mum.

So it is true, then. He is a deeply sinful creature who deeply deserves the scorn of the others.

"I can see that you agree, Oliver. Now the question is, do you know who has lived *without* sin?"

Ollie knows this. Perhaps this is his redemption. "Yes," he says quietly but bravely. "Jesus was without sin."

Nettleship gives Gordon a congratulatory glance for his tutelage.

"And the Prophet Muhammad, praise be unto Him." Ollie adds. He had promised Mum to be truthful to his heart.

Nettleson turns back to Ollie, startled, but before he can speak Ollie adds: "And the Imam Ali, who was the *perfect man*." Anne and Gordon stare at Ollie, astonished at his statements.

"That's enough blasphemy!" Nettleship roars. The resonant blast sends Ollie back into his chair. "Your head has been filled with satanic fantasies."

Gordon speaks up: "Walter, I have been teaching him for months. He knows that Jesus Christ is the Son of God and the only one who has lived without sin. I don't understand…"

"The boy has heard you, Gordon," Nettleship says, "but Satan is strong within him, whispering lies and insulating him from the saving power of Jesus Christ. God knows the evil climate in which this child was reared. Heresy and heathenism, immorality and whoring within his very home, wickedness and blasphemy of every kind. The child was plucked from the bowels of hell on earth. Did you expect that the demons in him would faint away upon hearing your words?"

Ollie knows that Nettleship is referring to Persia and his life there, but he cannot relate to these words. London had seemed more like hell than Bushruyih. And he was quite certain there were no demons inside him. *Wouldn't he know?* Still, he believed in demons and jinns and evil eyes, so maybe…

"Oliver, I want you to listen to me very carefully," Nettleship says, pressing his doughy face close to Ollie's. "Are you listening?" He pauses. "You are doomed to hell, my child. And there is only one thing that can save you from eternal damnation. The atoning blood of Jesus Christ, who died and rose again that you, Oliver Chadwick, might have eternal life and be spared the unending torment of hellfire and brimstone."

Anne suddenly breaks into tears. She is afraid for her son's soul. *Please God*, she prays, *help Ali to accept your Son and denounce the false gods of Islam.*

Nettleship continues. "We are here tonight, Oliver, because God has a plan for your life, but we have only this one evening to help you understand how Jesus can save you and help you follow that plan. Yes, I said *God*, not Allah or any other false god that Satan has concocted to deceive you. And I said Jesus, not Muhammad or any other anti-Christ that Satan has invented to lead you astray. The path of Muhammad is a shortcut to hell!"

Ollie is hyperventilating. Could it be true? *Yes, it could be!*

Nettleship leans forward and cradles Ollie's face in his hands. His angry roar now becomes a personal plea, heartfelt and tearful, a song of salvation. "Ollie, I don't want you to burn in the fires of hell. But your sins are so great that they are like heavy weights tied to your soul. Your belief in Muhammad is the greatest sin of all, because if Muhammad is in your life and your heart there is no room for Jesus Christ, and Jesus is the only one who can remove your sins and help you soar into the heavens, free of your burden, saved at last and forever from your bondage to Satan, protected from his claim on you."

Nettleship motions for the others to gather around Ollie. The bodies push in and hands reach out to touch him like the tentacles of a great beast. The weight of so many hands is like the weight of a mountain and he feels as though he is being buried alive. He gasps for breath. Could it be that he is a container for Satan and his demons? How could Ollie have thought that *he*, one of the greatest sinners of all, was the Promised One? This, perhaps, was his greatest sin!

Nettleship's soothing, pleading voice continues to wrap Ollie in hope. "The Bible is God's incorruptible, infallible Word of God, my son, and the Bible says that man cannot serve two masters. My dear boy, you cannot serve both Jesus and Muhammad, you cannot serve both God and Satan. You must make a choice. If you do not choose tonight, we may not be able to help you, because tomorrow you enter another hell, a school that will deceive you in many new ways, and you may be lost forever."

Ollie's face is flushed and his body trembles. The scorching heat of his guilt sears his heart. Had everyone in his past lied to him? About Muhammad and Ali and the Promised One and the path to heaven and the Qu'ran...?

"There is but one choice, Ollie. Accept Jesus as your savior. Reach out to him. Accept him as your only master and guide. Renounce Satan and his minions, Muhammad and his book of lies. Ask Jesus to forgive your sins and he will do it. He will take them and fling them into the fiery pit, throw them into the face of Satan himself. And you will be free. Will you do this, Ollie? Will you ask Jesus?"

Ollie shakes violently. His body aches with guilt. He is so afraid. So confused He will do anything to remove this terrible pain. To end this torment. "Yes," he says. "Yes, yes."

Then say the words, Ollie, say these words: "Jesus, come into my heart and forgive my sins."

Ollie sobs. "Jesus, come into my heart and forgive my sins."

"I accept you as the Son of God and the Lord of my life."

Beneath the layer of hands, Ollie reaches inside his shirt. "I accept you as the Son of God and the Lord of my life."

Nettleship looks up at the ceiling, perhaps seeing God there, and says, "I renounce Satan and his hold on me, and all other false gods and prophets."

"I renounce Satan and his hold on me," Ollie repeats, "and all other false gods and prophets." Inside his shirt he tenderly caresses the silver tubular charm that hangs from his necklace. It contains a verse from the Qu'ran: *And those who put away false gods lest they should worship them and turn to Allah in repentance, for them there are glad tidings.*

With a sigh, Nettleship says, "In Jesus name, Amen!"

The many hands all lift heavenward with a chorus of *Amens*, and Ollie breathes deeply, saved from suffocation.

Silently, Anne thanks God for her son's salvation while Gordon weeps for his own sins.

CHAPTER 5

The man is smaller than he had expected. The long caravan journey to Karbala had magnified Kujiri's imagined picture of the Shaykhi leader into a shimmering, larger-than-life mirage, and now the human scale of Shaykh Ahmad seems to belie the man's station. *How can so much wisdom and knowledge be captured in such a small frame? Can this frail person truly be the legendary Shaykh Ahmad?*

Kujiri had arrived in Karbala three days earlier. After burying his wife and the others in a sprawling cemetery near the Tomb of Imam Husayn, he had inquired about the Shaykhi school. For many years it had been his fondest dream to meet Shaykh Ahmad and beseech him for enlightenment on various topics. Eventually, Kujiri had met a man named Siyyid Kazim, a disciple of Shaykh Ahmad, and was invited by him to attend a gathering of students. At that time he was not told the Shaykhi leader also would be present at the gathering or he may not have survived the excruciating anticipation of meeting face-to-face the object of his arduous quest.

The simple stone building had given Kujiri no hint of the personage—so venerated and reviled—hidden within its crumbling walls. Kujiri had entered with no sense of the moment except historical—that here, at some time in the past, the great man himself had been present. Siyyid Kazim had ushered him quietly into a large room that now echoes with the voices of at least twenty students, all sitting on the floor and facing a small, aged man seated on cushions.

"Who is the teacher?" Kujiri had asked Siyyid Kazim.

"He is the man you have come all this way to meet—Shaykh Ahmad."

And now the enormity of the occasion overwhelms Kujírí. He sits down for fear that he may otherwise collapse. This man, this small and unimposing creation of flesh and bone, is the holy man that Kujiri has traveled hundreds of miles to meet. The man whose ideas had almost cost Kujiri's life at the caravanserai. The man whose teachings had polarized Muslims and provoked charges of heresy.

Jalal is homesick. The long journey with his father from Bushruyih to the madrisih in Mashhad had been an adventure, but now the boy finds it difficult to think of anything but his family and friends. Especially one friend—Ali Qasim. The friend who had vanished.

He remembers the night that 'Abdu'llah, Jalal's father, had given him the precious sword. Jalal remembers how anxious he had been for morning to come so that he could carry this treasure to the kelauntar's compound and show it to his best friend. He had barely slept that evening. At dawn, after prayers, he had grabbed the sword, in its rich velvet wrap, and had been ready to race from the house with it when his mother had stopped him, smiling as she always did, understanding his excitement but insistent on performing her motherly duties. "Not without breakfast!" she had said. And so he had set down the sword to eat with his family.

After breakfast he had walked (so difficult not to *run*) to the main gate. As he had approached it, the massive gate had been flung open and at least twenty men, all of them nervous and staring straight ahead, had marched hurriedly from the compound, muskets raised and swords clattering at their sides, followed by an ashen-faced kelauntar.

"Jalal! Come here!" the kelauntar had ordered. And Jalal had run to the side of Ali's father, who seized his arm painfully with an expression of—what? Panic, perhaps. Fear. Anxiety. "You must tell me the truth or I will have your father tortured and exiled. Do you understand?"

"Did Ali tell you that he was planning to leave Bushruyih?"

"What? No! Never!"

"Tell me the truth! What did Ali say to you in the past several days about his mother and the missionary? Be honest, now! Were they all planning to leave Bushruyih together?"

"No. He never said anything about them. Why? Is Ali all right?"

The kelauntar had sighed deeply. For a moment Ali had thought that this pear-shaped man might deflate into an empty bag and blow away, but at last the sigh ended and a fierce, angry expression swept over the kelauntar.

"Ali and his mother have been kidnapped by the English missionary," the kelauntar had explained unconvincingly. *If this were true, why had he asked about Ali's plans, or his mother's?* "Come with me!"

The kelauntar had marched Jalal, accompanied by the angry musketeers, to the mosque where a terrible sight confronted the boy. In the courtyard, lying on his back, was Omar, the caravanserai gatekeeper. Two men had removed Omar's shoes and begun to lift Omar's legs, passing his feet through leather loops hanging from a long pole. Two others had then rotated the pole by its handles, and this action had turned Omar's soles upward, tightening the ankle loops so Omar could not writhe out of them. Jalal had heard about this torture, the *bastinado*, but his father had never permitted him to witness it.

Two floggers had approached Omar's feet with glances at the kelauntar, who had nodded his consent to begin. Hundreds of willow wands, each of them soaked in water to keep them from breaking too early, were piled next to the floggers. Plucking a wand from the pile, each flogger had begun to thrash the tender white soles of Omar's feet. Cries and curses had filled the courtyard.

After both wands had been broken on the bleeding feet, the kelauntar approached Omar saying, "We know you helped them. If you tell us where they are going, we will stop the bastinado."

"I don't know." These had been Omar's only words, at least as far as Jalal can remember.

The floggers had begun again with fresh sticks. More questions had been asked, more curses and screams had tortured Jalal's ears. Over a hundred wands had been broken before the kelauntar had mercifully ended the torment. By this time Omar had passed out. The deep and throbbing pain, temporarily relieved by unconsciousness, would return as he awakened. His feet would swell until the skin burst; infection would spread. For weeks the slightest movement or touch would send bolts of fiery pain throughout his body.

As Omar's feet were being freed from the restraints, the kelauntar had grabbed Jalal by the shoulders and issued another threat. "I'm warning you, if you do not tell me the truth your father will suffer the same fate as Omar! Confess what Ali told you. I know you boys—you share everything. Tell me now!"

He had shaken the boy so hard that Husayn had dropped his sword. The dazzling blade had glimmered in the sunshine, scattering particles of light in every direction.

The sword had seemed to mesmerize the kelauntar, calm him, speak to him in some mystical way. "I believe you," he finally had said, and then he had placed the sword gently into Jalal's hands. "Ali would have loved it." The anger seemed to have been replaced with melancholy, but only for a moment.

"What's this I hear about Anisa?" A loud voice, coming from the fat-jowled vizier, had startled them. Followed by his showy attendants, the vizier had strutted to the kelauntar. "I'm told that you have allowed my future wife to leave Bushruyih. If this is true, I would not place bets on your future!"

"It's untrue that I *allowed* her to leave. The truth is that she has been kidnapped. But I've now obtained information about where to find her." The kelauntar had gestured to the limp body of Omar and the vizier noted the dalandar's shredded, bleeding feet.

This is where Jalal had grown confused, the part that he now tries so hard to understand. Had the kelauntar given Ali's mother to the vizier to marry? And since Omar had not provided any information under torture, how could the kelauntar have known the location of Ali and Anisa? If the kelauntar had believed that Anisa planned to leave willingly, why did,he tell the vizier that she was kidnapped? And if this was a lie, would it not lead him into further trouble with the vizier, who clearly had struck some kind of bargain with the kelauntar?

"They have only been gone for a short time," the kelauntar had said to the vizier. "I suggest that you and your attendants accompany us as we go to find them. Twenty men are ready to leave as we speak. You may want to be there when we mete out justice to the English missionary."

The vizier clearly had relished the thought of torturing and killing this arrogant foreigner who had intruded on his happiness. "Yes," he had said, "we will accompany you."

"Good. They will not have traveled far. But we must leave immediately if we want to make it back by evening."

Yes, Jalal is very homesick, but not for the kelauntar and his strange behavior. He misses his family and Ali, of whom only a mystery remains, for as the kelauntar and his twenty men had returned to Bushruyih on the evening of Ali's disappearance, neither the boy nor Anisa were among them. The vizier and his attendants had also vanished. In the days that followed, before Jalal had left for Mashhad, rumors had circulated throughout the hamlet. It had been said that the kelauntar had caught up with the English missionary and killed him. That the vizier had taken Anisa with him and returned to Tabbas for their marriage. It had also been said that Ali had chosen to stay with his mother. For Jalal, the true story of his best friend's disappearance remains a mystery and he prays that one day he and Ali will meet again.

His eyelids sag with fatigue. While he has been indulging himself with memories, a half-hour has past. Precious time! There is so much studying to do. The pressures of the madrisih are intense and the students compete fiercely for the attention and praise of the instructors. Jalal glances across the dim room. On another mat, lit by candles, is a manuscript that holds the rapt attention of an older boy, Taqi, Jalal's fourteen-year-old roommate.

Since arriving at the madrisih with high expectations, Jalal has tried to see the bright side. But his experience here has been wrinkled with disappointments, stained with unanswered questions. He had hungered for spiritual fulfillment but had been given table scraps of musty dogma. He had wanted deeper understanding but had been chastised for his questions. Islam was ceasing to be that rare and wondrous mystery that invited exploration. It was becoming a tedious recitation of trivia and empty ritual.

He longs for the appearance of the Qa'im. He now understands the tremendous need for the Promised One Who will reinvigorate the slumbering spirit of Islam, empower the righteous, and purify the world with Truth.

Jalal does not want to study this evening. Instead, he craves the one thing that all the teachers and students and lectures and debates seem to deny him. Nearness to God. Just that. The clever arguments in the manuscripts will not help him achieve it. But one thing might.

He blows out the candles, and in the darkness he talks to God.

CHAPTER 6

Mr. Russell is in a bad mood. It is rare when he is not. His pipe-thin body marches down the corridor with the stiffness of an octogenarian, though Russell is not yet forty. Whiskers sprout like crabgrass all the way to his jaw line, making a bushy frame for a tightly pinched face that many say has not smiled in years. His spine is straight and rigid whether he is sitting, standing or walking, and this inflexibility seems a manifestation of his unyielding and officious attitude toward the boys in his charge. As headmaster of Charterhouse, he has declared himself *supreme ruler*. No offense is unreported, no infraction unpunished. For this reason, Dr. Russell strides resolutely toward the classroom on another splendid mission of juvenile correction. He swings a four-foot bamboo cane thick as his index finger, the instrument of choice for administering discipline. He has reserved the exclusive right of caning for himself.

In the hushed classroom, Ollie sits in a creaking chair, studiously analyzing the Latin words of the catechism. There is a pattern to these odd words, but he cannot quite make it out. The other boys seem to have been educated in this language, but no one had bothered to ask Ollie if he knew Latin.

The oddly warped door to the classroom opens and all eyes turn toward the disturbance. Mr. Peele, the instructor, swiftly stands up from his desk, accompanied by a chorus of gasps. Dr. Russell enters with a scowl and begins searching faces. Like a wildfire, terror races through the room as the stern headmaster, cloaked in a tight black suit, slowly and rhythmically slaps the cane against the palm of his left hand. For many of the boys, this stiff and terrifying man has become the picture conjured by the word *Satan*.

"Mr. Peele," Dr. Russell says, barely opening his mouth, "I understand we have a bed wetter in the room."

"Really, sir, I had no idea," Mr. Peele replies.

"Yes, it's true, I'm afraid." Dr. Russell begins pacing around the perimeter of the room. "The laundry told me just yesterday. They do not take kindly to bed wetters, and neither do I. This morning we inspected the beds of our students, and I am most happy to announce that we have discovered the identity of this undisciplined chap." He fiercely slaps the cane against his palm. "Would you like to know who it is?"

Ollie sinks slowly into his chair, trying to grow smaller. He knows that he is the prey of this monster. Since arriving at Charterhouse three weeks ago, he has sunk into despair and hopelessness. Two weeks ago the trouble had begun. One morning Ollie had dreamed that he was on the *Prince Regent* and suddenly had fallen overboard. The sea had surrounded him, pulled him deep into its bosom, and oddly he was not frightened but found it warm and restful, even peaceful. But then he had awakened, confused at finding himself in bed but still wet from the comforting sea. Sitting up, his arms and backside drenched, he finally determined the trouble. *How could this be? It had never happened before!* Yet the more he had tried to avoid the trouble, the worse it had gotten. He was always careful to cover his sheets in the morning. He had smuggled towels into bed to soak up the trouble. On laundry day he had bundled his sheets with many others so that no one could trace them back to his bed. But now he had been caught.

Worse than the pain of caning is the prospect of public humiliation. *Oliver the bed wetter.* Everyone will know.

"Can there be anything as repulsive as fouling one's own bed?" Dr. Russell asks, taking a step closer to Ollie. "I can imagine that such a boy has little self-respect, for he is soiling himself as well, and in the process, sullying the reputation of the Charterhouse. Don't you agree, Oliver Chadwick?" Dr. Russell is standing directly in front of Ollie, who trembles frightfully. The headmaster had seemed to dislike Ollie from the day he had arrived.

"Yes, sir." Ollie chokes out a croaking affirmation, knowing that he has agreed to the rightness of his coming punishment. *It must be God's will!* He lowers his head, submitting himself to the purifying cane. *Jesus, forgive me for my weakness. Muhammad, give me strength.*

Suddenly, Dr. Russell swivels and bends, grabbing another boy by the nape of the neck. The small boy yelps! Ollie raises his head and watches as tiny Edmund Phipps, his twelve-year-old roommate, is marched to the teacher's desk.

"Here is your bed wetter!" Dr. Russell announces to the room. "Wee Edmund Phipps wants to be a proper English gentleman. But before he can earn our respect, he must learn to respect himself by casting off this repulsive and repetitive act of self-loathing. Mr. Phipps, perhaps a caning will help you remember the lesson of this day. Drop your trousers!"

Little Edmund Phipps begins to howl in fear. His face puckers into a tight fist that squeezes out tears as he says, "I didn't do it... I didn't!" Dr. Russell turns the boy around to face the teacher's desk, and Edmund slowly, with shaking hands, unbuckles his belt and begins to lower his pants.

The other boys are now laughing, partly out of relief. They start to taunt Edmund Phipps with name-calling: "Bed wetter!" and "Wee Wee Edmund!" Ollie watches in horror. *What is happening?* Could it be that Edmund Phipps is also guilty? Or that just this morning he wet his bed, perhaps for the first time, and had the misfortune of getting caught? Maybe they had found Edmund's soiled bed and had stopped searching before finding Ollie's wet sheets.

Ollie watches as Edmund exposes his white buttocks and bends over the desk, sobbing and gurgling. He watches Dr. Russell raise the stiff cane and smack the boy with a startling crack. Edmund screams in pain, and for a moment this halts the laughter. A fiery welt blooms where the cane struck.

Ollie stares in horror. Watching this torture is worse than preparing for his own punishment. He is certain now that a terrible mistake has been made, that Edmund is innocent and he is guilty.

Dr. Russell raises the cane, but before he can strike Edmund again, Ollie cries out, "No!" The headmaster lowers the cane and turns to see Ollie standing.

"What is it, young man?" Dr. Russell says.

"It was not Edmund, sir. It was me. I am the bed wetter."

"I see. And you are not just trying to save your friend? We do not honor that kind of misguided deceit in this school."

"No, sir. I am certain the bed they found was mine, sir."

The headmaster turns to Edmund and says, "Well then, young man, you are off the hook, so to speak. Your roommate has just confessed to the crime."

Edmund, sniffling, raises himself from the desk and pulls up his trousers.

"Oliver Chadwick, if you would be so good as to step to the front of the room, please," Dr. Russell says. Ollie complies. As he reaches Mr. Peele's desk, he looks at Dr. Russell. Up close, the man does not look like Satan at all. He is just a man. And the cane is just a piece of bamboo. Let him whack away! Nothing he can do will be as painful as Ollie's forced separation from his loved ones. The image of Jalal comes into his mind, and the image calms him. It is almost as if his friend is communicating to him, telling him to be brave, to be proud for having done the right thing. He knows that is what Jalal would have told him.

Without being asked, Ollie unbuckles his belt, lowers his trousers and bends over the desk. The air is cool on his bare buttocks. He thinks of Bushruyih, the wind and the sand, the courtyard garden. He thinks of Mum's loving smile—she has not forgotten him, he is sure of it. He thinks of…

Smack! The searing pain blisters his consciousness. Unbelievable pain! But he does not make a sound.

"I would have given Edmund four," the headmaster explains. "But for failing to speak up before your innocent friend was caned, I will give you eight."

Whack! Eight, yes, eight will be fine. Eight will take Ollie back to the painful Bushruyih sunburn, the scorpion sting on his thigh, the fall onto sharp rocks. *Smack!* Eight will take Ollie back to the heartache of abandoning his father, the anguish of seeing the gloomy hellhole of London for the first time.

Crack!

CHAPTER 7

Awaking. Drenched with sweat. Gasping for air. The nightmare clings to him. Even as his eyes dart from wall to floor to sleeping mat, Jalal cannot shake the feeling that he has fallen from heaven and landed back in the madrisih.

Taqi, his roommate, watches him struggle for breath. "Are you all right?"

"No," Jalal replies. "I am without hope. I don't know how to escape this prison."

"You mean the school?"

"I am suffocating here. They give me no room to breathe."

"They are just trying to give us a pattern for thinking."

"No, Taqi, they are trying to get us to repeat *their* thoughts without thinking for ourselves."

"Is that so bad? Your thinking may be flawed."

"How would *they* know? They don't listen!"

"You believe they are wrong?"

"I believe they are giving us answers to questions that don't matter, and I believe they have forgotten the important questions."

Jalal remembers the Shaykhi—the old man named Kujiri—and the memory comforts him. He revisits that memorable day—the day he learned about the ideas of the Shaykhis and backed down Mulla Ibrahim in the caravanserai. And then he understands what he must do to escape. Somehow, he must find a Shaykhi in Mashhad. Such a person could be the antidote for the anesthesia of the madrisih.

Just then a large man enters the room, startling both of the boys. The man is about the same age as Jalal's father but wears a green turban, the symbol of a Siyyid—a direct descendent of the Prophet Muhammad. His face is long and lean with many creases like the rays of the sun emanating from each of his eyes. *Those eyes!* Jalal can see an inner light illuminating them—no, probably just his own imagination. The man smiles, and when he speaks his voice is soft and gentle. "Jalal?"

"Yes."

The man stands, uncoiling his frame, which is much larger than Jalal had imagined. "My name is Siyyid Mahmud of Mashhad. I have a message for you."

Jalal has been holding his breath. Now he lets it out. "From my father?" he asks expectantly.

"When I told the mullas I was delivering a message to you, they assumed it was from your father. I'm afraid I did not correct them."

"But—if the message is not from my father…"

"It is from someone you have not met but who knows of you. I was asked to deliver it in person to be certain that you received it." He hands a sealed envelope to Jalal who eagerly takes it.

"I do not recognize the seal," the boy says.

"It is the seal of Siyyid Kazim." Mahmud can see that the boy does not recognize this name so he explains. "For many years Siyyid Kazim was a disciple of Shaykh Ahmad. Now that the Shaykh has begun a Pilgrimage—perhaps his final journey—Kazim is in charge of the Shaykhi school in Karbala."

"And he knows of me? But how?"

Mahmud shrugs. "Perhaps the answer is in the message."

Jalal breaks open the seal and removes the message. Crouching by a candle, he reads it carefully and silently, except for one word that escapes his lips: "Kujiri!" When he is finished, he sits down as if stunned. After a few moments, he looks up at Siyyid Mahmud and says, "You are a Shaykhi."

"I am."

"Kazim and I have a mutual friend by the name of Kujiri, who is now serving as the school's gardener. He told Kazim about me, and now I've been invited to attend the school when I am finished with my studies here."

The boy furrows his brow.

"You are not pleased with the invitation?"

"I am not pleased with the madrisih. I wish I could go now."

"All in good time."

"The message also said that you might be willing to tutor me in the Shaykhi beliefs."

"That is up to you. But to be honest, I am no authority. Just a seeker of truth—like yourself. But there are other Shaykhis in Mashhad as well. Not many, but a few."

"Can we start now? There are so many questions that didn't occur to me when I was with Kujiri. The ideas were all so new."

"Then let's take a walk."

Jalal jumps to his feet. As the the two walk down the dark corridor they approach Mulla Jani, one of the instructors to whom Siyyid Mahmud had spoken earlier. The mulla turns to Jalal and says, "I hope the message brought you good news."

"Oh yes," Jalal replies. "Very good news."

CHAPTER 8

In the weeks that follow his caning, Ollie begins to fit into the rhythms of Charterhouse. He has made two good friends at school: William Threader, who has proven to be a patient, masterful tutor of Latin, and Charles Dickens, a bright boy with a wizardly English vocabulary that Ollie admires. The once-cheerless environment of Charterhouse is becoming quite comfortable—except for the hauntings of Dr. Russell. (Just yesterday the fearsome headmaster slammed a boy's head between two books until his nose bled; the particular crime was unclear.)

Now it is nearly Christmas, three months since Ollie arrived, and the once-opaque "society" of Charterhouse is no longer such an enigma. In fact, Ollie finds a certain messy orderliness to the way that allegiances and alliances are drawn. On this bright December morning, Ollie is awakened by the clanging house-bell at 6:45, dressed in ten minutes, and in Goodworthy's room brushing the Upper's gown before the second bell at 7:00. One minute before 7:30 he is in his place at Chapel; he has learned the hard way not to be late, for God apparently has ordained a harsh punishment for tardiness, ranging from an extra hour's recitation of the Catechism to copying the entire Iliad with a worn quill.

This morning a special guest, Reginald Pennick—the rotund cleric who had helped Ollie gain admittance to Charterhouse—leads the service. Many years ago, before multiple promotions within the church hierarchy, Reginald served a full-time post at the school. During prayers, Ollie sneaks a glance at this stuffed-sausage of a man but quickly closes his eyes when he sees Reginald staring at him. After Chapel, Reginald catches Ollie's eye with a discrete wave, beckoning him to stay for a minute.

"Oliver, my boy, it's so good to see you again," says Reginald, smiling broadly. Ollie notices that the man's teeth are crooked and yellow. "I don't think we've seen each other since dinner at your great grandmother's home, am I right?"

"That's right, sir."

"Son, you don't have to call me sir. We're family friends. Please call me Reginald."

"Very good, sir—I mean, *Reginald*." Ollie doesn't like using this familiar name with a man he scarcely knows. And he doesn't like being called *son*.

"Much better. I do hope things are going well for you here."

"Very well, yes."

"Excellent. You know, I had many happy years serving the boys here at Charterhouse. I miss it, I certainly do. That's why I've asked to come here and lead Chapel now and then."

"I hope this will make you happy."

"Oh yes, just being around the boys makes me feel—well, very *alive*. The spirit of youth!"

Ollie looks at his shoes, embarrassed that he can't think of anything to say.

"Oliver, I want you to know that I promised Emily—your great grand-mother—that I would look out for you."

"I'm doing quite well, really."

"Yes, I'm sure. But from time to time you may need someone to… to whom you can turn. I have been given a small office on the grounds, and while I won't be here every day, I want you to know that my door will always be open to you when I am at school. I want to protect you from any, shall we say *unfortunate consequences* of life in a boarding school."

"'Unfortunate consequences?' I'm not sure—"

"Let's just leave it at that for now. I want to be your protector, if that's all right with you." Reginald doesn't wait for Ollie to answer before he says: "In return, I would ask a favor of you."

"A favor—yes, certainly… of course."

"I am preparing a manuscript that I hope to have published next year on the meaning of the resurrection of Jesus Christ. As I am going over my work, I'm afraid I find it necessary to make numerous small changes, and this means I need my revisions incorporated into a new manuscript. Would you be willing to do this for me? I can certainly pay you something for your time."

"I'm not sure, actually—"

"It would make your great grandmother very proud to know that you are helping with such a worthy work. I'm sure you wouldn't want to disappoint both of us by refusing."

Ollie wants to refuse, but he can't find the words. Maybe he should agree. Certainly it would make Mum proud. Before he can answer, Reginald fills the silence. "Very good. I know that Christmas holiday begins tomorrow and you're anxious to go home. But I'd like you to stop by my office behind the Chapel this evening so I can better explain the scope of this project. I'd very much like you to be thinking about it during the holiday."

"I suppose so, yes—"

Reginald looks up and sees Mr. Tubbs, the butler of Ollie's House, in the Chapel doorway. The two exchange icy looks, and then Tubbs is gone.

The bell at 1:15 warns the sweaty school boys to wash up for dinner. Time has flown too quickly, and with each tick of the clock Ollie feels increasing dread about this evening's meeting with Reginald. The drudgery of copying pages of boring prose, the uneasiness he feels when he's in Reginald's presence—these things make Ollie nauseated. *Why such a strong reaction?* Maybe he should feel honored instead of unsettled! It is possible that Reginald Pennick's manuscript will be a great theological work, and Ollie can be a part of it. Now that would be *something*.

Lunch begins promptly at 1:30. Ollie cannot eat. He is too stirred up by his thoughts. He walks the entire grounds, thinking and praying, asking God's forgiveness for his selfishness and cynicism, dedicating himself to his new mission. The sense of foreboding that had surrounded the evening's meeting with Reginald has been replaced with anticipation. He now looks forward to studying the manuscript for its deep insight and wisdom, to inserting with his quill Reginald's most subtle purifications in a perfectly rendered manuscript.

Oliver Chadwick, the *Pen of God*!

At 7:30 Ollie runs to his room to change clothes. Fifteen minutes later he charges out of his room and down the stairs. He wants to walk slowly to Reginald's office so he won't be out of breath. A voice calls to him as he steps outside his residence, the Perry House.

"Ollie, a word please."

Ollie recognizes the voice of Mr. Tubbs, the beloved butler of the Perry House.

"Ollie, I'm wondering if we could have a private chat—very important, or I wouldn't suggest it."

"Well, I'm actually—"

"My missus is visiting her sister tonight, so it turns out my place is available. I have a pitcher of fresh lemonade."

"That's a very kind offer, I'm sure, but—"

"It's of a very personal nature, so I'd consider it a great favor if—"

"Really, Mr. Tubbs, I appreciate the invitation, but I have a meeting this evening—in ten minutes as a matter of fact."

"Are you seeing Reginald Pennick this evening?"

"Why, yes, I am." Ollie steps closer to Mr. Tubbs. "Reginald has asked me to be his personal assistant in preparing a manuscript for publication."

"He's *Reginald* to you now, is he?"

"He asked me to call him by a familiar name since we'll be working so closely. Does it sound disrespectful?"

"That's not the word I would use, no."

"I really have to go. I'll see you later this evening I'm sure."

Ollie wheels and begins to canter across the school grounds, hoping he won't be sweating and out of breath when he arrives.

Reginald opens the office door with a wide smile and the fragrance of wine on his breath. "My, you are punctual, aren't you," he says with a dramatic sweep of his hand and a childlike giggle. "I like that. Do come in."

Ollie follows Reginald into the small office which contains a mahogany desk, a leather-inlaid table with four chairs, and a plush royal blue sofa. "Go on, have a seat over here on the sofa. It's the most comfortable place."

Ollie sits and sinks into the soft cushions.

"Here, let me pour you a glass of wine," Reginald says, grasping a decanter. "It's good for the digestion after a big meal. You can certainly put away the food for a boy your size."

"You know what I had for supper?"

"I just happened to pass through the dining hall. Here, drink up."

Ollie studies the wine glass, takes a small sip. It tastes quite good! He takes another sip and Reginald tops it off.

"I find that wine stimulates my spirituality," Reginald says. "You grew up as a Muslim, is that right?"

"Yes."

"Did you know that Jesus turned water into wine? It's in the Bible."

"I've read it." Ollie lets more of the sweet-tasting wine glide down his throat. It doesn't burn like whiskey; it soothes.

"Ahh—then you must know that wine is a divine nectar," Reginald continues. "Here, have a little more—nurture your spirit and draw nearer to God." He pours more wine into Ollie's glass. "God wants you to be close to him. Do you have any idea how I know that?" Ollie nods no. "Because He made you so attractive. The Persian people have a certain... a certain beauty that is undeniable. Your mother is extraordinary, of course, you know that."

Ollie is listening, but he is confused. *What about the manuscript?*

Reginald picks up a sheaf of papers from the desk and walks to the sofa, easing his plump body onto the cushions next to Ollie. His weight tilts the cushions and Ollie finds himself falling downhill toward the cleric, touching him. Embarrassed at the physical contact, he attempts to adjust his body so that it does not touch the old man, but he can't.

"Oliver," Reginald says firmly, "I want you to understand something." He puts an arm around Ollie's shoulders and his hand becomes a hook that keeps Ollie from separating his body from Reginald. "I want you to understand that God works in mysterious ways, and that whatever happens in this room is between us and God. I believe that God has drawn us together for a reason. You are going to be a source of great inspiration and joy for me, and this will enable me to decipher God's message of the resurrection for the entire world to understand."

Ollie can't make any sense out of this conversation. The room, the walls, the desk—all begin to move. He can't think of anything else to do, so he stands up, his legs rubbery. "The manuscript—the book that you are writing. Can I see it?"

"Of course you can." Reginald smiles benignly and hands the sheaf of papers to Ollie who sets them on the table with the wine glass and sits down on one of the chairs.

"Go ahead, son. Read the manuscript." Reginald stands and pours more wine into Ollie's glass as the boy begins to read. A few minutes of silence pass. Ollie unconsciously sips the wine as if it were tea. The words, the concepts on these papers are so new to him, so... so strange and provocative. As Ollie reads, the words grow blurry and he squints to make them out, runs his fingers nervously through his hair, rubs his left arm to stop the tingling.

How is it possible, Ollie wonders, that this information was not known to others, that the secret code of New Testament symbolism never had been deciphered before. The revelations in these papers stun Ollie, shock him. Here he reads of a Jesus who loved men, and chose only men as Disciples so he could be near them, not just spiritually but physically. Here is a Jesus who shuns marriage and intimacy with women, and whose own father disappears from the record of His life because Joseph cannot bear the unconventional truth about his son. Here is a God who ordained only men as His Prophets and created women merely to propagate humankind. Ollie discovers a Jesus who was transparent to history until he was thirteen—Ollie's age—the age of sexual awakening, when He became aware of his special message to man-kind. In these pages the crucifixion horrifyingly symbolizes the rejection and murder of God's natural order for men and boys by a society that for thousands of years had rejected it. And His resurrection suggestively illustrates the re-awakening of God's plan, the rising up of Truth over prejudice.

The underlying Truth, as Reginald reveals, is that God always intended men to love men, and boys of thirteen are especially blessed when introduced into the holy stream of man's love. Physical intimacy between males is a Holy and Spiritual sacrament on the level of baptism or communion, but the Church for obvious political reasons has suppressed this essential message. The result has been a stunting of man-kind's spiritual development.

Ollie's eyes drink in these intoxicating, blasphemous ideas—and the intricate drawings illustrating the Messiah's intimacy with his Disciples. Disgusting and arousing. Sacred. Profane. Ollie finds himself spinning while seated, his brain blunted by the wine, his feet prickly, his face slick with sweat. Reginald gently puts his hands on Ollie's shoulders, feels the boy's heat rising.

"From the time I first saw you, Oliver, I knew why God had brought you into my life. Your purpose is to reawaken my soul so I can continue my spiritual journey, and my greatest desire is to show you a window into another world that you cannot even imagine exists." Reginald plunges his hand down Ollie's shirt, touches the smooth skin of his chest, and sighs. "The world is not ready for what we have to share. That is why we must keep it a secret—between us—until the world is capable of understanding."

Ollie is frozen in his chair. He can't think, can't move. *This is a man of God*, he thinks. *A man of great spiritual authority. A man who knows so much more than me.* But then he remembers Mulla Ibrahim in Bushruyih, a spiritual leader overtaken by blood lust, a teacher who could not defend his own arguments without help from his students, a cleric who had made up his own Truth out of convenience or self-deception or hunger for power. And then Ollie understands that Christianity must have its *Ibrahims* as well. If Ollie could stand up to Mulla Ibrahim, he can stand up to Reginald Pennick. The touch of this old man on his bare skin disgusts him—*this cannot be of God!* He will not allow this to happen!

Ollie shakily stands and turns to face Reginald, who misunderstands the boy's intentions and pulls Ollie towards him, smothering him with a kiss, his mouth dry as a mummy, breath stale and wine-sour. Ollie suddenly stuns the old man with a sharp elbow in the chest. In pain, Reginald loosens his grip. Ollie twists his body, crumples to the floor, escaping to the desk.

Reginald wheels angrily and pierces the boy with a barbed, red-eyed stare. "You disappoint me, Oliver," he says. "But it doesn't matter, because God has ordained that I be your savior. Jesus cast out demons—so will I."

"This is not right! I will tell—"

"You will not tell anyone!" roars Reginald. "Because if you tell, you will be expelled from Charterhouse and banned from any other school in London. You will be abandoned by the Church—and by God Himself. You will be without the protection of any religion. You have no idea of my influence. God speaks through me!"

"Ollie understands the threat, and he fears this large, powerful man. He decides that he can consider his strategy later; right now he must escape from this room. If he waits, it may be too late. With a great lurch, Ollie leaps past Reginald and lunges toward the door, but the cleric is surprisingly agile and catches the boy's arm. With one great sweeping move, Reginald slings the boy across the room onto the sofa and pounces on top of him. "You must submit, Oliver. You are possessed of demons! I do this for the good of your soul." With those words, Reginald begins fumbling with Ollie's belt buckle.

The loud knock on the door is like a slap in the face. Reginald halts, sits up panting, eyes wide and still as a dead man's. Another loud knock. And then a voice, Mr. Tubbs' powerful baritone: "Reginald, is Ollie in there? I have an urgent message for the boy."

Reginald claps a hand over Ollie's mouth, silencing him. A pause. Then a louder, more frantic knock. "Reginald, I know Ollie is in there. Open the door."

Reginald thinks for a moment, then whispers to Ollie, "If you say anything about this to anyone..." Ollie nods that he understands. Slowly, Reginald removes his hand from the boy's mouth. "All right, Samuel, we're coming. We were in the middle of prayers, give us a minute."

Ollie stands, quickly adjusts his clothing, combs his hair with his fingers and wipes the sweat off his face with a sleeve. Reginald straightens the sofa and walks to the door, opening it slowly, just a crack.

"What is it, Samuel? Something important enough to interrupt our prayers I hope," he says.

Mr. Tubbs tries to look through the small doorway opening. "Like I said, Reginald,"—the word *Reginald* is tinged with acrimony—"I have an urgent message for Mr. Chadwick. From his great grandmother."

"Well, hand it in and I'll give it to him."

"I don't have the message with me, Reginald. I was just sent to fetch the boy. Please send him out, it's urgent."

Ollie pushes his way through the opening. The chilled air feels refreshing. Even in the darkness, Mr. Tubbs can see the boy's flushed face and wrinkled shirt. "All right, Mr. Chadwick, let's go get your message," says Mr. Tubbs. "Good evening, Reginald. I'm sorry for interrupting your prayers."

"Is your pension secure, Samuel? I'd hate to see you without a pension in your later years, if you know what I mean."

"I do. Good night again."

Reginald closes the door quickly.

Ollie silently walks five paces ahead of Mr. Tubbs, who doesn't say a word. When they arrive back at the Perry house, Ollie stops at the door. For a minute, maybe longer, he just stands there facing the house, afraid to face Mr. Tubbs, not ready to enter the door. At last he turns, staring at the ground. Mr. Tubbs is still there.

"As I recall, in our earlier conversation you promised that we'd talk when you returned," Mr. Tubbs says. "Of course, if you're not up to it—"

"No, I want to talk."

"My place?"

"I'd rather, uh, stay outside, if you don't mind."

"Not at all. I don't blame you. How about the Green?"

Ollie nods yes.

On the Green, the moonlight is bright and the air has a cool bite. Ollie sits down, his back to a mulberry tree. Mulberries remind him of Bushruyih. Mr. Tubbs sits on the ground.

"You knew, didn't you?" says Ollie. "You wanted to warn me earlier."

"Yes."

"But you let me go there."

"I am not one to force my will onto others, unlike another party we both know. But in my defense, I must add that I was just outside the office the entire time."

"Then you know I tried to escape."

"I do."

"He's a monster."

"Has been for decades."

"You mean he's done this before?"

"Many times, I'm afraid. A man like that—he's very clever."

"He said he was writing a manuscript about the resurrection."

"He wrote that manuscript forty years ago. I doubt that he's changed a word of it since. Another boy many years ago told me about the vile lies it contains. I think Reginald originally wrote it as a simple tool of seduction, but over the years he started to believe it. He's over seventy, Ollie—old and lonely and desperate.

"And dangerous."

"Yes, that too. He's ruined many a boy's life. But one of them in particular, well—"

"Tell me."

"I'll try. One particular boy was here four decades ago when I had just arrived myself. I was only ten or maybe twelve years older, but this boy and I got along famously. What a lad he was! Bright, confident—intending to become a Priest. Would have made a good one, too."

"But then Reginald—"

"Corrupted him, yes. As with you, the boy was not a willing participant. At first, the boy fell under the wizard's spell, but shortly he came to his senses and realized what a grievous position he was in. Then Reginald threatened him. The boy *so desired* the Priesthood! And Reginald held that cherished dream in his hands, offering it as a reward, wielding it like a noose."

"What happened?"

"At long last, the boy abandoned his dream of becoming a Priest and left school. He became a Presbyterian minister." Mr. Tubbs stares at the boy, who digests this last bit of information. And then the full meaning of the story rushes through Ollie like a flooding river.

"Augustus?"

"Yes, your grandfather."

Ollie puts his head into his hands. He can't breathe, and then he can't stop gulping air. The wine, the abuse, the revelations—it's too much. Suddenly, he is trembling uncontrollably. *Too much!*

Mr. Tubbs reaches out, tenderly touches the boy—but Ollie twitches, pulls away fearfully. "It's all right, Ollie," says Mr. Tubbs.

Ollie looks at him, realizes that this butler, this friend, is not the monster Reginald Pennick. He slumps into the old man's arms.

He cries.

And so does Samuel Tubbs.

CHAPTER 9

Breakfast is a lazy, unorganized affair on this first day of Christmas holiday at Charterhouse. Ollie picks at his food. Many of the boys—those living further from the school—had departed for home the previous evening accompanied by smiling mothers and father, aunts and uncles. Bored, Ollie looks up and sees the shuffling form of Mr. Tubbs fast approaching.

"Mr. Chadwick, sir," says Mr. Tubbs excitedly when he nears the boy. "There is a carriage waiting."

So soon! Ollie had thought the carriage would arrive later. It is not so far to Mum's house. "Thank you, Mr. Tubbs," he says, giving the old man a hug. They exchange a long, knowing look, and then Mr. Tubbs says, "You'd better be off now."

Ollie breathlessly races to his room, retrieves one small bag and a wool coat, and darts back down the stairs to find the carriage empty except for the grizzled driver who greets him with a formal "Good day, sir."

"Good day."

"May I get your things, sir?"

"I've only this one bag." Ollie climbs into the carriage, disappointed that neither Mum nor Anne has chosen to make the short trip. Suddenly he realizes how profoundly lonely he has been these past several months.

"Try to make yourself comfortable, sir. It's a bit of a ride to Chillington-hall."

"But I thought I was going home!"

"You are, sir. The Hall at Chillington has been in your family for generations now. A fine manor-house it is, if I may say so. Are you ready, sir?"

Ollie is confused. He has never heard any mention of Chillington. "How far is it?" he asks.

"It will be evening when we get there, sir. Your family is already there. Shall we be off?"

"I want to ride up there with you." Ollie clambers up into the seat next to the driver.

The driver jerks the reins and the steaming horses lunge forward, as eager as the driver to be moving. Mr. Tubbs, watching from the Perry House, waves goodbye, but Ollie doesn't see him.

Once out of London proper, the carriage slowly bumps along the rutted roads, groaning like an old man with arthritis. Ollie watches the thick-bodied carriage-horses, frosty plumes rhythmically exhaled from their cavernous nostrils. He listens to the comforting *clop-clop* of the hooves, the gentle moaning of a breeze in the bare branches, the occasional curse of a sheepherder and the staccato bleats of his animals. Ollie's nose is cold; he vigorously rubs it. The once-blue sky has turned steely gray. Heavy clouds begin to tumble in the wind. *Clop-clop, clop-clop.* The cold sun is finally erased by clouds, and with its disappearance all color is sucked out of the landscape. A gray wilderness surrounds Ollie, and the chill penetrates to the bone. *Clop-clop.* The freezing wind makes his eyes water and carries to him the stench of Reginald Pennick's wine-sour breath. In the knotted burl of a passing oak tree Ollie sees the pompous-pudgy face of the old Priest—sneering, leering. *Clop-clop, clop-clop.* A finger of wind snakes down his collar, teasing his chest like the old man's cadaverous hand. Ollie pinches off the collar to thwart the assault, but it is too late. His heart has grown cold, his soul has turned to ice. The damage is done. He tries to pray for forgiveness but can't name his offense. *Jesus, are you listening? Muhammad, help me!* Only the faint howl of the wind replies, and he knows that God has abandoned him.

Clop-clop.

The driver mercifully stops at a roadhouse for lunch. Bread and cheese, a mug of ale. Ollie can't eat. Even the warmth of the fireplace cannot thaw Ollie's frozen heart.

Into the carriage again. "A few more hours," the driver says. Ollie stares upward at the glacial sky. A snowflake lands on his eyelash, making him blink. For hours he sits there, jostled by the lurching carriage, dusted with snow, eyes blankly staring at the road ahead. Suddenly a large hare bounds across the road, startling the horses. The carriage rattles. Ollie watches the hare bounce into a dark hollow beneath a fallen pine, and only then hears the angry shriek of an eagle and sees the predator's sinewy talons brush the top of the rotting limbs that guard its prey. A narrow escape.

The carriage drives past the drama and Ollie looks back. *Stay there,* Ollie silently commands the hare, *and be safe.* The eagle soars overhead, searching for another victim. The fortunate hare stays hidden. And for the first time today, Ollie smiles.

Rolling meadows blistered with groves of forest continue to unfold themselves as the carriage clatters onward. The gray winter light turns lavender, then blue, as the hidden sun begins to set. At last they reach the village of Chillington, a cluster of thatch-roofed cottages that line a silvery stream not yet skimmed with ice. The hamlet is cloistered in a majestic forest of ancient oaks, beeches, and colossal pines. As the familiar carriage rambles through the village, the inhabitants stop and wave. Here are woodsmen, fishermen, shepherds and farmers, scarf-covered wives and mothers, children in coats and mittens, barking dogs and clucking chickens. Over their humble abodes, the Hall of Chillington has prevailed for centuries, a true Northern manor-house, magnificent yet rude in its massive plainness.

The gateway to the Hall is in the heart of the village and the carriage passes through it. A square, windowless central tower, having survived the old Border wars, still guards the rest of the manor-house, which shows the influence of many generations in its overhanging roofs, carved balconies, and numerous chimneys. The carriage pulls up a few yards from the front door. An elderly gentleman in a powdered wig and rich livery of blue and scarlet immediately opens the door and bolts to the carriage as if he has been waiting for this moment for years.

"We were worried sick," the old gentleman says to the driver.

"The roads were a bit mucky, what with the weather and all."

"And this must be young Master Chadwick," the old man says to Ollie, extending his arms to help the boy down. Ollie refuses the help and jumps to the ground.

"I am Oliver Chadwick," he announces.

"Yes, you certainly are," the wigged man replies. "If you would be so good as to follow me, then."

The two of them enter the famous Chillington-hall. In the main foyer, Anne rushes to meet her son, taking him in her arms and squeezing him so tightly that he pulls away. "My darling son, it's been so long! So long!"

"Hello, mother," Ollie says matter-of-factly. He had expected to be overcome with emotion upon seeing her, but now that the moment has arrived, he feels something else… detachment, perhaps. No, no—anger, that's it. Resentment for abandoning him to the care of Charterhouse. For not being there to protect him. For not having visited or written. For having put her speaking career ahead of their relationship. For having torn him away from his home only to abandon him to the wretchedness of Dr. Russell and Reginald Pennick.

Anne senses his remoteness. "Why, Oliver, don't you love your mother?" she begs. "I'm so sorry that I haven't been there for you, but you see, everyone said it would be easier for you this way, without a doting mother to interfere with your new life at school. But now that you're doing so well, perhaps we can get together now and then. Would you like that?"

Of course he would. But his stubborn tongue won't form the words.

"Oh, Ollie, you're angry with me, I know. But let's have a pleasant time together while we're here. I missed you so very, very much." She hugs him again. He can smell expensive perfume on her. Lilacs. At last he discovers some words that he can say.

"Where is Mum?"

Anne pulls back, stares at him painfully. Rejected absolutely. The corners of her mouth turn down and she sniffs back tears. She has been put in her place. "Why, Mrs. Chadwick is in her bedroom. Not feeling very well, I'm afraid."

Ollie looks up at the wigged man, Corcoran, and with the steely resolve of *Master* Chadwick says, "I wish to be taken to her now, please."

Corcoran glances at Anne, then nods silently to Ollie and says, "Follow me, please."

They walk through echoing chambers and up a wide, intricately carved staircase that would have impressed royalty. Behind them, Anne stands stiffly in her place.

Mum lies on a gargantuan four-poster bed draped in lace and silks. Propped up on flower-print pillows she looks so frail, yet she smiles when Corcoran leads Ollie into the bedroom.

"Oliver, my son, come to me," she says. Ollie hesitates for a moment—is he resentful of Mum, as well?—but then races to the bed and hugs his great-grandmother as if she is the most precious thing in the world. Of course she could not have visited him at Charterhouse; she has been ill. It's not as if she had forgotten him. Despite their physical separation, she had written him letters, warm and loving letters, full of encouragement and news.

"I've missed you, Mum," he says, his face buried in her neck.

"And I missed you too, Oliver. But now we are together for the holiday."

Ollie raises his head, looks at the old woman's rheumy eyes. The spark is gone. Something is wrong, something more than the gout. "Are you very ill, Mum?" he asks.

"Oh my, you are a curious one, aren't you? That's a rather personal question."

"I'm worried about you, is all."

Mum looks him straight in the eyes. She has known for a long time that her body is eating itself up, the malignancy spreading through her body. She can feel it, the gnawing pain like buzzards picking at her flesh, the debilitating weakness that increasingly overtakes her.

"I am ill, Oliver, that is quite true, and some day I am going to die. But not tonight, I promise you."

Ollie hugs her again. "I don't want you to die."

"There often comes a time when people embrace death, Ollie. For a just cause. Or for relief from pain. But let's not be so serious. Corcoran—will you fetch Ollie's gift?"

"Of course, madam," Corcoran walks to the closet and retrieves a wrapped package.

"Go ahead, open it," Mum says with a broad grin.

Ollie tears off the wrapping paper and opens the box. He gently lifts out several garments such as he has never seen before.

"Don't look so puzzled, my son. You must wear the correct attire when you undertake your first fox hunt in the morning. Go ahead, try them on. I paid a good penny to Edmund Gooch, the tailor, and I want to make sure they fit properly."

Ollie has heard the boys at Charterhouse talk with great fondness of fox hunting, but he is not quite sure what to make of it. Still, the prospect of riding a horse again excites him. *In the morning!* Yes, he'll be on the back of a horse in the morning. With thoughts of his beloved desert stallion flooding back, Ollie begins to put on the assortment of odd garments. White riding breeches. Canary vest with brass buttons. Sky-blue silk stock tie (Mum helps him tie the knot) with horizontal gold stock pin. Scarlet swallowtail coat with purple collar edged in gold. Black leather boots with tan colored tops. White string gloves.

Completely assembled, he moves to stand in front of a large dressing mirror, impressed with himself. Corcoran hands him a hunting crop with thong and cord snap, showing him how to carry it. Ollie is the picture of the English gentleman fox hunter and Mum stares at him, beaming. In the mirror's reflection, Ollie sees a portrait of a young man on the wall behind him. He wheels to see it more clearly. The boy in the painting, too, is similarly attired—*exactly* the same, in fact. The boy is holding a fox. Ollie turns to Mum. A question hangs in the air.

"It's your grandfather, Augustus Chadwick," Mum explains. "He was about your age when we had that portrait done. What a glorious time we all had!" Mum's thoughts seem to drift off into another time that makes her smile.

Ollie and Corcoran patiently await her return.

At last she sighs and, turning to Corcoran, says, "Please show Ollie to his room." Then she turns to Ollie. "You will find appropriate dinner clothes there. After you change, dinner will be served. Everyone is waiting. I will try to join you downstairs."

As Ollie leaves the room, Mum stops him with a whispery "I love you, Oliver Chadwick."

"I love you too, Mum."

Again Ollie glances at the portrait, his eyes focusing on the fox, an animal that is so much like, like—Reginald Pennick. So cunning in his crimson garments. So crafty in his moves. Yet so devious pursuing his desires. Yes, Reginald is a sly old fox. Vermin. And sometimes you simply had to get rid of the vermin. What Ollie needs now is an eagle. A bird of prey.

Mum, sensing the swirl of emotions that are rushing through the boy, tenderly places her hand on Ollie's arm to comfort him. Yes, he has an eagle at his command. He can almost hear the beat of Mum's wings, feel her steely talons on his arm.

"Mum," he says, "I have something terrible to tell you."

"Yes, dear. Anything. You know I'll understand… and protect you."

"It's about Reginald Pennick."

CHAPTER 10

She is burning up. Not with fever, but with rage. Consciously she knows what a pitiful creature she is, so utterly consumed with vengeance and so helpless to turn the rudder during the final days of her life. Seated alone in her bedroom, the words of her great-grandson still burn her soul. *Reginald Pennick. Augustus. Oliver. Betrayal. Revenge.*

In hindsight, it all seems excruciatingly clear. For decades, one man has stood at the center of her agony and her son's pain. A declared man of God. A charlatan who now threatens the one living person that she truly loves.

Mum's rage simmers, then boils over, exploding uncontrollably. She violently throws a vase into a mirror. Shards of glass and porcelain spray the floor. In a frenzy, she flings an end table against the wall, flips over a large chair, kicks the cushions across the room, madly strips the bed and slumps into the snarled pile of covers on the floor, exhausted and sobbing. This is where the maid finds her a few minutes later. She is no longer crying. Her eyes are dry and steely, her body rigid with a single-minded purpose. Her rage has been replaced with absolute determination. For some time she has known about one problem that requires her intervention, but now she has two individuals who must be brought to justice by her own hands.

The first one she will deal with immediately, and then she will deal with Reginald Pennick.

Ollie has never celebrated Christmas before, and thus has no expectations. The Chadwick family tradition for generations has governed every detail of Christmas morning. The merry Chillington-hall band—cousins and uncles and aunts and special friends and honored neighbors—arise early and gather in the Greatroom around an enormous Christmas tree decorated with candles, handmade ornaments, tiny packages, and real snow brought in by the servants. Mrs. Chadwick, they are told, is not feeling well and is resting in her room, but she wants them to carry on without her. As usual, the guests will take turns opening a special gift from the old woman, and then they may open gifts from each other as they see fit.

The servants pass out breakfast pastries and mugs of hot tea as everyone argues over the order of gift-opening. Three female cousins win the debate—no one knows how—and they go first, expressing mild pleasure at the garments Mrs. Chadwick has given them. Herbert Eaton, the *Times* reporter who wrote the first stories about Anne and Oliver, unwraps a new fox hunting gun, hoisting it aloft for everyone to see.

With dramatic flair, Gordon lifts his gift—an envelope humorously bound by an oversized ribbon and bow. "It's not a new gun, I'm sure of that," he says to faint laughter. Anne watches him delicately unwrap the bow and open the envelope, building the suspense. *What could Mrs. Chadwick have picked out for Gordon?*

Gordon's slender fingers slip into the envelope and remove a thin sheaf of papers. "My, my—I wonder what this could be," he says. Ollie is bouncing up and down with anticipation. *Such a mysterious and unusual gift! It must be something special.*

It is clearly a document, folded once. Gordon unfolds it, turns the front page right-side up, and begins to read. Everyone leans forward, awaiting a grand announcement. Gordon flips to the second page, holds up one hand and says, "Hold on, now—just a minute." He reads more. And then his face whitens. He glances at Anne, then quickly turns away.

"Gordon, what is it?" Anne asks.

Gordon stands quickly, folds the document and awkwardly addresses the group. "If you'll excuse me. Anne, please see that the party continues." He leaves the room.

The group is silent, staring at Anne. "Well, then—I suppose we'll have to wait to discover what that was all about. Who is next? Elizabeth, I believe it is you."

CHAPTER 11

In her bedroom, Mum sits on the sofa, waiting. The servants have cleaned up the room and made the bed. She can hear heavy footsteps on the creaking floor of the hallway. Closing her eyes, she smiles faintly.

Will he knock?

The door flies open and Gordon lunges into the room, his ashen face now red with anger. "I want you to explain this!" he exclaims.

"I've been expecting you. Please close the door and then come and sit down," Mum says calmly.

Gordon slams the door and stomps to an overstuffed chair. He slaps the document onto a table and slumps into the chair's soft cushions, comically sinking down further than he had expected.

Mum smiles and says, "Now then—I imagine you came to thank me for my gift? How sweet."

"Maybe I should remind you of the terms of our arrangement," he says, then takes a breath, trying to calm himself. "When I approached you with news of Anisa and Ali, you agreed to give me a sum of money to finance an expedition to rescue them."

"I paid you. It was a lot of money."

"And I honored my promise. I brought them home."

"You also insisted that I make a rather sizable donation to the Evangelicals to further their work. I considered that extortion, under the circumstances, but I paid."

"It was a good cause. Do I have to remind you that it was my missionary work with them that made it possible for me to find your granddaughter and great-grandson?"

"Unfortunately, as I looked into the matter of this donation, I discovered that only a small portion of that money was ever turned over to the Evangelicals. Guess where it went?"

Gordon shifts his weight. His eyes dart excitedly around the room before focusing again on Mrs. Chadwick. "All right, I took the rest. So what? I was the one taking all the risks. They helped me arrange transportation, that's all. You can't tell me it wasn't worth the money to get your family back."

"And you call yourself a man of God!"

"I have saved hundreds of souls from eternal damnation!"

"Maybe you should work on your own soul. I fear it's at risk."

"None of this has anything to do with that document," Gordon says. He picks it up, unfolds it, stares at the front page. "'Last Will and Testament of Emily R. Chadwick.' As I read this, I see that you've taken Anne out of your will."

"That's not entirely true. After I'm gone, she'll receive about £3,000 per year. That's quite a comfortable living. After all, she is my granddaughter. I wouldn't want her to be cast out into the streets. But I think I see your point. If you should marry her, as you intend to do in a few months, you will no longer be marrying into my money. Isn't that it?"

"We had an arrangement. I told you I was in love with Anne and we wanted to marry. You gave me your permission!"

"Ahhh—I see. Of course, it never would have occurred to me that your interest in marrying Anne was motivated by her being the Chadwick heiress. I'm just an old woman, the simple wife of a wealthy man—is that what you thought? An easy touch?"

"You can't do this!"

"Let me say this as plainly as possible. You still have my permission to marry Anne if you wish. The two of you can share her £3,000 per year. As for Ollie, he will get everything else when he's thirty. Until then, he will receive funds from a trust account managed by my attorney." She pauses, then says, "You know, I don't like you. I don't like anyone who attempts to make money off another's misfortune. I don't like liars."

"I rescued her." Gordon thumps his chest with his forefinger. "And Ollie! Don't forget that. You wouldn't have Ollie if it wasn't for me."

"Is there anything else?" Mrs. Chadwick says dismissively.

"You would do this to your own granddaughter to punish me? That is the most despicable... What do you have against Anne? From the very beginning you've disliked her. Yet you fawn all over Ollie."

"Anne is my granddaughter. Period. As a co-conspirator with you, she deserves no more than her annual stipend. The moment I met her, I knew that the two of you were in this together. I believe your rescue was a sham. From Ollie's descriptions, their life was no prison. The way she feigned affection when she met me was transparent. I think the two of you have been waiting for the old woman to croak so you can get your hooks into my money. Just like her mother."

"Oh, I see. No woman is ever good enough for a Chadwick man, is that it? All women are predators, just after your money."

"Chadwick men have a weakness for selfish women. I even had to protect my own husband, God bless him, from such connivances. Men are fools."

"So Anne is guilty of being the daughter of her mother."

"She's guilty of selfishness and conspiracy."

Gordon stands and begins to pace nervously. "I can't believe this. All right—I admit that at first I saw a pot of gold here. When I learned that Anisa was a Chadwick, I thought I could turn that into a few pounds. But the truth is, I fell in love with her."

"Then marry her. And get a job."

"I may just do that. In the beginning I probably would have married her for the money. But now—you're wrong about me. I love Anne. And she is a wonderful woman. She has never said one word about an inheritance. I honestly don't think she would miss it! We never once talked about it, that's the truth."

"Maybe you'd like to tell me about the year you spent in prison in Madrid. Was it for fraud, or something else?"

Gordon sits down, suddenly contrite. "That was before I found God. Jesus changed my life. Do you think that's not possible?"

"I think it's unlikely."

"Then I have no recourse but to prove that I love your granddaughter despite your money."

"And how will you do that?"

"By marrying her. Forget your bags of money. My book is due to be published late summer. I expect it will earn a great deal of money."

"Oh—perhaps I didn't mention it," Mrs. Chadwick says coyly. "Last month, at about the same time I changed my will, I bought the publishing company. George C. Boothby & Sons, I believe, is that right? It seems we've decided not to publish your manuscript after all. It just, what can I say, lacks credibility."

Gordon slumps into the chair like a deflated balloon. "Of course, you can keep the advance payment, don't worry about that. I hope it isn't all spent." Mum coldly smiles at the speechless Gordon, who appears utterly defeated. "Would you like some hot tea?"

Gordon's life has completely unraveled. "You are a mean, hateful woman."

"I am justice," she responds. "Justice can seem cruel."

He stands again with an unconvincing posture of defiance. "I will marry Anne despite your malicious scheming."

"Are you quite sure that Anne will want you?"

"What? Of course. She loves me."

"Hmmm—I wonder what would happen if she were put to the test."

"What do you mean?"

"Perhaps you didn't read the entire will." She takes the document and turns several pages. "There is a provision here that allows her to regain some of her inheritance—half of my estate, to be exact, the other half going to Oliver. But there are two conditions that must be met. The first one is that she must not marry you—in fact, you are named right here," she says, pointing to a line on the page and smiling. "The second condition is that she must marry someone else and remain married for ten years. You see, it occurred to me that I may be wrong about Anne, though it isn't likely. And if so, then here is the remedy. I believe that ten years of a sustained marital relationship is beyond the ability of most opportunists who would marry her for the money. And a fair sentence if she wants to earn her inheritance. I wonder what will happen when she learns of *this* provision. Will she still choose to marry you, knowing of a certainty that she will lose her inheritance for good?"

Gordon cannot respond.

Checkmate.

Mrs. Chadwick breaks the uneasy silence. "Gordon, I know you hate me. And I greatly dislike and distrust you. But I don't want you to think of me as unreasonable." Gordon has to laugh at this. *What could be more unreasonable than the plot this scheming woman has set into action?* "Despite your dishonorable motives, I do appreciate having my great-grandson brought home. Because of this I am inclined to make you an offer."

Gordon sits up, shifts to the edge of the chair. *What is she up to now?* "Let's say £30,000 for your trouble. That's in addition, I might add, to the outrageous sum I've already paid you. But now that I have Oliver, I can probably justify this as an investment."

"You will give me another £30,000? You must want something else."

"Here are my terms. I am prepared to give you a bank note for £10,000 immediately. If you accept the money, you must leave tonight without speaking to anyone, trusting me to explain your reasons as I see fit. You must leave England by New Year's Day and move to, oh, Paris would be nice. Or Madrid. You can be a missionary if you wish. But you must completely stay out of England for at least four years. You must let me know the address of your residence. Then on the last day of each year for the next four years you will receive another £5,000. Provided, of course, that you have honored our agreement."

Mrs. Chadwick reaches into a handbag and removes a bank note, handing it to Gordon. He takes it, studies it, looks up at the old woman. He stands, paces thoughtfully, and finally approaches her with eyes like slits in a mask.

"All right. I accept."

Her expression and posture do not change, but inside Mum is quivering with delight. She sees Gordon's decision as proof of her suspicions. Yes, he has shown that he is driven by the money. The payoff is a trivial sum to guarantee that Ollie is free of Gordon's influence.

Through the immense maze of Chillington-hall it is easy for Gordon to make his escape unseen by others. A waiting carriage whisks him into the foggy night.

As Gordon bumps along the frozen road to London, Mrs. Chadwick carefully places the Last Will and Testament on the hallway floor outside Gordon's room where Anne will see it and think that Gordon accidentally dropped it there. Like a spider waiting for a fly, the old woman waits and watches from a door at the far end of the corridor.

As Mrs. Chadwick had hoped, Anne at last approaches Gordon's room and knocks on the door. As Anne waits outside the vacant room, she sees the folded document on the floor, recognizing it as the 'gift' Gordon had received that morning. She looks at the first page, then hides it beneath her shawl and takes it into her own room next door.

Mrs. Chadwick returns to her bedroom. About ten minutes later there is a knock on her door. Lying in bed, the old woman calls out, "Come in, please!"

Anne enters and approaches the bed. "I've not been able to find Gordon anywhere. Do you know where he is?"

"Sit down my dear."

Anne defies the command. "Gordon received a gift from you this morning that seemed to trouble him. He flew out of the room and I haven't seen him since."

Mrs. Chadwick notices that Anne does not immediately ask about the Will, a sign of her deviousness. "It's time we talked, my dear," she says. "I confess there is something that I've been hiding from you. Only today did I get confirmation of some very disturbing news about Gordon."

"What is it?"

"I know how much you love Gordon, but there are some things about him that you didn't know. I've done some investigation, and this morning I confronted him with what I learned."

"Tell me—what is this all about?"

"I learned that Gordon has a wife in France." Mrs. Chadwick can be a convincing liar when she has a plan.

Anne is shaken. "That's impossible," she says. "He would have told me, I'm sure of it."

"He has kept it a secret for years. Several times he has asked for a divorce, but his wife has never agreed to it. I grew suspicious about his behavior some time ago and hired a man to investigate. The so-called 'gift' I gave him this morning was a document that proved he was married. He immediately came to my room to admit it and confess his love for you. Maybe I'm old-fashioned, but I will never be able to trust that man now that I know he deceived me."

Anne looks at Mrs. Chadwick suspiciously. *Why did the old woman lie about the gift?* "This is terrible," Anne says. "What will happen next?"

"Gordon could not confront you with this until he settled his personal affairs. He is returning to France. He said that he believes his wife is now ready to grant him a divorce. In fact, his wife had written him just last week expressing a change of heart. Gordon wants to settle this matter legally, then return and ask your forgiveness. He still wants to marry you."

"He does?"

"If you ask me, I'm against it. But I won't stand in your way. I just ask you to consider the consequences of marrying a man like that."

Anne stands up and walks to the mirror, too preoccupied to notice it is broken. She turns with an amazing calmness and looks at Mrs. Chadwick. "You would still let me marry Gordon?"

"My dear, how could I stop it? You are both adults."

Anne walks back to the bed where she stands stiffly, staring at Mrs. Chadwick who waits for a response. *Is Anne thinking about the Will? Is she taking the bait?*

"A man like that—you're right. I love him so much. But how could I ever trust him again?"

"There would be consequences," Mrs. Chadwick says again. *So many consequences, which Anne must be considering right now. Will she choose love… or money?*

"This is very hurtful," Anne says, though her expression doesn't show any pain. "And disappointing. I can't forgive those kinds of lies. If he calls again, I will not see him. I will never marry him."

Her anderun survival skills seem to have engaged. She cannot let any man have power over her. Survival means using any advantage, taking what you can get.

"A beautiful woman like you will find a good man, my dear. An honest man. Choose wisely, and you will be rewarded, I'm sure."

"Yes, I'm sure. I'll get over it. I think I'll go to my room now, this hasn't been easy for me."

"That's fine, dear. Go now."

Anne leaves. Mrs. Chadwick has her confirmation. She was right on both counts. Anne, too, is drawn to the money. She had never mentioned finding the Will, never confronted the lie about the gift. Still, Anne is a Chadwick, and if she can turn herself around, find a good man, and stay married…

Anne walks slowly down the corridor toward her room, traversing a large balcony that overlooks the foyer. Herbert Eaton, the reporter, standing below, writing a note to himself. He is not unattractive—a bit pale and shallow-chested, perhaps, but well-scrubbed and lacking the oily, slicked-back hair that Anne dislikes. He is pleasant enough, and during her interview for the *Times* article he was courteous and attentive.

As Anne studies him, he suddenly glances up, eyes brightening as he catches her shape in the half-shadow. "I say, there you are," he says, hurling his voice upward. "Did you find Gordon?"

"I'm afraid not. He appears to have abandoned me."

"What a pity. I wonder if you would like to take some air. All those pastries have fogged my brain."

"I'd be delighted."

The time for mourning has passed.

CHAPTER 12

With a heart aching unbearably for his son's companionship, 'Abdu'llah had set out weeks ago for Mashhad to visit his son, Jalal, at the madrisih. But the Turkoman had raided his caravan and only thirty of them had survived. 'Abdu'llah's arm was badly injured and has now turned septic. In a nearby village he seeks a physician but finds that the only man with any experience in medicine had been captured by the Turkoman—except for a young man of twenty, Assaf, who tends to the animals.

Assaf looks at the blackening wound, sniffs the putrefying flesh, and moans loudly, "This is not good, this is not good."

'Abdu'llah, too, knows the signs of gangrene. Soon the sepsis will be coursing through his veins, poisoning his entire body. "Is there nothing you can do?" he implores Assaf, who only shakes his head and mumbles. "Did the doctor have any medicines?" 'Abdu'llah asks.

"Yes, most certainly, but nothing that will handle this. The infection is too far advanced. But there *is* one thing…"

"What is it?"

"About a year ago we had a goat with an injured leg that was turning black like your arm. I knew it was only a matter of time before the goat died a terrible, painful death. My brother loved this goat and would not let me destroy it, so I cut off the goat's leg and hung charms around its neck."

'Abdu'llah understands the young man's suggestion. Amputating the arm would also excise the infection. The prospects seem grim.

"The goat lived," Assaf cheerfully adds.

"Thank you for the story. Do you have any clean dressings that I can use to wrap the wound?"

"Of course. And I will get you what medicines the good doctor has."

Assaf returns with a basket of rags, some bottles of strange powder, and a poultice that he wraps around the black wound. "I crushed some desert plants to treat your wounds. Maybe it will help draw out the infection." He takes a knife and points it at 'Abdu'llah's left forearm as if to cut the flesh.

"What are you doing?" 'Abdu'llah exclaims.

"I need to bleed you. Letting out the poison may help. If I cut your forearm below the wound, the blood will flow downward to the fresh cut instead of upward to your shoulder and chest where it can poison the rest of your body. You will need to keep bleeding until the infection is gone or you are dead," Assaf says bluntly.

The thinking seems logical. 'Abdu'llah grimaces as Assaf punctures the skin and the blood begins to flow.

"Can you tell me where I can hire a horse and a guide to take me to Mash-had?" 'Abdu'llah asks.

"You are abandoning the caravan? Then I will take you myself. I've been to Mashhad and I know the shortest route. And I know a doctor there—a *real* doctor."

Assaf packs provisions and meets 'Abdu'llah at dawn. In the rugged hills it is better traveling in daylight. 'Abdu'llah is pale and perspiring. It will be a long journey for a sick man.

"If you die before we reach Mashhad, what should I do with your body?" Assaf asks as they pass through the village gate. He is a practical man.

"Take my body to the madrisih in Mashhad and leave it with my son, Jalal of Bushruyih."

On the fourth day of their journey the infection has blackened 'Abdu'llah's entire upper arm and the pain has become almost unbearable. Assaf ties 'Abdu'llah to the saddle so he won't fall as they travel. That evening he cleanses the foul-smelling wound with fresh water, trims dead flesh with a heated knife, and packs the wound with more crushed plants that he finds on the hillsides.

On the seventh day, as the tired travelers begin to descend from a barren ridge, Assaf suddenly begins to shout and sing. "There it is—Mashhad!" he hollers, waking 'Abdu'llah from unconsciousness. "We can be there by night-fall."

Assaf takes the reins of 'Abdu'llah's horse and begins a steady canter to-ward the Mashhad city gate. It is dark when they reach it and Assaf leads

'Abdu'llah to the crumbling home of Pierre Renaud, a French homeopathic physician who has been marooned in Mashhad since the death of his wife and child to cholera. A loud bang on the door wakes the doctor.

"Yes, yes, I'm coming!" he yells in French-tinged Farsi. "I'll be right there." Dr. Renaud opens the door and finds the body of 'Abdu'llah lying slumped on the ground. "Assaf, what have you brought me?"

"His name is 'Abdu'llah of Bushruyih. He has a very bad infection."

The two men drag 'Abdu'llah into the doctor's house and Renaud rips open the unconscious man's garment, exposing the festering wound. "I'm surprised he is still alive," he says. "The gangrene has spread. Here's what you must do. Go find your friend Anoush of Zunuzi. He has recently buried some sheep who died from eating poisonous berries. Dig up the sheep and bring me back a pail of maggots."

Assaf scrunches up his nose at this suggestion.

"You must hurry, Assaf," the doctor says. "While you are gone I am going to open the arm from the shoulder to the wrist. I need maggots to put on the wound. They will eat the dead flesh. Off with you now!"

It is mid-morning when 'Abdu'llah at last wakes up, confused at his surroundings. "Am I alive?" he asks Assaf. A fat dressing surrounds his entire arm.

"Yes. We're at the doctor's house. He treated your wound last night."

The doctor enters the room and looks glumly at 'Abdu'llah. "The news is not good," he says. "I'm afraid the infection has spread quite far."

"I came all this way to see my son," he says weakly. "That's my only wish."

The doctor nods. "We can find him and bring him here if you like."

"No. He will worry, and that will interfere with his religious studies."

"Then what can we do?"

"Let me think. And rest."

The doctor hands 'Abdu'llah a cup of strong tea, then he and Assaf leave the room. 'Abdu'llah shifts painfully on his mat. This journey has not been what he had imagined. He can feel the cold fingers of death flowing through his veins. If only he could see Jalal one last time. And then it strikes him.

Why not?

He struggles to his feet, pale and dizzy. Yes, his legs still hold his weight. He finds a walking stick in the corner of the room and staggers to it. Leaning heavily on the stick, he steps falteringly out of the house and into the street. Now he must find the madrisih.

Jalal sits in a large chamber with many other students. They face 'Abid, their elderly and arrogant instructor. In the shadows behind 'Abid, a bent figure painfully leans against a cold column out of sight.

Carried by an ox-drawn cart, 'Abdu'llah has made it to the madrisih and is cheered at the sight of his son seated cross-legged on the floor. How big he has become! And how 'Abdu'llah wants to call out his name, rush to his side and wrap his arms around him. But he must not be seen. And so he merely watches and listens as the discussion begins to unfold.

"Mulla, I have been told of some holy traditions¹ of the blessed Imams that I find very difficult to understand. Can you help me?" The voice is Jalal's, and the familiarity of it shoots through 'Abdu'llah like a dart, chilling and thrilling him at the same time.

"Yes, Jalal, I'm quite sure I can help you."

"I have heard the mullas quoting a holy tradition on the subject of God's mercy in sending the rains. They have said that every drop of rain is entrusted to an angel of God who carries it down to earth. Is this tradition true?"

"It most assuredly is true," 'Abid replies.

"Thank you. On the subject of the ritual uncleanliness of dogs, I have also heard that there is a holy tradition that no angel will visit the house where dogs are kept. Is this tradition also true?"

"Yes, it's true. What is so difficult to understand?"

"Just this. How is it that rain falls on the houses that have dogs?" Jalal asks, "The rains, when they come, fall everywhere alike."

Trapped and perturbed in the insolence of this student, 'Abid abruptly stands. Despite his pain, 'Abdu'llah silently laughs.

'Abid has no answer for Jalal, and so he he angrily says, "These inane questions are beneath the dignity of our school. I would ask you, Jalal, to refrain from such purposeless riddles in the future."

'Abdu'llah can see that this was no purposeless riddle. In this simple exchange, his precious son had not only won the debate but had revealed the bankruptcy of a narrow, literal, unthinking reliance on scripture and tradition. Astonished and swelling with pride, 'Abdu'llah silently stumbles out of the shadows and departs without speaking a word.

His heart is full and at peace. Jalal indeed will become a great mulla—a mujtahid, perhaps. Suddenly flushed with pain and nausea, 'Abdu'llah knows that his time has come. No use wishing it were otherwise. The maggots in his arm are already gnawing to the bone; pieces of him have already died. The great mosque is but a short distance from here, and next to it the holy ground for which the corpses carried by many caravans are bound. He has come such a great distance already; surely he can make it that far.

Staggering slowly down the dusty street, 'Abdu'llah finally reaches the burial ground and finds a mulberry tree. Sitting against it, in the cool shade, he takes in his hand the only two possessions he has brought with him. The first is a letter asking to be interred here and for his wife to be notified. The second is a pouch full of tumans to pay for his burial. He prays for forgiveness, for his family's well-being, and that Jalal will achieve his destiny. *What is written, is written.* Suddenly the words are a comfort.

'Abdu'llah's last thought is simple and full of irony. How fortunate he is to have been allowed to walk with dignity to this holy place, while so many others have had to be carried like mummies slung over the backs of mules.

CHAPTER 13

Of all his London adventures, Ollie finds theatre excursions led by schoolmates the most intoxicating. Each night the curtain rises on sixteen stages throughout London to reveal worlds within worlds of astonishing entertainment that hook the boys like a narcotic. It is in the enormous pit of the Surrey Theatre, then, that the Ollie and his friends frequently find themselves bedazzled and giddy with laughter.

For Ollie, suffering through another dull Latin class, anticipation of tonight's theatre attraction is building because of a playbill announcing *Juan Fernandez; or, The Island Ape, starring Mons. Gouffé, the Man-Monkey*.

Ollie replays the advertisement in his head, amazed by the outrageous descriptions.

"The Man-Monkey will perform his most extraordinary Leaps, Features of Agility and Gymnastic Displays," the playbill promises. "He will conclude his Performance by Running round the Fronts of the BOXES and GALLERY, supported only by minute Mouldings."

How is this possible? Ollie wonders. *I must see it!*

So enthralled is the boy by this world of man-made enchantment that he has almost forgotten his studies. His mind whirls around the whimsical tales and vibrant showmanship of these evening forays, and begins to spin his own version of a pantomime: *Harlequin and the Enchanted Horse; or A Persian Marriage*.

Thank goodness his mother will be having a fine *English* wedding. And so soon! Gordon's mysterious disappearance had been mourned by few and explained by none, but Ollie knows the truth. He had seen his mother approach Mum's bedroom on Christmas day, and had listened at the door as they delicately sparred. He had found the pages from Mum's Will in his mother's room, and though the words were complicated, he had understood his own inheritance, Gordon's sudden departure, and his mother's desire to marry quickly and begin fulfilling the ten year requirement for her own inheritance. When Herbert Eaton had announced two weeks later that he and Anne were to be married, Ollie was not surprised.

Behind all of this he can see the hand of his great-grandmother, wise old Mum. He does not hate Mum for her scheming; instead, he admires her canniness and influence. He is learning from her how to use power to obtain his own goals, and the patience to see his own schemes unfold over time. By his own hand the fate of Reginald Pennick has been altered, though Ollie does not yet know how. As soon as Mum has recovered from her illness, Ollie is sure that the old woman will satisfy his need for vengeance.

In the meantime, life is good.

After Latin class, Ollie races across campus, rounds the crumbling corner of a building and suddenly stops. Ahead of him is the door to Reginald Pennick's office, but it is not the sight of this offensive place that makes him hesitate; stationed just down the cobblestone street is Mum's carriage, the horses calm and still, the driver hunched and snoring loudly in his seat.

Why is Mum here? Ollie wonders. He walks slowly past the carriage, peers into the vacant interior, then looks back at Reginald's office and understands.

Yes, today is visiting day.

CHAPTER 14

Mrs. Chadwick paces the dimly lit office, afraid to sit for fear of contact with the evidence of Reginald's sins against nature, sickened by the imagined cries of fragile boys and the images of their tear-streaked faces—oh God, Ollie and Augustus, and so many others. Her breaths are purposely shallow, as if the air itself may be tainted by the evil vapors emanating from this vile man of the cloth.

A portrait of Christ weeping tears of blood chills her; surely Christ had been witness to Reginald's repeated crimes, and surely He had cried tears of blood at the atrocities committed in His name by His servant.

Voices! She can hear the faint voice of Reginald approaching the office door; he is speaking to someone, unlatching the door, stepping in with a fresh-faced young boy of about twelve, his flabby arm grotesquely cupped around the boy's shoulders.

"I am so anxious to show you the manuscript, Harold," the priest says, barely getting the words out before gasping in terror at the apparition standing before him. "My good lady," he says, holding his hand to his chest after a moment of recovery. "You startled me, Emily. A man my age… we are lucky that my heart did not explode in my chest. Is there something I can do for you?"

Mrs. Chadwick steps from the shadows and a streak of light crosses her face. "Indeed there is, Reginald," she says calmly. "Perhaps you can show both of us your manuscript. I'm very interested in it—as was my son, Augustus, and my grandson Oliver."

The old priest's cheeks, flushed with anticipation upon entering the room, now blanch. "Harold," he says to the boy, "I have some business to attend to if you don't mind. The manuscript will wait. Off with you now!"

Confused, the boy turns and walks out the door with just a brief pause to turn his head and catch a last glimpse of the old witch who had startled Reginald.

Reginald's knees are quaking and he sets down his heavy frame on a frail chair that creaks beneath his weight. The moment he had seen Mrs. Chadwick's face he had known the purpose of her visit. He begins to speak, but the words bunch in his lying mouth. "Emily, I—I don't know what you think…"

Mrs. Chadwick's unblinking eyes scorch his face. "I know everything, Reginald. I know more than you can remember."

How can this bent wisp of a woman frighten him so? His gut rumbles and his head throbs. *Those venomous eyes!* His hand begins to tremble; he can't control it. Perspiration beads on his forehead and his mouth becomes dry and cottony.

"Honestly, Reginald, did you think I would never find out? Surely you knew this moment would come. As you thought about the inevitability of it, what did you imagine you would say?"

"Emily, please…"

"You betrayed your God, Reginald. And you betrayed your church. And Charterhouse. And my son and grandson, Reginald—and how many others?"

"I've prayed for forgiveness, Emily. I'm so weak—but I believe that God in his boundless mercy has forgiven me."

"How nice for you. And were you also going to ask forgiveness for raping this new boy? Maybe you could ask God's forgiveness in advance."

"I pray for the strength to resist my carnal desires, you must believe me."

"I don't really care if God has forgiven you or not. Reginald," Mrs. Chadwick says coldly. "I want you to pay very close attention to what I am going to say. Can you do that?"

Like a small child chastised by his mother, Reginald nods yes.

"You betrayed *me*, Reginald. First with Augustus, after you led me to believe that you would look after his best interests. And then, so many years later, with Oliver. How could you look me in the eye and do it a *second time*? Oh, Reginald—you have disappointed me so." She walks to the door and sighs deeply. "I thought I would be angrier than this."

Reginald shifts his body to see her standing in the open doorway and his spirits lift; perhaps he is getting off easy.

"Still, you deserve punishment," Mrs. Chadwick says. "God may forgive you, Reginald, but I do not. In one week the *Times* will tell your story for everyone to read. You will be famous at last!" She smiles and then squints her eyes. "Unless…"

The word hangs in space as she closes the door.

Unless.

Reginald cannot stand, cannot think, cannot even breathe. This is the executioner's axe. He may go to prison, and he knows the dismal fate of child molesters in English jails. Even worse… he could never bear the public humiliation. He has been utterly, completely undone by Mrs. Chadwick.

Unless.

CHAPTER 15

The corpse lies on the stone floor of the madrisih's courtyard, peaceful and still. Jalal crouches over it sadly, stretches out a warm hand to feel the coldness and tautness of its skin, and tries to imagine this heap of spent flesh as his father. No, this is not 'Abdu'llah; the lifeless husk at his feet is merely the shell that once contained his father, a useless snakeskin now shed and left behind. The real 'Abdu'llah, the soul of the great and loving father, is now free of its physical constraints, and Jalal can almost feel its presence in the warm breeze that tenderly ruffles his hair, and in the laughter of the mulberry leaves rustling overhead.

Though he knows in his bones the triviality of death in the cosmic scheme of eternal spiritual evolution, he is suddenly convulsed with emotion and begins spiraling downward into a despair of loss and loneliness. His tears flow, hot stinging tears, moistening 'Abdu'llah's dusty cloak and releasing an emotion that Jalal believed he had overcome.

Anger.

He is angry that after so long a separation, and such a hard journey, his father had died before reuniting with his son. He is angry that he, Jalal, had been deprived of one last embrace, one last chance to see his father alive.

Assaf stands over Jalal, watching. "He came here to see you."

"I know."

"Not just to Mashhad," Assaf explains. "Your father came to the *madrisih* to see you."

Jalal looks up and wipes his eyes with the ample sleeves of his tunic. "No, he didn't come here. He never made it."

"Oh, yes he did. I followed him here."

Jalal stands, confused. "I'm sure he wasn't here."

"Listen to me. Earlier today I left your father alone for a time. He was sleeping, and when I looked in on him again he was gone. Having lost him—well, you can see what a dilemma it created for me. If he died, I would not know where he was, and so I would not be able to deliver his body to you as he had wished. So I ran out of the house, guessing that he might be trying to make his way here."

"But you said that you found him in the burial grounds on the way here."

"In the burial grounds, yes… but not on the way here. I arrived at the madrisih just as your father was entering. It was not hard to distinguish him with that bandaged arm. I waited outside and finally he came out. He was smiling, but staggering. I wanted to go to him and offer my help, but it seemed wrong. Instead I followed him to the burial ground, and that's where I found him. At first I thought he had just gone to sleep, so I approached to find out. But then it was clear that, that he…"

Jalal steps back and sighs. "I don't understand at all. If he came to the madrisih, why didn't he see me? After such a long journey…"

At first Assaf doesn't know what to say, but then, concluding that the damage already had been done, he turns to Jalal and says, "He was so proud of you he didn't want anything to distract you."

The weight of this pronouncement pulls Jalal unsteadily to the ground where he sits, bracing himself with stiff arms and hands planted on the cold floor. He mentally plays out the scene the way it must have unfolded; his father hiding in the shadows, capturing one last glimpse of his son…

"Assaf—" Jalal says, "thank you for bringing my father to me.."

Assaf kneels beside 'Abdu'llah. "I only knew your father for a short time, but he reminded me of my own father, who was also killed by the Turkoman. Here, I have something else for you." Assaf holds out 'Abdu'llah's coin purse and a letter.

Jalal takes these objects, these last two mementos of his father, and feels his whole body cramping into a ball of pain. Fighting back tears, he opens the pouch, which contains a quantity of tumans, then reads the letter. "I will honor his wishes," he says, putting the letter down. "But tell me—you could have kept the letter and the money, there's quite a lot here. Most Persians would have seen their own good fortune in such a circumstance."

Sensing that he should leave Jalal alone with his father, Assaf silently turns to leave.

"Assaf, wait!" Jalal rises and approaches the young man. He opens his father's pouch, plucks out several coins, then hands the pouch to Assaf. "It will cost me nothing to have my father buried near the mosque, and I need very little for myself. My family in Bushruyih is well off. Take the rest, my friend. Consider it a gift from my father to his last companion."

For the first time the two of them stand facing each other, eye to eye. Assaf sees something in the face of Jalal, something that both stirs and calms him. Something swirling in the boy's dark eyes, like a universe of kindness and compassion and... and fearlessness. These eyes, these deep and unblinking eyes, so gentle but so heartbreakingly, breathtakingly lucid, like a window to the soul, glisten in the purple twilight and reflect an infinity of emotions.

Assaf shivers then drops to his knees without taking the pouch. He feels as if his soul has danced with the soul of Jalal. Looking up, all he can think of to say is, "Your father spoke of the Qa'im, saying that you... that you..."

"That I am expecting Him soon, yes."

Jalal touches Assaf's shoulder with a hand cooled by the stone floor.

Assaf places his own hand over it and holds it there. He cannot steer his gaze away from Jalal's eyes.

"Me too," he says, trembling at the boy's touch. "Me too."

CHAPTER 16

During these winter months Ollie has learned many things, but chief among them is the ability to distinguish between eighty-eight kinds of mud, for London is the "sucking mud-hole of the universe," as Herbert Eaton so delicately understates it. First there is the rich palette of hues, from cast-iron black and dark chocolate to chestnut brown, chalk-grey, and a kind of putrid green like freshly digested hay; and then there are the pungent aromas emanating from the ooze, a stinking sour stench perhaps, or a molasses-sweet perfume, or maybe the acidy scent of soupy leaves moldering in the muck. But the most telling characteristics of London mud are the look-and-feel of it, which can be swirling, puckering, pasty, cracked, or crumbling; rigid, ribbed, and troweled, or juicy, slimy, and bubbling; flaking and chipping, or slurpy and sticky.

The roads to the Surrey Theatre are overrun with gummy mud this evening and the carriage containing Ollie, Herbert and Anne drifts from side to side as the horses with slipping hooves and steaming backs pull the clogged wooden wheels through the clotting sludge. "Damn mud!" Herbert exclaims. "It'll overtake us before long, I swear—turn us all into fossils! They'll find our damn bones ten thousand years from now and some archaeologist will conclude that we were either on our way to the theatre or the garbage pit."

"You know I don't like it when you curse, Herbert," Anne says gently.

Herbert sighs and looks out the window at the sea of mud, his complaints now stuck in his throat and his mood not a bit cheerier for all of Anne's patient words. He grunts, as if to register one last protest, and Anne lets the malformed expletive pass unremarked.

Despite the bleak mud and the spitting snow, Ollie is ebullient, for his wish has come true. He has coerced his mother and his stepfather-to-be into attending the theatre with him on the spectacular evening that Mons. Gouffé, the Man-Monkey, will climb the walls and swing from the balconies in amazing feats of dexterity. He presses his body against his mother's, feels her warmth, and with a tender burrowing gesture urges her arm to wrap around him, containing him for a moment in a different world quite apart from London—a dry and sun-drenched world of sand and stallions where mud is not a liability but is baked into houses, and mulberry leaves shade your eyes from the luminous sky.

At last they arrive at the Surrey; Ollie notices the horses snorting and their chests heaving from the effort of plowing the roads with the gummed-up carriage. The three of them step from the carriage and Anne pulls a hood over her head, protecting her hair from the hard and stinging flakes of snow. Herbert expertly guides them through the maze of vehicles, past the smell of wet horses and leather, around the sink holes of mud, and into the theatre where a loud, piercing voice calls out, "Ollie, over here!" It is Thomas Dibdin the Surrey's pencil-thin manager.

Ollie waves excitedly at Dibdin, then takes his mother by the hand and begins to lead her toward the voice. They push through the crowd until they reach Dibdin.

"Ollie, my good fellow, isn't William with you this evening?" Dibdin asks.

"Not tonight. But I brought my mother, like I said I might."

Anne pulls down her hood and shakes her head, loosening her hair and revealing her face.

Dibdin turns to Anne and, try as he might, cannot hide his astonishment at her voluptuous beauty. "My dear boy, I had heard that your mother was a beautiful woman, but nothing could have prepared me for—"

Herbert doesn't like the way Thomas Dibdin is visually devouring his fiancée and so he extends a hand, pretending to accidentally bump the man with the points of his fingers. "Excuse me, sir. I am Herbert Eaton of the London Times, Anne's fiancé."

Dibdin takes the hand and mumbles a "Very good to meet you sir," with barely a glance in Herbert's direction.

"Oliver has mentioned you, sir," Herbert continues, "and I want to thank you for the courtesy and friendship you have shown him over these past weeks."

Dibdin glances at Herbert with a slight nod of acknowledgement, but turns back reverently to the glorious Anne. With the tip of his tongue, Dibdin wets his lips tentatively, instinctively, before speaking in a cracked voice: "My dear, if you should ever choose to have a career in the theatre, I do hope that you will consult with me first. I must say that you have a kind of charisma, a presence that is quite astonishing."

Anne is dazzled by the man's attention and flattery. For the first time in months she is speechless and just a little embarrassed.

Herbert has had enough of Dibdin. He grabs the bony man by an arm, tightly but not so tight as to be considered rude, and turns the man in the direction of the flowing crowd. "Yes, my good man, if Anne should ever choose the theatre, you will be the first to know. But now, I wonder if you could point me to our seats? That would be good of you."

Dibdin seems suddenly shaken from a dream. He looks up at Herbert, trying to make sense of the words that were just spoken, and finally does. "Yes, yes, of course, of course. But as a gesture of my fondness for Ollie, I would like to offer you three of the better seats in the theatre. I am the manager, after all."

With a sense of purpose, Dibdin leads the threesome to a box with a thrilling view of the entire stage and the enormous "pit" in which hundreds of theatre-goers stand to be near the stage. Ollie hopes that Mons. Gouffé, the Man-Monkey, will choose to swing from their balcony perch.

Thomas Dibdin takes his seat in a box opposite the Chadwicks. With his opera glasses trained on Anne, Dibdin settles into what he considers to be the best seat in the house. He has heard about this magnificent harem girl, and her exotic beauty—so hard to believe she is actually *English*!—but he had never imagined such a seductive apparition of heaven's angels.

The first major piece of the evening begins, a boisterous melodrama of Dibdin's invention called *The Burning Bridge*, with a plot thick as pudding. Through the opera glasses Dibdin scrutinizes Anne's response to the performance and is delighted at how her expressive eyes reflect every nuance of her experience. Like an exposed nerve she reacts to every plot twist, every actor's gesture, every word thrust into the audience. She laughs and playfully shouts her pleasure, gasps and pales visibly at each terrible histrionic tragedy.

At the preposterous conclusion of the piece, a female specter is called upon to rise from a lake, surrounded by a mist. To create this magical illusion, Dibdin has surrounded the ascending figure with a series of lamps behind gauze screens. As this rising cloud of gauzes nears the ceiling, a breeze blows a fold of the specter's dress across a lamp, igniting it in flame.

Anne's mouth falls open and her eyes grow wide and round as marbles. For the first time during the performance, Dibdin turns toward the stage and is astonished at the sight of Bertram Davidge, the actor playing the female specter, dangling and flailing about as he sheds his outer garments, revealing that he is in reality a Scotsman with his kilt on, already dressed for the next piece.

Anne howls with laughter and Ollie doubles over, his sides splitting from the hilarity. The Surrey shakes with the loudest laughter and applause of the evening. No one is quite certain if this has been planned or not; after all, it is a melodrama. Perhaps Dibdin is a genius. Or maybe Davidge is an idiot. What does it matter?

Dibdin breathes deeply, convinced at last that the fire has not spread to the rest of the Theater. As he trains his opera glasses again on Anne, he sees the beautiful woman illuminating the entire theatre with her smile and knows that she has been smitten by the theatre.

And so it goes on, this enchanting evening that fills Anne, the storyteller, with boundless amusement and wipes away the fatigue of her endless speaking engagements in countless echoing halls. "I'm so glad you invited us to attend, Ollie," she says over and over, enthralled by the color and music and drama and humor of it.

Through it all Herbert Eaton sits rigidly in his seat, arms folded, only an occasional smile wrinkling his face, scrutinizing everything with the cold, objective newsman's eye. Still, he intends to be a good sport about it for the sake of the beautiful Anne, who by the grace of God he has won, and also for Oliver, a gifted boy he has come to like very much. It would be so much easier to endure the evening, though, if it were not for the cloying caricature sitting in the box opposite them, that stick figure Thomas Dibdin who obsessively studies them—or *Anne*, as Herbert suspects—through opera glasses.

As the evening's pantomime, *Harlequin and Mother Goose*, nears its frantic conclusion, Ollie can feel his heart beginning to pound. The end of the pantomime means that Mons. Gouffé, the Man-Monkey, is about to appear. Ollie grabs his mother's hand and squeezes so tightly that Anne winces. The audience seems exhausted from laughter as the pantomime finally ends, and the applause, though friendly, seems weak. Ollie begins to wonder how the Man-Monkey will revive the crowd.

The curtain descends and a tympani begins a thunderous announcement of the evening's finale. Ollie moves to the edge of his seat, nervous with anticipation.

Herbert glances at Dibdin's box—empty!

Anne trembles slightly, her body vibrating with the beat of the drum.

The audience hushes.

Behind the curtain, Dibdin whispers into the ear of a mysterious figure that seems to be half-man, half-ape. The figure nods, and then the curtain rises with a fanfare. Dibdin walks limberly to the center of the stage. With a voice ten times louder than anyone could imagine being produced by such a frail body, he greets the audience and introduces the featured act.

"Ladies and gentlemen, it is my distinct pleasure to introduce this evening a true marvel of the animal kingdom, a creature discovered in the jungle, then captured, tamed and trained to perform such amazing feats that you will not believe your eyes. No mere man could accomplish such astonishing deeds of dexterity, and no ape alone could exhibit such intelligence and skill. But this creature is not a man, and not a monkey; incredibly, he is a blend of the best of both. And so on behalf of the Surrey Theatre, I present to you Mons. Gouffé, the Man-Monkey."

Suddenly all the lights in the theatre are doused, plunging the audience into darkness. Anne gasps. Ollie grabs his mother's arm. The tympani rumbles again, building in volume and climaxing with a crash of cymbals. A ring of torches on the stage suddenly bursts into flame and an odd-looking creature the size of a man appears from the shadows and takes its place center-stage. The creature's head looks like an ape and its body is covered by fur, but its proportions are those of a human. The creature walks with a slight crouch and the crowd murmurs.

"Do you think he's really half-monkey?" Ollie asks his mother.

"I don't know, Ollie."

"Do you think his mother or father was a monkey?"

"Hush now—let's watch."

"I think his father."

The Man-Monkey begins his performance. Two attendants, dressed in safari outfits, create a tower of four empty pint glasses. A small boy, about eight, in gaily-colored Indian vestments, waddles over to the creature who picks him up and places him on one hip the way a mother carries an infant.

Ollie watches carefully as the Man-Monkey places one distinctly human hand on the crown of the top pint glass and, in a gravity-defying move, slowly bends and raises his feet from the floor until his entire body is horizontal to the stage, supported only by the fragile glass tower and one bent arm. The Indian child, now sitting upright on the creature's hip, raises his arms, urging the audience to applaud.

Ollie is awe-struck as the Man-Monkey performs one miraculous gymnastic feat after another with ropes and poles and columns and swings. He balances weightlessly, strikes impossible poses, leaps and jumps with astounding agility, and lifts incredible weights with his teeth. The crescendo of the performance continues to build and the audience seems more astonished with each act.

The climax—a bewildering display of rapid-fire tumbling and leaps through fiery hoops, followed by a dizzying rope-to-rope swing across the stage and then *way* out over the heads of the mesmerized pit audience—produces roaring applause and shouts of jubilation. Mons. Gouffé, the Man-Monkey, lands softly on the stage and takes a well-deserved bow. The applause continues unabated until the creature suddenly holds up his hands and points toward Ollie's box.

Ollie shivers. *Is the creature pointing at him?*

Suddenly the Man-Monkey bounds to the end of the stage and begins to climb the wall, finding small crevices for his feet and hands. Up the wall he goes, and the crowd first hushes, then collectively gasps as he reaches for a gold-embroidered drapery suspended from the ceiling and pinned to the wall. With one hand, the creature vigorously shakes it loose from the wall, then leaps onto it and swings slowly, breathtakingly, to Ollie's box. Anne rocks back in her chair, startled. Ollie is so dumbfounded that he can't move. Herbert stands and steps back. The Man-Monkey catches the molding, hoists himself over a brass railing, and rolls into the box.

Looking up at Anne, Mons. Gouffé says, "Madam, is your name Anne?"

Wide-eyed and pale, Anne nods yes.

"Mr. Dibdin would like you all to join him for wine after the performance. He'll find you in the lobby"

With that, the Man-Monkey stands to face the appreciative audience with raised hands and then quickly disappears into the corridor.

The mad exiting crush of people like a river current carries Anne, Herbert and Ollie down the corridor, down a crumbling flight of stairs, and into the lobby. The Man-Monkey, though an imposter—Ollie had seen the spirit gum and make-up on Mons. Gouffé's face as he rolled into the box, and had brushed the fake-fur suit—had exceeded his expectations. A well-done sham could be as interesting and effective as the genuine article, he has discovered.

Their carriage skates through the encrusted mud and begins to rumble over the bridge that connects the south bank of the Thames to the north bank. The snow has stopped but colder air has gripped the city. In the distance, at the far end of the bridge, Ollie can see torches burning and dark figures silhouetted against their glow.

"Herbert, what's that up ahead?" he asks.

Herbert shrugs his shoulders. As the carriage draws near to the commotion, Ollie hears voices shouting, but he can't make out the words. Suddenly, Herbert yells, "Driver, pull up, will you?"

"What is it?" Anne asks.

"I don't know, but it looks like some kind of trouble. Stay here." Herbert's news instincts draw him out of the carriage. Turning up his collar, he starts to walk toward the crowd of seven or eight men, then turns to see Ollie following him.

Three men are pulling ropes connected to something heavy that is located down the steep embankment. Herbert holds up a card and says, "I'm Herbert Eaton with the London Times. What's the trouble here?"

One of the men, mud-spattered to his waist, says, "The Times, eh? This mean we're going to make the papers?"

"That depends on what you're doing here."

"A woman coming across the bridge saw a man leap into the river—suicide, probably. Never hit the water, though. Body hit the rocks under the bridge."

"Who was the man?"

"Between you and me, sir, I've got no idea, that's the truth. Haven't got the body up here yet. It's on the other end of the rope here."

Feeling a bit foolish just standing there, Herbert grabs one end of a rope and helps to pull up the body. Ollie joins him. After five minutes or so, a lumpy corpse finally appears on the level grade of the bridge. As men are fascinated by dead things, the rope pullers gather around it.

Ollie remains on the fringe of the group, not anxious to see the remains but able to hear the voices of the men. "Some sort of priest, I'd say, from his clothing," one of them says. "Any identification on him?" asks another.

And then Ollie hears Herbert's voice, calm but grim. "I know this man," Herbert says. "His name is Reginald Pennick."

Ollie pushes his way through the thick knot of men and sees the body lying there. More than any of the others, he understands what has happened, and
yet he does not feel sadness for the priest—or shock, or regret. He looks at the
limp, corpulent body and feels nothing except… What name can he give this
feeling that is starting to rush through his body, making his head swirl and his
feet tingle? Yes, of course.

Pleasure.

CHAPTER 17

Anne's April wedding to Herbert Eaton is distilled to its essence, a simple ceremony presided over by Judge Horace McIntyre, a close friend of Mrs. Chadwick. In the backyard of Mum's Belgravia mansion, attended only by close family and friends, the service lasts but fifteen minutes, including a short interlude for an unscheduled cloudburst. Despite the miniaturization of the wedding, the account of it dominates the first page of the *London Times* Society section; it is fully eight inches longer than the meager story of Reginald Pennick's suicide, which had been published on the fourth page of the News section several weeks earlier.

The heart of the wedding story is a revisitation of Anne's adventures in Persia and eventual "escape" (no longer a "rescue" by that scoundrel Gordon Cranston). The story had been carefully concocted in advance by Anne and Herbert in a crafty attempt to resurrect interest in the exotic tale and reinvigorate Anne's flagging lecture career. Long ago she had abandoned the "free" talks at Evangelical religious meetings to concentrate on maximizing the economic gain from her notoriety, but the attention span of fickle Londoners has proven to be limited and there is no shortage of exciting tales by returning explorers and soldiers, sudden political whirlwinds, local scandals, and bloody murders to replace the increasing staleness of Anne's exploits in the public mind. The tactic works, and within days of the wedding new letters begin to arrive inquiring about Anne's availability to speak at meetings throughout the city.

Appreciating now the value of publicity, Anne proposes that Mrs. Chadwick reconsider the publication of Gordon's book with several important revisions. The author of the new version, of course, would be Anne herself, but Herbert would be her ghost-writer. Herbert thinks it is a good idea and supports Anne's appeal to Mrs. Chadwick, who at last relents with a wordless and dismissive wave of the hand.

As the press of writing consumes Herbert, the act of recreating and revising her life rejuvenates Anne, and after supper she often takes the carriage to the Charterhouse, gathers up Ollie, and heads to the theatre. Increasingly, the fantastic images and shocking plot twists of the evening's entertainment begin to influence and embroider her version of adventures in Persia, which with each retelling becomes less fact and more fiction.

CHAPTER 18

It is the saddest day in Ollie's fifteen years; sadder even than the day he was uprooted from Bushruyih and separated from his father and Jalal. He can think of nothing that compares to the despair that he feels as Mum's coffin is lowered into a dark rectangular pit on the grounds of Chillington-hall. Though he had roamed these grounds freely during holidays, he had never before seen this small, secluded cemetery on the eastern side of the mansion.

The bones of many ancestors rest here, and a disturbing thought occurs to him: one day, perhaps, his own bones will molder in a grave on this very spot. Only the brilliant spring morning, with new life budding in the trees, gives Ollie solace.

To the left of Mum's grave is a weathered tombstone identifying the grave of great-grandfather Edward Chadwick. To Mum's right is another marker for her son, Augustus; Ollie knows that this grave is empty, for his grandfather and grandmother, Elizabeth, died somewhere in Persia attending to God's business. *Where will Anne's grave be*, he wonders, *and mine?* He wants to be buried near Mum.

Numbed by the death, he remembers little of the dignified ceremony except that no one cried—no one except Ollie, who cried silently. Perhaps this is the fate of those who grow very old and die in the fullness of time; few are left to mourn them, and the young ones remaining are glad to have the decks swept clean at last.

The old woman had just missed the publication date of *Midnight March to Freedom*, Herbert Eaton's version of Anne's story, but tomorrow the volume arrives in bookstores throughout London. To celebrate the long-awaited event, Anne has invited Oliver home for dinner, *home* being the Belgravia estate now solely occupied and managed with glowing pride by Anne and her husband on behalf of Oliver, the legal heir.

For months, Anne's speaking career has been slowly rising as the evangelical fever of America has slowly spread like a contagion throughout London. The smart gilt-edged first edition of *Midnight March*, with enticing pen-and-ink drawings by Harold Willoughby, London's foremost book illustrator, will surely turn the fever to her advantage. Already, the Evangelicals—who usually plead that they are "poor as church mice"—have been offering substantial fees for Anne's services. With a little luck, a retooled presentation emphasizing her "redemption" from pagan Islam, assisted by her prodigious storytelling talent, can turn her into the spokesperson for revival in London.

For a substantial fee.

With Anne's agile mind occupied by career-building, it is Herbert who has preserved and deepened a relationship with Oliver. Their common interest in writing—news writing in particular—has built a bridge between them that is now well worn from frequent travel. Herbert appreciates the boy's interest in his craft, and basks in Ollie's admiration of his talent and skill, though he realizes that his own abilities have limits.

On this particular evening, this celebration of the release of the magnificent George C. Boothby & Sons edition of the book, Ollie finds himself reliving past moments. As on that first evening nearly three years ago, the room is dominated by a long mahogany table and twelve brocaded chairs. He has eaten in this room many times—everything here is familiar—but his thoughts return to that very first dinner, with Mum at the head of the table. Reginald Pennick and Herbert Eaton had been seated to her right, Gordon and Anne—after the harem-girl's dramatic entrance—were to the old woman's left. Everything in this room is the same, the crystal bowl filled with fruit, the gleaming dishes and sparkling silverware, even the long-stemmed wine glasses filled with port. But it is all wrong! Mum is not seated at the head of the table; that chair is now occupied by Anne. Herbert has shifted to the other side of the table, now seated to Anne's left next to an empty chair, presumably Ollie's. The two chairs to Anne's right are filled with unfamiliar people, just as Herbert and Reginald were unfamiliar to Ollie that first evening.

Suddenly, Oliver is homesick for where he is. He longs to be in this very dining room, with this very table and these chairs and those long-stemmed glasses, but at an earlier time. A time before Reginald was a villain and Herbert was Ollie's step-father. A time when Anne was still a mother, not a lecturer, and the Charterhouse was still an English madrisih. A time when Mum was alive.

The sadness that overcomes him is almost unbearable. He steps away from the door to quiet his emotions before entering and decides to think of happy memories to lighten his mood. But what? For a few unbearable, frightening seconds, he can think of nothing. And then an unexpected image appears. A smiling, sun-sweetened face. A twelve-year-old boy.

Jalal.

Never has Ollie felt so alone. Mum has died, perhaps to escape the lies and half-truths in the book. And Anisa—his mother Anne—has exposed the wide gulf between them. He feels like crying, but a young man of fifteen should not cry, so he stands, crosses the room to a writing desk, and finds a piece of note paper. Dipping a quill into the inkwell, he readies himself to write. He will record his feelings, document the conversation with his mother, nudge the river of ink into answers. Writing helps him organize his thoughts, and as the first words appear on the page, he is surprised to find them moving from right to left.

In Farsi.

CHAPTER 19

Discriminating book buyers from all over London patronize Bumble & Stryker, a labyrinthine purveyor of new and used books for the erudite (and those who pretend to erudition.) The publication of a major new book is a seed from which germinates countless blooms of conversation among the well-rooted members of fashionable society.

Nobody who is anybody can afford to be uninformed of the latest literary sensation, for during the London Season—called simply "the Season" by those whose lives become sodden with the social froth of this annual rite—one's ignorance can be easily and publicly laid bare. Indeed, it is the intent of many during the Season to expose the deficits of others, no matter how petty, lowering by degrees the standing of rivals and elevating one's own position by comparison, as if there is a fixed amount of status to be continuously rebalanced.

Fool's Day is the favored time, then, for releasing a new work in the book stores of London, for it demarcates the home stretch of preparation for the Season, the Party That Lasts One Hundred Days. There is only a month to bone up on the latest volumes.

April is the month for sending and receiving invitations to a whirlwind of court balls and concerts, private balls and dinner parties, debuts and dances and sporting events, all of which earnestly begin in May. In the brief span of time until August 12, when Parliament adjourns (and, coincidentally, grouse season opens), London turns into a simmering stewpot of matchmaking. Titled girls—and the daughters of clergy, military officers, physicians and barristers—are queued up and presented, always by a lady of higher rank, to the Queen; without such an anointing, they are not eligible for introduction to potential suitors during the Season. Once presented, prospective brides may attend as many as fifty balls in one Season, sixty parties, and two dozen breakfasts and dinners. Presentation to the Queen ignites a fuse that burns bright and hot; if these girls are not married within one or two Seasons, they are considered failures. If unmarried by thirty, they become hopeless spinsters unlikely ever to marry within (or above) their station.

April is also a month of crushing humiliation for those ladies and gentlemen who find themselves suddenly among the Unforgivens, exiled from important events because of some social faux pas of the previous year, or a financial reversal, or perhaps the merest taint of scandal among one's cousins. When invitations to the expected "occasions" do not materialize in the post, and the invitations sent out are returned with the poisonous inscription *Regret Not Able To Attend*, the rejection can bring about an early winter of despair before the Season has even begun.

April is a popular month for suicides.

In Bumble and Stryker, Anne Chadwick is seated behind an elegantly carved walnut table stacked high with copies of *Midnight March to Freedom*. She is privileged to be one of two "authors" allowed to sign books for purchasers, and the queue for her autograph stretches out the front door and halfway to the butcher's shop. The book is a handsome leather-bound edition with the title embossed in gold foil and the attribution "By Anne Chadwick Eaton and Herbert Eaton." While hurriedly signing her name, the dulled quill in her hand spatters ink onto her dogskin gloves and she curses silently; a true "lady" would not be seen at this time of year with ink-stained gloves. She turns to a silent figure perched on a tall stool behind her and says, "Herbert, I need another pair of gloves, if you would be so kind."

Herbert Eaton stands wearily and ambles out in search of ladies gloves. He had put so much work into that bloody book, but no one wants *his* name signed on its title page. They only want Anne's. The Harem Girl. At least he is married to a woman that most men would give an arm to possess, and has moved from his moldy bachelor cottage to a mansion in Belgravia. Still, being assigned to the servant-girl's duty of fetching gloves is humiliating.

Inside the bookstore, Anne continues to scrawl her name in book after book. Despite her spoiled gloves and stiffening fingers, she smiles, looking up only occasionally at the buyers. At last she sets the quill down and massages her cramping hand; she can rest for a moment or two, surely. Perhaps find a knife to sharpen the dull quill.

As her eyes scan the table for a sharp implement, she feels a presence before her. How odd, that the socially attuned body can almost mystically sense the aura of the socially elevated ones. Without even lifting her eyes, Anne knows that the woman standing before her is rich and powerful; the gravitational pull of the lady's influence is immense. As the woman had approached the signing table, the others had backed away in hushed reverence, like the parting of the Red Sea.

"My goodness, child, you are a beauty, just as your grandmother told me," the woman says, her voice caressing the words like a lullaby. "Miss Chadwick—I suppose I should call you Mrs. Eaton now," the woman continues, "I am Lady Cowper. Agnes, if you like. Pleased to meet you."

Anne wilts. Slumps in her chair. Reddens with embarrassment at her speechlessness. She knows of Lady Cowper; who doesn't? As one of the Patronesses of Almack's Assembly Rooms, she is one of the de facto Queens of London Society. Almack's on King's Street is the glittering site of Wednesday night balls during the Season, and the premier curtain-raiser for society debutantes. Along with her doughty cronies—Lady Sarah Jersey, Lady Castlereigh, Lady Sefton, Princess Esterhazy, and the Countess of Leiven—Lady Cowper arbitrarily decides the social fate of countless young ladies who long for, live for, *compete* for the cherished prize of their approval. Rejection (horrors!) means unbearable humiliation and disgrace from which no recovery is imaginable. Life would be over.

If accepted, however, and upon payment of a subscription fee of ten guineas, these nubile nymphs are admitted into Almack's holy chambers for the Season, and by extension into London society's highest circles. It is a ticket to rub shoulders with the *ton*, that envied set of people who possess the threefold advantage of being rich, well-born, and fashionable. The lustrous Assembly Rooms are fertile ground for husband hunting, and the debutantes, who have been bred to beautify and dignify the male of the species with their doting presence, coquettishly strut and flirt and fan their feathers to attract a mate from among the most highly placed bachelors in London.

Unlike much of London bureaucracy, bribes to obtain acceptance are wholly ineffective, and the Patronesses are not easily swayed by social rank or personal wealth. Anne has heard that several years earlier, the Duke of Wellington had been denied entry to the Rooms—imagine!—because of the double solecism of tardiness (he arrived at 11:07 p.m.) and unacceptable attire (he had worn trousers rather than knee-breeches as prescribed by the Committee.)

Such is the power of the dowagers of Almack's.

Lady Cowper, slim and perky for a woman of sixty, with loose-fitting skin that suggests rapid weight loss for the Season, studies Anne for a moment and then cocks her head before saying, "I would like to purchase one of your books."

This breaks Anne's stupor and she murmurs a quiet, "Oh, my, yes—of course. I'm so sorry, I was just not expecting—I was… surprised, that is—"

"That's perfectly all right, my dear. Your grandmother told me so much about you—before her untimely passing, such a tragedy that was!—I feel as though I practically know you."

Anne is astonished and delighted that Emily Chadwick had spoken of her to such esteemed acquaintances. "We all grieved for weeks. I thought of her more as a mother than a grandmother."

"You didn't know your mother very well?"

"I was young when she was killed in Persia." Anne hands a copy of *Midnight March* to Lady Cowper, explaining, "It's all in the book, actually."

Lady Cowper does not touch the book in Anne's outstretched hand. "If you'd be so good as to sign it for me, dear," she says.

Embarrassed, Anne sets the book onto the table's surface and opens the cover. "Of course, I'm so sorry," she says, her cheeks pink-tinged with embarrassment. *Lady Cowper must think her such a jinglebrained mushroom!* She takes up her quill, dips it into the inkwell, and begins to inscribe her name on the title page.

Lady Cowper eyes the ink-spattered gloves on Anne's delicate hands. "Oh, my dear, this will not do at all." As Anne finishes her signature, Lady Cowper reaches out gracefully and takes Anne's writing hand in her own, gazing at it dolefully. "Not with the Season upon us."

Suddenly Anne understands the woman's meaning and again her cheeks rouge brightly with the ruby betrayal of her mortification. "I'm so sorry. I was… I sent my husband to—"

"Don't worry, my dear. Your hands are about the same size as mine." Lady Cowper opens her satin, pearl-rimmed purse and plucks from it a pair of white silk gloves. "These will do, I believe. I always have a second pair, just in case." She hands the gloves to Anne. "We can't have a new Member of Almack's signing her name in stained gloves now, can we? Some very important people will be seeing you today."

Anne removes her dogskin gloves and slowly takes Lady Cowper's. She begins to put them on before she comprehends what has just happened.

"Lady Cowper," she timidly says, "did I hear you correctly? Have I been accepted into Almack's?."

"It was one of your grandmother's final wishes, and after meeting you—gloves notwithstanding, under the circumstances—I see no reason not to honor her wish. Of course, there will be the matter of the subscription fee."

"Oh, that will be no problem I assure you."

"Of course not. You can bring it to the first Wednesday ball."

"Of course. There is one other little matter that just occurred to me. I was wondering about my husband, you see… whether he will be permitted to accompany me to the balls."

"Ah, yes, Mr. Herbert Eaton of the *London Times*. Forgive me, my dear—so many of the young ladies we accept are unattached and prefer to attend our events unaccompanied. Of course, we have our rules."

"Oh yes, I understand completely. If it is not possible—"

"I suggest you bring your Mr. Eaton to the Rooms. Let me see now—" Lady Cowper pauses and rolls her eyes toward the ceiling, as if consulting a calendar up there, then continues: "Wednesday afternoon would be a convenient time for us. We can interview him then. Naturally, I am only one vote, but if he makes a favorable impression on the Committee, then—" Lady Cowper raises a flat palm in a gesture of optimism.

"How generous of you!" Anne hands the book to Lady Cowper.

"I shall read it with great interest before the Season begins," the older woman says. "I'm certain it will be much discussed this year. You may keep the gloves, my dear, but do be careful with the quill."

Lady Cowper wheels and glides effortlessly out of the store, the very picture of dignity.

With the excitement of the afternoon, Anne has forgotten about Herbert's mission of mercy, so she is surprised when he enters the book store with a long flat box tied with a pale yellow ribbon. He is in a much better mood than when he left, a wide grin exposing uneven teeth yellowed by pipe smoke. The musty smell of ale that clings to him like an aura explains the length of his absence.

"Here they are, my sweet," he says, proudly holding out the box for her to take, which she does. But as her hands grasp the shiny package, Herbert notices the silky white gloves that she is wearing. Not an ink stain on them! Confused, he looks up at her and says, "I was quite certain that you needed a new pair of gloves. Or was it stockings?" He cocks his head and looks down at her ankles. The ale has addled his brain.

"Yes, Luv, I did. Until Lady Cowper loaned me a pair of hers."

"Lady Cowper!" he shouts. "Herself?" He is impressed.

"In person. I've been accepted into Almack's for the Season."

"That is wonderful news! What a Season this will be. And my book is out just in time. Boothby's timing is impeccable, isn't it?" His spirits are soaring so high that he risks a sardonic thrust of his verbal sword in retaliation for his injured pride: "I didn't know that Evangelicals were admitted into the Best Circle."

Anne flinches but chooses to ignore his remark. Instead, she parries: "After you meet with the Committee, my dear, I'm sure they'll permit you to accompany me."

"*Permit* me to—?" The phrase—the concept—steals the joy from him. He grows suddenly somber, his moods magnified by the two pints sloshing in his belly. "What am I to make of that? A group of old women passing judgment on *me*?" But then he remembers the well-publicized incident with the Duke of Wellington. Thoughtfully now he says, "And when will this audition take place?"

"I'm sure it's just a formality, Luv. Please be a good boy and try not to spoil this for me?" She leans forward and kisses him, stifling a gasp at the stale odor of alcohol that he exudes.

He can smell her sweet and humid breath, feel her soft lips so succulent and tender, her warm body pressing against him. The flesh is weak. As she withdraws, he can see her lips pouting as if the kiss had not ended, and her moist eyes smiling at him expectantly.

"Of course, of course," he says, or something like that. As soon as he speaks, he forgets what he said. What he wants now is another pint of ale to marinate his twice-wounded pride. "I'll be off, then. "I have some business. The carriage will pick you up at six as we planned."

He turns and hurriedly leaves Bumble & Stryker to the care of his wife. Marching blindly through the double doors to the street, he bumps into another pedestrian and mutters an insincere apology without looking up.

The jostled man, who follows Herbert with his eyes, is an odd sight on the London street. In contrast to the many clerks and businessmen who stride about in their severe waistcoats of black or gray and crisply pressed hats, he is attired in a flowing cream tunic and elaborately layered turban. He speaks quietly to a companion and the words, if heard by Herbert or any other Londoner, would be gibberish. The two men nod to each other, and then the first man looks into the shining window of Bumble & Stryker. There, on a carpet of burgundy felt, is a display of books called *Midnight March to Freedom*. The man cannot read the title—he can read only the simplest English—but he can clearly see the centerpiece of the display, a poster with a magnificent life-size portrait of the exotic Anne Chadwick imaginatively dressed as a harem girl; the publisher is counting on the woman's exquisite beauty to sell a considerable number of books.

As he stares at the poster, the jostled man's eyes glimmer in recognition of this beautiful woman. He tosses a question to his companion. Satisfied with the response, the man in the rippling tunic moves toward the entrance of Bumble & Stryker, past the line of autograph seekers who stare incredulously at his flamboyant costume, and into the sacred chamber of book signing. There he sees Anne Chadwick at the table. She is beaming with confidence, glowing with good fortune, her eyes turned downward toward the title page of a book as she scribbles her now-famous name in purple ink.

In another minute, if he does nothing, the man's heart will pound through his chest. He wants to approach Anne Chadwick, but as he steps forward his companion restrains him, whispers in his ear. The man nods.

Better to have a plan. The famous author will not be difficult to find again.

CHAPTER 20

To Ollie's dismay, *Midnight March to Freedom* is the literary sensation of the Season. In his room at the Charterhouse, as he finishes the last page of the book, he feels ashamed and depressed. For Ollie, the book is an embarrassment, a betrayal. He can barely recognize himself in its pages. The heroine, Anisa, seems a stock character out of some idiotic Surrey melodrama. And the villain, the kelauntar, is a lustful alcoholic and drug addict who abuses the women of his harem and robs from the village that he so corruptly governs. *Unfair!* This is not the father that Ollie remembers. The story of young Ali, the progeny of England, the prodigy of Persia, is all wrong. Jalal, the true prodigy, has been erased from the story and Ali assigned his virtues. *How can there be a story about Ali without mention of his other half, Jalal?*

The emotional account of Ollie's spiritual salvation under the god-empowered hands of believers at Walter Nettleship's house will set off shouts of *hallelujah* from the Evangelicals, but causes Ollie only pain. The written account of confession and conversion is not his experience at all, but an outsider's. It is religious propaganda. None of the feelings attributed to him are true. He had experienced fear, guilt, humiliation and anger, not peace and joy and spirit-filled intoxication as Anne had imagined, or perhaps invented. He had not publicly spoken in the language of angels, *or had he?* He certainly had not reached toward the heavens to embrace the one true God and denounce the false god of his father's profane religion. *Not that he can remember.*

On a particularly warm day in early May, Ollie walks across the grounds of the Charterhouse. Ollie is watched closely by two men in a closed black carriage. One of these men wears a billowing turban. The lower part of his face is covered by a ruddy beard colored with henna. With a finger pointed like a pistol, the turbaned man's companion, dressed in English attire, gestures toward Ollie. The carriage driver cannot understand the excited Farsi that the companion speaks, but it is clear that the man in the turban has been looking for this boy.

As Ollie walks, his coat hitched over his right shoulder, a faint shout in the distance makes him stop. It sounds like, "Mr. Chadwick!" Ollie turns toward the source and sees a tall, reedy man running toward him.

"Mr. Chadwick!" The shout is louder now.

Ollie waits for the man to approach. Reaching him at last, the man bends over and places his hands on his knees to catch his breath, then wheezes a hoarse, "Mr. Chadwick, I was hoping it was you." The Englishman is about forty and, judging from his poor physical condition, better suited for sitting than running.

"I am Oliver Chadwick, if that is who you seek," Ollie says.

"It is, indeed. May I have a word with you?"

"I'm afraid you have an advantage over me. You know my name, but I don't know yours."

"Forgive me. I am Eardley Pickwick. May we speak?"

"Unfortunately, I have a class shortly."

"Yes, of course. Just a moment of your time, please."

"I really must be going to—"

Just then Ollie is interrupted by a stream of Farsi that is so unexpected, so startling that at first he does not recognize it. The words slam against him with a force that moves him backward a step. Pickwick steps forward to make up the distance. It has been a very long time since Ollie has heard anyone speak Farsi.

The strange-sounding words buzz in Ollie's head for a few seconds, then sort themselves out. Still confused about their source, Ollie now interprets the Farsi into English. *How odd—to be translating from his native tongue into English instead of the other way around. He really has become a true English gentleman.* The message of the translation is tantalizing: "Mr. Chadwick, a friend of mine, a gentleman from Persia, is currently visiting London. He is familiar with your book and would like to meet you."

In Farsi, Ollie replies, "You speak the language very well for an Englishman."

The conversation continues in Farsi.

"Yes, I was born in London of English parents," Pickwick replies, "and I have lived here all my life, except for two years abroad. In Persia."

"And why did you visit Persia?"

"I am an adjunct professor of middle eastern studies at Oxford, with a specialty in languages. An Orientalist, so to speak. I spent two years in Persia doing research and perfecting my Farsi. Although, I've been told, it is still far from perfect."

"Excuse me, sir. Please don't think me rude, but I am now late for my class. If you'll excuse me, perhaps some other time—"

Pickwick urgently reverts to English, and the coarseness of the language catches Ollie's attention. "Mr. Chadwick, the gentleman of whom I speak has come all the way from Persia to meet you. He is in the carriage over there." Pickwick gestures toward the solemn black carriage standing perhaps a hundred yards away. "He has some news that will be of great interest to you."

"News you say? Of what?"

"Please, Mr. Chadwick. Come and meet with him in the carriage. He will explain everything. This conversation will prove to be much more important than your class."

Ollie stares at the carriage. Inside the closed cabin, through a window, he can just make out the shadowy figure of a man shifting in his seat. Ollie's curiosity is piqued, but the memory of his encounter with Reginald Pennick is still fresh in his mind. *Don't place yourself in isolation with a stranger*, he tells himself. *Be careful. Be smart.*

Ollie fights his growing curiosity. Maybe there is news of his father. Or Jalal. But caution wins the battle. "If your friend would like to meet with me, then I suggest the George & Vulture at, say, six this evening." The George & Vulture is a popular pub that is always busy at night, providing the security of a crowd.

Pickwick stares at the boy, restraining his frustration, but finally nods yes.

"Then I must be on my way. Good day, sir. I look forward to meeting you again this evening." Ollie spins and begins to walk toward his class, aware that Eardley Pickwick—if that is his true name—stands behind him straight as a pillar, watching.

Ollie is suddenly aware that his heart is pounding and his mouth is as dry as a woolen shirt.

CHAPTER 21

Ollie arrives early at the George & Vulture on Lombard Street. The inn is already clogged with thick-bodied Englishmen stuffing their bellies with beef and marinating their tonsils with stout ale and ruby wine. After a few minutes, three jowly gentlemen, solicitors from the look of their blue satchels ballooned with papers, vacate a table near the front window. Ollie deftly slips in behind them, staking his claim. A weary barmaid hustles over to him, wagging a fat finger and jabbering loudly about the inappropriateness of usurping that small square space while so many others are waiting for the comfort of a seat. But Ollie has learned the art of negotiation. He holds up a guinea and the barmaid's mouth clamps shut, her greedy eyes fixed on the gold coin.

"Thank you so much for reserving the table for me," Ollie says, smiling coyly. "My friends will be here shortly."

With a nod of sudden understanding, the barmaid plucks the coin from Ollie's hand and says, "You're very welcome, sir. What's your pleasure?"

"Some port, I believe." Ollie is in the mood for wine. Herbert drinks port while he writes. It must fuel one's powers of communication. And this evening Ollie will need all of his powers.

"Very good, sir." The barmaid scurries off.

From the table, Ollie has a fine view of the Tower of London and the courtyard. Such a big city it is. As he waits for Eardley Pickwick and friend to arrive, he senses its ominous nature.

"You bloody well know I can't afford a place like this!" A voice startles Ollie and he turns toward it, seeing a chum who is also interested in writing, a pasty-faced boy named Charles Dickens.

"Sit down, Charles," Ollie says. "No, not over there. Here by me."

Charles takes a seat next to Ollie. He looks around the room.

"I will pay for the evening, don't worry," Ollie explains. "You can save your money for the theatre. By the way, thank you for coming."

"What's this about, Ollie? I received your invitation, but I must say I'm puzzled as to the occasion."

"I'm, uh, meeting some gentlemen here this evening, and to be truthful, I didn't want to be alone. Or outnumbered."

"Well, this is my first time to the George & Vulture."

"My stepfather, Herbert, has brought me here several times. He claims the place is haunted by the ghosts of England's most famous journalists." Ollie points to a small table across the room. "You see, over there is where Jonathon Swift used to sit when he was editor of the *Examiner*. That was before he wrote *Gulliver's Travels*... or perhaps during."

Charles stares at the table, imagining the great Swift sitting there, swilling an ale and scrawling his masterpiece.

"At the far end of the bar—" Ollie gestures in another direction and Charles swivels his head—"Joseph Addison and Richard Steele of the *Tattler* used to debate their essays and, perhaps, find ample targets for their satire by merely looking about the room. Or so Herbert has told me."

The barmaid pushes her way to Ollie's table and sets down a glass of port. "Anything for you, sir?" she asks Charles.

"An ale, please," Charles replies. "But tell me—is it true that Addison and Steele used to come here? And Swift?"

"I wouldn't know, sir. Are they from the neighborhood?"

"*Jonathon* Swift, the author!"

"Ahh—*Gulliver's Travels*. Aye, it's true, sir—though I never met him m'self, bein' as how he frequented the place a century ago. This old inn has been the home away from home for a number of gentlemen who were good with the quill, that's true. I've been told that Daniel Defoe himself—*Robinson Crusoe*, you know..."

"Yes, one of my favorites," Charles interjects.

"...had a table in the back room. But that was a long time ago, too. And this table you're at—" the barmaid thumps the surface with her knuckles— "was the favorite of the great Samuel Johnson himself. I'll be back with yer ale, sir. Will there be others?"

"Two more," Ollie says, then watches the barmaid whirl and slice through the crowded room.

"It's a wonderful place!" Charles says, smiling for the first time. "A place for authors." He takes a deep breath, inhaling the ghostly smell of drying ink and famous prose.

"Yes, I agree. Quite wonderful," Ollie says. "But let me tell you about our guests before they arrive. I don't know much about them, but they will be here shortly and—"

Ollie is startled by the sudden appearance of the man from the carriage.

"I hope I'm not too early," the man says. "I thought it would take longer to get here." He turns to Charles, extends a hand and introduces himself. "I am Eardley Pickwick."

Charles takes his hand and shakes it vigorously. "Charles Dickens, pleased to meet you."

Eardley sits down, turns to Ollie, and utters a string of Farsi, expressing his dismay that Ollie has brought a companion to the meeting. Ollie lies, saying that he and Charles meet every Wednesday evening at the George & Vulture to discuss literary matters, so it is Eardley and his mysterious companion who are the interlopers, not Charles.

Charles listens quietly. He doesn't understand Farsi, but he senses the tension in this exchange, and it makes him uneasy. "Something to drink?" he asks Eardley, hoping to lighten the moment.

Eardley ignores Charles—or maybe not, for he switches back to English. "We have only a few moments alone, so let me be candid."

"Please do," Ollie replies.

"The real reason I came early was to explain my desperate circumstances. I hope this will remain confidential?" Eardley glances at Charles, who stares back for a moment before realizing the question was directed at him. Charles nods his agreement.

"During the past two years it was my misfortune to fall upon hard times," Eardley continues. "My debts mounted quickly, and fearing that my creditors might plunge me into debtor's prison, I tried to solve my dilemma by gambling. As you might guess, this misguided strategy produced—well, let's just say *unsatisfactory results*." Eardley nervously looks over his shoulder, ensuring that the second man has not yet arrived.

"Why are you telling us this?" Ollie asks.

"Because I must implore you to cooperate with my companion. You see, he came to England seeking an English tutor and translator who could help him in his diplomatic work. But I sensed from the beginning that his true mission was something else entirely. While I don't pretend to know his goal, it is clear that you are an important part of its achievement."

Charles is lost. He speaks up: "Is this other man from Persia, like Ali?"

"Yes. And he has promised me a substantial amount of money to help locate Ollie, the bulk of which will be paid if and when his mission can be accomplished. The sum is enough to satisfy my creditors! And he has promised me continued employment as well—if his objective is attained. The truth is, you see, while I told Ollie that I was an adjunct professor at Oxford, I have not been employed there for several years. I was dismissed for—well, that's quite another story. Unfortunately, there are not many employment opportunities at the moment for an expert in oriental history and languages, especially when one is shut out of academia. This, I'm afraid, is at the root of my financial dilemma. So you see, in a large sense, my fate is in your hands."

"And what would you have Ollie do?" Charles asks.

Eardley lowers his eyes sadly and mutters, "I don't know." Then he lifts his gaze to stare directly into Ollie's eyes. "But I beg of you, please give him a chance to explain, and keep an open mind. He seems like a very nice gentleman, and he's very rich."

The barmaid interrupts with a mug of ale. "Here ya go, sir," she says to Charles, spilling the foam as she pushes the pewter mug toward the boy. Then she turns to Eardley and says, "There's a gentleman wants a word with ya, sir, in the back room. Says you'll know what it's about. Anything in the meantime, sir?"

Eardley stands, nodding no. The barmaid departs and Eardley sighs deeply, the stress of the moment pinching his entire face into a pucker. Ollie can see perspiration on the man's brow. "I beg of you…" Eardley says to Ollie. And then he disappears into the crowd.

Ollie is afraid of the revelation that is only moments away. But *what* does he fear? Here, in the George & Vulture, he is surrounded by civilized humanity. Still, since the episode with Reginald Pennick, any eccentric or secretive behavior by an older man—particularly one in a position of power—arouses Ollie's suspicions. Ollie has vowed never to be in such a vulnerable position again. He gulps the remainder of his wine and motions for the barmaid.

"Yes sir, another wine?" the matron asks.

Ollie produces another bright, shiny guinea, holding it up for the woman to see. "Yes, one more, please. And *this* is for you—if you'll keep an eye on our table. We may require your service at a moment's notice."

The barmaid stares at the coin, her eyes gleaming. *Two guineas in one night!* Of course she will give the young man her special attention. She reaches out to seize the guinea, but as her hand nears it, Ollie flicks his wrist and the coin moves just beyond her reach.

"Remember, now. I need your attention."

"Yes, sir. I understand."

Ollie flips the coin to the woman, who bobbles it. The guinea falls with a clank to the floor. She stoops to retrieve it, then stands up with a grin. "If you should need *anything*, sir—" she says. And then she is gone.

"That's quite a lot of money to be throwing away," Charles says.

"It's nothing. My grandmother was rich."

"And now you are."

"In time, perhaps. Right now I'm just a school boy with a pocket full of guineas."

Ollie's eyes are drawn to the back room. The smoke and a forest of standing bodies hide the entrance to this room, but suddenly a gold and brown turban emerges from it, hovering above the freshly ironed hats and balding heads of the chattering Englishmen who obscure the wearer. The turban hesitates for a moment, then begins to float through the crowd.

Ollie's heart hammers his chest. He is terrified! How could he ever have believed that a public place could protect him? What a stupid idea it was to meet this man. Ollie presses his fingers against his chest, feeling the silver charm beneath his shirt and praying for protection.

The turban continues to float menacingly above the crowd, weaving in and out, left and right, making its way toward Ollie. But the face beneath it remains hidden in shadows, veiled in smoke, blocked by the other men.

Ollie shuts his eyes. He wishes he were safely at home in his Belgravia mansion. Yes, *his* mansion. He is the heir, the master. He is no longer a child. He must gain control of himself, take charge of this situation. This is his country, his London, his tavern, his barmaid—*he has seen to that!*—and his meeting. The gentleman in the turban should be the nervous one.

With great resolve, Ollie opens his eyes. The turbaned man is hidden behind the body of Eardley Pickwick who stands at the table and says, "Mr. Chadwick, I would like to introduce my employer."

Eardley steps aside. The turbaned man approaches the table and his face becomes fully illuminated. In a thick accent, the man says, "Good evening, Ali."

Ollie stares at the man in disbelief. His brain swirls, his body shivers, his heart clenches into a fist. This cannot be! Not in London! Not after his long escape across the Persian desert.

Ollie replies at last. There are so many things that he could say, but only three words come to him: "Good evening, father."

Startled, Charles turns to Ollie. *What a delicious twist! Who could invent such a plot?*

Eardley, too, is astonished.

But not as surprised as Ollie, who manages to control himself like a proper English gentleman. "Please join us. I'm eager to hear about your travels."

Ollie gestures and the barmaid appears almost instantly. "My friends would like something to drink," Ollie says. "Mr. Pickwick?"

"An ale please, dark."

Ollie turns to his father, Mirza Hasan Qasim. In Farsi he says, "Father? Perhaps you wish to abstain from alcohol."

Hasan replies in Farsi: "I'll have whatever you are drinking. Wine? Perfect. I find the wine in London not up to the standards of Shiraz, but sufficient."

"My apologies, Charles, if we speak for a few minutes in our native tongue," Ollie says, then coolly turns back to his father, again speaking in Farsi. "How did you find me?"

"Your mother's portrait on a book caught my eye. Such a beautiful woman. Mr. Pickwick contacted the publisher and the rest was quite simple. How do you find public life?"

"Intrusive," Ollie says. "Tell me about Bushruyih. I haven't seen it in over three years."

"Neither have I."

"You don't live there?"

"Shortly after you left, there was an unfortunate event involving the provincial vizier, who was attacked and slaughtered outside the village. I led a small, brave band of Bushruyih citizens into the desert where we found the Turkoman murderers and annihilated them, despite their superior force. I was so distressed at the death of the great vizier that I took news of the tragedy—and the justice we administered—directly to the shah. As a show of gratitude, the shah named me to fill the vizier's vacant position."

"So now you're the vizier of Khurasan?"

"No longer. About a year later, Persia found itself at war with the Russians. Perhaps you heard. No? Well, it suddenly seemed wise for our country to court the English as allies, even though Persians distrust Englishmen almost as much as Russians. I made another journey to Tehran and gained an audience with my uncle, the shah, suggesting that I might be useful in a diplomatic position. As you may recall, I had learned a few words of English from that traitor, Gordon Cranston, and I demonstrated my ability. The shah could not judge my lack of fluency, of course, and so my meager abilities must have been magnified in his estimation. At any rate, I gained my new post as a diplomat to England and began consulting with the British Attaché in Tehran, who helped me improve my English—in exchange, of course, for favors that I was now in a position to grant."

Eardley suspects that payment to Hasan for 'favors' had bought more than English lessons.

"A few months ago," Hasan continues, "with the war going badly, I was asked to come to London and appeal for more support. How fortunate for me that you and your mother also wound up in London. Now, please, tell me your story. I understand that your English family is rich and powerful. It appears that you descend from the Qajar empire on one side, and a British publishing empire on the other. For Persians, you would be considered the first-born of a strategic union between cultures. Who would have thought that your slave-mother would turn out to be a British heiress? That would have been useful to know."

Ollie looks at this man and no longer sees his father. Instead, he sees a cold and conniving Persian diplomat. *Had his father changed over the years, or was he always like this?* Maybe his mother's book, with its vivid portrayal of the villainous kelauntar, had more truth in it than Ollie had known.

"I am at a disadvantage," Ollie says. "It seems you already know my story. And since I know so little of yours, may I ask a question?"

"Of course."

"What do you want?"

Mirza Hasan Qasim stiffens in his chair. The accusatory tone of his son's question startles him. He had hoped that Ali would be glad to see him, but there is no sign of sentiment or love in this boy. *His mother must have poisoned his mind!* "All right, you want to know my intentions? They are quite simple. I am here to take you back with me to Persia."

Now Ollie stiffens. Surely this is a joke!

"Why would I return to Persia?" Ollie asks.

"To help your country," Hasan replies.

"My country is England."

"You were born in Persia, the son of a Persian prince. You are a *Persian*, not an Englishman."

"My country is England now. I was born in Persia, the son of a slave. My mother is an Englishwoman, and England is my home."

"Ali, in the name of Allah, and for the sake of Muhammad—praise be unto Him—please reconsider. Your country is at war with Russia."

"*In the name of Allah*, did you say? Maybe your agents failed to inform you that I am a Christian now. Whatever I do, I do in the name of Jesus. And for the sake of Jesus, I will remain in England." Ollie has not experienced such religious stirrings in a long time, but his father has confronted him directly with his past, which he now considers pagan. His emotions are roused, and he finds himself saying things he only half means. "I will never return to Persia! I will never leave England!"

At these words, Hasan seems to slump. The pomp has leaked out of him. He lowers his head for a moment, then raises his eyes. Ollie detects moisture in those eyes—tears, or maybe just the sting of cigar smoke—but says nothing. An awkward silence envelopes them.

Finally, Eardley clears his throat and mutters a nervous, "Well, then—"

In a quiet voice, Hasan interrupts. He says to Ollie, "I can see that an appeal to your patriotism was a mistake. Let me confess my real motive. I am a father who has lost his son. When you left Bushruyih, my heart was broken. Every moment of my life has been spent trying to find you. I sought my new position as a diplomat hoping it would give me certain advantages in gaining information about you and your mother. You were my only son. You *are* my only son. Now I've found you, and my heart aches as it did the morning I discovered you gone."

Ollie begins to soften. He can recall the gentleness and emotion with which the kelauntar agreed to send him to the madrisih in Mashhad. Perhaps there is a middle ground here. What would be the harm in reestablishing a relationship with his own father?"

"I never gave up hope of getting you back," Hasan says. "And your mother."

These words cut Ollie like a dagger. *And your mother!* Anisa the slave girl. Yes, it is becoming clear now. This is about *possession*. About Mirza Hasan Qasim's pride and the humiliation of losing his cherished objects. He wants them back! And he will stop at nothing until he succeeds. Now his son is not just a son, but a political advantage, a blood relation to a potential ally. How much of his father's story is true? All of it now is suspect. Looking back on this conversation with a fresh perspective, Ollie detects a pattern of deceit. Hasan had changed tactics too quickly, had sprouted tears too early, and most likely had bent and twisted every element of his story to suit his selfish interests.

Ollie grows angry but contains his emotions long enough to quietly say, "Father, you never had a son." What he means is that Hasan had always viewed Ali as a possession, but Hasan takes from these words a different and more provocative meaning—that Ollie is denouncing his father.

Hasan erupts, slamming a fist on the table. The glasses and mug jump. "It is not for the son to denounce his father!" Hasan fiercely proclaims. "You are mine! You were taken from me, and I will have you back." The outburst cracks Hasan's thin veneer of reasonableness, confirming Ollie's suspicions.

Eardley tries to patch the crack with a paste of soft words and sentiment. "Ollie, surely you can understand the heartbreak of a father," he says desperately. "He is only angry because he loves you. I'm sure you didn't mean what you said. Tell him that you'll reconsider. Maybe take a little time—"

"I meant what I said!" Ollie says firmly. "Now please leave!"

"The conversation is not over until I give the order!" Hasan insists. "There is another matter that may change your mind."

Ollie bristles at his father's arrogance. "As the host, I declare this meeting adjourned."

"No! The conversation is not over." Hasan's face glows red with anger. He is not accustomed to defiance. This is now a test of wills, and Hasan has underestimated the will of his son. Ollie is no longer the meek twelve-year-old who dwells in Hasan's time-sweetened memory.

Ollie motions to the barmaid, who within seconds materializes at the table. "These gentlemen have been invited to leave," Ollie explains. "Would you inform the proprietor that they may need to be escorted out?"

At first the barmaid does not understand, but when she peers into the angry face of Hasan it all becomes clear.

"I'll have something for you afterward," Ollie suggests.

The barmaid scurries off to get help.

Eardley, seeing his life suddenly crushed between the feuding parties, dissolves into a porridge of self-pity.

Charles seems invigorated by his companion's spunk, even though he understands little of the conversation.

Hasan leans over the table, glaring at Ollie. "You are not considering the interests of your mother in your decision," he says.

Ollie sits back in his chair. "What do you mean?"

"If you returned to Persia, you could spare her."

"Spare her—from what?"

"From humiliation. Do you know how she humiliated me with the lies in her book? Of course you do. But my mortification is nothing compared to what she will face."

"What do you mean?"

"No one in Persia will read your mother's book, so my humiliation will not exist there, where it would most hurt me. But consider what disgrace your mother will suffer when certain information is revealed within her own circle here in London."

The barmaid returns with two hulking men wearing scowls. "Are your friends ready to leave, sir?" the barmaid asks Ollie. For a moment, Ollie ignores the barmaid and the two men. Staring at Hasan, he asks, "What information?"

Hasan leans close to Ollie, whispers into his ear. As he speaks, a faint sneer deforms his lips.

When Hasan is finished speaking, Ollie leans back in his chair, visibly shaken. "You would do this?" he asks his father, who merely nods yes.

Ollie turns to the barmaid and says, "They are ready to leave. Please show them out."

The two hulks step forward threateningly, but Eardley and Hasan rise without further encouragement. As he begins to walk away, Hasan turns to Ollie with cold, passionless eyes, and again nods *yes*—an exclamation point to his warning.

On the street, Eardley turns to Hasan. "I was hoping it would go well," he says nervously. "I'm sorry. Perhaps he will change his mind."

"He won't. He's a Qasim—and all Qasims are stubborn."

"But maybe—"

"I will need you to do one more thing for me."

"Of course. And then?"

"And then I suggest you seek employment elsewhere. You remind me of a most unpleasant evening."

Through the window, Ollie watches his father turn his back on Eardley and arrogantly strut away. Eardley seems to deflate as he walks, disappearing into his greatcoat.

"Ollie, are you all right?" Charles asks.

"No, not really." Ollie tells the truth. He is scared, angry, frustrated—and very, very sad. He is at war with his own father, who holds his mother hostage. An unfair advantage. He continues to look out the window, pretending to watch Eardley melt into nothingness, but in reality Ollie is choking back tears.

His reflection in the glass gives him away.

CHAPTER 22

Ollie is drunk. The George and Vulture is a block behind him, perhaps two. Maybe three. He chokes back a burning finger of bile squeezed up from his stomach, stumbles over the jutting lip of a cobblestone, steadies himself against the sooty brick of a building—or is it a wall? He had set off for the river to clear his head—a simple excursion—but his rudderless brain has steered him into a murky backwater of dark, stinking alleys that twist like the entrails of a great beast. As he coughs and dizzyingly turns around, searching for some marker, some indication of where he is, an awful panic seizes him. He cannot remember which way is forward. Another alley converges on this point. *That way?* The stench of garbage and human waste surrounds him like a fog and he chokes, falls to his knees, heaves up a sour stew of old wine and chewed sausage, wipes a string of vomit from his mouth, and finally sits down in the filth, leaning against the cold brick wall where he passes out.

He dreams of his mother. She is on the deck of a ship, waving. At him—no, at a gathering of Evangelicals on the shore, admirers who wave back and blow their loving kisses in her direction. Ollie stands alone on a bridge, watching the ship, watching the crowd, watching his mother steam away. His mother—she is not alone. She stands with her arm around Jalal, who is still twelve years old. Standing behind them in her beautiful green gown is Mum. They are leaving, all of them. Abandoning him. So happy they seem! So eager to get on with their new lives in their new destination. Ollie waves frantically, trying to get their attention, but they don't notice. Or don't care. At last he can no longer see them—only the silhouette of the ship. He sinks to the floor of the bridge, sitting there for a moment silently, sadly, then lying down, his back pressing against the cold iron platform.

Oh yes, he is lost.

A seagull lands on him and starts to peck at his chest. It hurts! His hands flail, trying to slap the gull away.

Not a gull! A snake.

No, a *stick* poking him in the ribs. *Get it away!*

He grabs the stick, opens his eyes. The world is dark and blurry, his head swirling. The ship's bridge is gone. He is in a dark alley, holding a stick that wiggles and prods. A shadowy face looms over him. The filthy face of a boy.

"He's alive, I told ya."

The voice is young, a child's. There are more faces staring at him, half-moons in the dim light. And more children's laughter.

"Hey mister, whatcha doin' 'ere?

"Drunk, 'e is. Get 'is money."

The jostling stick grows dead in Ollie's hand. A mouse is in his pocket, wiggling. He grabs it. *A hand.* A tiny hand!

"Ouch!"

They are stealing his money! Slowly, Ollie's brain begins to engage. He grasps the hand firmly, but it fights to get away. Suddenly he is beaten by more sticks, a full-body bastinado. He lets the hand go and the faces retreat.

The thrashing stops. The boys are seven, maybe eight years old. A half-dozen of them. They point their sticks at him threateningly.

"I says, forge' 'im, 'e's not drunk enough."

"Will yer 'ave a look at 'im, eh? Them not so bad kit, 'e's got notes on 'im, I tell yer."

Ollie must be drunker than he thought. These filthy urchins are ragged and small. But aggressive. Maybe this is still a dream.

"Poke 'im in the bloomin' eye wiv a stick, see wot 'e does."

Ollie doesn't like the sound of this. With great effort, he pushes his back up the scummy brick wall and points a menacing finger at the Lilliputian mob. The boys take a step backward, jabbing at him with their sticks.

"I don' like th' looks of dis," one of them says.

"There're six of us and one of 'im, right? I says 'e's too drunk ter hurt us."

"Go fer 'is shins!"

The boys raise their sticks like lances and prepare to charge. Suddenly terrified, Ollie holds up his hands and shouts, "Nooo! What do you want, money?"

The boys look at each other. One of them, the tallest boy with a strikingly handsome face, speaks in a high-pitched voice. "Wot do ya fin'? We're not aht 'ere for the chuffin' fan of it." The gruff words spoken in such a soft, childish voice, are almost comical.

Ollie's head is clearing. Maybe he had slept for a while, shaking off his drunken stupor, before the boys discovered him. He licks his dry lips, looks around the shadowy maze of alleys and decides on a reasonable course of action.

"Maybe we can strike a bargain," he says.

"A *deal*, is 'at wot ya mean?'"

"That's right. If we don't fight, no one gets hurt. I have money. I'll give you money if you do something for me."

The boys consult—*argue* is a better word. Finally the tall boy addresses Ollie. "Ya sum kind of pervert or summit?"

Pervert? The boys have the wrong idea. "No, no, not that," he says. The boys seem puzzled.

"We could take yer bread 'n 'honey if we bleedin' wanted to."

"Yes, I'm sure you could. But some of you would be badly hurt. No sense in that." Ollie is astonished that this gang of youngsters is roaming the alleys so late. He reaches into a pocket and takes out a handful of schillings, keeping his notes and guineas carefully tucked away.

The boys' eyes grow big as they stare at the money.

"I'll tell you what," Ollie says. "I will pay you to answer questions. One schilling per answer. Does that seem fair?"

The boys consult again, their heads nodding up and down.

"Awright. But yer 'ave ter pay us after each answer."

"Then put down your sticks. My first question is, where are your parents?"

The tall boy objects. "That's six questions!"

"All right," Ollie agrees. "Then it's worth six schillings. Who wants to go first?"

The tall boy begins, and then each in turn tells his tale. Slowly, the boys begin to relax. Over the next hour they answer Ollie's questions, taking seats on the garbage-strewn alley floor, gradually moving closer to Ollie, all the better to take the schillings. Ollie, too, sits down, drawn into their stories of neglect and abuse. Two of the boys had escaped from grim London orphanages in which they were poorly fed, worked to the bone, and sexually abused by the adults in power. One of them had been abandoned at the orphanage door by his mother when he was four years old. One of the others lives with an alcoholic father who beats him when he is sober, and beats him harder when drunk. The two youngest boys live in brothels with their prostitute moms, who work nights. Until a month ago, the tall, handsome boy had lived in a nanny-house, an abode of working child prostitutes. Four of them already had worked in organized child gangs—pickpocketing, thieving, selling the sexual favors of girls barely older than themselves—and had escaped the iron-fisted tyranny of their "boss" despite his menacing threats. If they should ever be caught by him…

As the boys talk, the alley fills up with their pain and grief and hopelessness. None of them believes he will live to see the age of ten. Something—starvation, murder, illness, accident—is sure to get them. But not to pity, for death will relieve their misery. If only the act of dying were not so terrifying! All of them have only contempt for adults, the tormenters of children and defilers of innocence. In just a few years, these little boys have experienced brutality and exploitation beyond measure.

And yet they have survived!

"Look after yorself, right, that's the bleedin' rule out 'ere," the tall boy says. "No bloke will do it for yer. It's up ter yer alone. Even yor own mum won't 'ave a look after yer in the end, that's 'ow it is." The words produce a long silence.

And that's when Ollie realizes he is no longer lost. His despair over the dilemma presented by his father—should he go back to Persia to save his mother from embarrassment?—is ended. There is no dilemma. Adults can take care of themselves. But who will look after the children? He will *never* return to Persia. As for his mother—she has already steamed out of London on her own vessel, leaving him behind. *A curse on parents!* Let her deal with Mirza Hasan Qasim and his secret. Ollie will look after his own interests.

Ollie admires the grit and raw honesty of these boys. Without their pure selfishness they would perish in days, perhaps hours. This is what saves them. It is their secret to survival. *Selfishness.* Looking after themselves, in the direst circumstances, when no one else will.

The pause in the conversation has become awkward. One of the boys looks at his ragged companions and finally breaks the silence: "Wot now then, eh? We all gonna sit 'round an' sing hymns?"

The tall boy seems to break out of a coma. He looks up at Ollie. "Say, we've been answerin' yor questions for a wile now, but yer 'aven't been payin'. I fink yer owe us some schillin's." The tall boy is right. As the boys had become drawn deeply into their own terrible stories, they had slowly forgotten about the reward. Until now.

"All right, I have an idea," Ollie says. "Agreed, I owe you money, but none of us knows how much. Not for sure. So I have a proposal." He fishes a gleaming guinea out of his pocket and shows it. The boys lean forward expectantly. "This is the last of my money." Not quite true, but he has won their confidence. "I will give it to you on three conditions. First, you must agree to share it equally. Second, you must agree that this covers my debt to you. And third—please show me the way back to Lombard Street."

"Yer 'ave yorself a deal," the tall boy says. "By the way, my bleedin' name is Tim." He extends a small hand. "Tim Shaw."

Ollie takes Tim's hand, pressing the coin between their palms. "And I am Oliver Chadwick. Remember—share the guinea."

"Aye, it belongs ter all of us."

Ollie silently follows the boys through the maze of alleys, jumping over piles of rat-infested refuse, tripping over squealing cats. He had drunkenly wandered much further than he had thought into the bowels of London. Suddenly the boys stop. The tall boy gestures Ollie forward, out of London's entrails, back into the relatively civilized world of Lombard Street.

It is early morning. The sky is just a pale glow. Human life is emerging—the bill poster and his glue-pot, the scrubber, two or three cabs trolling for drunkards too soused to walk home, a scattering of shopkeepers rattling keys in their doors and dreaming of a new day better then the last one. Ollie steps into the street and takes a deep breath. Compared to the rancidness of the back alleys, even the soot-filled air of Lombard Street smells particularly sweet this morning. Ah, the fragrance of hot pies!

Ollie looks down at himself. What a mess! His clothes are stained with muck, his hands are black and sticky, and the foul taste in his mouth…!

Yet he feels oddly settled. He smiles. And then he turns to thank the boys.

But no one is there.

Chapter 23

The much-anticipated event is upon them—the first Almack's ball of the Season. For weeks, Anne has dragged Herbert and Oliver to dance lessons tutored by none other than Camille Dundas, who has finely tuned the steps of such important personages as Lord and Lady Grimston and Princess Wittycapstein. These exhausting preparations have given Mr. and Mrs. Herbert Eaton and their son a dance repertoire hand-picked for Almack's Assembly Rooms— waltzes, gallopades, and quadrilles. Anne is now quite certain that Herbert will not embarrass her on the dance floor.

Oliver accepts the tedious dance lessons as part of the necessary education of an English gentleman. Now sixteen, he has the height and bearing of a young man, with astonishingly good looks—the gift of his mother's genes— and moist, dusky eyes that mesmerize every young lady who passes him on the street, though he doesn't notice. He thinks through the complicated steps and gestures of the quadrille as he finishes dressing in the knee-breeches, white cravat, and *chapeau bras* dictated for male guests by the Patronesses.

The whirlwind of preparations during these past weeks has helped Ollie forget about the heated row with his father at the George & Vulture. But in the back of Ollie's mind is the nagging fear that his father will carry out his terrible threat. And if he does, Ollie will be to blame, for Ollie had decided to make no warning and launch no defense.

The time for departure arrives. Anne is exhausted from her day-long apprehension of her first ball. Herbert is irritated by his wife's incessant fussing. They march out of the Belgravia mansion toward the carriage where Ollie is already seated, sampling the cool night air. Anne has timed their departure so that they will arrive at Almack's shortly after ten. Earlier would make them seem over-eager; later would unnecessarily shorten the evening, and Anne wants the evening to last forever.

Ollie peers out of the carriage window and sees the dazzling figure of his mother glistening and sparkling in the moonlight. She is wearing Mum's brilliant diadem with *bandeaux* of the same costly jewels in her hair. A flowing tunic of white tulle, embroidered in silver, caresses a gown of rich white satin that molds itself to every curve and movement. Like an angel, she glides to the carriage, and like an angel, she remains an enigma to Ollie. He pictures her in Bushruyih, in the anderun, the favorite of the other wives, so selfless and kind, so tender and caring. But now, despite her shimmering beauty, her heart seems to have hardened. She is no longer his mother; she had given up that role to Mum upon arrival in London, washing her hands of him just as easily as she had washed off the Persian.

"Ollie," Anne says as she is helped into the carriage, "you look like a proper gentleman. Isn't this fun?"

Neither Ollie nor Herbert replies. Anne adjusts her gown as she sits on the cushioned seat. The horses jerk the carriage into motion. All the way to Almack's, the three are silent. Anne stares ahead, occasionally glancing out the open side windows but ever-so-careful not to let the wind muss her hair. She seems in another world, oblivious of her companions, rehearsing in her mind the coming events. She wants everything to go perfectly! Tonight is the pinnacle of her transformation from slave-girl to London *ton*. She will be a celebrity in the highest circles—not a visitor, but *one of them*, a peer. She is tense, but has never felt more alive. Her skin tingles and her stomach churns.

And then they enter the hallowed kingdom of Almack's, which extends out its guarded doors to King St. at St. James, where London's most fashionable thoroughfare links up with its most aristocratic square. Herbert steps from the carriage and gives his gloved hand to Anne as she gracefully disembarks. She pauses for a moment, studies the details of her husband and then adjusts his cravat into a perfect waterfall, patting him on the chest afterward like a patient puppy. "Oooh," she says, a kind of sigh, an admittance that the time has come to ascend the staircase.

Oliver follows behind, forgotten it seems. Orbiting around him are society's matrons and debutantes, giggling and chattering nervously, tripping embarrassingly on their long gowns, complaining viciously about their rivals, huffing and panting with the exertion of the climb.

Inside, the main ballroom is bejeweled with glowing oil-lamps and wax-lights that spread a soft, glimmering sheen over the entire assembly. The perimeter of the room is fringed with two rows of plump sofas that are quickly filling with guests staking out favored positions. At the far end of the room, on massive burgundy sofas embroidered with gold and silver threads, the imperious Patronesses hold court, and it is toward these imposing thrones that Anne and Herbert lead Oliver. Gracefully and politely they prance around the edges of the room, careful not to cross the unpopulated center marked off for dancing by red velvet ropes lest they violate an unspoken rule. Before the first dance, to cross this inviolate space is to call undue attention to oneself, and despite the peacock strutting and flirtatious preening of the guests, such a gaffe is considered pathetically untoward.

Oliver is dazzled by the human ornamentation that surrounds him—girls in gowns with fashionably low-cut bodices and haughty bustles made of silk and satin and velvet of every hue (some pale and delicate but others deep-hued and sensuous), their hair intricately interwoven with birds nests or fruit baskets or whole gardens of flowers, or wearing hats of crepe crested with waving plumes of feathers; and the matrons with rouged faces, false frontlets, and *ceintures* of costly brilliants, all of them ruthlessly plotting to keep their girls in the way of the "prizes" but out of the way of the "detrimentals." The men, too—particularly those seeking an ornamental companion from the highest circles—strut and fluff their feathers, posing to flaunt their cat-skin waistcoats and mirror-finish Hessian boots and diamond-studded watch fobs. And into this sumptuous stew is stirred foreign dignitaries in full military dress or formal native costume—an ambassador from Pakistan, a German general and Spanish admiral, diplomats from America, Russia, and India. Oliver is surrounded by the titled—Ladies and Marchionesses, Princesses and Countesses; Barons and Lords and Viscounts and Earls and Marquisses and...

Oliver is unaware of the male heads turning and the hungry eyes sliding surreptitiously to capture a tasty glimpse of the delicious Anne Chadwick, who in her simple form-fitting silver sheath and flowing cloak seems almost naked compared to the embellishment of the other women. *By choice?* Her stark beauty carves through the ornamental fatigue like a perfectly cut diamond on a velvet cloth and sends hormones purring. *How daring, to buck the fashions of the day. Isn't she the slave-girl from Persia?* Nor does young Oliver notice the countless furtive glances in his direction by the suddenly captivated debutantes whose mothers, so astute and observant, nudge them with sharp elbows—*Look, there is Lord Longhride's second brother!*--and point out better prospects among the older men—*I believe that Baron Rendlesham has his eye on you, my dear. Ohh, he just looked away!*

As he slips past, Oliver overhears snatches of conversation that betray the matrimonial motives of Almack's matrons. *My dear, you must not sit next to the Countess of Leuchars; she wears such a profusion of pink and yellow, it will make you look pale.* As always, these women seem to perceive a chronic shortage of prizes, and by the sudden brightening of their eyes and heaving of their motherly chests when one approaches, Oliver understands that a title and a good rent-roll are the chief criteria, not love or looks or even age (many of the main prizes are ten, fifteen, sometimes twenty years older than the young ladies who expectantly display their carefully packaged charms).

The receiving line for the Patronesses has diminished and Anne is taking the hand of Lady Cowper, who introduces her to the Committee. Herbert generously and idly stands straight and still while a great fuss is made about Anne Chadwick the author, the slave-girl, the heiress. Almost as an afterthought, Herbert is greeted by the Patronesses, who now seem eager to get the line moving again. Until, that is, Princess Esterhazy—a small, round woman, about fifty, born Princess Theresa of Thum and Taxis before marrying the Austrian Ambassador—sees the fresh handsome face and sturdy frame of Oliver Chadwick.

"And you must be the Chadwick son," Princess Esterhazy says, looking into Oliver's deep and dark eyes. Certainly the lad is eighteen or older, from the cut of him.

Oliver nods and smiles. Light seems to fall on the princess, and the other Patronesses now turn their heads to study the boy-man, peering at him as if he were a horse for sale.

"I understand you are half Persian," the princess says.

A question.

"Yes, my father was a Qajar prince."

"Ah, yes, so I recall from the book. I pictured you rather more... more childlike. You seem to be a fine young man."

"I aim to be a true English gentleman, though I know my Persian heritage makes me less so."

"Nonsense! There is something rather romantic about the Persians; of course, I've never met one. *Before*, that is. Be a good lad and come up here with us, will you?"

Princess Esterhazy pats the sofa cushion and scoots to her left, making room for him. The other Patronesses laugh. "To become a gentleman worth knowing, you should meet the rest of London society, and this is the vantage point, I assure you. Tonight you are my guest of honor. Mrs. Eaton, I will make sure none of these squabbling matrons get their "hooks" into your son this evening."

Anne looks on with astonishment. All she can think to say is, "Your Royal Highness, how good of you." She sees Oliver seated on London society's throne, cradled between Princess Esterhazy and Lady Cowper, looking suddenly younger than his age. As other guests greet the Patronesses, Ollie is introduced to them by the princess with a broad grin. The evening has begun with a surprise.

There are more to come.

Promptly at eleven, the orchestra strikes up a tuneful introduction. Guests swarm onto the floor for the first dance of the evening. Gentlemen claim their partners, the ladies they have been admiring since arrival, leaving not a few women alone in silent tears. The dance begins—a stirring gallopade, resembling more a race than an ordinary dance—launching the evening's revelry.

On the dance floor the gallant men and their ladies begin their frantic scramble. The brightly polished floor is slippery, the product of a new French compound rubbed into the wood. A few feet find the going adventurous.

Of all the dances he has learned, Oliver likes the athletic gallopade best. He turns to Princess Esterhazy and boldly offers his hand. Though it has been some years since the princess has danced the gallopade, she smiles and walks with him to the dance floor. The other Patronesses stare after her. Two of them begin searching for their husbands, not to be outdone by the princess, but the men are hiding in the tea room.

The gallopade begins to pick up momentum. Some of the more spirited dancers dash against the ropes, rebounding back into the action. The princess gaily lifts her feet, prances in time to the music, holds Oliver's hand and gaily shrieks as the crowd begins rushing, faster and faster. Some of the younger women now prance like headstrong fillies, pulling the men along, tapping their feet, slipping and sliding as centrifugal force flings them about. And then a gentleman of about forty, Lord Corvesa, loses his footing on the polished floor and crashes down, taking his partner with him. Three others tumble over the crumpled bodies with piercing shrieks. Princess Esterhazy is saved by the steady hand of Oliver. The orchestra stops. Every mother and chaperone in the room whose charge is not by her side suddenly races to the scene of the catastrophe. The princess, looking down at the prostrate dancers and seeing no injuries, lets out a low laugh, which grows into a comical chirp. The others begin to laugh with her.

"The gallopade is not for the faint-hearted," she says. "My gallant partner, Oliver Chadwick, saved me from a fall." She pats her hands together, and the crowd begins to applaud with her. And then, with a look of mock horror, the princess stares at the source of the calamity and says, "Lord Corvesa, what are you doing on the floor beneath Miss Caroline Pelham?"

Lord Corvesa sits upright and replies, "Madam, I was breaking her fall."

The entire room breaks into laughter and the orchestra strikes up a waltz. Oliver escorts the princess back to her sofa. "Thank you, my dear," the princess says to Oliver. "That was my first gallopade in eight years. And my last, I'm afraid. But memorable it certainly was."

"I have never enjoyed the gallopade as much as this evening, your Highness," he replies. And means it. "Would you excuse me? I would like some lemonade."

"Of course. But come back to visit us before the end of the evening, will you?"

Oliver marches to the long refreshment table and sips a glass of weak lemonade. As he turns, he is chilled by the sight of a turban moving through the crowd. But then the turbaned figure turns toward him. It is a man from India.

As the evening continues, Oliver invents a plan to erase the disapproving scowls from the faces of mothers who see their eligible daughters glancing at him. He invites the mothers to dance. By midnight, he has asked four of the stunned women and received no rejections. Heartbreakingly, two of them danced this evening but their daughters did not.

At half-past-midnight, at the refreshment table, Lady Cowper finds Anne and Herbert sampling some of the dry sandwiches that are staple fare at Almack's. No one comes here for the food. "Anne, my dear, I've been looking for you," Lady Cowper says in a most urgent voice. "I have someone I very much want you to meet." She turns and motions to someone. "He says he is an old friend of yours from Persia."

Anne wrinkles up her nose. She has no old friends in London.

"This is a very exciting moment. I know from your book what you went through in escaping from Persia. I am so pleased that I can reunite you with a dear friend who is now a diplomat visiting London for the first time."

Anne is very confused.

"And here he is, my dear, along with his interpreter, Eardley Pickwick."

Lady Cowper does not see the white expression of horror on Anne's face because she is busy waving her arms, beckoning the other Patronesses to join her. Anne looks at the familiar turbaned face and feels as if she is falling into the fiery pit of hell. She reels and leans against Herbert, who is confused by her behavior.

"Dear," Herbert says, "what is it?"

Anne cannot speak, cannot stand, yet she does not fall. She continues to look into the wretched face of the kelauntar, Mirza Hasan Qasim. *This cannot be happening. Not here, not in London.*

Ladies Castlereigh and Sefton join Lady Cowper at the table. "My dear friends, we have here an old friend of Anne's," Lady Cowper explains to the other Committee members, "from Persia. Mr. Hasan…" She cannot remember the odd name.

"Mirza Hasan Qasim, thank you very much," the Persian says.

Lady Cowper's arm-waving has attracted the attention of about fifty guests, including Oliver, who sees his father standing next to Anne. His heart drops in his chest. He could not have imagined such a terrible event—especially here, at Almack's. His mother's humiliation will be killing.

"Mr. Hasan," Lady Cowper says slowly, as if this will help the Persian understand her words, "will you tell us how you know Mrs. Eaton?"

Hasan speaks to Eardley, who translates for the crowd: "In Persia, I knew her as Anisa. She lived in the village of Bushruyih, of which I was mayor."

Lady Cowper looks confused. "Excuse me, perhaps the translation is not accurate," she nervously says to Eardley. "If I remember correctly, Anne was bought as a slave by the mayor of that village. Could you ask him to repeat his explanation?"

Eardley and Hasan have a brief exchange in Persian, then Eardley translates: "Yes, I am the one who purchased Anisa in Bokhara."

The blood rushes from Lady Cowper's face. "Oh my," she says. Looking at Anne with wide eyes, she continues: "Then… then Mr. Qasim is the same Qasim that you wrote about in your book?"

Trembling, Anne slowly nods yes.

"Oh my dear, I am so sorry. I had no idea."

Hasan speaks again, and Eardley offers a translation: "Mr. Qasim would like to explain that he purchased Anisa—Anne—on the slave market in

Bokhara to save her from a most miserable existence. He then most respect-fully brought her to his village of Bushruyih."

Now more than a hundred guests have gathered. A chain of whispers helps the latecomers catch up on the conversation. The cluster has thickened to the point that the orchestra, having just finished a quadrille, hesitates to begin an-other piece. The room is suddenly hushed.

Eardley continues. "Mr. Qasim wants everyone to know that he always had the most noble intentions toward Anne. That is why he took her as his wife."

Anne faints into Herbert's arms. *The truth is out!* Herbert lies her down on the floor and looks up at the Persian. "She was a slave in Persia! I am her husband!" he shouts.

Another quick verbal exchange ends with the Persian handing a paper to Eardley who then speaks: "Mr. Qasim has brought with him the legal marriage contract, which has been authenticated by officials in London, as you can see."

He hands the paper to Lady Cowper, who shakes her head and mumbles, *Oh dear, oh dear.*

The crowd buzzes madly, for the meaning of this revelation has suddenly become quite clear. If Anne Chadwick is the legal wife of Mirza Hasan Qasim, then she cannot, could not, dare not marry another man. And since she married Herbert Eaton, she must have committed…

"Mr. Qasim would very much like to take his wife back to Persia with him. He believes that she was misled by the treachery of a missionary, who swayed her into the deceitful and sinful life that she has been leading in London. He is prepared to forgive her."

Suddenly Herbert Eaton stands, facing the Persian with a fierce look in his eyes. "Look here, this woman is my wife and she is not going to Persia!" He pokes a stiff forefinger into the Persian's chest, backing him up and shouting, "You and your lies—you get out of here!"

Four men reach out to Herbert and pull him back.

Lady Cowper is still mumbling *Oh dear, oh my goodness,* and studying the paper in her hands.

The Persian straightens his tunic and speaks in English: "I am sorry, my friends. But it is true. She is my wife. I will not divorce her. The book is a lie."

Herbert shouts, "Get out of here, you heathen scum! Get out!" He is dif-ficult to restrain—it takes two more men.

Anne opens her eyes, moans at the sight of Herbert tearfully raging above her, then turns to see Oliver on the fringe of the crowd. She stares at him. He stares back, and his look of guilt tells her what she needs to know. He had known about his father's threat and had not told her.

Hasan takes Eardley Pickwick by the arm and walks toward the door, passing Oliver. Hasan does not look at his son—not even a glimpse—but Eardley whispers to him in passing, the words hissing from a sad face: "He promised to pay all my bills." A plea for forgiveness.

The Patronesses stand motionless and numb. The crowd begins to disperse as if the Eatons suddenly had been diagnosed with cholera.

Herbert drops to his knees, brushes his fingers through Anne's hair. His tears fall on her face. He truly does not care about himself, but he can feel the immense weight of Anne's humiliation. What will they do now that they are not, can not, *will never be* man and wife? He suddenly realizes how much he loves her. And misses her.

Oliver knows what he will do. First, he will go to the George & Vulture and get drunk. Then he will ruin Eardley Pickwick.

It's a start.

CHAPTER 24

By the time Oliver arrives at the George & Vulture it is closed. It has rained and steam rises from the streets like a fog on the moors. The opening ball at Almack's will go on until four or five, and Ollie can almost hear the excited buzz of the *ton* excitedly dissecting the awful scene between the Persian diplomat and the slave-girl.

He wants to go home, but can't face seeing his mother. He is shrouded with a cloak of guilt. *The poisonous look that his mother gave him—she had known!* And he had wilted under her gaze. Is *still* wilted. He walks hunched like an old man, saddened and contrite.

Why hadn't he told Anne about his father's plan for revenge? She could have prepared a defense.

But then he realizes that he is not as sad as he first thought. And not so contrite. Watching his mother's public humiliation was painful, yes, but now barely half-an-hour later he is not feeling quite so ashamed of himself. After all, he had not invited his father to Almack's, and did not know that he would attend.

And was it not his mother's choice to hide the fact of her Persian marriage? Certainly she could have anticipated the possible consequences of bigamy. Had she *really* thought that she could get away with it?

And what of her virtual abandonment of her son? Could she really have expected the loyalty and intimacy of his full confidence when she had so selfishly withdrawn from his life? No, she had forfeited her right to motherhood; she had relinquished those rights to Mum, who had seen through Anne's transparency at their first meeting.

How he misses Mum!

It is suddenly clear to Ollie that Anne has brought about her own tragedy. All he had done was to do nothing—to let the natural order of things evolve. If he had intervened on his mother's behalf, if he had warned her, if she had somehow avoided this fate, wrong would not have been righted. In a sense, by simply getting out of the way, Ollie had become an agent for justice.

A blur of movement in an alley catches his eye. The street urchins! Ollie is suddenly seized by a desire to see those youngsters again. *What was the tall one's name?* He rushes into the alley and is greeted by the stench of garbage and a wriggling mass of rats unintimidated by his presence. The gang has disappeared, but he knows they are close, hiding in the shadows.

"Halloooo!" he calls out. "I'm looking for Tim Shaw."

Silence—except for the gnawing of rodent teeth on beef bones and rotten cabbage.

"Tim, I know you're here," Ollie calls again. "I'm sure you remember me. Oliver Chadwick. We had a nice chat and I paid you to answer my questions."

More silence. Maybe this is not the right alley. He steps forward slowly. One of the annoyed rats turns irritably to look at him, then goes back to its feeding. Ollie takes another step and then hears a shuffle of gravel from further down the alley. He stops. His eyes are slowly adjusting to the dim light.

From the shadows a small boy appears, his face a pale biscuit in the devouring darkness. Then another boy appears, and another, all carrying long sticks. "Ollie, that you?" The voice is high-pitched, a little boy's.

"Tim?" Ollie asks.

"No, it's Willie." The boys come nearer. "Ya lookin' for sum more answers?"

"Maybe. Where is Tim?"

"Tim? Oh, Tim ain't wit us no more."

"Then where can I find him?"

"Find 'im? In 'eaven, I s'pose, wit the angels."

These words strike Ollie hard. *Perhaps he misunderstood!*

"Do you mean… he's *dead*?"

"Oh, 'e's dead, aw wite. Got sick, 'e did, coughin' up all kinds o' grunge, an' then 'e jus' up an' died. The gavvers took 'is body somewhere. Least the rats didn't get it." The small boy pokes a large gray rat with his stick. The rat hisses and then rumbles away from the garbage.

A great sadness settles over Ollie. How odd that he feels such grief for a boy he barely knew, and so little sadness for his mother. The grief grows until it almost overcomes him. This is not some kind of social falling-out that has happened, it is a life suddenly ended. The life of a small, pathetic creature who never had a chance.

"Where did they take him?" Ollie is glad that the darkness covers his moist eyes.

The boy shrugs his shoulders.

Ollie reaches into his pocket and produces a few schillings, then hands them to the boy. "I'm sorry you lost your friend," he says.

"I 'ope ter live as long," the boy says, taking the money.

The boys melt back into their harsh dark world. Ollie stands there, unable to move his feet. He cannot shake the unbearable grief, which is swelling up now like a taut bag over his head, suffocating him with an airless anguish. He wants to tear away this shroud of sadness and lash out at those responsible.

He wants justice for this wrongful death!

But there is no one to blame. *Too many* to blame. The villains are all nameless and faceless. They are blameless through their anonymity. They are found among the legions of corrupt and ignorant politicians, the malevolent orphanages, the oblivious and self-serving ton of Almack's. The blame is on this wicked and uncaring society that tolerates equally the hypocrisy and over-reaching power of the rich on one hand, and the wretched, deplorable condition of the poor on the other hand. Two hands, each full. A kind of balance. London's idea of a just society.

Ollie feels himself challenged. He is newly rich. He will become powerful. And yet he cries for little Tim Shaw. He cries, but he also remembers that a few hours ago he was seated on a fabulous burgundy sofa with Princess Esterhazy, dancing the gallopade to a full orchestra, sipping lemonade with captains of industry and generals and diplomats. Right now he would trade the sensuous delights of Almack's for a chance to stand beside the grim pauper's grave of Tim Shaw in a chilling rain.

Journalism! The craft of writing and publishing the truth. The opportunity to unveil hypocrisy and injustice, unmask inhumanity in all its clever disguises, and wave the magically curative wand of public scrutiny over the malignancies of London—this is Ollie's answer, his mission.

But first he needs to hurt someone. He craves vengeance. And the only personal target he knows is Eardley Pickwick, a vivid symbol of the sleazy, selfish, ruthless nature of humankind, and how easily one can destroy another through a simple act of greed. Ollie will bring this man down. His profound sadness has been replaced by anger. And exhaustion. Ollie hails a carriage and goes to his room at the Charterhouse—he still cannot face his mother.

On the weekend Ollie finally returns home. His mother has vanished, and all her things have been removed from the house. There is no note. No evidence that she had ever lived there.

Herbert, standing by several packed crates of his belongings, greets Ollie with a hug. "She's gone, Ollie. Left yesterday."

"Where did she go?" Ollie asks.

"I don't know." Herbert sniffs back tears.

"Is she very angry?"

"All of her speaking engagements have been cancelled," Herbert replies.

"So soon?"

"It seems the Evangelicals have not yet learned the Christian principle of forgiveness. But they are quick to see sin." Herbert pauses, takes a deep breath, then says, "I fear for your mother's well-being."

"She's strong. You have no idea."

"I hope you're right, Ollie."

Oliver looks down at the crates and frowns. "I don't want you to leave, Herbert. You don't have to go."

"It makes no sense to stay. This is not my home."

"Yes it is! I've lost one father, I don't want to lose another."

Herbert reaches out again and hugs the boy, who is now taller than he is. "It's best that I leave."

Ollie pulls away and says, "And go where? You gave up your apartments when you married Anne."

"I've made arrangements for temporary quarters until I can get my feet back under me."

"Stay here—temporarily, that is, until you have a permanent place. Why move twice? This is a very large house. If you must move out, then do it when you're ready."

"I don't know, Ollie. Our rooms here, they still have memories that—"

"But we have other rooms here. Rooms without those memories."

"Ollie…"

"I need you to stay with me, just for a while." Ollie looks at Herbert, and his face is suddenly a small boy's, lonely and afraid.

"Well, maybe just until I find a permanent place."

"Excellent! Then I think we should have a special dinner tonight to celebrate that we are still together… for a time, at least."

Herbert smiles sadly. He knows that Ollie has manipulated him into remaining in the mansion, but that's all right.

He wants to stay.

CHAPTER 25

It is a cold winter in London. Another Christmas is past, the bleak phantom of February haunts the cheerless whole of England, and only the promise of an evening's entertainment saves Ollie from suffocating under the tedium of school.

The rumbling carriage drops Ollie just outside the George & Vulture. He finds Charles inside, his upper lip moist with foam (the ale purchased on Ollie's account, as usual). He is entertaining the well-lubricated patrons with his uncanny impressions of the low population of the streets, the popular singers, the loathsome bureaucrats, the leading actors, and any Shakespearean play, including all the speaking parts in a chorus of voices.

"Where is William, have you seen him?" Ollie asks Charles, referring to a mutual friend. "I was late arriving, and he's usually early, always anxious for a free pint or two on the Chadwick estate."

"Not here, so far as I know. Of course, the Queen of bloody England could be here and I wouldn't know it."

William suddenly appears into the empty space between Ollie and Charles. "Sorry I'm late," he says, "but I have a wonderful surprise. The evening's entertainment is on me for a change."

Charles holds up a hand. "Something's wrong here," he says in a mocking tone. "I didn't even know that you carried money. Do you have any experience actually buying things?"

"You should talk!" William shouts, feigning offense. "When was the last time that you paid for an ale when your good friend Ollie was present? Or dinner at the George & Vulture?"

Ollie interjects suspiciously: "This entertainment you speak of—what is it? I'm not in the mood for another bear-baiting."

"It just so happens to be opening night of a new spectacular at the Surrey."
With a flourish, William produces a tube of tightly rolled paper and waves it
rhythmically like a conductor's baton. "Strike up the fanfare now!" And then
he hoists the tube aloft with his right hand and with his left unfurls a colorful
playbill for the Surrey's new show. *Escape from the Harem!* it screams in garish blood-red letters and a suggestive collage of images: a half-naked harem
girl precariously reclining against the gleaming blade of a giant curved scimitar, galloping camels chased by turbaned ghouls on hard-charging Arabians,
a sneering, evil-eyed villain with a beard like a briar patch and brows like
untrimmed hedges.

Ollie stares at the playbill, not fully comprehending it until he reads the
orange sub-heading: *Starring the hypnotic Anne Chadwick in a Reenactment
of her Astonishing FLIGHT from SAVAGE CAPTIVITY through the Mountains
and Deserts and across the Sea to Freedom and London society.* Ollie can feel
the blood race from his head. He slumps in his chair like an empty potato sack.

William looks at his dispirited friend. The broad grin evaporates. "I thought
you'd be happy to see your mother."

"William, you're a sap," Charles says.

Ollie looks up. "It's all right, William," he says. "I knew that my mother
had gone into the theater."

"We don't have to use the tickets," he says. "But I'll bet it's a rollicking
good show. Lots of animals on the stage."

"Shut up, William," Charles says. "I'll wager a bet that Ollie's part of the
story has been cut out."

"I certainly hope so!" Ollie snorts. "William, let me see that playbill again."

William hands the gaudy poster to Ollie, who stares at it.

"This bearded, satanic creature looks nothing like my father, though I'm
sure it's intended to be him. And this harem girl—"

"A bit more bosomy than your mother, I'll grant you that…"

Charles kicks William in the shin. "Do you practice your buffoonery?" he
chides.

William ignores the reprimand. "…but not as pretty by a long shot," he
adds, as if his previous remark had been interrupted. "After the incident at
Almack's—"

"You knew about that?" Ollie injects.

"Ollie, *all of London* knew about it," William replies. "Afterwards, your
mother went to Dibdin at the Surrey and offered herself to him."

Charles rolls his eyes heavenward. "My God, you have such a way with words,"

"What I mean is—your mother offered herself as an actress to the Surrey Theater," William says. "You knew, I'm sure, that Dibdin was quite taken with, well, with your mother's physical presence, and had been after her to star in something or other at his theater. He'd been dreaming up one spectacular after another with her in the starring roles, but I'll bet that he never thought he'd get her."

Ollie stares at his friend. "You know a lot about this."

"Of course. Dibdin is a friend of the family. It's how we got tickets in the old days. He thought you should be there for your mother's first performance in London."

"She's been performing since the day we arrived," Ollie says. "She's a very experienced actress. The tickets—they're from Dibdin?"

William nods yes. "Not that I'm unwilling to pay for our entertainment some evening. Just so happens that this evening…"

Ollie abruptly stands. "He's right, Dibdin is. I should be at my mother's first performance. What's there to be afraid of? If she wants to make a fool of herself, the least I can do is to be there to enjoy it."

"Are you sure?" Charles asks.

"Very sure."

"Excellent!" Charles jubilantly exclaims. "I'm always up for a night of theater." He glances at William, catches his eye. "Especially if there are lots of animals involved."

The clatter of the carriage over chunks of ice and crunchy wheel-ruts jars Oliver's brain, or perhaps his disorientation is from the disjointed recollections of another wintry night: a wooly Man-Monkey clambering up a balcony; a bloated priest rising from his watery grave. The idea of an evening at the theater is becoming a terrifying thing despite the mirth of Oliver's companions.

The Surrey Theater looms ahead like a mausoleum for dead memories and those hanging on by a thread: Ollie's mother, head tossed back, laughter spurting from her throat like water from a fountain; the flowing mane of a white stallion soaring above the tangerine sand of Bushruyih; broken shards of sunlight blinking through the rustling leaves of a Judas tree. Almost dead now are these dusty, fleeting images. And good riddance! They have no relevance for Ollie today. Better to sweep them out the door and let the cold winter breeze scatter the rubble.

Why, then, is his pulse racing and his head pounding? His mother is dead to him. Has been for months. He has grieved the loss of Anisa, applauded the death of Anne, mourned the disappearance of Mrs. Eaton, and buried the evangelical saint, fervently praying that she not rise again like the Messiah she feigned to worship. Yes, that's it! *She has been resurrected.* She has ghoulishly recreated herself in the outlandish form of an actress—a painted face masking her evil self, fanciful costumes camouflaging the decay of her soul. If Ollie sees her thus risen from the grave he will have to acknowledge that she will not die and will haunt him like a demon that cannot be cast out.

Nonsense. Get a grip!

The carriage rumbles to a halt. Ollie steps out, begins to walk toward the illuminated theater entrance. He slips on the frozen mud but catches his balance. Walking unsteadily toward the crowded entrance, he understands suddenly that he is the unholy progeny of a carnivore and a chameleon, a monstrous corruption containing the foulest characteristics of each. His destiny has been predetermined by the potent blood of his parents, a crimson river of deceit and treachery that will almost certainly sweep him into its surging path to perdition. His true inheritance is not the wealth of the Chadwick's, but the inevitability of damnation. The sins of the father are multiplied by the iniquity of the mother. He is a man without a country holding a passport to hell. He hates his parents not for who or what they are, but for the abomination that their union has produced.

In other words, he hates himself.

As proof of his powerlessness to fight the unalterable course of his life, he knows that he will do nothing to reverse his most spiteful act of vengeance. The pangs of guilt will not do it; neither will the personal shame of his actions. He has shrugged off these minor pains—all too easily, he knows—in exchange for the temporal satisfaction of revenge. The image of Eardley Pickwick squatting in a hovel amidst the thousands of other debtors in the Marshalsea fills him with an exquisite pleasure barely tinged with sadness. With his father departed for Persia and his mother mortally wounded, Ollie had unleashed his rage on the only target within range. At considerable expense Ollie had hired agents to investigate Pickwick's failed financial relationships, and then had organized the unpaid creditors into consolidating their claims against him. Having gone mostly unpaid by his faithless Qajar employer, Pickwick's financial dilemma had worsened. Eventually the court had sentenced him to the wretched debtor's prison. Pickwick had owed such a large sum that surely he would never again see London as a free man. On most nights Ollie sees this as justice; only occasionally does he wonder about the fairness of it, or the collateral damage to Pickwick's family.

Ollie yearns for the kind of personal transformation that religion says is possible, a salvation from his genetic preordination, but cannot fathom that a God Who has become increasingly reclusive can overpower the inexorable forces of nature that are shaping his character.

"Would you like us to send you home, Ollie?" Charles speaks softly. Both he and William are staring at Ollie's frowning face. "You don't seem up for this."

The three young men push through the clotting crowd of blue-bloods who have turned out to see the sequel of Anne Chadwick, the fabulously beautiful and publicly humiliated society dame. Many of these theatre-goers would rarely be seen on the east end, but this of course is a special occasion. A spectacle that flaunts scandal. Ollie can almost smell the morbid curiosity. Any other English woman who had been so visibly expelled from the *ton* would have merely wilted away, but not Anne Chadwick. Not Anisa.

At last the performance begins. Ollie can make no sense of it. The story begins with a loud battle scene with remarkably placid horses and a camel. A young girl is captured by slinking black-clad marauders and her parents brutally slain to the collective gasp of an audience that seems wholly unprepared for the violent opening act.

The next scene is a garish tableau in which the young girl is sold into slavery and forced to work as a servant. Her brutish owners whip her into submission, accompanied by the boisterous boos of the blue-bloods who are now warming to the tragedy. The girl spits venomously at her captors and resists their sensuous advances (cheers!) only to be viciously beaten (hisses!) But then an even more menacing figure appears on stage, a leering, demonic character who purchases the unbroken young girl, marries her, and rides off stage with his new wife chained and stumbling behind his horse.

The village of the next scene looks nothing like Ollie's cherished Bushruyih. The kelauntar is too obviously evil, the anderún too much like an etching from the *Arabian Nights*. For the first time Anne Cranston appears as the grown-up Anisa and the audience buzzes. This is what they were waiting for. But that boy caressed by Anisa is a complete mystery to Oliver, as if his mother had borne and raised another son in secret.

There is no loyal Jalal in this tale, no dashing Gordon Cranston, and the other wives of the kelauntar are ugly, evil women who spitefully mistreat the saintly Anisa and her son. This is not history, but fantasy. And into this fictitious world is inserted an unlikely zoo of animals. A lion (clearly in the wrong neighborhood) bursts into the anderun and threatens the women with a remarkably bored roar, performing it only after repeated prodding by his off-stage trainer. Anisa's son rides a baby elephant, undoubtedly left over from the invasion of Alexander the Great. Peacocks strut the stage, a mule defecates to the wild amusement of the audience, a camel spits in the face of a villager and then, as if knowing it has blown its lines, crashes through a wall attempting to escape.

Then comes a quiet scene, intended to hush the audience and prepare it for an exciting chase across the desert. As Anisa dramatically kneels in prayer, asking for the assistance of the English God that she has never forgotten, she looks heavenward—and slightly to her right. Her eyes open widely and she stares directly at Ollie. The radiance of her face shines through the thick make-up and her pleading eyes seem to implore him to… what? Is she really looking at him, or is she just acting? Had she arranged for him to be in that box so she would know where to find him? He cannot be sure that she is looking at him, but somehow senses communication between them.

As she looks upward, she says her lines: "I know I have sinned, my God, but please forgive me. I want nothing more than to return to my Christian home."

Her words penetrate Ollie to the bone. Is she asking for *his* forgiveness? He hates her, but desperately wants to feel her arms around him—the way she held that artificial Ali on the stage—and to hear her tell a story again. *The Enchanted Horse*. Oh, if only he could leap onto that horse and fly into the past, into the world he had left behind, before things had gotten so complicated. *Yes, I can forgive you, mother*, he thinks. *I can forgive you, if you ask.*

But then the trance is broken. On the stage Anisa looks away from Ollie and stands. As her eyes peel away, it feels like skin being ripped from his body. Anisa walks to a sleeping mat and looks down at the small figure of her artificial son and says, "I must leave you here, my son. It is too dangerous a journey that I embark on, and I cannot risk your life. Your father will take care of you. It is a man's world here—not a woman's. Be well, my son."

She reaches down and touches her son's forehead. Ollie can almost feel the warmth of her hand all the way up in his box seat. As she withdraws her hand, Ollie is startled. He now realizes that his mother has chosen to leave him. She is abandoning him forever. She is announcing to the entire world that she has given up her son in exchange for another life. And the audience—so dense they are, so willing to accept this decision as a noble and courageous act to spare a son.

A surge of anger rises up in Ollie. He had allowed himself to be tricked again by his duplicitous mother. Without thinking, he stands and shouts out, "How dare you abandon your son! You do not deserve to be called a mother!"

Charles and William look up at Ollie, startled. The audience turns toward him. Anne looks up as well, searching for the source of that outrageous remark, then gasps when she sees Ollie standing in the box above her. She sinks to her knees.

The curtain falls. It is the intermission, a pause before the perilous chase across the desert.

The audience applauds, still looking at Ollie, some of them thinking he was part of the performance, the others merely confused. A belly dancer and assorted musicians scramble onto the stage, diverting audience attention. During this musical interlude the desert scenery is loudly erected behind the curtain and Ollie marches out of the box, profoundly embarrassed by his actions. Charles and William chase after him.

"Ollie, wait!" William shouts. Ollie is headed for the stairway, fully intending to leave the theater immediately.

"Ollie, I'm proud of you," Charles says.

Ollie stops and wheels. "Proud of me?" he says scornfully. "Don't be an idiot. I came here to watch my mother embarrass herself, but I ended up the fool."

"I doubt if anyone here even knows who you are," William suggests. "And if we leave this very minute…"

The three young men look at each other. For William and Ollie, anonymous escape suddenly seems the wisest course.

"But the play isn't over," Charles complains.

"Then you stay and watch," Ollie says. "Tomorrow you can tell us what we missed."

Charles considers this for a moment, then looks up at his friends. "Actually, the play is quite bad, isn't it?" The others nod their agreement. "Then let's get out of here. On the way back, Ollie, you can tell us how it ends."

"I can tell you right now," Ollie replies. "It ends with the slave-girl on a stage in London struggling to restore her dignity, and her son bolting for the exit."

"The son must be a theater critic," William interjects.

"All right, then. I suggest we return to the George & Vulture," Charles says, "where William can make good on his promise to pay for an evening's entertainment."

CHAPTER 26

This particular summer day is unbearably hot. A dank mustiness hangs like a wet blanket in the air. But the sun is a welcome sight after five days of dismal clouds and a rheumy rain thickened by soot and coal dust into dark puddles of mucus. Now the high sun is burning away the humid cloud that had enshrouded the city and is raising the spirits of the residents—all, that is, but Herbert Eaton, who glumly looks out at the greenery that surrounds the Belgravia mansion and wonders at how this perfect day looks to the debtors of Marshalsea prison. One of these wretched souls has stubbornly occupied too large a portion of Herbert's consciousness lately.

Eardley Pickwick.

Herbert shoulders a large share of guilt for the fate of Mr. Pickwick. He had known of Ollie's plan for vengeance and had done nothing to stop it. This certainly makes him an accomplice before the fact. Morally, at least. Pickwick had been in desperate straights and easily duped into Hasan's plot to publicly humiliate Anne. Which act is the more abominable one—Pickwick's misguided attempt to earn support for his family, or Ollie's spiteful ruin of the man?

Oh, not that Herbert is above feelings of revenge. He had experienced unbearable pain and rage that night at Almack's, and for many nights after. He had not been able to work for weeks. And he had plotted his own revenge—against the puppeteer, however, and not the puppet. Unfortunately, the target of Herbert's wrath has disappeared into the haze of a distant land.

Herbert can understand Ollie's wrenching loss and can only estimate the young man's personal torture, but he cannot live with the outcome of Ollie's actions.

Looking about the immense Belgravia sitting room, with its artfully carved woodwork and expensive furnishings, Herbert feels doubly guilty. Has he not failed to correct Ollie's shameful act out of his own selfish desire to remain an honored guest in this magnificent mansion? Has he not been desperately holding onto a shred of his pre-Almack's destiny to be a master of this house? What if he should anger the young heir with a direct confrontation and be cast out on his ear? Herbert could not bear to dwell again in that cramped and cluttered apartment of his former life, not after glorying in the splendor of this Belgravia mansion. And the love and admiration bestowed upon him by the young Oliver Chadwick—how could he risk losing that? He and the young man have become father and son, bound together not by blood but by their shared loss and grief.

There is also, of course, the extraordinarily generous allowance that Ollie has arranged for Herbert, an amount that many wealthy men would not provide their firstborn sons. An amount that some would consider a bribe, and that even Herbert considers a strong inducement toward a positive relationship. To lose this support, to significantly reduce his standard of living would be… well, Herbert likes to think of it as unnecessary.

Such a quandary—caused, of course, by flaws in Herbert's character grotesquely magnified by the plight of Eardley Pickwick. Herbert cannot live with the unfairness of Pickwick's incarceration, but lacks the courage to confront Ollie directly. And so there is only one possible solution.

Herbert beckons a carriage—such a luxury to have one's own driver—and heads off in the direction of St. George's Church. The streets are more rutted than usual, he thinks. More holes and blown-down branches. The carriage rumbles steadily along, and Herbert is thankful for the thick embroidered squab beneath him. How often in the past he had suffered the bone-jarring jolts of the common hackneys and their greasy leather-on-wood benches.

Herbert disembarks just north of St. George's. "I won't be but an hour or so," he tells the driver. The sour air stinks of rotting fruit and overflowing refuse from numerous laystalls. Here is the main gate to Marshalsea prison, that horrifying walled village-within-a-city.

At the bleak gate, Herbert shows his newspaper credentials to the porter and says, "I'm here to see Mr. Eardley Pickwick. Can you direct me to him?"

"Of course, sir," the porter says. He consults a thick book, licking his dirty thumb each time he turns a page, then looks up and proceeds to give a bewildering set of directions that Herbert finally realizes must be written down.

Inside the locked gate, Herbert begins to walk through the filthy labyrinth of narrow streets and snaking alleys, turning left at the coffee house and right at the tap, walking past a row of grimy lodging houses, dodging a game of blind man's bluff played cheerlessly by tattered urchins who suffer the sins of their fathers, proving—undoubtedly—the truth of the Scriptures. Loud shouts are flung from one shattered window, and from the next a soothing antidote— the sound of a woman singing a soft, heartbreaking lullaby to an infant born in prison.

Herbert's destination finally appears, a slouching three-story house that sags like a dying mare. The front door, wrenched from its rusting hinges, is braced against the moldering wall as if holding the entire building upright. The entrance exudes a stale breath—a kind of hopeless sigh that Herbert fans away with a broad sweating palm.

He adjusts his cravat and enters.

Pickwick's room is on the first floor. Past a splintered archway. Down a damp hall with mossy, wounded walls oozing rivulets of pearly slime. Around a cramped corner to a cracked door.

Herbert knocks. Heavy footsteps plod across a creaking floor and the door swings open. "What is it?" the tenant asks irritably. He is pale and unshaven, scarecrow thin, and coughing. At first Herbert doesn't see that this broken man is Eardley Pickwick, but Eardley recognizes Herbert Eaton immediately. "Ohhh! I apologize for my rudeness. Please come in, Mr. Eaton. I think of you often."

Only now does Herbert identify the man—a horrifying revelation. Even in Herbert's nightmares, Pickwick had not appeared in such a miserable state. "Thank you, yes," Herbert replies, and walks into the room. He sees bare, cracked walls, a wide broken bed, two wooden chairs and an empty water basin. Tattered clothes are strewn about as if some violent act has been perpetrated here.

"I'm surprised. I never imagined that Herbert Eaton would be paying me a visit. I am honored, sir." Pickwick coughs again, producing a ball of phlegm that he spits into a soiled handkerchief. "Excuse me for that, sir. There's little heat in the winter, and the summers are given over to mold and mildew. A bit hard on the lungs, it is. Please have a chair."

Herbert glances more closely at the grimy chair offered by Pickwick and declines. "Prefer to stand for a time, I would." The tart stench of decay is turning Herbert's stomach. He swallows back a stinging rise of vomit. "I had intended to come earlier, but my schedule, you see…"

"Yes, yes, I'm sure you're a busy man."

"Yes, busy, very busy you see. But here I am now."

"And for what reason, may I ask? No! Let me try to deduce your purpose." Pickwick holds up a hand but coughs violently before he can speak again. Finally he sits down on the second chair. When he has cleared his chest, he hoarsely adds, "I imagine you have come seeking an apology, or perhaps some kind of vengeance. Well, as you can see, my offense against you and your almost-family has not gone unpunished due to the tenacious zeal of young Oliver Chadwick. God's agent, he is. I hold no grudge against him."

"You do not believe that the severity of your punishment—which, I might add, is for another offense altogether—is not unfair?" Herbert is astonished at Pickwick's apparent lack of acrimony.

"*Unfair* you ask? The two men with whom I share this squalid bed have less debt than I. None of us can earn enough while in prison to settle our debts, yet here we are, stuck until we pay them off, which for most of us amounts to a life sentence. This whole system is unfair. But I have the added guilt of turning a mother and son against each other, of causing the public humiliation of your fiancée, of conspiring with Satan himself—for that is who I consider Mr. Hasan Qasim to be. I am, sir, in my own estimation, fairly judged and punished."

These words of submission do not relieve Herbert's guilt; they only heighten his anxiety. "But surely your family—"

"My crimes—and my sins—have wounded my family deeply. More deeply than my punishment. Fortunately, I was able to divorce my wife, sparing her from this hell-hole. My daughter is now resting in God's bosom. You see, one of my other sins was to fail in providing for my family. I could not afford a doctor when Mary, my little girl, became ill at the tender age of eight. Eventually she died, and my marriage with her. My daughter's older brother—he now forbids me to call him *son*—has disowned me." Pickwick smiles sadly before coughing. Then he finishes: "Imagine a son disowning his father. You see, sir, I have no family anymore. If I had chosen a different employer than that scoundrel Qasim—if I had been paid for the honest work that I did for him—if I had not so willingly allowed him to deceive me—if I had been a wise man instead of a fool—"

"I must admit," Herbert interjects, "that you have suffered terribly for your transgressions. There was a time when I might have strangled you with my own bare hands. The pain inflicted on me was intolerable, or so it seemed. But the more I've reflected on this tragedy, the less I blame you. As much as I loved

Anne, I must admit that some of my feelings were motivated by ambition—and to a certain degree, also by an even more primitive biological force."

"She was—*is*, I'm sure—a most beautiful woman."

"Stunningly beautiful, yes. And ambitious, too, I'm afraid. Even more so than me. I will never know if she really loved me. You see, there was an inheritance at stake, and I was the shortest distance between Anne and the money."

It suddenly strikes Herbert as peculiar, this urge to confess so much to Eardley Pickwick, but he cannot stop himself. "I've thought a great deal about this, and as much as I miss Anne Chadwick, I believe that she had planted the seeds of her own destruction the day she decided to hide her previous marriage for her own selfish purposes. The truth would have come out at some point. I wonder how many other lies…"

Herbert does not finish the sentence. He does not have to.

"And so you came here to explain this to me?"

"No, that was not my intention at all. My aim was something else altogether. To make a proposal, actually."

"A proposal?"

"Yes. Before I came here, I firmly believed that you had been unfairly condemned to this living hell. I believe that even more strongly now. For that reason I would like to personally make your condition a little more, well, comfortable."

"To ease your conscience?"

"Perhaps. Does it matter? A man in your straights should take whatever lifeline is flung to him."

"I'm listening."

"I cannot undo what master Chadwick has done. It is not my place, and he would never forgive me. For that reason I can't settle your accounts and see to your release from this awful place. My personal risk would be much too great. But I have substantial means of my own, and I would very much like to rent for you an apartment on the Masters Side. The conditions there are much better—and healthier. You won't have to chum with others, squeezed into one pathetic bed as you are here for some ridiculous price."

"Two shillings and six pence per week for my part of a bed, it's true, most of which goes into the Keeper's pocket. Almost as much as I make in a week at the laundry."

"Outrageous! From now on, then, your living expenses will be covered for you. With some diligent effort on your part, you can save money, and over time perhaps settle—"

"Your conscience must be quite prickly."

"We are both victims of Mr. Hasan Qasim, and so is Oliver. I see this offer as a kind of settlement to even the consequences of Qasim's treachery. It is not fair that you should suffer so disproportionately, especially since Oliver and I have wronged you as well. Oliver by his misguided efforts to injure you personally, and myself by allowing it to happen."

"Then consider the score now settled. Money is unnecessary."

"But—"

"I appreciate your offer, but you must understand that I have no life outside the locked gates of Marshalsea. Comfort does not appeal to me. A quick end to this miserable existence does. Take my appreciation, my sincere gratitude for your generous offer, and go now. Please! Without another word."

Eardley Pickwick stands up. Herbert starts to protest but Eardley stops him with a shake of the head and a cold hand on the shoulder.

"I beg of you, go now," Eardley says, his eyes watery and his voice trembling. "And know that you are forgiven for whatever you believe you have done to me. Both you and Oliver."

Eardley escorts the speechless Herbert Eaton to the broken door and into the murky corridor. "Go now. And say a prayer for my little Mary, God rest her soul, and for my son's forgiveness. You've done your part and surely God will recognize and reward your intent. Go now."

And with that, Eardley Pickwick steps back into his bare room and closes the door. Stunned, Herbert turns the corner and begins to walk down the hall. At the far end, the doorway glows brightly, beckoning him to it.

What has happened here? A change, a transformation. He can feel it. And now he is embarrassed that he had acted so cowardly. *Rent an apartment?* Nonsense. *Make the man more comfortable in this foul place?* Ridiculous. An insult!

No, Herbert will take the necessary risks to do what is right, what he should have done in the first place. He will pay off Eardley Pickwick's debts and make sure the poor man is released from Marshalsea prison. He will somehow find gainful employment for Pickwick, and a doctor.

Herbert will save himself by saving Eardley Pickwick. Two victims will be resurrected. Oliver, unfortunately, is on his own. And as for Hasan Qasim, never before has Herbert Eaton so hated one man.

Herbert Eaton steps into the healing sunlight with two great missions: one of salvation, the other of revenge.

CHAPTER 27

It should be an exciting day for Oliver Chadwick, this first day at university. He has chosen Christ Church at Oxford in honor of Herbert's attendance there, and the academic cap and gown that adorn him lend the appearance of a serious student. But Ollie has tired of school and religion and, to be honest, England. College is a Chadwick tradition which he must honor, but the thought of long years of study in dusty libraries under the watchful eye of robed and dusty professors gives him no pleasure.

What continues to please him is the exploration of the world through the eyes of journalism; thank God for Herbert's influence, which has allowed Ollie to apprentice as a genuine news writer at the *Times*. What excites Ollie is not the prospect of a degree from Oxford, but the opportunity to write about events in the world, and new places, and new ideas as they form in the minds of creative thinkers.

He is restless, yes, but resigned to his fate as a student for the foreseeable future. Some day he will leave England and travel to America, the new land, and help the stodgy English understand what it means to be a *young* country just starting to find itself.

The carriage bounces lightly down the street. It should be an exciting day, but Ollie's mind is thinking years ahead. He seems so lost in thought that he does not notice the bleak institution on his right, or the painters covering the rust of the heavy iron gate, or the fresh gilt sign so recently attached to the main building's façade. Already young Master Chadwick has almost forgotten the singular charitable act that he had hoped would redeem him from his sins, including the irrevocable punishment of Eardley Pickwick. He has almost forgotten the child whose name is now emblazoned on the institution, the result of a bureaucratic barter in exchange for a generous gift that also assures important reforms.

Or perhaps Ollie has not forgotten at all but stubbornly refuses to acknowledge these and many other mileposts of his life.

The carriage is passing the institution. Oliver dreams of the future and tries to bury the past. It is one way to conquer pain—the simple act of sweeping aside the cause. If Ollie were to remember, the pain would surface and blister his consciousness.

Ollie has almost buried the past, but not quite. And so, before the carriage rounds the corner, Master Chadwick turns to look backward one more time, just before the newly named *Tim Shaw Orphanage* disappears from sight.

CHAPTER 28

Kazim scoops a handful of dirt. He packs it gently around the base of a rose bush in the garden outside the Shaykhi school in Karbala. A great sadness weighs on him. He looks up, wipes a trickle of perspiration from his forehead, and notices the subtle shape of a spirit approaching the school. The slow, trudging figure, made thin and watery by the rising heat waves, slowly advances.

Kazim sits back on his haunches, feels an odd buzzing in his head. An expectation of something. A recognition.

The solitary figure continues to advance and Kazim feels the sadness draining from his body. How he can identify a man he has never met he cannot understand, but he is quite certain that the approaching figure is someone who has been expected for quite some time.

He wants to rush out and embrace this person but instead merely rises and brushes the soil from his hands, his stomach rumbling with excitement.

The figure is now close enough to see that he is a young man wearing the garments of a mulla. The anticipation is killing Kazim but he holds his ground.

What if this is just some road-weary cleric passing by? *Don't make a fool of yourself!* He remains motionless.

The young cleric approaches and speaks. "Is this the Shaykhi school?" he asks with a smile.

"Yes it is." Kazim's throat is suddenly dry and he has to push out the hoarse words.

"I'm looking for a friend of mine, Muhammad Kujiri. I've traveled a great distance to see him."

"Then you must be Jalal. I've heard so much about you."

"*Mulla* Jalal," the young man says, smiling proudly. "I've completed my studies in Mashhad."

"Congratulations! I am Siyyid Kazim." The school master reaches out at last and embraces the young man, who seems suddenly surprised.

"I'm sorry, sir. I had no idea who you were or I would have shown more respect," Jalal says, dropping to his knees.

Embarrassed, Kazim pulls the young man to his feet. "I appreciate the gesture, but it's unnecessary. As I understand it, you will be joining us here."

"I've been waiting a long time. I hope I won't disappoint you."

"I'm sure you won't. There were times, you know, when Kujiri seemed to think that you might be the Promised One."

"The Qa'im? I can't imagine why—"

"No matter. He certainly held you in high regard."

"I'd like to see him. Is he here?"

Kazim looks at his feet for a moment, then with sad eyes gazes at Jalal, who understands immediately.

"When did he die?" Jalal asks.

"Last week. More than anything in the world he wanted to see you again, but he had grown very old and weak. Finally he passed away working in the garden, right here. But he's still here with us," Kazim says.

"You mean his spirit?"

"I mean Kujiri." Kazim looks down at the garden. "He is buried here, among his cherished flowers. He wanted the garden to be in its most glorious condition when you arrived."

Jalal looks down at the soft soil and says, "What garden can be more glorious than this?"

PART 3
NEW YORK 1841

CHAPTER 1

The image is bright and clear but upside down. The corpse seems tethered to the ground by a taut rope, as if it were being lifted feet first into the air, pulled upward perhaps by the hand of God but held earthbound by the connivances of Satan. Caught in the void between heaven and hell.

The red-haired man seems satisfied with his composition but fiddles with the focus of his lens. There! Now even the mop of hair that hangs from the dead man's puffy head is sharply defined. You could almost count the strands.

The photographer stares intently at the viewing glass, studying the bloated face, feeling safe behind the projected image as if he were somehow shielded from the reality of the gallows. Seeing the image inscribed by light on glass is very much like viewing a daguerreotype at an exhibition. It is one step removed from the physical object that bent light into its own faithful reproduction.

The hanging man suddenly gasps! Not dead, not yet. The photographer jumps! A great roar from the crowd announces the horror of it. The short fall through the trap door and sharp twang of the rope should have snapped the victim's neck, bringing about a mercifully quick death, but the noose had been misaligned. The poor victim is strangling.

Then all is still again. This is important, because the long exposure time for capturing the image on a metal plate requires the absolute absence of motion. That's why the dead make such good subjects; they seldom move.

The photographer waits to see if the hanging man moves again. Nothing. Good! He removes the viewing glass from the camera obscura, replaces the lens cap, reaches into a leather satchel and with graceful, practiced moves takes out a rectangular plateholder. Through a hinged opening on the top of the camera he inserts the plateholder, then pulls up the dark-slide to expose the magical plate itself.

A small breeze has blown up and the dead man begins to rotate slightly at the end of his rope. Frustrated, the photographer abandons his position of safety and marches to the gallows, steadying the man.

The breeze stops.

Now the photographer can make his picture. The sun is shining into the opening beneath the gallows floor where the dead man hangs. Perfect light. It is all about light, this photography business.

The photographer gently removes the lens cap, which acts as a shutter, and counts out five seconds. Experience tells him to add one more. One thousand six. Done! The lens cap is replaced. The dark-slide is plunged downward. Job finished.

"Thank you," he says to the patient New York City officials who quickly lift the dead man and slip him out of the noose. The crowd seems almost as entertained by the photography as by the hanging. They have seen executions before, but never a picture being made.

As the red-haired man packs up his contraptions, a tall well-dressed gentleman approaches with a question. "Do you make pictures of living things, too?" the man says, his words crispened by a faint English accent.

"So long as they don't move," the photographer replies. "Odd thing is, the few times I made portraits of living men, they looked dead. Something about holding a pose for twenty seconds that sucks the life out of you." He continues to pack things away. "Do you find documenting the dead to be macabre or merely distasteful?" Clearly the photographer has suffered his share of verbal attacks on his chosen line of work.

"Less macabre, I believe, than watching life expunged as an amusement. And what will you do with a picture of a hanging man?"

"It's for the newspaper. Dead murderers sell papers. I used to make drawings. "

"An artist, too?"

"My true calling. Look, I had permission to make this picture so if you're going to lecture me…"

"I wouldn't think of it, my good man." Ollie's affable interruption catches the photographer off guard. "I was hoping that you could lecture me. You see, I'm quite interested in this field of endeavor. It's quite new, I'm sure. Even in London we've not seen it yet, though it's been talked about. How on earth were you so fortunate as to fall into it here in New York?"

The photographer stands up and looks at the Englishman skeptically. *What does this fellow want?* In New York, everyone has a selfish motive. The ingratiating smile that greets him, though, seems genuine enough. He decides to play along for a time.

"As I said, I was an artist. Illustrations, mainly, for the *New York Times*. Portraits. Buildings. The occasional corpse. But when I heard about this discovery, my curiosity got the better of me." The photographer kneels down and continues to pack up his apparatus. "I was doing a sketch of Professor Morse at New York University. The paper wanted an article about that extraordinary man of science—quite an inventor, he is. They wanted a portrait to go with it. While I was sketching away with my little pencils the Professor suddenly looked up at me and said, 'I have a better idea.' My name's Jonathon, by the way. Jonathon Fury."

Jonathon picks up two small metal images, the output of his camera, and hands them to the Englishman who looks at them in wonderment, and says, "I'm Oliver Chadwick, also in the newspaper business—*London Times*." Ollie hands the pictures back to Jonathon. "Fury, that's quite an interesting name."

"Not my real name, to be sure. I was an orphan. Irish, which you can plainly see from my red locks. The family that took me in didn't want to keep me, but figured I should have a name. Just not *their* name, seeing as how they were going to give me to someone else eventually. So they took a look at my angry hair and said I looked *burnin'-up furious*. I was a fury, they said. What a good name! I've been Jonathon Fury ever since."

"And are you? A fury?"

"With a couple of pints in me."

"Could you use a pint now? I'm buying."

Under the load of two satchels, a large oak camera case and an iron center tripod, the pair trudges down the street to Wilkie's, a local tavern favored by bankers and shopkeepers. Inside, a tart-tongued barmaid fetches two mugs of amber ale for Oliver and his new acquaintance.

"You were saying about Professor Morse…" Ollie says.

"Yes, yes, quite a gentleman. Great things yet to come from him, I'm sure."

"He invented the process you are using?"

"Not actually. While he was visiting Paris in, let's see, 1839—he made the acquaintance of Mons. Daguerre, who had discovered the method of fixing the image of the camera obscura. After Morse returned to New York, Daguerre sent him a description of the process, which the Professor was able to duplicate. While I was sketching the Professor, he suggested that instead of a drawing I should make a *daguerreotype* of him—that's the word he used. In honor of the Frenchman. Once he showed me how light could be captured on metal, I begged him to teach me."

Ollie sips his ale. What a wonderful world America is—full of new ways to exhibit death.

"Does the newspaper pay well?" Ollie asks. He knows this is a very personal question, but he has a concealed motive.

"Yes, well—no. They pay me for each image that they print. It's not so much, really, but it pays for the plates and the chemicals."

Ollie is captivated by this marvelous invention. He leans forward confidentially and says in a conspiratorial whisper, "I have a business proposition for you."

Jonathon leans forward hungrily. The paper pays less for his pictures than he has let on. "I'm all ears," he says. "Does it involve money?"

"Quite," Ollie says. "And more than you are earning now. I'm here to write a series of articles on America for the readers of the *London Times*... which is behind the times, I'm afraid. Sans daguerreotypes. It would be absolutely ripping if you would hire on with me to illustrate my articles with your little pictures."

"How much, then?"

"Money? Oh, let me see." Ollie thinks about it for a moment, then leans forward and whispers into one of Jonathon's ears. The photographer seems impressed. "Of course," Ollie adds, "for that sum I'd expect you to assist me in other ways, too. We'd be a team, you and I."

He hands Jonathon some American money. "Here, a down payment. What do you say?"

Ollie's tale is only partly true. He intends to write articles about America, but he is self-funded. He has taken a year at his own expense to travel and write. To refresh his spirit. To recapture the journalistic spark that he had lost while languishing in sundry management duties at the *Times*. These are the reasons that he gives himself, whenever he bothers to ask. The truth is something else.

"And where shall we go?" Jonathon asks. "Are you looking for adventure, romance, mystery, political intrigue—we have it all in America."

"Yes," Ollie says.

Jonathon laughs. "So you want it all," he says.

"Right now I only want another ale. Barmaid!" Ollie cannot explain the true purpose of his long journey to America. Not yet—perhaps never. But it is here, in this vast new land, that he hopes to find and finally bury one who has been long dead. And who knows? Maybe Jonathon can find a picture in it. Corpses, after all, are the man's specialty.

Chapter 2

He opens the burgundy sheath and exposes the jeweled scabbard. Of the few objects he brought with him to the Shaykhi school ten years ago, this one—this gleaming sword—is his most cherished possession. Caught in its mirrored surface for all time is the reflection of his father. Each time Jalal gazes on the perfect arc of the blade he can see his father's kind smile, and sometimes—when he swings the graceful blade and carves the air into quarters—he can hear his father's gentle, resonant voice singing out.

This time, though, he does not send the blade into its dizzying routine. He merely looks at it. Truth is, he has done no more than look at the sword for the past year. A weakness and tremor in his limbs has made it difficult to hold and maneuver. The last time he had tried to practice with it, the blade had spun out of his hand and lodged in a wall.

On this day he is feeling shaky and light-headed; still, the magnificent sword feels good in his hand—but so heavy. Now that he can barely lift it. Slowly he places it back into its scabbard and wraps it in the elegant pouch.

As he attempts to stand, the convulsions begin. The sword drops from his hands onto the stone floor with a muffled crash. He falls on top of it, arms flailing, legs shaking. He bites his tongue. His eyes roll, showing only the whites. Agonizing pain shoots through his body. Still conscious, he tries to form words with which to make a plea for God's help.

At this precise time, Jahangir, a student who had arrived at the Shaykhi school six months earlier, appears in the doorway of Jalal's room. He has been sent there by Siyyid Kazim to fetch the respected Mulla for a meeting. As the young man stares in alarm at the convulsing figure on the floor, he hears an awful moan that sounds like the words *Oh God, what would you have me do?*

Mistaking the Mulla's terrifying seizure for a kind of mystical ecstasy, Jahangir does nothing to interfere. In his suddenly awakened state, with excited visions of the imminent appearance of the Promised One whirling in his head, the student has his own revelation; so astonishing is it that he drops to his knees and covers his face in mortification at his profane intrusion, for in his confused mind he has become witness to a sacred conversation between God and his earthly manifestation, the Promised One, the Qa'im. He shivers with the thought that all this time, secluded in this simple school, the Qa'im has been present but unannounced, has embraced the young student with his holy arms, has breathed upon them all with his holy breath.

Jahangir prays for forgiveness. He should not have witnessed this remarkable communion of God and his agent. Jahangir should be punished. Killed, perhaps. The time has not yet come for the Qa'im to be made known to men.

And then the convulsions stop. Jalal turns, lies flat on his back, eyes closed. A great sigh like the exhalation of angels emits from him.

The conversation with God is done.

Jahangir leaps to his feet and flees for his life.

CHAPTER 3

They stroll down bustling Nassau Street, *the city's brain* as it is called because along this busy thoroughfare are most of New York's newspapers and a burgeoning industry of printers and publishers.

"You can smell the ink," Ollie says.

"Smells like money to me," Jonathon Fury replies. And then he stops, pointing to a complex of brick buildings across the street. The corner structure, which flies an immense American flag, is the largest. "Tammany Hall," Jonathon explains. "Headquarters of the Democratic Party. Therein lies the black heart of politics. If you've got a vote to give, whether it's yours or some long-dead fellow's, Tammany Hall will exchange it for a promise."

Jonathon's slender finger points to three narrow buildings attached like vertical stripes to Tammany Hall. "And next to Tammany we have the offices of three of New York's best fish wraps, the *Tattler*, *Brother Jonathon*—no relation, mind you—and the *Sun*."

"I've read the *Tattler*. Wouldn't wrap *my* fish in it," Ollie remarks. "Which of these fine publications pays for your daguerreotypes?"

"None of 'em. My partner in crime, so to speak, is the *Herald*. Has a taste for the macabre. Just down the street a little further. They're all around us here, the public prints, the pamphleteers, the dime novels. Take another sniff! The smell of ink and paper covers up the stench of the rottenness and repulsive filth they prey upon and regurgitate for the masses."

"You don't seem to have much regard for your associates in the trade."

"Regard? None whatsoever. May God one day see the trail of slime left by James Gordon Bennett, and smell his foul breath that mildews everything fresh and fragrant in the city. But the Herald—it pays the bills. Would you like to see some of my personal work—the pictures that don't earn a penny? Not a hanging man or rotting corpse among them."

"Very much." Ollie is taken by this opinionated, fiery young man who is two or three years his junior.

"Fine. But first... a cigar. To celebrate our partnership."

"To celebrate your *employment*, to be more precise."

They briskly walk several blocks to Anderson's Segars at 321 Broadway, just across from City Hall Park. It is an expansive shop guarded by a large statue of Sir Walter Raleigh, the patron saint of tobacco. Jonathon catches Ollie's arm before he enters.

"Most of the newspaper trade frequents this shop," Jonathon explains. "If you want to meet someone in the trade, plant your feet in Anderson's and wait. Sooner or later everyone will make an appearance here. I've even seen Bennett himself ogling the beautiful cigar girl inside."

The aromatic breath of the store nearly knocks Ollie off his feet. From one direction wafts delightful whiffs of sweet and spicy fragrances, and from another the most pungent and bitter smells. The effect is an olfactory thunder that crashes in Ollie's nostrils and makes him sneeze. Twice.

"God bless you!"

Ollie blows his nose into a monogrammed handkerchief and looks around for the silky-voiced speaker. Across the room he sees an apparition of riveting beauty behind the counter, a gorgeous dark-haired young woman with streaks of sunlight painting her face.

"Uhh, please... I mean, thank you," Ollie says awkwardly and then stubs his toe trying to take a step forward.

This must be the way men felt when they first saw my beautiful mother, he thinks. *The breath knocked out of you. Words erased from the brain. All neural function jumbled.*

"May I help you with something?" the silken voice asks.

At this moment Ollie is beyond help, but he lies. "Yes, please. Something, yes... I'm looking for something."

Jonathon sees that Ollie has been seduced by the young maiden; he understands, for he has been rendered speechless himself by her attention, as have most of the men in the shop, some of whom don't even smoke or chew. He knows that the crafty owner, John Anderson, a handsome fair-haired man of about Ollie's age, had also fallen under the spell of Mary Rogers—some said they had been romantically involved—but the enchantment was finally broken by the tobacconist's commercial instincts. In a stroke of genius, Anderson had hired Mary as his now-famous "cigar girl." Almost immediately she had begun to draw the customers that previously had been so difficult to pull away from the more established shops. Mary's allure proved to be more addictive than the nicotine Anderson purveyed. The newspapermen who now frequent Anderson's Segars had published articles about the "beautiful cigar girl"; Jonathon had illustrated one of these gushing pieces for the *Herald*, producing an inspired woodcut that captured the wholesome coquettishness of the dark-eyed beauty. Other *segar* shops tried to duplicate Anderson's not-so-secret ingredient, but none of the girls they hired could match the charisma and magnetism of Mary Rogers, the media darling.

"Watch out, my man—she's a siren," Jonathon whispers to Ollie.

Ollie nods without hearing a word of Jonathon's advice and purposefully steps forward to the counter. He awkwardly extends his hand and says, "My name is Oliver Chadwick and I've only recently arrived here from New York. Pleased to meet you."

He thinks this went well—he had not stumbled or stammered.

Mary takes his hand and shakes it courteously, professionally. "I'm very pleased to meet you as well, sir, but unless I'm mistaken, this *is* New York. How is it, then, that you recently arrived from this very city?" She smiles coyly.

Ollie's heart is beating through his chest. What an idiot he is!

Jonathon walks up to the counter and rescues him. "Hello Mary," he says.

"Jonathon! How good to see you! Don't tell me you've gone through that entire pouch already," she says with a sly grin.

"Actually, no. I'm showing my new employer the high spots of the city. He's from London."

"Not that I couldn't tell from the British accent," she says to Ollie, purring the last two words provocatively before laughing. "We specialize in *fine cut*, if that's your particular interest."

Ollie looks at Jonathon for an interpretation. "*Chewing* tobacco," Jonathon explain.

"Oh. I'm afraid not. Perhaps a cigar for myself and my friend. Your finest—we've some celebrating to do."

"Then I've just the thing!" Mary says with just the hint of a smile. She reaches beneath the counter and fetches three fat cigars from an ornate humidor, holding them up like trophies. "Though I suggest *three*, not two. Otherwise how could I celebrate with you?"

Ollie is so thoroughly charmed that he merely smiles—a stunned, goofy grin, Jonathan thinks—and grunts, "Of course."

Mary begins to fit the first cigar into the opening of a silver-plated cigar cutter, but stops and looks up at Ollie. I'm sorry, may I?" she asks.

Such delicate fingers, Ollie thinks. *Such pure white unblemished skin*. He craves a touch but dares not. "Please, go ahead," he replies.

Mary expertly slices the end off the first cigar. The sound is deliciously crispy. "This particular blend has a smooth, rich, complex taste," she says as she begins working on the second one. "Packed with earthy complexity, a hint of cocoa bean with leathery notes, and a spicy finish. My favorite."

Mary begins to cut the third cigar as Ollie watches, astonished at the thought of this magnificent exemplar of femininity puffing on a cigar. Still, the thought excites him. Mary Rogers, he is quite sure, is full of surprises.

Mary offers a cut cigar to Ollie and Jonathon. With a saucy flick of her head she snaps back the flowing locks that had begun to veil her face like curling wisps of smoke, and then with the briefest of glances at Ollie says, "I'm glad you don't chew."

His mind races with the possible meaning of that.

Ollie and Jonathon insert the cigars into their mouths and Mary lights them. They puff and the fire catches with a crackling hiss. The aroma is strong but delightful. Something in it—a hint of bitterness, a trace of ripeness, an insinuation of citrus—transports him momentarily back to Bushruyíh and the pungent smoking rooms of the men. But then he is back in New York, in Anderson's, staring into the eyes of a princess who sensuously puffs a cigar.

"Like it?" she asks.

Looking at her, Ollie responds, "The most incredible thing I've ever experienced. I'm not sure one will be enough."

"We'd be happy to provide more if you wish," she says.

Feeling suddenly transparent, Jonathan clears his throat. "We should be going, Ollie. I still have a delivery to make."

"Perhaps we'll see you again," Mary says. Her eyes have not left Ollie since she took her first puff. "Are you staying in the neighborhood?"

"The Regis Hotel," Ollie says. "Temporarily."

"Ooooh" Mary coos. "Quite expensive there."

Ollie quickly recalculates his need to stay in New York City. "I may be here for a while," he says. "I'll be looking for other accommodations nearby. I'm in journalism, you see."

"Ah, yes, this is the center of the world for journalists, isn't it?"

Ollie wants to correct her. London, in his mind, is the true center. But instead he finds himself saying, "Yes, I suppose."

"My mother operates a boarding house on Nassau Street. Finest one in the district—wouldn't you say so, Jonathon?"

Jonathon, who has been studying the torn leather on his shoe, politely nods *yes*.

"We've just had a room open up," Mary says. "Perhaps you'd like to see it—but I'm being presumptuous, aren't I? Forgive me."

"Not at all!" Ollie exclaims. The idea has a great deal of merit in his mind, though he's only thought about it from one angle. "Nassau Street would be the perfect address for me."

"Then I suggest you show up tomorrow at, say, ten? I'll tell my mother to be expecting Mr. Oliver Chadwick."

Ollie loves the way his name sounds in her throat.

CHAPTER 4

Jalal loves this stone chamber, with lances of sunlight piercing cloudy air that smells of wisdom and sanctity, and the sound of sandals slapping across the hard floor as students scurry for the close seats. The sum of it is embedded into his consciousness after years of familiarity—*intimacy*, to be honest—with this small cube carved out of God's kingdom. The fragrance of roses like a thick cloak, the jumbled geometry of the space, the Persian carpets that have sacrificed their luxurious weaves for the salvation of so many soles—these things, and the hauntings of a generation of the now-dead, and the anticipations of the soon-to-die, make the room an almost-living thing. Where the teaching chambers in Mashhad left him lonely and cold, this one has always enveloped him with tenderness and love. Jalal will miss it terribly when one day he must leave.

A decade of congregation here has finely tuned his senses, and he can feel a warp in the atmosphere. As he enters, he is startled by subtle shifts in the attitude and position of the other students, a collection of small, insignificant things: a concentration of eyes as he enters; conversations that are more hushed than usual; a furtive glance—then another; a look of bewilderment, and another of astonishment. For the first time since he had arrived at the Shaykhi school and was introduced to so many strangers in this chamber, he feels uncomfortable.

Jahangir is standing amidst a thick knot of students. The young man's astonishment at the vision of Jalal's body-quaking *communion with God* has spilled out of his mouth as rumor. *"He is the Qa'im, I'm sure of it; I saw him physically trembling in the embrace of God."* Jahangir's initial fear of having witnessed the forbidden sight has been overwhelmed by his excitement at the possibilities.

The other students buzz quietly with disparate views on the matter, but who can dispute that Jalal possesses the qualities that one would expect to find in the Promised One? *Has he ever expressed anger or a discourteous word to anyone?* Never. *Is he obedient in keeping the laws of his faith?* Without exception. *Does he exhibit spiritual insight and clarity?* Beyond the ability of any of them. Jalal's character is beyond reproach and his leadership uncontested. There is not one among these students who would refuse to follow him on any mission. But some remain convinced that if the Qa'im were present in the school it must be the esteemed Shaykhi leader Kazim.

Jalal's entry into the chamber sets off a quiet frenzy of conjecture and confusion. The students don't know if they should look at him or not—*what if he is the Qa'im?*—or if they should wait until addressed. *When will he announce his station?* Many of them long to touch him, embrace him; such a privilege, to touch the Promised One. *But maybe he is not the Qa'im.* Perhaps Jahangir is mistaken, or has merely imagined his colorful vision, or is lying. *Look at Jalal—no! Don't look at him—he is holy, anyone can see that. The way he carries himself.*

Awkwardness and uncertainty permeate the chamber, for though Jalal is a close friend of most, the possibility that he is the Promised One changes everything.

Siyyid Kazim enters and takes his customary position in front of the students, who scramble for their positions on the floor. Kazim does not maintain discipline with threats and punishments. He is so loved and respected, and his attention so achingly desired by everyone present, that the merest wrinkle of his brow in disapproval or the slightest withdrawal of his gaze can cut to the bone; yet he never does this maliciously. He never raises his voice or his hand, and always admonishes his students with kindness and encouragement. Still, he is not soft or compliant, but firm—absolutely firm in his convictions. And his reasoning—often challenged, because the appropriateness of challenging convention is part of his message—is usually faultless. He exudes both confidence and humility, and in him this is no paradox.

Kazim begins to speak, so softly at first that students in the back don't hear him until an irritated few silence the crowd. Embarrassed by their own inattention, the noisier ones immediately stop chattering and focus their attention on Kazim, who seems unusually weary, as if the weight of centuries were resting on his shoulders.

"It has come to my attention that certain powerful mujtahids in Persia have called for our extermination as heretics," he says. "Yet these men, who profess to great spiritual wisdom, refuse to debate us openly on the issues. One can only presume that they fear the public humiliation of having their arguments reduced to rubble."

The students laugh. Threats against them by the orthodox Islamic clergy are not new, but the attacks are growing fiercer as the time of the Qa'im approaches.

"They question our political aspirations," Kazim continues, "yet we have none. They distort the goal of our mission, which is nothing more than to prepare our world for the appearance of the Promised One so it will not repeat the tragedies of the past." The students understand that Kazim is referring to humankind's perpetual rejection and persecution of God's messengers of previous eras, from Moses and Jesus to Muhammad.

As Kazim passionately rallies the disciples to their vital task, a young man unknown to Jalal enters the chamber from the rear and takes a seat near the threshold. He is younger than Jalal and like Kazim wears a green turban signifying that he is a Siyyid, one of Muhammad's direct descendants. A finger of golden sunlight finds the lap of this seated youth, whose face remains partly veiled in shadow.

Siyyid Kazim has been focusing his attention on the students seated at his feet. Now he lifts his eyes to survey the entire room, hoping to engage all of the students with his passionate discourse. But as his eyes fall upon the unidentified young man, he suddenly stops speaking. For quite some time he stands there, motionless and speechless. The pause becomes awkward.

"Please, continue," someone urges.

Another voice calls out, "Yes, please go on."

At last Kazim turns his eyes to this last speaker. "What more can I say?" Kazim replies. "The Truth is more manifest than the ray of light that has fallen upon that lap!" With a long, crooked finger he points to the mysterious youth in the back.

Jalal has seen the glowing stripe of sunlight illuminating the visitor's lap, but none of the others have noticed. They seem confused by Kazim's cryptic remark, distracted by the puzzle of his words. Jalal is suddenly seized by a most astonishing possibility; *has Kazim introduced the Qa'im?*

The notion engulfs him. It races through his veins like fire shooting up a fuel-soaked string.

Still under Kazim's hot gaze, the student who last spoke attempts to divert the conversation away from his own perplexity. "Why is it that you neither reveal the name of the Promised One nor identify His person?" he asks.

Kazim takes a step backward and then threateningly points his bony finger at his own throat. The meaning of this unspoken gesture is clear to everyone: if Kazim were to divulge the identity of the Qa'im, they both would be put to death. A great hush overcomes the assembly. Many of the faces turn toward Jalal. These men believe that he may be the long-awaited One and feel chastised now for their open gossip about him. Others devotedly remain with eyes fixed on Siyyid Kazim, their candidate.

Only Jalal glances at the youth in the back of the room, but the visitor is gone.

CHAPTER 5

The vast wings of canvas snap in the breeze with a sound like the crack of rugs being shaken—the comforting sound of cleansing. Freshly cut timbers hold the sagging weight of the tent aloft while a rousing Christian hymn raises the roof from below. In upstate New York, Alice Crenshaw prepares a vastly different group to learn news about the imminent return of their Promised One, Jesus Christ. Alice loves the crisp woodsy smell of the sawdust that billows beneath the feet like a tawny cloud tamping down the worldly dust, buoying the spirits, and clinging to boots like divine sparks.

Smells like heaven, she thinks.

Alice is leading the hymn with a passionate soprano voice that keeps the crowd of one hundred fifty repentants from wandering too far from the melody. The thunderous piano chords played by the local minister's wife are eerily dissonant, the sour sound of humidity corrupting the taut strings.

The stirring hymn ends. Alice takes a seat behind her sweating, corpulent father, who waddles up to the makeshift pulpit and grips the outside edges as if he is going to wrench it from the ground and fling it into the audience. The sheer mass of Reverend Theodore Crenshaw's body exerts a gravitational pull on everyone seated before him, causing them to lean forward in their creaky seats. Their expectations soar.

This is the main event, the featured act. This man is the instrument of God and out of his mouth will come words of healing, enlightenment, salvation. And so it is a slight disappointment when the voice of this imposing figure comes out thin and reedy instead of rich and powerful. But the disappointment is quickly swept aside as his words flow like molten lava over the hushed audience.

"Dearly beloved," he begins, "you and I are living in the final days. I know that you have heard these words before: '*Jesus is coming soon!*' You have heard them frequently—so frequently that they have lost their meaning. What does 'soon' mean? Within the next hundred years? The next thousand? My friends, these words have been repeated for one thousand eight hundred and forty-one years. How can we take them seriously any longer? Like the shepherd who cried wolf too often, we clergy have misled you, and for this I apologize."

Alice leans forward. In the humid night air, her flowered cotton dress sticks to her back. She wipes an irritating bead of perspiration from her forehead and settles in for the show; she has heard this sermon many times before, but the potency of the message still thrills her. Since she and her father heard the startling revelation of the farmer William Miller, who had decoded the Bible prophecies of Christ's Second Coming, she has known that her mission is to help deliver this message to the world. How can you know when Jesus is returning to earth and not want to shout it out?

"I also want to give you some good news. The long wait is over. Throughout history, millions of Christians have expectantly awaited the return of their Savior only to die without seeing the magnificent event unfold. But for you, my friends, it will be different, for I can promise that you will see the Second Coming of Jesus Christ with your own eyes!"

The crowd buzzes. Cries of *hallelujah!* merge unhappily with murmurs of scorn. Alice smiles. The reaction of people to this news is so predictable.

"I can even tell you in which year you will witness this glorious event," the Reverend says. "Do you want to know?"

Yes, the crowd shouts.

"Are you prepared to accept the *responsibility* of this knowledge?" Reverend Crenshaw is shouting now. Spit sprays from his lips and perspiration flies from his bald forehead.

"This truth comes not from me, but from God's own Word, the Holy Bible, in which this greatest of all mysteries has been kept veiled from humankind until now. So listen carefully to me, for I am about to reveal the time of Christ's Second Coming, and after receiving this news you will have to decide what to do with your remaining time. Will you ignore this news, or believe it not? Will you repent and do good works? Will you continue in your profitless daily existence unchanged?"

Reverend Crenshaw plucks a handkerchief from his pocket and wipes his face. The audience nervously anticipates his next words.

Alice detects something wrong. Her father has never paused at this point in his sermon. And now he is looking over his shoulder at her, pale and slick with sweat. The evening is humid, but not so much that...

The Reverend's knees buckle, but he catches himself. The audience seems not to notice as he slowly straightens himself and attempts to speak again.

"The truth comes not from me, but from God's own Word..." he says before pausing again.

He has never repeated himself before. Alice leans forward. And then the Reverend clutches at his heart and sags to the floor, divine sparks scattering in the air. Alice, the local minister and two others rush forward to her father, who lies gasping on the ground. The Reverend takes Alice's hand, and then sighs.

"I'll be all right," he says, but of course Alice does not believe him. With a smile, he looks up at her and says, "I feel better lying down. Perhaps some of the men can move me to the back of the tent and you can continue the sermon. I would very much like to hear you."

"Me?" Alice says. "No, father, we should tell everyone to go home. They'll understand. We need to get you to a doctor."

"Nonsense. I'm not going to die. I'm also not going to finish the sermon. That's for you to do. I think my preaching days are over, my dear. Remember this—we have not yet delivered the news to these people. Don't keep them waiting."

Alice kisses her father on the cheek. "promise you'll be all right?"

"As God is my witness. And tonight, in this tent, He surely is."

Alice watches as the men lift up the side of the tent and roll a small wagon over to her father. As they lift him onto it, Alice turns to the horrified congregation. The crowd quiets as she begins to speak.

"As you could see," she says, "my father has poured his life into this work. He has promised me that he will be all right, so please don't worry. He also asked me to finish delivering his sermon. So let me ask you now—would you prefer to go home, or will you permit me to continue my father's work?"

Go on, they shout. *Continue. Tell us the date.*

"I asked if you would permit me to continue my fathers work. I was thinking about my father, the Reverend, when I said that. But in truth, you have given me permission to finish my heavenly Father's work as well. For that I thank you."

Alice clears her throat and watches the wagon, with her father in it, exit the far end of the tent.

"My earthly father has promised to reveal the time of our Savior's return in majesty and glory. And so he shall reveal this secret—through me. Some of you, however, may wonder at how we came to this astonishing truth. Through what clarifying lens did we look to see God's secret timetable when no one else for thousands of years has been able to solve its mystery? The gentleman to whom we must give credit for this glorious discovery is William Miller. Before I announce the date of Christ's return, let me share the irrefutable method by which this date was at last deciphered. Do you believe the Bible is the Word of God?"

The question prompts an explosion of *yeas* and *hallelujahs* shouted above a deafening applause.

"Let it be noted that God has revealed to his prophets these events in diverse figures and at different times. He has revealed these things to Daniel and Peter, to Isaiah and St. John the Divine. And these prophecies have been recorded in His infallible Holy Book in such detail that it makes me shudder when I consider the magnitude of such an announcement. Yet the details have been cloaked in mystical and symbolic language to keep them from discovery until these Final Days *hallelujah!*"

That final shouted word echoes throughout the tent and is hollered back as a chorus of praise and astonishment. Alice is speaking with a preacher's cadence and a voice grown suddenly husky and vigorous. The lilting soprano is gone, and the quaver in her voice sends chills through the audience.

Reverend Crenshaw has never heard his daughter preach; always she has sung solos, and led the hymns, and counseled the repentants who came forward to receive Christ's healing salvation. *Where is this captivating voice coming from? Such authority, such power, such—holiness!* It's as if God were speaking through Alice with His Own Voice attuned ever so slightly by the woman's frailer instrument of speech. She seems possessed by angels.

"That we can now see the dates of God's great plan, and comprehend what was previously incomprehensible, and divine the mysteries that He has chosen to keep locked from sight—*these* are the surest signs that we are in the Final Days. We know these things not because of our own intelligence or cleverness, but because God Almighty has unlocked the lofty gates guarding his master plan, and has chosen to reveal his secrets to us so that we may prepare for the greatest event ever to unfold on this earthly plane. *Praise God!*"

Praise God! she hears a hundred times over. The people are standing, waving their arms, crying tears of joy. Some are kneeling and kissing the earth, raising their faces with divine sparks flying all around them.

Alice wipes her face with a cotton handkerchief. It won't be the last time this evening. She is soaring above the crowd, cradled in the hands of Jesus, speaking without conscious thought, vibrating in the breath of God.

She loves it.

CHAPTER 6

Jonathon Fury closes the door to the small, windowless room which is lit by a solitary gas lantern. He stuffs the remnants of a tattered curtain into the half-inch opening beneath the door, sealing the room from any outside light. "The room must be as dark as possible," he explains to his companion, Oliver Chadwick.

"And if it isn't?" Ollie asks.

"Fogs the picture," Jonathon replies curtly. "And after all the effort you put into coercing Mary to pose for this portrait, that would be a shame."

Ollie is mystified by the array of chemicals and apparatus spread out on the narrow table in front of them. The making of a daguerreotype seems roughly equivalent to alchemy.

"Don't touch anything!" Jonathon warns. "Just watch."

Jonathon lifts a small glass vial from the table and moves it toward a cast iron fuming box that is suspended like an inverted pyramid above a glass alcohol burner. "The first step—pour a small amount of mercury into the fuming box."

Ollie watches the mercury dribble into the black box.

"Now we light the burner and turn off the lantern," Jonathon continues. Ignited, the glass burner hisses and glows. With a whoosh, the lantern goes out. The room is now much darker, illuminated only by the radiance of the burner.

Jonathon centers the base of the fuming box over the burner and slides a thermometer into a side slot. "We heat the mercury to approximately 175 degrees Fahrenheit," he explains. "Doesn't take long."

From a wooden box, Jonathon removes the exposed daguerreotype plate, consults the thermometer, and adjusts the burner slightly. "There, just right," he says. He places the plate face-down on top of the fuming box. "The image will develop by exposure to the mercury fumes. It still amazes me. Usually takes two or three minutes."

From a dark jug Jonathon pours a smelly solution into a glass tray. "Hypo-sulfate," he explains. "We'll need this for the next step."

Except for the hissing of the alcohol burner, the room remains silent until Jonathon inspects the plate. "Just right!" he says proudly. "Experience has put a clock inside my head." He immerses the plate face-up into the hypo-sulfate. "This removes all the remaining light-sensitive chemicals from the plate. Take a look at your picture!"

Ollie lowers his head over the tray and gazes at the image that has magi-cally appeared on the metal plate. There, beneath the rippling chemicals, a face stares up at him. "My God, it worked!" Ollie says. "It's her! A perfect, miniature Mary Rogers."

"Of course it worked," Jonathon says glumly. "I'm an expert. That's why you hired me." Jonathon moves the plate to another tray and pours a clear liquid over it. "Distilled water," he explains, "to further remove any unwanted chemicals."

Jonathon moves the plate to a gilding stand, leveling it with thumb screws so it is suspended horizontally above a brass spirit lamp. "The final step… gold chloride." He lights the spirit lamp and gently pours the gold chloride onto the developed image. "Heat bonds the gold to the silver of the image and makes the picture richer in tone."

Finally, Jonathon lights the lantern and the room once again glows bright-ly. Ollie can see the magnificent image clearly now. The face of Mary Rogers almost speaks to him. If Jonathon were not there, he would kiss that beautiful countenance, caress those tender cheeks, stroke that silky hair.

"Is it acceptable?" Jonathon asks.

"Quite."

Ollie can hardly wait to present it to the woman he dreams about.

CHAPTER 7

Could it be more perfect? The address—126 Nassau Street, on the east side between Beekman and Ann Streets—is well situated by accident or fate in the center of the publishing universe; the living accommodations are delightfully ordinary; and the landlady's daughter is exceptionally captivating—in fact, Mary Rogers has caused Ollie to momentarily disregard the grim undertaking that has brought him to this New World.

Except for a small placard on its front, the Rogers boardinghouse bears the familial look of its surrounding siblings. It is a featureless three-story red brick building with a flat roof, seemingly stenciled into place from a popular blueprint.

Nassau Street is a graceful, winding road that stretches from Broad Street to Park Row, stopping just a block from City Hall Park and the tobacco shop. Along its gentle curves are a muddle of merchants, workshops, boardinghouses and private residences. Here the rich and very poor, the Poles and Italians and Swedes and English, the Negroes and Asians, all work and play next to each other; for all the violence and wickedness in this rich stew of a city, the evil of social segregation has not yet poisoned the neighborhood.

To the south of Nassau Street and the Rogers boardinghouse is Wall Street, the center of commerce, and to the northwest—in back of City Hall—is the treacherous Five Points district, Manhattan's notorious festering slum. Surrounding the boardinghouse are the city's most lustrous landmarks: Trinity and St. Paul's Church; Theatre Alley; and just two blocks distant, Broadway "shining like a track of fire," as Mary Cecilia Rogers glowingly describes it.

Coursing like a virulent fever throughout the city, however, are countless gamblers and seducers, criminals and confidence men, whores and street-corner preachers, operating their beguiling or guile-less crafts against a backdrop of shrill street-cries and pious hymns, black gutters and gilded carriages, broken wine bottles and polished communion cups.

At sixty, twice-widowed Phebe Rogers and her daughter had come to this new Babylon as refugees from a hard Connecticut farm existence. Only last year frail Phebe had leased the building that is now her boardinghouse from Peter Aymar, a small-time real estate baron who a decade earlier had speculated his life savings on constructing a dozen of these Nassau Street structures. Happily, he had chosen his location wisely.

Almost at once, young single men who had come to the city in search of work began to flock to the Rogers boardinghouse; the presence of beautiful Mary Rogers and the home-spun hospitality of Phebe proved to be a winning combination. Together with Alice, their servant girl, the mother and daughter team created a serviceable home away from home for tradesmen of modest means. Still, earning a living proved difficult and Mary quickly took up part-time work at Anderson's to help make frayed ends meet.

On this particular humid Sunday, Ollie is seated on a striped divan in the Rogers' cozy sitting room. His heart thrums with anticipation. Soon he will leave this stuffy room with his love, Mary Rogers, and picnic on the shore.

Opposite Ollie, half-sunken like a bobber into an ocean of over-stuffed chair, Arthur Crommelin reads the *Tattler*. With sandy hair, brown eyes and moustache, tan skin and expressionless brown eyes, 30-year-old Arthur looks to Ollie like a sepia-toned daguerreotype. Of a dead man.

To Ollie's left, seated at an upright piano on which a calloused forefinger awkwardly picks out a popular tune, is William Kiekuk, a swarthy sailor with unruly black hair and darting eyes that seem always to be surveying a sea's vast horizon. Apparently Kiekuk is lodging here between voyages. No one is quite sure for how long.

With a loud clatter the *Tattler* is smashed into an unkempt heap and Arthur Crommelin comes to life, staring now at Ollie. "Never been to London," he says.

"Is that right?" Ollie perfunctorily responds.

"Never wanted to, actually. Old and dusty there, from what I hear. New York is the *new world*, the *future*, don't you think?"

"Much newer, to be sure. The *future?*—I don't know. For whom?"

"You, for example. A man from London. Certainly you came here to get away from something, or to find something. When your business if done, will you return to your homeland or stay on to make your fortune here? I'd wager that you'll stay on."

Ollie stares at Crommelin. *The man has no idea what he's talking about,* he thinks. *Homeland?* England is not Ollie's native soil. *Will he return to his true homeland?* Ollie can't imagine that. *Stay on and make his fortune here?* A loud snort—the result of stifling a chest-deep laugh—erupts from his throat. He has already made his fortune—the easy way. Inheritance. Ollie looks at Crommelin, the bobber waiting for a nibble to announce a fish on the hook.

"My travels are for business. Newspapering. When I'm done here I'll go home."

"So tell me, will you write about Phebe's boardinghouse? About us? Will people read about us in the London papers?"

With a straight face Ollie teasingly replies, "You never know. If I were you I'd be on my best behavior. You know that news writers prefer stories about scoundrels and scandals."

Crommelin doesn't catch the mocking tone. He squints defensively.

"Arthur, I'm joking," Ollie finally explains.

"Yes, of course," Crommelin replies without the slightest upward curl of his lip. His dead, unseeing eyes begin to wander the room, focusing at last on Kiekuk. "Hey, sailor—I thought your sister lived in New York. Why give up a free bed with the family?"

Kiekuk continues to approximate a familiar tune on the piano. Without turning he mumbles, "Same reason as you. The girl."

Crommelin stiffens and Ollie cocks his head. *Did he hear that correctly?*

"That's nonsense, and you know it," Crommelin asserts somewhat self-righteously. "There was never anything between…"

"Oh get off it!" Kiekuk shouts. "Everyone knows you wanted to get into her knickers."

"This is ridiculous." Crommelin mutters.

Ollie is shaken by this sharp turn in the conversation. *They are talking about the woman he loves!*

"Ain't no fantasy that Artie-boy here was pretty thick with Mary Cecilia," the sailor says. "Like a bull in heat. Until she put the ring through his nose. Wrapped him around her pretty little pinky, she did. And he still comes sniffin' around, hopin' for…"

Crommelin suddenly bolts to his feet. Ollie fears that the man, now red-faced with clenched fists, is about to attack the piano player. "Fellows, please…" he implores.

Crommelin does not move, but stares viciously at Kiekuk. When he finally speaks, he spits frothy comets of saliva into the air. "Who are you to degrade my love. You!—a seaman who knows only lust and sees only body parts."

The sailor smashes his fist on the keyboard. "Maybe I don't care what's on her mind," he growls, "but I know it isn't you. She's done with you, Arthur. She has the corker now." Kiekuk storms out of the room, out of the house.

Ollie stares at Crommelin who stands frozen in place, obviously hurt and humiliated. He knows he should find words to dress the man's wounds, but he is too riled himself to act rationally. Instead, he throws salt. "You were lovers, you and Mary?" he asks.

Crommelin slumps into the billows of his chair. "She's a maddening creature. A disease," he says softly, defeated by his duel with the sailor. "Once she infects you, your knees weaken, your heart crumbles, your brain turns to…" He searches for an appropriate metaphor. Seeing the proper Englishman on the divan, he finally has it: "Your brain turns to Yorkshire pudding."

The tension eases. Ollie actually laughs, and Crommelin follows. And then Mary Rogers enters the room. Arthur Crommelin stands first, then Ollie.

"Arthur, you're still here," Mary says with a disarming smile. "I thought you were going out this afternoon." She crosses the room and gently kisses Crommelin's cheek, a sister's kiss, a friend's. The formality of it—the lack of intimacy and passion—kills Arthur.

"And so I am," he says, then stands.

Instead of acknowledging Arthur's intended departure, Mary turns her attention to Ollie. Her eyes glisten as the tip of her tongue moistens her painted lips. Crommelin can feel the heat rising between them, and he stiffens.

"Ollie, my mother would dearly love to come along with us," Mary coos. "She's been slaving away in this house for too long. Do you mind?"

Ollie is disappointed, but he will not show it to Arthur Crommelin. He wanted Mary to himself today, but he will not display his feelings to Crommelin. "I'd love for her to come," he replies cheerfully—a fine bit of acting. "Imagine, two women at once. What do you say to that, Arthur? Am I a lucky man?"

Arthur looks at Ollie with a sad stare and says, "Here's to Yorkshire pudding." And then he leaves.

CHAPTER 8

New York City is directly connected to the Jersey side of the Hudson River by invisible streets of water on which steamboats glide back and forth eight times a day during the summer. Standing on the deck of one of these boats, Ollie is mesmerized by the play of sunlight on Mary's face, the sensuous curve of her bonnet, the stray wisps of black hair flickering in the wind. She squints into the sun, which makes her look sleepy. She watches the approaching shore with a purposeful gaze, as if something there awaits her.

"You've never been to the Elysian Fields before, then?" The voice, like a rusty hinge, startles Ollie. He turns to see Phebe Rogers standing to his right. The short, plump woman has been uncharacteristically silent until now. Always friendly and even 'motherly' to Ollie when the two of them are alone, she becomes tense and tight-lipped when Mary is present.

"I've never been across the Hudson," Ollie replies.

"Beautiful spot," Phebe says. "Don't get there as much I'd like."

"Then I'm very glad you could accompany us today." Though Ollie would have preferred to have Mary, his angel, all to himself, he likes this old woman and feels comfortable with her company.

He misses Mum terribly.

The steamboat lands near a hotel that serves travelers who are staying on for a visit to nearby Hoboken. Ollie, Mary, and Phebe disembark, carrying baskets of food. A short walk down a well-traveled path leads them to a peaceful clearing—five acres of cool breezes and green grasses surrounded on three sides by trees and on the fourth by the river.

The Elysian Fields.

The stony path continues upward past large oak trees and locusts. On its winding route beneath one of the high cliffs that oversee the Hudson it passes a quaint tavern, Nick Moore's House. The clearing is furnished with swings and other amusements for use by the hot and tired inhabitants of the city who have come here for healthful relaxation.

"Over here," Mary says, taking Ollie's hand and scrambling to a plush grassy spot by the river. "It's perfect here. I'm famished, how about you?"

"I'm hungry, yes."

Mary releases Ollie's hand—*he doesn't want her to let go*—and opens one of the baskets, removing a folded tablecloth. After unfurling it into the breeze, she gives it a saucy snap and drops the square cloth onto the grass.

"Our table!" she announces proudly.

Phebe is out of breath when she catches up to the younger ones. She sets down her considerable bulk next to the tablecloth and pops open a parasol, providing instant shade. "I burn easily," she explains.

Kneeling almost reverently in front of the larger basket, Mary teasingly rubs her hands together and says, "I wonder what we have for lunch today." She begins removing the packed food. Two loaves of bread, one white and one dark. Baked cod and sliced beef. Butter, apple jelly, pears, and grapes. "Lunch, anyone?" she says.

"There's nothing to drink, dear," Phebe says. Her words are said curtly. She barely softens them with the tangy tone of that final endearment.

"I didn't forget, mama. It's so hard to carry beverages all this way—so heavy! I'll run up to Nick Moore's and get us some beer."

She stands, and Ollie stands with her. "No, let me go," he says.

"Don't be silly."

"Then I'll go *with* you."

"Ollie, I want you to enjoy yourself here. This spot on the river is my gift to you. Look after my mother. I won't be long."

Before Ollie can object she is racing up the path alone.

Ollie looks down at Phebe, who is already biting into a torn slab of white bread smeared with apple jelly.

"I hope I didn't give you the impression that I am trying to avoid your company," Ollie says.

"I'm an old woman," Phebe replies. "My daughter is young and beautiful. I'm not offended by your preference. Mary is *everyone's* preference."

Ollie sits down next to Phebe. "May I ask you a question?" Phebe nods. "Arthur Crommelin…"

"That's not a question, but I know what you mean."

"He's very keen on Mary."

"Everyone is keen on Mary, but Arthur more than most. Mary and he were engaged. For almost six months, seems to me."

The words stun Ollie. "Engaged!" he says. "But what happened?"

"Some things Mary keeps to herself. But I suspect that she never really loved him. The man has no humor."

"I've noticed."

"He's so—intense. I think his intensity finally just wore her out."

"If she didn't love him, then why'd she agree to the engagement?"

"We were new to New York. She was flattered by his attention. And I think she needed an excuse to escape the overwhelming attentions of John Anderson."

"Her employer?"

"The very same. John was obsessed with her. Still is. But he's practical as well, a good businessman. He learned that she's more valuable to him as a cigar girl than a lover."

"I know I'm prying, but—I don't really know how to ask this…"

"Then don't," Phebe says. "Unless you're prepared to answer sensitive questions about your own love life."

Ollie considers this, decides to change the subject. "If you don't mind me asking a different question—I've noticed that you and Mary seem rather distant lately. Does it have to do with me?"

"You?" Phebe seems genuinely surprised at this suggestion. "My dear Oliver, I can truly say that you are not the problem. I wish you had come to us a month earlier."

"Then what is it?"

"Oliver, you are a generous, well-educated young man with wonderful manners. You've brightened the life of my Mary, who unfortunately is prone to making unwise personal decisions. At the present time we are having a—well, let's call it a disagreement about one of these decisions."

"She wants to move away from home?" he guesses.

"Oh, eventually that will happen," Phebe says. "But no—that's not it. I'm afraid that Phebe has become engaged again, this time to Daniel Payne, one of our borders."

Ollie rocks backward and catches himself on his elbows. "Payne?" he asks, hoping that he has misunderstood.

"Yes, Daniel Payne, the corker."

"He was in the house the evening I moved in, but he's been absent since. I thought maybe he had moved out."

"I pray to God that he will *never* return—though he owes me money. Has a problem with the sauce, that one. Gets awful mad and abusive when he's drunk. Problem is, when he's sober he's a real charmer. Especially with the ladies."

"But why—?"

"Why did she hook up with this boozer? Because he asked, I suppose. And because she needed a way to brush off Arthur Crommelin, who could not believe that his relationship with her was over."

Ollie thinks about his encounter with Crommelin this morning. "He still believes that he has a chance. So you're angry with Mary because she's engaged?"

"Because she's engaged to a scoundrel who will ruin her life. But she won't listen to reason—not from me, that's for sure. Makes my blood boil to think of her marrying that lunatic."

"Where has he been?"

"Said he was going to visit his brother, but I'd wager he's in a drunken stupor somewhere sharing a bed with some harlot from Five Corners. The man has no scruples, but Mary can't see the lies. He'll be back one of these days and…" Phebe stops suddenly.

"And then what?" Ollie asks, sitting up and leaning toward her.

Phebe avoids his gaze. "Forgive me for being a selfish old woman. I've never seen Mary as happy as she's been the past few days. By coincidence or not, that happens to be when you came to us. I would like to see that happiness continue."

Ollie is reeling from the sudden impact of Phebe's tale. His emotions are snarled and he can't untangle them. Disappointment, yes. He is profoundly disappointed that his precious angel is engaged to another man. Saddened, too, as well as disillusioned. The illusion of Mary's purity and innocence has been exposed. *What more is there to learn about her sordid relationships?*

But Ollie feels a tingle of excitement, also—that such a worldly woman would be interested in him, a man of meager experience. And he is becoming intoxicated with the mystery of Mary Rogers, sensing that there is far more to her than what Phebe has explained. The more unattainable Mary becomes, the more desirable she is to Ollie.

"You said that she's been happy since I arrived at the boardinghouse," Ollie says, fishing for more details.

"My, yes. Everything is 'Ollie this,' and 'Ollie that.'"

"You believe she fancies me, then?"

"That's an English way of saying it. Don't tell me you haven't noticed."

"Do you believe that she loves this Payne fellow?"

"No, quite the opposite. I think she's even taken to disliking the brute. But he has some kind of powerful hold over her."

Ollie leans over and kisses Phebe lightly on the cheek. Her perfume—the fragrance of lilacs—reminds him of Mum, and suddenly he feels close to this old woman. He wants to tell her his own story, for he has at least as many secrets as Mary, but he holds his tongue and only says, "I love your daughter, Phebe."

With suddenly moist eyes, Phebe looks at this young man. "Of course you do, Ollie," she says. "Save her, then."

Ollie lies back on the grass. A massive white cloud passes in front of the sun. Ollie sees in this cloud the image of something familiar.

The Prophet Muhammad.

"There you are, dear!" Phebe cries out. "Did you get the beer?"

"Yes, mama."

Something in Mary's voice concerns Ollie. He sits up as Mary kneels down with a basket full of brown bottles.

"Just what the doctor ordered," Mary says. But her voice is thin and brittle. She looks pale. The sparkle in her eyes is gone. She guiltily avoids Ollie's eyes.

"Are you all right, Mary?" Ollie asks.

"Oh yes, just fine. I believe the heat may have gotten to me, though. I was a little sick up there, but I'm feeling better now."

Ollie can sense it—she is lying. He is challenged now to solve the mystery of Mary Brown. And to save her.

"My, my—look who's here!" This sarcastic tenor voice belongs to Jonathon Fury. Ollie turns his head to see the bright red mane of his employee flashing in the summer sun.

"Jonathon—what are you doing out here?"

Jonathon lugs two satchels and the large wooden camera box over to the table cloth and wipes a river of perspiration from his forehead. "My employer had no work for me today, so I decided to make some pictures out here. The light is wonderful. Fancy meeting you here."

"Well have some food, will you?" Ollie says. "We brought enough for an army."

"I was going to have a bite and a beer at Nick Moore's House, but your invitation is very appealing." Jonathon looks down at the food. "Yes, all right then. Thank you. I insist, though, on paying for my meal with a daguerreotype of the three of you in the Elysian Fields. A moment to remember, and remember it you shall."

"Very well," Ollie says. "But after lunch. We eat first."

Jonathon glances at Mary, who furtively turns away. Something is bothering her—something bigger than the others could even guess—and Jonathon knows what it is.

CHAPTER 9

As the Shaykhi students flow toward the great hall, anxious whispers like hissing serpents slither through the corridors and coil in the corners of the room. The gossip is intoxicating. Some of the students passionately believe that Jalal is the Promised One; their belief has blinded them to other possibilities.

A smaller group has staked its belief in a reclusive student named Naseem, a young man so pious that he is often asked to lead prayers. A frail ascetic with no close friends, Naseem's only apparent indulgences are the self-imposed mortifications to which he submits. Yet for some of the Shaykhis there is something otherworldly in the bleak stare of this ghostly young man, a glimmer of the divine in his bearing, and an unconventional wisdom that has helped resolve the personal problems of many of the students.

Siyyid Kazim enters the room and the students rush to be near him. Jalal takes a place in the back of the gathering. Their teacher turns his tired eyes onto the group and begins to speak.

"Some of you have been here for many years, listening to our teachings and studying the writings," Kazim says deliberately. "You have seen how the local 'ulama have attempted to strangle us with their deceits and propaganda. How I wish that Shaykh Ahmad were still with us, for I must admit my own failings in countering these endless attacks. I apologize to all of you for my waning strength."

A chorus of support rises up from the students who are unaccustomed to hearing such expressions from their leader.

Kazim paces for a moment and then turns back to the students. "What concerns me even more, however, are the attacks that come from inside."

This remark sets off an uproar. *What kind of betrayal or treachery does he speak of?* Some of the students jump up and look ominously around the room, searching for a sign of guilt in the others.

"Listen carefully, then, to what I have to say," Kazim continues. "There is one among us who is guilty of a delusion that is capable of dividing us forever. One of you has put forth blasphemous claims, falsely announcing to a few that he is the Promised One. And more than a few recklessly believe him—despite the fact that he possesses none of the required attributes we have been studying. Have you learned any of the things we have taught?"

Fortunately, this is a rhetorical question. The students lower their eyes in shame.

"I speak directly to the imposter now," Kazim continues. "No one here seems to have questioned why the Qa'im, that most spotless soul, should have to punish himself with painful injuries to his body as you do. The Qa'im will be *wrongly* punished by many others, and cannot be *justly* punished by anyone. Your acts betray you."

The round eyes of the students turn to the back of the room where Naseem prayerfully sits as if not hearing his teacher's words.

"Remove yourself from our sight," Kazim says. "There is no place for you here."

Naseem slowly stands, raising his head arrogantly rather than shamefully. "One day you will discover your mistake," he says before walking out.

"I already have discovered my mistake," Kazim says as he watches the imposter leave the room. "And I have corrected it."

The stunned gathering is silent, as if the students are recalculating a shift in their collective equilibrium. *What is next?*

"Cleansing our own house is only one step," Kazim says. "Now we must address the attacks from outside our community. You have all heard, I believe, of Siyyid Baqir." Heads bob up and down but there are several blank expressions. "He is a most formidable ecclesiastical dignitary. He now lives in Isfahan, but his authority extends far beyond the confines of that city. If we could win his support, we would have a measure of protection."

Jahangir, the one who had witnessed Jalal's seizure, stands bravely and addresses the teacher. "I've head of this man," Jahangir says. "He was once a friend of Shaykh Ahmad but withdrew his support after the Shaykh died. How could any of us approach such a powerful man?"

"So many questions," Kazim says. "Would that one amongst you could arise and with complete detachment deliver a message on my behalf to this learned Siyyid."

"What message?" Jahangir asks before sitting down.

Siyyid Kazim walks into the middle of the group. "Imagine that this messenger would obtain from the Siyyid a solemn declaration testifying to the unquestioned authority of Shaykh Ahmad, and to the truth and soundness of his teachings."

Several of the students, who were about to volunteer, now have second thoughts.

"And imagine, then, that this same messenger—after securing such a testimony—would travel to Mashhad and obtain a similar pronouncement from Mirza Askari, the foremost ecclesiastical leader in that holy city."

Kazim surveys the room. His thinly veiled solicitation produces no volunteers. He waits, smiling faintly and nodding his head before striding back to the front of the room. Then, before he can continue, a student stands.

"I will go!" Mirza Muhit says bravely. Muhit had been one of the boldest and most vocal believers in Naseem, the imposter. "I will be your messenger."

Kazim stares at the young man, who wilts beneath the teacher's gaze. "Beware of touching the lion's tail," Kazim says. "Do not belittle the delicacy and difficulty of such a mission."

Muhit sits down, unable to bear the intensity of Kazim's hot gaze and disquieting words.

Siyyid Kazim sweeps his eyes over the seated students, landing at last on the face of Jalal. "Arise and perform this mission," he says. "I declare you equal to the task."

Jalal stands, astonished and embarrassed. *Surely there are others more worthy.* A hundred eyes stare at him. A thousand thoughts explode in his head. Clearing his mind with a prayer, he walks through the parting crowd and kneels at the feet of Siyyid Kazim, kissing the hem of his teacher's robe.

"In the name of God, I will go," Jalal says.

CHAPTER 10

Mary studies the daguerreotype and decides that it is a portrait of someone else. "Not me," she says. "This woman is beautiful, and I'm not. This person is young, and I'm a hundred years old. At least I feel like it."

"I suppose you're right. Far too young and pretty," Ollie agrees, looking at the picture. "But she's wearing your clothes."

"I'd better check my closet, then."

"You don't mind if I carry a picture of another woman, do you?"

"Of course not. But if you see her in person, tell her I want my dress back."

They are in the sitting room of the boarding house, which is otherwise vacant. Ollie takes the metal plate on which the image of Mary is emblazoned and places it in his pocket. "I had a wonderful time today."

"Me too." Mary rests her hand on Ollie's knee. "I like spending time with you, Ollie. Tell me about your life in England. It must be a terribly exotic place compared to New York. All that history."

"Well, yes, London has history all right. But I'm afraid my own history is rather humdrum." Ollie dodges the colorful events of his life; what sense is there in dredging up a story with so much heartache? "My father is an editor for the *London Times*, and I'm a news writer."

"That's what you do. I'm interested in your life before that."

"Not much to talk about, really. Public boys' school, Oxford University, home in Belgravia, terrible at sports but love horses. Never been married. Never been kissed, actually."

Mary laughs. "I don't believe that for a minute!"

"Well, once—by my great-grandmother."

"What! Not by your own mother?"

Ollie is boxed in. He doesn't want to talk about his mother, but he doesn't want to lie. "My mother left me when I was younger."

The smile disappears from Mary's face. "I'm sorry," she says. "I really am."

"It's all right. It was a long time ago."

"But the pain never really goes away, does it?" Mary says. "It's always there, in the background. A dull throbbing."

Ollie looks at Mary. She seems to speak from experience, but— "It is like that a bit, I suppose. You're lucky to have your mother with you, Mary. Even when you're quarrelling, Phebe seems to love you a great deal. Do you have siblings?"

"I don't know. I mean, I don't think so."

"Your mother is quite a lot older than you. I thought… maybe you were the baby of the family. She must have gotten a late start."

"Late, yes."

"Have you always been together?" It is easier for Ollie to ask personal questions than answer them, and suddenly he realizes that he knows almost nothing about Mary and her family, except for Phebe.

"Since I can remember," Mary replies. "My, you're full of questions. Seems to me we were talking about you, and all of a sudden here I am gushing about my own family."

"I was raised by my great-grandmother," Ollie confesses. He had not meant to reveal even this much about his past, but feels compelled to offer something in exchange for another piece of Mary's story.

Mary hears these words and turns to Ollie with moist eyes. "Me too," she says. "I mean, my grandmother."

Ollie is confused. "But your mother, Phebe, and you—"

"Phebe is my grandmother," Mary says. "I've been raised by my grandmother, Ollie, just like you were raised by your great-grandmother."

Of course. Phebe is old enough to be Mary's grandmother.

"And your mother—?"

"Phebe's daughter. It's a sordid little tale. I don't even know why I'm telling you this. No one else in New York knows."

"Your mother was pregnant."

"Well of course she was pregnant. She gave birth to a daughter!" Mary is suddenly agitated. She stands up, turning her back on Ollie who stays seated on the divan. "The problem was that she never got married."

"Did you know your mother?" Ollie asks.

Mary nods *no*. "She chose to abandon me to my grandmother's care rather than face the scandal. To be honest, I prefer to be my grandmother's daughter rather than my mother's bastard child." She turns and stares at Ollie, bluster camouflaging pain. "So there you have it."

"Your grandmother stood by you."

"Yes, but sometimes when I look at her I see her wondering when my bad blood will steer me in the direction of hell. In my grandmother's eyes, I'm cursed by my mother's carnal act. Almost certainly I will end up like her, and then poor Phebe will have another generation to raise."

"So she's opinionated about your... relationships."

"Opinionated? No, I would say *scared*. Waiting for disaster."

"But you seem to love her."

"Oh, yes—more than you know. Without her... I can't imagine... No one else looked after me. No one wanted me. Mother—*Phebe*—was always there, atoning I think for her daughter's sin. Poor woman—she's atoned long enough. She needs some peace."

"But you're such a help to her."

"I'm her biggest worry." Mary stops and thinks for a minute. "Is your great-grandmother still alive?" she asks.

"She died about ten years ago."

"Did she worry about you?"

"Yes."

"Then she's at peace."

Ollie considers this. It is difficult to think of Mum *at peace*. Would she approve of Mary? He thinks so. Would she approve of the way Ollie has turned out? He is not so certain—perhaps once he has tied up the remaining loose ends, the way Mum did. She always finished things.

"I'm very tired, Ollie," Mary says, kissing him on the forehead. "I'm going upstairs now." And then she is gone.

An hour later, as Ollie lies in bed, the door to his room slowly opens. He can hear the click of the latch and the squeak of the hinges.

"Ollie?" A whisper. "May I come in?"

"Of course."

Mary Rogers softly walks across the room and slips into Ollie's bed. "I was feeling terribly alone. Would you just hold me?"

Forever, Ollie thinks.

CHAPTER 11

Jonathon stares at Ollie incredulously. "Are you mad?" he asks. "The girl is engaged. What were you thinking of?" During the following silence he puts the exposed metal plate on the fuming box above the heated mercury, then adds, "Nobody likes Daniel Payne, but he's mighty mean when he's drunk. If he ever finds out—"

The darkness of the room makes Ollie feel almost anonymous. It's easier to talk about private matters in this small dim place. *That's probably why so many Catholics relish the confessional.*

"I wasn't really thinking about that," Ollie confesses. "Her engagement, I mean."

"Did you think about it at all?

"Not in any conscious way, no."

"Don't be so intellectual about it. If you had any scruples, you would have booted her out."

"I couldn't do that."

"Why not?"

"I love her."

"Listen to me now—that wasn't love you were feeling last night."

"Don't make it sound so tawdry."

"Don't make it sound—? Jonathon! Listen to me. The woman is pledged to another man. She comes to your bed last night. But you're not the man she has promised to marry. What does that tell you?"

"I think she loves me too."

"Are all Brits so stupid? Let me be blunt. Mary Rogers is a very attractive girl. I'm attracted to her myself—physically, that is. Ask any man who comes into Anderson's. They're all like moths flying around a flame. That girl will burn you if you get too close. She's had other lovers, Ollie. Ask *them*."

"Every woman has a past. I don't care about hers."

"So it's true, then. Your brain has actually gone dead."

"Isn't that bloody picture done yet?"

Jonathon moves the plate from the fuming box to a tray of hypo-sulfate solution. "While I wait for our great journey into the heart of America to begin, the newspapers are forgetting all about me. My career in New York is in de-cline. I'm taking a great risk waiting for you to sort out your few things. What if you sort *me* out?"

"For God's sake."

Jonathon moves the plate to another tray and flushes its surface with dis-tilled water. "It's a legitimate concern. Of course, I'd have less concern if you agreed to pay me an adequate sum in the event that you terminated my services."

"That's bribery!" Ollie protests, but in reality he feels relieved that the conversation has turned from his obsession with Mary Rogers to the slightly less delicate topic of money. "How much would be adequate?"

In the darkness, Jonathon smiles. "I'm sure you'll make a suitable offer." Jonathon places the plate onto the stand, lights the spirit lamp beneath it, and opens a bottle of gold chloride.

"All right then," Ollie says. "In the event I terminate you, I will pay you an additional four weeks salary."

"Six weeks," Jonathon says. "And transportation back to New York if we're somewhere else." Jonathon gently pours the gold chloride over the im-age.

"All right. But if you take other work while we're in New York, I get half the proceeds."

Yes, Ollie's brain has gone dead, Jonathon thinks. He would have given Ollie more than that. "It's done, then."

Jonathon lights a lantern and the room begins to glow with a warm light. "Agreed. No complaints, but I reserve the right to give advice from time to time."

Ollie sighs, then nods and picks up the gilded plate. "What is this?"

"A picture I made at the Elysian Fields. The day we all met there."

"Is that the tavern, Nick Moore's House?"

"It is. The owner spied my camera and asked me to make a picture of the establishment. Even brought out his patrons to be in it—that's them standing in front of the place."

Ollie looks up at Jonathon. "And were you paid for your services?"

"Of course. I'm a professional."

Jonathon picks up the plate and studies it carefully. As he had suspected, in the picture he finds indelible proof of Mary's sordid secret—the reason she contrived a trip to the Elysian Fields last Sunday.

CHAPTER 12

The boarding house is full tonight, and the sitting room is brimming over with testosterone. Arthur Crommelin reclines in his customary overstuffed chair—*why is he here? He doesn't reside here any more*—and Ollie has staked out one end of the divan. William Kiekuk nervously plunks out a succession of wrong notes on the piano, just as he did on Sunday. *Does the man have nothing better to do than irritate people with his lack of musicianship?* Three other male guests hunker down in hard-backed chairs. No one will sit on the divan next to another man.

Stomachs growl. Supper is late this evening.

The men read newspapers and trade inane remarks, awkwardly passing the time. Ollie begins to wonder if all of these men could be Mary's suitors.

No, of course not. She's engaged.

Another man struts into the room and finds all the chairs occupied. He marches to the divan and sits down, turning to face Ollie.

"Don't believe we've made the acquaintance," the man says. "Daniel Payne."

Ollie extends his hand. "Oliver Chadwick," he says, and the men shake hands.

Daniel is about thirty with a ruddy complexion and sandy hair. He has a firm handshake and muscular build.

Ollie studies the man's face—the puffy nose is lined with spidery red veins and the rheumy eyes are bloodshot. Untamed brown eyebrows sprout in all directions, and several bent hairs dangle precariously above the left eyelid. He looks like he's been drinking, but acts stone sober.

"So you're the one from England?" Daniel says. "Heard about you."

Ollie nods politely but says nothing.

"And I'm the lucky S.O.B. who won the hand of Mary Rogers!" he says. "You probably heard about me." Daniel looks around the sitting room, taunting the losers.

"Indeed," Ollie says.

"*'Indeed'?* What kind of talk is that? We're plain folk here. All of us're different in some ways, but all of us the same in two ways—we're all plain folk and we all love beautiful Mary, isn't that right fellows?"

No one responds. Ollie feels anger welling up inside him.

Arthur Crommelin leans forward, not an easy task in the overstuffed chair that has nearly swallowed him whole. "How nice to have you back," he says to Daniel. "Now shut your trap or there'll be no supper for you."

"Look who's talkin'," Daniel replies with a smirk. "And what are you doin' here, Arthur? You been cast aside, but here ya are waitin' for some table scraps ta fall. Ain't no scraps fallin' around here while Daniel's in the house. Where the hell is supper anyway?"

Arthur decides it isn't worth a fight. He sinks back into soft cushions.

William Kiekuk smashes a fist into the keyboard. The thunderous sound grabs everyone's attention, which is what he wants. He swivels on the piano bench to face Daniel Payne.

"Daniel, I don't know what you got on Miss Mary, but it must be somethin' powerful, 'cause I know she wouldn't hitch up with a drunk like you otherwise. I was prayin' some ol' whore would slit your throat an' we'd never see your ugly face again. But here you are. Proof, I guess, that there just ain't no God after all."

Daniel glowers at Kiekuk and clenches his fists, then takes a breath and smiles discordantly. "I know what you're doin', Kiekuk. You're bein' jealous, you an' Arthur both, 'cause I won and you both lost."

At that precise moment, Mary Rogers walks into the room and Kiekuk sits down.

Daniel turns to her and says, "Hello, Darlin'. I missed you somethin' terrible." He walks over to her, kisses her on the lips and gives her a hug. From over his shoulder she stares blankly at Ollie, then closes her eyes until Daniel releases her.

"Hello, Daniel," she says with a soft, unconvincing smile. Then she turns to the group. "Gentlemen, I'm sorry I was late this evening. Mother held the meal until I arrived, but dinner is now served. If you'll follow me."

The image of Mary kissing the distasteful Daniel Payne riles Ollie, but he restrains himself. *She needs time to untangle things,* he tells himself.

But then what? Will Daniel pull a knife on Ollie in a drunken rage?

The men take their places at a long dinner table. Daniel sits next to Ollie. Beatrice, the kitchen helper, begins to carry out the food on big trays.

As Daniel takes a big scoop of potatoes, he turns to Ollie and says, "So Oliver, I hear that you enjoyed Sunday at the Elysian Fields? Mighty nice place out there, ain't it? Very romantic."

Ollie is surprised that Daniel knows about the foray to New Jersey.

"Oliver was kind enough to take mother and me," Mary says, interrupting. "Thank you again, Mr. Chadwick. Mother said she had a wonderful time talking to you."

"Got a friend who was out there the same day, told me about it," Daniel says, staring at Ollie.

"Your friend should have joined us. We had plenty of food. In fact, my assistant, Jonathon Fury, joined us as we were having lunch."

"You have an assistant, then?" Daniel says, stabbing a fork into a large slice of beef roast on a passing platter, then slapping the juicy slab onto his plate. "How nice. Most of us poor slobs have to do our own work."

"You're a corker, I understand."

"I am. Not a job up to yer standards, I'm sure, but the pay is good."

Ollie backs his chair away from the table and leans over to pick something up from the floor behind Daniel's chair. He straightens up, pulls his chair in closer, and hands a small metal flask to Daniel. "Well, you must earn enough to keep yourself in whiskey. I believe this is yours."

Daniel takes it, glances at a stern Mary Rogers, then with his first sign of embarrassment says, "Like to keep a bit o' tea with me durin' a long work day."

Ollie deduces that Daniel has promised Mary to lay off the booze. "Filled with tea, then?" he says.

"That's what I said!"

"Of course. Pass the corn, please," Ollie replies. Then he reaches to a coffee pot. "Perhaps you'd like some black coffee. It can take the edge off that strong tea."

From the corner of his eye Ollie can see that he his verbal dart has wounded the hateful Daniel Payne. The bluster leaks out of the man.

Daniel again looks at Mary and then lowers his eyes. He stands and says, "Excuse me please. I'm tireder than I thought. Think I'll catch some sleep." He walks around the table to Mary, stoops to kiss her hair tenderly from behind—he seems to inhale her fragrance but she does not acknowledge his gesture—and leaves the room.

No one will say anything about Daniel's behavior while Mary is present.

Ollie can plainly see that Daniel, for all his bravado and verbal bullying, deeply loves Mary. Clearly the man is struggling to control his drinking problem, probably at the instigation of Mary, and his failure is a cause of pain for both of them.

Mary avoids Ollie's eyes.

Does she love this brute, Daniel Payne? Impossible. But there is something between these two.

Something.

CHAPTER 13

Sunday, July 25, begins as a perfect summer morning. It is hot and humid, but a gentle breeze blows through Ollie's window refreshing him as he lies in bed. His life is adrift, but deliciously so. The mysterious mission that for years has driven him so fiercely now seems less urgent. Mary Rogers has tamed it.

He thinks about Herbert Eaton, his best friend and mentor, the man who stood by him through the pain of Anne's duplicity and even now looks after the Belgravia mansion to which Ollie will one day return. Ollie does not miss much about London, but he misses Herbert terribly. And he now understands something about love—about how Herbert, after the pain and humiliation of Anne's betrayal, can still love the woman. True love is undying. After all these years, Ollie knows that Herbert still holds out hope that one day Anne will be granted a divorce and return to him. And if that should ever happen, Ollie knows that in an instant Herbert will forgive all.

Can Ollie ever love so unconditionally? He hopes so. He believes that he does now love in such a way. He cannot imagine a circumstance or a world in which he would not love Mary Rogers.

The sound of his loved one's voice now floats through the open window and makes him shiver with delight. He can't make out the words, but the musical voice is like wind chimes. He lets it dance in his ears for a moment, then rises from the bed and walks to the window overlooking the front yard. There he can see Mary Rogers with her back to the house. She is speaking to someone just out of sight. The willowy elegance of the girl, her lissome grace and womanly gestures, cast a spell of such exquisite bliss that Ollie nearly swoons from the enchantment. He memorizes this picture, this magical square of space framed by the window.

But then the unseen person to whom Mary speaks moves toward her and the spell is broken, for there, intruding into Ollie's tranquil portrait of Mary, is the despicable Daniel Payne. He is agitated. With frantic gestures he seems to be pleading his side of an argument to a jury of trees and clouds. He menacingly points a finger at Mary but she doesn't back down. Instead she raises her hands in a question then turns in exasperation. At last, with her face toward the window, Ollie can make out her words: "That's it. I'm running my errands."

Mary races into the house, apparently to gather her things. Daniel kicks angrily at the dirt and marches off. Ollie can hear footsteps on the stairs— *Mary's?*—and then a gentle knock on his door.

He scrambles for a dressing gown and then says, "Come in."

Mary enters the room. Her face is flushed, which makes her even more beautiful in the morning light. "Good morning," she says.

"It's a very good morning now that you're here," Ollie replies. He takes a step toward her but she coyly backs away. He stops.

"I wanted you to know that I would be gone for much of the day," Mary explains. "Errands to run and such." Except for the pinkness in her cheeks, there is no sign in her manner of the argument with Payne. How quickly she has put it behind her.

"Care for company?" Ollie asks.

"I wouldn't think of taking up your day with a visit to my aunt and my other menial chores," she answers. "But I also thought that you might be interested in knowing I broke off the engagement this morning."

She says this so casually! As if announcing a shopping list.

For Ollie, though, this is momentous news. He grins and rushes toward Mary, smothering her with an embrace.

"He was very hurt," Mary says when she is released from Ollie's smothering hug.

"I'm not surprised. Did he threaten you?" Ollie remembers the menacing finger pointed at Mary.

"He was angry, but Daniel would never hurt me. He loves me too much. He's more likely to hurt himself."

"Still, the man has a great deal of pride—"

Mary pulls away and speaks harshly. "I said he'd never hurt me. It's over now. He'll go on a bender and in a week he'll come and get his things, and then he'll be gone. That's all there is to it."

Ollie is startled by her brittle change of demeanor. He can see that hurting Daniel's feelings was difficult for someone as sensitive and caring as Mary. He takes a deep breath—the way Herbert always did with headstrong Anne—and chooses to say nothing. Mary stares at the floor for a moment, then looks up at Ollie and puts her hands on his chest.

"I'm sorry I spoke to you that way," she says. Then she kisses him on the cheek. "I'll be back this evening. We have so much to talk about."

Mary turns and leaves. Ollie moves to the window and watches her walk across the front yard in her white dress, leghorn hat, and parasol.

So be it. A day alone.

Ollie decides to enjoy the sunshine.

Sunday mornings in New York are unusually quiet. Work has stopped, all commerce has ceased, even the shops and taverns are closed. The incessant beating of the presses on Nassau Street is mercifully stilled by the closing of the newspapers on the Sabbath. The streets, on other mornings choked with people, are deserted except for the occasional early stroller or churchgoer. Ollie likes the solitude. The silence, filled only with birdsong and the rustling of leaves, transports him back to the grounds of Chillington-hall.

Feeling loose and free now, he lunches at a small tavern on Warren Street, then visits Scott's Bazaar on Dey Street. After an hour or so of inspecting the odd conglomeration of merchandise, he walks up Broadway to James Street and yields to an urge to read the newspapers at Mr. Bickford's. He finds an old issue of the *London Times* and searches for Herbert's byline but finds none. His mentor writes very little news these days.

Ollie finds a copy of the *New York Herald* and begins to work his way through it. Here, on these crackling pages, is chronicled the sleaze and vice of a city teeming with lust and crime. On page one, a picture of yet another hanged murderer—*Jonathon's work?*—and on page two a collection of small stories about murders, robberies, prostitution, beatings, rapes, and other inventions of evil.

Page three catches his eye. At the top begins an article by James Gordon Bennett, the slime-mongering owner of the paper. It describes the progress of a self-declared Prophet in Illinois named Joseph Smith who has founded an "empire guarded by his own militia, the likes of which may greatly outnumber the State's own military and most certainly provides the superior kind of training that is so often lacking in American militias." Ollie detects a sly derision in the article as he continues reading:

> *The astonishing Mormon mixture of worldly prudence and reli-*
> *gious enthusiasm, of civilized reason with ancient ideas of reli-*
> *gious observance and military organization, is without parallel*
> *in the history of nations since the time of Mohammad. In two*
> *years the Holy City of God, Nauvoo, has risen from a few houses*
> *to possess 10,000 souls, besides much cattle.*

So—America has its own Qa'im—or perhaps just an apprentice. From what Ollie can tell, this Joe Smith does not claim to be a Manifestation of God, the return of Jesus, or the Promised One of Islam. He claims to be only a modern-day Christian Prophet who has delivered to the world sacred texts long hidden until this most auspicious moment in time.

Ollie makes a mental note to visit this village of Nauvoo on his journey to the center of the nation. What an interesting piece this would make for the *London Times*. He envisions his headline: *America Invents Its Own Religion*.

Ollie smiles at Bennett's language. "Without parallel in the history of nations since Mohammad…10,000 souls, besides much cattle." It sounds like one of the garish posters promoting the *Surrey's* latest spectacular. Only the depiction of the mighty Mormon militia rings true. Is not the history of religion always tied to a warring God? Ollie can imagine how the Mormon's neighbors are reacting to an exotic new "temple" and an army of self-righteous zealots rising up among their farm fields.

Oddly, next to this "religious" piece is the salacious account of a "sex trial." An infamous New York abortionist, Madame Restell, had been convicted on July 20 of "administering to one Ann Maria Purdy certain noxious medicine drugs or substances unknown, she being at the time pregnant—thereby procuring her miscarriage by the use of instruments—the same not being necessary to preserve her life, and not having been advised by two physicians to be necessary for such purpose."

Ollie notices that the accompanying drawing of Madame Restell is attributed to *Jonathon Fury*. The man is an artist—and an editorialist. The macabre etching shows a somber woman about Ollie's age. Her hair is parted unbecomingly in the middle and she is clothed in dark bunchy garments. A smirking, bat-like demon with outstretched leathery wings hovers in front of her belly, and in the demon's gruesome grip is a dead infant.

According to the article, on the same day as her conviction Madame Restell's attorney filed an appeal on grounds of entrapment and "procedural illegalities." The appeal was immediately granted and after one day in prison Restell was released pending a new trial. Anti-abortionists called this legal maneuvering "quite literally a miscarriage of justice."

Ollie reflects on the eerie juxtaposition of these two articles. How many religions, he wonders, have been aborted by the threatened adherents of other faiths? How many "prophets" have been slaughtered during the formative stages of their work to preserve the viability of the religions from which they were born?

Ollie has lost track of time. It's now late afternoon. He leaves Mr. Bickford's and heads back to Broadway. As he walks toward downtown, he enters the fringe of a gathering crowd. Ollie watches couples holding hands, stealing kisses, laughing and dancing. He longs to be with Mary, but now his heart is as heavy as the storm clouds that are accumulating in the west.

Before he can settle down, Ollie knows that he must complete the mission that brought him to America. He will have to leave New York soon. Will Mary wait for him?

A loud clap of thunder raises everyone's eyes to the clouds. Some begin to drift home but many remain on the street, tempting the weather to rain on their promenade.

The storm hits within minutes of his arrival at the boarding house. The rain slices downward like knives, obscuring from sight even the homes across the street.

I hope Mary is safe at her aunt's, Ollie thinks. He goes upstairs and changes clothes, coming back down just in time for Phebe's dinner. Only three boarders are present—Ollie, Arthur Crommelin, and William Kiekuk—the others presumably having been caught somewhere trying to get home.

"We have so many seats empty, why don't you and Phebe join us tonight?" Ollie suggests to Beatrice, the servant-girl, who is carrying platters of food. The invitation is accepted and the five of them sit down for a quiet dinner.

"I'm sure everyone is quite safe," Phebe says, sensing Ollie's concern. "It's just a summer storm. As for Mary, she'll be home in the morning, I'm sure."

The rain continues to pound down. Ollie goes to bed early, but an hour later he hears footsteps on the stairs. Hoping it is Mary, he gets out of bed and opens his door.

"Whatcha lookin' at?" barks Daniel Payne. He is soaked.

"Thought it was Mary," Ollie says.

"She's not home? She was supposed to be home by nightfall."

"We think she stayed with her aunt because of the rain."

With a huff, Payne enters his room and slams the door.

CHAPTER 14

Ollie sleeps fitfully. The rain continues to pour until early morning. At daybreak, as the sun begins to peek through the scattering clouds, Ollie rises and finds Phebe in the kitchen preparing breakfast. The old woman volunteers nothing about Mary, so Ollie asks.

"I fell asleep early. What time did Mary get home?" His tone is casual. He doesn't want to betray his concern.

"Oh, she never got home. Prob'ly spent the night at her aunt's as we thought. I expect we'll see her before long. She's due at Anderson's by ten, and she won't be going there in that little white cotton dress."

Breakfast is quiet. Daniel Payne enters the dining room without a word, eats silently, and begins to leave.

"Payne!" Ollie shouts. "Any idea where Mary might have gone?"

"Her aunt's is what she said."

There is a long pause, and then Payne steps closer to Ollie, his jaw firmly set. His whole body seems tightly clenched, like a fist. "You seem mighty concerned."

"Lot's of things could happen to a girl out there alone, that's all."

"Well it's my worry, not yours. She's my girl."

Ollie wants to call his bluff and explain that he knows about the break-up, but he remains silent. "What are you doing about it?" Ollie asks.

"I'm goin' to her aunt's to fetch her. Costin' me two hours pay, want you to know. That's what I'm doin' about it."

"Look, there's no reason to lose pay. I can go."

"You stay outta this! It's none o' yer business. An' you stay away from Mary, too. She wants nothin' to do with you!"

Payne wheels and struts away. The man, Ollie decides, is desperately trying to save face. Or else he has utterly denied Mary's decision to call off the engagement. What will Payne do when Mary returns and he has to own up?

Ollie feels powerless to do anything but wait. He walks down the street and back but never leaves sight of the boarding house. He tries to read a copy of *Last of the Mohicans* pulled from the sitting room bookshelf and is astonished at the scribbling on the title page: *To Beautiful Mary, Anderson's most exquisite import. Your captivated servant, James Fennimore Cooper.*

Is there anyone who did not know Mary Rogers, the segar girl?

Ninety minutes after leaving, Daniel Payne returns pale and shaken. Ollie greets him expectantly at the front door.

"She never arrived at her aunt's," Payne says. Then he smashes his fist into the door casing and says, "If she's seein' someone else, I'll…" He doesn't finish his threat.

"Her aunt has no idea where she went?"

Payne shakes his head.

"Well we've got to find her," Ollie says.

"What d'ya think I been doin'? Her aunt's house is only fifteen minutes away. I been askin' questions in the neighborhood."

"And?"

"No luck. Thought I'd get a picture of her to show. Her mother had a drawing."

Ollie remembers the daguerreotype. "I know where there's a picture." He races up to Mary's room and finds the daguerreotype on her dresser but suddenly realizes that he can't give up this precious image to Daniel Payne. He turns and walks down the stairs prepared to lie. In the sitting room he finds Phebe handing a small drawing to Payne, who looks up at Ollie with a pleading expression.

"I'm not good at thinkin' this kinda thing through," Payne says.

"All right," Ollie replies, placing the daguerreotype into his pocket. "Phebe, we need to think of all the places she might have gone."

Within minutes, Ollie has a plan. Daniel will travel to Harlem at the northern end of Manhattan, then to Williamsburg in Brooklyn. Ollie will recruit Jonathon to help and they'll make inquiries in the Hoboken area and on Staten Island. They'll talk to hospitals, ferry pilots, carriage drivers, shopkeepers, anyone who will listen. Mary could not have just *disappeared* on a quiet Sunday.

Ollie's first stop is at the offices of the *Sun* where he places a missing persons notice for Tuesday's edition.

> Left her home on Sunday Morning, July 25, a young lady, had on a white dress, black shawl, blue scarf, leghorn hat, light colored shoes and parasol light colored; it is supposed some accident has befallen her. Whoever will give information respecting her at 126 Nassau Street shall be rewarded for their trouble.

CHAPTER 15

Exhausted and discouraged, Ollie, Jonathon and Daniel Payne converge on the boarding house late Monday night having uncovered no concrete leads. A handful of people "thought" they "may" have seen a young woman who "looked like" Mary Rogers, but no one was sure.

"Tomorrow perhaps we'll have our army," Ollie says before slouching into the divan. "I placed a missing persons notice in the *Sun*. Someone must have seen *something*!"

"I spoke to a friend of mine at the Police Department, man named Hayes," Jonathon says. "Told him that Mary was missing. He said if she doesn't turn up in another day or two we should let him know, but probably she's…"

Payne looks up. "Shacked up—is that what he said?"

"In a manner of speaking, yes." Jonathon looks at Ollie, unfazed. He believes Mary incapable of such a thing.

"Let's think this through," Ollie suggests. "She said she was going to her aunt's, but she never arrived. So either Mary was intending to surprise her aunt—any ideas on that?—or she lied to both of us and was going somewhere else."

Daniel jumps angrily to his feet. "Whad'ya mean *both* of us? When did she tell *you* about her aunt?"

Ollie hadn't meant to betray his conversation with Mary. "I ran into her on the way out Sunday morning. She was getting ready to go somewhere and I merely inquired about her destination. Small talk, that's all."

Payne buys it. He sits back down, puts his face into his hands. "She's been killed, I know it. This damn city!"

Ollie snaps back, "It's too early to write her epitaph! I suggest we all get some sleep." He wants to get away from this tiresome brute.

"Maybe you can sleep!" Payne hisses. "*We were going to be married!*"

Fatigue and Payne's self-pity are too much for Ollie. "Payne, you're a damn liar," he says coldly. "The two of you broke up this morning. For all I know, you abducted her to get even!" The words spill out. "How do we even know that you visited her aunt? We have only your word for it. What were you doing all day yesterday?"

"What do you mean *we broke up*?" Payne looks shaken. "Who told you *we broke up*?" He is trembling, not out of anger this time but out of panic or anxiety. "Who told you that?" he roars, then bolts for Ollie and grabs him by the shirt.

Jonathon tries to separate the two but Payne's grasp is too strong.

Ollie stares at the contemptible Daniel Payne and sneers. "Mary!" he yells. "Mary told me herself. She told me everything!" Ollie is out of control, and he knows it. But he doesn't care. Fear and anger have boiled over. The probable outcome of Mary's disappearance is too much to let go unavenged. If Daniel had anything to do with it…

"She… she wasn't serious," Daniel stammers, letting go of Ollie's shirt. "Didn't mean it, I'm sure she didn't. She's said things like that in the past, but always took 'em back." He walks across the room. "But she never told no one else." He turns back to Ollie. "So if she told you… you must be very close." He squints at Ollie. "You her lover? I knew there was someone else. You the reason she was leavin' me?"

He starts to march across the room with Ollie in his sights, but Phebe suddenly enters. Payne stops and all three men turn to acknowledge the old woman. Phebe's eyes are red and moist, but she seems alert to the situation.

"Am I interrupting anything, gentlemen?"

No one answers. All three men take their seats.

"I fear the worst for my daughter," Phebe says. "If any of you care about her, I hope you will work together to find her. Fighting among yourselves will not bring her back to us."

The men politely nod their agreement.

"I would like to introduce Mary's aunt, Mrs. Downing," Phebe says. From behind her, an elderly woman in a cotton shawl and gray dress enters the room.

"Good evening," Mrs. Downing says.

The men all rise to greet her, but Payne continues to stare at the floor.

"Sit down, please," Mrs. Downing continues, then narrows her eyes and recognizes Payne. "Is that Daniel Payne? My, it certainly is. It's been some weeks since you and Mary paid me a visit."

Ollie glances at Daniel, who squirms noticeably.

"Mrs. Downing," Ollie says. "I was under the impression that Daniel visited you today about Mary?"

"Today? My goodness no. I've just returned from out-of-town this afternoon—been gone for several days."

Ollie turns to Payne threateningly. "Daniel, don't you find that a bit odd?"

Payne slumps into his chair. "Look," he says, "maybe I didn't talk to her aunt. But I didn't need to. I knew that she didn't go to Mrs. Downing's house. That much is true."

"And what did you do to Mary?" Ollie says, leaning close.

"Nothing! My God, the police'll be askin' me the same questions. *I don't know what happened to her!*"

"Here's what I know," Ollie says. "You're in a lot of trouble."

Payne stands and nervously approaches Phebe. "Honest, I didn't do nothin'. I admit I followed Mary after she left the house, and that's how I know she didn't go to her aunt's. She caught a carriage and headed in the other direction, toward the Hoboken ferries. By the time I got a carriage, she was out of sight. So I wandered around for a while, thinking', just thinkin', about how I'd fouled up. That's why Mary was leavin' me. I just wanted to make things up to her, that's why I went to Mrs. Downing's house and waited outside, hopin' she'd show up. No one was home. I waited and waited. And then the storm came and I waited some more. Then I came back to the boarding house."

"I don't believe a word of it," Ollie says.

"He lied once, he could easily be lying now," Jonathon says. "Still, it's hard to disprove his story."

"Or prove it," Ollie adds. "The police will have fun trying. A man follows the lover who jilted him and she turns up missing." He thinks for a minute, then turns on Payne and spits out a venomous, "What did you do to her?"

Payne shrinks into his chair with a pitiful "Nothin'."

Ollie turns to the two women. "I'm sorry for my outburst," he says.

Phebe breaks into tears and Mrs. Downing wraps an arm around her, leading her into the kitchen.

With the women gone, Payne stands suddenly with a hard look in his eye. In a maddeningly calm voice that is miles apart from the emotion of a few seconds earlier, he stares at Ollie and says, "It was not me. Why don't ya ask Arthur Crommelin why he's not here tonight?" He begins to circle Ollie. "Or William Kiekuk? They never miss a meal at Phebe's, 'cept tonight. Ya want a jilted lover? Find Crommelin. Ya want a man who knows he can never have little darlin' Mary? Find Kiekuk. Now that I been thinkin' about it, that new fella—what's his name? Ollie?—been sniffin' 'round Miss Mary. Never know what a perverted Brit might do if he can't get what he wants. Then there's a thousand frustrated suitors at Anderson's, too. Could be any of 'em."

Payne plucks a metal flask from his hip pocket, unscrews the top and takes a swig of whiskey. "Miss Mary ain't here tonight. Think I'll have me a spot o' tea." He takes another swig. "She'd better have a damn good excuse for stayin' out late!" He storms out of the room.

Ollie looks at Jonathon, stunned by Payne's irrational behavior. "What do you think?"

Jonathon says, "He's crazy enough to have done something to her."

"And not so crazy that he rather artfully made almost everyone under this roof a suspect," Ollie adds. "The man has no proof of his whereabouts the day Mary disappeared."

Jonathon stares at him and says, "So what did you do all day Sunday, Ollie. And can you prove it?"

Ollie thinks about this, then stands stiffly and heads for the staircase. "We're convicting everyone we know, yet as far as I can tell there is no evidence that a crime has been committed. Be back here in the morning. I'm sure we'll have callers in response to my notice in the Sun."

Jonathon watches Ollie climb the stairs, then reaches into his breast pocket and removes a daguerreotype, the one he had made just before discovering Ollie and Mary at the Elysian Fields.

He stares at the picture, wondering if he is looking at the image of a murderer.

Chapter 16

Tuesday comes like a bolt of lightning. At seven o'clock a visitor interrupts breakfast with "great certainty" that she had seen the "missing girl" with several men in a Five Points tavern and, by the way, how will the reward be paid? By the end of the day, twenty-seven individuals had seen Mary Rogers from one side of town to another; clearly the girl was kicking up her heels on her day off. She was seen kissing an elderly woman, being followed from a bar by a gang of "black-skinned foreigners," holding hands with an older gentleman sporting an eye patch and a handlebar moustache, sipping beer and munching chestnuts and running across a park "as if in terror" and…

John Anderson, Mary's employer, is the last one to call. "Are you the one, then, who placed the notice in the *Sun*?" he asks Ollie.

Dazed by the continuous stream of contradictory testimony, Jonathon nods dumbly and offers tea.

"No thank you," Anderson says. "When I received the note yesterday from Mary's mother saying that Mary was indisposed, I had no idea…"

"We continue to hope for the best," Ollie replies.

"One of my customers showed me the missing persons notice this afternoon and I recognized the address. My God, I hope she's not been…" He cuts off his words.

"We know only that she's missing," Ollie says.

"Nothing else? Surely the police…"

Jonathon interjects, "The police have been contacted but say they can do nothing until there's evidence of a crime. Apparently it's not a crime for a young woman to leave home for a few days without telling anyone."

"But not *Mary*!" Anderson objects. "She would never intentionally cause her mother concern. Will you keep me informed? I'm dreadfully worried about her."

"Of course," Jonathon says.

On his way out, Anderson turns and says, "My customers are asking about her. What should I say?"

"Ask them to pray for her," Ollie says.

"Yes, of course. Thank you." Anderson leaves.

Ollie puts his fingers to his temples, massages deeply, then glances at Jonathon and says, "As I recall, John Anderson and Mary were once involved with each other. More than business."

"Yes."

"We've wasted a day sitting here, haven't we?"

"Yes."

"Then tomorrow we'll go find her. You and I." Ollie shuffles off to bed. Jonathon is afraid they *will* find her.

CHAPTER 17

It's perverse, he thinks, but a daguerreotypist must always be prepared to make a record, and if Mary Rogers should be found today—in whatever condition—he will document it. And so Jonathon hauls his cases and bags from the ferry to the Elysian Fields, stopping more than once to wipe his brow in the heat. It's not yet nine o'clock and already past eighty degrees. Humidity in the seventies.

He is here because his instincts and his photographic clue have led him here, and he is here alone because Ollie could not bear to revisit the scene of a much happier day. The Fields vibrate with green, every hue of it, the dark shades deeper and the lighter tints even more shimmering after the soaking rains of Sunday night. Verdant life sprouts everywhere.

Jonathon trudges along the path, deciding on a course of action. He can think of none. *Being here*, that is his plan. Sometimes a newsman can do no more than to be at the scene of a crime, and he is sure a crime was committed near this spot.

He settles into the spot on which he had found Ollie talking to Phebe last week—was it really just last week?—and finds that it is blessedly shaded by a large oak. He lies down, gathering his thoughts. First, he decides, he will interrogate the owner of Nick Moore's House, Frederika Loss. This should get to the heart of the matter. He will show the daguerreotype that he made last week, the one she herself had asked him to make, and observe her face for the telltale signs of guilt. If Jonathon is right, Mrs. Loss has knowledge of what happened to Mary Rogers. If not, surely she must *suspect* the truth.

Even the breeze is hot today.

Jonathon decides to rest for a few more minutes to rejuvenate his heat-drained body. With his eyes closed he begins to pick out the individual sounds that make up the aural web that surrounds him. He hears the flute-like sounds of children singing and laughing, a squirrel chattering, a noisy crow and an angry blue jay. A young couple twenty yards away discusses money—Jonathon can make out some of the words on the wind. Someone runs by scuffing the soft earth and breathing hard, clearly out of breath. He could make up a story about each of these sounds. The world pulses with the music of life.

He could just lie here and listen.

From further away he hears a woman yelling. Calling for children? No—something else, but too far away. Coming closer, though. The voice seems excited, agitated.

Another voice becomes tangled with the woman's—a man's booming voice, easier to understand. "Found!" he yells. No, that's not it. "Drowned!" That's what the man is yelling.

Jonathon's eyes snap open. He sits up. "A drowned body!" he hears. And his blood turns cold. Looking around he sees about twenty people running toward the docks. He stands and grabs his bags, then races after the gawkers. He runs, stops to catch his breath, runs again, stops again, his lungs exploding from the exertion of carrying his heavy load. The scene of the drowning is much further away than he had imagined.

At last he jogs around a small bend on the shore and finds a cluster of hushed people knotted together on a small patch of sand. They are looking at something—the body, presumably. Jonathon comes up behind the group but cannot push his way through. A rocky ledge blocks his way to the right, and the Jersey River laps at the shore to his left. He takes off his shoes, rolls up his pants legs and wades into the river, flanking the crowd.

Finally he can see the object of all this commotion. The blackened, swollen body of a woman lies in a heap on the sand. The river's erosion and facial bruises on the woman's face make her impossible to identify at a glance. A man kneels at her side. He is holding her arm, inspecting her tattered dress. Jonathon knows this man.

"Arthur?" Jonathon says.

Arthur Crommelin looks up and sees Jonathon standing in the water. "Jonathon," he says, "it's Mary."

Jonathon wades back to his bags and rudely begins to push his way through the crowd. "*New York Herald*!" he shouts. "Let me through… *New York Herald*!" He hates himself for this, but it's his job. Documenting. Recording the events of life and death. Breathlessly he begins the well-practiced process of setting up the tripod and the camera, preparing the plate for exposure. He knows that if he stops to think about the victim as Mary Rogers, he will break down in front of the entire crowd. He must keep it impersonal.

As Jonathon prepares to make a daguerreotype, Crommelin chants a litany of disjointed facts. "Had to come here," he says. "I knew she would have come here." Jonathon only partly listens. *Do your job!* "Called for the coroner..." *The camera should be higher.* "So glad I was here when they found her..." *Where's the damn plateholder?* "They saw her floating in the water... between two tides... hired a boat and brought her to shore." *Move them all back—their shadows are on her!* "I'm so sorry Mary."

Jonathon makes four pictures; he had brought only four plates with him. When his work ritual is done, he packs up his paraphernalia and faces the horror of telling Ollie and Phebe that Mary has been found. He also begins to wonder why Arthur Crommelin was here. *Looking for Mary, like me,* he supposes. Something drew Arthur to the Elysian Fields—*perhaps the same thing that drew me here*, he thinks. But if that were true, then Arthur would also know about—

More voices now. A handful of policemen, two jurors and the Hoboken coroner, Dr. Richard Cook, whom Jonathon knows.

"Fury!" Cook shouts. The paunchy coroner has a red face, pork chop sideburns and a fringe of grey hair surrounding a sunburned head. "What're you doing here? This is a drowning, not a hanging." Cook smokes a thick cigar. The pungent smoke masks the stench of the corpses he is called on to inspect.

"The victim's a friend of mine."

The coroner looks at the bags of daguerreotype equipment next to Jonathon. "It's a gruesome job you have there, son."

"You should talk," Jonathon replies.

"Business must be bad. Makin' money off your dyin' friends now, huh? When I die, I don't want you anywhere near my body." Cook looks down at the corpse. "Holy Mother!" he says. "She's quite a mess, ain't she? This ain't all river damage."

The uniformed police push back the crowd. Crommelin protests and Jonathon explains that the man is a close friend of the deceased.

"She certainly had a lot of friends present when she popped up here," Cook says. "Peculiar, wouldn't you say? Who is she?"

"Mary Rogers—New York City."

"Name sounds familiar."

"The cigar girl at Anderson's…"

"No kiddin'? Met her a few times at the shop. Sold me this cigar. Beautiful girl. What a shame to end up like this." Cook stoops over the body and vigorously puffs his cigar, creating a thick veil of protective smoke around his face.

Jonathon fights back his breakfast as Cook begins to inspect the corpse.

CHAPTER 18

Ollie cannot speak. Every breath is difficult. He is being choked by his heart, which seems to have expanded monstrously. His body is numb. The room in which he sits has collapsed into a dark tunnel; only the faces of Jonathon and the policeman are clear and bright. He knows that words are being spoken, but they seem scattered and disconnected, devoid of meaning. Since the words "they found Mary's body," everything has disintegrated into nothing.

Hell cannot be worse than this.

He should have been ready for this news. He should have known that New York City devours young women and spits them out into early graves. He is to blame, of course, for believing that his love would surround her with protection.

And then it hits him. Mary is gone forever.

The despair is like falling endlessly—heart in his throat, nothing to touch—into a dark and bottomless well. He gasps at the weightlessness. Utterly disoriented, Ollie tries to stand and leave the room but falls backward onto the divan.

He needs to hate someone for this. Hatred is a ledge to hang onto. And *anger*—anger is the lifeline to pull him up from this pit.

Revenge! He needs to feel its healing touch.

But he is dead. Numb. Without the intense pain of Mary's death he can't arouse the passion he needs to save himself.

"It can't be Mary—can't be her." The words are a woman's. Phebe's. She is crying. "Who did this terrible thing?"

Ollie will not cry. He will get even.

"We don't know much right now," the policeman says. "The coroner is still performing his inquest. But he sent these articles with us."

The policeman and Jonathon spread out the remnants of Mary Rogers on a table. First, a section of dress, then flowers from Mary's hat, a garter, the bottom of Mary's pantalette, and a shoe.

Phebe sighs and puts her face in her hands. "Mary's things. It's true then, there's no mistake." She begins to sob.

"One last thing," Jonathon says, holding out a curl of Mary's hair snipped off by the coroner.

Phebe looks at the lock but refuses to take it. "No, no—not my baby's hair," she says.

Ollie silently reaches out for the lock and Jonathon hands it to him. As Ollie touches the river-coarsened strands, searing pain breaks through the terrible numbness, shocking him to life. My God, *the pain feels good!* It scorches his heart and lungs, strikes like hot lightning in his gut, stabs at his head. Tears try to burst out but he fights them back into a crampy balloon of grief that is swelling in his throat.

And then he finds himself in bed. The rest of the evening has evaporated. He is alone with his thoughts and the relentless torment of guilt. If he must hate someone for this tragedy, why not hate himself? Had he not damned Mary with his selfish act of physical intimacy? Had he not set in motion God's punishment for both of them the minute Ollie corrupted Mary's purity? What greater punishment is there than to lose someone you so deeply love?

So much for the mercy of God!

The words of St. James, which had been so indelibly inscribed in his consciousness, now ring hollow in his ear: *But the wisdom that is from above is first pure, then peaceable, gentle, and easy to be entreated, full of mercy and good fruits, without partiality, and without hypocrisy.*

What kind of mercy is this, that God imposes the harshest sentence for an act of tenderness? Is it not the greatest hypocrisy to propagate a message of love and then rebuke its expression? Ollie can see that the angry, vengeful God of the Old Testament has not been transformed into a God of Love as St. John had written, but had remained a spiteful, merciless persecutor of humanity.

Ollie shivers as he recognizes the blasphemy of his thoughts. What possesses him? To blame God for Mary's death is a fool's conceit. In the cold grip of loneliness he wrestles with his conscience until sleep overtakes him. And in this world of sleep, Ollie and another boy, each twelve, lay on a blanket of warm Bushruyíh sand, heads nearly touching, eyes fixed on the clouds. Ali Qasím squints as the sun emerges from behind a luminous mountain of nervous vapor, then his eyes widen.

"Do you see it? Right there!" Ali points toward a small pinched cloud near the peak of the white mountain. His friend Jalal, his only true friend, raises his head and tries to follow the aim of that rigid finger.

"It's Mary Rogers, in the clouds," Ali exclaims.

But by the time Jalal finds the cloud that is Mary, it is no longer her, but someone else.

"No," Jalal says, "it's not Mary. It's your mother. She's come to look after you."

CHAPTER 19

She is past the quarter-century mark and unmarried. Not that she wouldn't make any man a fine wife—sturdily built she is, and hard-working, with a god-fearing soul—but she has lacked the opportunity to meet a suitable mate. So busy! Always preparing for the next tent meeting. Praying for the souls of the nation. Studying the scriptures with her father. Helping him with his sermons. And now delivering them as well.

Alice Crenshaw senses the purring of hormones and the ticking of the clock. Until now she has held captive the hormones, wild demons caged by her iron will, though they speak seductively to her, mostly at night, and excite her with outrageous ideas and wicked deceits. There is a heaven, they tell her, right here on earth. A heaven of such exquisite pleasure that one can be plunged into a world of bliss and ecstasy. And there is a natural duty for her to fulfill, too, they say—a responsibility to bring new life into the world. These are the things she dreams of when her conscious mind is numb with sleep and unable to provide reliable discipline.

The ticking of the clock, though, is what panics her whenever she hears its maddening cadence, which is more frequent these days. One clock is exasperating, but now there are two, and the incessant drumbeats overlap and haunt her with their opposing messages. The first one, the clock that has measured most of her years, tells her that she is running out of time to marry and have children. With her strict moral code these events must occur in exactly that order. She is now past her prime—most brides are much younger. Her best child-bearing years are behind her.

She should not even be thinking such wicked things! She is a Bride of Christ. She has dedicated her life and soul to His cause. Why, then, does she long for the touch of a mere mortal? *It must be the demons whispering in her ear.*

The second clock ticks even louder. Each tick brings her and the world of humanity nearer to Christ's Return. In two years or less He will come again. *She will be united with Him. Nothing else matters.*

Will she never, then, experience the rapture of physical intimacy or the joy of motherhood? *Of course not!* Her rapture will be into the arms of Jesus, rescued from physical torments and taken into his enveloping protection.

Because of her calling, Alice's intimacy with men is limited to the spiritual plane. She sees men kneeling in the sawdust, weeping for their sins, begging for salvation, holding her hand in desperation as she dispenses God's mercy the way a farmer's wife dishes out breakfast. She is surrounded by men who are broken, despairing, hungry for forgiveness. And in her they do not see a woman but a saint, an angel, untouchable and somehow sacred. The blessing of her calling is the curse of her physical existence.

It is early morning and as Alice walks down a wooded trail, relishing the pleasure of solitude and self-pity, she feels the heat of the sun on her back like the warm hand of God pushing her along. Even Christ was tempted, she tells herself. Even Jesus had doubts: *"Why hast Thou forsaken me?"* Surely a feeble, sinful creature such as Alice is allowed a moment or two of uncertainty.

She is tired. And so glad there is no sermon to give this evening. Instead, she will be attending a meeting at which her old friend William Miller, the man who deciphered God's calendar, will be speaking.

Miller's revelation has spawned scores of evangelists, and they have swarmed like locusts across New York State. Added to an existing army of revivalists of other persuasions, Miller's followers have found themselves plowing well-tilled soil. The residents of New York have been scorched by the fires of hell and saved by God's mercy so many times that the upstate region is now comically referred to as the "Burnt-Over District" by the city papers.

Alice has heard the disparaging comments, but to her way of thinking fresh new growth regenerates and purifies every burnt-over field, so let them laugh. Let them mock her work and Miller's. They won't be laughing when Christ returns in the clouds to call His faithful to Him.

She lies down in a meadow and looks up at the sky.

In the clouds.

He will come in the clouds.

And then she sees it. The big cloud just now passing in front of the sun. *It is Jesus, in the clouds.* His perfect image, standing with arms held out, inviting her to him.

No, it is not time for Him to come. Not time for her to leave. Not until 1843—God's timetable.

She stares at this Jesus in the clouds and begins to understand. As the cloud reshapes itself in the wind, Jesus takes on the shape of a face. A man's face. It's a sign! Jesus is sending her a man to be with her in the end days.

Oh God, oh merciful God! Could it be true?

She stares at the cloud, the kind face, the man. The cloud passes and the heat of the revealed sun now embraces her.

She closes her eyes and imagines the man from the cloud cradling her with his warm body.

Thank you Jesus!

Opening her eyes, she searches the sky for the man's face, but the cloud has transformed itself again. The man is gone.

But she can remember his smile.

CHAPTER 20

By the early weeks of August 1841, Mary Rogers is the talk of New York. In a city overridden by vice and murder, it is a wonder that the specter of Mary has so captivated the public, but no accident. The darling of the newspaper district has been resurrected in print by the scores of journalists who smoked her segars at Anderson's and dreamed of secret trysts in the back room.

All scraps of information, every shred of evidence, each sniff of a new suspect is digested and regurgitated in cold type. Coroner's reports and foggy eyewitness accounts become first-page news. The *Herald* and the *Evening Post*, having worn out the threadbare facts, freely invent new ones to stir the story and prick the prurience of their readers. The reformist *Tribune*, in the "cause of pursuing justice," screams a battle cry over Mary's desecration. The raucous penny press recasts Mary as the temptress in a sordid tale of sex and violence. In the pages of the *Enquirer* she has devolved into a sexual and seductive harlot with "unnatural vivacity."

Theory is transfigured into reality, fiction transforms into hard news, and journalism—hauled about by the scruff of the neck by James Gordon Bennett—completes its metamorphosis into public entertainment. The urban mystery tale of Mary Rogers has been serialized in the best tradition of Charles Dickens, and the public, panting for more, hangs on for each new installment.

Ollie can no longer read these accounts. The *Sun* has decided that a gang of dark-skinned fiends kidnapped and molested the Beautiful Cigar Girl, performing "countless vile acts" on her body. The *Enquirer* has assured the public that Mary was the victim of the dangers of sexual freedom, her life and death a cautionary morality tale played out on the promiscuous streets. As if Mary were a side of beef on the butcher's hook, the newsmen probe her most private parts with their imaginations and report on her likely (or unlikely) sexual experience. They publicly violate Mary's corpse over and over with fabricated descriptions and fictional events.

Ollie has become obsessed with finding Mary's killer. He has pored over the police reports—not the embroidered versions in the public prints, but the official ones—and pestered the investigators with pointed questions and imaginative speculations. He has woven together his own theory of the crime, and it points inerrantly to William Kiekuk.

How could the police not have seen it?

So obsessed is Ollie with justice—no, *revenge*—that for a week he has followed Kiekuk on the man's spiflicated rounds, searched the sailor's seedy room a mile from the boardinghouse, and interrogated the rejected lover's boozed-up buddies. If Kiekuk is guilty—and Ollie is quite sure he is—the fellow at least exhibits the virtue of remorse. The poor drunkard often breaks into sobbing fits at his watering holes, shamelessly confesses his love for Mary Rogers to anyone with an open ear, and on occasion has threatened to throw himself off the nearest bridge, so extreme is his anguish.

Who but a guilty man would consider suicide?

The police, of course, have investigated everyone who knew Mary, especially the boardinghouse clan of Arthur Crommelin, Daniel Payne and William Kiekuk, but found no one to charge. The unsolved mystery continues to captivate the public, and now there are those who believe that the bloated body found in the harbor was not Mary Rogers at all, but someone else. *The segar girl must have planned to disappear. She was deep in debt, or guilty of some heinous crime, or maybe she had stolen a king's ransom and needed to vanish fast. Perhaps she murdered the anonymous look-alike victim to throw the authorities off her trail!*

By late August Ollie is choked with righteous indignation. Kiekuk remains a free man, uncharged in any crime and preparing now to ship out for parts unknown. The police have arrested a dozen suspects—gang members, Africans, an Irishman, several smalltime hoodlums, a couple of Asians, a Czech. All were released without a charge. *Of course they were! Kiekuk's the guilty one.*

On this particular sultry evening Ollie is more fixated than ever on the despicable William Kiekuk. He follows him from his boardinghouse to a sailor's dive, the *Open Bow*, just off the harbor, where Kiekuk meets up with a couple of swarthy, sweating compatriots seated with soggy elbows on a beer-sticky table. Ollie enters the tavern and finds a shadowed bench in the corner of the stinking hall. With the sour, putrid breath of a buzzard, the tavern enshrouds him. *Hard to breathe!* Rancid tobacco, the sharp stench of unwashed bodies, the musty smell of cheap perfume dabbed onto the sagging necks of sickly whores—it all mingles into a reeking, nauseating assault on his senses. He almost pukes. *How can these people be laughing so uproariously in this foul atmosphere, and dancing so closely?*

So intently does Ollie watch Kiekuk's self-embalmment that he does not notice that he himself has been followed. Another man at the far end of the splintered-wood bar has slipped into the tavern unseen and now watches Ollie's every move.

Kiekuk chugs a whiskey, chases it down with a warm beer. Then does it again. His broken-toothed friends copy him, laughing.

Ollie does the same, not to be outdone by the evil Kiekuk. Besides, there is courage in the bottle, and he will need it tonight.

At the other end of the bar another man slowly sips a mug of ale, eyes glued to the Englishman.

The evening deteriorates rapidly. Fists fly at the fireplace end of the cavernous room, and bottles break, but Kiekuk and his party scarcely notice. The glassy-eyed sailor seems now to be swimming in self-pity. Draped by a filthy, ragged sleeve, a fat arm fatherly pats him on the shoulder, an awkward gesture of tenderness from a red-eyed companion. Ollie cannot hear their words over the din, but it appears that William Kiekuk is once again coughing up the phlegm of his misery at the death of Mary Rogers. One of his punishments, it seems—the endless regurgitation of remorse—has been self-imposed.

What more could a vengeful Ollie do to this wretched creature?

Remorse is not nearly enough. Ollie needs blood. An eye for an eye.

With whiskey-fueled courage, Ollie lifts his body from the hard bench and strides purposefully toward Kiekuk and his friends. He lurches once to the left, than again to the right—too much booze, perhaps—but he manages to tack into the harbor of his vile target, stumbling into Kiekuk's chair.

The sailor turns to see Ollie standing beside him. It takes a moment for him to recognize this man, but when he does the flats of his palms angrily drive into the wobbling table, pushing him from his chair into a bent-over standing position. His quavering body forms a speechless question mark that Ollie answers with a confidential whisper.

The man at the end of the bar decides to make his move. Is he too late? He pushes aside a drunken man and woman, dodges a barmaid, and approaches Kiekuk's table. With a firm hand he grabs Ollie's lapel and pulls him away from the sailor.

Ollie turns to the man with a stupid grin. "Jonathon Fury! Can I buy you a drink, mate?"

Jonathon turns to Kiekuk, who is falling into his chair with an ashen face. It is too late.

Jonathon plucks his drunken employer from the smoky tavern and into the street. "What did you say to him?" he demands.

"What do you say to a murderer?" Ollie responds.

"Kiekuk did not kill Mary. The police have absolutely cleared him."

"What do they know?" Ollie says, inadvertently leaning again Jonathon. "They're idiots. All of 'em, idiots."

"Ollie, what did you do? Tell me. What did you say to Kiekuk in there?"

Ollie pulls away from Jonathon Fury, straightens his tie—as if this will make him less inebriated—and smugly says, "Frankly, it's none of your business."

Jonathon stares at him hotly. Ollie cannot bear the heat of his gaze.

"All right, all right," Ollie says. "I told him the one thing William Kiekuk could not bear to hear."

"And what is that?"

"Ahhh—if you understood the man's passion, you would not have to ask. Could you call a carriage?"

And that is all Jonathon would ever learn.

The next morning, William Kiekuk is found dead on the shore of the Elysian Fields. Clearly a suicide. In his pocket is a smudged note with the words: "To the World—Here I am on the spot where Mary was found. God forgive me for my misfortune and my misspent time."

By afternoon Jonathon has another picture.

Dead people make the best subjects.

When he hears the news, Ollie smiles and immediately thinks of Reginald Pennick. And Mum.

He learned so much from Mum.

CHAPTER 21

Months of harsh elements and nonstop walking have eroded Jalal's body but not his spirit. The sinewy muscles of his thighs and calves are as hard as leather straps, the blisters on his feet have calloused into a scaly coat of armor, and his face and neck have been toasted by the sun and roughened by the gritty wind. He has already journeyed a thousand miles over rough roads and difficult mountains, passing through many hamlets and cities before finally approaching his first destination, Isfahan.

He knows that he may be killed in this ancient city. His message is not a popular one here, and the mujtahid that he must confront is powerful. Many infidels have been put to death in this place.

No matter. He has one purpose and nothing will deter him.

Isfahan stands on the north bank of the Zayandeh River. The road from the south is paved with stones and lined with animated vendors. As Jalal passes, he is accosted by sellers of fruit, bread, maust, and cooked lamb. His stomach aches with hunger, but he has not pushed himself to his physical limit for months only to delay the fulfillment of his mission with a meal. A *kalyan-furúsh*, or purveyor of smoke, rushes out from his makeshift stall to offer any of a dozen bubbling water pipes to the tattered man in white— "Refresh yourself, what's so important that you can't enjoy a moment with the kalyan?"

Jalal ignores him.

The banks of the Zayandeh River bloom with webs of chintz and colorful cottons being washed and bleached or left to vibrate in the drying breeze. The *Siose Pol*, or Bridge of 33 Arches, crosses the river and links the upper and lower halves of Chahar Bagh, the main road. Beggars chase Jalal as he crosses the long bridge, but he ignores them and they finally turn back, looking for more attentive prey.

Jalal passes through a guarded gate at the north end of the bridge and enters a beautiful terraced avenue lined by enormous *chahar* or palm trees, for which the road is named. He would love to escape the high sun and sit in the cool shade of these palms, even for a moment, but he presses on.

The avenue is long, and on both sides are four immense gardens each containing the ruins of an ancient palace. The *Eight Paradises*, Isfahanís call these gardens. Each one is entered from the avenue through a handsome gate that is located directly across the road from its counterpart, giving the avenue a pleasing symmetry. The eight gates are elegantly constructed, with galleries and chambers above the doorways and large arches decorated with lacquered tilework and enameling.

But everything is crumbling.

Jalal recalls the old proverb, *Isfahan nesfeh jahan*, which means "Isfahan is half the world." If so, Jalal wonders if the *other* half has been better maintained.

He continues to walk, finally passing through the Gate of Ali Kapi, a colossal archway with rooms on both ends and an enormous veranda, supported by twelve wooden columns, that runs the length of it. The imposing gateway opens up onto the Meidan-i-Shah, or Royal Square. Jalal scans the horizon of this immense space.

His eyes land on the most conspicuous landmark, undoubtedly the object of his quest. The blue-tiled dome and quartet of stately minarets pronounces itself the seat of spiritual authority in Isfahan, obliterating the claims of other mosques. This is the Royal Mosque, the province of the mujtahid.

Beneath the dome he seeks out an old mulla who is muttering to himself. Jalal says, "I am looking for the mujtahid. Can you tell me where to find him?"

The old man looks at the disheveled and tarnished person in front of him, grunts and turns to walk away.

"Please!" Jalal says.

The old man turns back to stare at the dusty traveler. "The mujtahid is a very great and wise man," he says dismissively, "a divine with enormous prestige, not to mention wealth, which I believe is a sign that spiritual vivacity is sometimes rewarded by material bliss. At least I hope that is true. He gives audience only to those who truly deserve his attention. So what, may I ask, is your business with the mujtahid?"

"I came to enlighten him about an important subject."

This, of course, stuns the old man, who tries to restrain a chuckle but snorts loudly instead. "I see," he says. "Well, then again, Siyyid Muhammad-Baqir has not appointed me to scrutinize or approve those soliciting his counsel—or wishing to counsel him." The old man continues to stare at the traveler, impressed by the young man's confidence and demeanor. "You will find him with his students in the inner courtyard. Follow this corridor." The man gestures to a tiled hallway.

Jalal nods appreciatively. "Thank you," he says. "May God grant you special favors for your assistance in His work." And then he leaves.

The old man watches Jalal disappear down the corridor. Curiosity gets the better of him, though, and he decides to follow the strange young man to see what might happen.

Jalal finds the mujtahid seated crisply in front of his clean and well-groomed students. The untidy traveler, looking like a beggar compared to the others in their rich apparel, walks to the edge of the group.

The old man stands in the shadow of a column, watching.

Siyyid Muhammad-Baqir immediately sees the intruder standing before him. This young man appears so unkempt. So insignificant. So unimportant, in fact, that the mujtahid dismisses the intruder from his mind and continues imparting wisdom to his disciples. But then, during a pause in which he attempts to draw a breath of air, the mujtahid is interrupted.

"Listen carefully to my message," Jalal says. "Your response can ensure the safety of the Faith of the Prophet of God… and refusal to consider it will cause the Faith grievous injury."

A collective gasp rises from the students. *Who would dare speak such words to the great mujtahid?*

The old man in the shadows smiles in astonishment. This bold traveler may not live to see sunset, but his courage is refreshing.

Everyone expects the mujtahid to rebuke the intruder, but an even more extraordinary event transpires. The mujtahid merely stares at the young man in the dirty white robe for a good long time, and then, unruffled, speaks calmly.

"I cannot consider your message unless you state it. What message do you bring that is so urgent that you must interrupt my class to deliver it?"

"I have been sent here by Siyyid Kazim," Jalal says. "I have been asked to learn why in the beginning you showed such consideration and affection for the late Shaykh Ahmad, and have now detached yourself from the body of his chosen disciples. Why is it that you have abandoned us to the mercy of our opponents?"

The mujtahid stares at Jalal for a moment. On the deeply creased parchment of his face, arched eyebrows form hasty diacritical marks over his eyes. After an uncomfortable pause he says, "So you are a Shaykhi. I should have guessed it. And you believe that I have altered my previous allegiance to the teachings of Shaykh Ahmad and his disciple, Kazim. I suppose I have, but for good reason. In these later years we have noticed so many conflicting statements and obscure, mysterious allusions in their writings that we felt it advisable to keep silent for a time. We chose to refrain from either censure or applause."

The mujtahid has put Jalal on the defense. *Is it not reasonable to choose neutrality when questions exist?* The traveler knows that the mujtahid's explanation could easily end the discussion—except for one thing.

Jalal takes several steps toward the mujtahid—not a threatening move, but a display of intellectual engagement. "I can appreciate your difficulty, Jalal replies. "Perhaps I can help remove your confusion. If you will set forth specifically such passages in their writings that seem to appear mysterious or inconsistent with the precepts of the Faith, I will—with the aid of God—undertake to explain their true meaning."

This gentle thrust leaves the mujtahid tantalized by the prospect of quizzing this young man. "You make a reasonable suggestion," he says. "But since you've just completed such a long journey, I'm sure you need some rest. We can leave this matter for another day. Let us show you our hospitality."

"I appreciate your offer, but I won't be able to rest until I've my mission."

The mujtahid is moved by the traveler's sincerity and perseverance. *If only there were a chance that one of his students might mature into such a model of devotion.* He can think of no candidate in this current crop of acolytes.

The learned doctor sits and turns to the beak-nosed student in the front of the group. He orders this boy to gather up some books of Shaykh Ahmad and Siyyid Kazim.

The old man in the shadows marvels at this turn of events. He steps into the sunlight. The mujtahid notices and waves for the old man to join the group. "This is my father, Mulla Muqaddas," he explains.

"We have met," Jalal replies. Turning to the old man, he says, "My name is Jalal from Bushruyíh."

Muqaddas smiles at Jalal and says, "I wondered if it might be you. I've heard you are one of the brightest lights in the Shaykhi school."

Jalal is startled that someone in such a distant city—particularly the father of the great Siyyid Muhammad-Baqir—has heard of him.

Just then the boy returns with an armload of books and the debate begins. The mujtahid plucks out of the manuscripts the most esoteric and intricate ideas of the Shaykhi leaders and artfully stages questions about matters that had deeply perplexed many of the most learned men in Persia. He craftily advances complex rebuttals and probes mercilessly for the slightest error or inconsistency in the logic of the young traveler's exposition. For hours they debate the Shaykhi view on the eternal presence and vigilance of the holy Imam, the resurrection of the body, the *Fourth Support* of Islam. Time and again the great doctor loses in argument to the young messenger from Karbala, but always with a look of astonishment and enlightenment, not anger or frustration.

When at last the call to evening prayer interrupts this marathon conversation, both debaters look up to see that the group of students has quadrupled in size. Instead of exhaustion, the mujtahid appears exhilarated as he stands up, knees creaking painfully, and addresses the assemblage.

"I will soon issue a written declaration testifying to the high station of the two great teachers that Jalal has traveled so far to defend."

CHAPTER 22

It has been three weeks since Ollie received the letter of resignation from Jonathon Fury. The simple note, written in Jonathon's fluid hand, had been short and pointed: "I regret that I can no longer remain in your employ for reasons best left unstated. Jonathon." The reasons may have been unspecified, but Ollie knows that Jonathon holds him responsible for William Kiekuk's suicide.

Ollie understands the accusation but feels no remorse. If he had held a magnifying glass to the guilt and pain of that wretched sailor, and provoked a coward's exit from this life, so be it. Had Ollie not served the cause of justice? Was not the note found in Kiekuk's damp pocket an implicit confession? That smug, self-righteous Fury has no right to judge.

Still, Ollie misses the fiery-haired companion. He feels particularly alone in this scum-pond called New York City. Though abrasive and argumentative, Jonathon always brought a practical outlook to every confrontation.

Ollie had tried for a week to locate Jonathon without success. He had sent a note to Jonathon's apartment but it was returned. He had contacted the *Herald* and newspapermen from other papers, but no one had seen the man in the past couple of weeks.

On this particular Tuesday morning, Ollie wakes and remembers that he has not collected his mail since Mary had disappeared. The *London Times* had arranged for his personal mail to be sent to the offices of the *New York Times* for safekeeping, since Ollie had no known American address at the time of his departure from home.

After breakfast Ollie walks to the offices of the *Times*, a journey he has made a number of times in the past, hoping that there will be a letter from Herbert Eaton with news of home. It has been a long time since he has heard from his mentor. He braces himself for disappointment—on all but two occasions there has been no mail at all, and on those two the correspondence amounted to nothing more than reports from his solicitors in London concerning various mundane matters of land ownership and the state of other family assets. None of his letters to Herbert have been answered.

It is shocking, then, that his timid request for mail is greeted with a cheerful, "Why yes, Mr. Chadwick, we do have something for you." But the letter placed into his eager hands does not bear the distinctively bold handwriting of Herbert Eaton, nor the officious printing of the legal aid in the solicitor's office. The carefully written address, in purple ink, has clearly been applied to paper by the hand of a woman. On the back is the seal of Anne Chadwick.

Ollie seizes the letter and leaves the office building at once. His heart is pounding and his imagination swirls, but he cannot read this letter in public.

He catches the eye of a carriage driver and climbs aboard, instructing the man to simply drive—anywhere at all. Just keep moving. In the comparative privacy of the carriage, Ollie fumbles with the envelope, hoping to open it without damage, as if it were some kind of holy object. At last he is able to unseal the flap and remove the two pages of contents, astounded by the artful calligraphy of his mother's script. She has written this letter slowly, carefully, as if believing that she must seduce her son into reading its message by caressing each word with the elegant strokes of her quill.

The first words make him weep—"Ollie, my Son..." Yes, he was right in seeking out a private reading place. The moisture in his eyes clouds his vision. He cannot read more until he wipes away the tears. And then his mother's message becomes clear.

> I pray to God that this letter will find you, and find you well. Herbert, with whom I have recently become reacquainted, was good enough to give me your address in America. What can I say, my son, but that the years have delivered unto me an awareness of my own past follies, and that this enlightenment has come with a heavy price. My remorse is overpowering and my sense of guilt so total that last week, upon the return of Herbert from a long trip abroad, I sought him out and begged for his forgiveness. The fact that he forgave me without pause demonstrates how foolish my past actions were. How different might our lives have been if your father had not exposed my dreadful secret, and that I was still married no matter how unjust that union might have been.

And yet, if I had lived in a sinful relationship with Herbert, surely I would have been justly punished in some other way.

I have earned for myself some fame as an actress, and no small amount of material comfort, but none of this compensates for the terrible loss I feel as a mother. I believe that my sincerity in asking for Herbert's forgiveness and understanding was rewarded by the news he brought back with him from abroad. He has learned that your father has died, no doubt at the hands of some party he had wronged. While I do not celebrate the death of any of God's creation, I think that your father certainly brought about his own destruction, and his death has opened up new possibilities for me just as his life had closed them off.

I so hope that you will be pleased with the news that Herbert and I are going to be married—I almost said, "at last." I have never stopped loving him, just as I have never stopped loving you, my son. My deepest desire is that the three of us can some day soon be a family.

I know that all this is being heaped upon you suddenly, so forgive me if I relate one other piece of news, something which I hope you will greet with the same kind of happiness I have in writing it. I will be sailing to New York City in October, arriving on the 18th, God willing, to perform a wonderful British play there. Herbert will join me in early November.

I cannot know how you will respond to this news, and I make no assumptions about your desire to see your mother again. And so, if you choose not to greet me at the harbor, I will understand, though I pray that I will see you standing there as I disembark in that exciting new land. This is a dream that will sustain me until I arrive.

Enough for now, my son, my only son. I pray that we will be together soon.

With my deepest love,
Your mother, Anisa

Ollie has been filled with hate for so long that forgiveness erupts like a fountain. Of course he will meet his mother at the harbor. Of course he is delighted that Herbert, his closest friend and mentor, will become his step-father. After so much tragedy, this letter brings him great joy. The news of his father's death does not sadden him or please him. It's as if the man had evaporated from Ollie's life after the nightmarish scene at Almack's.

That evening he dreams of curling up in his mother's lap and listening to her velvety voice as she recites the story of the *Enchanted Horse* and its magical flight home.

CHAPTER 23

It has been gnawing on him, this fierce beast of guilt. Jonathon would love to continue his self-righteous conceit—that Oliver is wholly to blame for William Kiekuk's suicide—but he knows better. He knows that he is equally to blame for this tragedy, for there is no difference between the sins of commission and the iniquities of omission when both lead to terrible pain and catastrophe.

In the dim gaslight of the darkroom, as Jonathon removes a plate from the fuming box, he is filled with regret. He alone, perhaps, holds the secret that could have prevented Ollie's misguided behavior. It's time to correct his omission, no matter what the consequences. Slipping on his rumpled jacket and buttoning it on the run, he catches a carriage and gives the driver the address of the boardinghouse.

He can feel the daguerreotype in his breast pocket. He has carried it there for weeks, always intending to find the right time to reveal it.

This may not be the best time, but it is a better time than later.

Phebe is mourning with relatives in Connecticut. The boarding house has been left in the maladroit hands of Beatrice, the servant girl, who is growing more distraught by the minute as unfulfilled responsibilities cascade into calamity, or so she believes.

Following breakfast, Ollie steps outside for a walk just as Jonathon Fury is racing across the street towards the house. Both men hesitate for a moment—*how will the other one react to this sudden reunion?*—but then both wave acknowledgement.

"I've been looking for you," Ollie says matter-of-factly, trying not to show his great pleasure at seeing Jonathon again.

"Our last time together was not a pleasant one," Jonathon replies.

"Yes, I know. But surely you can't hold a grudge against me for confronting Mary's killer. Certainly she deserved some kind of justice, a concept that seems entirely foreign to the police."

"I can't argue against justice," Jonathon says quietly. "But the matter of whether justice was served is what I came to see you about."

Ollie won't be drawn into a philosophical argument. "It's a tired old topic, my friend," Ollie says. "Anyway, I have some very good news to share with you. My mother's coming to New York."

"I thought you were estranged?"

"No longer. She wrote to me and apologized. Wants to see me. Ohh—and she's getting married to Herbert, my mentor. I'm very anxious for you to meet my family."

Jonathon pauses. This conversation is not going as he had planned. He hesitates to bring up the subject of the daguerreotype's secret for fear that it will dampen Ollie's spirits.

Ollie takes Jonathon by the arm and starts to walk toward the street. "Let's walk," he says. "It's such a beautiful day."

And so they walk together for over two hours. Where before Ollie protected his history like a dam holding back a deep reservoir of personal experience, his story now streams out like a whitewater river. Astonished by the details, Jonathon scarcely speaks. He had not known that Ollie was half-Persian, that his mother was enslaved by the Turkoman, or that his father was a member of the Qajar dynasty. He learns of the harsh days at the Charterhouse, the narrow escape from the lair of Reginald Pennick, the betrayal by his own father and his mother's downward spiral from spirituality to infamy. The man who has been his employer—this brittle English journalist—becomes a human being.

The two men stop at a park and claim a wooden bench. "It occurs to me," Ollie says, "that I've monopolized the conversation. Forgive me. I don't know what came over me."

"Forgiven. But I had no idea who you were and where you came from."

"Maybe you can tell me who I am. Sometimes I don't know."

Jonathon starts to speak, but Ollie holds up a hand to stop him. "No more about me, please. But since I've shared some of my secrets with you, perhaps you'll reciprocate. I know about your orphanage experiences and how you learned the art of daguerreotype, but almost nothing more. I know the book-ends, but none of the books. Now please, tell me about your life after the orphanage."

Jonathon is not prepared to discuss his life. He never is. But he knows he cannot refuse after Ollie's candid outpouring.

"My life is no match for yours, I'm afraid. Rather dull stuff. Grew up with my step-parents, went to the seminary, and left before graduation. Trouble is I have an abundance of questions and far too little faith. My religious questions were never answered. The way I see it, though, my education opened my eyes to the real Truth, that religion is designed for small minds and deep pockets.

"I traveled around a bit and sketched many immigrants. Such wonderful faces! Inevitably my conversations with them led to that old topic of religion, for many of these people practiced faiths that I had barely heard of. I wish that I could say I found a faith to believe in, but I didn't. I found an abundance of piety and empty ritual, and more discouragingly, I became even more con-fused. So many faiths, so many practices, so many beliefs.

"I've grown weary of mystical speculation. I've come to appreciate facts. And the material world. If I worship anything, it's the superficial. The surface of things. The way that light plays on a church steeple is now a spiritual experi-ence for me. I care not at all what goes on in the sanctuary below. I see fulfill-ment in reality, and disappointment in religion. So many people are awaiting the coming of their Savior. So many are hopeful, but will be disappointed. My religion is art, and I am seldom disappointed.

It occurs to Jonathon that by releasing his own flood of self-revelation he has created the perfect opportunity to fulfill his mission of Truth. Almost as if to redeem his self-indulgence, he bends his words to suit his new purpose.

"You are a writer, Ollie," Jonathon continues, "but sometimes a picture can reveal a truth that words cannot describe—or verify. Would you like an example?"

Ollie nods his head, not sure what to expect.

Jonathon removes a daguerreotype from the breast pocket of his coat. "Here is a picture that you have never seen, yet it reveals a truth that concerns you deeply. Take a close look."

Ollie takes the metal plate and studies it carefully.

"It's Nick Moore's House," Ollie says. "The tavern at the Elysian Fields."

A bittersweet twinge. Memories of a happier time.

Jonathon looks at Ollie's moist eyes as they stare at the picture. "I took this picture the day I met you there. You were with Phebe, and a short time later Mary joined you."

"Yes… a wonderful day. Some day I'll write about it. Haven't been able to yet."

"And when you do," Jonathon says quietly, "will your words tell the truth? Will they tell the truth as well as this daguerreotype does?"

"I don't understand you. There is no one I know in this picture—not Mary or Phebe, not me. What does this picture have to do with me?"

"This little picture," Jonathon says, "reveals the truth of Mary's life—and death."

"Nonsense!" Ollie says. He doesn't like the new direction that this conversation is taking. "It has nothing to do with Mary. It's just a picture of a tavern with a bunch of stupid people standing in front of it staring at your camera."

"There's more, if you look harder," Jonathon urges.

"I think we should start back. I'm not interested in this historical record of people I don't know."

"You know one of them. At least you know who she is."

Jonathon looks at the picture again and shakes his head. "I don't know any of them," he explains.

"One of them is the person that Mary came to see that day. The reason she went to the Elysian Fields."

"She went there to relax with her mother and me."

"A secondary benefit of the excursion," Jonathon suggests. "But her main reason was to meet someone about a matter of great importance. Quite literally a matter of life and death."

"What can you possibly be talking about?" Ollie asks.

"I arrived at the Elysian Fields to take a picture of Nick Moore's House," Jonathon says. "I know the proprietor, an immigrant I befriended once. I don't mind making an extra dollar here and there—by the way, I've calculated your share. When I arrived at the tavern, I saw Mary inside. She was seated at a table across the room talking to another woman, a woman I knew from a sketch I once made. The woman's name is Madame Restell."

To Ollie, the name has a familiar ring to it. And then suddenly he recalls the sketch by Jonathon Fury in the newspaper that he came across at Mr. Bickford's reading room. The evil woman with a smirking, bat-like demon clutching a dead infant in front of her belly.

Madame Restell, the abortionist.

Ollie holds up the picture, studies the faces. Yes, there—the third face from the left—that could be Restell.

Ollie looks up at Jonathon. His face asks the question, and Jonathon replies, "I leave it to you to decide what business Mary may have had with Madame Restell, but after she left the room—I suppose to compose herself before rejoining you—I asked the other guests to join me outside for a picture. Who could refuse being the subject of a daguerreotype? This image is the result."

Ollie slumps. "Mary was pregnant?"

Jonathon looks at his friend and speaks again. "Daniel's child, I'm thinking. When we were looking for her, I returned to the Elysian Fields. I spoke with one of the guests who told me that Madame Restell and Mary were there the day that Mary disappeared. He's the old gentleman on the far right side of the picture. He's always there. But he wouldn't tell the police what he knew for fear that he'd be implicated."

Ollie looks up with sad eyes. "You think that Mary went there for an abortion the night she disappeared?"

Jonathon nods. "And it went badly. I don't think they killed her on purpose, but when she died they must have dumped her body—"

"My God!" Ollie yells. "Kiekuk."

"Nothing to do with it. Was with his friends the whole time, just as they told the police."

Suddenly Ollie stands angrily. "And you knew about this! Why didn't you tell me? Why did you wait until now?"

Now Jonathon slumps. Sighs. Looks up pleadingly. "I'm sorry," he says. "I came to apologize. I think I was afraid of hurting your feelings—about Mary being pregnant. It was wrong."

"My God," Ollie says again. "We killed him."

Hearing those words so coldly stated pierces Jonathon's heart. The two men remain speechless for a long time.

The next afternoon, Ollie and Jonathon place flowers on William Kiekuk's simple grave and Jonathon recites the Lord's Prayer for the first time in five years.

He has not forgotten a word of it.

CHAPTER 24

The pain in his chest threatens to burst into the rest of his body. Ollie knows that the pain is not physical; it is the anguish of deep sorrow and remorse, the festering of blame and unfulfilled revenge, the open wound of unanswered questions—all of this infected by the blasphemous notion that God, above all the human villainy, is the One Most Responsible for the tragedies of Mary Rogers and William Kiekuk. What a scheme He has devised! Evil reigns and unfairness prevails. *Blessed are the meek, for they shall inherit the iniquities of their parents and serve as chattel for the selfish ones who rule without the hindrance of conscience or compassion.*

Ollie holds the entire system to blame from the captains of industry in their regal castles ruling their slum-bound serfs, to the priests and bishops who just as rigorously control their minions through the never-yielding harness of sin and conveniently re-legislated laws of God. It is a system obviously condoned by God, else why would the same abuses of power continue to exist over such a vast expanse of time? *And God created the heavens and the earth, and the earth was filled with suffering for all but the most ruthless.*

How different God looks on this side of the world.

It is early Sunday morning in the dark sitting room of the Rogers boarding house. It is God's day, and Ollie wishes he did not believe in God. He would pray for the courage to be an atheist, but how can one ask for help from the very Entity one wishes did not exist?

Of course, his fevered thinking is wrong. The Truth is that there is a God, and God would not create suffering, therefore suffering must be an invention of humankind. Why God does not intervene to prevent suffering is an open question at the moment—but perhaps it is because He has not been asked, or not asked with the correct protocol.

Ollie considers his current spiritual life and finds that he has none. He has not read the Bible in months. For a year or more he has not listened to the words of God, except for Jonathon's quiet recital of the Lord's Prayer at Kiekuk's gravesite. The God-intoxicated child who longed to be a mulla has slid into a shadow-world where God is most often invoked by swearing, a habit that has replaced prayer in Ollie's life. It is so satisfying to enjoin God to condemn some foul person or hateful action to the fires of hell. As if God is there merely to serve the whims of His creation.

Discipline.

God is disciplining Ollie. This occurs to him in a blinding flash of insight. It is simple reward and punishment. So far, mostly punishment. That it is unfair for Mary and William to have been sacrificed to abet Ollie's discipline makes no sense in a material world, but who among men can judge spiritual justice? If Ollie is to experience the rewards of God's labyrinthine system, he must read the signposts and navigate a new course. Perhaps take up prayer again, or read the scriptures. Or go to church. Then maybe the pain will disappear and God's reward magically will manifest itself.

During this tortured reasoning Ollie suddenly shudders with the understanding that the fate of his mother is in his own trembling hands. Anne Chadwick, right now on a steamer from London to New York City, is a necessary player in the unfolding drama of Ollie's discipline. *Punishment:* she perishes on the journey. *Reward:* she reaches New York, reconciles with Ollie, and the two live happily ever after.

Is it this simple? And this terrible? *My God*, he thinks, quickly turning the curse into a prayer. *I am such a fool!*

It is Sunday morning, one week before his mother arrives. Is it possible to redeem his entire life in one week? Are seven days of piety sufficient to halt—or even simply ease—the inevitable punishment?

No, his thinking is too self-serving, a mockery of God's justice. He must not think of himself, only his mother. *Her protection.* Everything he does must be done for her sake, not his. There can be no reward for selfishness. Only more punishment. And yet he cannot keep his thoughts from wandering to the pain *he* will surely experience if she is taken from him again, especially after the heart-wrenching loss of Mary Rogers.

He must go to church!

Quickly he dresses, races to the street and summons a carriage. He directs the driver to Jonathon's small apartment on Ruth Street and with pounding fists on the vibrating door wakes his red-eyed companion from a sound sleep.

"What on earth—" Jonathon moans upon opening the door.

"Get dressed, man. We're going to church," Ollie explains.

"Church? Are you out of your mind?"

"It's Sunday. Now hurry up!" Ollie pushes the owly young man into his bedroom.

"Church," Jonathon mutters. "I should get extra pay for this."

"You'll get something extra, all right. In heaven. Now hurry up!"

Jonathon scrambles to find suitable clothes, begins to put on a shirt. "What church do you have in mind?" he asks.

"Thought you might have a suggestion," Ollie replies.

"You're in a hurry to go to church, but you don't know what church you're going to. Am I understanding this fully?"

"Yes, indeed you are. I'm sure you know a good church. You were a religious man in your former years as I recall."

"I know many of the churches in New York mainly because I have made pictures of their exteriors. What's your preference? Catholic or protestant? Certainly not Jewish."

"And surely not Catholic," Ollie says.

"Episcopalian, Presbyterian, Methodist, Lutheran, Baptist, Congregational, Dutch Reformed or Unitarian?"

"Rather like a menu, isn't it? From which plate did you eat?"

"Baptist."

"Then Baptist it is."

"Big or small? Plain or fancy?"

"Don't care, really. Just take me to the Baptist church that most impressed you."

"The people or the building?"

This stops Ollie. He thinks for a moment before replying, "Jonathon, take me to the damn church where you think God is most welcome."

"I no longer believe in God."

Ollie rolls his eyes, exasperated.

Jonathon pulls on his pants. Suddenly livened he says, "But if there were a God, I think he would feel most welcome where there's some vigor. I know just the church."

The carriage ride, under Jonathon's direction, takes just over an hour and transports Ollie out of the city proper. New York City is still overwhelmingly rural compared to London, pastoral as far north as Fourteenth Street and mostly swamp beyond. Grand brownstones and gray factories rise next to fields and groves, and slums fester within earshot of farmland. Lavish Victorias and sporty phaetons patrol the rutted streets alongside dilapidated hay wagons.

The carriage route takes them up Broadway, past the rebuilt Trinity Church and its majestic spire, past Astor's Opera House, Washington Hall, Gothic Hall, the New York Hospital, and under the arched stone bridge at Canal Street. Past the bridge, the graded streets degenerate for a time into uneven horse paths, but after Union Square the carriage turns up Fifth Avenue to again find pockets of New York opulence.

Within several blocks the carriage enters a swampy shantytown of muck and garbage, ragpickers and half-feral pigs. The carriage wheels slip sideways in the slime, causing the horses to lean heavily into their task of wrenching the carriage through this fetid pestilence. Then at last the slum is behind them and the road hardens. Within fifteen minutes they are all the way to 174th Street, trotting easily over the High Bridge and its huge stone arches to arrive at the other side of the East River.

Jonathon points out a plain wooden church on a hilltop above a small settlement. "The Lord is welcome here," he says, "and the Devil visits at his own peril."

The carriage pulls up outside the church, which is surrounded by farm wagons and tethered horses. Already the building is bloated with bodies— a wall of backsides block the front door, window sills serve as improvised pews—and still more people are arriving. Had not Ollie known that this was a church service, he might have guessed it a siege. Within minutes the fragile structure is completely surrounded by people—families with crying infants, tobacco-spitting grandpas, matrons with breadbasket bosoms and boxes of food. Children run and dance in the coarse grass, old men listen in vain at the windows and doors. Only muted shouts and gasps emit from the clap-board heart of this gathering humanity.

And then the building explodes, or so it seems. Red-faced people begin to stream out the doors, children leap out the windows, all of them motioning for the onlookers to join them in a march toward a meadow behind the church. The early October breezes are cool, but the churchgoers seem overheated. At last the preacher, a solemn and sallow matchstick figure, awkward-limbed and stiff-jointed, grimly steps down the three creaking stairs to the ground and slowly marches to the front of the outdoor assemblage. Jonathon and Ollie take seats in the grass among the others.

Reverend Starkweather may look like a dead man already embalmed, but his voice—oh, that resonant voice, by turns a raspy roar, a sensuous whisper, or a ghostly wail quivering with the vibration of angels—that voice instantly exerts an extraordinary influence over the crowd. It burrows into their minds, obliterating logical thought and allowing deeply buried emotions to surface. And the man's face, that cadaverous face, begins actually to shine and he takes on a most pleasing, almost handsome countenance. As he speaks, the stiffness in his limbs transforms into the supple grace of a dancer, and the October clouds above seem actually to separate and bathe the preacher and his throng in a holy light.

"Brother William Miller," the preacher is saying, "by the power of God Almighty, has unlocked the most impenetrable mystery of the universe. The time of the Second Advent of our Lord Jesus Christ. The return of our Savior. Sometime during the year 1843, Jesus Christ shall return to earth in His glory, Hallelujah!"

A chorus of shouted Hallelujahs rises to the heavens.

Ollie is stunned. He has not heard of this man named Miller, but the man's message is abundantly familiar, for 1843-44 corresponds to the Islamic year in which the Qa'im, the Promised One of Islam, is to appear. He shivers at the prospect that two Manifestations of God might appear almost simultaneously. The cherished teachings of Islam, nearly erased by his Christianity, begin to flood Ollie with tender remembrances that mingle oddly with the apocalyptic revelations of Reverend Starkweather.

"Those of us who have been converted," Starkweather is saying, "will never taste the sting of death. We will be gathered up into His loving arms—" Starkweather gracefully swoops his arms around a mass of air that becomes, for many of the wide-eyed listeners, an armful of Christians— "and spared the unspeakable horrors that are in store for those left behind. And yet, how can we know for sure that we will be among those who are taken up with Him into the clouds? My brothers and sisters, listen to me, for that auspicious hour draws nigh. True conversion must not be only of the spirit, but of the body as well."

Ollie is suddenly seized with such a sense of foreboding that he begins to tremble. He can see laid out before him his miserable life, his turning away from God, his failure to abide by God's system of justice. He can see the swollen and bloated face of Mary Rogers in the dark waters of the Hudson, and the limp corpse of William Kiekuk staring up at him with accusing eyes, and the pathetic body of Reginald Pennick dredged up from the riverbank, all of them sinners condemned not by their own sins but by Ollie's lack of discipline.

Most terrifying of all, he can see the delicate hand of his mother reaching upward from the deep abyss of the sea in one last desperate attempt to be saved… and to save him.

"My dear friends," Reverend Starkweather is saying, "your bodies must experience your redemption just as surely as your souls, for your bodies will be taken upward to the bosom of Jesus on that great resurrection day. Ask God to wash away your sins and claim your body for his higher purpose."

And then, in a grand demonstration of his command, the Reverend reaches skyward and begins to shudder, imploring God for a sign of his own redemption. His legs quake and his eyes roll back in his head. He chants an unintelligible string of syllables and tearfully falls to his knees. An elderly man near the tree-stump pulpit stands and yells "Glory!" then goes rigid and falls over stiff as a board. A few mothers begin to roll upon the ground as if writhing in pain. A frightened young girl foams at the mouth and shakes until her sharp bones nearly break through her skin. Others jump up and down hysterically with their eyes closed, babbling in some unknown tongue, or laugh giddily, or vomit into the grass, or sob heartbreakingly because the miracle of their redemption has for some reason been withheld and they fear the torment of being left behind. The cries and chants and shouts commingle and soar upward to buffet the clouds that one day will serve as Jesus' throne.

A searing pain inside Ollie's head has become unbearable. He scratches at his face and tears at his hair, trying to rip out the source of his misery. Then his entire frame begins to quake uncontrollably. His joints feel as though they will fly apart. His teeth chatter, bloodying his blasphemous tongue. He falls onto his back, gasping for air and struggling to beg God for redemption.

Terrified, Jonathon leaps onto his friend and tries to dampen the shaking with his own body, but finds himself pulsating wildly.

Between bone-jarring convulsions, strange words flow from Ollie's lips. Jonathon believes them to be hysterical gibberish, but they are not. The language is Farsi, and to a Persian the words mean, "Dear God, forgive me and protect my mother." And then Ollie passes out.

In the carriage on the way home, Jonathon is still too weak and frightened to talk about the events in the meadow. He had brought Ollie to this church half-jokingly to demonstrate the absurdity of religion, and now he feels responsible for his companion's horrifying experience.

Ollie is speechless, too, but at peace.
The pain is gone. And his mother is safe.
He is sure of that.

CHAPTER 25

If the publishing district is the city's brain, then the waterfront is clearly New York's beating heart. There is more activity here, more racket and sweat and transport of wealth than Wall Street and Broadway will see in many years. Penniless immigrants and foreign dignitaries all enter the New World through the splendid tawdriness of the city's piers.

Jonathon and Ollie walk along the waterfront, eyes searching the gray dusk that has settled over the jittery silver water. Jonathon carries a large satchel and a wooden box—his camera obscura; Ollie carries a tripod. They pick their way past a forest of barrels and crates and steamer trunks that will soon be harvested only to grow again within a few hours.

It is a loud, smelly and dangerous place. The crashing of wooden crates, the clamorous begging of gulls and the angry squawks of herons provide a raucous background chorus for the grating calls of the stevedores who spit their shrill curses in every direction like obscene versions of *Hallelujias!* and *Glories!* Scummy water slaps the shore beneath the docks with rhythmic hisses, heaving up its stinking cargo of dead fish and slimy weeds. Rowdies and thieves nervously pace the quays eyeing treasures to be looted, pockets to be picked, or purses to be snatched when fine ladies dance across the slippery boards to their carriages.

Ollie spots a young scamp on the pier, and the boy's mop of hair and cocksure posture brings back painful memories of little Tim Shaw in the dark alleys of London. The scrawny lad is slyly hawking newspapers on the pier while he surreptitiously inspects a row of trunks, mentally cataloging their probable contents and value. Suddenly the boy finds one he likes, turns coyly to a bearded man on the periphery, and nods.

Within minutes, Ollie guesses, the trunk will be gone, pilfered during some kind of stevedore distraction.

Ollie ignores the unfolding plot; it is not his battle. Instead he stops and surveys the harbor. Coming into view is a three-masted steamship, powered by wind when available and an enormous paddlewheel when the air is stagnant.

Jonathon removes a mariner's telescope from his coat pocket and focuses on the incoming ship. "It's the Surrey," he says, identifying the ship that is transporting Ollie's mother to New York. Jonathon's tone, though, is less enthusiastic than Ollie had expected.

"Belching a lot of smoke, isn't it?" Ollie asks. "Give me a look."

Jonathon hands the telescope to Ollie, who jerks it over the horizon until he finds the ship. The Surrey is in sorry shape. The front mast is broken and the sails are in tatters, hanging like rags on a clothesline. A mob is gathered on deck, frantically waving as a towering column of smoke rises behind them into the October sky. Ollie turns to Jonathon with a fearful look.

"There were powerful storms in the Atlantic this week," Jonathon says. "Heard that two fishing boats were lost in a squall. I'm glad to see the Surrey made it—have to admit I was a little concerned."

"All that smoke," Ollie says. "Where is it coming from?"

"Could be the boilers are a bit bruised up. Still, she's making it in all right, though with a limp."

Ollie puts his eye to the glass again. "They're waving their arms," he says, "Too far away to be recognizing loved ones on the shore. They look frightened, Jonathon."

"They're in the mouth of the harbor. What could happen here?"

As Ollie continues to study the excitement on the Surrey's deck, an explosion from behind startles him. He jumps, drops the telescope into the nervous water, and wheels suddenly to see a cloud of thick gray smoke rising from the dock. Stevedores are racing to the source of it.

"My God!" Ollie says to Jonathon. "I thought for a moment the ship was blowing up. Sorry about the telescope."

"Never mind. Let me set up the camera to get a shot of the Surrey as she comes in. There may be just enough light."

As Jonathon begins to assemble his apparatus, Ollie turns back to the dock and sees the boy slowly meandering through the stacks of crates.

Of course. *A diversion!*

Ollie scans the pier and finds the fancy steamer trunk that had attracted the newsboy's interest. Just then two men, hauling what looks like a large piece of carpet, race up to the trunk and groaningly lift it onto their makeshift skid. Off they go, dragging their treasure behind, the carpet and its freight sliding easily over the slick boards. Ollie smiles at the thieves' gall, thankful that his mother's trunk was not among the tantalizing selections on the quay.

As the two men reach the end of the pier and begin to pull the trunk behind a large bush, three leatherheads—waterfront police—swarm around the thieves with drawn pistols and clubs. The exhausted hooligans abandon their prize and try to run, but are easily caught and wrestled to the ground.

Ollie turns his gaze back to the urchin, who watches dispassionately for a moment, then begins to wave his papers in the air, grandly playing the part of a legitimate news hawker. Suddenly one of the leatherheads races down the wharf and with a huge hand seizes the boy's arm.

"You best come with me, lad," the leatherhead says.

On an impulse, Ollie strides over to the pair and says, "What seems to be the trouble here?"

"This boy is a known acquaintance of the two we just arrested over there," the leatherhead says, pointing to the scruffy duo now seated on the wet boards. "Lootin' the waterfront, they were. A sorry lot."

"Yes, I did see those two making off with a trunk just now. But I think you must be mistaken about the boy—I had quite a conversation with him just moments ago, and I've been watching him for some time. Can't say he's behaved in any suspicious way, certainly not as concerns the trunk in question. If he's a friend of those thieves, than it's bad luck for him, indeed, but I'm sure you won't arrest him for the mere misfortune of his acquaintances."

"You'll vouch for him, then?"

"Most certainly."

"And you are—?"

"Oliver Chadwick of the *London Times*, at your service sir. And your name, if I may ask? For my story, of course, about your diligent protection of the waterfront."

"Edward McClanahan," the leatherhead says proudly, releasing his tight grip on the boy's shoulder. The boy rubs the spot painfully. "You be watchin' yer step, lad. Keep yer nose clean if you wanna stay outta the Tombs."

The leatherhead lumbers away and the boy looks up at Ollie apprehensively. "What's the price, then?" he asks.

"The price? Oh, you mean for my act of kindness."

The boy continues to stare at him suspiciously. "No one does nothin' on the docks 'less he wants somethin' in return," the boy says.

"Ah, yes," Ollie replies with a smile. "One of your newspapers, please."

Surprised, the boy hands over one of the papers and Ollie gives him a silver dollar. The boy's eyes brighten. "Got no change," he says.

"And I need none," Ollie says. "But if I were you, I'd find another line of work. The 'Tombs' don't sound like a very nice place."

"Oh, they don't put kids like me in the Tombs. He was jus' tryin' to scare me's all. If they get their mitts on me, it's the orphanage. Been there before."

Jonathon hollers from the edge of the dock, his camera pointed at the Surrey. "I'm going to make a picture now!"

Ollie smiles benignly and looks down at the newspaper he has just purchased. It is last week's edition.

And just then a terrible blast rolls across the water. Ollie turns to see the Surrey engulfed in flames, its varnished wood feeding the fire like dry tinder. Great billows of smoke pour out from its ruptured boiler. Bits and pieces of the ship are still flying through the air. A few people leap into the cold water, which itself is ablaze with burning scraps of wood. Ollie can hear the hysterical screams of those still alive. A woman, her dress in flames, jumps overboard and bounces limply off a large floating plank.

There is another terrible blast—then still another—and many more in rapid succession, like a thousand muskets firing across the water. The ship is suddenly surrounded by a colorful halo of sparks and whistling rockets as a store of Chinese fireworks in the hold suddenly detonates. The ghastly shrieks of the dying passengers and crew are drowned out by thunderous explosions. The awful tragedy is eerily beautified by the dazzling spectacle of shooting stars, sparkling crowns of red and green, booming concussions, and delicate sprinkles of sputtering embers. The dancing lights haunt the gray water, making it appear strangely alluring.

A huge crowd has gathered on the docks—stevedores and rowdies and people who had been cheerfully awaiting the arrival of loved ones. They are strangely hushed by the almost holy splendor of the aerial display. They stand there watching, motionless, mouths agape, as if in a trance. The newsboy has dropped his papers and stares.

So awestruck is Jonathon by the thrilling exhibition that he has not yet appreciated the likely fate of Ollie's mother. Almost instinctively he replaces the dark slide into the frame holder. He has recorded the event.

Then the fireworks are gone. Smoke smears the horizon. After such a furious outburst of sound and color, the sudden silence and gloom are unbearably fearsome. Almost in unison, the crowd gasps as the full import of the catastrophe sweeps over them. Women wail and frightened children sob. Men curse and scream for God's mercy.

The Surrey tilts, its aft rising in the water until the entire ship slowly submerges head-first like a diver into a pond.

Now the tragedy strikes Ollie, too, and he begins to moan. The newsboy looks at him quizzically.

Jonathon approaches Ollie and says, "I'm sure there will be some survivors. Your mother is probably among them."

"Is it possible?" Ollie asks.

The newsboy speaks up. "I saw people jumpin' off the ship."

"Yes," Ollie says, "it's possible I suppose. If they can make it to shore."

"Come on then," the urchin shouts. "They'll wash up over here!"

Just ahead three men push a bumboat into the waves and jump in, trying to row out to assist any survivors. The wind starts to swirl and the waves now carry bits of wreckage onto the shore—boxes and broken boards, smashed crates, dresses and bed linens, burned baskets, a violin case, framed paintings, steamer trunks… and a human leg. Then more flotsam sweeps ashore, and several bodies. First a child of three in a woolen suit, shirt and tie. Then a grandmother in a flowing red dress fanned out on the rippling water like a blood stain. And following her so many others. One by one they are pushed out of the water, given back by the generous sea, but too late. Only one moves, a young man of twenty or so, and he flops like a dying fish before shuddering into stillness.

More cargo and bodies wash ashore with astonishing speed, and a teeming mob of scavengers descends upon every morsel as if it were a juicy steak, rifling through each crate, fighting over every sodden article of clothing, searching the corpses for silver and jewelry. A wretched hag strips a dead woman naked then waves the victim's undergarments overhead like a flag of victory.

Ollie and Jonathon wade through the frigid water looking for Anne Chadwick. Ollie prays for a miracle, and still expects one.

Splashing behind them is the newsboy, who catches up to Ollie and says, "How'll I know yer mother?"

"Find the most beautiful woman you've ever seen—that'll be her. And she'll be alive," Ollie says bravely. His legs are numb from the cold.

The three of them move solemnly along the shore, inspecting every female body that has washed up from the cold water. So many!

The tide is efficient.

"Over here!" the newsboy yells. "She's alive!"

Ollie and Jonathon sprint to a body the newsboy has discovered. The woman's face is covered by damp stringy hair, but the woman moves her arm and coughs. Ollie sweeps back the hair and looks hopefully at the pale face.

"Not her," he says. Then he yells, "Someone—over here! A live one!"

Two fishermen rush to the woman and begin to pull her further up on the shore.

Ollie and Jonathon continue their search. Bodies like beached whales lie everywhere. Later they will learn that over one hundred and twenty people perished in the catastrophe.

It is Jonathon who finds her. Though he has never seen Anne Chadwick's likeness, he knows it is her. She lies serenely on her back. The foaming water cradles her like fine lace. Her hair, as if slowly blowing in a desert breeze, floats gently about her exquisite face. Jonathon becomes choked with emotion. He stares at this peaceful countenance for a moment and recognizes that Ollie's mother bears a striking resemblance to another beautiful though younger woman found in the cold water only a few weeks ago—Mary Rogers.

"Ollie," Jonathon calls, but he has lost his voice and Ollie cannot hear him. He shouts this time: "Ollie, over here!"

Ollie and the newsboy turn to see Jonathon tenderly holding a woman's body in the lapping water. The incoming waves move the woman's arms, creating the illusion of life. With a burst of hope and thankfulness to God, Ollie rushes to the woman. Approaching her, his heart swells as he recognizes his mother, but as he kneels beside her in the bone-chilling water he can see tears streaming from Jonathon's eyes.

At that moment Ollie knows he has both found and lost his mother.

A dagger of pain slices through Ollie's chest and he sobs.

The newsboy kneels down beside Ollie and says, "She's so pretty. Why does God take the pretty ones and leave so many of the ugly and mean?"

Ollie realizes that he knows the answer to this question. The pain in his chest mercifully vanishes, transformed into rage by the truth of that answer. This entire charade, this travesty played out apparently for the amusement of a chimerical God, Ollie sees as an act of Divine Betrayal. Ollie had prayed for his mother's protection. He had received forgiveness and redemption. But what good is redemption if it is followed by more punishment? This ghoulish spectacle of death is God's way of dramatically thumbing His nose at Ollie.

Looking up at the smoke-filled sky, Ollie faces into the wind and shouts, "Damn you!"

CHAPTER 26

How he had lucked into such a pleasant circumstance he cannot begin to fathom, but six years of living on garbage, sharing cold and filthy quarters with ravenous rats, and suffering the abuse of "employers" such as the scumbags arrested on the pier—these life experiences have taught the newsboy not to question any good fortune. And here he is, sleeping on a plump mattress with fresh linens, embraced by the lusty fragrance of fresh-baked bread. The spectacular tragedy of the harbor, which now seems like a century ago, curiously has become his bounty, as if there has been a sudden warp in life's system of balance that allows his startling good fortune to have been paid in advance by the misfortune of others. Kind of like Jesus paying for the sins of humankind by dying on the cross.

The newsboy feels untethered from his old fate. Born again!

He remembers the Bible stories that the somber evangelicals in the Five Points Gospel Mission forced him to endure before ladling out their thin soup into chipped bowls. One of these tales, the story of God asking Abraham to sacrifice his son, had seemed silly at the time. But now the newsboy can relate to Abraham's son, Isaac, for whom he was undoubtedly named, and the tremendous relief that Abraham's son must have felt when God decided that His thirst for blood could be slaked by a slaughtered ram. Had not everything changed for Isaac in that quirky moment? Why should it not also change for Isaac the urchin?

The delicious aroma of bread pulls him from bed, urges him out of his pajamas—*imagine that, clean pajamas!*—and into a pair of fine woolen trousers, an ironed cotton shirt, and sleek leather boots. He looks down at his clothes, and as he has been every day for the past two weeks, he is still astonished to find no patches and stains, no gaping holes, not a single missing button. He runs a boar's bristle brush through his black locks—once a snarled nest of matted hair, straw and vermin—and finds them beautifully shorn to a fashionable length and style.

The bread beckons, and Isaac gallops down the creaking staircase to the kitchen where he finds Mrs. Rogers at work on a breakfast of tea, sausages and potatoes.

Ollie looks up with a gleaming eye and sees the boy in the doorway. Good morning to you son, he says, and then he is back to his craft of finely rasping a pair of rolls to a perfect smoothness. Just like when I was in school, he adds, I was the supreme toaster, no one finer in all of London. And then he smears the rolls with a glaze of butter, and over the coals of the pot-bellied stove toasts the rolls to a uniform golden-brown hue. Food for the gods, he says.

Isaac finds himself swathed in the warmth of the kitchen and stuffing himself on a home-made breakfast that is even better than yesterday's. He imagines that Mrs. Rogers is his grandmother, or a saint, or possibly both, and she feeds his fantasy with fried potatoes and hugs. He knows about the old woman's loss, and knows that once again he is the beneficiary of someone else's misery with a heavy price paid in advance. He hopes that his presence helps fill her void as well.

We must get the boy into a good school, Ollie is saying to Mrs. Rogers, no matter what the cost. I agree, the old woman replies, the lad is bright. Yes he is. And then Ollie is looking at the boy and smiling. Do you want to stay here with us, Ollie is asking, and Isaac, mouth stuffed full of toasted roll, nods yes with wide eyes and leaping heart. Then I must attend to some matters, Ollie says, turning to Mrs. Rogers, such as informing the authorities and making the arrangement, shall we say, a legal one. Is it possible? When money changes hands, everything is possible.

Is this what a family feels like, Isaac wonders, never having experienced such a thing, and then he is saying aloud, Can I stay here then? Of course, dear, Mrs. Rogers replies. For how long? How long would you like? A long time. Then a long time it shall be.

With a pat on Isaac's shoulder Ollie bounds out the door. To make things right, he says. Ollie is an odd one, moody at times, such as when the subject of God comes up. No talking about God, he will say, or Jesus. Most of the other civilized adults in Isaac's life went on and on about God this and God that, as if the whole purpose of life was to know God and what he intended for you to do. But Ollie grows angry at the subject of God, or religion, or priests or ministers. You don't know God, he will say, and then steam will pour out of his ears. Isaac can still hear Ollie's piercing condemnation of God in the wind, and he supposes that the death of Ann Chadwick has something to do with Ollie's anger. Because he wants Ollie to be happy, Isaac never mentions God or religion when Ollie is around—not that he would otherwise. The boy has never had time for such nonsense, not when physical survival was the only thing that mattered.

But now he wonders if there is a God. Not that he would ask Ollie.

Two weeks later Isaac is enrolled at Lenox, a private boy's day school. Ollie takes him there and Isaac is proud to hear this strong proper gentleman announce to the stodgy principal that he is Isaac's guardian. The term has a legal ring to it, and Isaac wonders if this is what Ollie meant by *making things right*.

Guardian. The term makes Isaac feel protected.

Don't worry, Ollie tells Isaac as he leaves the boy there, no one will know anything about you here. Okay. A carriage will pick you up every day after school. Okay.

The subjects at school are difficult, especially for a boy with no formal education, and Isaac is afraid that failure will mean banishment to the streets. *Wouldn't that be a fitting way for life to rebalance the scales? And Ollie would certainly have a perfect right, as an agent of life's system of balance, to correct the wrong.* So Isaac spends his evenings learning to read and write.

Mrs. Rogers and Ollie and Jonathon are amazed at Isaac's hunger for knowledge, not understanding the fear that motivates the boy.

The many evenings spent learning with his guardian binds Isaac closer to Ollie. Isaac is fascinated by the letters that Ollie writes to Herbert Eaton in London, and the letters he receives in return. The idea of having someone in a distant place who is interested in your life seems so... What's the word, Isaac? So *exotic*. Can you spell it? E-X-O... Keep going. Is Herbert your father? He's my guardian; you see I have a guardian too. He looks after you then? He comforts me with his words, but he is suffering terribly now because the love of his life has died and so it is my turn to comfort him.

One night Jonathon says to Ollie, I'm so glad we're working at last. Yes, it's good, isn't it? When Isaac asks what work they are doing, Ollie remains silent but Jonathon says, Ollie's writing a series of newspaper articles on American Revivalism in New York City for the *London Times*, with pictures by yours truly. The *fraud* of Revivalism.

By spring the series is nearly finished, and so is Isaac's first year of school. One evening, as Isaac studies a well-worn text book in the front room of the boarding house, Ollie approaches him and closes the book on Isaac's lap. I have something very important to talk to you about, he says to Isaac. What is it? I was wondering if maybe, perhaps, you would like to make our arrangement more permanent. But you're already my guardian, isn't that permanent? Yes but a guardian is one thing and a father is quite another. You mean—adopt me? Yes, that's what I mean, what would you think?

Two weeks later Isaac becomes Ollie's son and legal heir. For Isaac, heir means nothing but son means everything. On this same day Ollie announces that he must leave for a few weeks, perhaps a few months, to continue the series of articles.

But you've written everything there is to write about Revivalism in New York City, Isaac says. Do you really have to go? I have a mission to complete, the very reason in fact that I came to this country. Will you write to me then, Father?

The word *father* stabs Ollie unexpectedly. He had come to New York City as someone's son, and he is now leaving as someone's father. I'll write often, he says, embracing Isaac.

On a cloudy Sunday morning Ollie and Jonathon pack their carriage and head off down Nassau Street for the wilderness of New York State.

CHAPTER 27

It is not hard to find camp-meetings in New York State. As Ollie and Jonathon travel from one to another, they can see why this broad expanse between the Atlantic and Lake Ontario is called the *Burnt-Over District*; roving revivalists have raked this batch of sinners over the coals of hell's fire so many times that people here are no longer converted but *re-converted* out of fear that the first or third or sixth time didn't take. Like an overworked farm field, this once-fertile spiritual territory would have been depleted of new Christian prospects if it were not for the compost-heap of Adventism, as Ollie sees it. William Miller's schedule for the End of the World has given the evangelists what they needed most, a ticking clock, and with it they are growing one more bumper crop of repentants ripe for harvesting.

Ollie cannot bear the lies of God's agents, the preachers; or the smug righteousness of the hymns; or the gullibility of the audiences; or neuroticism celebrated as a spiritual gift. He sees it all as a fraud hoisted upon humanity and he seeks to call it out, or at least disrupt its influence, until people can see God for what He really is—a devious, vindictive, capricious Being who finds amusement in the pain and suffering for which He created mankind. Every exhortation shouted by the master manipulators behind the pulpits, each *Hallelujah* and *Glory* erupting from the mouths of the misled, every tear and heartfelt plea for mercy from a merciless God—all of this fans Ollie's passion for exposing the hoax of religion.

Jonathon sees Ollie's torment, which had first manifested during a local event. While one preacher had been urging repentants to come forward that they might be saved from eternal damnation, Ollie suddenly had stood up and shouted for the preacher to ask God's forgiveness, and his wife's, for his affair with the pianist. From the evangelist's sudden embarrassment and the intense flush of the pianist's face—which was almost as red as Jonathon's hair—the charge had seemed credible. Having successfully shattered the fragile moment, Ollie had identified himself as a reporter for the *London Times* and asked for an interview. The preacher had abruptly left the pulpit and the sinners in the audience had been left to deal with the Almighty on their own, although some had been seen retrieving their "love offering" from the collection bucket.

When Jonathon had asked how Ollie had learned about the affair, Ollie had merely said, "I have my great-grandmother's gift." From that moment, Jonathon had known that the camp-meetings they attended were not selected at random.

Disruptions at subsequent venues had taken other forms, and if it were not for the sly smile that creased Ollie's face during such upheavals Jonathon would not have suspected his friend's guiding hand in these events. Over time, larger numbers of unbelievers had begun to populate the tents—Universalists, deists, atheists, even Protestants who believed William Miller, the man who had cracked the code of Christ's Return, to be himself a devil in disguise. The camp-meetings at times had disintegrated into hot debates and shouting matches as unbelievers in their many shades sparred with the Adventists and rivaled the preachers' fervor with their own indignant zeal or pure contrariness.

At some camp-meetings liquor stands had begun to appear on the roads leading into the grounds, attracting curious onlookers and fueling the discontent of the local citizenry. On one such stand a sign had appeared: WHISKEY FOR SALE—DRUNKS 5¢, CHRISTIANS FREE.

Cheap booze inevitably had led to gangs of shellacked rowdies taunting the sinners who had ridden through the gauntlet on their way to the Kingdom of God. At one camp ground, horse-drawn omnibuses mysteriously had appeared and the drunken mob had clambered aboard them to convey their curses into the center of the meeting. But the liquor had done its job, and cursing had been transformed into egg-tossing—an act that Jonathon thought required some forethought—and then vandalism. The laughing tormenters had overturned food tables, torn down the colored folks' tent, set fire to a stack of hymnals, and provoked retaliation with a discordant version of *Onward Christian Soldiers* before merrily stumbling back onto their omnibuses to escape the wrath of a thousand believers suddenly awakened from their stunned stupor.

How Ollie had been able to orchestrate and finance such shenanigans, if indeed he had, Jonathon could not figure out. At each camp-meeting, they would generally arrive during set-up and Ollie would leave Jonathon to his craft with the simple instruction to document the event in pictures "as you see fit, you're the artist," and then would disappear for several days. There had never been a shortage of dramatic images to capture by daguerreotype or drawing—the muscular wrangling of tents, the freshly-scrubbed children in flowered bonnets, the bent-kneed repentants, the countless expressions of grief, panic, devotion, fear, love. How Jonathon had wished he could also capture the sounds that filled the woods around these camp-grounds—the moans and wails, the rapturous songs of praise, a crow's cackle during silent prayers, the camp bells that announced each activity, the innumerable voices like the sound of many waters.

Though he had counted himself among the unbelievers, Jonathon had found comfort in these camps. He could ignore the hellfire and brimstone just as he could frame a picture to eliminate distracting elements. It almost made him wish he believed in God.

With many camp-meetings behind them, Ollie and Jonathon approach yet another one, but this time Ollie seems quietly nervous. Apprehensive. Unlike most of the others, this meeting has already begun so they will be entering the grounds during a service. Jonathon knows this because the chorus of *Don't You See My Jesus Coming* serenely wafts through the virgin timber that surrounds the camp.

The two of them ride their horses westward down a narrow road that finally breaks over a small ridge. From here they can look down upon the campground. Drawn about in a circle are the white tents, like patches of snow in a field of greens and yellows. Behind the tents are the provision stalls and cook-shops. Curling smoke rises like incense from many small fires. Tall stands of hemlocks and vines cast their melancholy shadows over the gathered multitude, which must number several thousand. The enormous tabernacle tent sits in the center with its sides drawn up to entice summer breezes to cool perspiring faces and, God willing, to encourage the Holy Spirit to enter and take possession of desperate hearts.

Jonathon notices that there are no liquor stands or gangs of thugs along the road.

They continue to ride, pushed forward by several hundred late-arriving salvation seekers traveling by foot, horseback and wagon. After making arrangements at the stables to care for their horses—50¢ per day for the pair—

Jonathon follows Ollie to the big tent. It is stuffed to overflowing. Ollie pulls
Jonathon into the tent and they take two vacant seats on a freshly-sawn plank.

On the platform, a rude pulpit made of rough boards stands in front of a
row of wooden chairs in which sit assorted dignitaries, local church leaders,
and the traveling evangelists, musicians and singers. One of them is a plain but
kind-looking woman several years younger than Ollie. She is looking at him
and he instinctively smiles at her.

Suspended behind the pulpit are two immense sheets of canvas, each perhaps ten feet square. On one is painted the figure of a man with a head of gold,
breast and arms of silver, belly of brass, legs of iron, and feet of clay; this
is the dream of Nebuchadnezzar. The other floating image is a depiction of
the wonders of the Apocalyptic vision—the monsters and dragons, the scarlet
woman observed by the Seer of Patmos, exotic Orientals, mystic symbols—all
translated into bizarre and absurd caricatures but exhibited here like the freaks
of a traveling sideshow.

For his rapt audience, the preacher is earnestly dissecting the image of the
man with clay feet. Each section of this Frankenstein's monster represents a
kingdom on earth, he says. And then he proceeds to take the body apart, kingdom by kingdom, until nothing is left but the feet of iron and clay, which are
doomed, he says—DOOMED!—to be broken into pieces on the tenth day of
the seventh month of Jubilee *Hallelujah!*

Throughout the oration Jonathon tensely awaits some kind of interruption
by Ollie, but it never comes. The man sits there quietly, listening, moving only
occasionally to wipe his brow with a handkerchief.

At last the preacher begins his altar call, inviting all those repentants in the
tent to come forward and be saved while there is still time, and if you are not
yet persuaded, please come back this evening to hear one of the most powerful
preachers ever to bring the message of the Second Coming of Jesus to the great
state of New York, our dear brother *Gordon Cranston*. At seven o'clock this
evening, the preacher says.

Ollie suddenly stirs, agitated. As a hundred or more sinners rise from their
seats and march toward the pulpit, Ollie also rises. Jonathon winces, expecting
some kind of profane outburst. He closes his eyes, leans away, hoping that the
distance will disassociate him from Ollie.

But Ollie says nothing. He simply walks out of the tent. He is finally about
to complete his mission.

CHAPTER 28

Ollie and Jonathon had slipped into the tent a half-hour earlier to take the seats vacated by the elderly couple. Two women are seated on the speaker's platform. One of them, Dorothy Atkins, is the session's soloist, a gifted soprano who had been "saved" two years earlier and loved to tell about it between songs. The other one is Alice Crenshaw, a rare female preacher who was serving as the "host" of the afternoon session after speaking in the morning.

For Alice, the urgency of the Second Advent message, which through repetition had benumbed her exhilaration, has been overshadowed by a more material concern. At twenty-six, she is still unmarried. Still a virgin. Has never known a man more intimately than as a "spiritual sister." But she remembers Jesus' promise to send a man to be with her in the end days. Remembers the face in the clouds. The smile. How could she forget it? Since that day she has been looking for that smile, certain that it would appear on the face of the man who had been promised for her. For months she has searched every face in every crowd, always sure that Jesus would keep his word.

And now, suddenly she finds that smile in the sixth row, just to her left. Had this handsome man recognized her, too? Maybe it doesn't work that way. Perhaps only she knows his destiny.

She is glad that she is not preaching this afternoon. Imagine if she were in the middle of an emotional appeal to the sinners and then looked down to see that smile—why, she would lose her place, almost certainly. Mumble something inane. Make a fool of herself in front of him.

What to do? The preacher is droning on and on about the destruction of great kingdoms and other obscure things that suddenly have no relevance to her; would he never finish? She tries praying for tranquility, but her heart is beating too hard. She tries to logically plot her next steps, but her whole body had been inflamed with desire and she can't think. She has shifted in her seat, dabbed her flushed face with a handkerchief, crossed and uncrossed her legs at the ankles, and recited the Lord's Prayer as a distraction, but got the words mixed up.

Her life is at a crossroads. It will never be the same. *Do husbands and wives know each other in heaven*? she wonders, and decides they do, otherwise what was the point?

It's impossible to keep her eyes off the man with the smile, though the smile has now disappeared. She tries to look elsewhere, but her eyes are controlled by demons—or angels. They keep getting pulled in his direction.

He is so handsome!

Once, just as the speaker gets to the feet of clay part, the man seems to scan the speaker's platform and she quickly averts her eyes—*had he seen her staring at him?*—and finds it deliciously painful to prevent them from rebounding. When she can restrain her gaze no longer, she furtively glances at the man again, but by this time he is studying the big canvas picture.

For how long had he looked at her?

At last the piano starts to play and the dignitaries on the platform stand and begin to hum the plaintive melody—all except Alice, who cannot find her voice. It suddenly occurs to her that the end of the service, let alone the End of Time, is near. And this means that the man will soon leave the tent. Perhaps she will never see him again. *My God,* she prays, *what should I do?* Her stomach turns over and her palms grow sweaty. And then, as the tearful repentants begin to stream toward the pulpit, the man leaves the tent. Just like that.

What should I do? she pleads to God, looking for a sign. And then she hears the preacher speak these words: "Tarry not, for time is too short for indecision. Be bold, and claim what God has promised for you."

In that moment, Alice knows what to do.

Ollie strides from the tent, his mind stirred into a boiling stew by the very mention of the name Gordon Cranston. Memories begin to simmer on the flame of his emotions. Cranston the missionary. Cranston the lover. Cranston the patient teacher, the selfless rescuer, the fortunate mate-to-be of an heiress. All of it lies and deceit. Every devious action calculated to advance a plot hatched in London.

This long-awaited day will finally relieve Ollie of the awful bitterness that he has carried for so many years. This evening the true face of Gordon Cranston will be exposed to the thousands who have come to hear his lies. Of all the devils who wear the cleric's mantle—Walter Nettleship, Reginald Pennick, the unfaithful camp-meeting preacher and so many others—Gordon Cranston is the king of religious whores. And he is still perpetrating his spiritual atrocities on unsuspecting victims!

His strides have shortened and now he stops, takes a deep breath. The comforting scent of pine and freshly cut wood calms him. What a perfect venue for the completion of his mission.

A quiet voice from behind startles him. A feminine voice. "Excuse me, sir," it says.

Ollie turns to see a plain but pretty young woman looking up at him. She looks vaguely familiar.

As he catches her eye, she looks down at her shoes. "Sorry to bother you," she says.

"No bother," Ollie says with a smile.

Alice looks up and sees the smile. Yes, there can be no doubt. What had the preacher said? Oh yes, *Tarry not. Be bold.* She has no idea what to say next but opens her mouth, confident that God will control her tongue. "I believe, sir, that you have come here to find someone."

There. It's done.

But as Alice immediately considers the words she has just heard herself speak she is horrified. *My God, what manner of introduction is this? He will think I'm a lunatic!"* She fights to retain her faith in God.

Misunderstanding her, Ollie is astonished at the statement. How could this woman possibly know about Gordon Cranston? Even Jonathon is ignorant of his plans. "Actually," he mumbles, "the truth is yes, I came here to find someone."

Ollie's friendly tone restores Alice's confidence. *The man did not go racing off!* Rejoicing in this small miracle, she finds the strength to reply. "I was quite sure of it. Very sure." *Well—that was inane.*

"I don't believe we've met before," Ollie says. "May I ask how you knew my intentions?"

There is the hint of an accent in his speech—English, perhaps?—and it has a most soothing yet provocative effect on Alice. *A man of the world!* Would it be too bold to wrap her arms around him and smother him in kisses?

"God," she says.

"Pardon me?"

"God. He sometimes shows me things, and he showed me you."

Ollie's eyes widen. This was not an answer that he expected. The woman makes no sense. Or perhaps she is an oracle. For just an instant Ollie feels that God is calling him out, letting him know that his actions are being noted.

Alice senses his confusion and says, "I'm sure that makes no sense, does it? But you see, I've been asking myself why I recognize you but you don't recognize me. I believe that you were led here by God for a reason that you don't yet understand."

Ollie finds this thought most unappealing. He certainly knows why he came here. The idea that God led him here for some other purpose—well, that's pretty much out of the question. Nothing will prevent Ollie from his ultimate act of revenge.

"My name is Oliver Chadwick," he says, changing the topic. "From London, by way of New York City."

"I'm very happy to meet you, Mr. Chadwick. I'm Alice Crenshaw, one of the speakers at this grand event."

They politely nod to each other. "My mother frequently spoke at meetings of Evangelicals in London," Ollie says, knowing that Alice will misconstrue this as a prideful boast.

Alice replies, "I'm the only offspring of my father, a long-time preacher in these parts. Originally from Vermont. I learned from listening to him, never expecting that one day he would become unable to preach and I would take his place. Kind of an unwitting protégé, I guess you'd say."

"Miss Crenshaw, why did you seek me out just now?"

This startles Alice. She was just easing into comfortable small-talk and then, bam! He put her on the spot. She hopes God has more words for her to speak. But instead of words, she receives insight. As she looks into this man's eyes, deeply for the first time, she can see things. Disturbing things. She can see unhappiness hidden beneath the handsome countenance, anger swirling in the wake of his smile, a quiet desperation smoldering behind his eyes, and pain—such intense pain that she can feel it herself.

"I apologize for my abruptness," Ollie says in the uncomfortable silence. He fears that he has offended this poor woman, and he hadn't meant to. He rather likes her. "I'm just tired from a long ride here, please forgive me."

Alice rubs her arms as if wiping out the pain that had been transferred to her. In a flash she understands what is going on, and it is so much more wonderful than she had imagined.

"There is nothing for me to forgive, Mr. Chadwick," she says. Her tone is lower, more soothing and confident. She smiles and her smile warms Ollie, as if the sun had just emerged from a cloud. "I'm afraid I was mistaken. You see, I had thought that you were sent here for *me*."

Ollie looks at her quizzically.

"But now I see that the truth is quite the opposite," she adds. "I was sent here for you."

CHAPTER 29

In the food tent, Jonathon can see Ollie and a young woman he recognizes from the speaker's platform. With a casual gait, he approaches the table and says to the woman, "Good evening, I'm Jonathon Fury, nice to meet you." The words sound more spiteful than intended, he thinks, then worries that his chief motive may be jealousy.

Ollie steps into the breach and says, "Alice Crenshaw, this is my assistant. Actually, the finest daguerreotypist in the country."

"Nice to meet you," Alice says, "but I'm afraid I don't know what a daguerreotypist is. I assume, though, that if you work with Ollie it has something to do with the newspaper business."

Jonathon smiles broadly and, he hopes, not too insincerely. "I make pictures to illustrate his stories," he replies.

"Drawings?" Alice asks.

"No, something altogether new," Jonathon explains. "In fact, I have my camera just outside the tent. Perhaps you will allow me to demonstrate."

Jonathon leads the pair out of the tent and reveals that the camera obscura is already set up on its tripod. In great detail he explains the technology of the camera and shows samples of the stunning images he has made at previous camp-meetings.

"I wonder if you would allow me to take your picture," Jonathon says.

"Oh goodness no," Alice says. "I'm not anything that someone would like to look at."

Ollie interrupts. "I think you're beautiful. I would like to have a picture of you, to remind me of this occasion."

"Well then, maybe—" she says.

"Excellent!" Jonathon shouts, and begins to give her instructions.

As Alice shyly cooperates, Ollie studies her face. She is not a mesmerizing beauty like his mother or Mary Brown, but she has kind and attractive features. Plain, yes, but fresh and wholesome. And then it strikes Ollie—*she shuns make-up. And jewelry.* That's the difference. Her beauty is not aided by paint and powder, nor framed by glittering beads or fabulous wigs. Everything about her is genuine Alice. And now, the way that the late afternoon sun burnishes her face with a buttery glow, she seems somehow angelic.

"Thank you," Jonathon says, abruptly halting Ollie's reverie. "I'll leave you two now. I want to get a few more pictures before the light is gone and the evening service starts."

As Jonathon leaves, Alice turns to Ollie and says, "Would you like to sit with me this evening? I don't have to be on the platform."

"I'd like that very much," Ollie says instinctively, then realizes that he has sabotaged himself. How can he humiliate a friend of this wonderful young woman while he is sitting next to her at the service? What would she think of him? He cannot do such a thing, at least not this evening. Fortunately, Gordon Cranston will be speaking for the next three nights. Ollie will find the right time.

"I would like to stretch my legs a bit. Will you walk with me?" Alice asks.

"Of course." Ollie realizes that he seems to have no will of his own while he is with Alice. He is drawn to her goodness. She lives in a world of superstition that he has rejected, but he senses a refreshing pureness of spirit that he has never encountered before.

They walk through the camp-grounds. He hears praying from some of the tents, children laughing, scripture being recited. An old woman sings a hymn, her voice cracking in emotion. The camp-grounds contain everything that Ollie has come to despise—the piety and emotionalism, the delusions of divine grandeur, the intellectual manipulation, the fraudulent belief in a kind and beneficent God—yet with Alice at his side these things seem less detestable. How can he hate what seems to bring an abundance of joy to a woman of such decency?

She takes his arm, and the warmth of her hand is like a candle illuminating the darkness of his soul. For several minutes they just walk, without words, and she seems completely at peace, as if the weight of the world had been lifted from her and she could float above the tents. How Ollie would love to float with her, but he is tethered to the ground, to the rock of revenge, and all he can do is wonder at her happiness.

It has been wearing on him, this matter of Gordon Cranston, and how Alice had come to know him. Ollie knows it may break the dreamlike mood, but he has to know. "Alice, have you known Cranston for a long time?"

"Oh my, what a question," she says. "Now I have to think, and I was having such a good time simply enjoying the present company without thinking."

"Sorry," he says.

"No, that's all right. Let me see now. Gordon is an Englishman, did you know that?"

"I did, actually."

"Worked as a missionary for some time, then lived in France for a while. Apparently he found France disagreeable for some reason and came to the New World for a fresh start. He met my father one evening when the Reverend was a guest speaker at a church service in Boston. He was so moved by the sermon that he answered the call and came forward, though he was a minister himself. He said that he had fallen out of favor with God and had been in league with the devil. Had done some horrible things, he said, that had injured people he loved, and when God visited upon him terrible trials in France, he saw that he was deserving of it and came near to taking his own life in remorse."

Ollie listens carefully. When Alice pauses, he asks, "He seemed sincere?"

"Oh my, yes. I was there that evening. He sobbed and sobbed. And the next day he came by and talked to us some more. Wanted a fresh start, he said. He didn't know how to make amends to those he had hurt except to help a multitude of others come to know Jesus. Daddy—the Reverend—gave him the job of helping prepare his sermons. Gordon knew his Bible, I can tell you that much. Before long he was delivering sermons himself, and people were responding to his message. Daddy said he had a gift."

"A gift," Ollie repeats.

"He works for no pay, just expenses. But still, there is a sadness in him. As though there is unfinished business that he must attend to. I hope I'm not being too bold, Oliver, when I say that I see the same kind of sadness in you."

Ollie looks at Alice without speaking. Too many thoughts are spinning in his head. Is it possible that a rogue like Gordon Cranston could be transformed? "Did he ever say who it was that he hurt in England?"

"Did I say they were in England? I guess I did. No, he never mentioned them by name. But wait a minute, we're at my tent. Let me get something."

Alice rushes into the tent and after a moment flings back the flap and emerges with a book. "He gave me this book," she says, handing it to Ollie.

"Said he knew the folks in the story from his days as a missionary. He never said as much, but my guess is that the people in it have something to do with his sadness."

Ollie takes the book, *Midnight March to Freedom* by Anne Chadwick and Herbert Eaton. "Have you read it?" he asks.

"Oh yes. Amazing adventure. It's supposed to be true."

"Really?" Ollie says. "Mind if I borrow it?"

"Not at all."

Ollie is anxious to remove the book, with its many references to Anne and Ollie Chadwick, from Alice's possession.

He is not sure why. But some things are best kept secret.

CHAPTER 30

Jonathon finds Ollie tending to his horse, a muscular chestnut bay. He watches for a moment as Ollie caringly strokes the animal with the palms of his hands, then begins to firmly massage the massive leg muscles with his strong fingers. Big muscles, big pain, Ollie had once told Jonathon. They can't speak, you know, so it's up to us to look out for them.

The horse sighs.

Jonathon is fascinated that his troubled friend can be so tender with animals and so cruel to people. From their conversations on the trail, he gathers that Ollie despises the self-proclaimed *men of God* in particular because they are supposed to look out for their suffering flocks, but too often end up fleecing them instead. Big pain, big opportunity. He suspects, though, that Ollie's bigger problem is with God Himself.

Inspired by Ollie's thoughtfulness to his horse, Jonathon steps across the straw-covered ground and begins to deeply massage his black mare. The horse winces.

"Start out gently," Ollie says. "and you'll find where the pain is. She'll let you know when you can work it a little harder."

"How'll she do that?"

"She won't kick you."

"Oh."

Jonathon gently skims his hands over the animals flesh. "Seems like a pretty nice girl."

"Keep doing that and she'll be in love," Ollie replies.

"I was talking about Alice."

"Alice? Yeah, she's nice. A good conversationalist."

"Uh-huh. She seems to like you."

"She's a preacher. Wants to save me, I suspect."

"Maybe." Jonathon finds a sore spot in his animal's rear leg and begins to work it gently. "Are you going to tear her down like the other preachers?"

Ollie sternly faces Jonathon. "What are you talking about?"

"I'm talking about the preacher back in Albany."

"He deserved it, you can't say that he didn't."

"And the liquor stands and the mobs."

Ollie silently turns back to his horse, his fingers kneading deeply into the throbbing muscles.

"I'm talking about the vandalism," Jonathon says. "The drunks cursing in front of the children. The innocent people hurt. And the manipulation. Ollie, can't you see it? The very thing you hate in these preachers you're guilty of yourself."

Ollie's horse screeches in pain, then kicks and stomps as Ollie's fingers probe too deeply, too angrily. Ollie backs away with a flushed face and wheels to face Jonathon again. "I have my reasons," he says, restraining himself.

"Sure you do. Everyone has reasons."

Now that Jonathon has finally spoken up he can't stop. His pent-up anger explodes with sarcasm. "So what's your reason here? Maybe I know. You've never shown up a woman preacher. Got some goods on her?" God, it feels good to lash out like this. "When will you take it to her, Ollie? Tomorrow morning when she's at the pulpit? Or maybe you'll wait, it'll hurt worse the more she likes you. What is it this time, she a whore?"

Ollie lunges at Jonathon. They crash into a wooden railing and fall into the prickly straw, wrestling, Ollie on top. Jonathon rolls him off and jumps to his feet, but Ollie grabs a leg and pulls him back down, cracking Jonathon's head on a spot of bare ground. Ollie clambers back on top, sitting on Jonathon's chest and raising his fist to strike a blow to the face. But he hesitates as he sees Jonathon open his eyes and look up at him.

Jonathon says, "Hit me then. Take it out on me like you do the preachers."

Ollie lowers his fist, grabs the front of Jonathon's shirt with both hands and shakes the man like a rag doll.

When it is over, Jonathon says, "It's still not enough, is it? Never will be. You can't punish God by punishing His creation."

Ollie releases Jonathon's shirt, bends over to look him in the eye, then says, "Don't ever call her a whore!" He stands up and storms out of the stable.

Jonathon shouts after him, "Trust me, it's easier if you don't believe in God!"

Outside the stable Ollie dusts himself off. The sun is setting and people are starting to migrate toward the tabernacle tent for the great Gordon Cranston show. Still breathing hard, Ollie wonders at his own behavior. What was it that set him off like that? Jonathon's insubordination? The ambush of accusations? Perhaps the insult to a lady's honor?

What is certain is that his emotions are careening recklessly, and why not? The opportunity to fulfill his mission is finally at hand, yet he has stupidly allowed his rage, the fuel of his revenge, to be softened by a woman preacher. His only friend in this wilderness of souls has accused him of dreadful but true things, and Ollie feels the stirrings of remorse, yet he is compelled to continue. He fears that Jonathon may be right, that there is no end to the course that he is on, and no satisfaction to be derived from it, yet he doesn't care. He is Frankenstein's monster, assembled in some blasphemous workshop from these conflicting parts, horrified by his own ugliness, fearful of his profane purpose, possessing a terrible capacity for both tenderness and great cruelty, and driven at last by his own painful paradoxes to find and destroy his Creator. And he is powerless to stop.

He knows that he must battle on, but he also knows that if he does not act now, this evening, he may lose his resolve. Alice has proven to be a powerful antidote for his rage.

Carrying Alice's copy of *Midnight March to Freedom*, he walks to the tabernacle tent, which is almost full. He sees Alice standing outside the main entrance, obviously looking for him. With a pencil plucked from his pocket he quickly writes a short note on the title page of the book, then finds a boy about to enter the tent and bribes him with a shiny coin to deliver the book to someone inside. Finally he approaches Alice, who looks at him brightly at first, then detects his turmoil.

"I was afraid you wouldn't come," she says honestly, pulling a shaft of straw from his hair and taking his arm. "You look like you've been wrestling with an angel."

The gathering dusk has brought a chill. Alice's hands warm him, make him remember other loving hands in other places at other times. He is comforted by her presence, but he knows it will only last for a short time. Already he mourns her loss.

Tonight will be very difficult for him.

Alice takes a deep breath, gulps the night air, and scans the magical landscape that surrounds them, a sight that has eluded Ollie in his distress. As if trying to pull him into the beauty of his surroundings, Alice smiles and continues to drink in with her eyes the near-mystical setting. Lamps, pine torches, fireflies and stars mingle into a light-filled otherworldly vision. The surrounding tents glow like moons, illuminated from within. The grounds are sprayed with the soft light of tree lanterns and the flickering blaze of fire altars, six-foot high platforms topped with earth and pine-knot bonfires that warm the fluttering leaves of overhanging trees. Like serpents in the moonlight, tree roots rubbed raw by the feet of the crowd seem to wriggle with a phosphorescent gleam. In this wild yet solemn night-scene anything and everything seems possible.

Alice leads Ollie into the tent. The air inside is heavily spiced with the woodsy scent of sawdust and freshly cut timber. Spruce boughs tied together as a furry green cross hang behind the rough-sawn pulpit. A piano with a slightly flat E above middle C softly plays a hymn intended to calm the incoming crowd, which unfortunately ignores the music in favor of their own bubbling stream of expectant laughter and friendly greetings. If one knew no better it would seem as though this were a reunion of one immense family.

Alice finds a spot on a bench twelve rows from the speaker's platform "for the twelve apostles," she says. The chairs on the platform are taken, and Ollie's eyes center on the man to the right of the pulpit, Gordon Cranston. How many years has it been since this cowardly Judas had abandoned Anisa and Ollie for a handful of silver paid over the years? How long has Ollie waited for this moment? Gordon seems barely to have aged. He is still strikingly handsome, though perhaps ten pounds heavier, with a dab of silver in his hair.

Ollie is suddenly aware that his hands are shaking. He is nervous! His hunter's heart is pounding; the long-awaited prey has finally stepped into the clear.

"Are you all right, Ollie?" Alice asks.

"Yes—just a bit excited."

"I know what you mean. I always expect miracles." But she is talking about something altogether different.

Ollie watches as a boy approaches Gordon with Alice's copy of *Midnight March to Freedom*. Gordon smiles at the boy but is clearly puzzled as he takes the book and opens it to the title page on which is scrawled Ollie's message in Farsi. *Anisa is dead. I have come for you*, it reads.

Ollie watches Gordon's eyes widen then dart from left to right as if seeking out the author of the thinly veiled threat. Gordon is clearly shaken. As if praying, he closes his eyes and pinches the bridge of his nose with his thumb and forefinger.

Ollie surveys the tent and sees Jonathon squeezing into a seat in the fourth row. Suddenly the solemn piano begins to pound out a rousing song. Gordon and the others seated by him leap to their feet and begin clapping their hands, keeping time to the mesmerizing beat of the thundering bass chords. The audience rises almost in unison and within a few seconds several thousand voices begin to sing the words. The sopranos wail, the tenors harmonize, and the baritones beat out the stirring words:

> You will see your Lord a-coming
> On the resurrection morning,
> While the band of music
> Will be sounding through the air.

The song ends with cheers and hallelujahs, and the crowd settles into their hard benches once again. One by one the dignitaries on the platform stand and take turns thanking the crowd for coming, exhorting them, making announcements, leading a hymn, singing a solo, giving testimonies of how Jesus turned their sinful selves into sanctified temples of God just in time, for *Judgment Day is right around the corner!*

As the final speaker begins to introduce Gordon Cranston, the main event, a drunken man in soiled overalls staggers down the center aisle and begins to yell, "Gladys! Gladys, where are you? Get your damn butt outta this tent ya hear?"

Jonathon looks across the sea of penitents at Ollie, wondering if he had orchestrated this disruption. Standing at the pulpit, the speaker—a frail, boyish minister from a neighboring town—raises his hand and meekly invites the man to be quiet.

"Religious snake oil!" is the reply. The drunkard, a fierce bull of a man, begins to lurch toward the platform like a prosecuting attorney about to make his case. He launches into a loud and profane tirade about religious charlatans and the weak minds of those who are swayed by them. Unprepared for such an outburst, the speaker backs away from the pulpit. A woman in the audience, presumably Gladys, falteringly stands up as the drunkard passes her row and begins to sneak out, pausing at the back of the tent where she can make a quick escape if needed. All faces are turned toward the ranting drunk who slowly makes his way toward the pulpit.

Suddenly Alice stands and steps into the center aisle to intercept the tormenter. Surprised, he stops a few feet from her. Alice opens her arms as if to embrace him. His vaporous red eyes burn into her and he gestures as if to holler something at her but no words come out, just a raspy rattle. He tries again to speak but his words seem swallowed up by Alice's outstretched arms. He turns to hurl angry words at the crowd but emits only a feeble screech. The tent is absolutely silent. The man grips his throat, terrified with the realization that his voice has been stolen. Again he tries to speak but only a strangled column of air escapes his throat.

Dumbfounded, the drunkard lumbers menacingly toward Alice. Ollie rises to protect her, but before he can step into the aisle the man falls into Alice's arms weeping like a baby, his enormous hands limp at his side. Alice calmly strokes the back of the man's wooly head, whispers something into his ear, and the man slumps to the ground as if felled by a musket shot.

"As the prophet Isaiah wrote, 'the LORD hath poured out upon you the spirit of deep sleep, and hath closed your eyes,'" Alice says, kneeling over the man. "And the wicked shall be silent in darkness; for by strength shall no man prevail."

It takes five men to lift the fallen drunkard. As they carry the sagging body to the front of the tent, Alice stands and in a joyous voice says, "Did not Paul admonish us? He wrote 'be not drunk with wine, wherein is excess; but be filled with the Spirit, speaking to yourselves in psalms and hymns and spiritual songs…"

The piano begins to play *Amazing Grace* and three thousand voices join in song as Alice, her voice rising above the impromptu choir, finishes reciting the scripture: "'making melody in your heart to the Lord; giving thanks always for all things unto God and the Father in the name of our Lord Jesus Christ; submitting yourselves one to another in the fear of God.'"

As the song ends, the sleeping man is laid on his back before the first row of benches and Alice takes her seat next to Ollie.

"What happened?" Ollie asks her.

Alice does not answer; she is looking upward, toward heaven, silently mouthing words to some unseen presence.

A prayer, perhaps.

As if replying to Ollie's question the boyish preacher, having courageously stepped back to the pulpit to lead the singing, confidently says, "It seems that God did not want our service to be interrupted by blasphemy."

Hallelujahs fill the tent.

At last Gordon is introduced to the crowd. As he approaches the pulpit he is clutching the copy of *Midnight March to Freedom* as if it were a Bible. He stares out at the expectant audience and, glancing at the sleeping man, says, "Before Jesus ascended into heaven he spoke to his disciples saying, 'These signs shall follow them that believe; In my name shall they cast out devils.' Sister Alice, God be with you."

A chorus of *Amens* soars through the dusty air.

"The Apostle Paul wrote, 'Behold, I show you a mystery. We shall not all sleep, but we shall all be changed. In a moment, in the twinkling of an eye, at the last trump: for the trumpet shall sound, and the dead shall be raised incorruptible, and we shall be changed.'"

Glory! Hallelujah!

Gordon's voice rises an octave as his eyes turn toward heaven and his right hand reaches out as if to take God's hand. "'For the Lord himself shall descend from heaven with a shout, with the voice of the archangel, and with the trump of God: and the dead in Christ shall rise first: Then we which are alive and remain shall be caught up together with them in the clouds, to meet the Lord in the air: and so shall we ever be with the Lord!'"

A thousand rapt believers leap from their seats and raise their hands, shouting in celebration of the Great Truth.

Ollie notices that Gordon's left hand still grips the book.

To quiet the rapturous crowd, Gordon closes his eyes and begins a prayer. Within seconds the tent is hushed. "Our dear Father in heaven," he prays, "help us to prepare our hearts for the imminent return of your Son Jesus, and guide our thoughts in these final hours to be wholly consumed by your love and purpose for our lives. Help us to show the same spirit of love to those around us that Jesus showed to all humanity. Forgive us, Father, our sins, which are many, and help us to forgive those who have wronged us. In this time of great expectation, give us strength to endure the torments and ridicule of unbelievers as Jesus endured His persecutors. In the name of Jesus—may His triumphant return not find us asleep – Amen."

Amen.

Gordon's prayer, Ollie knows, was a thinly veiled appeal to him for forgiveness. He smiles smugly as Alice gently takes his hand. He is surprised at its warmth.

This would be a good time to confront Gordon in front of the entire assembly, Ollie thinks, but the touch of Alice's hand restrains him. Soothes him.

Remember this man's betrayal, and how he ruined your life, Ollie tells himself. But he cannot bring his anger to a boil. *Give it time,* he decides. *The pompous arrogance of this impostor will incite you soon enough. Give him time to dig his own grave from which there will be no resurrection.*

"Until a few minutes ago," Gordon says, "I was expecting to present to you the overwhelming evidence of the impending Second Coming of Christ, an event which has been awaited so longingly for centuries and which is now only months away. Yes, there is no doubt that in less than a year our Savior will return to fulfill His promise, praise God!"

Praise God!

"I was going to lay out the indisputable evidence for you so that you can begin to prepare yourselves for the wonderful and terrible upheaval to come… but I have changed my mind. You see, time is too short. The time of persuasion is over; it is now time for preparation. If you do not believe that Jesus is coming, I have no time for you, so you may as well leave right now."

Gordon pauses. The audience begins to buzz. About fifty people rise, huffing and nodding their heads before heading for the exits, but the remainder— thousands of them—cling to their benches.

"This evening I have learned that my mission has been changed," Gordon says, gripping the rough pulpit with one hand while he grips the book with the other. "From this moment it is my responsibility to get believers ready for the return of Jesus. There is so little time, my friends, and so much to do. But the hard work begins with our hearts, for God will not allow us to be caught up in the clouds to meet the Lord so long as we harbor resentment and fail to forgive those who have wronged us. My friends—beloved of God—hear me on this. Jesus came the first time to show us how to love and how to forgive. How can we expect to be forgiven if we cannot forgive! Wives, I am talking about forgiving your husbands, and husbands your wives."

Gladys, the wife of the raging man, begins to weep at the back of the tent and another woman embraces her.

Gordon continues. "Brothers, set aside your feelings of anger for the wrongs of your siblings, and daughters, forgive your parents their shortcomings. Neighbors, forgive your friends and acquaintances so that you may be forgiven, and let your forgiveness be known!"

Throughout the audience, people sob as they consider their unholy grudges.

"Are we not all deficient in some way? Have we not all wronged someone during our lifetime of struggle? Did not Jesus forgive his accusers and murderers by asking God to forgive them for they knew not what they had done? My dear friends, know of a certainty that we must *make* peace before we can *find* peace. And since we have all wronged someone, we must ask them for forgiveness, just as we ask God to forgive us our trespasses."

Ollie listens to these words, confused by the apparent conviction of the speaker. This is not the arrogant and deceitful Gordon who had haunted the dark chambers of Ollie's mind for so many years. This man, bearing the name of Gordon Cranston and garbed in the aging body of the traitorous missionary, cannot be Gordon, for no man could be so transformed. From the twelfth row Ollie can see tears in the eyes of the preacher. He can hear the wretched man's plea as if it were a private conversation between the two of them.

"Only moments ago, God spoke to me," Gordon continues. "His message was that tonight I must become His agent for change in your hearts. God's messenger, I am quite sure, did not know that he was conducting God's business this evening."

Gordon holds the book to his chest. Ollie shudders at the implication that he is a messenger for a God whom he despises.

Alice sees the book and recognizes it as the copy of *Midnight March to Freedom* she had given to Ollie, a book originally loaned to her by Gordon. A book written by... by... Alice Chadwick. *Chadwick.* Oliver Chadwick. Ollie—Ali— The pieces come together in her mind. Gordon, a missionary to Persia. Ali, the heroine's son abducted from his father and reared in London.

"Before I can begin to fulfill this sacred mission," Gordon explains, "I must purify my own heart, for I have grievously wronged others in the past. I betrayed those I had come to deeply love through an act of such exquisite selfishness that my own life became a penance for my sins."

Alice turns to Ollie and can see the raw emotion in his eyes. In a horrifying instant she understands Ollie's purpose in coming to the meeting and can see the future. Through the touch of Ollie's hand she can feel the quivering demon of revenge awaiting its time.

Yes, she was sent here to help Ollie.

The warmth of Alice's hand begins to move upward through Ollie's arm and radiate into his chest and shoulders.

"I have learned that one of those whom I so gravely wronged is now dead," Gordon says. "And so I must live my life without her forgiveness."

Ollie watches the man as he seems to fight back tears. *Is this an act? If so, it is a performance that Anisa would have admired.*

"The other victim of my selfishness is among you tonight—perhaps filled with hatred for me and thoughts of revenge—and to you I now speak directly. The truth is, I deserve your retribution, but I beg for your forgiveness. Not that I should be left unpunished, but that you will free *yourself* from the prison of your passions. You see, my friend, I have been serving a sentence imposed by a much higher power."

Ollie's body is now penetrated by the soothing warmth of Alice's healing touch, but even steeped in this narcotic balm his demons fight for survival. He cannot forget. He does not *want* to forgive.

Gordon turns to a boy in the first row; Ollie can only see the back of the boy, but he appears to be about twelve years old.

"In God's infinite wisdom," Gordon says, "He chose to punish me sweetly… in such a manner that I will never forget my transgressions. I would like to introduce you to my son."

Gordon gestures to a woman of sixty who is seated next to the boy. She whispers into the boy's ear, then walks with him to the platform and helps him up the three steps to the pulpit. The boy walks awkwardly and when he turns to face the audience displays the enlarged forehead, slanted eyes and distant gaze of a boy severely afflicted with a condition that will one day be called Down syndrome.

Gordon wraps his arms around the boy. "This is Peter," he says. "Named after the apostle, because he is my rock. Peter's mother died in childbirth in France, where I had fled to escape from those whom I had disappointed. Peter has the intelligence of a much younger child, but the gentleness and kindness of a Saint. What he lacks in mental ability, Peter makes up for in spirituality."

He stops to wipe his eyes, then continues. "In some ways, he is a painful reminder of my sweet and loving wife and the transgressions for which I will never atone. In other ways Peter is my mentor, for he possesses such a pure heart and forgiving nature that I find myself continually striving to achieve his virtues. Now that Peter is twelve years old—his birthday was just three weeks ago—he is the same age as the boy I betrayed once in Persia, and again in England many years ago."

Ollie is now bathed in Alice's warmth, but the swaggering demons still groan and strut, unwilling to depart after so many years with their gracious host. Though stunned by the appearance of Gordon's son, and moved by his dramatic tale, Ollie clings to the motivating purpose of his life. He will not let God, the Selfish One, alone have the pleasure of punishment.

And then it occurs to Ollie that Gordon has removed his ability to embarrass the man in front of his admirers by the very act of Gordon's public confession. The humiliating truth has been turned to Gordon's advantage.

The demons stir and begin to chatter. *The man is clever,* they say. *Do not trust him. He deserves your vengeance—did he not agree? He has beaten you for now, but humiliation has always been too kind a punishment.*

Ollie tenses as he realizes that, for the first time, he has imagined Gordon's death. His hand jerks, and Alice senses his struggle. She grasps his hand now with both of hers and prays, prays hard. "I forgive you," she says quietly."

"What?" Ollie whispers.

"I forgive you."

"For what?"

Alice looks at him. He has not felt loved since Mary Rogers, but through Alice's gaze he feels love again—the embrace of her eyes, the kindness of her voice.

"I forgive you," she says, "for whatever you are about to do, unless it is to forgive, because for this you need not be forgiven."

The warmth from Alice's hands is almost unbearable. He feels as if he is burning up. He must be ill. A fever!

Gordon whispers something to Peter, then hands the book to his son. The boy looks out at the sea of faces, then cautiously navigates the steps to the sawdust floor and begins walking down the center aisle. "Ali, I don't know where you are," Gordon says, "and I am not sure I would recognize you now that you're a man. But I offer you my son. The sins of the father have been visited upon the son. Forgive my son and you shall forgive me."

The crowd is silent, absolutely captivated, unable to guess what will happen next. All eyes watch the boy as he slowly makes his way down the aisle, kicking up clouds of dust, surveying the faces with heavy-lidded eyes.

Ollie watches Peter intently, and on the screen of the boy's face he sees the countenance of a young Jalal, and Tim Shaw, and his son Isaac, and then astonishingly his own face appears, as if reflected in a mirror, and he realizes at last that through forgiveness he can be forgiven, by accepting the Son he accepts the Father.

The demons groan and Ollie understands now that his dizzying fever was in truth the fires of hell, but now the fever has broken and the demons are fleeing. A great earthquake of revelation overtakes him, with Alice's hands at the epicenter, and he feels a kind of peace and joy that he has not felt since he was twelve and the world was a spiritual place of great expectation and prophets appeared in the clouds.

Peter stops at the twelfth row and closes his eyes. The crowd gasps, wondering what is to occur. Peter turns to his right and looks into Ollie's eyes and Ollie stands, not consciously, but drawn to his feet by some unseen force. He simply finds himself standing and facing the boy. Alice releases Ollie's hand and the sudden disconnection shocks him, makes him feel like a man who cannot swim and is suddenly cast into deep water. He desperately reaches for Alice's hand, understanding that they are meant to be together, that she completes him in some mystical way.

And then he looks at Peter who says, simply, "Forgive me."

He is falling—no, flying; weightless and calm, able to see the distant horizon and the sun which is beginning to rise—and he reaches out to Peter. He embraces the boy.

"It is finished," Gordon says. "I can go about my mission now. Who among you has the courage to forgive? Stand up. Stand up now. Join Ali and Alice and my beloved son in releasing yourself from the bondage of hatred and retribution." The piano begins to play. "Vengeance is mine, saith the Lord. Cleanse yourself, throw off your shackles, and soar into the clouds of your reunion with Christ."

Hundreds rise to their feet, many of them sobbing and holding hands. Gladys races from the back of the tent to her sleeping husband, kneeling by his side in tears. Gordon begins to walk down the aisle toward Peter. He turns to his left, facing a forest of standing people and shouts, "Forgive!"

And suddenly many of them fall to the ground, perhaps a hundred, as if in a trance. Gordon turns to his right and again shouts "Forgive!" and another hundred go down like trees in a great wind, Jonathon among them. On both sides of the aisle, the still-conscious begin to lift the sleeping ones up and carry them to the front of the tent, laying them down in rows like corpses after a battle, removing benches to make room for the stream of incoming bodies. Gordon marches through the great tent; hundreds more fall to the ground. "Take them to the front where they can bury their grudges and awaken fresh in the Lord."

The crowd begins to sing as Gordon returns to the pulpit. Ollie, pulling Alice behind, pushes through the crowd and finds Jonathon unconscious and lying on his back. He kneels down by his friend and says, "Forgive me, please."

As thousands of voices rise in song, the sleeping ones begin to awaken.

"It's like resurrection morning," Alice says, awestruck as the corpse-like bodies begin to stir and sit up, confused at first but soon joining the chorus.

Jonathon awakens and looks up at Ollie. "Are you all right?" Ollie asks.

Pulling his knees to his chest, Jonathon sits up and looks around. He does not answer.

He is too embarrassed.

CHAPTER 31

The Rochester train station is spare, with just one large enclosed room and a worn platform that leans to the west. With a loud series of asthmatic huffs that wheeze out dark clouds of coal-stained smoke, the train groans to a halt.

Through a smeared window, Isaac can see a crowd of about fifty gathering on the platform. C'mon grandma, he yells. Mrs. Rogers plucks a fully stuffed bag from beneath her seat and stiffly follows Isaac down the aisle to the end of the cramped passenger car. Feeling the fresh slap of October air in his face, Isaac clambers down the folding stairs, frantically looking for his father.

An excited voice: Isaac, over here. A whiplash turn of the head. A broad grin like a glint of sunlight. Running. Arms wrapped around him. You've grown, son—three inches at least. A massive outpouring of words and laughter. I hope you haven't forgotten this old woman, Mrs. Rogers says, letting her stuffed bag thud to the platform. Of course not, can't you tell how much I've missed you both?

A feminine clearing of the throat. Oh yes, Ollie says, let me introduce my fiancée Alice Crenshaw. Mrs. Rogers faces the beaming woman and says, Ollie's written so much about you dear. Thank you, Alice replies, and I feel like I know both of you as well.

There is movement, everyone walking, and then Isaac is in a carriage and Ollie drenches him with news and information about his new home town. The Rochester Daily Advertiser was the first daily paper not only in Rochester but in all the United States west of the city of Albany, Ollie explains, and this is important because newspapers chronicle the ever-advancing civilization. Essential work. Nearly twenty-five thousand people live here, so while it's not New York City, it's a thriving metropolis with twenty-two flour mills. And look, right now we're riding over the aqueduct, stupidly built of soft local stone that melted away but now is refurbished, the largest stone arch bridge in America as far as I know, at least that's what the locals boast.

Back in New York City Isaac had started wondering if Ollie had abandoned him. Wasn't that the story of Isaac's life? As if he should expect his good fortune to last. Oh, there had been a river of letters from Ollie describing the exciting new land west of the big city, and tents full of gullible sinners ripe for "saving," but Isaac believed that each day of separation had eroded his tenuous connection to Ollie. Fortunately, with each passing day, Phebe Rogers had become more of a grandma, filling Isaac's parental void with her aromatic cooking and funny stories. She had become the one constant in his life—always there when he had come home from school to ask about his adventures and soothe his frayed nerves.

But then the *Letter* had arrived, and in it Ollie had told of his spiritual re-awakening, his newfound love, his desire to put down roots in a clean city on a freshwater lake. He had apologized for his misleading advice about God and begged Mrs. Rogers—whom he had started calling Mum in his writings—to forgive him; he had not meant to replace Mary in his heart, but Alice Crenshaw had *just happened* to him, as if it were God's will, *and Mum, I know you will love her when you meet, because you have such a generous heart. And you'll meet her soon, because I want all of you to be with me here in Rochester where I've rented a house until Alice and I are married next year.*

The carriage takes them out of the city and up into the surrounding hills. From this elevation Isaac can see the gently curving Genesee River, sparkling in the afternoon light, and beyond the sloping fields a forest of church steeples rising upward like saplings full of promise. The carriage turns sharply onto a winding road that approaches a magnificent Greek Revival farm house, the centerpiece of a fifty acre estate complete with its own barn, smithy, and orchard.

A whitetail buck, its dinner of fallen apples interrupted by the clattering carriage, leaps across the road and is almost struck by the horses.

Is this your home, Isaac asks Ollie. No, it's *our* home, yours and Mum's as much as mine, Ollie says. I bought the property from a man who was down on his luck, as they say, for a fair price—the Christian thing to do—and renamed it Chillington-hall. An odd name, Isaac thinks, but he likes it. Formal. Foreign sounding—English, perhaps.

The carriage pulls up in front of the farm house. This is it, Ollie says, your new home. Let's get your things put away. The trunks are pulled off the carriage by two hired hands, young men in their twenties who seem used to rough and heavy work.

Grinning manically, Ollie ushers Isaac to a bedroom at the top of the stairs containing a narrow bed, a writing desk, a night stand with an oil lamp, and a wooden den chair. You'll have to help me make this into a comfortable room for you, Ollie says, anything you need you let me know. Ollie hugs the boy, runs his fingers through Isaac's coarse mop of hair and says, I'm so glad you're here.

Ollie closes the door behind him and Isaac looks out the window at the vast field behind the house. Small mounds of snow glitter like diamonds waiting to be picked. The sun is low and the edge of the mysterious woods beyond the field casts a deep shadow. Three deer munch grass in the field just one leap from the protection of the forest. Isaac feels at peace here, decides to lie down on the bed. So soft, like a cradle. His head sinks into the pillow.

A loud rap on the door startles Isaac. It is very dark in the room, the moon now the only source of light. How long has he slept? The door opens a crack and Lucas, one of the hired hands, peers through, his face in shadows. Dinner is served, Lucas says.

Leaping out of bed, shaking his head to whisk away the cobwebs. He throws on his clothes and opens the door. The hallway is dim but he can smell food and follows the scent down a creaking staircase to a landing.

Voices.

He moves to their source and finds an entrance wide as a double door into the dining room. Standing there, unnoticed at first, he can see a large dining table covered with a familiar cream-colored table cloth, the one that Mrs. Rogers often used in the boarding house. Imagine! She had thought to bring her own table cloth. The old woman sits at the head of the table with Ollie to her left. An empty chair sits between Ollie and Alice Crenshaw. Across the table from Isaac's father, beyond a gleaming silver candelabra and the china bowls of yellow squash, mashed potatoes and beef gravy, is Jonathon Fury and, to his right, closest to the doorway, an unfamiliar man who looks almost as old as Phebe Rogers. The man has a Santa Claus belly and a ruddy complexion.

Jonathon is the first to see Isaac standing in the doorway. Isaac my boy, do come in. Yes, thank you. Ollie looks up at his son, grinning. Right over here, son, between us. Ollie gestures to the empty chair and it is soon occupied by a famished twelve-year-old. I would like to present my son, Isaac, Ollie says proudly to the unfamiliar man across the table. Ollie, this is Alice's father, the Reverend Theodore Crenshaw. Really, Oliver, the boy can call me Ted.

Ollie pats the boy on the shoulder. I'm sorry I was late, Father, Isaac says, and his words cause everyone at the table to stop what they are doing and stare at the boy because his words are gibberish to their ears. Maybe he speaks in tongues, Reverend Crenshaw suggests, knitting his brows into a look of extreme consternation. No, explains Ollie, he spoke to me in Farsi.

I wanted to surprise you, Father. Do you like hearing your native language? Isaac says in Farsi.

The unexpected blessing overcomes Ollie and his eyes well up with tears. I do like it, especially from my son's lips. But how—? Mrs. Rogers waves her hand to interrupt. The boy is absolutely incorrigible, she says with a warm smile, then adds, He made a new friend, a merchant from Persia who sells rugs—I think he sought the fellow out—and the man agreed to give him some lessons in exchange for help in the store.

Four roasted grouse are delivered to the table, and Reverend Crenshaw says the blessing. Oh God, bless this food for our use, we give thanks for the bounties you bestow upon us. It takes a full three minutes—which is what happens when a preacher is allowed to say the prayer, for they never seem to be able to say goodbye to God, Ollie tells Isaac later—and then the bowls and platters are emptied onto plates and scooped into hungry mouths.

I'm not used to being waited on, Mrs. Rogers says—a timid complaint—and Ollie just laughs. You must get used to it, Mum, he says. The food and the laughter and the hugs are so wonderful that Isaac wants the meal to never end. Heaven can be no better than this, he thinks. Maybe this is heaven.

At last, though, weary and with a full belly, Isaac climbs the stairs carrying a lit candle and a handful of matches for the oil lamp. He stumbles into bed and almost immediately awakens with the sharp glare of sunlight in his eyes. He sits up—for a moment he cannot remember where he is—and then sinks again into his bountiful pillow.

He is home.

CHAPTER 32

The homemade ice cream is exquisite. Everyone groans from the stuffing that their bellies have endured on this last night of 1842. Only three hours until the new year—a most auspicious year, for Jesus will interrupt the calendar sometime in the next 365 days to restore his Kingdom on earth, or so some believe. A fire crackles in the fireplace around which are gathered those closest to Ollie: Alice and the Reverend Theodore Crenshaw, Isaac, Phebe Rogers, Jonathon Fury, and a man recently arrived from London for the holidays, Herbert Eaton.

The Reverend, glancing at Mrs. Rogers, wonders if she notices that he has taken off some of his girth. She is quite a handsome woman, he thinks, even though she is six or seven years his senior. And this kind-hearted woman is a sorceress in the kitchen, too. Who can blame an old preacher from dreaming of a wife?

Herbert Eaton and Ollie murmur quietly to each other, apparently sharing with each other an unending supply of news from their months apart. During a pause in Ollie's conversation with the man he calls his stepfather, Isaac looks up at Herbert and says, "Did you know Ollie's real father?"

"I did, yes," comes the reply.

"I didn't know my real father, or what happened to him."

"Well, I had an opportunity to meet Oliver's father one evening in London," Herbert says. "I found him to be a rather disagreeable fellow, not at all like Oliver, whom I had come to know and love as a son, the same way I'm sure that he came to know and love you."

"And what happened to him? Ollie's father?"

"The truth is, we will probably never know for sure. He returned to Persia after refusing to divorce Oliver's mother, the woman I hoped to marry. After some time I decided to travel to Persia myself, perhaps to reason with him, to convince him to grant a divorce. But while I was there I learned that he had been murdered in some kind of Persian court intrigue."

Herbert turns to Ollie, who is startled by the news; obviously, despite their many words, they have not talked of this.

Isaac remembers meeting Anne, of course, and can still see her radiant features surrounded by the foam of the incoming sea. "Such unusual timing," Isaac says.

"I don't quite follow."

"That Oliver's father should be killed during your visit to Persia."

Herbert looks away sadly, rubs his palms together nervously, and replies, "I have experienced my share of guilt over that same irony, you can be sure."

Ollie studies his mentor with kind eyes. "You should set it behind you."

The Reverend, who has slid into a semi-reclining position in his soft chair, straightens himself and says, "Fortunately, God is merciful."

"How is that?" Herbert asks. "I don't mean to be rude, sir, but I fail to see how these acts of violence that separate us from our loved ones can be an act of mercy."

"They are not," the Reverend replies. "They are also not the acts of God, but of those who have chosen through their own free-will to depart from God's will and sink into a life of sin and degradation."

Jonathon stops fidgeting with his daguerreotypes and interjects, "And where can we find God's mercy, then? He is merciful to the murderers—I can see that—by allowing them to perpetrate their crimes. But where is his mercy to the God-fearing folks who are left behind in the wake of their violence?"

"Jonathon my boy, life is filled with violence and great sadness. Has been ever since Adam and Eve sinned in the Garden. God's mercy, you suggest, must be immediate and material. I suggest his mercy is the gift of eternal life and our eventual reunion with those we have loved and lost, though it takes some patience to appreciate this view."

"And a belief in God," Jonathon says.

"Yes, that too," the Reverend says. "But we are living in a very special age, one in which Jesus will return—within a few months now—to bring the Kingdom of God to Earth, hallelujah."

"Hallelujah," Alice adds.

"We are entering the year in which Jesus will indeed show us God's mercy, as well as his terrible wrath. If you want to see God's mercy, Jonathon, turn unto Him and wait for a few more weeks or months. For me, I would not want to be on the other side."

"How can you be so sure that Jesus will come in 1843?" Isaac asks. "Haven't Christians been awaiting His return every day since He died?"

The preacher instinct rises in Alice and she speaks up. "Perhaps it's a good thing to reflect on this as we prepare to enter the year of the Second Advent of Jesus Christ," she says. "The answer to your question, Isaac, is simple arithmetic. But before we can do our adding and subtracting we must first solve a riddle. Do you like riddles, Isaac?"

The boy nods and smiles.

"Well this riddle has stumped men and women for thousands of years. You see, for a long time mankind has believed that Jesus was telling the truth when he said that he would come again."

"You mean, of course, that *Christians* believed."

"Thank you, Jonathon," Alice says. "Of course that's what I meant. Now Isaac, one of the great mysteries of Christianity is the precise time that Jesus will return. The Bible seems to give us the answer, but the answer is delivered as a kind of riddle."

"Why wouldn't God simply tell us?"

"I can't say for sure, but he seems to have sealed his prophecy so that men would not be able to figure it out until the time was right, and then the answer would be so clear that… well, the man who did unravel this mystery was named William Miller. My father and I lived near him in Vermont.

"He must have been very smart," Isaac says.

"Oh yes, and he studied the Bible long and hard for many years before the answer was made known to him. You see, there are many prophecies in the Bible, but they must be interpreted correctly. Our dear brother William Miller has determined that Jesus will come again between March 21, 1843, and March 21, 1844, according to the Jewish mode of computation of time."

Isaac huddles up against Alice. "So we don't have long to live?"

"We don't have much longer to endure this cruel world, is how I look at it," Alice replies. "But since we have been also assured that husbands and wives will know each other in the next life, Ollie and I would like to make an announcement. Ollie?"

Ollie looks a bit befuddled, but then he catches on to Alice's introduction and stands up with a glass of eggnog in his hand. "Alice and I have decided to get married sooner rather than later."

"With the end of the world coming, that seems like a good idea," Jonathon cynically adds. "Congratulations, my friend. Exactly when is this event to take place? And please don't use Biblical language to obfuscate."

Ollie laughs. "To be perfectly clear about it, we will be wed on March 20th, the day before the first possible date of the Advent.

"We want to be husband and wife when we are taken up in the air to meet Jesus," Alice adds.

"Then I shall have to plan a return visit," Herbert says. "What a wonderful excuse to see you all again."

The group continues to talk until nearly midnight, but by the passing of the old year the Reverend is snoring in his chair, Mrs. Rogers has gone to bed, Isaac is asleep on the rug in front of the fire dreaming of Jesus holding him in his gentle arms, Herbert Eaton and Jonathon are deep in conversation, Alice is praying, and Ollie is reading the book of Revelation, St. John's vision of the End of Times.

> ...and the holy city shall they tread under foot forty and two months. And I will give power unto my two witnesses, and they shall prophesy a thousand two hundred and threescore days, clothed in sackcloth.

Ollie does not understand who the two witnesses are, but it is clear to him that forty-two months is equal to 1260 years. And that a thousand two hundred and threescore days is also equal to 1260 years. The number, duplicated in the Book of Revelation as if for emphasis, makes him shiver.

How odd, he thinks, that the Islamic year 1260, the year in which the Qa'im has been long expected to appear, coincides with the year 1844 in the Christian calendar. And that the Bible seems to prophesy in Islamic years.

Chapter 33

At three o'clock in the morning on the first day of 1843, Ollie awakens to the creaking of floorboards downstairs. It would be wise to check the main floor, he decides. Lighting an oil lamp, he begins shuffling to the door. All is quiet now. He slowly walks down the hallway, the oil lamp casting an eerie glow around him. He softly steps down the eight stairs to a landing, turns right, but before he can navigate the five remaining stairs to the front room a soft voice startles him. A half-whisper.

"Would you be so good as to douse the light?" Herbert says.

Ollie can see the outline of the man. He is seated in a chair that has been pulled over to look directly out a window.

Ollie puts out the light.

"Come over here, then," Herbert says.

Ollie steps down to the main floor and walks to the window, pulling another chair alongside Herbert and sitting down. "Indigestion?" he asks Herbert. "I've had a spot of it myself tonight."

He can smell the sharp odor of alcohol.

"It's snowing. You can see it better in the dark," Herbert says. He is still dressed in his shirt and pants.

Ollie looks out the window. The moonlight through the clouds is faint but still illuminates a scattering of snowflakes. "Beautiful," he says.

"Remember that night in London?"

"What night."

"We went to the theater to see that dreadful pantomime—"

"The Surrey, you mean?"

"Yes, the Surrey."

"Mons. Gouffé, the Man-Monkey."

"That's it—the wooly beast who invaded our box. It was snowing that evening as well."

"And afterward we were crossing the bridge and—"

"The body in the river. Very dramatic that was. The Priest Pennick, wasn't it? Yes, I'm sure of it." Herbert pauses. His right arm rises and Ollie can see a bottle float to Herbert's lips—brandy smuggled into an otherwise booze-free house.

Herbert swallows deeply then coughs and sighs. "Did you know, Ollie, that your mother and that furry Man-Monkey—or rather the unpretentious bastard who played the part—did you know they became lovers? Oh yes, they did."

Ollie is not surprised. He had known that his mother had backslid into sinful ways after the humiliating evening at Almack's, though he had never heard the details.

"Can't blame her, really," Herbert says. His speech is slowing down, becoming slurred. "Her life—I'm sure she thought her life was over. The *ton* would never accept her as a genuine… a genuine member of London society after such a—" he seems to be searching for a word— "such a *scandal*. The only way she could survive—such an inventive woman—the only way, I'm sure, was to play the part. Become an actress. And you know theatre people. No morals at all. Anything to claim center stage."

Herbert takes another slow sip of brandy.

"You must have hated her for that."

"Oh no, no," Herbert says, turning to look at Ollie for the first time. He smiles gently in the dark. "I never stopped loving her—your mother." Herbert turns away and stares out the window again, pausing for such a long time that Ollie wonders if he has fallen asleep. Just as Ollie extends a hand to touch Herbert's arm, the man speaks again, startling him. "It was your father I hated, truth be told. Ruined all our lives."

"I suppose you must blame someone for your misfortune," Ollie says.

"And whom, my son, do you blame for your misfortunes? You've had your share."

"I've learned not to blame. I've learned to forgive."

"Forgive *me*, then, because I'm not up to hearing that evangelical balderdash this evening. You hate just as I hate. I can see it in you."

"You're wrong."

"Oh yes, I can see it. You've always had hate in you. You hated your mother. You hated your father."

"I forgave them."

"Did you hate *me*, Ollie?"

"Never. I loved you. I love you now, you know that."

"After Mary Rogers was murdered—after your mother drowned—who did you hate then? You can't tell me that you suffered these tragedies without hating *someone*."

Ollie stands and walks to the window. "Oh yes, I hated someone," he says. "With such intensity, such passion that it drove me mad for a time."

"Yes, I understand that kind of madness."

"The fact that I could not directly attack the object of my vengeance drove me madder still."

"Yes, it was Gordon, wasn't it? That's why you came to America. That's why you followed this… this dreadful sawdust trail of tent meetings. To seek your revenge."

"Yes, I wanted to hurt Gordon, it's true. To humiliate him." Ollie turns to face Herbert. Even in the dark he can see that Herbert's eyelids are sagging and moisture is filling his eyes. "But my true target was much bigger," Ollie continues. "Much *much* bigger."

Herbert's eyes widen in understanding. "You blamed *God*."

"And all those who spoke for Him."

Herbert blinks once, twice. He thinks about this. "Yes, I can see it," he says. "It makes sense in a terrible sort of way. And here I was, plotting my revenge against a mere mortal."

"What do you mean *revenge*?" Ollie stares hard at Herbert, who looks away.

"Do you think you're the only one driven mad by your tragedies?"

"You traveled to Persia," Ollie says, trying to reshape his memory into a useful pattern. "Mother wrote that you went there to beg my father to divorce her." He kneels down in front of Herbert, who is suddenly avoiding his gaze. "But you were prepared for revenge in case he refused, weren't you? Tell me, Herbert, when my father said *no*—when he laughed at you as I'm sure he did—what did you do?"

Herbert takes a swig of brandy, but Ollie swipes the bottle from his hand.

"Tell me, Herbert. How did my father die?"

Herbert's eyes finally jerk sideways to look at Ollie. He stares into Ollie's dark face, speechless, lips quivering, holding back a flood of emotion. At last he reaches upward with both hands, cradles Ollie's face, and begins to cry.

"I love you, Ollie," he says. "You're all I have left. *Don't make me do this*."

Ollie continues to stare.

"Herbert, tell me."

Tears stream down Herbert's face. His nose is running. He wipes his face on his shirtsleeve.

"Yes, as your mother told you I traveled to Persia. I went with a companion—Eardley Pickwick."

"Pickwick!" The mention of this name startles Ollie. "But he—"

"—was released from the Marshalsea prison when I paid his debts." Herbert sniffs and leans back in his chair. "At first I only meant to help the wretched man. But later he became useful when I traveled to Persia."

"Of course—he spoke the language."

"The longer I was separated from your mother, the deeper my pain grew. Like you, Ollie, I was nearly driven mad with hatred. To me, your father was a devil. I longed for his destruction. In Tehran he was easy to find."

Herbert leans forward now. The tears have stopped. Putting his story into words seems to bring back his passion for vengeance.

"Eardley was able to arrange a meeting. But I knew even before I left London that your father would never agree to a divorce. Your homeland, Ollie, is a savage place. It cost me considerably less than I expected to hire an assassin. And when it was done, no one mourned him." Herbert stares coldly into Ollie's eyes. "Not even you, I suspect."

Ollie sits back on his heels.

The coldness drains from Herbert's eyes and he begins to sob. "Forgive me, my son."

Ollie stands and looks down on his mentor. "It is not my forgiveness you need," he says. And then he leaves Herbert alone in the dark.

CHAPTER 34

It is early March, 1843. During the previous evening, cold air had passed over the warmer waters of the big lake to the north, picking up moisture and heat. Eight inches of unspoiled whiteness now blankets Ollie's farm this morning.

This is a big day indeed, with the wedding at the house and dress-up clothes and a grand meal afterward. An exciting day!

Ollie and two neighbors are shoveling a path to the front door. Rev. Samuel Ezekiel Albinson, an old friend of Rev. Crenshaw, has just arrived by carriage and is kicking his way through the windswept mounds of snow to the front door. He curses softly as cold particles of snow creep into his loose-top boots, then notices Isaac listening and begs forgiveness. "Cold feet bring out the beast in me," he explains.

Jonathon is madly setting up chairs on the front porch and perching his large camera obscura on the awkward tripod, its feet stuck into a snowbank in the front yard. "It couldn't have held off for another day, this snow," Jonathon says to the Reverend as he passes by.

"Can't talk," the Reverend says, "got snow in my boots. It'll be pneumonia for sure." He moves stiffly, stomping his feet on the porch before entering the house.

"Isaac! Are you dressed?" Jonathon shouts.

"Underneath, yes," Isaac says, meaning that beneath his outer garments he's ready for the wedding.

"The only one who's ready, I'm sure." Jonathon replies. "Ollie! Leave the shoveling, will you, and get the bride and the others. I want to make this picture before the guests begin arriving. This is the most disorganized event I've ever seen."

Ollie chucks his shovel blade-first into a snowbank and gallops into the house. "Be just a minute," he says, grinning. "Have patience, my friend. You'd think it was your wedding, the way you're so nervous about it."

"Just trying to keep things moving around here."

Isaac picks up the shovel.

"Leave the shoveling, will you?" Jonathon shouts at the boy. "And peel off that coat. As soon as the others appear, we're going to make a group picture and that'll be done. The rest of the day is someone else's worry. And hurry up the others, will you? That's a good lad."

Isaac enters the house and closes the door. Jonathon levels the camera, but just when he seems pleased with the shot, the front leg sinks more deeply into the snow, lowering the camera's front. He fiddles, moving the legs, pushing them firmly into the snow, playing with the focus, then consulting his watch.

Another carriage shows up—friends of Rev. Crenshaw and Alice.

"This is what I was afraid of," Jonathon barks to himself before stomping up the front stairs to the porch and pushing open the door. "The guests are arriving, I hope you're satisfied!"

"We're coming, dear," Mrs. Rogers says. Her words are spoken in a melodious, disembodied voice. She is nowhere to be seen. But then, as if expertly choreographed, the entire wedding party materializes at once and even Jonathon can't help but smile as he sees their beaming faces.

"All right, then," Jonathon says. "Onto the porch—and no boots. We'll make the picture and then you can get on with the wedding."

Jonathon leads the group outdoors, gestures to the chairs, and gives instructions as to where each person should stand or sit. He pushes his way through the snow to the camera and blows a faint dusting of snowflakes off the ground glass, which instantly fogs. "Damn!" he says. But the fog lifts quickly and he fine-tunes his focus.

Ollie and Alice are standing behind the two chairs, Alice in a striking black silk dress with white fur trim. Isaac stands to the right of Ollie in a smart wool suit and dark tie, and Rev. Albinson, looking far too much like an undertaker in his tall black hat and black suit, stands to the left of Alice.

"We're ready for the bride and groom," Jonathon says.

Rev. Crenshaw, gently assisting Phebe Rogers by the arm, guides her into one of the chairs, then sits down beside her. He has lost perhaps thirty pounds, and his groom's face is radiant in the outdoor light. Phebe, though five years older than the Reverend, looks ten years younger in her gray silk gown and white fur.

"This is the last time any of us will be able to call you Mrs. Rogers," Rev. Crenshaw says to Phebe with a wry smile. "From now on, Mrs. *Crenshaw*!"

Jonathon covers the lens with a cap and slides the plateholder into the camera. "You must be very still now," Jonathon explains, then uncovers the lens. He counts off the seconds and then replaces the cap onto the lens with a sigh. "Very good. Thank you very much."

"One more," says Ollie. "With you in it."

"But I'm the photographer," Jonathon says.

"You've shown Isaac how to do your magic. I insist."

Isaac grins and leaps from the porch into the snow, slashing his way to the camera. With a look of resignation, Jonathon marches up onto the porch and peels off his coat and boots, taking Isaac's place in the grouping.

"You must be very still now," Isaac says, irreverently repeating Jonathon's instruction. "How many seconds today?"

Jonathon holds up fingers. Isaac nods and makes the picture. Everyone laughs when it is over, even Jonathon, for he has never had his own picture taken. "I don't like it much," he says, "having to stand still."

CHAPTER 35

No sooner have the Crenshaws settled into the Reverend's comfortable house but another wedding seems to sprout from the moist April soil, this event much simpler than the last. Alice has decided upon a small family wedding and on her special day she descends Ollie's creaking staircase in a brownish-green pelisse—a spartan day-dress with a high neck and long sleeves—and a dark green bonnet. A veil clouds her face like a puff of her father's cigar smoke.

For just a moment, the veil whisks Oliver back to Bushruyíh and the magnificent image of his veiled mother reposing on silk cushions in the anderun.

Reverend Crenshaw presides over the short service, with Jonathon as Best Man and Phebe Crenshaw as Matron of Honor. Oliver and Alice stand before the Reverend as Isaac sings the *Twilight Hymn*. The boy has perfect pitch and an angelic voice that astonishes Oliver, who has never heard the boy sing. In this atmosphere of expectation for the imminent Return of Christ, the words of the hymn provoke shivers in all present:

> Yes, when the toilsome day is gone,
> And night with banners gray,
> Steals silently the glade along
> In twilight's soft array,
>
> I love to steal awhile away
> From every cumbering care,
> And spend the hours of setting day
> In gratitude and prayer.
>
> I love to meditate on death!

When shall his message come
With friendly smiles to steal my breath
And take an exile home?

I love by faith to take a view
Of blissful scenes in heaven;
The sight doth all my strength renew,
While here by storms I'm driven.

When the hymn is finished, the Reverend turns to his daughter and reminds her that she is the Bride of Christ. "In Revelation 19:7 we are told that the bride makes herself ready for the marriage and the marriage supper by providing herself a garment of good works," he says; this is the only part of the sermon that Isaac will remember in future years.

"My dearest daughter, all Christians do not work for Christ, therefore all will not be the bride. The absence of this garment will cause an unfaithful Christian to be 'put away' as it were, in the darkness outside the wedding feast. It is the darkness outside the feast where the unfaithful will be, while those who have been faithful will be enjoying a communion and fellowship not shared by all. Be faithful always."

To Oliver the Reverend says, "My son, you have brought great joy to my daughter and to our home. This marriage may last only a day, perhaps just an hour, because Jesus is coming soon to take us all from the earthly storms that are driving us, as that stirring hymn reminds us. But in heaven your marriage is eternal. You will be together always."

Afterward, Jonathon photographs the wedding party. He does not believe that Jesus is coming, and he suspects that Ollie and Alice will cherish the picture in their old age on earth. Anyway, if Jesus *does* come and abduct his friends from earth, Jonathon is quite certain that he will be left alone to care for the farm. This picture, then, will be a memorial to his friendships after they are gone.

A wet April quickly becomes a hot and muggy summer. Now that school is out, Isaac is free to pester Ollie with his newfound passion—learning Farsi, his father's native tongue. On evenings when Ollie is not traveling to gather material for his articles, Isaac demands lessons. He wants to be like his father. He wants to communicate with him in the language that was Ollie's boyhood language. He wants nothing to be lost in translation.

At first he finds his mouth and tongue ill-suited for the foreign sounds he tries to duplicate, but before long he has mastered the odd nasals and glides, the unfamiliar labial stops and palatal affricates and high-back rounded vowels. His early vocal gymnastics make Ollie smile, but bemusement soon changes to pride as Isaac's harsh New York accent melts into the caramelized textures of the Farsi tongue. An incessant exchange of utterances becomes a secret language between father and son. The intimacy and exclusivity of it strengthens a bond that neither of them has ever experienced before. By autumn, Isaac and Ollie are speaking to each other primarily in Persian, with Alice defensively picking up a few words here and there to fling into a conversation, often inappropriately.

Isaac's linguistic immersion floats above the strong ebb and flow of religious emotion. Expectation of the rapture causes tension, even among those who long for it. At times the anticipation manifests joy and euphoria, but sometimes—usually in the stillness of night—emotion turns to anxiety, even fear. The thought of being snatched up bodily, plucked like a ripe orange from the tree of life, separated from all that is familiar and known, to face the fearsome countenance of God—this can be terrifying. What will it feel like? Will sins be exposed to everyone? *What if I am left behind?*

Mornings, of course, can be even worse than the nights.

On a Wednesday morning in late October, as Isaac prepares for school, Alice suddenly awakens alone in bed. Panic-struck, she screams and runs from the bedroom, pale and trembling. Seeing Isaac downstairs, she cries out, "No, Isaac—not you, too!"

Alice stumbles down the stairs and Isaac rushes to her. "Ollie's been taken!" she shouts. "He's been taken and we've been left!" She seems still to be dreaming.

Isaac grabs her shoulders and shakes, but she starts sobbing and repeating the words, "My God, Isaac, we've been left behind!"

Isaac turns at the sound of a door creaking open. Ollie, who has been drinking tea on the porch, has entered.

"It's all right, Alice," he says. "I'm here."

Confused, Alice turns to Ollie and says, "You've been left, too?"

"We are all here, Sweetheart. All of us," Ollie replies. "The time has not yet arrived for any of us to be taken."

Alice stares at her husband and tries to gather her thoughts. Isaac releases her. She rakes her fingers through her matted hair and shakes her head as if this will encourage clarity. "Oh," she says weakly.

And then they have a nice breakfast of tea and eggs.

Several weeks later, on a Thursday evening, the Crenshaws come to the Chadwick's farmhouse for dinner, an occurrence that takes place several times each week. Phebe brings a freshly baked chocolate cake. After dinner, Phebe retires to the living room to read her magazine while the Reverend reports statistics about the number of recent local converts to Alice and Ollie.

"Five more souls to join us on the day of rapture," the Reverend declares. "Old man Fogarty is still a hold-out, however, despite the efforts of his entire family to save him. Tough old coot. Satan's got a firm grip on him."

"That's wonderful news, Papa," Alice says. "I mean about the five converts, not about Ben Fogarty." She looks unusually plump and happy. She leans and burrows into Ollie's chest on the sofa. Ollie wraps his arms around her.

"Any day now," the Reverend says somberly. "It will happen soon, I can feel it in my bones."

"Maybe it's your arthritis," Jonathon says, teasing the old man.

"You should take this more seriously, Jonathon." The Reverend puffs out his chest and his voice takes on the officious intonation of the preacher. "In these last days, I tell you all, we should be tireless in our efforts to save every soul that can be saved. I'm afraid that we may be holding up Christ's return because there are souls to be saved that we have not yet reached. Alice, we need you back in the pulpit."

"Papa!" Alice cuts off her father with a gentle word. "God has called me to another purpose right now."

"My dear, no other purpose can be so noble as to use your gifts for evangelism..."

"Papa, listen to me!" The smile is gone from Alice's face. She pulls away from Ollie, arches her back, and then takes Ollie's hand. With a tender glance at her husband she says, "I'm going to be a mother."

Ollie is as surprised as the Reverend.

Isaac grins radiantly.

"Are you sure?" Ollie asks.

"I saw Doctor Malcomb. There's no doubt."

Ollie sits, dazed, as the Reverend springs from his chair and lumbers to his daughter, embracing her.

"That's wonderful news, my dear. But it's early—I'm sure that God will give you the strength to…"

Alice interrupts him again. "The Doctor said that I have a very frail framework—as he put it—and a constitution that, for whatever reason, will make bearing this child somewhat risky for both the baby and me. He cautioned me to eliminate physical and emotional stress wherever possible. I think that traveling and preaching is out of the question for now."

As if just now coming out of a trance, Ollie stands and shouts, "Did you hear that Isaac? Jonathon? I'm going to be a father!"

He steps to his son and his friend. They shake his hand and pat him on the back as the Reverend retakes his seat, somewhat sadly.

The Reverend says, "Such joyful news, and yet—"

"And yet what, Papa?"

"And yet… what's the point? Surely we'll all be taken into the arms of Jesus before the child will be born."

The group's joy drains away.

"Oh Papa, surely there is a reason that I was given this gift."

The Reverend's expression turns even sourer. "Oh God, why do you test us in this way?"

"In what way, Papa?"

"This child of yours is conceived in sin. You know the Psalm. It says, 'Behold, I was brought forth in iniquity, and in sin my mother conceived me.' Until baptism, a child is condemned to suffer the consequences of humanity's sins. If Jesus should come before it is born, it cannot come with us."

Alice had not considered this complication.

"But Grandpa," Isaac says, "it doesn't seem fair that an unborn child could be condemned to hell. How can a child that's not even born be held accountable?"

The Reverend is too invested in his theology to invoke common sense, yet he makes an attempt at logic when he replies, "The unborn child, the infant, and young children have not had the time or the life experience necessary to understand the requirements of salvation. Would you agree? I thought so. They are unable to understand the awesome responsibilities of making a covenant with

God. Therefore, the spiritual condition of the unborn, the infant, and young children is the same as any unconverted person who has never had the opportunity for salvation."

Unhappy with this opinion, Isaac curses in Persian. Ollie glances at his son, wondering where Isaac could have learned such a thing, then remembers the time he ran his shin into a railing in front of the boy.

"Papa, baptism is surely a way to salvation for children, is it not?" Alice pleads.

"Yes, of course, but this child is not yet born." There is a long silence. "Wait a minute. Are you suggesting…?"

Ollie immediately understands the direction of his wife's thinking. He interjects, "I want my child to be baptized tonight."

With an enormous sigh, the Reverend puts his hands to his temples, rubbing them so hard he leaves fingerprints. His brow wrinkles and his face reddens as if he is lifting a heavy weight. Then he says, "This is a rather technical issue."

Phebe, silent until now, loudly puts down her magazine and says, "For goodness sake, Theodore, baptize the child. God is the judge here, not you."

"I agree with Phebe," Jonathon says. "Never believed in all this dunking and sprinkling, but unless baptism can be a sin, I don't see what harm it can do. In fact, if you really believe that Jesus might come any minute, you might hurry it up a bit."

And so the Reverend agrees to improvise a baptism ceremony for the unborn child. That evening, the group surrounds Alice, who remains seated on the sofa next to Ollie. The Reverend pulls some random scraps of scripture out of his memory, a few of which relate to the unfolding event. And then he unbuttons Alice's dress over her abdomen, exposing white skin. Taking a handful of water from a teacup, he drizzles her belly and she coos "Oooh!" as the cool water drips onto her warm flesh. After a few more words from the standard Baptism ceremony and a short prayer, the service is over and Phebe fetches plates of dessert—the "most important part of the ceremony," according to Jonathon.

CHAPTER 36

The following week is a time of dreams. In a ramshackle house two farms removed from Ollie's homestead, a nine-year-old girl, Winnie Talbot, is awakened at four oclock in the morning. Running into her parent's bedroom, she shakes her mother.

"What is it dear?" Edith Talbot asks. "Another dream?"

Winnie nods.

"A scary one?"

Winnie shakes her head. "Just sad," she says.

Winnie's father, Ed, has had enough of the girl's nightmares. God has cursed him with a daughter who suffers from a kind of madness. Even though his wife and many of the neighbors (especially the religious ones) think of Winnie as an oracle, Ed knows better. His mother was mad, and his grandfather—both of them subject to prolonged periods of melancholy, like Winnie, during which they would sit and stare speechlessly for days or weeks.

"I'm glad your words have come back, Winnie," Edith says, stroking her daughter's hair. "Care to tell me about it?"

"There was a man standing under a palm tree."

Edith considers this. Confused, she says, "And the man was sad?"

"No," Winnie says. "He was happy. But I was sad."

"Why were you sad, Winnie?"

"Because he is going to die."

"When, Winnie—when is he going to die?"

"On the last day of the year."

"Then why is he happy?"

"Because the one he has been waiting for will come soon after."

Edith Talbot has no idea what this dream means, but surely Reverend Crenshaw will know. And possibly old lady Peterson on the far side of town, and Felix Shims at the Methodist Church, and... Many people who will want to know that Winnie has had another dream.

At the precise time of Winnie's dream, it is noon in the Ottoman Empire. Once each year, Siyyid Kazim, the leader of the Shaykhis, visits the tomb of the Imam Husayn, and this is that special day. Traveling with more than twenty students, he stops at a large palm tree to perform the Muslim noonday prayer. The faithful gather around him while a grizzled shepherd, who was sitting on the stony ground near the tree when they arrived, watches from a few paces away.

"Join us if you wish, my friend," Siyyid Kazim says to the shepherd, who seems astonished at the presence of the Siyyid and nods timidly.

After devotions, Kazim stands and stretches. The students sip from their water gourds. Kazim is not yet fifty, but his bones feel as if he is eighty. A constant pain in his stomach keeps him up most nights, and life itself seems to be seeping out of him one drop at a time.

The shepherd shyly approaches Kazim. "I believe that I have a message for you," he says.

"For me?" Kazim says, surprised..

"If you are Siyyid Kazim, yes."

Kazim is bewildered. How could this shepherd know his name? "Who sent this message?' he asks.

The shepherd bows suddenly. "The Prophet Muhammad," he answers. "I cannot understand why He chose such a lowly creature as me. I must be mistaken."

The shepherd's words catch the attention of the group. Siyyid Kazim takes the man's hand and lifts the shepherd to his feet. "You were seated here before we arrived. You were expecting me. How is that possible? Even I did not know that we would offer our prayers at this spot until we stopped here."

The shepherd's dark eyes, folded into deeply set wrinkles carved by years of squinting, seem to brighten. "It is too much for an old man to believe that God would speak to me. I waited here to prove that my dream was just an old man's fantasy."

"I have had dreams, too," Kazim says. "Tell me about yours."

After a deep breath, the shepherd begins to speak. "Three days ago I was tending my flock in the field over there." The shepherd points beyond the palm tree to a stony meadow. "As my sheep were grazing, I reclined against a large stone and fell asleep. A dream came to me, and in this dream I saw Muhammad, the Apostle of God, who spoke to me. The prophet said, *Give ear to My words, and treasure them in your heart. For these words of Mine are the trust of God which I commit to your keeping.*"

The shepherd is suddenly overcome with emotion. He drops to his knees and says, "Forgive me if this dream if not of God!"

Kazim kneels beside the old man. "You said the message was for me," he says. "You must deliver it."

The shepherd rubs his face with dusty hands, shakes his head, and calms himself with a whistling exhalation through cracked lips. "The Prophet told me to stay near this tree. *On the third day after this dream*, He said, *a descendant of My house, Siyyid Kazim by name, will alight at the hour of noon beneath the shadow of the palm tree. As soon as your eyes fall upon him, seek his presence and convey to him My loving greetings.*"

Kazim touches the man's shoulder, and the warmth of his hand seems to soothe the shepherd. "What were His greetings?" Kazim asks gently.

"I am to say, on behalf of the Prophet, *Rejoice, for the hour of your departure is at hand. When you shall have performed your visits to the tomb of the Imam Husayn and returned to Karbala...*" The old man stops, looks up at Siyyid Kazim with great sadness and then continues: "*...there, on the day of 'Arafih, you will wing your flight to Me.*"

A gasp rises from Kazim's followers. This old man has announced that Siyyid Kazim will soon die, on the day of 'Arafih, which—though they do not know it—corresponds to the last day of the year on the Christian calendar.

The shepherd continues. "I do not understand the last part of the Prophet's message. He said that I should tell you, *Soon after, He who is the Truth shall be made manifest. Then shall the world be illuminated by the light of His face.*"

Having pronounced his ominous message, the old man sits on the ground. Grieved at the news of their master's death sentence, the students begin to weep.

"There is no doubt as to the truth of your dream," Kazim says to the shepherd and then turns to his weeping followers. "And as for you—why do you weep and groan? Did you not hear the good news? The appearance of the Promised One is at hand. Why are you sad? Would you not wish me to die, that the Promised One may be revealed?"

The weeping stops. Siyyid Kazim tenderly embraces the old shepherd.

One of the students says, "It's not fair that after all your work you will not live to see the prophecy fulfilled."

Smiling, Kazim turns to the young speaker and says, "From what other seat would you rather witness such a glorious day?"

In Rochester, by lunchtime on the day of Winnie's dream, Edith Talbot has spread the news of her daughter's most recent vision to most of her friends. The Evangelicals are buzzing with excitement; surely the dream means *something*. By three o'clock, a group of churchmen track down Reverend Crenshaw and corner him in his kitchen. "What is the meaning of the oracle's dream?" they all ask at once. The churchmen look to the Reverend as their advent advisor, a fount of mystical wisdom about the end times.

"I don't like the word *oracle*," the Reverend says. "Winnie's a child of God—a bit odd, but many of the prophets of old were a bit off plumb, too. Sometimes I think that those with special, uh, *mental aberrations*—as it were—possess a gift, or an openness to receiving God's word."

"Yes, yes, of course," says Pastor Phelps of the Congregational Church. He is impatient. "But does this dream have anything to do with the Return of Christ? The year is almost gone, and we're still waiting!"

Reverend Crenshaw, now sixty pounds lighter than his previous self, rises nimbly to his feet as if about to take the pulpit. He begins to pace.

"I believe the dream does pertain to His return, yes. Why would God be communicating to us now if not to speak about the Second Coming? It is logical that this dream is meant to reveal something profound about that great event."

"So who is the man beneath the palm tree?" demands Felix Shims, a deacon at the Methodist Church. "And why is he happy if he's going to die on New Year's Eve?"

"And who is this person who is coming after this fellow dies?" asks the Baptist minister.

"Here's what I believe," the Reverend says. "The palm tree represents Christianity. Did not Christ ride into Jerusalem on Palm Sunday, symbolically introducing Christianity to the world?"

The churchmen all nod yes. This makes sense.

"And the man beneath the palm tree, beneath that symbol of Christianity, must represent all Christians!"

The churchmen murmur approval. Why had they not seen this?

Felix Shims, however, is troubled by the Reverend's interpretation. "Are you saying that Christianity is going to die at the end of this year?" he says.

"My dear friend," the Reverend replies jovially, "in this dream, *death* must surely represent the death of this wicked world in which we live. The Christian beneath the palm tree is happy because the end of this world means the beginning of the reign of Christ. Did not Winnie say that the man was happy because the one he is waiting for—and I can only suggest that he is waiting for the return of Christ—will come soon after?"

"Astonishing!" remarks the Baptist minister. "It makes sense."

But Felix Shims is not satisfied. "Wait just a minute here, Reverend," he says. His brow is furrowed. "If the world comes to an end on New Year's Eve, then how can Christ come *soon after*? My understanding is that Christ's return is what brings about the end of the world. Doesn't that mean that He will have to come *right before*, rather than *soon after*?"

The churchmen grow silent. Perhaps they had agreed with the Reverend too soon.

Reverend Crenshaw scratches his head. "You raise a good point, Felix," he says, buying time to think. In a flash it comes to him. Of course!

"But then again, would you not all agree that we must die before we can be resurrected?" the Reverend asks.

Everyone agrees.

"And that our old nature must die before we can be *born again* in Christ?"

Again, there is no dissent.

"Then, my friends, does it not hold that the world must die before Christ returns? Is he not the life *giver*? This is the true meaning of the dream. On New Year's Eve, the world will die—spiritually or symbolically or in reality, I don't know which—but the world will die, and we will know it when it does. And shortly thereafter, Christ will return in the Glory of the Father to bring life abundant to believers in Him."

Spontaneous applause greets his creative output. Not until after supper will it occur to the Reverend that he has set a precise date for the end of the world.

Chapter 37

Through the window of the Rochester Inn, Ollie can see the November snow descending in a suffocating fury. Ollie sits across a pine table from newspaperman Thomas Sharp. It is not the icy wind whistling through the cracked window pane that causes Ollie to shiver; it is the harrowing tale being spun by the editor of the *Warsaw Signal*.

"Since the death of your friend Horace Carter, you've been living in terror," Ollie summarizes as Sharp stops his monologue to sip his coffee.

"Unfortunately, I can't prove that the Mormons were responsible for his death, though I've tried."

"You could be wrong."

"You don't know these people the way I do. Horace was a Mormon, then left the Faith. This is unforgiveable to them. Their secret Avenging Angels track down apostates and spill their blood on the soil, believing that only this can redeem their traitorous souls in the eyes of God."

"If they are the murderous lot you make them out to be, why have they not killed you? Why stop at intimidation?"

"Believe me, there are nights when I wish they would burst into my room and spill my blood, just to get it over with. I feel like a man who's been marching for months toward the gallows. On the streets I sometimes see them staring. Some nights I hear footsteps outside the window. But that's not the worst of it."

"What could be worse?"

"Their intimidation has had the desired effect. It has rendered my pen impotent."

"I think you over-dramatize your surrender. In the past weeks I've read your articles and I would not characterize your writing as timid."

"Ahhh, but you don't know the words that were *not* written!"

"I do know, however, what you *did* write. I've followed your articles… dare I say *religiously*? You criticized the formation of the Nauvoo Legion."

"To no avail. It may now be the most powerful army in the land. Who could have known that when Joseph Smith moved his band of outcasts to Nauvoo, that mosquito-infested hell-hole would become a military headquarters."

"You decried the Nauvoo city charter that authorized the Legion, and Joseph Smith's land transactions. You've denounced their prophet himself… and his excessive power."

"Excessive power seems almost too modest a description for someone who is mayor, lieutenant-general of the Nauvoo Legion, presiding judge of the highest city court, land speculator, and political boss. But I have not protested a new ordinance passed by the Nauvoo city council that allows the city to review all state arrest orders! This puts more than power in the hands of Mr. Smith. It makes him essentially *exempt from civil law*!"

"Then you must write your conscience," Ollie says.

Thomas Sharp pulls a wrinkled piece of paper out of his coat pocket and puts it on the table. His eyes urge Ollie to read it. "I have written my conscience," Sharp explains. "But I lack the courage to publish it. I believe that my health depends on my silence in this matter."

Ollie reads some of the written words aloud: "Now we ask our citizens; what think you of this barefaced defiance of our laws by the City Council of Nauvoo, and if persisted in, what must be the final result?"

"Violence." Sharp replies, answering the question he had written. "I believe violence may be inevitable. I have it from a most trustworthy source that Joseph Smith is going to write a letter to several of the candidates for the United States presidency. He will be asking them if they are willing to validate and sustain Mormon rights with federal power."

"I can't believe that any candidate would agree to such a thing."

"Probably not, but Mr. Smith has the entire Mormon vote to pledge. If they all refuse, however, I understand that Smith is prepared to declare himself a candidate."

"Joseph Smith? President of the United States?"

"His ambition knows no bounds. And for every decision he makes, he can testify that God revealed to him indisputable divine guidance."

Ollie stops to think about this. "Have you wondered if the man truly is a prophet?"

"Oliver, he is a polygamist. His followers kill people for heresy."

Ollie again stops to think. This description sounds like the great mujtahids of Islam. These wise men certainly were not prophets, and they represented a counterfeit religion. Only Christianity, of which Mormonism most certainly is a clever perversion, bears the stamp of authenticity.

"Your grudge with the Mormons is a political one," Ollie says at last. "My dispute with Joseph Smith is purely religious."

"Personally, Oliver, I don't care if your dispute is over the color of his eyes. The anti-Mormon movement needs every man of influence it can find. Your stories appear in many newspapers. You could help make the case for controlling this madman."

Ollie stares across the table at Thomas Sharp. "If you publish this story"—he holds up Sharp's wrinkled article—"I will help."

"You drive a hard bargain. It's my life on the line, you know." Sharp extends his hand, almost tipping over the oil lantern that burns brightly in the center of the table.

Ollie takes the man's hand and shakes it once, firmly.

CHAPTER 38

Over the next month Ollie weakly honors his agreement with Thomas Sharp by publishing several articles critical of the Mormons. In Ollie's mind, though, the Mormon issue fades daily as the world seems to rapidly pitch toward the Second Coming. Every conversation and each prayer anticipates that auspicious event. Reverend Crenshaw has assured everyone that Christ will return by the end of the year—before the start of 1844, he has promised. Though no one will put a date or time on His Glorious Return, the Rochester Christians almost universally look to New Year's Eve as the perfect occasion.

In the week following Christmas, emotions begin to erupt. The clock is ticking down. Many Christians report that they can't sleep. Many non-Christians suddenly declare their belief in Jesus and beg forgiveness for their lives of slumber and sin. Prayers rise like a continuous mist from the city and surrounding villages. Work all but ceases. Procrastinating wives and daughters sew white ascension robes. Apocalyptic nightmares cause brave husbands and sons to tremble and scream. Many farmers say their animals are growing restless. A waitress in Rochester breaks down sobbing and has to be sedated by Doc Anderson. The bell ringer at the Baptist church begins singing a hymn and can't be stopped.

On New Year's Eve, the whole family gathers at Ollie's house for the Big Event. Except for Jonathon, they are all wearing white ascension robes. The afternoon passes slowly with the offering of many prayers and the singing of many solemn hymns. Isaac can feel his gut tightening in anticipation of the Appearance of Jesus in the clouds. It could come at any time now.

As the sun sets and darkness envelopes the farm, Phebe offers to make some supper. "I'm sure everyone is hungry by now," she says.

"Phebe, we have no need for food, my dear," Reverend Crenshaw says. "Come and sit by me. These old bodies of ours will soon be called up to a place where food has no meaning."

Ollie cradles his wife on the sofa. "You're trembling," he says. "Afraid?"

"I don't think so," Alice replies. "A little maybe. Excited mostly."

"When He comes," the Reverend explains with great confidence, "we will wonder why we were ever nervous about it, so wonderful it will be."

Phebe takes her husband's hand and squeezes it. "Still, I'm a little scared."

"So we will be able to enter heaven without dying," Isaac says. "Just like Ezekiel."

Jonathon is preparing his camera for the event. He is quite certain that he will not be going anywhere with his friends. In fact, he is quite sure that no one will be leaving the farm this evening. At the start of the New Year, 1844, he will take a picture of the friends he is with, just as he has for the past two years. And if by some chance his friends vanish, he will make a self-portrait and title it "*I Was Wrong*."

For a few minutes the crackle of the fireplace is the only sound in the house. Reverend Crenshaw takes out a pocket watch, studies it, and then puts it away. "Less than four hours on this earth," he says.

A loud knock on the door interrupts them.

Phebe shrieks. Isaac scurries across the floor to sit by Ollie. They stare at the front door. Is this how it will happen? A knock on the door to collect them for their journey to heaven?

Another knock! Louder.

Bravely, Ollie stands and walks to the door. "Who is it?" he asks.

"Edith Talbot. And Winnie," a voice replies.

Ollie opens the door and the two Talbots enter with a cold wind. Nine-year-old Winnie, the local oracle, stomps her feet to clear off the caked snow.

"We got here as soon as we could," Edith says excitedly. "Didn't know where else to go." She turns to Reverend Crenshaw. "Thought you would be here tonight, Reverend. Glad you're all here."

Ollie escorts them into the center of the room. "Please, take off your coats," he says.

"No, we don't have time."

"For goodness sake, Edith, what's this all about?" the Reverend says.

Edith turns to the old man. "It's Winnie, sir. She's had another vision."

The Reverend stands and approaches Winnie, then turns to look at the faces of his family as if to say, "*It's beginning.*" Winnie is absolutely calm, but the Reverend's eyes reveal a nervousness that was not present before.

"You don't have to be afraid, Reverend. It's wonderful," Winnie says.

"How is it wonderful, Winnie?"

"I saw a cloud in the night sky that was filled with lights. It flashed bright, and the lights rolled around inside it. And then the dark sky started to glow, and a wind started up. I could feel it on my face, and even though it was cold outside, the wind was warm. I looked away for just a second, and when I looked back a hundred angels were starting to gather around the cloud. Maybe a thousand. I think they're getting ready for Jesus."

These words penetrate Reverend Crenshaw and the strength goes out of his legs, which buckle. On his knees he raises his hands and shouts, "It's true. He is coming at last!"

They do not feel the frigid air as they race out of the house into the moonlit night like white ghosts. Jonathon trails them with his camera and tripod.

Storm clouds have eerily gathered on the horizon like a bunched-up shroud. The clouds roll ominously and threaten to obscure the full moon just beyond them.

"Quickly now," the Reverend urges, "Up onto the barn." He and Isaac lift a wooden ladder from the side of the barn, setting it upright against the roof. "Careful now." The Reverend climbs the ladder first. Once he is on the roof he turns and helps Phebe off the ladder, then Alice. Edith and Winnie are next, followed by Isaac.

Edith places her left foot on a patch of ice and begins to slip, but Isaac catches her dress and she regains her footing.

It seems to Ollie that being a few feet closer to heaven is not much of an advantage. Besides, heights bother him. "I'm staying down here," he replies. He turns to see his friend setting up a camera and flash pot. "With Jonathon," he adds.

The roof dwellers find places to sit. The Reverend turns to the oracle and says, "Winnie, do you see any clouds that look like the ones in your vision?"

The girl scans the horizon. "Not yet," she says, "but they're changing real fast."

"And they're quickly coming towards us," Alice says. For the first time, seated there in the winter chill, she feels cold. She wishes that Ollie were there to put his arms around her.

For five minutes, nothing happens. The sky watchers begin to shiver.

"Anything, Winnie?" the Reverend asks hopefully.

The girls shakes her head no.

"Let me get your coats!" Ollie yells, but he is shushed by the others. He looks up at the sky. Just to the east is a growing mountain of clouds. It looks like a thunderhead, rare as that would be in winter.

"There!" Winnie says, pointing to the thunderhead. "There!"

All heads swivel to look in the direction of her finger. The cloud formation is both frightening and awe-inspiring. It tumbles and tilts. And then it happens.

A single flash!

Then more lights. They're in the clouds. They dance.

The Reverend stands up. "It's time!" he shouts. "Just like Winnie said!" And then he helps Phebe up. Alice is still grasping her knees, too mesmerized to stand. Isaac helps Edith and Winnie to their feet.

Below, Ollie stares at the spectacle and says to himself, "It's really true."

Jonathon looks up at the sky as another flash ignites the center of the thunderhead in a yellow-blue burst.

"Winter lightning," he says. "Very rare." No one hears him.

No one is listening.

As the thunderhead lights up again, Alice starts to stand. She is just saying, "I'm ready, dear Lord…" when a terrifying clap of thunder tears through the night, startling her. She starts to fall. Steps backward to catch herself. Skids on a patch of ice. Tumbles over the edge of the roof, arms outstretched, robes flying majestically, body suddenly crunching against the frozen ground, eyes still open, smiling.

Horrified, Ollie rushes to her. Scoops her into his arms. Sees the spattered blood and lifeless eyes. Knows she is gone.

With gasps and moans the others scurry back down the ladder. The reality of death has erased their thoughts of eternal life. The spectacular meteorological exhibition continues, but by the time Alice's body is carried into the house the show is over.

Alice is the only one who is taken that evening, but not in the way they had thought. Everyone else is left behind, and the torment is as terrible as they had imagined.

Jesus did not come in the clouds.

At least not in Rochester, New York.

At the time of Alice Crenshaw's fall from the roof, Siyyid Kazim lies on his sleeping mat surrounded by nine of his students. Perspiration drains from his fevered body, soaking his white garments. One of the students, Jahangir, reaches for Kazim's hand and is startled by its heat.

"Your fever grows," Jahangir says.

"Perhaps the fire within me," Kazim replies hopefully, "is purging the last of my imperfections before I depart this world."

"I have been praying that you will be healed!" Jahangir replies.

"You should be praying that you will accept God's will."

"It cannot be God's will that you die before the Qa'im appears. That would be unfair. No one has worked harder to prepare us for His…"

Kazim angrily interrupts the young student. "And who are you to question God's fairness?" He painfully raises himself up on one elbow to look into his student's eyes. "Have you the foresight to see the end in the beginning? My death, which God told a shepherd would happen on the day of 'Arafih, is the beginning of the end. And what day is this, Jahangir?"

"The day of 'Arafih," Jahangir sadly replies.

Kazim collapses onto his mat but continues to converse with the young student, though his words now come in short bursts between gasps for breath. "Of which offense do you accuse God, then? Of being in error when he revealed the time of my death, or of being unfair to take me before the Qa'im appears? Which is it?"

"God is Perfection," Jahangir replies. He struggles to focus on the logic of this argument when his Master is dying. "He can be neither in error nor unfair."

"In that case—" Kazim's words grow more feeble—"do not pray for God to place himself in error by healing me, for the one thing that God cannot do is contradict his own perfection. And do not judge God's fairness by the standard of your shortsightedness."

Kazim smiles, takes a deep breath, and says, "God be with all of you in the times ahead."

Tears fill Jahangir's eyes and he wipes them away with a coarse sleeve. By the time that Jahangir looks again upon his master, Siyyid Kazim is dead, a teacher to his last breath.

CHAPTER 39

Like a hungry crow on a corpse, grief plucks out Oliver's eyes, blinding him to the naïve hospitality of his family and friends. In the fog of the funeral and the cold days that follow, he staggers through the barest routine of survival.

The Reverend, himself a derelict of sorrow, prays insufferably that God will remove from him the burden of sin that surely had caused God to punish him in this unbearable way. Jonathon wonders at how a "man of God" can turn a daughter's death into such a narcissistic rumination.

Through sheer will, Isaac and Phebe keep the family troupe going, as if the oldest and the youngest members of this glowering cast somehow had been exempted from mourning. They cook and serve meals to the distraught. They clean the houses, feed the animals, travel to Rochester for supplies, thank the well-wishers for their kind thoughts, even try to raise the spirits of the emotional invalids in their charge by singing cheerful duets after dinner (to no applause) and importing parlor games into the sitting room (Oliver and the Reverend decline to participate.)

Isaac is particularly troubled by his father. Ollie seems more than sad; he seems to be simmering with repressed rage. Isaac fears the day that this molten flow will erupt. But Ollie is not the first to blow.

At the end of the third week of "self-pity," as Phebe calls the unrelieved bereavement, she snaps. It's not that she minds helping out on the farm and taking care of her loved ones, but when Oliver sullenly eats her beef and potatoes, made with her own weary hands, and then swoons into an even deeper spell of foul temper, Phebe throws a cast-iron skillet across the room and screams. The piercing shriek startles them all, even Phebe; no one has ever heard Phebe as much as raise her voice. The sound is a fingernails-on-a-blackboard, child-yelling, coyotes-howling kind of screech that boils the blood and sends shivers down the spine. The cats disappear and the dogs cock their heads in dismay.

"Stop it stop it stop it!" Phebe yells. "I can't take this any longer! What's the matter with you? *All* of you?"

The force of Phebe's voice rocks Oliver back in his kitchen chair.

"You can't mourn forever!" Phebe says, breaking into a sob. "I lost two dear ones as well, you know. First my dear granddaughter, then my stepdaughter. You're not the only one in pain around here."

She marches over to Ollie. Fixes her gaze on him. Bends so her red face is close to his. "You might lift a finger to help around here. Seems to me that Isaac and myself are the only ones left alive in this family." She straightens up; her back is hurting. "Maybe the Reverend was right, that Winnie's dream about the man under the palm tree meant that the world would die on New Year's Eve. My world died, and yours too, I expect, when Alice fell off the roof. But if the Reverend was correct, we would then be born again—and to my reckoning, that means we'd come back to life. Well, I'm still waiting for the two of you." She shifts her gaze from Oliver to the Reverend.

"Woman, you're speaking madness," the Reverend interjects, "and very possibly blasphemy."

"Oh, go to hell, Reverend!" Phebe says.

The Reverend gasps as Jonathon smiles to himself.

"Or maybe you're already there," Phebe continues. "You're no better than this one"—she points to Ollie—"and maybe worse. Who do you think you are—Jesus Himself? Who made you so cockamamie important that only *your* sins could be responsible for Alice's death. Maybe you should take on the sins of the world and have yourself crucified!"

The Reverend is speechless. He simply stares wide-eyed at his wife.

Phebe goes on: "And who's to say that your daughter's death was punishment for *anything*? People die every day. New babies are born. The sun rises every morning. And I'm *so sorry* that Jesus didn't come on your schedule."

With a thud, Phebe sits down. And as she does, Oliver rises ominously from his chair. None of this speechmaking has improved his mood. In fact, he appears ready to burst into flame.

"You speak of God as if he is just," Ollie begins. "Well, where is God's mercy in the death of my mother?" He turns with reddened eyes to Phebe and says, "Where is God's love in the death of Mary Rogers?"

Then finally he turns to the Reverend and says, "Where in the name of heaven is God's righteousness in the killing of our good and pure Alice Chadwick?"

The Reverend is bright red and twitching. He bursts from his chair with the words, "I, sir, will not tolerate your blasphemy! Come, Phebe—we're leaving at once."

The Reverend grabs Phebe's hand, yanks her from a kitchen chair, and whisks her into the living room where they hurriedly pull on boots and coats before plunging through the front door into the cold night.

Isaac wants to abandon his father, run after the Reverend and Phebe and ask for safe harbor. He is frightened by the darkness that has overtaken his father. But in the end his loyalty is to the man who saved him from the harsh streets of New York City. In those days, Isaac remembers, he was a miserable and unlovable wretch—maybe more unlovable than Ollie is now. Yet Ollie stood by him, adopted him, cared for him. Now it seems time to reciprocate.

Ollie is standing by the kitchen window, staring into the night. Isaac walks up behind him. In Farsi the boy quietly says, "I love you, father."

Olie turns and looks at his boy. He has grown so tall! The others may have abandoned Ollie—and why should they not have?—but his son has stayed. Ollie wraps his arms around Isaac and says, "I will always love you."

It is the only love that remains in him.

CHAPTER 40

The Rochester winter of 1844 is colder than most, as if nature itself were mourning Alice's death. For weeks, Ollie has not spoken to Reverend Crenshaw and Phebe; if possible, he has grown still more bitter and rancorous.

Forbidden to visit his "grandparents," Isaac has continually disobeyed his father. The Reverend and Phebe had always treated him like their own flesh and blood, and he misses the fresh pies and hot meals, so he secretly visits them after school. On this chilly February night, as he lies awake in bed, Isaac tells himself it is foolish to feel like the longsuffering product of a broken home when this family, after all, is nothing but an artifice created by chance circumstances and New York adoption law. But in the end he always decides that the truth of the matter comes from the heart, and he knows that in their hearts all of these people—Ollie, the Reverend, Phebe, and yes even Jonathon—truly love him.

Ollie has walled himself in—or *out*, as the case may be. He has left the religious community of Rochester behind and begun a campaign of "cleansing," as he calls it, to rid the town of charlatanism, hypocrisy, and superstition. His chief targets are the clergy and the overtly pious. Three weeks previously, in a manic outburst, Ollie had stomped into St. Martin's Catholic Church during mass and before a filled sanctuary had publicly washed his soiled hands and face in a basin of Holy Water while muttering that the only articles of faith worth honoring were the articles he would soon be publishing in the newspaper. True to his word, less than a week later he published charges of corruption of minors against Father Flaherty; claimed that witnesses had seen Rev. Jacobs, the Temperance leader who preached at Union Methodist Church, imbibing spirits in the parsonage; called out Deacon Smythe of Colony Baptist

Church for using profanity when issuing orders to his colored mill workers; accused Rev. Longley of the First Congregational Church of an adulterous re-lationship with a blonde congregant "who is fond of wearing scarves about the neck and little else when in the solitary pastoral care of the Reverend."

No one knew how Ollie had persuaded the editor of the *Rochester Chron-icle* to publish such clearly slanderous charges. Some suggested bribery, but most citizens and many churchgoers privately speculated that Ollie certainly must have gathered some evidence on which to base his allegations. (No one suspected that Ollie had bought the failing newspaper and retained its editor for a handsome salary.) This unspoken conclusion was given additional weight when, despite fierce denials, none of the accused chose to sue the slanderer in open court. One of them, in fact—the much-loved Rev. Longley, who ap-parently was more loved than anyone thought—suddenly left his church after fifteen years of ministry "to attend to a grievously sick relative in Boston." The others, including the uncharged clergy of twenty or so other churches, seemed more intent on scanning the faces of their congregations for traitors or, worse yet, the countenance of Oliver Chadwick, who just last Sunday rose from his seat in the third to last pew of Trinity Lutheran Church and asked Pastor Yn-gqvist if he would be using this week's offering to cover his personal gambling debts. (Pastor Yngqvist had angrily and unwisely answered no, which many took to mean that he had always covered his gambling debts from his personal income. The irony of the Pastor's defense was not lost on the congregation, which had endured an hour-long diatribe on the wickedness of gambling the previous week.)

In a scathing series of three articles, Oliver had dubbed William Miller— the father of the Adventist movement—"a new edition of Mormonism." He wrote that Miller and Joseph Smith were "two kings speaking lies at the same table."

In just over a month, Oliver had become feared by the religious main-stream and cheered by the rest. No one knew where or by what means Ollie gained his information, and this caused a great wave of paranoia to set in among the Men of God. They grew suspicious of everyone they knew, but at the same time their overall behavior (some believed) grew more Christian and their vices fewer.

Jonathon had abandoned the farm for New York City, disgusted by Ollie's malicious behavior. And as Reverend Crenshaw also began to fear Ollie, the old man seemed to cast a suspicious eye on young Isaac as well. "I'm not a spy for my father," Isaac would often plead, and the Reverend would usually nod politely as if to agree, yet the Reverend was now often absent when Isaac came to call, and when the Reverend was present he was often mute, or nearly so.

Of the family that Isaac had held so dearly, by springtime he remains in contact with only two. Phebe and he continue to find ways to communicate and sometimes meet; these are glorious moments filled with love and tenderness. Ollie, on the other hand, has adopted severe authoritarian measures in his attempt to impose discipline on his disobedient son. He now drops Isaac off at school in the morning and picks him up after school, ensuring that the boy has no clandestine contact with the Crenshaws. A harsh regimen of chores keeps Isaac occupied at all other times.

There are still moments, however, when Ollie and Isaac share the kind of intimacy they enjoyed before Alice died. These times occur primarily at night when the two of them speak only Farsi to each other. At such times Isaac often asks about Ollie's early life, and Ollie tells stories about his beautiful mother. With each telling, Ollie's memory of Anisa, of Anne Chadwick, glows a little brighter and the bitterness that he had felt toward her diminishes ever so slightly. He wants to keep the memory of her alive, as he does the memory of Mary Rogers and Alice Crenshaw Chadwick. His remembrance of them, and their love, and their senseless deaths, is the fuel that sustains his vendetta against a Power that he surely cannot beat, but which he can fight.

And fight he will.

In early May, Oliver receives a surprising letter from Jonathon Fury.

> My heart has been cold since returning to New York and I realize now that I had too easily given up the friendships I enjoyed in Rochester. While I cannot in good conscience approve of your behavior at all times, I have come to the inevitable conclusion that I am not responsible for your actions, but only for my faithfulness to a friend, a virtue which I have sorely lacked and failed to demonstrate. I write now for two reasons: to ask your forgiveness; and to invite you to a most special occasion, one which I believe you will thoroughly enjoy.
>
> On May 22, Professor Morse, whom you may recall introduced me to the mysteries of the daguerreotype, is unveiling a new invention which he promises will revolutionize the world. I will be making a picture of this historic occasion, and I believe that

you might be interested in attending for the purpose of announcing this grand event through the newspapers. If you choose to attend, I trust you will see fit to bring Isaac, as I miss him terribly and would greatly appreciate seeing him again.

Your friend, Jonathon.

Oliver sets the letter aside, tries for a moment to dismiss it from his mind, then picks it up and reads it again. Until now he had not recognized how lonely the farm house had become with Jonathon gone.

CHAPTER 41

On May 18, the God-fearing citizens of Rochester are happy to see Oliver leave their city. Jesus may not have returned yet, but the departure of the "antichrist" (as some churches have nominated Oliver) is seen by many Christians as the next best thing. According to Pastor Yngqvist of St. Luke's Lutheran, watching Oliver board the train sends him into "a Rapture of a different sort." Perhaps with this pot-stirrer stirring the bigger pot of New York City, Jesus will consider coming to Rochester.

In the few days before his departure, Oliver had sold the *Rochester Chronicle* to his loyal editor for a pittance and a promise to continue printing Oliver's articles. He had also put the farm up for sale. It was clear to Isaac that he and his father would not be returning. The "militant religious reformer" had set his sights on a bigger battlefield.

It is late afternoon when Oliver and Isaac exit the train in New York and catch a carriage to the Regis Hotel. On the way, the carriage passes the old boarding house on Nassau Street. Isaac cranes his neck to see his old home, a place of great happiness that he will never forget, but Ollie does not seem to notice.

At the hotel they are greeted by Jonathon Fury, who bursts into a sunny grin when he sees Isaac. "My goodness, old man," Jonathon says to Isaac, "you've grown inches in the few weeks since I left."

The two embrace emotionally.

Oliver feels a twinge of guilt; he can't remember the last time he had hugged his son.

"It's good to see you, Jonathon," Oliver says. His manner is reserved—not aloof, but cool.

"Likewise."

"I trust the City has been generous to you."

"It has."

An awkward pause threatens to linger too long, so Isaac interrupts. "Father says that you have a friend with a new invention." The remark is directed at Jonathon. "He says that your friend will be announcing it shortly, and you'll be the official doc... docu..."

"Documentarian," says Jonathon, helping out. "Actually, I am hoping that your father will document the event in words and I will do so in a historic daguerreotype." Jonathon turns to Oliver. "Your coming to New York is an affirmative response, I hope."

"It is, my good man." Oliver reaches out and takes Jonathon's hand to shake it, but instinctively pulls him close and embraces him tightly, finishing with a double pat on the back to dismiss any implication that he meant it too personally.

"I'm so glad," Jonathon says. His face shows that he means it more than his words suggest.

The three of them dine in a fancy restaurant with genuine china, white tablecloths, and a crystal chandelier. Jonathon shares all the big city news and gossip that he can remember, and Ollie smiles and laughs more than Isaac can remember. It seems like the good old days, and Isaac basks in the hope that this camaraderie will last forever.

"Tell me about this grand event of yours," Oliver says to Jonathon as he gestures to their Hungarian waiter for more wine.

"Not my event. Shortly after I got into the city, I contacted my old friend, Samuel Morse. That's how I learned of his wonderful invention. It has to do with the telegraph."

"Of course, I've heard of that. Is there a practical use for it?"

"That's what Morse has been working on. Somehow he convinced Congress to give him the money to build a short telegraph line between Washington and Baltimore."

"Such a distance! How on earth can a signal be transmitted so far?"

"Well, he seems to have contrived a way for this to happen, and on May 24th he proposes to demonstrate for Congress the first telegraph message transmitted between two cities. It seems quite impossible, I agree, especially since the two cities are not even visible to each other, but with Morse I've learned that nothing is ever out of the question."

"Two different cities—what!—forty miles apart?"

"From what I understand, he ran his telegraph line along the connecting railroad track."

"Well, now, that's the first sensible thing I've heard about this whole affair. If the message can't be transmitted by telegraph, then he can just put it on a train and deliver it the old-fashioned way."

They all laugh. "I thought perhaps it would be best for us to be with my friend, Morse, in the capitol when he transmits the message," Jonathon says. "It will be quite a historic occasion."

"Yes, in Washington. We should be with the inventor as the message is sent, I quite agree. Where in the capitol will this take place?"

"In the chamber of the Supreme Court."

CHAPTER 42

After a difficult journey through the mountains, Jalal finds the flat plain to the north quite agreeable. Lacking a mule, they carry all their belongings on their backs. Following his previous successful missions for the late Siyyid Kázim, he has now undertaken the last and most important undertaking assigned to Kazim's students—to finally seek out the Qa'im Himself. A recurring dream of the holy city of Shiraz had been haunting him. And so Jalal had set out for Shiráz.

The journey is nearly over. It is afternoon and Shiraz appears like a quivering desert mirage, a small yellow and white smear against a fringe of purple mountains. As the men walk toward it, the city begins to take form, and as the sun descends, the city appears as an island in a sea of emerald. The panorama is magnificent: vast plain and wrinkled hills, cypress groves and gardens blooming with jasmine and roses, towers and walls, domes and spires, all bathed in the mellow late afternoon light. The stony road is surrounded by a fluttering sea of red and white poppies blown by a fresh breeze that whisks away the sour heat of the day. An orange sun throws long blue shadows from the tall minarets and slender sarv trees. This is the city of Hafiz, the lyric Persian bard of the fourteenth-century.

They approach the Kazerun gate, one of six entrances to the city. Jalal is fatigued. Every muscle aches and his knees throb. He drops to the ground, sits for a minute, and then lies down. The sand, still warm from the sun, cradles him. He cannot keep his eyes open. Through his eyelids he can see the shadows of birds flying above, hear their songs and the flutter of their wings. Slowly he opens his eyes. The scarlet-rimmed clouds drift slowly above. For a moment he is twelve again, lying in the warm Bushruyíh sand, and the voice of his best friend cries out, "Do you see it? Right there! It's the Prophet Muhammad, in the clouds."

The sound of sandals on pebbles brings him out of his reverie. He sits up and sees the silhouette of a stranger approaching, a young man with the brilliant orange light of the sun behind him. He stands to greet this apparition, and as the young man nears, Jalal can see the green turban of the Siyyids, direct descendants of the Prophet Muhammad.

The young man silently embraces him. The touch is gentle and soothing, sending waves of calm and comfort through Jalal's aching body. It is the kind of embrace that Jalal imagines receiving from Ali, should God permit that they be reunited. And then they are standing before each other, Jalal with many questions.

The youth's face seems familiar. "Are you a disciple of Siyyid Kazim?" Jalal asks.

The youth replies that he reveres the Siyyid's teachings. And then he overwhelms Jalal with expressions of affection and loving-kindness. For some time they talk; Jalal is mesmerized by the soft, melodious voice and the gleaming eyes of this youth, who cannot be more than 25 years old. At last the young man invites Jalal to his home.

From the gate, the main road is lined with gardens and on the east a residence for dervishes. On the west side, the Garden of the Throne, formed by terraces stacked on terraces, stands on rising ground overlooking the city. The magnificent fountain at its summit pours out cascading streams of water over slabs of marble.

Jalal finds himself ignoring the beauty of the city, so entranced is he by the sweetness of this youth, the dignity of his bearing, the genuine affection he has shown to a stranger. After some minutes of walking, the youth stops at the door of a modest house and knocks. An Ethiopian servant opens the door and smiles warmly at the young Siyyid.

The young man crosses the threshold and motions for Jalal to follow. He is seated immediately onto a Persian carpet and the servant offers a ewer of water so that he might wash the stains of travel from his hands and feet.

The young man takes the container and pours water over Jalal's hands. The traveler is surprised by this act of servitude; instinctively he recoils, but the host is gently persistent. After Jalal dries his hands, the youth gives him a drink that is both sweet and bitter, warm and cold, oddly refreshing and impossible to identify; it has a taste that he cannot recall ever experiencing before. He is overcome with a sense of well-being and wonders at the marvelous alchemy that is present in the beverage, then slowly becomes aware that the source of his euphoria is not the beverage—which he now recognizes as a simple blend of lemon water and honey— but the presence of his host.

The time for prayer comes quickly. The green-turbaned youth stands beside Jalal and prays with him. An hour after sunset, the Siyyid looks up at his guest and asks a most surprising question. "After Kazim, whom do you regard as his successor and your leader?"

The mention of Kazim startles Jalal. He searches his memory for a connection between this youth and the Shaykhi leader, and then it comes to him. Yes, he has seen this young man before—at the Shaykhi school. The mysterious young man who had sat at the rear of the chamber with the shaft of sunlight illuminating his lap. This is the young man to whom Kazim had so surreptitiously paid his respects.

"At the hour of his death," Jalal begins, "our departed teacher insistently exhorted us to scatter far and wide in search of the Promised One."

"Has your teacher given you any distinguishing features of this Promised One?"

"Yes, of course!" Jalal responds with a litany of physical and spiritual, intellectual and spiritual characteristics delineated by Kazim. He pauses, wondering if he has missed anything, when suddenly the youth declares, "Behold, all these signs are manifest in Me!"

So astonished is Jalal that he can only smile and politely point out that surely there must be at least one of these characteristics that is not present in his host; otherwise how could these signs collectively distinguish the Promised One?"

The youth's arguments are convincing but not conclusive. They serve principally to incite Jalal's instinct to debate, searching for at least one missing sign.

Without success.

The youth stares at Jalal without a smile, and the traveler immediately feels a surge of remorse. His host had showed him nothing but love and hospitality, only to be repaid by arrogance and condescension.

Even as he admonishes himself, though, Jalal is preparing for a more stringent test. During his interminable travels, he had devised an examination that he was convinced would sift out pretenders and identify the true Promised One. In this test, Jalal would ask the claimant to spontaneously dictate—with no hesitation, and in a style and language entirely different from prevailing standards—a commentary on the Surih of Joseph. This chapter of the Qu'ran had perplexed for centuries the supplest religious minds. Even Kazim had refused when asked by Jalal to write such a commentary, saying, "This is beyond me. But that Great One who comes after me will reveal it for you without being asked, and that commentary will be one of the clearest evidences of the loftiness of His position."

As Jalal is deciding how to proceed, 'Ali Muhammad gently says, "Now is the time to deliver the commentary on the Surih of Joseph."

Unasked, 'Ali Muhammad takes up a pen and begins to record with astounding speed his spoken words. Without pause, without hesitation, he delivers a flawless exposition on the bewildering chapter of the Qu'ran. Jalal sits enraptured by the melodious words of this mysterious revelation, and the unbroken flow of writing, and the sweeping force of the secrets and wisdom imparted by this youth. He is transported into another world, in which the threads of material knowledge and spiritual truth are woven into the music of heaven, and the seen coexists with the unseen, and time ceases to exist at all.

But when the pen stops writing, and the youth's voice no longer sounds, Jalal crashes back into the world of Shiraz. Still dizzy with ecstasy, he tries to stand, but falls sideways. His host steadies him.

"I must go to my companions," Jalal says, though he is not sure why; perhaps he is afraid that if he stays he will die of bliss.

"Please sit, my friend," the young Siyyid says. "If you leave in such a state, whoever sees you will certainly say, 'This poor man has lost his mind.'"

Jalal sits down again.

It is two hours past sunset on May 22, 1844.

CHAPTER 43

In Washington, D.C., thirteen-year-old Annie Ellsworth is being driven home from school in her father's carriage. Not every school girl in the capitol is so privileged, but her father is the Commissioner of Patents. Annie would not understand that such a position is unique in its ability to attract large "honorariums" for speeches that are never given, provided that patents are. What Annie does understand is the power of God to heal, bless, forgive, and protect. From her earliest years, Annie has been connected to God. As her good friend Samuel Morse has told her, she and God each hold a telegraph key and communicate over a direct line.

Some of Annie's school mates call her "spooky"; she never loses her temper, or cheats at games, or gossips, or does any of the naughty things that every other thirteen-year-old does. She prefers to read her Bible rather than discuss boys; she'd rather pray than eat. Annie's mother—no saint (if such a station is based on behavior)—worries about her daughter. In truth, she worries that Annie will disclose her mother's petty vanities and vices to God, and that retribution is just around the corner. It is not easy being the mother of an angel, especially when one is a bit of a devil.

On this glorious spring day, Annie has a problem. "Sammy"—as she calls her parent's friend, Samuel Morse—has asked Annie to decide on a message to be sent over the telegraph. It is quite an honor, as this will be the first message ever to be sent by telegraph from one city to another. Because she is such a serious young girl, she has taken this responsibility to heart. She wants the message to be exactly right, to communicate something very important to the world, but so far she has not come up with the right message.

At about the time that Jalal resettles himself onto the comfortable carpet in the young Siyyid's house in Shiraz, Annie is arriving home. The carriage pulls up outside her house, scattering a flock of pigeons. She watches them fly away and then, while looking up into the empty sky, she sees the image of a man in the clouds and she knows what Sammy's message should be.

She races into the house and writes the message onto a piece of note paper, folding it in half and placing it into an envelope that she addresses to "Samuel Morse." She puts her name on the back and takes the envelope to the carriage driver, instructing him to deliver it immediately. The driver, who has often taken Mr. Morse to his favorite hotel after visits with the family, delivers the message to the hotel desk. Samuel Morse is handed the envelope when he returns to his hotel after dinner. He is amused by the envelope, understanding at once what it contains.

"In this envelope," Morse explains to his dinner companions, Jonathon Fury and Oliver Chadwick, "is the message that I will send from Baltimore to Washington. It has been chosen by the most remarkable young lady I know."

"What is this historic message?" Oliver asks.

Samuel Morse waves the envelope back and forth, as if trying to divine the message without reading it, then puts the envelope into his coat pocket. "I don't know," he says. "But I like surprises. Let's wait until Friday."

In the transforming bliss and harmony of his host's modest Shirazi room, Jalal feels connected to all spiritual beings, as if he can commune without effort with all who reside, either permanently or temporarily, in a spiritual plane that transcends the limits of the material world. The universe seems open to him now, fractured to its core so that he can see and hear what was previously unseen and unheard. His spirit seems to mingle with his host's, and with thousands of others who seek nearness with their Beloved and pray for insight, and through meditation tune the subtle vibrations of their bodies and souls to the melodies of God.

Jalal sits spellbound by the utterances of this young man, humbled by his depth of knowledge. Time floats effortlessly past, without meaning or boundary. A river of wisdom rushes by him, and Jalal recognizes that even with cupped hands he can capture only a few drops.

After a peaceful silence, the young Siyyid looks up at Jalal and says, "You are the first to believe in me! I am the Gate of God, and you are the gate of that Gate."

In the Supreme Court chamber, all is ready for the grand demonstration. Distinguished gentlemen from Congress greet Samuel Morse with hearty handshakes, though most are privately skeptical that this telegraph gadget will deliver as promised. The whole idea of it simply defies logic.

Jonathon Fury has set up his cumbersome camera in a strategic position from which he can capture Mr. Morse and the telegraph key at the most opportune moment. Oliver Chadwick and Isaac sit in hard wood chairs beside the camera; now sixteen, Isaac's insatiable curiosity makes him perhaps the most interested occupant of this room, except for Mr. Morse.

With a loud clearing of the throat, Samuel Morse begins his presentation with "heartfelt thanks" to Congress for providing the money required to construct the telegraph line from Baltimore to Washington. Next, he delivers a pedantic, too-long discourse on the physics of electricity and the logic behind the dots and dashes that will soon be embossed onto a strip of paper by the telegraph device. The inventor immodestly refers to this system of symbols as "Morse code."

Before he is finished with his lecture, a number of witnesses are checking their pocket watches and rolling their eyes. At last he introduces his "very special guest," Annie Ellsworth, who is attired in a flowery dress and matching hat. Seated next to her parents in the first row, she now stands to applause, blushes, then bows politely and retakes her seat.

"Miss Ellsworth has selected the message that we will be communicating to my colleague, Alfred Vail, in Baltimore. After Mr. Vail receives it, he will send the same message back to me here in Washington, and that will conclude our demonstration. The message is in this sealed envelope, which I have not yet opened." Then, turning to Jonathon and Oliver, he says, "Are you gentlemen ready?"

They nod.

Morse opens the envelope, studies the message, and then smiles at Annie. He leans over the telegraph key and begins a series of clicking sounds that are undecipherable to anyone save himself. When he is finished, he folds his hands in front of himself and speaks to the group. "Alfred Vail already will have received my message, and I expect he is translating it for the group assembled there. In a short while, he will retransmit the mess—"

At just this moment, the telegraph begins to click and pull through its strip of paper. For the first time, everyone in the chamber is attentive. After a few seconds, Morse tears off the paper strip and holds it up, focusing his eyes on the embossed bumps.

"Ladies and gentlemen, our demonstration has been a success. Mr. Vail has transmitted to us the very same message that I sent him only moments ago."

A smattering of applause greets these words. It was not a very dramatic demonstration, but the device seemed to have worked. Unsatisfied, though, Oliver raises his hand.

"Mr. Chadwick?" Morse says obligingly.

"Yes sir, I was wondering if you could tell us what the message was."

"Oh, my yes, of course. My compliments to Miss Ellsworth for a most fitting message, indeed. Let me read it to you." He holds up the strip of paper again, looks at it, and reads.

"What hath God wrought?"

Samuel Morse assumes that the message was meant to underscore the revolutionary nature of his technological achievement. Jalal would have seen quite another meaning.

CHAPTER 44

On Thursday evening, June 7, the *Nauvoo Expositor* press begins to churn out its very first weekly edition, a collection of virulently anti-Mormon articles and scathing attacks. A month earlier, William Law and his brother Wilson had hauled the old press to Nauvoo after buying it with a few dollars of their own and a larger sum invested by confirmed Mormon haters. The Law brothers had not always been critics of the Prophet; until recently, William had been one of Joseph Smith's counselors, but he and his brother could no longer tolerate the Mormon practice of polygamy and the increasingly political nature of Smith's "Kingdom of God." In a shouting match, William had called out the Prophet and declared war on the movement he now believed was a public menace. He chose the printed word as his weapon, and this set the stage, he believed, for a duel of newspapers in Nauvoo. He could not have been more wrong.

The smell of ink and newsprint is thick at the *Expositor* office as William inspects the first sheet to come off the press. His black-smudged fingers flip the page over, leaving a thumbprint in the corner. "That old type you bought is a bit worn out. Look at the "i" and the "t" in particular," he says to his brother, handing Wilson the page.

"What'ya expect for the price?" Wilson replies.

A noise startles them—footsteps just outside the side window, which is covered by layers of newsprint. William turns, frightened. "You lock up?" he asks his brother.

"Tight as a drum."

"All right, then. We keep makin' papers tonight. Tomorrow the whole area will see the dark side of Joseph Smith."

"As if they haven't already."

"I take Nauvoo and Quincy. You head out early and drop off stacks in Carthage and Warsaw. Mr. Sharp over there in Warsaw'll give you a hand, he said. Good man."

"Ol' Joe is gonna be spittin' tacks… like the way he did when you testified against him over in Carthage and they brought him up on charges of adultery."

"I swore under oath, Wilson. Had to tell the truth as I saw it. Way I see it now is there's over three hundred of us former Mormons right here in Nauvoo who want to get things cleaned up, and that's only the ones who've raised their hands. Lots more behind them, you can bet on it."

The Law brothers do their job. The towns within horse wagon range are flooded with the first edition of the *Nauvoo Expositor*. Joseph Smith is one of the first to read it; five different people bring it directly to his home.

He doesn't like what he reads.

Right there on the front page it says that the newspaper's chief purpose is to *explode the vicious principles of Joseph Smith, and those who practice the same abominations and whoredoms which we verily know are not accordant and consonant with the principles of Jesus Christ and the Apostles.* The first inflammatory articles go on to charge Smith with bringing innocent females to Nauvoo under the pretext of religion, but in reality to add them to his harem. Another piece castigates Smith's candidacy for president by saying, *You are voting for a man who contends all governments are to be put down and the* one *established upon its ruins. We cannot believe that God ever raised up a prophet to Christianize a world by political schemes and intrigue.*

And there is more. The *Expositor* faults the political system of Nauvoo, criticizes specific church doctrines, and advocates in strong language widespread reforms.

John Taylor, a city councilman and high-ranking church leader, is the first to have brought the newspaper to Smith's home, and he now watches the Prophet's stormy reaction. To calm the Prophet-mayor-general-presidential candidate, Taylor tries to make a joke: "Looks like the Law brothers have found themselves a writer. Much better English than they speak."

Joseph Smith is not amused. His response, which carries with it the weight of religious and Nauvoo law, is succinct. "Call a meeting of the council for tomorrow morning!"

And so on Saturday morning, the Nauvoo city council convenes with one item on its agenda: the *Nauvoo Expositor*. "It stinks in the nose of every honest man," John Taylor says in one of the council's more even-handed exchanges.

After a lengthy discussion, Joseph Smith becomes visibly frustrated with the pace of the deliberations and stands up. "Such men and newspapers," he says, "are calculated to destroy the peace of the city, and it is not safe that such things should exist, on account of the mob spirit which they tend to produce. I would rather die tomorrow and have the thing smashed, than live and have it go on, for it is exciting the spirit of mobocracy and bringing death and destruction upon us!"

Upon finishing this tirade, unfortunately, it is dinner time and the council decides to postpone further discussion until Monday.

By Monday morning, Prophet Smith is even more agitated. He dislikes having to argue his points to a council that would not exist if he had not created it.

"I am uncomfortable with destroying this business," Councilor Warrington, a non-Mormon, confesses to the assembly. "I strongly suggest that we fine the *Expositor* $3,000 for every libel published in these pages. And if this does not curb its slander, then we should declare it a public nuisance."

"A ridiculous proposition," Joseph Smith counters. "Mormons would then have to travel to the county seat at Carthage to prosecute these cases, and their lives would be endangered. I urge all of you to agree that the best remedy is to declare the *Expositor* a public nuisance without a troublesome judicial process. As the city council, we have that right."

By six-thirty that evening, the council diffidently passes an ordinance declaring the *Nauvoo Expositor* a public nuisance and issues an order for the mayor to have it destroyed. The mayor, Joseph Smith, duly agrees to fulfill his obligation.

Less than two hours later, a mob of citizens, assisted by the Nauvoo Legion under the command of the major general, march to the unstaffed office of the *Nauvoo Expositor*. They smash the press, scatter the type throughout the street, and set the building on fire. The duel of the newspapers had lasted four days.

Inside the *Expositor's* office, in a wooden file cabinet, one of the last items to burn had been an official *Nauvoo Expositor* stock certificate in the name of Oliver Chadwick, now the owner of 50% of the ashes.

The Prophet's actions that evening galvanize the non-Mormons of Hancock County, who view this sanctioned vandalism as a final act of contempt for their laws.

Upon hearing the news, Oliver catches a train for western Illinois. The Ellsworths, particularly Annie, having taken a liking to Isaac and graciously offer to look after the inquisitive boy until Oliver returns.

CHAPTER 45

The June humidity paints Ollie's face with a wet brush. Loosening his moist collar, Ollie peers over a shot of whiskey at Thomas Cole Sharp. "I want to see him with my own eyes," he says. "I want to see this person who claims to speak with angels."

Just an hour earlier, Ollie had arrived in Carthage, the Hancock County Seat in western Illinois. He had quickly learned that Sharp's prophetic skills were a match for Prophet Joseph Smith's, for the Mormon leader—as Sharp had foretold—had surrendered with his brother Hyrum on charges of inciting a riot by burning the offices of the *Expositor*. It seems the *gentiles* were out to get the Prophet.

"Just about everyone in these parts wants to catch a glimpse of him," Sharp replies. "He's being held over there in the Hancock House, same place as where Governor Ford is staying."

"Sounds more like he's a celebrity than a prisoner."

"Both, I'd say. The governor pledged to keep them safe if they surrendered themselves."

A hot breeze wafts through the stuffy Carthage Saloon bringing little relief to the twenty or so damp and dour faces huddled over wobbly tables. A thick tobacco haze like a swamp fog hovers in layers, stinging the eyes and sniping at the nostrils.

"Will the charges stick?" Ollie asks Thomas Sharp.

"Don't know. My main concern right now is bail."

"How so?"

"Whatever amount of bail they set, these Mormons have the money to pay. I worry that Smith will be released before noon."

"If your account of the riot at the Expositor is accurate…"

"Of course it's accurate!"

"Yes, of course. And based on that account, there may be a way to keep these imposters in custody."

"Then tell me at once!"

"Who is the primary judicial officer in Carthage?"

"Well, umm… tonight?"

"And tomorrow."

"I suppose that would be the Justice of the Peace, Robert Warner. He's also captain of the Carthage Greys."

"That's very good. The Greys are vehemently anti-Mormon. And where might I find Mr. Warner?"

Thomas Sharp swivels his wiry body on the hard wooden chair and cranes to look at a pudgy fifty-year-old man with a misbuttoned vest, thick spectacles, and stringy gray locks that curl over a sweat-stained collar. Robert Warner is seated at a table with three finely attired companions.

"Right there," Sharp says.

"I think another criminal charge is in order," Ollie replies. "One for which no bail need be set."

"What charge is that?"

"*Treason*—for declaring martial law at Nauvoo."

Thomas Sharp's eyes widen as Ollie stands and walks over to the Justice of the Peace. He watches as Ollie introduces himself, cordially shakes hands, is offered the last remaining seat at the table, then leans closer to Warner. The older man's smile disappears as Ollie speaks. He listens intently for several minutes and then his smile returns. Warner pats Ollie on the knee and grasps his hand, pumping it vigorously. Ollie stands up and returns to Thomas Sharp.

"It's done," Ollie explains

"*Well* done, my good man," Sharp says, patting Ollie on the shoulder. "If I might add… you seem to be rather enjoying your role as…"

"Instigator?"

Thomas Sharp nods.

"Mr. Warner wants me to meet a few of the other prominent residents of the community to discuss tactics."

"That's good. While you're at it, perhaps you can stir the coals a bit. Now that Joseph Smith is in custody, the boil seems to have come off the pot."

Oliver drains his whisky glass and sets it down loudly on the table. "We can keep this so-called Prophet in jail until the trial, but if he and his lawyers are clever enough, they stand a chance of evading justice."

"You know how I hate these Mormons, Oliver, but that's the best we can do. It's in the courts now—"

"—where politics can hold sway," Oliver reminds his friend. "I'm thinking of another form of justice."

"I don't quite understand."

"Thomas, 'an eye for an eye.' Is there a more perfect form of justice?

Sharp shakes his head. "I still don't understand," he says.

"Joseph Smith is in custody for inciting a riot which burned down the *Expositor*. Perhaps an act of civil disobedience might balance the scales."

Sharp sits back in his chair, alarmed. His voice rises as he says, "My God, man, are you talking about a lynch mob?"

"Keep your voice down!" Oliver leans toward Sharp and whispers, "If someone stirs the pot…"

"You?"

"If this "Prophet" is an imposter and a threat to property and lives, as you claim, then he deserves to be punished for his blasphemy and deceit. And if he is in truth a Prophet, a spokesperson for God, then in my opinion that is even worse. He and his Nauvoo Legion have taken up arms. I say, let the battle come to him."

"And how do you propose to…"

"At ten o'clock this evening I am meeting with a number of prominent citizens to discuss 'tactics.' I intend to remind them that this is a unique opportunity to remove the source of their despair. If they choose to take the logical course of action, then it is out of my hands."

"A reasoned plan to lynch a criminal is not a mob action. It's… it's a *conspiracy*." Thomas Sharpe is feeling the sting of his scruples awakening.

"Semantics," Oliver says dismissively. "If the majority this evening votes to ensure that justice is carried out, you could also call it *democratic*. Majority rules. The rightness of a deed, as you know, usually determines the term that defines it. Surely, as a newspaperman, you understand that words have a power to change the character of a thing. This evening a jury of Joseph Smith's peers will reach a verdict in his case and perhaps carry out their sentence at once. Who's to say that a politically-charged courtroom governed by rules that place the preponderance of power in the hands of the cleverest attorney is a fairer forum for administering justice?"

"I do believe you've gone mad," Sharp says. He sighs, jiggles his shot glass and downs the last few drops of whiskey. "I want to hear no more of it."

"Understood. All I ask is that you report what happens. I'm sure you will choose the most appropriate words."

"You seem confident in your ability to persuade these citizens to…"

"Not *persuade*, Thomas. Individually, I'm sure they're of a like mind. All I have to do is unite them. Their unity will be all the permission they need to see justice done."

The next morning, Thomas Sharp breakfasts alone at the Carthage Eatery. Oliver is nowhere to be found. A commotion in the street brings Sharp to his feet. He sweeps aside a frilly curtain to peer out the single dusty window. A group of Greys with rifles are escorting Governor Ford, Joseph Smith and his brother Hyrum down the rutted trail that carves through Carthage.

Sharp reaches into his pocket and plucks out a couple of coins, flings them onto the table, and races from the eatery.

The road is suddenly lined with people yelling and taunting the Smiths as they walk solemnly toward the south side of the town square. Sharp follows, and within several minutes they are standing before two long lines of militiamen.

A decorated soldier in the uniform of the Greys steps forward. Sharp recognizes this man by his enormous grey handlebar moustache; it is General Minor Deming, commander of the Hancock militia units.

In a voice that is too thin and nasal to have the ring of authority, Deming introduces the governor to the militia, and then presents the Smith brothers. The Carthage Greys, on the far end of the formation, begin to raise their rifles and shake their fists menacingly.

Pushing his way nearer to Joseph Smith, Sharp believes that he can detect a look of terror on the self-declared Prophet's face, and is pleased by it.

General Deming orders the men to stand down, but the Greys hiss and shout obscenities at the prisoners, ignoring the orders of their commander. Governor Ford raises his hands and pleads for silence and discipline, but is insulted by cries of "Down with all imposters!"

Three of the Greys fire their rifles into the air.

"I'll have you all arrested for insurbordination!" the governor fires back.

He is greeted by jeers and a loud voice saying "While you protect the imposters!"

At last the constable, David Bettisworth, himself a longtime Grey before retiring into his new position, and a brave man deeply respected by the militia, walks to the center of the chaos, looks down at his boots, and spits a brown stain of tobacco juice into the street. As he looks up at his former mates, everyone grows silent.

"Thank you, gentlemen," the constable says. "Nice to see you this mornin'. Now if you'd be so kind as to let us finish our little ceremony here, I'll be takin' the Smith brothers off to jail. I know you don't wanna be missin' this now."

The constable turns to the Smiths and motions for them to walk toward him. Sharp is now standing five paces from Joseph, and he can see the fury in the man's face. It must be humiliating, he imagines, for a Prophet of God, the mayor of Nauvoo, the commander of the Nauvoo Legion, and such a powerful political figure, to be ordered around by this common constable—to publicly obey a civil authority he does not respect, in fact despises, like a trained puppy.

Joseph and Hyrum reluctantly step forward and slowly walk the fifteen paces to the constable.

"What have we here?" the constable says to them. "Ya have something to say to me?"

Joseph looks at Hyrum. Their agreement is to surrender to the constable. But Joseph cannot force the words from his lips.

"Ya waitin' for a Revelation from God or what?" the constable says.

The two columns of militiamen burst into laughter.

Joseph looks up at the clouds, then back down at the constable. He says, "My brother and I surrender."

Spontaneous applause echoes throughout the town square. The Greys throw their hats into the air, and more rifles are fired in celebration as the constable takes Joseph by the arm and leads him and his brother toward the small two-story Carthage jail.

Sharp turns around and sees Oliver for the first time today. Ollie is chatting with the Justice of the Peace Robert Smith and General Deming. Their conversation seems intense, and then both of these men begin to nod as Ollie speaks. Once during this dialogue Ollie catches Sharp's eye, but turns away quickly.

That afternoon, Joseph and Hyrum are taken before Robert Warner in the stuffy stone courthouse. The Justice of the Peace sets bail at $500 each on the riot charges, and this amount is quickly posted by the Mormons. As Joseph and Hyrum rise to leave, however, Warner orders them arrested on charges of treason.

Stunned, Joseph glances at his attorney, who approaches the bench. After an angry exchange, the attorney walks over to Joseph, whispers a few words, shrugs in a gesture of futility, then turns back to the bench as Warner speaks.

"I am issuing an order to have the prisoners committed without bail until June 29th when a material witness for the charge of treason, Francis M. Higbee, can appear in court," Smith announces.

"Your Honor, that's four days!" the attorney pleads.

"We are adjourned," Warner replies. "Good day, gentlemen."

Sharp can see the Justice of the Peace glance toward the corner of the room with a conspiratorial smile; this is where Ollie is seated next to Jacob Cunningham Davis, a 31-year-old Illinois state senator from Warsaw, whom Sharp knows blames the Mormons for his failure to secure a nomination for Congress. On Ollie's other side is Levi Williams, a colonel in the 59th Regiment of the Illinois militia, and an occasional Baptist minister. Sharp knows that Levi, in his mid-thirties, is fiercely anti-Mormon and is not above using violence; six months earlier, Levi had ridden at the head of a mob that kidnapped a Mormon and his son near Warsaw, bound them with chains, threatened them with knives, and finally spirited them off to Missouri where the mob had the Mormons arrested on trumped-up horse stealing charges.

Ollie and his two new friends rise, pat each other in a congratulatory manner, and then greet another man on the way out of the courthouse. Sharp knows this man, too. Mark Aldrich is a land speculator and town promoter, one of the original developers of Warsaw. Now forty-two years old, his development schemes have frequently put him at odds with Mormon interests.

Thomas Sharp is amazed at how quickly Oliver has insinuated himself into this circle of influential, Mormon-hating residents of Hancock County. He does not have to ask Oliver how the previous evening's meeting had gone; the conspiracy clearly is underway.

The next morning, Ollie walks to the Carthage jail with Davis and Aldrich. They speak in urgent whispers to Franklin Worrell, a ferret-faced man who commands seven guards. Worrell glances at the three visitors, accepts a fistful of currency, and ushers the men to the second floor where Joseph Smith is kept.

Ollie walks over to the Joseph's cell and sees Joseph lying on a low cot; Joseph senses a presence and sits up, staring coldly at the Englishman.

"And who might you be?" Joseph asks.

"A Prophet," Ollie says.

Joseph narrows his eyes, considering this. "Prophets bear messages from God. What message do you bring?"

"God wants you to know that he is thankful for your service, but now it is time for you to join him."

Joseph looks nervously at his visitor; this sounds like a death threat. "Are you the messenger or the executioner?" he asks.

Ollie reaches into his coat pocket and removes a small pistol.

Joseph looks at it; this seems to answer the question.

Ollie handles the pistol carefully as he says, "In a short time, many will come for you. It will become very… *unpleasant*." He stretches out this last word so the intended meaning is clear. "You may want to avoid the unpleasantness. This can be your key to the next world." He passes the pistol through the bars.

With trembling hands, Joseph takes the gun. He looks up at his visitor, who is staring fiercely at him.

"If you are an imposter," Oliver says in a low whisper. "I can save your life. If you are truly a Prophet, however, there is nothing I can do for you that I have not already done. Which are you, then? A Prophet or an imposter?"

Joseph points the pistol at Ollie. "Rather than answer your question, maybe I should shoot you."

"That would answer my question," Ollie says softly. "But the truth is, I am already dead. And there is only one bullet in that gun. I suggest you use it wisely."

Joseph puts the pistol into his pocket and turns his back on Oliver. "You've come to torment me."

"I've come to look into the eyes of a Prophet."

Joseph wheels and stares into Ollie's eyes. "Then *behold!*" he says.

"I am not disappointed, then."

Ollie turns to leave, taking a few steps toward the staircase. As his left foot stretches out for the first step, Joseph stops him from descending with these words: "Would no imposter ever play out his role to the final curtain?" Joseph is toying with his visitor, refusing to let him reap the reward of certitude.

Ollie retracts his foot and studies the prisoner one last time. He dislikes this man, has made up his mind about him. "I am disappointed after all," he says. "Goodbye, Mr. Smith."

And then he is gone.

At four o'clock that afternoon, Oliver is seated on the porch of Will's Smithy, about a hundred paces from the Carthage jail. He has been listening for a single gunshot from the pistol he gave Joseph—but *nothing!* The blank he had placed in the chamber of the pistol would have left a mark and a ringing in Joseph's ears, but would have revealed volumes—more volumes than the famous golden plates that Joseph claimed he found after an angel's tip.

Expressionless, Oliver watches a mob of a hundred men appear down the road. They are marching toward the jail. Thirty or so have blackened their faces grotesquely, but Oliver knows who some of these men are: Jacob Davis, Levi Williams, and Mark Aldrich. The Carthage Greys have been stationed conveniently a half-mile from town by General Minor Deming, too far away to interfere meaningfully. And in any event, they are certain to take no serious action against their relatives and friends.

The mob approaches the Carthage jail. Oliver watches Thomas emerge from a saloon across from the jail, ever the observer. The mob is now fifty feet from the front door of the jail. Five of the guards flush from the building, pointing their rifles at the mob.

A voice shouts, "Turn around. Go home."

Another voice calls out, "There'll be no lynching here today, boys."

But the mob presses closer, now twenty feet from the guards, who point their rifles just over the heads of the insurgents and fire. Even from this distance, Ollie can see that some of the guards are smiling as they shoot.

The mob forces its way past the guards, wrenching away their rifles, throwing them to the ground with great showmanship.

After several seconds there are more shots fired, and Oliver knows what has happened. In his mind he can see Levi Williams leading a group of men up the stairs, and then firing into Hyrum's cell. Where will the Prophet's brother have been struck first? The chest? The face?

More shots are fired, and Ollie watches the stout form of Joseph Smith suddenly perched on the second-floor window sill. He fires his gun at the mob below but is caught in a cross-fire. Two bullets strike him in the back, one in the collar bone and a fourth in the breast. He teeters for a moment, one leg and arm outside the window, and then plunges to the ground, landing on his left side.

A voice shouts, "Dead!" Another voice inside the jail yells, "Dead here, too."

At last the Carthage Greys appear. The mob disperses quickly but no one is chased by the militia.

Thomas Sharp writes furiously in his notebook. The plan has worked. Joseph Smith is dead and Thomas Sharp surely will find just the right words to describe what happened at the Carthage jail.

CHAPTER 46

Oliver Chadwick feels no joy, no exhilaration, no pleasure in the death of Joseph Smith. In fact, he feels devoid of emotion. The rhythmic rocking of the train reduces time to a thin rail, and he is transported backwards to London, to a time when Mum had wrapped her protection around him and avenged those who meant him harm. *What do you think of me now, Mum?* His grandmother had shown him unyielding strength and an uncompromising sense of justice. She had exquisitely calculated her punishments and administered them without mercy, for she knew that no mercy was deserved. *I wish you were here, Mum; I miss you so much.* She always acted for Ollie's advantage; she was the only dependable person in his life. His rock. *Give me some of your confidence, Mum, some of the conviction you had in your own decisions.* He is afraid that he is not strong like Mum. Otherwise why would doubts bedevil him?

He feels no remorse for his role in the killing of the Prophet, but questions its strategic merit. If Smith becomes a martyr, than perhaps he will have inspired the hated Mormons to heroic deeds. Rather than stunting their growth, he may have removed an obstacle to growth.

Still—charlatan or Prophet, Joseph Smith deserved his punishment. The rest is knowable only when looking backwards, and Oliver knows that the punishment meted out to that fat old Anglican priest, Reginald Pennick, had produced positive results. Free of the need to avenge the prurient sins of the priest, Oliver had focused on his education and career. His life had been salvaged. For just a moment, Oliver thinks about the other boys corrupted by Pennick and their likely fates.

Mum, give me strength.

After arriving back in Washington, a carriage takes Oliver from the train station to the Ellsworth house. He is exhausted but anxious to see his son. A servant opens the door and greets Oliver warmly, inviting him into the sitting room. He sits there quietly for a moment, rubbing his eyes. He hears footsteps on the creaky floor and looks up, surprised to see Phebe standing in front of him. She looks much older.

"I'm so glad to see you, Oliver," she says, taking his hands in hers.

"Phebe—I didn't expect you to be here."

"Well, fate intervened, it seems. The Reverend died last week. Heart just gave out. *Broke*, if you ask me. I sent a letter, and it was forwarded here to Isaac. The Ellsworths invited me to be with Isaac in their wonderful home for a few days. No time to be alone, they said, and I agreed. With Alice and Theodore dead, and you and Isaac and Jonathon back east, there's just no reason for me to stay in Rochester."

Annie Ellsworth and Isaac suddenly burst into the room.

"Father!" Isaac shouts, running to Oliver and throwing his arms around him. "I'm so glad you're home. You heard about Grandpa?"

Oliver nods.

"Grandma can live with us, can't she?" Isaac pleads. "I told her she could."

"Of course," Oliver says. "She's always welcome."

Annie slips over to Oliver's chair and stands beside Isaac, touching him just barely. "We read about that awful tragedy in Carthage," she says. "We were so worried about you."

"Afraid that you might have been hurt," Isaac adds. "They've arrested some people in the murder."

Oliver doesn't like to think about the events in Carthage as murder. He winces slightly, shifts in his chair.

"One of the people they charged is your newspaper friend—uh, Sharp... Thomas Sharp," Isaac adds.

Oliver hadn't heard about this.

"What's odd," Isaac says, "is that this fellow Sharp wrote the first story about the mob at the jail. Turns out he might have been one of the conspirators. I'll get the *Times* for you."

Isaac turns to collect the latest *New York Times* from another room, but Oliver stops him. "No, son—I just want to spend some time with all of you right now. I can catch up on the news later."

Oliver gives Annie a hug and kisses her on the forehead—*such a beautiful girl*, he thinks.

Suddenly he is overcome with a desperate need to escape—not from this loving group, but away from this country, back to the land of his great-grand-mother.

Within a month, Oliver has purchased tickets to London for Jonathon, Isaac, Phebe and himself. *Time to show my son where I came from*, he tells himself.

As the patchwork family prepares to board their sailing vessel in New York, Isaac looks around at the docks. He recognizes some of the wretched inhabitants and most of the dark alleys, but no one recognizes him. He has changed—become civilized and educated. He feels no sentiment for this place, only appreciation to his father for rescuing him.

PART 4
PERSIA 1844

CHAPTER 1

With His own hands, Siyyid Salih, who has taken the title of the *Rasul*, or "Herald", pours a cup of aromatic black tea for Jalal and the other seventeen *Living Letters*, the term He uses to designate His disciples. During the previous weeks these men and one woman have become an extended family. But today many of them seem tense, as if they know a calamity is about to shatter their ranks forever. This sense of foreboding is not apparent in the Rasul, however, Who seems almost supernaturally calm with a generous smile on his face.

Danush, the youngest of the Letters, is the first to recognize that the apprehension darkening this occasion is due to the fear that this cozy band of believers will soon be split up. Some likely will die as they undertake their missions, but this provokes less anxiety than the inevitable separation from each other—and especially from the Rasul.

The Rasul addresses the disciples. "Oh My beloved friends! Ponder the words that Jesus addressed to his disciples as He sent them forth to propagate the Cause of God. 'Let your light shine before the eyes of men.'"

CHAPTER 2

The London weather is just as Oliver remembered it: dismal. A hard rain pelts him and his three companions as they exit the customs-house and slosh through the mud to a somber black carriage. The driver, stooped as if hammered down by the angry rain, turns to greet them and for just a moment this bent, sodden creature looks like Mum's driver, the one who had fetched young Ollie and his mother on their first evening in London. But of course this is not that old man, who had died some years ago, but the man's son, Evan, who appears through the rain like the old driver's ghost.

Evan nods politely, his wide-brimmed hat spilling water. He opens the carriage door and the four travelers scramble into the dry security of the dark enclosure. "I had expected Herbert to be here," Oliver says to Evan.

After a lack of communication over the past year, Oliver had finally sent a letter to Herbert announcing his imminent return. There had been no reply, just as there had not been to any of the other half-dozen letters that Oliver had sent.

"A bit under the weather, the Master is," Evan replies. "And such miserable weather to be under at that." Evan slams the door, climbs into his unsheltered seat, gathers the reins of the horses, and launches the vehicle on its way. To himself, mostly, he mutters, "Been under the weather for months now."

The weary party is silent for the first few minutes of the ride, but then, as if assuming Mum's role as tour guide, Oliver begins an unbroken commentary about the unfolding panorama, and with each familiar sight, each word, he feels more at home. Even the London muck brings back fond memories. Before long Isaac and Jonathon are asking questions and joking with each other. By the time they arrive at the Belgravia mansion, the rain has stopped and a swirling fog is rising from the ground.

"It's a bit larger than I had imagined," Jonathon says, referring to the mansion that sits a few paces from the halted carriage. He had known that Oliver was a man of means, but the ostentation of this estate stuns him. The sprawling Rochester farm had been simple and rustic, nothing like this two-story cathedral of opulence.

"Large, yes, I suppose, for a city home," Oliver replies. "But nothing compared to Chillington-hall. We'll go there for Christmas. Come, let me show you to your rooms."

Phebe steps out of the carriage, hoists her skirt above the mud, then notices that the skirt is already rimmed with the stuff and lets it fall back into the sticky brown-black goop. "I'm afraid I'll drag in a mess," she says.

Oliver turns and smiles. "Never mind that. We have people to clean it up. You're just seeing to their employment."

Oliver takes Isaac by the arm, guides him through the massive carved entrance and up the winding staircase.

"Herbert, are you here?" he shouts. There is no answer. He continues to escort Isaac up the stairs, down a long, dark hallway and into a bedroom. There he sees the same rosewood chest in the exact spot that it had occupied when young Ollie had first gazed at this room; the bed, situated just the way he had left it many years ago; the same view of the neatly groomed lawn, edged by thick trees that appear more grey than green in the dwindling light.

I was such a naïve lad, Oliver thinks as he swoons into the swelling comfort of nostalgia. *Everything was so new then, and now it's my past.*

For Isaac, though, everything *is* new. Overwhelmed by the voyage, the new land, the mansion, he sits on the bed approvingly and grins, then yawns. He lies down and immediately goes to sleep.

When he wakes it is dark. The thick clouds have finally parted and a thin rail of moonlight runs through the room. Disoriented, Isaac sits up and hears faint but angry voices. He walks across the room, stumbles over his luggage, and opens the door. Candles paint flickering ovals on the walls of the corridor. The voices are coming from the far end, from behind a partially open door that sprays lamplight onto the hallway floor.

The voices are too muffled to make out words, so Isaac quietly walks down the hall toward their source. As he approaches the door he can identify the louder voice as Oliver's. Another voice, softer and trembling, he cannot identify. Oliver is chastising someone; his words are harsh. Then the other man begins to weep. Isaac is frightened. What sort of behavior would merit Oliver's wrath?

"I left you to manage the household," Oliver is saying, "and look at you!"

The man continues to weep.

Oliver says, "I am disgraced by your behavior. Did I not allow you to continue on here, in a life of luxury, even though you murdered my father? I loved you once—thought of *you* as my father—but you betrayed me."

Isaac cannot understand these horrible words. Is there a murderer in this house? Slowly, boldly, he pushes the door open and peers in. Oliver is towering above an older man who is seated, face in hands, on a large bed. As the man lifts his face to look into the eyes of Oliver, Isaac recognizes Herbert Eaton.

Oliver hoists an empty scotch bottle from a nightstand, holds it ominously over Herbert's head and says, "If you want to die, there is a faster way than drinking. I will not have Isaac see his *grandfather* in this drunken state. I forbid you to leave this room unless you are sober. Not a hint of it on your breath, do you understand?"

Herbert nods pathetically.

"And you must be cleaned up. Hair washed and brushed. Eyes clear. Fresh clothes on your person, not these foul-smelling garments that reek of vomit. Until then…"

Isaac steps into the room. He cannot bear to see Oliver and Herbert arguing.

Oliver is startled by his presence, and Herbert turns away, embarrassed.

"It's all right, father," Isaac says, "I'm not a child, and you needn't keep secrets from me. I'm your son, after all."

Oliver sighs and puts the empty bottle back onto the nightstand. "I didn't want you to see him in this condition," Oliver explains.

Isaac walks around his father to see Herbert's red, bloated face. The man's rheumy eyes are bloodshot and full of tears. His hair is matted in the back and sticking out like straw in the front. His dressing gown is wrinkled and stained.

Herbert wipes his nose on a sleeve and sniffs.

"Hi, grandpa," Isaac says. "I've missed you." And then he leans in and embraces the old man with both arms. "Been a tough time, huh?" he whispers. He knows about despair, and tough times, and how they bring out the worst,

The warm touch and gentle voice bring fresh tears to Herbert's eyes, and he fights to keep from sobbing.

Oliver watches his son tenderly pull away from Herbert, then wipe the moisture from the old man's cheeks.

"I don't deserve you," Herbert says, attempting a smile but producing only a sad wrinkle.

"What time is it?" Isaac asks, turning to Oliver.

"Seven or so. Almost dinner time."

Isaac says, "I'm starved." He turns back to Herbert and smiles. "But there's time for a hot bath and a bit of grooming first. I'll help you."

"No, no, I can manage," Herbert replies bravely. "I'll call for hot water. You two get ready for dinner and I'll see you downstairs."

"Are you sure? I don't mind." Isaac says, taking the old man's hand.

"I am absolutely positive!" Herbert stands for the first time and manages an actual smile. "Must preserve some dignity, you know."

"All right then. Come on, father. He'll be fine." Isaac leads Oliver out of the room, closing the door behind him.

"I'm sorry you had to see that," Oliver says solemnly.

"You said he murdered your father. What does that mean?"

"It doesn't mean anything. Herbert's my father."

"But your real father was a Persian."

"Am I not *your* father?"

Isaac understands Oliver's meaning. And he knows the discussion is over. Isaac retreats to his room and dons fresh clothes for the evening meal.

About eight o'clock, he rambles down the stairs and finds Jonathon, Phebe, and Oliver seated at an enormous table. They are dressed in their finest clothes and chatting amiably. As Isaac enters the room, they look up and smile. Oliver, who is seated at the head of the table, gestures to a chair on his left and Isaac takes it.

"Now, then, all we need is Herbert and we can begin dinner," Oliver says. Oscar, a gray and wiry server, pours wine and delivers plates of tiny morsels that Isaac cannot identify but which awaken his taste buds.

About fifteen minutes later, as the server is pouring more wine, Oliver says, "Oscar, would you be so good as to remind Herbert that our guests are waiting on him? The pheasant will be cold by the time he arrives."

Oscar nods, puts down the shimmering green wine bottle and stiffly walks out of the room.

The wine glasses are empty again by the time Oscar returns and announces, ashen-faced, "I'm afraid there has been an accident, sir."

At these words Isaac flees from his seat, races up the stairway and dashes to Herbert's room. The door is open. Inside he can see the tub that had been placed there for Herbert's bath, and the red water in which the old man lies slumped, head back, mouth and eyes open, one arm hanging like a broken tree branch above a pool of blood and a straight razor.

Isaac stands there for a moment disbelieving his eyes. When he tries to run to Herbert, he is restrained by Oliver, who is now standing behind him.

"Let him be, son," Oliver says. "He's at peace now. And I trust he's with Anne."

It is not the occasion that Oliver would have chosen for introducing his American family to Chillington-hall, but life does not always offer choices. And so here they are, standing solemnly on the cold grounds of Chillington-hall, watching Herbert's coffin being lowered into a freshly dug pit near Mum's tombstone and the empty graves of Augustus and Elizabeth, whose bones still lie somewhere in Persia. Oliver can imagine that a small gathering like this one, sometime in the future, will watch his own coffin lowered into a dark hole near Mum's grave. And then some day further on, Isaac will find rest here as well.

Oliver thinks about his mother, Anne, who had been buried in a small cemetery in New York City, and he vows to have her moved here. It is only right.

The comforting thing about cemeteries is that they bring families together.

CHAPTER 3

By horseback, through the scorching heat of summer, Jalal has traveled three hundred miles from Shiraz to Isfahan, the first city in the route of the great mission prescribed by the Rasul. Everywhere the ravages of Persian tyranny and misgovernment have been visible. Along the road lay the scorched skeletons of many abandoned villages, and for long stretches the only vegetation has been scrubby tamarind trees and thorn bushes. Jalal has been traveling to many cities to debate the mujtahids and announce the cause of the Rasul. It is hard work. Most mujtahids have been hostile and unwavering in their ignorance.

Now, as he rests in the courtyard of a madrisih in Teheran, he looks up to see one of the teachers, a Shaykhi, glaring at him.

"When I heard that you had come to our school, my heart was full," the instructor replies. "You were the brightest of Kazim's students. I had hoped that you would promote the best interests of the Shaykhis, perhaps even help raise us out of obscurity here in the capital. But you seem to have abandoned your teacher's doctrines and set out on a suicidal mission that will also bring about the complete extinction of the few Shaykhis here in Teheran."

"Then you will be pleased to know that I have not abandoned the teachings of Shaykh Ahmad or Siyyid Kazim. Did they not both urge us to seek the Promised One, whom they said would appear in our time? And would not their teachings take on a different character after the fulfillment of their prophecy?"

The two men begin to debate the message that Jalal has brought to Teheran. It ends as the instructor expresses his disdain for this weary messenger by kicking sand on him and raging out of the courtyard.

By early afternoon, an animated crowd has gathered to watch a local mulla, known to be a shrewd and fearsome debater, lose point after point in his argument with Jalal. The crowd clearly backs their local cleric, hoping to see the itinerant heretic publicly humiliated. Finally, though clearly beaten, the local mulla proposes that the debate be called a draw "because heresy is powerful; it has the assistance of Satan, and so I have been clearly disadvantaged in this debate and remain unpersuaded in my views."

Many of the observers leave wondering why *truth* does not have the assistance of God to balance things out.

Jalal finds these public discourses increasingly unsatisfying. The outcome is often unclear and he fears that the sand-kicking Shaykhi instructor may have had a good point. Perhaps these public pronouncements cause more damage than good.

Famished, he begins to walk toward a large open-air market. The meaty aromas of kabob make his stomach growl, but for the first time he begins to worry about his ability to pay. Perhaps he will forego this meal and turn the pain of hunger into a meditation on sacrifice.

As he turns away from the meat vendors, Jalal literally bumps into a man dressed in very odd clothing. The only foreign-looking clothes like these that he can remember were worn by a Christian missionary in Bushruyih, a man who had tutored English to his best friend's mother.

The man nods politely and in perfect Persian says, "Forgive me, it was my fault. I was following you."

Startled, Jalal asks, "But why?"

"I'm hungry, aren't you," the man says. "May I buy you a kabob? I will explain while we eat."

As they devour the tender kabobs, the foreigner continues. "My name is Eardley Pickwick," he says. "Originally from England."

Jalal nods.

"I am presently a translator for the court. It seems that diplomatic relations with my country have created a demand for persons fluent in both Persian and English. As I was born and raised in England, I have the advantage of understanding my people's customs and politics."

"Are you Christian?"

"Let's just say… I've seen the error of all religions, so I have none at present."

"How did you come to be in Persia?"

"Originally, I was brought here as a translator for another English gentleman, but when I discovered his true purpose—to which I strongly objected—I terminated my employment. Of England, I hold no fond memories or attachments, and I found that my services were needed here, so I stayed on."

Jalal is finishing his kabob. He was hungrier than he had thought. Pickwick buys him another and they continue talking.

"You promised to explain why you were following me," Jalal says.

"In a very few days you have caused quite a stir in Teheran. I heard about you, and finally found you. It was not difficult. I should say that you are not well liked by the clerics here."

"I come to bring them truth, and they feel threatened by it."

"Let me be blunt. After hearing you debate that insufferable mulla this afternoon, your ideas affected me deeply. Particularly your claim that God has delivered a new Qu'ran."

"Those were not my words, nor my meaning."

"Close enough. As a translator—and as a man who only today discovered he was in search of religion—I was hoping that you might let me have a look at this document... if it is in your possession, of course."

This Englishman is quite transparent; Jalal quickly surmises that there is a hidden motive behind Eardley Pickwick's request. The man is an opportunist. But then again, God sometimes uses unsuspecting people to further his cause.

"Thank you for the kabobs," Jalal says.

"You're very welcome."

"As for your request, I've been instructed to deliver a copy of that tablet to the shah, but twice I've been turned away because I do not have 'credentials.' Unfortunately, I am just a poor mulla, not a dignitary."

"Ahhh!" Pickwick says with delight. "Then perhaps we can assist each other. What a happy coincidence that I can deliver your tablet to the shah."

"You have access to the shah?"

"Actually, to one of his advisers, who I am sure will deliver it personally to the shah at my request."

"In that case I'm sure it would be permissible for me to present the document to this adviser, who is perhaps your employer."

"I can arrange that."

"But I must deliver it to your employer myself. I must place the document in his hands and ask him to give it to the shah. Nothing less is acceptable. If you are permitted to see the document after I deliver it, I have no objection. In this way, perhaps both of us can be satisfied."

"Very well. I will make the arrangements."

"I am staying at the…"

"Yes, I know," Pickwick interrupts. "Stay there until I contact you again. You must remain available."

That evening, Jalal finds sleep evasive. It seems that God had delivered an answer to his prayers, and yet he feels uneasy.

By mid-afternoon of the next day, Jalal has written and posted a letter to the Rasul revealing the outcomes of his mission so far. He is exhausted. Every joint and limb throbs with fatigue. But the day is not done.

Eardley Pickwick finds him strolling through the gardens in front of the madrisih.

"Come with me," Pickwick says.

"Now?"

"Right now."

Within an hour they have been escorted into the citadel, past four levels of guards, down a maze of walkways, through the doors of Golestan Palace, and into the glittering Hall of Mirrors. Pickwick mistakes Jalal's silence as awe. "I'm sure you are overwhelmed by the majesty of these surroundings," Pickwick says. "I was quite stunned the first time I gained entrance."

Jalal is not awe-struck; certainly not by this meaningless and crass display of opulence. Most of it, he knows, is a mirage fluttering above a desert of national debt. Jalal also is not overcome by the political clout of the figure he is about to meet. By comparison to the events of this morning, this journey to the heart of the Qajar dynasty is a distasteful diversion. He longs instead for the sincere fellowship of the Rasul, and imagines the *true* majesty of…

Pickwick whispers into Jalal's ear, "Bow deeply when you first greet the grand vizier," he says.

The grand vizier!

Perhaps Jalal has misjudged this Englishman. It is common knowledge that the grand vizier is the power behind the throne.

They approach a short, squat man who stands with his back to them. The man swims in heavy ceremonial robes. A tall conical cap towers above his head. As the grand vizier hears footsteps approaching, he turns and gestures graciously for his guests to forego the normal formalities.

"So you are the man who has been preaching in our streets about a new religious Revelation," Haji Mirza Aqasi says. His eyes run up and down this dust-covered figure in white. He seems amused. "I understand you have something for the shah. A tablet—am I correct?"

"The author of this tablet instructed me to deliver it personally to the shah."

"May I see it?"

Jalal reaches into his satchel and removes the scroll. "It is very important that the shah receive this document at the earliest possible time."

"Yes, yes, I understand. Everyone's message is the most important one in the world. Well, I can assure you that I will hand your message to the shah myself." Aqasi holds out his hand for the scroll but Jalal merely stares at him. `

"I must have your word on this," Jalal says.

Aqasi bristles with anger.

Pickwick reflexively backs away; he has experienced the concussion of the Aqasi's explosions.

After a deep breath, though, Aqasi smiles weakly and says, "You have my word. The shah will have your tablet no later than tomorrow. Come now—the scroll."

Jalal hands the scroll to Aqasi. As possession of it changes hands, he sees a fleeting flicker of fear on the grand vizier's face immediately followed by a smirk of victory.

So this is the *new Qu'ran*, is it?" Aqasi says.

"It contains a message for the shah. I am sure he will understand it."

"I am certain of that." Suddenly the grand vizier wheels to his left and marches from the room without another word.

"The audience is over," Pickwick says.

Late the same evening, Pickwick is summoned to the personal chamber of Aqasi who has been studying the tablet.

"You did well to obtain this treasonous tract for me," he tells Pickwick. "It is even worse than I had feared. The author has the gall to ask Muhammad Shah to convert and assist his cause. In his view, the shah's authority to govern is subservient to this new religion. Even worse, this imbecile attacks me."

"By name?"

"By title. This is treason—and blasphemy."

"Do you want to have the messenger arrested?"

"The man is intoxicated by this heresy. He will never reveal the author's identity,. Let him go. Perhaps he will lead us to the mastermind of this plot."

"You think it is political rather than religious?"

"Everything comes down to power. And in Persia, religion is power. If we ignore it, this ripple of insurrection will become a tidal wave that can sweep us from power. On the other hand, if we can identify the fool behind this tablet and support the clergy in actions against him, we can *consolidate* our power and place the mullas clearly in our debt." He shows a sinister smile that chills Pickwick. "The Qajars and the clerics have not been on the same side for a long time."

Pickwick despises this man and dreads his role in the persecutions to come, but he fears leaving Aqasi's service even more. He has learned too much about Aqasi. And Aqasi knows that Pickwick had assisted Herbert Eaton in the assassination of Mirza Hasan Qasim. Eaton had escaped. Pickwick had not; he struck a bargain with Aqasi.

"May I read the tablet?" Pickwick asks calmly.

"Of course," Aqasi says. "There are no secrets between us."

CHAPTER 4

Danush, the youngest disciple, has become the Rasul's closest confidant. On most occasions, words are not required for Danush to understand the Rasul's emotions and needs. Danush feels warmed by the Rasul's presence and is continually astonished at his master's composure in the face of a gathering threat.

Despite the Rasul's admonitions to keep his identity secret, some of the Letters have revealed too much. Shiraz has become the focal point for those seeking the one who claims to be the deputy of the Qa'im. Rumors have pointed toward a young merchant in Shiraz, known to his small band of disciples as the Rasul.

Already the young man's tablet has stimulated wide discussion and fierce debate. The message is seen by some as a justification for open rebellion against unpopular governors. Others see in it the work of Satan and the need to defend the traditions of Islam at all costs. A few respond to the tablet's call for spiritual renewal and seek ways to join the "new religion." Riots have broken out in some towns and villages.

It is the season of the Hajj—the annual pilgrimage to Mecca and Medina. In the village of Jidda, the Rasul and his disciples Danush and Mubarak set out by camel on a journey of several days. About ten kilometers from Mecca they don the pilgrim's attire and walk to the shrine, joining a hundred thousand other pilgrims at Masjid al-Haram, the sacred sanctuary of Islam. In this huge courtyard thousands of worshippers orbit around a large black cube known as the Kaaba, the object towards which all Muslims throughout the world turn during prayer. This flat-roofed building rises fifty feet from a narrow marble platform on mortared bases of blue-gray stone. Tradition holds that the Kaaba was built by the prophet Abraham as a landmark for the House of God. At one corner of the Kaaba is a sacred stone that some believe was delivered by the angel Gabriel.

The floor and roof of the Masjid al-Haram are filled with pilgrims. The Rasul and his companions push their way into the courtyard. The sweaty, swarming pilgrims sweep them into their orbit, but the Rasul moves purposefully toward the Kaaba. Suddenly separated from the Rasul by the crush of bodies, Danush and Mubarak lose sight of Him. He seems to have been swallowed by the sea of humanity.

Panic seizes Danush and he begins to swim frantically through the crowd, looking everywhere for the Rasul but seeing only a mass of white-clad pilgrims. The hot sun glares off their garments, blinding Danush momentarily. For a moment he is carried forward by the crowd, his feet lifted off the ground and his arms flailing helplessly. Finally he finds a seam and pushes again toward the Kaaba. Mercifully, a gentle breeze stirs the air.

Danush cannot yet see the Rasul, but he can hear his voice above the din of the crowd. Yes, it is the Rasul's voice; it carries in the breeze. The words are faint but he can make them out. The Rasul is saying, "I am the Qa'im whom you were expecting."

The ceaseless rotation of the crowd slows, and then stops, as if the call to prayer had just sounded. Around Danush the faces of the pilgrims appear curious but confused. The murmur of the crowd, once the roar of an ocean, is now a gentle lapping on the shore. Danush pushes forward again and finds the Rasul holding the ring knob of the Kaaba door.

"I am the Qa'im whom you were expecting," the Rasul repeats.

Now the crowd grows still as the Rasul's words are translated into the various languages spoken by the pilgrims who have come from many lands. And then a hush overtakes the courtyard. There is no outcry, no cheers, no hysteria, no charges of heresy or blasphemy—only stunned silence, as if the pilgrims cannot comprehend what has just been said.

A tall pilgrim near the outer wall of the courtyard begins to push urgently toward the Kaaba. He wants a close look at this man who has brought the pilgrimage ritual—the last of the Five Pillars of Islam—to a complete halt. This pilgrim has studied the Rasul's tablet and unexpectedly had found himself transformed by its message. He had come to Masjid al-Harám at the beginning of the month of pilgrimage hoping that the author of those wondrous words would appear and reveal himself as the Traditions had foretold. A Christian by birth, and never a Muslim, he had disguised himself as a pilgrim to penetrate this holiest of Islamic shrines.

The silence of the courtyard is eerie. A sparrow flutters overhead and the sound of its wings causes many eyes to look up.

A third time the Rasul says "I am the Qa'im whom you were expecting."

Still there is no response. The tall pilgrim continues to push toward the Kaaba, but he is too late. As the crowd begins to understand what has happened, and begins to buzz with awareness and sudden opinion, the Rasul steps into the crowd, is embraced by Danush, and then disappears into the anonymity of the crowd.

The tall pilgrim reaches the Kaaba too late. He takes a deep breath, imagines that the air filling his lungs might be the same air that had caressed the holy body of that young man. His body shivers in the heat. Was he the only person here who understood the event that had just transpired? Should not these thousands of pilgrims have been expecting this momentous occasion?

The tall pilgrim feels a firm grip on his right arm, then another on his left. Someone shouts at him in Arabic. He speaks Farsi but understands enough Arabic to know that his ruse has been discovered. In his haste to achieve the presence of the Qa'im he had entered a holy area prohibited to non-Muslims.

Two more men approach him, shouting Arabic curses. A coarse voice speaking Farsi interrogates him. He cannot claim to be a Muslim. His knowledge of Islam is too academic. If he has been truly transformed by the message of the Qa'im, he cannot lie.

And so Eardley Pickwick admits his deceit. His pilgrim captors roughly escort him outside the courtyard and throw him into the dirt. One of them pulls a knife from beneath his pilgrim garb and holds it menacingly above Pickwick. These Muslims consider such a grievous offense to be punishable by death.

As the man with the knife lowers it and places the sharp edge beneath Pickwick's chin, the Englishman considers showing his court credentials. That may save him. But as he feels the cold blade on his throat, he also feels tired and sick. He has seen too much. Sinned too much. He has little left to offer, even if he were spared. He has no life in England to which he can return, and he despises his life in Persia. He has become a servant of evil in serving Aqasi. Maybe this end is not so bad. He may be bound for hell, but then again, if he sheds his blood for this newest Manifestation of God, perhaps there will be amnesty for the first martyr.

He looks up at his executioner and smiles. The knife moves. He can taste the blood in his throat.

Only God knows his sacrifice.

CHAPTER 5

Aqasi faces a dilemma, a political spark that he fears may ignite the dry kindling on which his brittle nation is built. Emissaries of a new self-proclaimed prophet have been popping up everywhere, announcing a "new Qu'ran," stirring the people into a state of perturbation. Some imbeciles have become followers of this "Rasul" despite stern warnings from the mullas about the imposter. Tensions are growing. Until now Aqasi has believed that this mild religious tempest works in his favor, for he can drift effortlessly above the fray on prevailing currents like an eagle awaiting an opportunity for a meal. While this instability preoccupies the mullas, the shah's court can in many subtle ways increase its power unchallenged by the religious authorities.

But now the instability has pricked the finger of Aqasi, drawing blood. As he considers the problem, he wrinkles up his nose in disgust. Another mess to clean up. And this one is politically delicate. A famous mujtahid who has converted to the Rasulí cause has been arrested in Shiraz and tortured for his heresy. A great uprising has occurred in the city. To quell the rioting, Aqasi has decided to order the governor to have the Rasul arrested in Bushire and tried by the clergy in Shiraz. In that way, he can wash his hands of the Rasul's certain fate.

Six days later the populace of Shiraz is astonished at the sight of the Rasul on his horse, riding free and unfettered, leading the governor's mounted escort directly to the seat of government.

The governor of Shiraz, Husayn Khan, has heard of the public spectacle created by the Rasul's cavalcade through the city streets, angrily described by some as a "triumphant return." Infuriated by the timid behavior of his guards, who were sent to bring the Rasul back in chains, the governor channels his anger toward the impudent young merchant who is now seated in a hard wooden chair at the center of an imposing chamber. Among the divines present is the city's leading mujtahid, Mulla Turab, a lean, white-bearded man with penetrating eyes and a hawk-like beak for a nose.

The governor is incensed by the Rasul's calm demeanor. Unable to restrain himself, he shouts, "Do you realize what a great mischief you have created?" His voice echoes in the solemn hall.

The Rasul looks up at the governor but remains silent.

"Are you aware what a disgrace you have become to the holy Faith of Islam, and to the august person of our sovereign?"

The Rasul patiently looks at the governor, as if waiting for all the questions to be asked before responding. His silence provokes the governor to bolt from his seat and stomp to the Rasul's chair. After circumambulating the captive, and failing to melt the man into submission through the sheer heat of his presence, the governor speaks into the Rasul's ear: "Are you not the man who claims to be the author of a new revelation that annuls the sacred precepts of the Qu'ran?"

The Rasul lowers his head, then looks up at the governor and calmly replies, "'If any bad man come unto you with news, clear up the matter at once, lest through ignorance you harm others, and be speedily constrained to repent of what you have done.'"

Taking great offense at this remark, the red-faced governor shouts, "What! You take it upon yourself to accuse us of evil and ignorance?"

With the flat of his hand, the governor swats the captive in the face. The Rasul's green turban flies onto the floor. The governor marches back to his ornate chair and sits down, angry and frustrated.

Dismayed by the governor's rude behavior, Mulla Turab stands abruptly and orders one of the other mullas to place the turban back onto the head of the Rasul, which is done immediately. And then Abu-Turab invites the Rasul to take a seat next to his own. The governor does not dare to chastise this powerful cleric, but he is confused by the Shaykh's sudden kindness toward the imposter.

Turning toward the governor, Mulla Turab speaks with great authority: "This youth has quoted a verse from the Qu'ran," he explains. "Apparently you did not recognize it."

The governor, a secular Muslim who has not consulted the Qu'ran in many years, shifts uneasily in his chair.

"This particular verse has made a profound impression on me," Abu-Turab continues, "for it tells us that even if a bad man brings us news, we ought to investigate the truth of it. The wise course, I feel, is to inquire into this matter with great care, and to judge this young man by the precepts of the holy Book."

"Inquire, then. I will not prevent you," the governor replies. In truth, he is relieved that Mulla Turab has taken the matter into his own hands. There is less chance now that the governor will err and shatter the fragile balance of power between the government and the clergy.

For ten minutes Mulla Turab questions the prisoner, sometimes so intimately that no one else can hear their exchanges.

As the governor grows restless and appears ready to terminate the interrogation, Mulla Turab stands and faces the governor. "I am completely satisfied," he announces. "The young man has denied the claim of being either the representative of the promised Qa'im, or the intermediary between Him and the faithful."

The governor sits up straight, astonished that the imposter would so easily recant his claims.

"I see no reason to inter him," Mulla Turab explains. And then he turns to the Rasul and says, "We request, however, that you present yourself on Friday in the Mosque of Vakíl where you can proclaim publicly your denial."

On Friday, as promised, the Rasul arrives at the Mosque. He enters the cavernous chamber just as Mulla Turab is ascending the steps to the pulpit-top. As the mujtahid turns to face his congregation, he sees the Rasul standing below. He smiles with the pride of a man who has shut down a rebellion.

"I would like to welcome Siyyid Salih, whom I see among you today," he announces.

Immediately the gathering begins to buzz excitedly, for they all know the name of the heretic who falsely calls himself the Rasul.

Mulla Turab extends his hand toward the Rasul and says, "It is time for you to publicly repudiate your claim."

The Rasul steps onto the first stair and prepares to address the congregation.

"Come up higher," Mulla Turab urges.

The Rasul takes another two steps up and turns. "Praise be to God, who hath in truth created the heavens and the earth," he begins.

An impatient voice calls out, "Enough idle chatter. Declare the thing you intend to say!"

Mulla Turab steps forward and shouts, "Hold your peace! And be ashamed of your impertinence." Stroking his long white beard, Mulla Turab then leans toward the Rasul and whispers, "Be quick about it. This crowd may get excited."

The Rasul looks out on the expectant, angry faces of the congregation and begins again. "The condemnation of God be upon him who regards me as a representative of the Twelfth Imam," he says, and this beginning seems much more satisfying to the mob below. He continues: "The condemnation of God also be upon whoever accuses me of having denied the unity of God, the Prophet-hood of Muhammad, the truth of any of the messengers of old, or the guardianship of 'Ali, the Commander of the Faithful."

The Rasul turns and climbs the rest of the stairs to the pulpit-top, warmly embracing Abu-Turab. As the young man begins his descent to the floor of the Mosque, Mulla Turab shudders with the sudden realization of what has just transpired. This young man has masterfully succeeded in silencing his most formidable opponents with a denial of what he is *not*. He is not the "gate" or representative of anyone—this much the young man could freely admit because his true station is much higher.

His real claim is to be the promised Qa'im. In reality, then, this public statement has been less a denial and more a clarification of what he *is*, though few will understand.

Mulla Turab is about to demand that the Rasul expand his denial to include any claim of being the Promised One, but as he watches the young man reach the floor of the mosque and prepare himself for the traditional Friday prayer, Mulla Turab smiles instead, and his thoughts inexplicably turn to protecting the young man from harm.

CHAPTER 6

Latin is now the official language of the Chadwick mansion in Belgravia, except for conversations of a personal nature between Ollie and Isaac. These are held in the rich, chocolaty Farsi tongue with a spicy dash of Arabic stirred in for good measure.

Through disuse, Oliver finds that his Latin has atrophied. The words now lie limp and lifeless on his tongue. Isaac, who has just begun his Latin studies and is years behind the other young men at the Charterhouse, struggles to find a pulse in the dead language; *arduum sane munus*—a truly arduous task. Phebe complains that English is becoming a lost language in the household, and Jonathon—who had finally picked up a few words of Farsi—now finds himself humorously intermixing it with the basic Latin vocabulary that has been pounded into his head by the insistent drone of conversations limited to fifty or sixty Latin words.

Through the summer months, while his schoolmates vacation, Isaac drills under the instruction of a dusty old tutor of Latin, Wilfred Brown, who speaks with a breath as stale as the language itself and believes, quite honestly, that he has been imbued with a supernatural understanding of the peculiar enunciation used by the original speakers of that dead tongue.

"They did not speak Latin with the broad, rude flatness of us Englishmen—oh yes, and you Americans, who are even ruder in your diction," he often tells Isaac. "They brought a music, a lilt, to their articulation, which is embedded into the language itself but is not apparent in the written form. Now watch the shape of my mouth and my tongue as I conjugate these verbs…"

How Wilfred Brown has divined these lost sounds remains a mystery, but Isaac suspects that a sufficient volume of Italian wine (in which the old man's brain perpetually marinates) might serve as a kind of cosmic medium that enables communication with past ages. By listening to his tutor, Isaac has concluded that ancient Romans frequently *slurred* their words, and sometimes stuttered and belched, and most often sounded as if they were, to be blunt, quite drunk.

In an experiment one afternoon, Isaac discovers that he can most successfully duplicate the original accent of the Romans after consuming four glasses of wine.

As Isaac suffers these lessons in a dim, musty room on the nearly vacant grounds of the Charterhouse, Jonathon Fury rejoices in the atmosphere and architecture of London, finding that the city's coal-infused fog often paints his daguerreotype subjects with a tincture of mystery that he considers quite artistic. He prefers making personal photographic experiments to the more practical work of illustrating news articles. Thanks to Oliver, however, the daguerreotype has quickly become a staple of illustration in the *Times* of London, and Jonathon its chief practitioner. Predictably, Jonathon is back to photographing public hangings and dour dignitaries at civic events.

Phebe has happily seized her role as mistress of the mansion, thriving on the power to procure food and other goods for the household by edict; much easier on the feet. While New York was big and modern and brutally brash, it seems now—in comparison to London—a cheap imitation of a city. This is the real thing. One can *smell* history in the damp air, and *touch* it on any excursion beyond the grounds of the Belgravia mansion. Only in the kitchen does Phebe long for the old days in her boarding house when she could cook and bake with her own strong hands. Her intractable English kitchen staff has demonstrated the uncanny ability to suck the flavor out of any dish, even when it is made from Phebe's own time-tested recipe. Still, it is improper for the lady of the house to perform such menial tasks as cooking, so Phebe diverts her creative energies into tinkering with the furniture, a more ladylike avocation. She has discovered a knack for rearranging the manor's movable objects into ever-changing constellations, much to the dismay of the males in her family who would prefer that the stars remain fixed for navigational purposes; the unpleasant result of these "reconfigurations" has been numerous stubbed toes, a few bruised shins, and torrents of profanity not always in Latin.

Still, it's good to hear English around the house.

Oliver has not re-acclimated to London. He had thought that returning home would restore some of the warmth and comfort of his memories, but now he recognizes that he had seldom been warm and comfortable in London. This is where he had been jarringly sent away to school, segregated from his family like an amputated limb; where his mother had rejected him for the companionship of tawdry theater people, and his doting grandmother had abandoned him by dying; where a man of the cloth had molested him; and where he had been humiliated in front of London high society by his own father.

Why a return to London had ever seemed like a good idea still confounds Oliver as he makes his way by carriage to the George and Vulture to meet Jonathon for lunch. In the months since his return, Oliver has seldom dined out, preferring to seclude himself in his mansion except for an occasional mission: a Turkoman-like raid on the local clergy. He has exposed the folly and hypocrisy of a half-dozen London priests; but even before his conquests, these small-time sinners had been too remote from God for Oliver to extract any satisfaction. It is *God* that he wants to punish. These vain, deluded agents of God in sparkling hats and satin robes do not even provide good sport!

As summer draws to an end, Oliver mellows. His rage at the clergy has grown tepid. Only as he prepares for bed each evening—as he studies the photographs of Mary Rogers and his wife, and the illustration of his mother on the cover of her book—does he feel the sting of anger. If he did not find pleasure in this pain he would hide the pictures, but instead he keeps them on his nightstand to remind him of his goal to punish God. Unfortunately, he has found no worthy targets on this earthly plain.

All this changes, however, one evening in late August when Oliver picks up the day's edition of the *Times* and reads:

> MOHAMMEDAN SCHISM. -- A new sect has lately set itself up in Persia, at the head of which is a merchant who had returned from a pilgrimage to Mecca, and proclaimed himself a successor of the Prophet. The way they treat such matters at Shiraz appears in the following account (June 23): -- Two persons being heard repeating their profession of faith according to the form prescribed by the impostor, were apprehended, tried, and found guilty of unpardonable blasphemy. They were sentenced to lose their beards by fire being set to them. The sentence was put into execution with all the zeal and fanaticism becoming a true believer in Mahomet.

Not deeming the loss of beards a sufficient punishment, they were further sentenced the next day, to have their faces blacked and exposed through the city. Each of them was led by a mir-gazah (executioner), who had made a hole in his nose and passed through it a string, which he sometimes   pulled with such violence that the unfortunate fellows cried out alternately for mercy from the executioner and for vengeance from Heaven.

It is the custom in Persia on such occasions for the executioners to collect money from the spectators, and particularly from the shopkeepers in the bazaar. In the evening when the pockets of the executioners were well filled with money, they led the unfortunate fellows to the city gate, and there turned them adrift. After which the mollahs at Shiraz sent men to Bushire, with power to seize the impostor, and take him to Shiraz, where, on being tried, he very wisely denied the charge of apostasy laid against him, and thus escaped from punishment.

Oliver knows that most readers of this article will dismiss the outrageous claim of this "merchant from Shiraz," but Oliver shudders with the possibility that the Promised One, whom he and his best friend Jalal had dreamed of finding, had appeared at last. While Christians will certainly scoff at this "fairy tale," Oliver hopes it is true, for if it is, then he has identified his quarry. If this Persian merchant speaks the truth, then Oliver knows how to punish God.

He will return to Persia. He will go home.

CHAPTER 7

The stream of visitors into the city of Kirmanshah, in the western mountains of Persia, takes everyone by surprise. Only three evenings previously, Tara and a small group of female companions—escorted by a ragtag band of armed believers—had entered the city under the watchful gaze of the residents.

Tara, the only female Living Letter, is a poetess renowned throughout Persia, but she is hated by the mullas for her views of women's rights and challenges to their authority. Only weeks earlier she had been banished from Ottoman territory. News of this had arrived several days earlier, and two houses had been prepared for the travelers by local sympathizers. Each afternoon and evening since her arrival, from behind a curtain, Tara has recited her mystical verse to the enraptured, poetry-mad Persians, aroused each gathering with the teachings of the Rasul, and debated with unfeminine ferocity the city's hostile clergy. These sessions, which had begun indoors, have now been forced outside by the size of the crowds.

For the past two weeks a young woman of sixteen named Zarrin has been visiting her cousins in Kirmanshah. Like Tara, Zarrin is fiercely independent, having already refused a distasteful marriage arranged with great pride and fanfare by her father. It is her defiance, in fact, that has brought her to this city. Humiliated by Zarrin's rejection of his hand-picked mate—a garlic-breathed merchant twice her age—Zarrin's father had banished her from the village, at least until the sting of his abasement passes.

Herded into a veiled pen near Tara's curtain, Zarrin joins many other cloaked women in listening to the now-famous poetess. She is joyously transported by the passion of these verses and eagerly plucks the ripe revelations of the Rasul from the lips of Tara. Far from radical, as the clergy has labeled these teachings, Zarrin finds them to be seductively reasonable; it is the mullas' sexist corruption of Islam that she finds extremist and absurd.

Several times during previous blistering debates with the mullas she had loudly cheered as Tara had vanquished her adversary with irrefutable arguments and elegant proofs. Each time that Zarrin had shouted, the other women had muzzled her with deafening hands, fearing retaliation.

Zarrin has never witnessed such an audacious public display of feminine power or such clear debunking of the mullas' unsupportable propositions. Mortified and enraged by their inability to put this woman in her place, the defeated mullas always resort to curses and threats, juvenile taunts and coarse interruptions, but nothing diverts the attention of the crowds from the charismatic Tara.

By the fourth day of these outdoor events the audience has grown so large and partisan to Tara's cause that even Zarrin begins to fear retaliation. She knows that the mullas will not continue to tolerate this unceasing flow of "heresy," especially delivered, as it is, by a woman.

As Zarrin peeks through the purple and red drapery that shrouds the women's section, she sees that for the first time there are no mullas present. She is certain they have not surrendered, and so she concludes they must be contriving some terrible revenge. Her heart begins to pound.

When the audience applauds a reading of one of Tara's poems, Zarrin exits the women's enclosure and orbits around the back until she finds Tara seated on a plain wooden chair behind her curtain. Tara smiles at the younger woman.

"Be careful, please," Zarrin whispers. "I believe the mullas are meeting somewhere to plot against you."

"No, my dear," Tara whispers back. "They have finished their plans and are coming for me as we speak."

Zarrin's eyes flash. As she begins to gasp, a hand from behind firmly cups her mouth, capturing the sound. An older woman has followed Zarrin and calms her now with a gentle *Sshhhh*!

Smiling, Tara asks Zarrin, "My sister, what is your name?"

The hand slowly releases Zarrin's mouth as she gives her name.

"Remember what you have seen and heard these past days," Tara whispers. "Carry it in your heart, and tell others. I may not be free after this to speak out."

"Then you must flee now!" Zarrin says.

"My mission is to teach, so I will teach as long as they let me. Now you have a mission, too. When I am silenced…"

The whisper is drowned in a sea of shouts as a gang of mullas invades the gathering. From behind the curtain, Zarrin and Tara can hear the clerics yelling scornfully at the men who are seated on the other side of the curtain. The screaming comes nearer, and then hands ripple the curtain.

A whiny voice calls out, "Cover yourself, woman!"

The meaning is clear. In a few seconds they are going to abduct Tara, who even now makes no effort to cover herself.

"Go, child!" Tara says to Zarrin. "Don't let them find you with me."

Zarrin flees just before local divines pull down the curtain. The sight of Tara's naked face horrifies them. One of the mullas, a man of great bulk, averts his eyes. The other two continue to drink in Tara's beauty, unable to turn away. The fat mulla, seeing his awestruck companions paralyzed, chastises them: "You see, she tempts even you, the most upright and virtuous mullas in Kirmanshah."

"Are men so feeble, "Tara says, "that they cannot look upon a woman's face without lust? Yes, it is certainly better to veil this woman rather than expose your own perversity."

Her eyes lower to focus on the fat mulla's paunch. "I think you had best veil your supper as well to obscure the path to gluttony."

Concealed just a few steps away, Zarrin chuckles.

Squinting to blur his vision and avoid irresistible temptation, the fat mulla angrily lurches toward Tara, pulls her black chador over her gleaming face, and orders his friends to seize her, which they do, the evil spell of seduction having now been broken.

From beneath her garment, Tara speaks again: "I will pray that you overcome your affliction. May God grant you even a *small* measure of self-control over the wicked impulses that seem to dominate you."

This taunt is too much for the fat mulla, who throws Tara onto the ground and viciously kicks her. The others, perhaps mellowed by their glimpse of Tara's mesmerizing beauty, pull him away.

Sitting up without help, Tara responds, "Perhaps you are ignorant of the Tradition that says, 'The strong is not the one who overcomes the people by his strength, but the strong is the one who controls himself while in anger.'"

Ignoring her, the fat mulla roughly stands her up. "Take her away," he commands. "The mujtahid will determine her punishment." Tara's arms are chained and she is led through a gathering that is now nearly two hundred strong.

A young man, who had been moved profoundly by Tara's vivid account of the Rasul's new revelation, removes a dagger from his cloak. He moves threateningly toward the mullas who are escorting Tara through the multitude of Tara's admirers. Immediately, the crowd begins to buzz with anticipation and twenty other men begin to follow the knife-bearer.

Hurriedly, the mullas remove Tara from the hostile environment.

Zarrin watches with tears in her eyes. Four short days is all that she had been allowed to hear Tara's stirring message of hope, and yet it had taken only minutes for that message to penetrate her heart. She remembers the words that Tara had spoken directly to her: "Carry it in your heart, and tell others."

Zarrin prays that she may gain the courage of Tara.

CHAPTER 8

The British Ambassador to Persia, Justin Sheil, sometimes feels more like a social secretary than a diplomat. The dashing official with jet black hair and straight teeth—an oddity for an Englishman—had barely celebrated his thirty-fifth birthday in Teheran when the letter arrived at his office. Once again he is being called to perform the tedious task of introducing British visitors to the Qajar court. At times like this (and there are many of them) Sheil sees all too clearly why he was sent to Persia. A debt had been repaid to his influential father, a famous general now retired, in a manner that can do little damage to the Empire. All Sheil is required to do here is keep England visible and not stir the pot. He is the shah's English babysitter, dangling baubles to distract him when necessary, pointing out ways that Persia can please its chimerical benefactor, and occasionally slapping the royal wrist to remind the shah that he is humiliatingly outranked by a *woman*, of all things—*Queen Victoria*, the ruler of an Empire immensely more powerful than beleaguered Persia.

Today, however, Lt. Col. Justin Sheil calmly escorts his three British guests to the palace. If not for the sway of the *London Times*, which had sent the letter of introduction, Sheil might not have bowed to this request. As it is, the *Times* may find reason to mention Sheil's name.

Sheil makes small talk with Oliver Chadwick, who is dressed in a fine grey frock-coat, as are his companions, Jonathon and Isaac. They could be three English gentlemen strolling through a London park on a fine Sunday afternoon. Before entering the glittering hall of mirrors, the trousers of the three Englishmen are adorned with scarlet coverings from the knees to the ankles, customary emblems worn by all foreigners who have an audience with the shah.

Looking frail and bad-tempered, Muhammad Shah slumps on his tiered marble throne. Standing before him, watching the four Englishmen approach, is the sour grand vizier and a thin, gaunt boy of fifteen dressed in garish robes that look like a sappy costume from an English school's version of Ali Baba and the Forty Thieves. This boy is Nasir al-Din, a boy who some believe will become the shah one day. The boy's outfit is obviously meant to impress the visitors.

Another man stands facing Aqasi, his back to the audience. This man is attired in a simple green robe and wears no turban.

With a detectable bored tone, Sheil goes through the usual tedious formalities of praising the shah and introducing the very important visitors from England, stressing that Oliver represents the most influential newspaper in the British Empire, the *London Times*. It is mention of the paper that piques Aqasi's attention, and his dark-rimmed, soulless eyes hungrily study Oliver.

It has come time for Oliver to speak, and Sheil makes it clear that he should address Aqasi, not the shah directly. Having seen Aqasi's animated response to mention of the *Times*, Oliver decides to speak in English to strengthen that association.

"I am deeply honored that you have agreed to meet with us," Oliver says.

The man in the green robe translates this into Persian. Aqasi nods without smiling and says in Persian, "We are always honored to have guests from your country. I know of your newspaper. It has not always been kind in its description of our country."

The man in the green robe, still facing Aqasi, translates into English. Oliver understands the remark before the English words are spoken and uses this extra time to consider his response. It is true, he knows, that the *Times* on occasion—*frequently*, to be honest—characterizes Persians as either barbarians or children who need the guidance of a benevolent parent such as England. He had not expected Aqasi to be so knowledgeable about the *Times*. The grand vizier is no fool.

"I apologize for the misrepresentations," Oliver says. "But please know that I am not the author of any of these distortions." The translator translates, and Aqasi nods. An apology from an Englishman is rare, indeed; it is sweet music to a Persian's ear.

"I have come here in part to pledge my support in correcting these false impressions," Oliver continues, "and reporting back to England that the ancient wisdom and majesty of Persia has been born once again in the Qajars."

As the translator translates, Sheil winces with disgust. The sickly shah, however, who until now has looked as though he might slip into a coma, suddenly perks up. Oliver thinks that a slight smile may be curling the edges of his lips.

Aqasi says, "Your assistance in correcting your newspaper and its readers would be most welcome." He is seeing some advantage to be gained by this Englishman's attitude, if he can be trusted.

Before the interpreter can translate Aqasi's words, Ali begins speaking in Persian. "You may wonder as to my motives. It is quite simple. I am Persian. I was born in Bushruyih where my father was the kelauntar and a distant relative of Muhammad Shah. My heart is Persian, even though my employer is English."

At first Aqasi is shocked, but then he smiles. "So you are Persian?" he says—more of a statement than a question. "And your friends?"

"I'm afraid not. Jonathon is a trusted associate, and Ishaq is my son." He uses the Persian equivalent for the name *Isaac*.

"I see, but how is it that Ishaq does not bear a family resemblance?"

Ishaq boldly speaks up in Persian. "I am Ali's adopted son. I was born in America," he says. Nasir al-Din looks up at Ishaq, astonished at the young man's facility with the Persian language and intrigued by Ishaq's American heritage.

Aqasi nods at Ishaq and then turns back to Ali, saying, "I cannot recall your father's name. He must have served under our administration."

"My father was Mirza Hasan Qasim. I am his son, Ali Qasim."

Aqasi remembers the arrogant, undisciplined, troublesome Hasan Qasim. The man had been murdered, and Aqasi was glad. "I knew him," Aqasi says.

"My father and I were not on close terms."

"I found him unreliable and selfish."

"So did I. And yet he is not the only unreliable one you have known."

"You have only just arrived, and yet you know something that I do not?"

Oliver nods yes. "But only because you do not speak English. You see, the task of properly characterizing your interests to the English people is not well served by your translator, who has unreliably translated your words, and mine, in—shall we say—an undesirable way."

The translator shifts his body nervously, glances at Aqasi.

"My translator is an Englishman. He should know English."

"I am both Persian and English. Your translator embarrasses you."

Suddenly the translator, Gordon Cranston, wheels to stare at Ali. His face is quivering. His eyes betray fear. Speaking English so Aqasi cannot understand, Gordon pleads, "Oliver, please, he may have me killed!"

"What are you doing here, Gordon?"

"The authorities in New York found out that I was embezzling the offerings of my tent meetings. I had to flee—surely you understand. I couldn't return to England, not with the papers your grandmother had me sign. The attorneys would have turned me inside out if they found out I was in London. I hated India—always did. Persia was my second home."

Ishaq recalls the dramatic scene in the great tent in New York State, and Gordon's afflicted son, the one with Down Syndrome, and the mass "falling over" of hundreds of penitents. He looks up at Gordon and says, "What about Peter, your poor son?"

Gordon stares at his feet. "He was not my son," he says. "I bought him from an institution that lacked certain scruples and trained him like a parrot for my act. Oliver, please help me. I truly fear for my life."

Revolted by this pitiful man, Jonathon dismissively rolls his eyes and says, "And I thought my days of taking pictures of dead men were over. This time, though, I might not mind."

"Oliver, please," Gordon begs.

Ali looks at Aqasi. "Your translator has asked me to help improve his language skills so he can better serve you," Ali says.

"Can this be done?" Aqasi asks.

Ali pauses. He looks at Jonathon, then at Isaac. Their gracious natures prompt tiny affirmative nods. He looks at Sheil, who has completely lost the thread of this conversation and seems eager for a graceful departure.

Ali turns to Aqasi and says, "I'm sorry, but I am not inclined to help him." A sorrowful gasp escapes from Isaac. Ali looks at Jonathon, then at Aqasi again, adding, "Unless it is your desire for me to do so, in which case I would be honored to serve in such a capacity."

The shah grunts in pain. Aqasi stares coldly at Ali and says, "The shah must be returned to his chambers due to an ailment. I will let you know my decision tomorrow."

The audience is finished.

CHAPTER 9

The rotting corpse of the caravanserai exudes the sweet-and-sour stench of rancid garbage, unwashed bodies, and camel dung. Fleas and lice and biting flies gnaw the flesh of the inhabitants, raising scabby welts. Clouds of dust and sharp bits of straw hang in the heavy air, stinging eyes and clogging nostrils. The clamorous cacophony of barking dogs, braying mules, grunting camels and squalling infants mixes raucously with the shouts and cries of belligerent travelers, quarrelsome charvadars, and screaming food vendors who prowl the courtyard uncensored, seeming to put every vague thought into words. Of all the foul caravanserais between Bushire and Tehran, this is the worst, an open pit filled with a steaming compost of humanity.

Within an hour dusk envelops the caravanserai, and the darkness seems to smother all human sounds, leaving night to the primitive songs and clanging bell choir of the animals. Lying against the south wall of his wretched den, Ali wonders at the choices he has made in life. He is independently wealthy, and yet he is spending this night on the hard floor of a rat-infested, flea-plagued cell rather than lying comfortably on a silky goose-down bed in an opulent Belgravia mansion.

Amidst Jonathon's snoring and Ishaq's stirring and the hungry rustling of rats in the straw, Ali searches his Wolesley valise and finds the precious images of Mary and Alice, silvery daguerreotypes that gleam eerily in the shaft of moonlight slicing through the single barred window of the room. And then he remembers why he has forsaken his privileged London life and traveled back to Persia, back in time, back to the vineyard of the Lord where His Prophets are rooted in the fertile, sacred soil; where God must plant and tend His grapes until that most propitious time when the Fruit is ripe for harvest. Ali remembers now, and his anger begins to flow again like lava. He wants to be that molten lava; he wants to scorch the vineyard and burn the grapes before the harvest, because only then will the Vinetender feel the anguish and torment of losing that which was so loved and which held so much promise.

Clutching his precious pictures, Ali goes to sleep.

The next morning, as the three English gentlemen eat a hastily made breakfast of bread and eggs, two Persian soldiers push their way into the small room made smaller still by the numerous trunks and portmanteaus lined against the walls for safekeeping.

"We are looking for Ali Qasim," the first soldier exclaims brusquely.

Ali stands. He is dressed in rumpled linen trousers and a cotton bush shirt, the kind usually worn by adventurers in Africa. At his feet lies a pith helmet, soiled and roughened by the desert winds. "I am Ali Qasim," he says.

The first soldier coldly eyes the foreigner and says, "The grand vizier sends his greetings and wishes you to be moved to an apartment that is more fitting for his new translator. Please come with us."

Ali glances at Jonathon and Ishaq. They are all anxious to abandon this caravanserai, but Aqasi's message does not bode well for Gordon Cranston.

"What has become of the grand vizier's previous translator?" Ali asks.

The soldier was not expecting this question. "He has been assigned to another post," he says.

Ali is quite certain the soldier knows nothing about Gordon's fate. "We have quite a lot of personal belongings," he says, gesturing to the baggage in the room. "And there is more in a guarded wagon outside."

The first soldier pulls aside the curtain to reveal another six or seven soldiers. "It will be our honor to move your possessions."

The new apartment is large and airy, with a separate sleeping room for each of them. A wide veranda overlooks the palace a mile away. A functioning *badgeer*, or wind tower, gently stirs the air.

That evening, all three of them are summoned to Aqasi's chamber for dinner and conversation. Clearly, Aqasi has something in mind. Seated on the floor before the grand vizier, Ali says, "I was informed by your escort that you want me to be your translator."

"You had offered your services and I accepted."

"As I recall, I had offered to tutor your current translator."

"He is no longer my translator. A wise man pointed out his deficiencies to me, and I have assigned him to another position in the government."

"He is well, then?"

"Of course he is well. No harm has come to him. I hope you do not believe the vicious accusations of your newspaper that we are barbarians."

"Of course not."

Just then, young Nasir al-Din enters the room and shyly whispers into Aqasi's ear. Aqasi turns his attention to Ishaq. "Your name is Ishaq, as I recall."

Ishaq courteously nods yes.

"Nasir al-Din will be the shah of all Persia one day, perhaps soon." Aqasi looks up at Nasir al-Din and smiles, but the smile lacks sincerity.

Ali thinks it camouflages something more sinister; but then, perhaps it is just the grand vizier's natural scowl that produces this effect.

"Though the prince is but fifteen years old," Aqasi continues, "he will be the sovereign ruler of our nation. You are deeply honored to be in his presence."

The four Englishmen bow reverently.

"Nasir al-Din would like to entertain Ishaq alone. He is quite interested in America, and would like to learn something of your language as well so he can communicate directly with the leaders of other English-speaking countries."

Ishaq and Ali are stunned by this invitation to befriend the monarch-to-be. "I can, I mean, yes… I am deeply honored," Ishaq says in Persian, "and would be happy to assist Nasir al-Din in whatever endeavors he seeks for me to, um, help him in."

For the first time Nasir al-Din speaks so he can be heard by all. Addressing Ishaq, he says, "How many wives do you have?"

Ishaq turns red. How *many*? What kind of question is that? He turns to Ali for help. Ali whispers to him in English, "Persian men can take a number of wives, and kings can have as many as they like. Although one is more than most men can handle."

Ishaq looks up at Nasir al-Din and replies in Farsi, "Actually, I have no wives at all."

"Not even one?"

"None."

Nasir al-Din, who is but fifteen, nods politely and says, "I have only one wife, but I'm told I should have more. Why have you not taken wives?"

Ishaq is startled that this youngster is already married. He replies, "I have been too busy traveling the world. Would it be fair to my *wives*—" he smiles at his use of the plural—"if I were not able to see them for years?"

Nasir al-Din contemplates this remark. "I see what you mean," he says finally. "In such a case, perhaps *concubines* are a wiser choice."

Ishaq knows about concubines from the Bible. He blushes uncontrollably and looks down at the floor.

Ali addresses Nasir al-Din: "Perhaps you would like Ishaq to tell you about America."

"Oh yes—America. I hope to go there some day. And England, too."

Aqasi has had enough of this adolescent banter. He motions Ishaq forward and sends him with Nasir al-Din into the bowels of the palace. "I will see that your son is brought back to your apartment when their conversation is ended," he explains to Ali. "Now then, tell me—are *you* married?" Aqasi smiles for the first time. Perhaps this is his way of making a joke.

"I was married once, but my wife died in America. Would you like to see a picture of her?"

"You carry a painting of your wife with you?"

"Not a painting. An actual *picture* of her. Of the *real* her."

This is awkward. There is no Farsi word for daguerreotype or photograph, no concept of the process or the result. Aqasi does not understand what he is describing.

Ali stands, reaches into a pocket, and produces the daguerreotype of Alice. "May I show you?" he asks.

Two guards step forward at Ali's movement, which appears threatening. Aqasi waves them off and motions for Ali to bring him the object, which he carefully takes and studies.

"This is a wonderful painting. So lifelike. It deceives one into thinking this is the actual person."

"But you see, this is not a painting at all. This picture of my wife is her actual image—it is her, you see—her image captured on a metal plate by my associate, Jonathon, using a process that only he and a few other individuals have mastered. In a sense, this is my wife. It is the light reflected from her face that is etched onto this silver plate…"

Aqasi is astonished. "Not a painting at all," he says. "But your wife… captured onto this plate." He looks up with at Jonathon with admiration. "And you know how to perform this magic?"

Jonathon has followed the gist of this conversation in Farsi, but has not understood the question. Ali translates into English and then Jonathon says in very imperfect Persian, "Yes, I make these pictures. I have—umm—a special *box* that helps me do it."

Aqasi's mind is soaring. "Can you put Nasir al-Din and me on your plates? Can you make pictures of the shah?"

Ali replies: "Yes, Jonathon can make pictures of anything. *Everything!* Your palaces, your thrones, your army. Anything at all."

"Then we must start tomorrow," Aqasi says. "We have many things to make pictures of. Now I wonder, Jonathon, if you would leave us so that we may have a private conversation."

Ali translates for Jonathon, who nods and stands.

Aqasi calls for an escort. "We must see you home safely, Jonathon. It would not do to have any harm befall the court's—" he does not know the word for what Jonathon does—"the court's *picture maker*."

"Photographer," Ali suggests in English.

"Yes, the court's *photographer*," Aqasi repeats, saying the last word in English.

After Jonathon has departed, Aqasi motions for Ali to sit directly in front of him, close enough to pat his knee. He speaks quietly now, as if he wants no one to overhear their conversation. "You have been worried about Mr. Cranston, am I correct?" he asks.

"I trust that your words were true, that he has not been harmed."

"I employed Mr. Cranston out of convenience. It is not easy to find someone fluent in English and Persian who does not work for the British government. I'm afraid, however, that Mr. Cranston's interests were less in translation and more in enriching himself. While I needed him, I was willing to ignore his petty larceny, but when you arrived he became expendable."

"Do you expect me to serve as your translator?"

"You are a British citizen. I cannot force you to take this position. But if you do, perhaps I can help you achieve your goal."

"And what do you believe my goal is?"

"I have no idea, but I'm quite certain you will tell me, because unless I know what you want I cannot help you get it."

Aqasi calls for more hot tea. During this pause in the conversation, Ali wrestles with his strategy. The grand vizier clearly is a perceptive and intelligent man. He remembered everyone's name after one mention and is even now playing out a strategy that Ali struggles to comprehend. Perhaps Aqasi's goal is simply to form an association with a British reporter so that coverage of Persian affairs will be more fair and balanced. *No, that seems too simplistic.* Maybe Aqasi sees in Ali an opportunity to study how the English think. *No, Cranston provided the same opportunity.* Could it be that Aqasi merely wants to replace Cranston, whom he seems to despise, with a more capable translator?

Ali decides to lay out his cards. After all, hadn't Aqasi mentioned a willingness to help Ali achieve *his* goal?

"I can be of much more use to you than merely translating conversations," Ali says.

"In what way?"

"I understand that this religious fanatic who calls himself the Rasul is causing quite a stir throughout your country. There has even been mention of him and his disciples in the *London Times*. I suspect that you would prefer this person to be eliminated, but that is risky business. Politically risky. We all know what happened to Pontius Pilate in the case of Jesus."

"What is your interest in this imposter?"

"I hold him responsible for the death of my wife."

This statement astonishes Aqasi, who thinks about it briefly then laughs out loud. "Are you saying that a young merchant from Persia killed your wife in America? It hardly seems possible."

"Yes, I know, but I believe it to be true in a different sort of way. I don't believe that he personally killed my wife, of course. But I do believe that the larger force that he represents is responsible by setting into motion events designed to cause my wife's death. That's all I can say right now."

Aqasi takes a sip of tea. He had never imagined that the imposter might be the spearhead of a larger conspiracy that extends throughout the world. Countering the threat posed by the Rasul suddenly takes on even greater urgency. He says, "Perhaps you and I have the same enemy."

"My thinking exactly."

"And what would you do about him?"

"My goal is the same as yours—to destroy him. I will stop at nothing to achieve my goal. In America and England I have destroyed or at least nullified many lesser figures that represent the same force. But this imposter, as you call him, is the head of the snake. Perhaps my efforts can help insulate you and the Qajars from direct implication. At the very least, you will have my untiring efforts to bring this man down."

Aqasi can feel the venom in this man, and he likes it. "And in return?"

"I will need some resources and, of course, the influence of your office to get certain things done. I will need you to thoughtfully consider my proposals for action, and act when you agree."

"And money?"

"I don't want your money. I find pleasure in spending my own fortune for this cause. I will spend it all if I have to."

Ali pauses, and then says, "There is one other thing. I want you to restore Gordon Cranston to his post as your official translator. I will not have the time to serve in that capacity, though I am deeply honored to be asked."

Aqasi has already made his decision. What does he have to lose? If something goes wrong, he can always blame this Englishman for tampering in Persian affairs. Besides, he believes that vengeance is a powerful motivator.

"I cannot restore Mr. Cranston to his post without first punishing him for his crimes," he explains. "Without punishment, what would prevent him from betraying me again?"

Ali nods. "What kind of punishment?"

"The punishment for theft is to cut off the hands."

Ali considers this. He looks sternly into Aqasi's eyes and says, "Only his left hand. He will need his other hand for writing translations."

Aqasi smiles. He likes this half-Persian, half-English man. How very useful to have struck a bargain with the most ruthless and devious halves.

CHAPTER 10

Alí has moved quickly. Within a few weeks of entering the Qajar court as Aqasi's translator, he has sketched out the seen and unseen lines of power, and more importantly, *future* power, for the shah's imminent death will cause an earthquake that is sure to shake the very foundations of Qajar rule. If Ali is going to accomplish his purpose, he will need the full support of the new rulers, whoever they may be.

Of the many things he has learned, the most important is that Aqasi is despised by the aristocrats in Tehran, who had been shut out of contact with the shah because of the grand vizier's paranoia. He has also learned that Aqasi is deeply resented by the majority of the Qajar court, who rail at the grand vizier's influence over the sickly shah. Almost everyone of power has been squeezed, humiliated, or punished in some way by the arrogant and wicked little man. The Prime Minister has even broken his promise of paying the shah's army on time. Still, the shah's continuing allegiance to Aqasi covers the Vizier with a shield that no one dares to penetrate—until the shah is dead.

At first, Ali had wondered at the grand vizier's rapid acceptance of him. Almost immediately Ali had become much more than a translator, and yet how could such a cold and untrusting person so quickly accept a complete stranger as a confidante? *Perhaps this is a trap!* This fleeting thought had been quickly dismissed. The rambling old man does not seem to have a network of trusted co-conspirators; through his own treachery and brutal tactics he has isolated himself from everyone but the shah.

No, this ghost of the legendary grand vizier sees in Ali what he needs the most: a thirst for vengeance to match that of Aqasi; undiminished cunning to plot against a most clever and insidious foe, the Rasul; youthful vitality to see the plot through; and a British passport to exert or manipulate influence if needed.

Aqasi calls for tea. "Ours is a tiresome business," he mutters inconclusively. "Particularly in dealing with this imposter, the Rasul. So tiresome."

Ali sees his opening. "Tiresome yes, but the number of his followers grows daily. Even the mullas seem uncertain of what to do. Since he was arrested and released in Isfahan, the public seems confused as to where we stand on this issue."

Aqasi paces. "Perhaps we should kill him and be done with it."

"That is always an alternative, but a risky one. Do we want a martyr?"

"Your suggestion, then, would be—?"

"He is obviously giving orders to his disciples. Without coordination, how could his teachings spread so quickly? I also fear that this movement could become armed and militant. I think we need to isolate this troublemaker so he can't communicate with his followers. I suggest we move him to Mah-Ku."

Aqasi stops pacing. He looks at Ali. Mah-Ku is a dreaded and desolate fortress in the rugged mountains of Azerbaijan. In other words, the perfect place for solitary confinement.

"I agree. I will send an order immediately to seize the imposter and remove him to Mah-Ku. There he'll be as good as dead."

"For our purposes, better than dead," Ali adds. "Azerbaijan would also seem like a good place for Nasir al-Din. A remote corner of the nation." Ali is dangling this casual suggestion as bait for the old man.

Aqasi considers this statement. "Yes, yes, a very good place. After all, the young man needs practical grooming in the affairs of state." He smiles conspiratorially at Ali. "Perhaps I could arrange for Nasir al-Din to assume the governorship of Azerbaijan. I understand there is a vacancy."

The plan unfolds at lightning speed. Within days, young Nasir al-Din is on the road to Tabriz.

Ishaq arrives one morning to find his eccentric friend, Nasir al-Din, suddenly gone. For the past month, Ishaq and Ali have been living in very different worlds. Ishaq has been allowed complete access to the palace harem, in which Nasir al-Din lives, a protected territory that not even Ali is permitted to enter. Ali, on the other hand, is often huddled in secret talks in the quarters of the despised Aqasi, or traveling about the country on some official business.

The ripe grapevine of the harem has buzzed with speculation that Aqasi has lost his mental faculties and the machinery of the government is increasingly being guided by Ali. Knowing his father well, Ishaq has concluded that Ali is maneuvering the apparatus of the Qajars to further his own agenda, a senseless and single-minded vendetta against the Rasul.

After a week of boredom, Ishaq approaches Jonathon, who has been busy making photographs of the ruling Qajars and documenting their opulent lives, about taking an unannounced journey of their own.

"I need to leave Tehran for a while," Ishaq confides. "Would you come with me? I'm sure there will be many wonderful pictures to take."

"I think I would rather take pictures of dead men hanging from nooses than one more portrait of a Qajar prince," Jonathon replies.

By mid-March, 1848, Ishaq and Jonathon have made their way slowly on horseback to the town of Zanjan, halfway to Tabriz. A cold wind forces them to seek shelter at a drafty caravanserai. They enter the frosty courtyard, followed by a hired guide and two other strangers on mules fifty yards behind. Only a handful of other travelers are present, all huddled around small fires and wrapped in woolen blankets. Ishaq sees a vacant stall and dismounts, intending to unload the pack mule that carries their supplies. As he and Jonathon unfasten the unwieldy collection of boxes and bags from the mule's back with no help from their guide, two strangers approach.

"You are not Persian?" the oldest stranger says in Farsi.

"We are not," Ishaq replies. "We are from England."

"But you speak Farsi."

"Yes, a little."

"Are you merchants?"

"No, simply travelers. We are looking for pictures."

This comment confuses the oldest stranger. "Pictures?" he says.

Jonathon finds a small daguerreotype of Golestan Palace in a satchel and walks it to the older man, gently handing it to him.

The man takes it and smiles. "I see. It is very good. Did you paint this?"

Jonathon turns to Ishaq for help. His Farsi is not good enough to explain.

"It is not a painting, and not an etching," Ishaq explains. "It is the actual image. My friend captures the light from the thing itself and places that light onto a metal plate."

The man is now very confused.

"Jonathon, show him other pictures," Ishaq instructs.

Jonathon finds pictures of various Qajar princes and shows them to the oldest stranger. "These are the men themselves, not paintings."

The stranger recoils, hands back the plate that he is inspecting. "This man is in this picture?" he asks. "It is not possible."

"No, no," Ishaq says. "it is the light that reflects from their faces that makes these pictures."

Jonathon scrambles to the mule again, opens a wooden box and takes out the camera. "I point this box at a person, and their image appears on a little metal plate," he explains.

The stranger dismounts and walks to the camera, cocks his head, touches the camera's exterior. "You could make a picture of me?"

Jonathon smiles, nods. "It would be my honor."

"This place is cold. You must come home with me." The stranger smiles, revealing crooked teeth. "I will give you warm rooms and hot food. This is no place for civilized men. Besides, Naw-Ruz is almost here. You must celebrate with us."

Naw-Ruz, the Persian New Year, is but two days away. Ishaq considers the man's offer and nods appreciatively. "And in return, we will make pictures of you and your family. The men, at least."

The man's home is spacious. Over dinner with the man, his two sons, and the lazy guide, Ishaq and Jonathon learn that their host, who is called Hamid, is a merchant in Zanjan. His wife and daughter are in the anderun. Occasionally, Ishaq can hear them moving about. After so many days in the shah's harem, where the wives and daughters of the shah freely showed their faces to Nasir al-Din and Ishaq, it seems odd to confront the customary segregation of men and women.

After much conversation, Hamid reclines on one elbow, smiling, and bluntly asks Ishaq, "Are you Christians?"

The question is unexpected. At first Ishaq does not know how to respond, but finally says, "We were born Christians."

"You have not converted to Islam?"

"We have not."

"Please forgive my curiosity, but what brought you to my country? Surely it was not just to make pictures of princes and palaces."

Ishaq looks at Jonathon, who merely shrugs his shoulders. Ishaq decides to be honest.

"My father heard of a new prophet who is called the Rasul and we came here to find him."

The man's eyes brighten.

"So—" Hamid exclaims. "You are Rasulis! That is wonderful. Rasulis from another land!"

Before Ishaq can clarify that his father came to hunt the Rasul, not serve him, Hamid has called in his wife and daughter. The two women enter unveiled.

The taciturn guide howls with indignation and runs from the room.

Hamid arches his eyebrows. "Perhaps he did not like my wife's food."

Jonathon does not catch the sarcasm. "I think he was astonished at seeing a woman's face."

"Yes," Hamid agrees. "Even most Rasulis would react in such a manner. But you are from England. Christian ladies can show their faces, can they not?"

"Of course," Jonathon says.

"Over the years, Islam—at least in my country—has corrupted the teachings of the Prophet Muhammad, I think to justify the hunger for power of the male clergy and to dominate our women. Fortunately, as you know, the Promised One has appeared to correct these wrong-headed interpretations and return us all to the true Religion of God, in which men and women truly are equal. I confess that until my daughter became a Rasuli and was tutored by a woman named Tara, I also remained ignorant. But when Zarrin returned home to us, the light shone from her face and her words caused my wife and me to recognize the truth of the Rasul."

Until now, Zarrin's face has been turned away from Ishaq so he could only see its profile. But now, as she gently turns to face him, Ishaq can see her face, and he is paralyzed by her bright eyes. She smiles at him, and he grows deaf to the words that Hamid utters.

"Zarrin helped us understand that in this new dispensation, women no longer need to hide their faces. Although, at the present time, this would be an unsafe practice outside our home. I am sorry about your guide... I assumed he was also a Rasuli."

Ishaq cannot take his eyes off Zarrin. He has heard nothing, and even if he had, could not speak right now.

But Zarrin can speak. She lowers her eyes and says to Ishaq, "Welcome to our house."

Hamid looks at the two youths and smiles. *At least this young man is a Rasuli*, he thinks. "Have you heard that the Rasul has been imprisoned in the fortress at Mah-Ku? Such evil in the world!"

These words shake Ishaq from his trance. "Yes, I heard that." He is embarrassed that this kind, trusting man has jumped to conclusions, and that Ishaq's father is in fact the source of the *evil* that has caused the Rasul to be sent to that awful place. Overcome with guilt, Ishaq prepares to confess his true station as the Christian son of the master persecutor of the Rasul.

Suddenly, however, the hired guide, shivering and mumbling, re-enters the room. Apparently the promise of a warm room and clean sleeping mat can override certain religious convictions. Trying desperately not to glance at the women's faces, the guide gestures submission, asks forgiveness for his rude behavior, and asks that he be allowed to sleep indoors.

Out of courtesy, Hamid's wife and daughter cover their faces and the guide audibly sighs, relieved that temptation has been removed and order restored to the world.

For Ishaq, however, the sight of Zarrin's dark, sparkling eyes above the black veil is even more tantalizing.

CHAPTER 11

After five weeks, Ishaq still lingers in the town of Zanjan, unable to separate himself from the intoxicating Zarrin. Tired of the "preening and love-sick coo-ing" of Ishaq, and having exhausted the meager photographic potential of the town, Jonathon Fury has left with the hired guide for Tabriz. For the first time since arriving in Persia, Ishaq is truly on his own, though he is not lonely.

He is, however, amazed at the efficiency of the Rasuli grapevine. News of the Rasul and his followers travels with nearly impossible speed across vast distances, yet Ishaq has never seen the fleet-footed bearers of these messages; for all he knows, God Himself transports this news from one remote place to another on the spiky backs of thunderbolts.

On one dazzling April morning, while sipping sweet tea in Zarrin's home, the unveiled young lady suddenly purses her lips and glances heavenward, as if she has just received a telepathic message from the mountains of Azerbaijan.

She says, "On Naw-Ruz, Jalal arrived at the prison-fortress in Mah-Ku to visit the Rasul."

This means little to Ishaq. He knows that the Rasul has been imprisoned in the remote prison, but he has never heard of Jalal. "Who is this person you speak of?" Ishaq asks.

"Jalal. A very great man. He was the first to recognize the Promised One, and he now travels the country spreading the Rasul's message. He traveled a thousand miles on foot, from Mashhad to Mah-Ku, to demonstrate his great devotion to the Rasul. Some day perhaps I will have the opportunity to show my love and devotion, too, just as Jalal and Tara have done so many times."

Ishaq performs a quick calculation in his head. "It must have taken this man eight or nine months for such a journey. A colossal waste of time, I'd say, since he could have traveled that same distance in a fraction of the time by horseback."

Zarrin's sharp, accusing gaze makes Ishaq immediately wish he had not said this.

"Of course, I'm sure he used this time wisely," he suggests defensively, "perhaps spreading the word among the many villages he passed through."

Zarrin smiles as if agreeing with his epiphany and forgiving its tardiness. Her smile brightens the room and causes Ishaq to tremble with its force. He is completely under her spell and finds himself wondering about Persian weddings.

"There is a meeting of Rasulis this evening," Zarrin says. "A secret meeting, of course. Would you like to attend?"

That evening, after dark, Zarrin and her family lead Ishaq to a small house on the far side of the village. They are all warmly greeted at the door. Inside are about thirty people. The women, including Zarrin, are all veiled. *Customs change slowly*, Ishaq thinks.

Many eyes furtively glance at Ishaq. He certainly does not look like a Persian, after all, and he probably has earned some kind of celebrity status through the Rasuli grapevine—*an Englishman who believes in the Rasul*. Suddenly Ishaq thinks that he comprehends what it must have been like for the early Christians, that small cult of believers who had met secretly in homes and caves to share news, deepen their faith, encourage each other, and plot strategy to survive and spread the gospel.

Without prompting now, the room grows quiet and an elderly man begins to chant a prayer in a thick, quavering voice. Ishaq recognizes it as one of the Rasul's revealed prayers, though he has not heard it chanted before, only recited.

After the chant, Zarrin—the youngest woman in the room—boldly stands and greets the assembly. "My friends," she says, "I have more news from Mah-Ku."

The room swells with anticipation. "

The warden at Mah-Ku has asked the Rasul to marry his daughter."

Heads nod excitedly. Voices buzz.

"The Rasul kindly refused this invitation," Zarrin continues.

"I've heard of this warden. His name is Ali Khan, and he is known for his cruelty. It is unimaginable that this scorpion would invite a prisoner to join his family."

"Unimaginable no longer," Zarrin replies. "The shah—or more likely his evil enforcer, Aqasi—has spies within the Mah-Ku fortress, just as we do. News of the warden's transformation inflamed the Qajar court, which also learned that many of the once-hostile villagers had become Rasulis. A few days after Jalal left Mah-Ku, Aqasi ordered the Rasul moved to the castle at Chiriq, which is the cruelest and most remote prison in the land. Aqasi's next move will probably be to order a trial for the Rasul in Tabriz."

This last remark lights a fuse. There are calls for militant insurrection, for an armed attempt to rescue the Rasul.

Ishaq is left wondering at the role that his father has played in these provocative decisions to punish the Rasul. He suspects that Ali has become the architect and Aqasi the feeble-minded sponsor. During the shouting, he finds himself reciting the Rasul's prayer for removal of difficulties. Perhaps, without recognizing it, he has become a Rasuli. He prays that he will find the strength to reject vengeance.

Zarrin calms the crowd with a solemn chant of another prayer, and then addresses the gathering from behind her veil. "My friends," she says, "followers of the Rasul are a people of love and forgiveness. God will guide us. If we are called to bear arms, to fight, to give up our lives, I believe it will be only to defend our faith. But I will defend to the death my loyalty to this new revelation, and my right to hold these beliefs."

Ishaq listens to this young woman and quivers with excitement. He has made his decision—two of them, in fact. He can no longer deny that he has become a disciple of the Rasul; and he has recognized at last that he is hopelessly in love with Zarrin.

CHAPTER 12

Despite Ali's best efforts, his foe is gathering strength. As he marches with false confidence across the great hall toward Aqasi's elegant chambers, Ali knows that he is about to be rebuked by the grand vizier. A young man of twenty-eight is quietly defying the harshest restraints that Ali has imposed. Not just *defying* them, but turning them against his persecutors.

In his opulent sitting room, Aqasi greets Ali coolly. The old man has adorned his richest and most regal attire for this occasion, a transparent attempt to intimidate the younger and quicker-witted Ali. Instead, the younger man inwardly sneers at the garish layers of feathered fabric and sparkling jewels. He remembers the clownish costumes that draped the counterfeit Persians in the Surrey's London production of *Midnight March to Freedom*; those foppish actors were less comical than the human peacock standing before him now.

"Be seated," Aqasi insists.

Ali sits down while Aqasi struts imperiously, fanning his feathers.

"I'm certain that you know the developments in Chiriq," Aqasi says, meaning it as a question.

"Of course I do," Ali replies. "The imposter possesses an uncanny ability to transform adversity into advantage."

"The warden at Chiriq is the shah's brother-in-law. But like that fool Ali Khan in Mah-Ku, this idiot has also succumbed to the imposter's spell."

"He is a fool, yes, but as he is the husband of the shah's sister I find it most difficult to chastise—"

"I am not interested in excuses!" Aqasi shouts. "Half the population of this country is related to the shah. Our bigger problem, though, is in the neighboring town of Khuy. I believe you went there to stir up the populace."

Ali knows what is coming. "Yes," he says, looking down at the blue and burgundy carpet on which he sits.

"And I suppose you've heard just how well that little mission turned out."

"On the surface, not well."

Aqasi snorts, then laughs. "*Not well* did you say? Let me tell you just how *not well* it has gone. The most prominent clergy in Khuy, along with a legion of the most eminent Siyyids and government officials, have declared their allegiance to this imposter."

"I've heard that."

"Then I suppose you also know that many of the residents of that town have followed the lead of these influential clerics. And as if that weren't enough, hundreds of followers of this troublemaker have converged on Chiriq, overwhelming the caravanserais. They are sleeping in the streets and in the shadow of the great mountain that guards the castle."

Ali nods solemnly. All this is true.

Aqasi pauses and sighs for effect. He stoops to gaze into Ali's eyes. Despite the political disaster that is unfolding, Aqasi has not had this much fun since Ali, with his more agile mind, had stealthily undermined his authority.

"As I recall," Aqasi says at last, readying a dagger thrust of words, "you persuaded me to save the imposter's life when I was prepared to kill him. Would you say now that this was bad advice?"

Ali hesitates. He knows that many men have been executed for smaller errors of judgment. He decides on a bold move.

"The advice was sound," he says.

Aqasi stares at him, dismayed. "How is that possible?" he asks.

Ali stands, regaining the advantage of height. "First," he says, "the populace of Khuy is of no consequence. They are fleas on the back of the nation and can be easily flicked off. And keep in mind that the majority of the residents are still against the Rasul. Second, the gathering of the Rasul's lunatics is not a problem, but rather a convenience. They have now identified themselves and like dumb animals have herded into a pen that is easier for us to watch and control. Third, the prominent officials of which you speak are themselves in virtual exile by virtue of their location in the outlying village of Khuy. Not only are they no threat to us, but they too have betrayed their treason. They will be taken care of in short order."

Aqasi squints, a tell-tale sign that he is feeling outmaneuvered again. "Are you saying that this was part of your plan?"

"I am not that smart," Ali replies. "I am only saying that my advice has led to a precipitous moment. Many of the traitors and those who are susceptible to apostasy and treason have identified themselves. Now we can deal with them—and with the imposter. It is time."

"For his execution? I recommended that long ago."

"Not yet. It is time for a formal public trial. And then execution."

"A trial!" Aqasi snorts again. "This clever fellow has turned other trials on their ear. It is too risky!"

"Please, hear me out. This trial will be held in Tabriz. I will personally stage it so that the imposter must either recant his claims or be found guilty—punishable by death."

"It has not worked before, not with this lunatic."

"I am not finished explaining my plan. Since the trial will be held in Tabriz, the president of the tribunal will be the governor of the province, the crown prince Nasir al-Din."

This startles Aqasi who sees the crown prince as a threat to his own candidate for the throne. "Nasir al-Din, you say? And how will this serve our interests?"

"Surely you can see the two possible outcomes, both to our advantage. If the Rasul is found guilty, we are rid of the imposter forever. Any negative consequences will befall the crown prince. But if the Rasul once again makes a fool of the tribunal, the fault will lie with Nasir al-Din. Since most people in positions of power are threatened by the guile and audacity of this imposter—and his apparent plan to destroy the government and Islam—poor Nasir al-Din may then find it difficult to rally support for his claim to the throne."

Aqasi stares at Ali. He likes the plan. Though he had anticipated great pleasure in punishing Ali, it can wait. "All right," he says. "Move the prisoner to Tabriz."

CHAPTER 13

According to Ali's spies, who have been posing as Rasulis throughout Persia, many followers of the Rasul have begun to flow toward the village of Shah-Rud. Ali suspects that an urgent meeting has been called to plot the movement's strategy. One of Ali's spies, Karim—the man who had been booted out of the Shaykhi school by Kazim—had gladly agreed to spy on the Rasulis, hoping one day to reap his revenge upon Jalal, Kazim's favorite.

Meeting with Ali in a steamy tea-house in Tehran, Karim explains, "The arrangements for those who were called to this meeting have been made by Mirza Ramin. Do you know this man?"

Ali nods, then frowns. This individual presents a dangerous dilemma. Ramin is the son of the late Mirza Firouz, one of the shah's favorite courtiers, who had served as vizier of the mountainous province of Nur with such kindness and compassion that many of the inhabitants had practically worshipped the man despite his great wealth. The popular vizier is now dead, but since childhood his son, Ramin, has shown even greater compassion and generosity. Even as a young man, the residents of Nur had called Ramin the "Father of the Poor." As he had grown up, he had given away vast sums to the less fortunate and had seen that they were fed and clothed, refusing the many political appointments that were his due.

Ali focuses his attention on preventing a Rasuli leader, *Jalal*, from attending the Rasuli conclave. Of all the Rasul's disciples, he fears this "Jalal" the most. He is a man who ironically shares the same common name as Ali's boyhood friend, a friend who never would not have been duped into abandoning Islam. He has heard many tales of the fanatic's epic journeys, his conquest of Islam's brightest minds, his charismatic leadership—and Ali is disgusted by it. Afraid and dismayed, both. The man sounds like a replica of the Rasul, but more dangerous, perhaps, because he is free to roam.

Ali looks up at Karim and says, "Do you know where Jalal is?"

The mention of Jalal's name causes Karim, who had been comfortably reclining on one elbow, to suddenly sit up straight, spilling tea on the carpet. "Jalal, yes, I know where he is!" Karim replies. "In Mashhad. He has built a Rasuli teaching center there."

"Good. I am guessing that you will not mind undertaking a mission to arrest and detain this troublemaker."

"It would be my greatest pleasure," Karim says. "Will he be tortured?"

"That will not be necessary. Just see to it that some trouble arises in Mashhad, and that Jalal is implicated."

"What kind of trouble?"

Ali can see that Karim is no giant of creativity. "All right," he says, "here is what you should do."

Karim leans forward with intense concentration.

"Go immediately to Mashhad. Use the post horses to get you there quickly—I will give you a letter of authorization. In Mashhad, seek out the Rasulis. Begin insulting them one by one until someone retaliates. There is always someone who cannot control himself. You do not mind a few minor bruises?"

Karim grunts, indicating he doesn't mind. After all, this is his opportunity for revenge.

"Then go to the mujtahid, Mirza Ahmad—I will alert him—and issue a complaint. The Rasuli who strikes you will be captured and severely punished, to the delight of the mullas. Afterward, see that the offender is taken back to Jalal, showing a connection between them. I will instruct the Prince Hamzih, who is camped with his army outside the city, to arrest Jalal on your notice. The prince will detain the man until after the Rasuli gathering. I cannot risk having all the Rasuli leaders in consultation at the same time."

"But the prince is known to admire Jalal."

"He can be as courteous a he wants, but I assure you, the prince will follow my orders."

Karim joyfully departs, and Ali returns to a more secret mission, one that only he knows about: cataloging the countless hidden assets that Aqasi has acquired through years of corruption and deceit.

Ali is sure that this information will be valuable one day.

CHAPTER 14

Badasht is a tiny hamlet in which eighty-one Rasulis have congregated in three magnificent adjoining gardens rented by Mirza Ramin. One of the gardens he has set aside for Tara, the second for Danush, and the third for himself. There is no garden for Jalal; he has been detained indefinitely by Prince Hamzih.

This remote location has been chosen because of violent agitation in the surrounding province of Khurasan. The evangelism of Danush and Jalal has stirred many hearts in this region, and also much anger. Seeded by the malevolent deceit of Ali and his paid collaborators, and cultivated by a frightened and jealous clergy, the roots of avarice and deception have grown deep and wide.

The simple people of Khurasan repeatedly have been told outrageous lies about the Rasul and his followers. Some mullas preach that slaying one Rasuli will cancel all the killer's sins. In many quarters it is forbidden for Muslims to talk to followers of the Rasul, since Rasulis have the power, it is said, to work dark magic on them.

A firestorm of frightening rumors circulates throughout the land: that Rasulis can mix something into tea that will cause insanity; that if children do not behave, the Rasulis will come and eat them; that Rasulis have tails and horns; that Rasulis had abolished all moral laws and marry their own sisters and daughters; that all Rasuli women are shared by all the men; that the Rasulis are plotting to overthrow the government; and, absurdly, that Rasulis had killed the Imam Husayn at Karbala centuries earlier. Such preposterous lies have found fertile ground among the many uneducated and superstitious inhabitants who still live in a magical world filled with demons, jinns, and evil eyes.

On the minds of Tara and the conclave's host, Ramin, is one overriding objective. Both have concluded that the new revelation of the Rasul requires a complete break with Islam and the abolition of its laws; that this new dispensation has ushered in a new religion, not merely a new sect or reformation of Islam; and that the time has finally come for this momentous but perilous announcement. Both also know that many of the Rasuli leaders gathered in Badasht may not be prepared for such a bold stroke—in fact, some may intensely disagree—and so the first days of the conference are spent in study, prayer, and spiritual preparation.

On each day, the Rasulis witness the abolition of a long-established law or tradition, and the introduction of a new law with authority flowing from the Rasul's teachings. Slowly, then, the foundations of Islamic ordinances are cast aside and Rasuli minds, still struggling with the pace of change, are allowed time to understand and accept the new precepts. Even so, many of the more conservative members of the conference vigorously oppose the radical step of separating themselves from their long-cherished Islamic faith.

Danush, who is closest to the Rasul, resists the radical decision to declare a truly independent faith. He slows down the proceedings, encourages dissenting voices, weighs in by favoring a slow, reasoned process, and in the process irritates the willful Tara, who lobbies intensely for an immediate and complete break with Islam and its countless obsolete conventions. Privately, Tara repudiates the authority of the younger disciple, telling a small circle of admirers, "I see him as a pupil whom the Rasul has sent me to edify and instruct. I regard him in no other light." The denunciations of Danush are just as strong. "Tara is the author of heresy," he confides to the more conservative faction. "Those who advocate her views are the victims of error."

Near the end of the conclave, Ramin grows ill and is confined to his large tent. The sides are drawn up to let the gentle breezes through, and slowly the Rasulis begin drifting to his side. When most of them have assembled around their host, one of the Rasulis who had aligned himself with Tara arrives with a message for Danush. Tara, he explains, requests that Danush meet with her privately in Tara's garden.

"I've severed myself completely from her," Danush angrily replies. "Tell her I refuse."

"She will insist," the messenger explains.

Danush silently looks away. The muscles in his jaw quiver with tension.

Responding to this intractable attitude, the messenger unsheathes his sword and lays it at the feet of Danush. "I refuse to go without you. Either accompany me, or cut off my head with this sword."

"As you wish!" Danush says, swiftly bending to pick up the sword.

The messenger eyes the blade and tauntingly stretches his neck. Danush glares at the man, nervously fingers the handle of the sword, moves the tip of it in a threatening circle near the man's throat.

And then, like a sudden flash of sunlight in the midst of a storm, Tara enters the tent. She is adorned in flowing garments. And she is unveiled.

For a moment the Rasulis stare at her, and then they begin to shout and scream. In Islam, to behold the face of a woman is inconceivable! For many of them, even to gaze on Tara's shadow is reprehensible, for they regard her as the incarnation of Fatimah, the daughter of the Prophet Muhammad, the noblest symbol of chastity.

Despite the cries and curses and madness engulfing the tent, Tara serenely seats herself to the right of Danush, a place of honor. The men gazing upon her beauty are seized with anger, fear, bewilderment, and guilt. An anguished Rasuli named 'Abdu'l-Khaliq cuts his own throat and flees from the tent, soaked with his own blood. Many others are struck dumb. Danush, who has remained seated, clutches the messenger's sword as if ready to strike a fatal blow to Tara. His face contorts with inexpressible rage.

Tara is unmoved by this intimidation. She remains seated, calmly surveying the uproar prompted by her unveiling. Slowly her face shows a glimmer of joy, then unadorned triumph. When she suddenly stands, the tumult ceases momentarily as the Rasulis anticipate another surprise.

Despite their intense agitation, no one wants to miss the next act of this unfolding drama.

To those who have remained, Tara quotes the Qu'ran: "Verily, amid the gardens and rivers shall the pious dwell in the seat of truth, in the presence of the King." Danush and a few others notice that as she quotes this verse, she furtively glances at Ramin.

Then, with a face radiant with emancipation, she announces a clarion-call to a new order, saying: "I am the blast of the trumpet. I am the call of the bugle. Like Gabriel, I would awaken sleeping souls."

Tara has served notice. The objective of this gathering has been achieved with a stunning spectacle by an impatient woman. Her proud uncovered face indelibly etches on the minds of every witness that a new religion, like Islam and Christianity before it, has emerged.

CHAPTER 15

Men of God are the same everywhere. mullas and priests drenched in self-ish imaginings proudly parade in pomp and arrogance, murdering and tor-turing the disagreeable ones with knife-sharp edicts, and wresting power and wealth from the ignorant masses while a mute God blesses their corruption with His silence. Religion, Ali sees clearly, is God's infernal side-show, a Sur-rey production with harlequins, man-monkeys, smoke-smudged apparitions, and dusty curtains cleverly concealing painted props wheeled out by drunken stagehands for the next dazzling fantasy. Religion is a shimmering entertain-ment, a raucous melodrama with suffering messiahs and smirking devils. It is a divinely staged sleight-of-hand diverting audience attention as pockets are picked and parents are plucked from their children and God-fearing wives with unborn children are merrily slaughtered for sport.

Ali knows that he cannot win his war against the Almighty. He knows that he is damned. But on his sure descent to hell he intends to inflict the utmost pain on God's manifestation, and if that figure is the Rasul, then Ali will torture and humiliate this Emissary and His followers so that God will finally appreci-ate the depth of Ali's rage and pain.

Sustaining such intense hatred is difficult. Ali fears that he will falter, and so he has adopted the proven rituals of religion to nurture his passion. Every evening he reads the scripture of his mother's letters, the tender and troubled notes of Mary Rogers, and the endearing but deluded sermons so lovingly written out by his wife. The holy verses, whispering to him from the graves of these wronged ones, feed his passion. Every morning he gazes on his angels, who stare back at him from silvery metal plates and the bravado of a solitary book illustration. As long as these precious faces are rooted in his mind, the way that images of Christ on the cross are fixed in the consciousness of Christians, he is sure that he will not forget the suffering of these beautiful wronged ones.

It is in prayer, however, that Ali finds the most exquisite whetstone for the blade of his rage. He prays not to God but to the spirits of Anisa and Mary and Alice, begging their forgiveness, invoking their assistance. As he prays, he feels their sweet breaths on his face and their gentle fingers stroking his cheeks. He speaks to them through stinging tears. In their pained silence he hears the faint sobbing of grief—is it his own? No, he is sure it is theirs—and he knows that their agony won't stop until his vengeance is complete. He will sacrifice his soul for them. He must be relentless in his persecution.

The news that Ali has just received from Mazandaran is mixed, causing his gut to growl like a lion. As directed, his agents had stirred up fear and anger in the villages surrounding Badasht, and the less fearful and angry were paid to be more so. As the Rasulis had finally left their lengthy conference, many were attacked by villagers and were forced to scatter. Unfortunately, the wealthy and influential Mirza Ramin somehow had helped the other ringleaders escape. Tara and Danush had eluded the mobs, and as if this were not enough bad news, Jalal had been released by Prince Hamzih, who had become so enamored of his prisoner that he had refused to confine the man any longer.

Now Ali will have to order the arrest of Tara and Danush to prevent their malignancy from spreading. It would have been so much easier if they had been killed by the mobs as planned.

News among the scattered Rasulis flies on winged horses, and often the news is disheartening. Several weeks ago Jalal had learned that Danush had been captured and is now in the custody of the cruel mujtahid of Sari. And Tara, who had sought protection in a farmhouse on the outskirts of Vaz, has also been seized by government agents. But today a messenger brings sunshine, a package from the Rasul, who is incarcerated in the mountain fortress of Chiriq. Jalal wonders at the monumental effort of smuggling this package out of that remote castle.

With tender hands he opens the package, finding a green turban and a letter in the Rasul's exquisite hand. Tears moisten his eyes as he reads: "Adorn your head with my green turban and with the Black Standard unfurled before you

hasten to assist My beloved Danush." And then, near the end, "…the appointed Day of God will indeed be at hand in less than the twinkling of an eye."

He shivers with the import of these words. His new mission, perhaps his
final mission, which will be carried out beneath the mythic Black Standard,
will help to usher in the Day of God. His mind leaps to a heart-quickening
mirage observed long ago when in the shade of the mulberries he and Ali,
his cherished Ali, had first glimpsed the quivering shapes in the desert heat—
the Black Standards, they had believed—and with boundless enthusiasm had
galloped toward them as the Islamic prophecy had urged: *Should your eyes
behold the Black Standards proceeding from Khurasan, hasten toward them,
even should ye have to crawl over snow, inasmuch as they proclaim the advent
of the Promised One, the vice-regent of God.*

Never had it occurred to him that he might be the bearer of the Black Standard; that he, Jalal, wearing the green turban of the Rasul, the emblem of the
direct lineage of Muhammad, would lead the long-prophesied march announcing the imminent Day of God.

He drops to his knees, trembling and humbled, and then falteringly places
the turban on his head. He feels that he is unworthy of this honor, that he is too
weak to lead such an important mission. His tremors have been worsening. His
body has been convulsing more frequently. He is worn down and his strength
is sapped. He had been so sure that his days of travel were over. His body sags
beneath the weight of responsibility but his spirit is buoyed by the promise that
the appointed Day of God will be manifest *in less than the twinkling of an eye*.

Certainly God will give him the strength that he needs for one last sprint.

.

Chapter 16

Ishaq enters the home of Zarrin and is greeted by her parents. Zarrin sits in the corner by herself.

"What is it?" Ishaq asks Zarrin's father. "Your message said it was urgent that I come." He looks around at the worried faces.

Zarrin's father stands and embraces Ishaq. "Have you heard that Jalal has begun a march with over two hundred men beneath the Black Standard? My son Zakaria left yesterday to join him."

"I'm sorry about Zakaria," Ishaq replies.

"No, no, we are very proud of Zakaria. If I were not so old and feeble I would join him."

"Then what is the urgency?"

"It is Zarrin."

Zarrin glances fiercely at Ishaq. Their eyes meet.

"I had hoped that she would become your wife some day," Zarrin's father says. "I know that love binds you together, and you have our blessing."

Ishaq blushes. He is caught off guard to have such an unexpectedly candid discussion played out in front of Zarrin's parents.

"However, Zarrin is intent on joining Jalal," Zarrin's father adds. "We have told her that such a dangerous mission is no place for a woman, even a Rasuli woman, but she will not listen to us."

Ishaq looks at Zarrin, who turns away. "Is this true, Zarrin?" he asks.

"If I were Tara, my family would cheer my decision," she replies. "But I am only little Zarrin. It seems that old prejudices die hard, even in Rasuli families. I wish that my father would understand that I am not a woman—I am a Rasuli. Why am I prevented from serving my Faith like my brother?"

"She talks like a madwoman," her father says. "We cannot reason with her. I thought that maybe you could talk some sense into her."

Ishaq sits down next to Zarrin. "If you were to join the march of the Black Standard unveiled, it would most certainly stir up the villagers and endanger the other Rasulis."

"Then I will veil myself."

"If you travel with them veiled—a lone woman among hundreds of Rasuli men—rumors of immorality will fly. It will play into the hands of the agitators. And many Rasulis are not yet ready, I think, for a woman to march with them into certain adversity. It could undermine their confidence."

"My confidence comes from God," Zarrin says, then leaps to her feet and races from the room.

Zarrin's father sighs, slaps his thigh, and asks his wife to serve their guest some tea. "My thanks to you, Ishaq. She is a strong-willed girl, but your arguments were irrefutable. She will sulk for a while—perhaps a long while—but I'm sure she understands the wisdom of staying home. Now then, I hope that Zarrin's zealous behavior has not lessened your interest in having her as your wife."

"In my culture, such matters are first addressed between the man and woman themselves, and then the family. Zarrin and I have never discussed marriage."

"In our culture, these matters are arranged by cooler heads."

"I understand that she rebuffed such an arrangement before."

Zarrin's father lowers his eyes and says, "She is a *very* strong-willed girl." He looks up at Ishaq with glistening eyes. "But I know that her heart burns for you. So what is your answer?"

Before Ishaq can reply, a slender young man appears beneath the arch that leads to the sleeping rooms. At first Ishaq does not identify this person, but then sees that it is Zarrin. She wears a man's turban and her brother's tunic and sandals. She could easily pass for a frail boy of sixteen.

"Zarrin!" her father bellows.

"As a boy, I will raise no eyebrows on either side," she calmly replies. And then, looking straight at Ishaq, she asks, "What is your argument now?"

Zarrin's father storms out of the room. Her mother enters with a steaming samovar. She nearly drops the tray when she sees her daughter, and then leaves with a disgusted huff.

Ishaq stares at the glowering, determined face of Zarrin. "Do you love God this much, or is this just defiance?"

"Have you learned nothing at all about me? My heart is as full of love for God as my brother's. I am as willing as he to give my life for the Promised One. I do not think that God favors the love of a man over a woman's. I do not think that God prefers the prayers of a man or rejects the devout service of a woman in any endeavor. The Rasul made a woman one of his Living Letters. Is there any clearer sign that this new dispensation is open to men and women equally?"

Ishaq goes to Zarrin and takes her hands. He is trembling with fear, but also with pride. "This march of the Black Standard," he says softly, "it's very dangerous, you know. It goes through the heart of a dark land. You will be surrounded by ignorant Muslims and hostile mullas. The government will be nipping at your heels and provoking aggression everywhere. You will be attacked and many of you will die. How can I let you go? I cannot bear to lose you."

"Then come with me."

"I can't."

"Yes, you can. I know that you are not afraid of death, and that you love God as I do. Join us!"

"You don't understand."

Zarrin backs away, feeling rejected. "I have no right to expect this of you. If it is not in your heart…"

"No, that's not it. I do believe in what you wish to do. But I can't be with you. Eventually you will take up arms and fight the villagers, and then if you survive, you will fight the army. I can see it coming."

"So you do fear death."

"I don't know… maybe. But that is not why I can't go with you."

Zarrin looks at him, sensing that he wants to explain but can't find the words.

A silence engulfs them. And then she speaks up, saying, "You are afraid that you may witness my death."

This thought chills Ishaq to the bone. "Yes, I am afraid of that, but would it be worse than waiting for news of it? I'm not sure. No, the reason I can't be with you… the reason is…"

She waits. He licks his lips and swallows air, searching for the courage to explain. At last he speaks, so softly she can hardly hear him. ""It's my father."

Confused, Zarrin says, "Your father? You've never spoken of him."

"My father is… he's in the Qajar government. He's the architect of the persecution of the Rasulis."

"That can't be. The evil man you speak of is Aqasi, and he has no children."

"Aqasi is a feeble old man. My father is Ali Qasim of Bushruyih, the power behind Aqasi."

Zarrin struggles to reconcile such evil with the kind young man that she loves. The sincerity in Ishaq's eyes convinces her of the truth of his claim.

"Then you must go to your father and persuade him to stop his persecution. Surely he will listen to you. When he understands that his own son is a Rasuli, I'm sure he will—"

Ishaq turns away.

"So this is why you cannot join us. You can't fight against your own father."

Ishaq turns again to face Zarrin. "My father is a brilliant and kind man in many ways, but he is tormented by the demons of hatred. He found me on the streets and saved my life, gave me a home, protected me. I owe him everything. I despise what he is doing, but I just can't declare war on him. I can't betray his love."

"Can you betray God's love for you?"

"That's not fair. It's not the same thing."

"All right, then do what I ask. Find your father and reason with him."

"He is beyond reason."

"You are his *son*! Show him your love. Then show him the love of God reflected in you. He will understand."

Ishaq desperately clutches Zarrin to him. He knows that he cannot prevent her from going to join Jalal. "When are you leaving?" he asks.

"At dawn... with three others. I'll be safe."

"I'll leave for Tehran at dawn as well. I will speak to my father, I promise. I will make him understand."

As he holds Zarrin tightly, he knows it is for the last time.

CHAPTER 17

On the march out of Mashhad they number two hundred and two men, including Assaf, the local physician, who had accompanied Jalal's mortally wounded father into the city more than twenty years ago. The ragtag army is a mix of the young and the aged. Many are recently converted mullas or students of religion. Others are carpenters, merchants, artisans, masons, blacksmiths, and peasants. They march not as uniformed soldiers in disciplined formation, but as a swarm of bees clustered around the honeyed comb of the Black Standard. They carry provisions on their own bent backs, in horse-drawn wagons, and on the backs of braying mules. Most carry weapons—swords and spears and old muskets—for defense against thieves and angry mobs. Some ride saddled horses, but most walk, as Jalal does, on their departure through the city gate.

An hour from the city, Jalal is confronted by Prince Hamzih, who had previously held him captive in a military encampment outside the city. The prince had been won over by Jalal and in releasing his captive had defied orders directly from Aqasi's office and offered his own white stallion to Jalal.

"Do you believe in the Rasul?" Jalal had asked the prince.

The prince had replied, "I believe in *you*."

Over the next days, in the villages of Sabzavar and Mazinan more recruits join the march, and in Miyamay the villagers are so moved by Jalal's call that over thirty villagers join them. As they camp outside the village of Astanih they are joined by Rasulis from many other parts of Persia. One of them is a slender youth with dark eyes and hollow cheeks. Jalal is intent on greeting each of the new enlistees, but as he approaches this frail boy, the youth turns away.

"What is your name, my son?" Jalal asks.

A thin, reedy voice replies, "Hasan."

Jalal hesitates for a moment and then says, "Followers of the Rasul must, above all things, be truthful, and so I ask again—what is your name?"

The figure turns slowly to stare into the eyes of Jalal, who is struck by the sudden ferocity of the youth's gaze. "My name is Zarrin," she replies.

Jalal stares at the young woman. "You wish to march with us?"

"I've come very far to be with you."

"It will be dangerous. Many of us will not survive."

"I am not afraid of death. And if we must fight, I will hold my own in any battle. I am not a poet like Tara, but I long to prove that I have her courage. I trust you agree that the Cause of the Rasul is open to both men and women equally."

Jalal smiles, then looks down and sees a scabbard hanging from Zarrin's belt. The hilt of a sword protrudes from it.

"Do you know how to use a sword?"

"My brother taught me."

"We use our weapons only in defense, is that clear?"

"Of course."

Zarrin suddenly realizes that she has just been accepted into the ranks of the Rasulis. She will be allowed to march beneath the Black Standard.

"Thank you!" she shouts.

"You may dress as a woman," Jalal says. "There is no shame in being a woman."

"I have only men's clothing with me. And I choose not to wear the chador any longer, unless you insist."

Jalal replies, "Tara removed her veil, and so may you. Dress as you wish."

"Zarrin!"

Another voice intrudes, and Zarrin's brother pushes his way up to her. "Zarrin, what are you doing here?"

"Hamid, what do you think?" Zarrin replies. "I have joined the march."

Embarrassed, Hamid turns to Jalal and says, "I apologize for my sister. I will hire an escort to see her home."

"Hamid, I am staying," Zarrin says. "Jalal has given me permission to join you and the others. It is settled."

"Is that true?" Hamid asks Jalal.

"I have no authority to refuse anyone whom God has called. Do you see the man over there?"

Jalal points to an elderly man who is seated beneath a tree.

"Abbas is eighty-three years old," he continues. "Both he and his son have joined us. And though I ride a horse, Abbas refuses. Instead, he walks alongside my horse all day. I have never seen him without a smile. It is not my right to deprive him of this joy in serving the cause of the Rasul simply because he is old. And it is not my right to deprive your sister of the joy of service because she is a woman."

Hamid accepts this. Looking at Zarrin, he asks, "Does our father know what you have done?"

"Yes."

"And Ishaq. Does he know?"

"He knows." She turns to Jalal and explains: "Ishaq and I are to be married. He is from England—and America—but his father is from Persia."

She looks down at her sandals. "Hamid, there is something you should know about Ishaq."

"What is it?"

Zarrin looks up at Hamid. "Ishaq's father is a very powerful man in the Qajar government. He is the true power behind Aqasi."

The name Aqasi invokes a sudden horror.

"Aqasi is our worst enemy!" Hamid says.

Jalal interjects, "Zarrin, do you know the name of Ishaq's father?"

"His name is Ali Qasim. Ishaq has gone to reason with him—to persuade him to stop persecuting us."

Jalal's gut rumbles. He feels dizzy with possibilities. *Ali Qasim*—surely there are many men with that name in Persia.

"Do you know where Ali Qasim is from?" Jalal asks.

"Yes, I think—Ishaq told me, if I can just remember. Yes—Ali Qasim of Bushruyih."

The blood rushes from Jalal's head. There can be no doubt! Jalal's most cherished childhood friend, Ali, has become his arch enemy. What kind of tortured journey could turn such a righteous youth from piety to persecution?

A tremendous sadness envelopes Jalal. He stammers a vague excuse to leave Zarrin and Hamid. He walks briskly to the far side of the Rasuli encampment. He sits down next to a large rock. He glances up at the sky and tries to imagine the face of Muhammad in the clouds, as he and Ali had seen so many years before—a comforting sign for two best friends who had pledged themselves to finding the Promised One. Jalal never could have imagined that their searches would be for completely different reasons—one to serve, and the other to destroy.

Beside the rock, beneath the blank sky, Jalal cries.

CHAPTER 18

Ishaq stands on the wide veranda of his father's Tehran apartment. Jonathon's and Ali's sleeping rooms have been vacant since he had arrived ten days ago. As Ishaq views the panorama of Tehran and the great palace stretched out beneath a deepening purple sky, he thinks about Zarrin and her fearlessness. Will he have the same courage when finally called upon to confront his father?

Ishaq wonders at how one can both love and despise another person. Perhaps these were the same confused feelings that Ali had had for his mother. In Ishaq's case, however, the perplexity is magnified by conflicting loyalties to his father and to his God. To honor one is to betray the other. How does one make such a difficult choice?

In the end, it is Zarrin who makes the decision clear. If Ali continues his campaign of persecution, Zarrin surely will be killed. The march of the Black Standard will be characterized as an armed insurrection by Ali, an excuse to exterminate the participants and, frighteningly, all other Rasulis—even the Rasul himself.

In the end, Ishaq must challenge his father.

But how far will he go? Is he prepared to confess his own conversion to this new Faith and risk total alienation from his father? And if so, will Ali's irrational rage overwhelm fatherly love? After all, Ishaq and Ali are not tied by blood but merely by choice, and choices can change.

A servant brings food and places it on the thick carpet. Ishaq walks into the receiving room, sits, and diffidently eats the lamb and rice. He sips the steaming tea and burns his tongue. The pain is sharp, exquisite, *deserved*. The sting of it reminds him that such muddled thinking is the disease from which his father suffers. If Ishaq allows his mind to wander those dark corridors, he will become his father.

The food and the thinking have made him weary. Ishaq stumbles into his room and lies down on a sleeping mat.

He opens his eyes—he must have fallen asleep because sunlight is streaming into the room. The legs of a man are standing beside him. Ishaq lifts his gaze to see Ali solemnly looking down at him.

"Father?" Ishaq says.

"It's good to see you, son."

Ishaq sits up, rubbing his eyes. "I've been waiting for you," he says.

"Yes, I know. I've been traveling. Much has happened. Last night, Muhammad Shah died."

This news sends a shiver through Ishaq. There will now be a wrenching battle for the throne. As always in this land, there will be treachery and bloodletting. For a time, no one will be safe.

"What will happen?" Ishaq asks.

Ali sits down by his son. "I knew that the shah could not live much longer so I made all the necessary arrangements for a swift transition of power," he says. "Within several days Nasir al-Din will declare himself the new shah. Soon after, he will leave Tabriz with the Azerbaijani army, which, as you know, is the most fearsome fighting force in the land and is controlled by Mirza Taki Khan, with whom I have an alliance."

"But Mirza Taki Khan is an avowed enemy of Aqasi!"

"Aqasi has few remaining friends or allies. The new shah and ten thousand troops will soon enter Tehran. Mirza Taki Khan will be named the new grand vizier."

"And Aqasi?"

"He is in his summer residence. The Russian minister plenipotentiary has already sent him a note recommending that he stay there. I expect that Aqasi, the old fool, will try to rally the dwindling band of Iravani guards to escort him back to Tehran, but he has no real hope of staying in power. Besides the Russians, I have also persuaded the British to support Nasir al-Din over Aqasi's candidate. It is now just a matter of pageantry."

Ali speaks calmly, as if these historic events—largely of his making—are of little consequence.

But Ishaq is frightened by the news. "What will become of *you*, then? Of *us*?"

"There's nothing to fear, believe me. They understand that I have no political aspirations. And they have clearly seen my… my *usefulness*. In return, they have given me their support in vanquishing a common enemy, the growing Rasuli insurrection."

These words stun Ishaq. He had been distracted by all the political news and had forgotten his own mission, but now realizes that the unfolding events have strengthened Ali's hand in persecuting the Rasulis. He stands suddenly and walks to the window, looking out at the city now bathed in sunlight. The view, he knows, belies the storm that is building—unless he can reason with his father.

Ali approaches Ishaq and says, "Something is bothering you."

"I just don't understand why you are so intent on murdering the Rasulis. They've done nothing to you… or to the government. Nothing, that is, that they have not been falsely accused of."

"Murder is a harsh word," Ali says. "but a good one. It can be applied in many circumstances. The murder of hundreds of innocent victims on a drowning ship. The murder of a wife and an unborn child."

"Those are old stories, father." Anger is overtaking Ishaq, and he can't repress it. "Old stories that anyone else would have gotten over. And they are *false* stories—about how God is to blame, as if you were the judge and jury. How high and mighty of you! But then, that's your pattern, isn't it? You tried the Rasul in Tabriz. And now you're trying to carry out the sentence."

Ali steps back, ashen. "Ishaq, do you actually believe that the Rasul is the so-called Promised One?"

Ishaq knows that he has inadvertently exposed his beliefs. There is no turning back now. Timidly, Ishaq says, "I do."

Ali turns and paces. Then he wheels, ready to fling a quiver full of accusations, but is interrupted by Ishaq.

"So do you, father." Ishaq's words are more forceful now. "You believe He is the Promised One… or you wouldn't be so bent on destroying Him. You want to punish God, and you see the Rasul as His Manifestation, so you are set on punishing Him."

The flurry of Ishaq's words take the steam out of Ali's intended accusations. Instead, Ali decides to defend his position.

"I don't know if the Rasul is who he claims to be, but I hope that he is. If he is *not*, then I will burn in hell for destroying a young man. And if he *is* the Promised One, I will burn in hell alongside Pontius Pilate—but I will have my revenge."

"You are willing to sacrifice an innocent man?"

"If he is an imposter, he is not innocent."

"What about all the Rasulis who will be slaughtered?"

"They have enlisted of their own free will."

"So why not murder all Muslims, or Christians, or Zoroastrians. Maybe we should slaughter all the Hindus and Buddhists, too."

"Don't be ridiculous! But do I have to remind you of all the wars that have been fought because of religion?"

"Do I have to remind you that your war against the Rasulis is now part of that wicked history? Is it any wonder that we need fresh guidance from God!"

"These other religions, despicable as they are, have become too deeply rooted to destroy. But this new one, this Rasuli religion—I can keep it from adding to the contamination."

"What if the Rasulis have been simply duped by the charisma of an imposter— they deserve to die for that?"

"It is their *actions* that make them guilty, not their beliefs. Did you know that the Rasulis have launched an insurrection in Mazandaran? They are parading through the villages beneath the Black Standard, recruiting for their cause."

"Father, they want peace, not war. They only want to state the Rasul's message and give the people a choice to accept or reject it. Why is this so threatening? No, it comes down to revenge, doesn't it? How many lives are you willing to sacrifice to satisfy your bloodlust?"

Ali marches to Ishaq and slaps him hard.

The stinging blow brings tears to Ishaq's eyes. Ishaq realizes now that he has taken the worst possible approach to this conversation. He should have heeded Zarrin's advice: *Show him your love. Then show him the love of God reflected in you.*

The tears in Ishaq's eyes multiply. "I love you, father, but I see what hate can do, and I don't want that for me or my wife."

"Your wife?" Ali cocks his head and squints. "Ishaq, are you married?"

"Not yet. And probably never. Zarrin, the woman I love, is a Rasuli, and she has gone to join Jalal's march in Mazandaran."

"I've heard of Jalal. A clever one, I'll give you that."

"If you continue your persecution of the Rasulis, I fear for Zarrin's life."

"It is out of my hands, son. If the Rasulis persist, they must be dealt with. I can't control the villagers."

"You can stop provoking them!"

"There is nothing I can do. I hope that this girl comes to her senses and returns home."

Ali speaks these words coldly. Having invoked his future hell-mate Pontius Pilate, Ali is now washing his hands of any responsibility.

"She will not return," Ishaq says angrily. His body is trembling. "She will be killed, and I will not blame God for her murder. I will blame my father."

Ali tries to appease. "You don't mean that, Ishaq."

"Yes, I do. But I will only blame you for a brief time, because, God-willing, I will die with her."

"You plan to join the march?"

"As soon as I can."

Ishaq rushes to the other side of the room. In a mad flurry he begins to pack his things. Ali stares at him for a moment as if calculating his son's threat, and then leaves without a word.

Once packed, Ishaq carries his bags into the receiving room and finds his father waiting with two armed guards.

Ali speaks to the larger guard. "Take him to the palace harem. He must not be allowed to leave."

"You are imprisoning me?" Ishaq asks incredulously.

"*Protecting* you. If you think back, you will realize it is not the first time."

The guards seize Ishaq by the arms.

"Be gentle but firm," Ali instructs. "He will try to escape. If he does, I will have your heads. While he is in custody, see to it that he has everything he wants. Anything at all. He may be released only on my order, or in the event of my death. Is that understood?"

The guards nod.

"Then take him away."

Ali does not look at Ishaq as he is led from the apartment, even when Ishaq yells, "You should have just left me on the piers!"

CHAPTER 19

In a cold drizzle, Jalal gathers the Rasulis around him for the Morning Prayer. When it is finished, he turns his gaze upon the two hundred hungry, shivering men—and the one pale woman. Yesterday, over twenty of them had left the march after Jalal had spoken of the certain perils to come.

With his sword at his side, Jalal leads the men toward Barfurush. For an hour they march in silence. The rhythmic sway of Jalal's white stallion begins to induce a familiar effect, a faint tremor in his arms.

Please God, not now, he pleads. *Not as we prepare to enter the city.*

But each rocking step of the horse seems to intensify the trembling. He grips the horn of his saddle with both hands, trying to suppress the shaking, but to no avail. He tries to control his breathing, but the shuddering continues.

Zarrin has been riding behind Jalal on a dark brown roan provided by Assaf, the physician. She has been studying the frail leader in flowing white garments who has already become a legend among Rasulis. She alone detects the faint quivering of his arms, the desperate grip on the saddle horn. Old Abbas trots merrily along the right side of Jalal's horse, so Zarrin urges her roan to his left side.

Jalal appears almost to be in a trance. His eyes are focused on some indistinct object ahead, as if this unwavering gaze is the sole means of staying saddled. He does not seem to notice Zarrin at his left.

For an hour they trudge through intensifying rain. About three miles from the city gate they find the road blocked by several hundred armed citizens shouting obscenities and waving weapons in the air. Jalal stares at them impassively. All of his strength and concentration is on controlling his tremors. If he gives in to fear or anger now, emotion will fuel the convulsions.

Please God, not now!

Faced with this fanatical mob, some of the Rasulis unsheathe their swords.

Her heart pounding, Zarrin draws her blade and holds it high in the air. The others raise their swords.

Rain clatters on the cold steel. The mob's curses stop suddenly as the militia prepares to be attacked.

Jalal blinks and turns his head to Zarrin. He must direct his men! His right arm is trembling too violently to be useful now. He sweeps his left arm out and with a shaking hand grips Zarrin's arm, forcing her to lower her weapon.

"Not yet," he whispers hoarsely. "Our swords must not leave their scabbards until the aggressor forces us to protect ourselves."

Zarrin slides her sword back into its scabbard. The others do the same.

Interpreting this as a sign of weakness, the militia again begins cursing and advancing toward the Rasulis.

Zarrin can feel the fierce vibration of Jalal's body as his arm connects with hers.

Is he afraid? she wonders. *Despite his words, does he fear death?*

"They are advancing!" Zarrin says.

"Not yet," Jalal replies. And then he releases her arm.

A volley of shots! Four Rasulis fall dead.

More shots.

Assaf the physician yells and grips his leg, slumping to the ground.

Jalal watches a tall, slender man in a brown turban lean against a tree, raise his musket, and fire at the marchers.

Old Abbas, who has been standing to the right of Jalal, is thrust backward by the force of the shot. Blood sputters from his chest.

Jalal's entire body is quaking now. Zarrin suspects that he has been overcome by madness or disease or fear. She is about to draw her sword and take command when she notices Jalal turning his eyes to the rain clouds above and moving his lips, as if praying.

More shots ring out.

Jalal bows his head. His body quakes uncontrollably, but he manages to whisper, "Now it is time."

How this shaking, quivering man can lead the Rasulis into battle, Zarrin cannot fathom. But as Jalal firmly grips the hilt of his sword, the trembling stops. With a steady hand, he unsheathes the gleaming blade from its jeweled leather scabbard.

Zarrin has never seen such a magnificent instrument! Even in the gloom of this rainy morning, it seems to shine with its own light. On the vivid black jowher of the blade she can see engraved in gold the name *Jalal*.

And then the blade flashes in a sudden shaft of sunlight, singing with the voice of angels. Jalal has begun the charge. Pointing his blade at the tall fanatic who had murdered Abbas, Jalal gallops into the thick of the mob and finds the man cowardly hiding behind the six-inch trunk of a tree.

The attackers are stunned at the boldness of the Rasuli charge and begin to fire their muskets.

Whipping the reins against the neck of her roan, Zarrin struggles to keep up with Jalal as bullets buzz past like angry bees.

In flowing white robes, Jalal jumps his steed over a fallen log and races toward the killer of Abbas. Without slowing, Jalal swings his sword—the gift from his father—in a powerful arc. The stroke cleaves in half the trunk of the tree, the body of the man, and the barrel of his musket. The tree falls, crashing into a group of villagers.

After many more days of hard marching, the Black Standard breaks the crest of a hill. Below, a small building is situated in a courtyard surrounded by a short octagonal wall. This simple square building, Jalal knows, is the shrine of Shaykh Hujjat, a revered cleric who had recorded many traditions of the words of Muhammad. This is where the Black Standard will come to rest. This is where the Rasulis must make their stand.

Jalal knows that many fanatics inflamed by fear and hatred, and even perhaps military troops, will soon be attacking them from all sides. The shrine quickly must become a fort.

Jalal turns to his companions and says, "We have arrived."

CHAPTER 20

Nasir-al Din Shah, the boy-king, wears the garment of arrogance well. Like a snake, he has shed the old skin of boyhood to reveal the bold new stripes of authority. Of the many titles that orbit around the throne of Persia, Nasir-al Din Shah has selected one of which he is particularly fond: the Pivot of the Universe.

The shah has chosen Gordon Cranston to be his interpreter on the recommendation of Ali. In proposing this appointment, Ali deceitfully had explained that Cranston's left hand had been chopped off by Aqasi in retaliation for the interpreter's stubborn defense of Nasir-al Din's claim to the throne.

Cranston is wary of Ali's motives but appreciates reinstatement to the shah's inner circle.

Lamps are lit in the shah's great chamber as dusk descends. The shah is seated on a burgundy carpet with Ali, Cranston, and Mirza Taki Khan, the new grand vizier. The mood is solemn. Troubling news from Mazandaran has just arrived.

"Who is this Jalal?" the shah asks Ali.

"One of the Rasul's disciples, and from all reports a brave warrior and charismatic leader."

"I should not have let you persuade me to spare the life of that imposter, the Rasul. If he were dead, his followers would scatter and soon forget him."

"I beg your indulgence," Ali responds. "but to make a martyr of the Rasul before his followers are humiliated or defeated would only create a rallying point for their fanaticism. They must be weakened first."

The grand vizier leans toward Ali and says, "A small band of these Rasulis soundly humiliated a group of devout Muslims near Barfurush. So tell me again who is being humiliated and defeated?"

"Our agents tell us that Jalal and his Black Standard have taken refuge in the shrine of Shaykh Hujjat, which they have been busy fortifying against attack. That doesn't sound like a conquering army."

"Yes, but even now men from the surrounding villages are joining ranks with the Rasulis at the shrine. And Jalal has also managed to get Danush freed. Danush has now joined them at the shrine. It sounds more like a festival to me. Even Mirza Ramin has visited."

"Mirza Ramin—the nobleman?" the shah asks.

"The same," Ali replies. "He is a devout follower of the Rasul. In fact, he organized a conference for them near Badasht. Despite his reputation for kindness and compassion, he is a very dangerous man."

"But he is greatly respected throughout Persia," the shah says. "Even my father respected this man, and loved his father, the vizier of Núr."

"It is this respect that temporarily spares him," Ali says.

The grand vizier snorts impatiently, rises, and walks to a window that reveals a vast purple sky. He wheels and stares at Ali expectantly. "How do you propose to handle this?"

Ali rises also, not wishing to remain in a posture of subservience. "With your permission, I will gather an army of five thousand men from Mazandaran and overwhelm their makeshift fort. We will crush them with overpowering force. It is to our advantage that Danush and Jalal are both there, for we will destroy them together."

"Five thousand men!" the young shah says, laughing. "I would think a thousand would be sufficient. The reports says that there are—what?—three hundred Rasulis in the shrine?"

"Now that Danush and his escort have arrived, three hundred and thirteen to be precise," Ali says, confident in the reports of his agents.

The grand vizier blanches. "My God!" he groans. "The Traditions say that the coming of the Promised One will be accompanied by the *three hundred thirteen men* who fought with the Prophet Muhammad at the Battle of Badr!"

"Get a grip on yourself," Ali says in English.

Gordon, the only one but Ali who can understand, laughs quietly.

"They carry the Black Standard," the grand vizier continues. "The prophesied three hundred thirteen now occupy the shrine of Shaykh Hujjat, the preserver of the Traditions. These are most ominous signs."

Ali returns to speaking Farsi. "These are myths! But you can see how cleverly these fanatics have hijacked the symbols of Islam to influence the weak-minded and the superstitious. If a great intellectual mind like yours can even momentarily flinch at the mention of such things, imagine the profound effect on the simple minds of the villagers. We must take no chances in destroying these fanatics at once. I'm sure that I don't have to point out that this will be the first military campaign under Nasir-al Din Shah's regime."

The shah rises. With boyish enthusiasm he says, "If five thousand men is a good number, then ten thousand is better. Let all of Persia see the might of the new shah. Ali, you will personally recruit the men. But see to it that these infidels are killed quickly."

Ali bows to the boy before him and says, "I will need ammunition and supplies."

The shah nods.

"Once the army has surrounded the shrine," Ali says, "we will quickly exterminate these vermin."

Bearing the shah's royal badge, Ali leaves the palace for Mazandaran the next morning. With the cooperation of Abdu'llah Khan, a powerful general in the army of Mazandaran, he is able to recruit over 12,000 men. Within a month, 'Abdu'llah has moved the troops to the small village of Afra near the shrine of Hujjat.

On the first evening of the army's encampment at Afra, 'Abdu'llah sits with Ali in a majestic tent that had taken thirty men the better part of the day to erect and then adorn with lush carpets, animal furs, and countless ornaments of battle and plunder.

Sipping tea, 'Abdu'llah looks up at Ali and says, "Do you believe he is the Qa'im?"

"I believe he threatens the kingdom. I leave religious conjecture to the mullas."

"The army we have assembled makes for wonderful pageantry, but is unnecessary to accomplish the mission. I propose that a smaller detachment—perhaps two thousand men—be stationed just outside the Rasuli fortress. We will sever the supply line to the shrine, depriving them of food and water. Trust me, before long they will surrender without a battle."

"You speak of a siege. I had envisioned an attack."

"These Rasulis have fortified themselves well. Even with our overwhelming numbers, I cannot guarantee success on a first attack. How would it appear if twelve thousand Persian troops were repulsed even once by a small band of farm boys and mullas?"

Ali laughs. "I'm impressed by your shrewdness. Your approach is more prudent."

The plan begins to unfold by the following afternoon.

Inside "Fort" Hujjat, as the inhabitants have been calling the reinforced shrine, the Rasulis watch apprehensively as hundreds of Persian troops circumambulate the shrine and imperiously set up camp barely a hundred yards from the fortified gate. The army wagons leave deep ruts in the soft Mazandaran soil as huge barricades are built up. The army detachment has even brought its own flock of sheep and goats to provide meat and milk for the troops.

Ten days after the start of the siege, Abbas the physician approaches Jalal and says, "We can endure the lack of food for a time, but there is no more water. We cannot last even another two days."

Jalal stares out at the grassy field on which the government troops are camped. In the front of the camp, seated at a table visible to the Rasulis, a captain eats lunch and hoists a glass as if toasting the Rasulis. The officer drinks deeply, and then tauntingly flings the remainder of the liquid onto the ground.

"God willing," Jalal replies to Abbas, "a downpour of rain will overtake our opponents this very evening, followed by a heavy snowfall. The rain will fill our cisterns and assist us in repelling our opponents."

Abbas looks up at the cloudless sky and sighs. *God willing*, he thinks. And then he prays for the strength to understand and obey God's will. His lips are parched and his skin withered and scaly from lack of water. Some of the men have already become disoriented. Even the animals have grown weak from dehydration.

At three o'clock that morning, a thunderclap, sounding like cannon fire, stirs the slumbering Rasulis. Within minutes rain begins to spatter on the roof of the shrine and the packed floor of the courtyard. The rain is cold and slushy, but the men begin to sing joyfully as the rain pelts them. They hold open their mouths, snatching the life-giving water out of the air.

The rain becomes a downpour, and then a violent waterfall, sending them for cover. The courtyard is becoming a shallow sea.

In their enemy encampment, the deluge seeps into the soft Mazandaran soil, turning it into a mushy bog. Tents blow over, a flash flood destroys the camp's munitions, and wagons sink into the mud. Frightened horses tear free from their restraints and race frantically through the camp. The sheep and goats flee in terror, many of them making their way toward the slightly higher ground of the fort.

The following morning dawns gray and colder. The exhausted, shivering troops, stuck in the mud without shelter, spend the day digging out while the Rasulis gather the sheep and goats that miraculously have strayed near the front gate. Cold but rejoicing nevertheless, the Rasulis eat and drink, dry out near warm fires, and huddle prayerfully inside the shelters.

That evening, a heavy snowstorm—unusual for this province on the shores of the Caspian Sea—blankets the entire region. The cold slush virtually immobilizes the army. Just after sunrise the next day, as the shah's army is rising stiffly from a cold and miserable night in the muck, the gate of Fort Hujjat flies open and two hundred Rasulis explode from it like a cannon ball with shouts of "Ya Sahibu'z-Zaman!" *The Lord of the Age!*

Jalal and Danush lead the charge on horseback, with Zarrin close behind on her roan. The remainder of the Rasulis charge on foot. Jalal holds his gleaming sword overhead.

The attack is so unexpected, and the cries of the Rasulis so fierce, that the shaken soldiers scatter like ants, most of them running through the sticky mud toward the much larger detachment in Afra.

The commanding officer, Mohit, stands to face the onslaught. With sword drawn, he stares down Zarrin who gallops toward him. As she nears, readying her sword, he ducks and slices his blade through the roan's front leg. The horse falls and Zarrin pitches face-first into the mud, still clutching her sword. She sits up and sees Mohit only several steps away. His face is spattered with snow and mud, and he is raising his sword, but as he tries to move forward he finds his feet trapped in the sucking mud. Cursing his luck, he watches Zarrin stand. Angrily he prepares to hurl his sword at her, but from behind Abbas spears him in the back.

Within minutes, all two thousand troops have abandoned their encampment. The Rasulis continue to charge, following the soldiers to nearby Afra. Believing themselves to be in no danger, the officers of the Afra camp had made no defensive preparations. As the bloody remnant of the forward detachment races into the camp, the Afra detachment erupts in panic and the men begin to scatter. Confused and afraid, many of them run to the River Talar and drown trying to escape an invading force that they are certain must be far larger than their own.

'Abdu'llah, who is only partially dressed, calls upon his officers to stand and fight, but they flee instead. All the officers are killed, and 'Abdu'llah dies alone with a club to the head.

Jalal finds one man neither running nor facing him with a weapon. The man stands on the edge of the forest staring fearlessly at Jalal, who approaches him on horseback. The man is dressed neither as a soldier or an officer.

Jalal urges his horse up to the stranger until the man is standing next to his thigh. It is not right to kill a man who is not armed, and who may not be part of the opposition.

"Who are you?" Jalal demands.

The man remains silent.

Jalal has no time for this. He raises his sword high and brings the hilt of it down on the man's head. Quickly, he hoists the unconscious fellow onto the back of his horse and ties him down.

In less than an hour, twelve thousand government troops have vanished from the encampment. Not a single Rasuli has been killed.

Some of the Rasulis want to continue the chase, but Danush instructs them to cease the attack and return to the fort. "Our purpose is to protect ourselves, not cause unnecessary harm," Danush explains.

Suddenly weary, the Rasulis return to their cheering companions who had been left to guard the fort.

Inside Fort Hujjat, Jalal lowers his captive from the back of the horse and carries the man into the shrine. He tends to the man's head wound, chastising himself for such preventable violence. When the man regains consciousness, Jalal offers him tea. The man sips it silently. Finally, the man looks at Jalal and speaks for the first time.

"What will you do with me?"

"It depends. Who are you?"

"I am a villager from Afra."

Jalal studies the man, whose robes are not those of a villager.

"And I am the shah," Jalal replies, smiling. "Now tell me the truth."

"All right, I am a representative of the shah."

"What is your name?"

"In England I am known as Oliver Chadwick. In Persia my name is Ali Qasim of Bushruyih."

These words stun Jalal. He stands and faces away from his captive. Ali Qasim! Yes, he had known that Ali had returned. Still facing the wall, Jalal says, "Let me introduce myself. I am Jalal."

This time Ali is stunned. He has been captured by the man he both despises and admires.

"The name my parents gave me is Jalal."

Ali searches his memory. He had known a boy named Jalal—his best friend, in fact, whom Ali had tearfully left behind and who still haunts his dreams.

Jalal turns. "Jalal of Bushruyih," he adds.

Two twelve-year-old friends face each other at last from across the great gulf of time.

CHAPTER 21

Alí stares at his boyhood friend. The legendary Rasuli warrior before him is the spiritually gifted boy who had been the envy of all the young men in Bush-ruyih. He is the intellectually precocious child who had vanquished the mujta-hids in debate and had saved the life of an old Shaykhi. He is the dreamer who had longed to be the first to discover the Promised One. He is, had been, Ali's dearest friend, but now is Ali's adversary. And yet this bearded captor in the soiled white robes does not strike fear in Ali's heart. The clear eyes, the affable smile, the gentle touch—these are not the expressions of a fanatic or a savage.

Ali is calm and relaxed. Two other individuals enter the shrine and light candles to illuminate the gathering darkness. Jalal introduces the first as Da-nush. The second one, who appears to be a young man, is introduced with the name of a woman, Zarrin.

Zarrin! This must be the young woman whom Ishaq loves. Surely no other woman by that name has joined the pursuit of Jalal's death wish.

Jalal introduces his captive to the others, saying, "This is my friend, Ali Qasim of Bushruyih, who is known in England as Oliver Chadwick."

Zarrin easily makes the connection with Ishaq, but she, too, remains silent.

Jalal continues speaking to Danush and Zarrin. "When we were boys of twelve, we both hoped to become mullas. Religion was at the center of our lives, and the Prophet dominated our thoughts. The years since have been very difficult for my friend, I assume, or he would not have abandoned his desire for nearness to God and cast his lot with our persecutors."

Zarrin casts a ferocious look at Ali and says, "You are in a position of great authority in the Qajar government."

Ali nods and replies, "I see that Ishaq has told you about me."

"He said that you might help us," Zarrin says, her voice brittle with tension, "but apparently you have decided to kill us instead. Why, then, should we not kill you?"

She moves her hand to the hilt of her sword but Danush calms her with the touch of his hand.

"Perhaps you should," Ali replies.

"Did Ishaq tell you about me, and that I was with Jalal?" she asks.

Ali nods again.

Zarrin bites her lip. She feels betrayed and masks her pain with sarcasm. "I'm sure you will understand if you are not invited to our wedding," she says.

"You will never be married," Ali replies. "When you chose to follow Jalal, you chose the path of certain death. I'm afraid that you will never leave this fort alive."

"Maybe you've forgotten how we crushed your proud army!" Zarrin snaps back.

"You have extended your lives by mere days. Very soon, news of your feat will be reaching Tehran. The child who is now shah will be infuriated because his precious pride has been injured. He will order a fresh army to descend upon your fort with such royal vengeance that buzzards will be picking your bones within a month. In a year, no one will remember you or your cause, except in ridicule. What you do with me doesn't matter because the wheels of your destruction have already been set in motion."

Zarrin is enraged at this man's defiance. "We hold your life! Do you not fear death?"

"I have already died many deaths," Ali says. "I died the day that God unjustly took my beloved. I died again when he drowned my mother—and yet again when he killed my wife and unborn daughter. Do you think one more death frightens me? No more than death frightens you. Is it difficult to understand that we both seek martyrdom? You in the service of your God, and I in my struggle to punish Him."

Danush sees that Jalal has been deeply touched by Ali's pain. "Zarrin, we must leave now. These two old friends have things to talk about."

The two men are alone again.

"The day you disappeared," Jalal says quietly, "I thought that angels had descended and plucked you from earth to serve God in some other realm. You had such goodness in you, such purity of heart. I envied you."

"Don't be foolish," Ali says, smiling for the first time. "It was I who envied you."

"I'm sorry that you blame God for your difficulties."

"Difficulties? Such a mild term for betrayal and murder."

"If you believe that God betrayed you, then you must still believe in God."

"In His existence, yes. But I've discovered His true nature."

"Yes, and so have I. But it seems our conclusions are probably irreconcilable."

"*Definitely* irreconcilable. Even your celebrated powers of debate will not persuade me that God is anything but cruel and unjust."

"Then I will not try. You may leave now."

"You're letting me go?"

Jalal nods. "But I wish you'd stay the night so we can talk."

"And so you can soften me up, change my mind? It won't happen."

Jalal sighs, looks at his muddy boots, and smiles softly. "I've missed you, Ali. For many years you came to me in my dreams, but then one day you stopped. Now that I've found you again, can you blame me for wanting to reminisce about our happy times together?"

Ali turns away. "I'll stay," he says.

They talk into the night, about flying horses and the sparse shade of mulberry trees and the buried plunder of Turkoman raiders, but not religion. About the excitement of caravans entering town and the feel of maust on the tongue and the delicate fragrances of the kelauntar's gardens, but not God. They recall the fleeting glimpses of female eyes that thrilled them, and the hilarious lunacy of old mullas, and the lively games of youth. On this frigid winter evening, they lie again on a blanket of warm Bushruyih sand, two twelve-year old boys, heads nearly touching, eyes on the clouds. And finally, as they sleep, Ali fleetingly comes to Jalal again in his dreams.

At dawn, Ali mounts a tired mule and turns to Jalal. "It would be so much easier if you and Zarrin would leave the fort. I can protect you. Come with me."

Jalal smiles and says, "On the other hand, we could use another able body here. I fear that we'll be outnumbered soon."

Ali and Jalal stare at each other through an impassable chasm.

Jalal says, "Remember when we both claimed that we would be the first to discover the Promised One?"

"Apparently you won."

"Don't give up," Jalal replies. He slaps the mule. It trudges toward the gate, which slowly yawns open.

From a small bundle wrapped tightly around his waist, Ali takes out two daguerreotypes and a folded dust cover, the beacons of his obsession. The faces shine in the early morning light. After an evening of remembrance, these are the memories that matter.

He must never forget that.

CHAPTER 22

After trading the mule and a handful of coins for a sturdy horse, Ali rides for Tehran and arrives at his airy apartment to find that Jonathon Fury has returned from his travels. Jonathon is cleaning his equipment as he dines on rice, stewed eggplant, and skewered beef.

Jonathon looks up, shocked to see Ali.

"My God," he says in English, "we all thought you had been killed in Afra." He leaps to his feet and wraps his arms around his grimy friend. "You look exhausted. Are you hungry? Eat before you faint!"

Ali sits and begins to eat.

Jonathon, too agitated to sit, remains standing.

"The new shah thinks you are dead, too," Jonathon says. "To be honest, he seems quite angry. Apparently the campaign in Afra didn't go as expected, but I suppose you know that. By now, everyone in Persia seems to know that a handful of Rasuli peasants vanquished a massive royal army. This fellow, Jalal, has captured the attention of the people. Depending on their outlook, he's either a saint or a devil—either way, something quite supernatural."

Ali swallows a mouthful of rice and says, "He's neither—I can attest to that."

"You've met him?"

"He captured me after the battle at Afra."

Jonathon sits down close to Ali. "And you escaped?"

"He let me go."

Jonathon considers this.

Ali continues to eat.

"Maybe you can follow his example and let Ishaq go," Jonathon says.

Ali closes his eyes. "If I release him, he will go to Fort Hujjat and die there. I heard news on the way back that the shah has called for Prince Mihdi to muster troops for an all-out assault on the Rasulis. This time they will not fail."

"That must make you very happy," Jonathon says, his voice tinged with sarcasm.

Ali doesn't know if the annihilation of the Rasulis makes him happy or not. Since his evening with Jalal and Zarrin, he has lost his zeal to punish these unfortunate misfits. Should they die because they were misled?

"Have you seen Ishaq?" Ali asks.

"He's well, but concerned for Zarrin. He doesn't know if she survived the battle at Afra. He's convinced that *you* did not."

"And how has he responded to my 'death'?" As soon as Ali asks this question, he realizes that he may not want to know the answer.

"He simply called your death an act of God's justice."

Ali steels himself against this revelation. "One day he will understand," he says.

"Understand what? That his father engineered the massacre of his fellow believers? This he already understands."

"They haven't been killed yet. In fact, they've inflicted more harm on our troops than they have suffered."

"Makes you wonder whose side God is on, doesn't it?"

"The God I know is on neither side. He is simply amused by the carnage."

"I think you should go to see Isaac."

"No."

"Then I'll go and tell him you're alive."

"You do what you have to do," Ali says. "I'm going to see the new shah. Attacking the Rasulis again is a strategic mistake that plays right into their hands."

"Yes, I'm sure he'll be eager to hear your opinion after that humiliating defeat in Afra."

This last dart stings. Ali stands up, glowers at Jonathon and flings a dart of his own: "So good to have you back from your travels."

Ali grunts his passage through the arched doorway and struts down the corridor to the outside door. He pushes aside the mute guard and marches to the palace, where he gains easy entrance. He finds Nasir-al-Din Shah and the grand vizier seated. They are conferring confidentially in the shah's chambers. Both men look up in surprise as Ali enters.

"I see you survived the debacle in Afra," the grand vizier says snidely. "As I recall, you promised us a quick end to the affair. You were so right."

"The general was an incompetent imbecile."

"Abdu'llah Khan was a cousin of the shah," the grand vizier states, glancing at the boy-king, "and was appointed to lead this mission by the shah. Are you saying that the shah made a mistake? Or could it be that *your* strategy was flawed?"

Ali sees the trap in these words. "I admit that it was wrong to insist that we attack Fort Hujjat with such a large force."

"They're calling it *Fort* Hujjat now?" the shah asks.

"Yes," Ali replies. "And based on the lessons of my previously flawed thinking, I now recommend a different strategy."

"No longer the warmonger?" the grand vizier asks. "What now? Maybe we should give the Rasulis medals for valor in the face of overwhelming odds."

Ali ignores the unveiled mockery. It is clear that the grand vizier is attempting to elevate his own position by derisively magnifying Ali's missteps.

"As I said." Ali continues, speaking directly to the shah, "the strategy of directly attacking the Rasulis has failed. Their fortifications are strong, and they are not afraid to attack fiercely as a method of defense. There is no reason to believe that attacking them again will produce a more satisfactory result. And if a new army should be defeated—or even merely fail to crush the fanatics on the first assault—the Rasulis' stature would grow to heroic proportions."

"If this is so," the shah asks, "what do you suggest?"

"Exactly the opposite of my previous recommendation. I now suggest that we try the Rasul for heresy and execute him. His death may deflate the Rasulis."

"You told us that making a martyr of the Rasul would rally these fanatics," the shah says, confused. "Now you say we should martyr him?"

"How can we take advice from a man of such contradictions?" the grand vizier says. "I wonder if your change of heart, Ali, comes from your son's embracing of this heresy. I understand that the woman he intends to marry is with the Rasulis at Hujjat."

Ali is stunned that the grand vizier knows so much.

"You've talked to my son?" Ali asks.

The shah interrupts. "I spoke with Ishaq, yes. He was quite candid in admitting his convictions. Too bad—I rather liked him."

To Ali, this sounds like a threat.

"My recommendation stands," Ali boldly says, sidestepping the issue of his son. "Do you approve?"

"Unfortunately, no," the grand vizier replies flatly. "It's too late. Within a day or two Prince Mihdi-Quli will have an army of five thousand on the doorstep of this *Fort* Hujjat, and this time we will be ready for the enemy's tactics. They've tipped their hand. The prince, I might add, is a much more astute leader than 'Abdu'llah Khan."

"I see," Ali says. "I trust you will have no complaint if I go to observe the magnificent victory."

"If you get there in time," the shah says, "you might pick up a sword and help out."

"As you wish," Ali replies, and then bows graciously. "Now, then, I will go to release my son from custody."

The grand vizier dramatically raises a large hand and says, "Ahh—but no. Ishaq will remain in our custody."

"But it was I who ordered him held!" Ali protests. "Surely I have the authority to release him. He has committed no offense."

The shah stands in a rustle of silk robes. "He is an admitted Rasuli. We are at war with these fanatics. I consider him to be an enemy."

Ali is shaken by this turn of events. "When can I expect him to be released?"

The shah and the grand vizier look at each other. They look back at Ali.

And then the grand vizier replies, "Released?"

CHAPTER 23

Once the tutor of the crown prince, Ishaq is now his hostage, and Ali is responsible. Another blunder in a tragic series of miscalculations. Ali fears that the opportunistic grand vizier will send Ishaq to the feared *Black Pit*, a cesspool dungeon in which the worst criminals and unrepentant heretics are sent to rot in filth and chains. This had been the grand vizier's implied threat.

Ali's confidence is shattered. He sees now that his perfect pitch for politics has dissolved, leaving him as tone deaf as Aqasi in his waning years. Ali's epic plan for punishing God has miscarried, and the misshapen mess lies at his feet. God, it seems, has decided to fight back.

Ali cannot bear to face Ishaq with such a burden of guilt. He must do something to win back his son's love and trust. Though he still despises God, Ali decides in a flash of inspiration that his atonement will be the rescue of his old friend Jalal and Ishaq's beloved Zarrin. If he has to save the entire legion of Rasulis at Fort Hujjat to accomplish this, he will.

Animated by his new purpose, and suddenly shivering with loneliness, Ali races to the apartment and asks Jonathon to accompanying him back to Afra. Jonathon is easily convinced. Before dawn the two men set out on fast horses, changing them at post stations on the way. They carry few possessions, although Jonathon has strapped a canvas bag, which contains his camera and a few other accessories, to his horse. He would rather go without food.

After four frigid days of travel through the mountains, they finally arrive at noon in the village of Malik-Kala, which lies about two miles east of Fort Hujjat. They hire an introverted old blacksmith to make repairs to a broken horseshoe and inquire about the location of the army of Prince Mihdi-Quli, but the blacksmith remains tight-lipped until Ali produces a letter bearing the seal of the shah. The forged document grants Ali unlimited powers in managing the government's campaign against the Rasulis.

The blacksmith sighs and unburdens himself of the dramatic events that he has recently observed. "This morning the army was surprised by the Rasulis," the blacksmith reports.

"This morning—are you sure?" Ali asks.

"I heard them about three hours before dawn," the blacksmith replies. "They must have crossed the river between here and the shrine. I looked out and saw them coming into the village. Must have been two hundred of them, led by a man in white robes on a white horse that glowed in the moonlight. I knew at once they were Rasulis, and I thought they might be attacking our town, but they passed through on the way to Vas-Kas, where the prince and his army were camped."

"So the army was not in Afra?"

"Not after the previous army was beaten there. This time they camped further away—out of reach. I'm a damned fool, but I followed the Rasulis—at a distance. It's not every day that a fellow from Malik-Kalá gets to see the shah's mighty army demolish a renowned band of heretics. And so I followed the Rasulis to the encampment of the prince, and what I saw and heard will give me nightmares for the rest of my life."

"The Rasulis were defeated?" Ali asks nervously.

"There was a defeat, true," the blacksmith says, "but it was the prince's army that was crushed. I hope you will tell the shah that there was nothing I could do to help."

"Yes, yes," Ali says, "but how could this happen? Surely the army must have been prepared for an attack by the Rasulis."

"They must have believed they were too far away from the Rasulis' lair to be attacked. Four miles, you must admit, is quite a distance to venture from a safe harbor! Suddenly I heard the cry 'Ya Sahibu'z-Zaman!' It rang out on all sides, like spirits shrieking. I fled to my village to hide."

Ali wonders at the strange events that have led him to silently cheer for his enemy, the Rasulis.

CHAPTER 24

Over the next three weeks, the armies of three renowned military leaders—
'Abbas, Mihdi, and Sulayman—merge into a massive army that converges on
Fort Hujjat. The young shah and his new grand vizier have taken matters out
of Ali's hands and ordered a massive build-up. The army is commanded by
forty-five of Persia's most experienced officers. The army immediately severs
supply lines to the fort, begins constructing barricades and war machines, aims
cannons at each of the fort's eight sides, and conducts exercises designed to
impress and frighten the Rasulis.

Despite the army's imposing display of strength, the soldiers are less than
confident. Stories of a mythic Jalal, wielding a magic sword and calling upon
the forces of the universe with the cry of *Ya Sahibu'z-Zaman*, terrify the superstitious troops. They know that other powerful armies have been defeated by
this fearsome foe, and so the soldiers sleep fitfully and work nervously as the
final preparations for war continue.

Jonathon photographs the army and its officers. Ali broods over his lack of
options; he is now mostly an observer.

It is too much to hope that the Rasulis can overcome the awesome fighting
force that has been assembled here.

On the first day of February, Jalal peers over the north wall at the main enemy
encampment. He suspects that the army's assault will begin in a day or two.
He performs his ablutions late in the afternoon, clothes himself in fresh white
garments, and places the Rasul's green turban on his head. He calls the Rasulis
around him.

"This evening we will attack the enemy," he says to them, "but this battle will be unlike any we have fought before. Who will join me?"

Zarrin is the first to raise her hand, and then hundreds of others solemnly raise their fists into the air.

Shortly after midnight, as the morning-star rises, Jalal mounts his white stallion. Behind him are three hundred and thirteen volunteers. Another hundred will remain to defend the fort.

Danush and Zarrin are already mounted. Their horses stomp the ground and snort plumes of fog in the icy air. Except for the sounds of the eager animals, silence envelopes the fort.

Jalal takes a deep breath. He looks up at the morning-star, a reminder of the spiritual dawn that he believes is about to break. He motions for the heavy gate to be opened.

Slowly he urges his horse to the portal and looks out. Small fires burn in the enemy encampment. Tents glow in the moonlight. Everything is quiet. He can hear the faint rustle of his companions closing ranks behind him.

Jalal lifts his sword overhead.

The heavens suddenly cry with shouts of *Ya Sahibu'z-Zaman!*

Roaring like a lion, Jalal charges the first barricade, followed by Zarrin and another hundred Rasulis. The sleepy guards glimpse a fleeting white phantom charging through the moonlight with the cry "The Lord of the Age!"

The terrified soldiers scatter as Jalal smashes through the first barricade, and then the second. At the third barricade, bullets begin to fly past Jalal from every side. Staccato claps of musket fire mix with the shouts of the Rasulis and cries of panic from the soldiers. In the confusing cross-fire, some army bullets strike other soldiers, and many fleeing troops are accidentally cut down by those trying to stand their ground, but Jalal remains untouched.

While Jalal is launching his frontal attack, the other two hundred Rasulis circle around the army and now begin an assault from the other sides. Their shouts terrify the stunned troops.

Prince 'Abbas flees from his tent, musket in hand. He dodges two Rasulis but is knocked down by a fleeing soldier who ignores his orders to stand and fight. The prince finds a tree and climbs into its branches to hide and observe the maelstrom that is sweeping through his camp.

Suddenly the munitions tent catches fire and the heavens explode in dazzling flames, illuminating the battlefield. The soldiers can now see their attackers, and army bullets begin to find their targets.

Still the Rasulis rush the soldiers from every side.

Jalal slashes the ropes of a tent. It collapses, exposing two frightened men. Jalal raises his sword to attack, but in the flickering light of the flames he recognizes one of these men—*Ali!*

Ali looks up at Jalal with a flash of recognition. He now sees that his death will come at the hand of his childhood friend. His mind flickers with the pale image of twelve-year-old Jalal's playful face above him after dropping a handful of sand in Ali's hair.

How did we end up here? he wonders. *When did we become enemies?*

Ali wants to call out to Jalal, call upon their friendship, beg for mercy, but he cannot.

I loved you, Ali remembers. *I still love you, Jalal.*

A sudden peace sweeps over him. If he is to die, let it be here, now, with his best friend. Let his tormented life end, and the pain with it. Let him sacrifice his life for their friendship.

Ali bows his head, accepting his fate.

Jalal calls to the nearest Rasuli fighter, a young man of Ishaq's age, and says, "Stay here. See that no harm comes to these men by our hands." And then he gallops off.

Ali drops to his knees and begins to sob. He cannot tell if his tears come from relief or sorrow.

Fifty yards from Ali, Zarrin finds herself surrounded by four men. Still mounted, she charges one of them and cuts him down with a slash of her sword. Suddenly her horse rears up. Its hooves crash down on another soldier.

Seeing her still in danger, Danush races to assist, but another soldier has cut off Zarrin's left hand with a swing of his harquebus. Hearing shouts as Danush draws near, the two soldiers turn and flee.

"You're wounded!" Danush says to Zarrin. "I'll take you back to the fort."

"Never!" she shouts as she tries to apply a strip of clothing as a tourniquet to her forearm. Danush dismounts and ties it for her. And then he sees the man killed by Zarrin's sword.

"It's Prince Mihdi!" he says.

Zarrin looks at Danush and says, "He should have known better than to pick on a woman."

As Jalal chases a group of terrified soldiers near the tent of Prince 'Abbas, his horse becomes tangled in the ropes of the tent. In a desperate attempt to free itself, the horse becomes further ensnared.

Seeing Jalal in peril, Zarrin gallops over to him and leaps from her saddle, trying to sever the web of ropes with her sword.

From his tree, Prince 'Abbas sees the white figure on his tangled mount just thirty yards away. He raises his musket and fires.

The bullet blasts a hole in Jalal's neck. Blood spurts from the gaping wound, splattering Zarrin below.

Prince 'Abbas jumps to the ground and flees. Looking up in horror, Zarrin sees Jalal falling slowly from his horse. With her one good hand, she helps him to the ground as Prince 'Abbas jumps from the tree and flees.

Three other Rasulis approach them. Zarrin puts Jalal's head in her lap and presses another torn strip of her garment against the gushing wound.

From a distance, Ali watches as the Rasulis lift up Jalal and begin to carry their unconscious leader toward the fort.

Within another ten minutes, the army has been routed. Of the enemy, only Ali and Jonathon remain on the battlefield. They are still guarded by the young Rasuli.

"I'm not sure what to do," the Rasuli says to Ali. "Will you come with us to the fort?"

"You go," Ali says. "We'll stay here for a while."

As the Rasuli walks toward the fort, the flames begin to die and darkness descends upon Ali and Jonathon. Ali is sure that his old friend will die. He is surprised at the depth of his sadness. But Zarrin—surely that was her with the bloody stump of an arm—Zarrin is alive! There is hope.

In the shrine, Jalal is lain on a mat and treated by Abbas the physician. After an hour, Jalal regains consciousness, finding Danush seated next to him behind closed doors.

"You have hastened the hour of your departure," Danush says, smiling sadly. "Please God, I will soon join you."

"Are you well pleased with me?" Jalal asks.

The doors that conceal the two friends do not open for an hour. Finally Danush exits the room to find Zarrin and six others waiting hopefully.

"I've bid my last farewell to him," Danush says sadly.

The Rasulis enter the room and Zarrin finds the body of Jalal lying there as if he were asleep. He is smiling faintly.

Zarrin leans close to Jalal and whispers, "I should not have left your side."

CHAPTER 25

The grand vizier paces furiously, his face a boil of rage. The young shah rubs his eyes. Ali fears that the boy-king, unaccustomed to successive humiliations, may begin weeping.

"Considering this latest defeat, perhaps it is time to consider my latest recommendation," Ali says to the grand vizier. "This band of God-intoxicated rebels cannot be beaten militarily."

Suddenly the shah leaps to his feet, his face contorted with fury. "I will not be humiliated again! If I am, both of you will pay, am I understood?"

Ali and the grand vizier both nod meekly.

"That is why I beg you to entertain my recommendation," Ali interjects. "It eliminates the risk of another military defeat."

"All right, I can agree to a negotiated settlement," the grand vizier replies, "but will the Rasulis? Right now, I'm sure they are feeling invincible."

"What do you have in mind?" the shah asks.

The grand vizier paces, thinking as he speaks. "First, a siege. No attack, just total isolation. With no food and water, the Rasulis will soon agree to anything."

"And you think the Rasulis will not attack us, as they have done before?"

"We will double the size of the army. Half the men will visibly perform maneuvers by night, the other half by day. There will be no period of vulnerability. We have learned the Rasuli tactics. If they are as smart as you say, they will not attack if they cannot surprise us."

"And when they have been softened up, what will be our offer?" Ali asks.

"If they lay down their arms and leave the fort, we will escort them to safety. They will be allowed to return home. Compared to starving, this will be an irresistible offer, I assure you."

"And we will honor our word?" Ali asks.

The grand vizier looks sharply at the shah, sighs, and then nods agreement.

"Thank you," Ali says, then leaves the room.

The shah, still standing, walks thoughtfully to the grand vizier. In a hushed voice he asks, "Do you really intend to let our enemies go free?"

The grand vizier smiles for the first time in this conversation and says, simply, "Of course not."

The first two regiments to arrive at Fort Hujjat are under the command of Prince Mihdi, who had been soundly beaten in a previous battle led by Mihdi's princely rival. Seeing an opportunity to regain his reputation and take revenge on the Rasulis, the prince decides to abandon the idea of a siege in favor of an all-out attack on the fort. If he can overcome these legendary Rasuli warriors, he is sure that his honor will be restored.

For two days the prince bombards the fort to dishearten the Rasulis, but it is he that grows dispirited as the incessant cannon fire fails to silence the voices of prayer and joyous chanting that emanate from the fort.

At last, exasperated by such unquenchable fervor, the prince erects a large tower. At its top he stations his largest cannon. With earth-shaking explosions, the cannon fires directly into the heart of the fort.

Finally the terrorized Rasulis are silenced.

The prince laughs heartily and congratulates his engineers and officers, but their celebration is short-lived. As they gather to toast the minor victory—the first triumph in the long campaign against these stubborn heretics—the gates of Fort Hujjat fly open and nineteen Rasulis on horseback charge the prince's army with the chilling cry of *Ya Sahibu'z-Zaman!*

Prince Mihdi's soldiers, shocked at such a daring daylight attack, immediately begin to flee. Like wildfire, panic blazes throughout the camp as the terrified troops, many of whom had lived through the previous horrifying rout, expect another unavoidable catastrophe. The small band of Rasulis quickly topples the tower, demolishes the new barricades, and returns to the fort with a number of the army's stoutest and best-fed horses.

The next morning, Ali and the grand vizier arrive at the encampment with several more regiments. Finding the prince's demoralized army in total disarray, and hearing Rasuli chants echoing victoriously through the frigid air, the grand vizier strips Prince Mihdi of his command and angrily threatens exile.

It is clear that Ali was right. These Rasulis, despite their small numbers, cannot be defeated militarily. The grand vizier places Sulayman in charge of the army and orders the siege to begin.

For months the siege goes as planned. All supply lines to Fort Hujjat are severed. The wells outside the fort are heavily guarded. Maneuvers day and night discourage the Rasulis from attacking the shah's army, which continues to grow.

Inside the fort, the Rasulis are forced to consume the flesh of their horses. They boil and devour the small amount of grass they can harvest at night outside the walls of the fort. Meager rainfalls leave most of the men dehydrated. Toward the end they are eating the leather of their saddles and handfuls of dirt to fill their aching bellies.

And then one sunny morning, when starvation seems inevitable, an emissary of Sulayman approaches Fort Hujjat. As the gate opens, Danush recognizes Jalal's friend Ali.

"You are Danush," Ali says. "I bear a message from Prince Sulayman. May we speak confidentially?"

Danush ushers Ali into the fort.

"The prince believes that the hostilities between you and the shah have been unduly prolonged," Ali says softly. "Both sides have fought long and suffered grievously. The prince, on behalf of the shah, fervently wishes to achieve an amicable conclusion to this violent conflict."

Ali hands Danush a Qu'ran and turns to the opening Súrih. There, in the margin, is a scribbled note.

"The prince wrote these words in the Qu'ran." Ali reads the prince's writing aloud. "'I swear by this most holy Book that I cherish no other purpose than to promote peace and friendliness between us. Come forth from your stronghold and rest assured that no hand will be stretched forth against you. You and your companions, I solemnly declare, are under the sheltering protection of the Almighty, of Muhammad, His Prophet, and of Nasir-al Din Shah, our sovereign.'"

Danush takes the Qu'ran and kisses it. He inspects the handwriting and finds the prince's seal on the page. He then peers intently into the eyes of Ali.

"Do you believe that Sulayman and the shah will honor their word?"

Remembering his palace conversation with the grand vizier and the shah, Ali says with conviction, "I do."

Within an hour the Rasulís march from their fortress under the protection of the shah. Sulayman has pitched a tent for Danush near the public bath of the village of Dízva overlooking the encampment. This tent is not far from Ali's.

By late afternoon Ali has fallen into a deep sleep. Content with the results of the day, he sleeps soundly through the night, his first uninterrupted sleep in months.

A windy morning brings with it a new horror. As Ali emerges from his flapping tent, he surveys the army encampment and notices that none of the Rasulis are out of their tents.

Thinking this odd, he finds a soldier and asks, "Have the Rasulis already left for their homes?"

The soldier laughs and replies, "They have left, all right. Some have already arrived in hell, and the others in chains."

"I don't understand," Ali says. "They were to be safely escorted home."

"A change in plans. The prince ordered them captured. Some resisted and had to be killed."

Sulayman's betrayal knocks the wind out of Ali.

How could he be such a fool?

Sulayman's action, of course, could only have been ordered by the grand vizier, the true betrayer. Sulayman would never have dared to do this on his own.

"What about Zarrin—the *girl*?" Ali asks the soldier.

"In chains, along with Danush. By now they are in Barfurush."

Furious, Ali runs to the encampment and finds Sulayman jovially having breakfast under a canopy. Ali storms over and flings the prince's table into the air. Food flies. The prince bolts to his feet. Ali grabs him by his military jacket. Three soldiers rush to protect their prince, but Sulayman gestures them away.

"You swore on the Qu'ran!" Ali shouts, spit spraying onto Sulayman's red face. "May you go to hell!"

Ali lets Sulayman go. The prince sighs, then smiles wickedly. "My orders come directly from the grand vizier. It is out of my hands. I suggest you go back to Tehran and take up the matter with him. Now if you don't mind, I would like to finish my breakfast."

Sulayman's attendants have already reset the table.

"What do you intend to do with them?" Ali asks.

"Some of them are men of means. They will fetch a nice ransom from their families. The others—sold into slavery, I imagine. Or executed."

Ali steps closer to Sulayman again, but this time the three guards close in on him. Physical intimidation is futile, he knows. He must get control of his anger and think clearly.

In a calmer voice, Ali asks, "What about Zarrin?"

"What an interesting question," Sulayman replies as fresh quail eggs and oranges are deposited on the table in front of him. "She has violated many of Islam's holiest precepts by impersonating a man and appearing in public without a veil. God knows what other sins she may have committed while in the company of these immoral Rasuli savages. I'm afraid she will be punished rather severely."

Traveling immediately to save Zarrin in Barfurush, Ali confronts another obstacle. The torrential rage of Sa'id, the mujtahid—inflamed by the humiliations heaped upon him by Jalal and Danush—sweeps aside Ali's impotent attempts at argument. As if he were swatting a fly, the mujtahid flicks Ali to the sidelines and immediately tries Danush and Zarrin for blasphemy and a host of other charges.

Finding them guilty, the mujtahid and the prince move the bound captives to the courtyard of the mosque where a large and angry throng has assembled. In fiery rhetoric, Sa'id catalogs the offenses of his prisoners. The bloodlust of the crowd boils hotter with each word he speaks.

"Despite the irredeemable nature of these despicable heretics," he concludes, "I wash my hands of all responsibility for any harm that may befall them. I leave God's justice to you."

The mujtahid gestures to the prince, who unchains Danush and Zarrin and pushes them into the cheering crowd. Like ravening wolves, the mob, guided by stern-faced mullas, strip Danush naked. With a hatchet, a sneering man hacks off his ears. A group of men urinates on his green turban and places it back on his head. A child smears human excrement on his face and body.

In horror, Ali watches as the stooped, bleeding body of Danush is entombed in heavy chains and then paraded, stumbling, around the courtyard. When at last he falls, a group of cackling women pounce upon him with knives and axes, dismembering his still quivering body.

And then the crowd turns to Zarrin. She, too, is stripped before the jeering mob and forced to kneel. A muscular man grabs her hair with one hand and pulls her knees off the ground. A bleeding chunk of scalp tears free. With his other hand the man swings a knife, carving off both breasts.

"She wanted to be a man!" he shouts.

The crowd howls gleefully.

Ali is sick. He vomits on the pavement, but no one notices.

Three men lift Zarrin to her feet. Somehow she is still conscious. Hands with daggers slice open wounds in her belly, her buttocks, her thighs. Burning candles are inserted into the gaping holes, sizzling in the bloody sockets. A blacksmith with a sharp spike pierces her nose and threads a chain through the hole. The children take turns leading her like an animal across the courtyard.

Through it all Zarrin remains silent—not a whimper, not a cry. And then a long-bearded mulla with a heavy axe approaches the pitiful girl now stooped on the bricks. With a thick grunt he beheads her.

On his hands and knees, Ali sees two rivers of blood converging.

And he remembers why he hates God.

CHAPTER 26

During the weeks that follow, the grand vizier launches a major campaign of persecution leading up to the trial and execution of the Rasul. Anyone professing allegiance to the heretic is arrested and tortured. Many are killed. The remaining Rasulis are forced underground.

On a warm July morning, the day before the Rasul's execution, Ali leaves the palace in Tabriz to visit the house in which the condemned young man awaits the firing squad. Already the city is teeming with residents excited about the coming event. It becomes clear to Ali that the Rasul must be moved at once to the army barracks, the most secure location for containing possible disturbances.

At the house, Ali orders that the young man's green turban and sash—the twin emblems of noble lineage—be removed before he is marched barefoot to the barracks. Walking several paces behind the armed guard, Ali is astonished at the hundreds of people who crowd around the captive, jeering and throwing stones.

At the barracks, the Rasul is placed in a cell with three other Rasulis, including the Rasul's amanuensis, Siyyid Husayn. Throughout the day, Ali silently observes the Rasul from a distance, wondering if this man of small stature and mild face can possibly be a Manifestation of God. He has no obvious physical gifts. He seems to have no unusual powers except emotional detachment from his fate; his face seems to glow with joy, not fear. Perhaps he is delusional!

At dawn, Ali arrives at the barracks where thousands of agitated residents already are gathered in the streets. The city's population is convulsing under the expectation of this "Day of Judgment," which Tabriz seems honored to host.

At the barracks, Ali orders the head footman to escort the Rasul to the city's leading mujtahids, who will issue the death warrants. Accompanying a contingent of soldiers to the condemned man's cell, Ali finds the Rasul speaking with his amanuensis.

The footman enters the cell and rudely pulls Siyyid Husayn aside so that the Rasul may be more easily removed. But the Rasul turns to the footman with a warning: "Not until I have said to him all those things that I wish to say can any earthly power silence me."

So stern is this warning that the footman takes a step backward. He turns to Ali, who nods encouragement to take charge.

"You must come with me now," the footman instructs the Rasul. "The mujtahids are waiting for you."

The Rasul follows the footman out of the cell as if this were only a brief interruption.

Ali has arranged for the Rasul to be paraded around the city quarters and through the bazaar until the signed death warrants have been collected. In this way the government will demonstrate its total domination of the accused.

Thousands line the streets to watch the "imposter" pass by. And when he is brought at last to the large courtyard for execution, over ten thousand eager spectators are present. They fill the back half of the courtyard, crowd the roof of the barracks, and line the tops of nearby buildings.

Ali has staged a marvelous spectacle for them. Under the command of Sam Khan, a Russian, seven hundred and fifty musket-carrying members of the Bahahudran regiment march into the quadrangle and align into three ranks. The regiment is comprised chiefly of the remnants of Russian deserters, most of them Christians, who had defected to Persia during the second Russo-Persian war. Ali had feared that Muslim regiments may have balked at killing a direct descendant of Muhammad.

The crowd cheers enthusiastically as the firing squad assembles.

Ali looks up and watches Jonathon Fury race across the quadrangle with his boxes. Upon reaching Ali, Jonathon begins to set up his camera.

"Back to photographing corpses?" Ali says in English.

Photographing *history*," Jonathon replies.

Sam Khan approaches the Rasul, who faces the vast display of muskets.

"I am a Christian," Sam Khan explains to the Rasul. "I have no argument with you." He appears frightened, as if his actions might call down the wrath of God. "If your cause is the cause of truth, enable me somehow to free myself from the obligation to shed your blood."

The Rasul quietly replies, "Follow your instructions. If your intention is sincere, the Almighty will relieve you from your perplexity."

From a distance of twenty paces, Ali watches this brief conversation without hearing. He is confused by the expression of serenity on the face of the Rasul, and the look of fear on the commander's.

Sam Khan closes his eyes. A great sigh emanates from his lips. He turns and orders two men to drive a spike into a wooden column in the courtyard wall. Following Ali's orders precisely, he instructs these men to fasten a rope to the spike and suspend from it the condemned man.

As the Rasul hangs between life and death, Ali finds his heart pounding. This is the moment that he has been longing for—*the punishment of God!* It is finally at hand, and Ali pants with anticipation.

Joining Ali to the side of the firing squad, Sam Khan gives the order for the regiment to raise and aim its weapons. Three ranks, each containing two hundred and fifty executioners, comply with his command.

Such an execution has never occurred in Persia. There has never been a firing squad. At the previous day's practice, no victim had been suspended from the wall. No live ammunition had been fired.

Today, the nervous troops are perspiring heavily. No one knows what to expect.

And then Sam Khan gives the order to fire.

The troops do not fire by ranks, but all at once. The roar is deafening. Smoke from the muskets fills the quadrangle and billows into the air, eclipsing the sun and plunging the hellish scene into darkness. Many spectators cry out in fear.

Sam Khan grips Ali's arm in the gathering gloom and begins reciting "The Lord is my Shepherd…"

Having ignited this turbulence with their volley of bullets, the troops now stagger into each other, eyes stinging and throats burning from the acrid discharge. A wind finally begins to whisk away the smoke.

A soldier in the first rank is the first to announce an even more astonishing sight. "The Rasul has disappeared!"

The Rasul is gone. The taut rope, having been severed by the bullets, now lies on the ground as limp as a dead serpent.

Bewildered and afraid, the spectators now begin to shout, "He has vanished! The Rasul has been taken from our sight!"

Rubbing his smarting eyes, Ali orders Sam Khan to launch a search of the barracks. He doesn't know how the Rasul has accomplished this trick, but there will be no escape.

Ali races to the Rasul's cell with the head footman, imagining that some clue to the matter may have been left behind. His mind is reeling and he is angry. Revenge has been plucked from his hands.

When the two men arrive at the Rasul's moldering cell, they are shocked. Behind the open cell door, composed and unsullied, the Rasul sits next to his amanuensis. He has emerged unscathed from the shower of bullets and is calmly speaking to his friend.

An astonished footman enters the cell. The Rasul looks up and says, "I have finished my conversation with Siyyid Husayn. Now you may fulfill your intention."

The trembling footman, certain that he has witnessed a miracle, wheels and runs from the cell.

Ali calls for the guards.

Sam Khan is the first to arrive. Upon seeing the Rasul in his cell, Sam Khan falls to his knees and says, "I have been relieved of my perplexity."

"I don't understand," Ali replies."

"You never will. My regiment will be leaving the barracks immediately. If you ask us to repeat this ungodly assignment, I will refuse."

Guards rush in and frantically secure the door.

Ali follows Sam Khan into the quadrangle. "You believe in Him, don't you?" Ali calls out.

"Under the penalty of death—I do." Sam Khan pauses. "God saved Him from your predictable treachery."

With a look of disgust, Sam Khan marches toward the remnant of his regiment.

Ali's mind is a riot of conflicting thoughts. Perhaps the spectacle of the firing squad was not a miracle at all. The Christian troops may simply have shot to miss.

All of them?

Nothing has changed.

Yes, everything has changed! God still betrays those who love Him, and the Rasul is still His stooge.

Yet God has protected the Rasul.

Ali tries to focus his thoughts. The entire barracks shudders in chaos. Spectators are still screaming and soldiers still aimlessly race back and forth.

In his mind, Ali can still see the smoke from the musket fire, the ropes rent into pieces by a hail of bullets, the Rasul peacefully completing his interrupted conversation.

Impossible!

And yet he and thousands of others have witnessed this implausible event. Who but God could be the author of such an audacious drama?

Ali will not play the scripted part of the defeated villain. This scene will not be the conclusion to this unfolding tale. He races through the scattering soldiers and finds Khamsih, the colonel of the body guard.

"Sam Khan and his Christians have fled in fear," he explains. "I need a man of courage to lead a Muslim regiment in completing this execution."

Khamsih, a portly man of immense ambition, bows to Ali and says, "You can trust me."

News of the second attempt flows through the crowds. Within two hours, Khamsih has assembled in the quadrangle another regiment of seven hundred fifty men.

"We will not fail as the Christians did," he explains to his men. "If even one of you misses your target, every one of you will become food for the bullets of another firing squad. Am I clear?"

Jonathon again is stationed with his camera next to Ali. "Maybe the real event will go better than the practice round," he says.

Ali ignores him.

Khamsih angrily storms to the Rasul's cell and removes the condemned man, striking the Rasul in the face before marching him to the execution spot.

Ali stands to the side, again watching the spectacle unfold.

A rope is slung over the spike. The victim is hoisted into the air and suspended from the rope.

As the troops prepare their muskets, the Rasul turns his face. Ali is certain that the Rasul is looking directly at him. The Rasul's serene, almost loving gaze makes Ali shiver in the hot noon sun.

"The day will come when you will have recognized me," the Rasul says to the crowd. "That day I shall have ceased to be with you."

Ali cannot stop looking into the Rasul's eyes. There is no fear or anger in them, but sadness. And love. This is not the countenance of a mocking God, nor the reflection of a betraying God. The kind face shimmers behind watery waves of heat that slowly ascend toward heaven.

Khamsih barks an order and the troops immediately stand at attention, muskets to their sides.

The Rasul's face, through the mirage of the rising heat, wrinkles and shifts, and then becomes the beautiful face of Ali's mother, who is smiling radiantly. Ali feels a tight knot growing in his chest. Anisa is not frightened or angry but seems delighted to see her son again. Ali wants to speak to her, even takes a step forward, but then the glimmering face transforms into the exquisite visage of Mary Rogers, with her penetrating gaze and coquettish grin. She is alert and happy and forgiving, as if her death had been the smallest of inconveniences.

The day will come…

Khamsih gives another order. With a rustling sound like a gust of wind in the forest, muskets are raised into position. The glare of the sun heats the bricks of the quadrangle pavement. Heat waves continue to rise in ripples.

The image unfolding before Ali shifts again, becoming the soft and lovely face of Ali's cherished wife. She has tears in her eyes, and Ali believes they are from pain or sadness until Alice smiles and her face dissolves into the round red face of an infant. Ali knows immediately that this is his unborn daughter.

…when you will have recognized me.

Protected, all of these loved ones. Safe and waiting. Revealing their love and understanding and forgiveness. Inviting through their tears and smiles a joyous reunion.

Khamsih orders the firing squad to take aim.

The face revealed in the mirage changes again. Ali sees a fox he had hunted at Chillington-hall, the meek surrender of its face as Ali raised his weapon to kill the guiltless creature. He remembers the unexpected bloodlust during the chase, and the intensity of the confrontation.

A sudden and horrible revelation sweeps over him. Ali has been blaming the prey for the hardships of the forest and the hunt.

Like a ruptured kaleidoscope, a flurry of images bursts into his mind. Free at last of guilt and anger, Ali sees himself as a child with his mother. At the breakfast table with Mary and Phebe. In bed with his pregnant wife on a cold wintry night.

A sudden peace descends upon him like a gentle rain.

He can choose to spare the fox.

Ali finds that he has closed his eyes. When he opens them, he is flung back into the horror of the barracks square. The executioners are pointing their muskets at the Rasul.

That day I shall have ceased to be with you.

He watches Khamsih's mouth beginning to open for the final order…

He desperately turns to the firing squad and shouts, "Nooooooo!" But his voice is drowned in the roar of musket fire.

Clouds of smoke rise again, but this time a swirling wind whisks away the gray mist, revealing the body shattered by hundreds of bullets.

Ali drops to his knees as the massive crowd begins to cheer. The applause masks his weeping.

The wind suddenly becomes a gale.

As the body is lowered, it is buffeted by the powerful wind that is stirring up the city. A dense whirlwind of dust begins to obscure the sun, plunging all of Tabriz into darkness. Ali imagines that this is God mourning the loss of his Promised One.

Moments ago, Ali would have rejoiced at inflicting on God such enormous pain, but now he prays for forgiveness.

The storm and the eerie darkness last from noon until night.

At dawn the next day, the body is lashed to a ladder by order of the grand vizier and paraded through the streets, then dumped into a moat outside the city gate. Sentinels are ordered to guard it day and night.

At the moat, Jonathon is permitted to photograph the body as evidence for the shah. While Ali watches, Jonathon positions his camera near the body. This is his first close look at the corpse, and he is astonished to find that the body is horribly mangled and yet the Rasul's face is untouched.

After removing his camera from the moat, Jonathon approaches Ali, who appears extremely agitated.

"Your work is finished," Jonathon says in English. "If you can find a way to get Ishaq released, I suppose you will go home now. Are you all right? You look terrible."

"Jonathon, I can't let the Rasul's body lie in this moat for the dogs."

"They'll shoot anyone who tries to take the body, you know that. Those are the orders of the grand vizier."

Ali's eyes glisten with moisture as he says, "If I'm killed, will you try to get Ishaq home safely?"

"I'll be there with you. If you want to save Ishaq, both of us will have to survive this adventure."

Ali's plan is simple. Under the cover of darkness, he and Jonathon will station a cart about fifty yards from the body and then creep silently into the moat, waiting for the guards to pass. When it is safe, they will wrap the body and carry it out of the moat to the cart.

"Not much of a plan," Jonathon says.

"Maybe this time God will be on our side."

Jonathon shows up that evening with two Rasuli friends who have volunteered to assist the mission. They station a cart as planned, and then silently enter the shadows of the moat system. The sentinels are positioned near the Rasul's body and show no signs of leaving.

"What now?" Jonathon whispers.

"I have another plan," Ali says. "When the guards are distracted, remove the body quickly."

Before Jonathon can stop him, Ali stands and briskly walks toward the guards, who immediately raise their weapons and order him to stop.

"I am Ali, representative of the shah!" he calls out. "Lower your weapons and let me approach."

Confused, the sentinels lower their muskets.

Ali walks up to the captain and says, "The grand vizier has changed your orders. There is no longer any need to guard the body. You may go home."

"Let me see the authorization," the captain demands.

Jonathon knows that Ali has no such authorization.

Ali rears up in his most regal posture. "Are you countermanding me, captain?" he roars. "I order you at once to abandon your posts so that the dogs may dine on this infidel's carcass."

The captain begins to shrink, but then puffs up his chest and says, "Without a written order, I must stay on guard."

Ali looks down at his feet, then looks up, glaring at the captain. "Then here is your direct order." He slams his fist into the captain's jaw.

Three sentinels pounce on Ali, who fights furiously, kicking two of them away. Another two join the melee. The rest of them stand and watch.

While all eyes are on the noisy fight, Jonathon and the Rasulis slip out of a deep shadow and slide the body away, replacing it with sacks of straw. In the gloom, it is hard to distinguish the sacks from the body.

Finally, one of the soldiers cracks the butt of his musket into Ali's skull, stunning him. The soldiers begin to argue about what to do next.

"We execute him!" the captain shouts. "Take him up and shoot him."

Five of the men carry Ali's limp body out of the moat.

Jonathon and the Rasulis are near the cart when Jonathon faintly hears the shouted order. He stops and looks at his friends."

"I can't let them do this," he whispers.

"He has chosen to sacrifice himself to save the remains of the Promised One," says one of the Rasulis. "We should complete his mission."

The Rasulis gently place the body into the cart as Jonathon stares into the blackness.

A shot reverberates in the night.

And then they quietly push the cart away.

CHAPTER 27

Their slippers make a scuffing sound on the marble floor as they walk to the shah's chamber. The meeting with the British consul had gone as expected: muted outrage over the execution of the Rasul, and tepid warnings about the Qajar crackdown on the Rasulis. All of it, the grand vizier explains to the young shah, is mere diplomatic rhetoric.

"Gordon, did you detect any hostile inflection that you may not have communicated to us?" the grand vizier asks the interpreter.

Green-robed Gordon Cranston trails by several steps, but now the shah and grand vizier stop and turn, awaiting his reply. "None whatsoever," Gordon answers. "But I found it interesting that Colonel Sheil specifically asked about Ali. Does he know something?"

"I doubt it," the grand vizier says. "Both of them are British, that's all. I think he was just making small talk."

"At some point Sheil will notice that Ali has disappeared completely from the shah's court," Gordon says.

"I suppose. And then we will have to tell him that the Englishman chose to return home with our best wishes after many years of service to the shah. I am glad Sheil did not inquire about Ali's son, though."

"What will you do with Ishaq now that his father is…"

The grand vizier turns to face the shah. "That matter I leave to the Pivot of the Universe," he says.

The boy-king stares at the grand vizier for a moment, then looks at Gordon and says, "Ishaq betrayed me when he chose to follow the Rasul. He will be killed, as we have killed the other Rasulis."

Yes, thousands of them, Gordon thinks. "But Ishaq was your friend, your teacher. His father helped you win the throne. You would execute him as if he were just a common criminal?"

"His father also became my enemy," the shah replies.

"Still, Ishaq never took up arms against you. He did not fight with the Rasulis at Hujjat. He never preached rebellion."

"Only because he was in custody."

"So his offense is that he was imprisoned?"

"Enough! His heart betrayed our friendship." The boy-king looks genuinely hurt.

"I believe he is still your friend," Gordon says.

The shah glares at Gordon, and then spins with a flurry of robes and begins to walk away. After a few steps, though, he turns again and says, "I am a merciful shah. I will spare him a painful hanging. An assassin will silently kill him while he sleeps. He will not suffer."

The shah storms down the long corridor followed by the grand vizier.

Persian mercy, Gordon says to himself.

In the harem—his prison—Ishaq sleeps deeply, dreaming of the meadows of Chillington-hall. For weeks he has mourned the loss of Zarrin, and now, having had no news of his father for many days, he allows himself a short nighttime visit to Ali's bucolic estate. It is a way of connecting with a man that he despises yet also loves intensely.

The moon is full, and its blue light streams across Ishaq's slumbering body. As he dreams, a dark figure creeps into his sleeping chamber and hovers over him, watching Ishaq's chest slowly rise and fall in shallow breaths. The man sits there for a moment as if considering his next move. And then the man reaches out his right hand and covers Ishaq's mouth.

Ishaq awakes suddenly, but the hand prevents him from crying out. Ishaq reaches for the man's arm and struggles, but the man is strong. Looking up at the man, Ishaq can see his eyes glimmering in the moonlight. They are familiar eyes—creased and squinting.

"Isaac!" the man whispers loudly. "Stop fighting me."

"Gordon?" Isaac says.

"Keep your voice down," Gordon says. "We are leaving."

"Leaving—why? What's going on?"

Isaac discovers that he is speaking in English. It has been a long time since he spoke his native tongue.

"Don't ask questions. It's urgent that we leave immediately."

Isaac sits up and stares at Gordon. His mind is still at Chillington-hall, but his eyes are seeing his moonlit sleeping quarters in Tehran.

"The guard will never let me leave."

"Let me worry about the guard."

"I'm not going anywhere unless you explain what's going on!" Isaac says firmly.

"The shah has ordered an assassin to kill you—perhaps this very evening."

"What? The shah would never do that."

"Believe me—he wants to exterminate every Rasuli in Persia."

Isaac considers this for a moment. "What about my father? Will he be leaving, too? Or is he behind this scheme."

Gordon realizes Isaac is unaware of his father's fate. He knows there is no time to explain. "Your father has switched sides," Gordon says. "I can't explain now, but he became a follower of the Rasul."

Isaac sighs. Tears fill his eyes. "I prayed every night that he would come to understand the truth," he says. "God has answered my prayers. Will my father be joining us?"

"You will see him again, I promise," Gordon says, though he adds in thought, *but not in this life.*

"Where is he?" Isaac asks.

Gordon feels time running out. "Isaac, I want you to listen very carefully. We are escaping an assassin. God willing, this is your own *Midnight March to Freedom.* If we do not leave right now, I may not be able to help you. Now do as I say!"

He hands Isaac a chador.

"This is a woman's!" Isaac protests.

"Put it on," Gordon insists. "And hurry. We must be leaving."

Isaac, embarrassed, pulls on the chador and follows Gordon out of the room and down the corridor. As they approach the night-guard, Gordon whispers to Isaac, "You must walk like a girl now. And keep silent, no matter what. I will do the talking."

"I don't know how a girl walks," Isaac says.

"Then just walk on your toes. Now follow me, and make sure the veil covers your whole face."

Gordon and Isaac walk toward the night-guard, a large dark-skinned man with fists like clubs and a curved scimitar hanging from his waistband. Isaac is now fully awake and beginning to appreciate the seriousness of this situation. His heart thumps wildly in his chest.

"Asghar, let us pass," Gordon says in Persian to the night-guard.

"It's very unusual that the shah wants one of the women to be brought to him," Asghar replies. He has been thinking about this since Gordon entered. "The shah usually comes *here*... when he comes at all."

"I gave you the signed authorization with his seal," Gordon says. "We must not keep him waiting."

Asghar studies the letter that Gordon had previously given him. "Why did he send *you*?" Asghar asks suspiciously.

"Because I was there. Because the shah can ask anyone he pleases to do anything he wishes," Gordon says angrily. "Now let us pass."

"Which girl are you taking?" Asghar begins to reach for Isaac's veil.

Gordon grabs the guard's arm and pulls it away. "Do not insult the wife of the shah!"

Asghar looks at Gordon and nods. "But I should ask the shah about this. It's a very unusual request."

"Don't be a fool! Do you want to keep your head? Look what happened to me the last time I questioned the shah." Gordon holds up the stump of his left arm. "Now let us pass!" he bellows.

Staring at the stump, Asghar finally backs away.

Gordon guides Isaac out of the palace and down a narrow street.

At last Isaac speaks. "How did you get that letter with the shah's seal?"

"Forged. I'm often in his chamber, where he keeps his seal."

The two of them walk for half-an-hour until they arrive at the caravanserai. Inside the courtyard, in one of the dusty rooms, Isaac is finally allowed to re-move his veil. Out of the blue shadows another man emerges—Jonathon Fury.

"Hello, Isaac," Jonathon says.

Isaac rushes to his old friend and embraces him heartily. "It's so good to see you," he says. "Do you have any news of my father?"

Jonathon looks at Gordon, who shrugs. "I didn't have time to tell him," Gordon explains.

"Tell me what?" Isaac asks.

"Isaac, your father was a true hero. He helped us save the body of the Rasul after the execution, but he was killed by the sentinels. I'm very sorry."

Isaac pulls away from Jonathon. "So he's dead?"

Jonathon nods.

Isaac thinks about this for a moment.

"But he helped us," Jonathon says at last. "As much as he could."

Isaac sighs. This is a lot to digest. "I think they will be looking for us once they find we're missing," he says.

"You and I will be leaving in the caravan tomorrow," Jonathon explains. "But Gordon has decided to stay here."

Looking at Gordon, Isaac says, "That's ridiculous. When they learn that you helped me escape with a forged letter, they'll kill you."

"There's nothing left for me in England or America," Gordon says. "My greatest loves and my greatest sins have been here in Persia. Besides, when they torture me, I will be able to tell them that you fled on horseback through the mountains of Azerbaijan."

"But why? You could escape with us."

Jonathon grasps Isaac's shoulder and says, "He's made his decision, Isaac. You and I are headed south for the port of Bushire. Of course, you will need to wear the chador as a disguise until we arrive there."

"No, I can't!" Isaac complains.

"You can," Jonathon replies. "Your father did."

At dawn, the small caravan leaves the caravanserai and heads for the south gate of Tehran. Gordon watches it disappear in the dust, and then walks toward the palace.

He has been despondent and guilt-ridden for many years.

But this morning he smiles.

EPILOGUE

CHILLINGTON-HALL

A sparkling glaze of ice coats the rolling landscape near Chillington. The carriage clatters over the snow-rutted road that passes through the tiny hamlet, which is surrounded by a majestic forest. The residents—woodsmen and fishermen, wives and children, dogs and chickens—all stop and wave. They recognize this carriage. It belongs to the owner of Chillington-hall. In the heart of the village, the carriage horses find the gateway to the Hall and become more animated, knowing that food and water will soon be provided.

The carriage finally pulls up a few yards from the entrance to the enormous manor-house. Outside the imposing door an elderly woman and gentleman are stomping their feet and clapping their hands to stay warm. When the carriage has stopped, they hobble over to it and open the carriage doors.

"Oh my goodness, my goodness, look who's here!" Phebe says. "It's been so long! Come now and get into the warm house. We have tea brewing."

The old gentleman begins to unstrap a large trunk from the back of the carriage. "Yes now, come along, we'll get your things."

And then Isaac Chadwick steps out of the carriage and gives Phebe a warm hug. "It's been a long time, Grandma," he says.

The old woman coos and steers the young man into the house. The smell of fresh-baked bread reminds Isaac of his days in Mrs. Rogers' Nassau-Street kitchen. He feels like a child again.

Supper is wonderful, obviously made by Phebe herself. In the morning, Phebe and Isaac put on warm jackets, gather bouquets of flowers, and walk to the small cemetery to fulfill the main purpose of this trip to Chillington-hall.

Many of Ollie's ancestors are buried here.

Standing on the edge of the cemetery, Isaac can see the marked grave of

Emily Chadwick, Ollie's great-grandmother, inscribed with Ollie's endearment, *Mum*. To Mum's left is Ollie's great-grandfather, Edward, and to her right the empty graves of Ollie's grandfather, Augustus, and his wife, Elizabeth.

There is a grave here as well for Anne Chadwick, Ollie's mother. The group's attention, however, is on a new headstone, this one also marking an empty grave. Isaac has ordered this simple inscription: *Oliver Chadwick, Wonderful Father and Man of God, 1813-1850.*

Phebe lays her flowers on the grave. Isaac motions for her to leave him here alone for a moment, and she does.

Kneeling before the marker, Isaac places his bouquet gently on the grave and then removes a small metal object from his coat pocket, hanging it by a silver chain from the headstone.

He smiles and walks off, leaving Jonathon's precious last photograph of the Rasul as Oliver's most fitting tribute.

THE BLACK PIT

The memory of the Rasul is the motivating force that keeps many of them alive—these wretched, tortured Rasulis now thrown into the *Black Pit* three stories below the ground. The foul stench is overwhelming, and the filth unbearable. Rats rule the depths of this dim and dank cesspool, chewing the eyes and feet of the dead or unconscious. These men could have saved themselves by recanting their faith, but none did, and this is the price for their belief.

The Rasulis occasionally pass time by chanting, but the guards—at least those who can bear the slime and the stink—beat them mercilessly for it. No outward expression of Rasuli belief is allowed in this dungeon of dungeons. And so the men live in their minds, repeating endlessly the words of the Rasul lest they forget, and whispering among themselves the promise of the Rasul, that within nine years of his declaration, another one would come. The One Who will become Manifest. The Promised One of all ages. The Second Blast of the trumpet.

They buoy themselves with whispered reminders that their suffering is the soil from which this other One, as yet undeclared, will arise and revitalize their faith, and bring righteousness and unity into the world.

One hundred Rasulis and nearly fifty common criminals—thieves, assassins, rapists, and highwaymen—crowd the dark pit, most of them naked and without bedding. One of them, however, has been singled out for the cruelest treatment. He sits with an enormous chain around his neck. The weight of it grinds into his flesh and forces his head and shoulders to bend painfully. This man had been a Persian nobleman, the son of the vizier of Nur, a man of such charity and character that only his popularity among the people had prevented him from execution as a Rasuli.

It was well-known that he had organized the infamous Rasuli council at Badasht and had been a confidante of Jalal and Danush. When the government was finally emboldened by its execution of the Rasul and the slaughter of twenty thousand Rasulis, the grand vizier had finally found the courage to arrest Mirza Ramin.

Of all the suffering in the Siyah Chal, this man suffers the most, and yet it is he who lifts the spirits of the others through his example and his whispered words of enlightenment.

It is now evening, and the darkness here is even darker. Only a torch at the end of a long passageway throws a sliver of light into the pit. Men cough and spit and vomit. They try to sleep, but the cold and the stench is killing. The sick moan and the new prisoners sob.

One of the men is desperately searching his memory for some small reminiscence, some remembered image that will transport him out of this hellish hole and into a happier world. A year in heavy chains and five months in the Black Pit, with no expectation of release, has shattered his memory, but one vision comes to him. It is an English manor-house surrounded by meadows and thick forests. A paradise of open air and sunshine, of glistening snow and galloping horses. He holds onto the image, and for a moment the sweet fragrance of fresh-baked bread replaces the stench of the pit, and he smiles.

His memory is now refreshed, and he remembers the beginning of the end. A dark night. A fight. Being dragged out of a moat, and facing an angry sentinel. The roar of a musket, and the biting pain of a bullet striking him in the chest. He believes that the bullet must have been guided by God, for it had struck head-on the small silver cylinder that he had worn around his neck since a child, the cylinder that contained a verse of the Qu'ran, and the bullet had shattered into pieces, painfully scattering the hot fragments into his skin, but failing to complete its fatal mission. He remembers that the sentinels had been frightened by this "miracle" and had taken him, bloody but breathing, to the local governor who had turned him over to the grand vizier, a man who believed that death was too kind a sentence for a traitorous Englishman.

Ollie remembers, too, one of the verses from the Surih of Joseph that been sealed in that silver charm. *Thou art my Protecting Guardian in the world and the Hereafter.* He cannot believe that God would have saved him for no purpose, and this belief gives him hope.

He turns his eyes toward the man drooping under the heavy chains. He wonders at how this man can now turn his eyes upward in the darkness, as if seeing a vision of his own; and how he can smile, with glistening eyes, despite the pain and illness with which he is afflicted. He watches the man's face, which is glowing, not with light but with the radiance of certitude. He watches as this man breathes in deeply the stench-filled air as if it were the fragrance of roses, and then sigh with a knowingness like the breath of God. And as the man sighs, a refreshing breeze seems to blow over Ollie, and suddenly he knows, *he knows*.

And he remembers, many years ago, two twelve-year-old boys in the warm Bushruyih sand. He can feel the sand now, see the face of Jalal eclipsing the sun. He can remember how both of them so desperately longed to be the first to discover the Promised One, how they had seen the Prophet in the clouds, and how he had believed that his steadfast friend had been rightly blessed with the honor.

He turns with recognition to the man in the heavy chains, and understands at last that *both* boys had been blessed. Two boys, two Prophets.

Many years ago, a cloud had found Jalil.

At last, Ollie's cloud has come to him.

ABOUT THE AUTHOR

Gary Lindberg has spent his entire adult life as a screenwriter, movie director and producer, author of fiction and nonfiction, and book publisher. He is the author of four Amazon #1 bestselling novels and three books about the unknown history of Elvis Presley. He cowrote and co-produced the Paramount motion picture *That Was Then, This Is Now* starring Morgan Freeman and Emilio Estevez. Currently, he resides in the Minneapolis area.